OCEANS APART

TWO BOOKS IN ONE

BETWEEN SUNDAYS

Other Life-Changing Fiction™ by Karen Kingsbury

9/11 Series

   One Tuesday Morning
   Beyond Tuesday Morning
   Every Now and Then

Lost Love Series

   Even Now
   Ever After
   Every Now and Then

Above the Line Series

   Above the Line: Take One
   Above the Line: Take Two
   Above the Line: Take Three
     (spring 2010)
   Above the Line: Final Cut
     (summer 2010)

Stand-Alone Titles

   Oceans Apart
   Between Sundays
   This Side of Heaven
   When Joy Came to Stay
   On Every Side
   Divine
   Like Dandelion Dust
   Where Yesterday Lives
   Shades of Blue
     (fall 2009)

Redemption Series

   Redemption
   Remember
   Return
   Rejoice
   Reunion

Firstborn Series

   Fame
   Forgiven
   Found
   Family
   Forever

Sunrise Series

   Sunrise
   Summer
   Someday
   Sunset

Red Glove Series

   Gideon's Gift
   Maggie's Miracle
   Sarah's Song
   Hannah's Hope

Forever Faithful Series

   Waiting for Morning
   Moment of Weakness
   Halfway to Forever

Women of Faith Fiction Series

   A Time to Dance
   A Time to Embrace

Cody Gunner Series

   A Thousand Tomorrows
   Just Beyond the Clouds

Children's Titles

   Let Me Hold You Longer
   Let's Go on a Mommy Date
   We Believe in Christmas
   Let's Go Have a Daddy Day
     (spring 2009)

Miracle Collections

   A Treasury of Christmas Miracles
   A Treasury of Miracles for Women
   A Treasury of Miracles for Teens
   A Treasury of Miracles for Friends
   A Treasury of Adoption Miracles

Gift Books

   Stay Close Little Girl
   Be Safe Little Boy
   Forever Young: Ten Gifts of Faith
     for the Graduate

KAREN

NEW YORK TIMES
BESTSELLING AUTHOR

KINGSBURY

OCEANS
APART

TWO BOOKS IN ONE

BETWEEN
SUNDAYS

ZONDERVAN®

ZONDERVAN.com/
AUTHORTRACKER
follow your favorite authors

ZONDERVAN

Between Sundays/Oceans Apart
Copyright © 2009 by Karen Kingsbury

Between Sundays
Copyright © 2007 by Karen Kingsbury

This title is also available as a Zondervan ebook product.
Visit www.zondervan.com/ebooks for more information.

This title is also available as a Zondervan audio product.
Visit www.zondervan.com/audiopages for more information.

Oceans Apart
Copyright © 2004 by Karen Kingsbury

This title is also available as a Zondervan ebook product.
Visit www.zondervan.com/ebooks for more information.

This title is also available as a Zondervan audio product.
Visit www.zondervan.com/audiopages for more information.

Requests for information should be addressed to:

Zondervan, *Grand Rapids, Michigan 49530*

ISBN 978-0-310-32597-0

Published in association with the literary agency of Alive Communications, Inc., 7680 Goddard Street, Suite 200, Colorado Springs, CO 80920. www.alivecommunications.com

Interior design by Michelle Espinoza

Printed in the United States of America

09 10 11 12 13 14 15 • 23 22 21 20 19 18 17 16 15 14 13 12 11 10 9 8 7 6 5 4 3 2 1

OCEANS
APART

DEDICATION

Dedicated to Donald, who continues to be my prince, my safe harbor, my best friend. You give me wings enough to fly, but keep me grounded in everything that matters. I smile when I think of our long walks and nighttime talks, the way you make me laugh after a hard day or your way of putting a layer of sensibility over any situation. You are an amazing man, Donald, gifted in so many areas, yet content to serve. I am blessed beyond words to be your wife, gifted with the joy of your presence in my life. Fifteen years have flown by in a heartbeat, and I can only pray God blesses us with so many more. I love you forever and always.

To Kelsey, my love and laughter, my silly-heart and only daughter. Can it be that you are fourteen? That you are standing on the brink of high school and cheerleading and driving and dating? You are gorgeous, sweetheart, inside and out. I cherish our together times, whether washing our faces at the same mirror or figuring out a math problem late at night. The glow in your eyes is the same one that belonged to that pixie-faced four-year-old. The only difference is this: now we don't have forever stretched out before us. Being with you is knowing intrinsically the speed of time, and my helplessness at slowing it even for a day. And so I celebrate you, Kelsey, and all we've shared, all we have yet to share as you dance closer to the front door. I love you and thank God for you, sweetheart.

To Tyler, my dreamer. How wonderful that God has blessed you with passion and purpose, a plan so big you can't help but breathe it and borrow from it and become it every day of your life. Our time in New York City was something I'll remember forever. And I'm convinced you will always know where your talent came from—

whether you're singing on Broadway or playing out a scene in LA, shine for Jesus, Tyler. Shine for Jesus. And no matter what happens, if you squint through the lights, you'll see me and your dad cheering for you from the first row. I love you, Tyler. I couldn't be more proud.

To Sean, my humble leader. Watching you among your peers, I am struck by the reality of how quickly you've worked your way into my heart. You've only been in our family for three years, and yet every child in class looks up to you. Of course, God had you in our hearts long before you came to live with us, and His plans for you continue to play out. Whether you're flying across a basketball court or reading devotions in the morning, your enthusiasm for life and your love for Jesus make you shine like a bright flame. Keep them, Sean. And know that I love you deeply.

To Josh, my gentle warrior. I'm convinced if I looked up *confidence* in the dictionary, there would be your smiling face. You have more determination than a dozen kids combined, and the belief that no matter what task is set before you, you'll not only complete it but redefine it. I'm amazed at your talents, whether in soccer, basketball, mathematics, or artwork. Don't ever forget our family verse, sweetheart. To whom much has been given, much will be expected. I can't wait to see how God uses you in the years to come. Keep Him first, Josh ... the way you did when you joyfully went to your room and pulled out half your piggy bank savings so people in Southeast Asia would have Bibles. I love you and I'm so proud of you, honey.

To EJ, my overcomer. Before this year, you struggled some. Yet I always knew you were the first chosen one, EJ, the child God first led us to adopt. And because of that, we knew He had a plan for bringing you into our family, a plan for seeing that through to completion. Now you are blossoming, becoming the most beautiful flower in the garden. Your eyes glow with the light of Christ, and you sit a little taller each day as the compliments pour in. "EJ, what great seat work," "EJ, what great manners," "EJ, what great sports skills." I need only look at you to feel the sting of tears— and the glory of God's goodness all around. I thank Him for your willingness to see the process through, and I love you, honey. Isn't God the greatest?

To Austin, my miracle boy (or Brett Favre, as you're calling yourself these days). Can it be that you are in kindergarten already? What other six-year-old would ask for shoulder pads for his birthday? Not so you can play on a team, but so you can spend hours in the yard decked in your Packers jersey—by yourself or with your brothers—so dedicated to the thrill of sports that no team or game schedule is needed. I watch you growing and becoming, and I think back to that day six years ago, the morning when we placed you into the arms of a surgeon and prayed God would give you back to us. Your heart surgery was a miracle, but the greater miracle is the life you've lived since then. Strong, determined, refusing to settle for anything but the best. And yet . . . with all that testosterone you got from Daddy, you have a heart full of my tenderness. I can't slow the ride, Austie, but I can enjoy every minute. I love you and thank God that He allowed you to live.

And to God Almighty, the author of life, the greatest author of all, Who has—for now—blessed me with these.

ACKNOWLEDGMENTS

As always, when I write a novel many people play a crucial role in making it come together. First and foremost I must thank God for giving me the gift of story. When I write, I feel as though I'm reading, merely taking notes on the picture God puts in my head. I simply show up at my computer and download my heart. Not a minute goes by when I don't realize that this ability is completely from God.

Also, thanks to my family, especially my husband, who makes amazing sacrifices so that I can give God's best to the ministry of writing. At the same time, he's first to remind me when life slips out of balance. In that light, thanks to my mom, Anne Kingsbury, who is simply the best assistant I could ever have. You are loyal and loving and you see my heart for ministry like no one ever has. My father, Ted Kingsbury, and my sisters, Susan and Tricia, have also been a wonderful support, helping me with research projects and special assignments. Thank you for everything.

Thanks, also, to my wonderful editor, Karen Ball, who always takes my work to a higher level; and to the folks at Zondervan who team up to make a book like this one everything it is today. You are a hardworking group, and I'm privileged to be working with you.

A number of friends have also taken on other roles—prayer support, kid support, public relations, and general enthusiasm about my work with life-changing fiction. And so thanks goes to Ann Hudson, Sylvia Wallgren, Melinda and John Chapman, Bobbi and Erika Terret, Robin Jones Gunn, Rick and Robin Dillon, Cindy Weil, Randy and Vicki Graves, Richard Camp and his family, Kathy Santschi, Joan Westfall, Betty Russell, Phyllis Cummins, the

Shampines (Kerry, D.J., and Brad), the teaching staff at our wonderful elementary school, the students at Don's high school, the college kids who think of our house as theirs (Thayne, Justin, Aaron, Jenna, Michele, Darren, Kara, Marc, Mark, and lots of others), and my dear friends at Christian Youth Theater. When life gets hard, I count on you and cherish the fact that you keep me cheering, even on deadline.

Of course thanks go to my agent, Rick Christian, at Alive Communications. I'm honored to work with someone so gifted.

In addition, my heartfelt thanks to pilots Eric Schoneberger and Scott Wakefield for lending their expertise to this book. It rings with authenticity because of you.

Also, a special thanks to the winner of my Ebay auction that raised money for the Christian orphanage in Haiti where we adopted our three boys. You won the right to have me name a character after your son, Max. I hope you enjoy the way that turned out.

Finally, thanks to the Evans family for making the winning bid in a recent Biola University auction. The Evans family won the Forever in Fiction item, and as such were also able to have a character in this book named after them. This arrangement led to the naming of Loren Herman Evans, our pilot's father. Many of this character's traits were fictionalized for the purpose of the story. However, a few similarities exist between the fictional Loren Evans and the real man, a man dedicated to the Lord and to his family, a man who loves hand-cranked homemade ice cream and a mean game of croquet, and who pretends to be retired when he's not playing golf and traveling. You are well loved, Mr. Evans. May God bless your family's gift to Biola, and may you enjoy having your name forever in fiction.

Of Butterflies and Second Chances

I tell of hearts and souls and dances . . .
Butterflies and second chances;
Desperate ones and dreamers bound,
Seeking life from barren ground,
Who suffer on in earthly fate
The bitter pain of angry hate.
Might but they stop and here forgive
Would break the bonds to breathe and live
And find that God in goodness brings
A chance for change, the hope of wings
To rest in Him, and self to die
And so become a butterfly.

—Karen Kingsbury

ONE

Fear was an owl that rarely lighted on the branches of Kiahna Siefert's heart.

Especially in the light of day.

But it was nine o'clock on the sunniest morning of spring, and Kiahna couldn't shake the feeling—the strange gnawing in her soul, the way the skin around her neck and chest felt two sizes too small.

What is it, God . . . what are You trying to tell me?

No answer echoed back at her, so Kiahna kept busy. The passenger briefing was nearly finished, and the pilots were in their seats. She anchored herself against the service wall and found her smile, the one she used every time she flew.

Flight 45, Honolulu to Tokyo, was a nine-hour flight. With a layover in Tokyo, the roundtrip gave Kiahna eighteen flight hours. Five times a month she made the two-day turnaround, and after a decade with the airline, her pay was better than any she could get anywhere else. Out the door at seven and, with the time change, home before dinner the next day. Kiahna had earned the route after ten years with the airline, and it was perfect for one reason.

It allowed her most days to be home with Max.

"Movie today?" The man was a light traveler, briefcase and a carry-on, a regular in first class. Whatever his worn leather bag held, it took him to Japan at least once a month.

"Yes, sir. Mel Gibson's latest."

"Good." He smiled and kept moving. "Gets me over the ocean quicker."

One by one the passengers filed in, same as always. But still she couldn't shake the feeling.

It took fourteen minutes to seat the cabin, and Kiahna worked the routine. The flight was nearly full, which meant the usual readjusting to make people and bags fit comfortably in the cramped quarters. She greeted passengers, sorted out seat assignments for confused travelers, and poured a drink tray for first class.

A family with four children was seated over the wing, and already their baby was crying. Kiahna found a package of crackers and coloring books for the couple's older children. With every motion she tried to sort out her feelings.

"Kiahna?"

She jumped and turned to face her partner. Stephanie was working the back part of the cabin. "We're waiting."

The announcement. She'd completely forgotten. A quick breath. "They're all in?"

"For two minutes now."

Kiahna snapped the drink tray into place on the small service counter and edged past the other woman. The announcement was hers that morning; she should have remembered. She took hold of the microphone and began the routine.

"Welcome aboard Flight 45. We're expecting a full cabin this morning, so if you have two carry-ons with you today, please store one of them in the space beneath the seat in front of you." She paused, her mouth still open.

What came next? There was more to say, something about oxygen and masks, but the words scrambled in her mind and refused to come. She stood unmoving, her heart slamming against her chest.

"Here"—Steph took hold of the microphone—"I've got it."

Kiahna's arms shook as she backed away, up against the closed front cabin door. What was wrong with her? She'd given that announcement a thousand times; she could be in a coma and say it.

Steph finished, and the copilot came on. "Flight attendants, prepare for takeoff."

They pushed their jump seats down and buckled in. Usually this was Kiahna's favorite part. A few minutes of power and thrust while the airplane barreled down the runway and lifted into the air, minutes where she wasn't needed by anyone for anything, when she could think about the day and all that lay ahead.

This time, though, was different.

All Kiahna could think about was the part of her day that lay behind, the part with Max.

At seven years old, Max was both brilliant and beautiful, a wonder boy streaking through her life like a comet at breakneck speeds. He wore red tennis shoes, and his best friend was his yellow Labrador retriever, Buddy. At school, Max had a reputation for being the fastest—and sometimes the silliest—boy on the playground. And his mouth ran faster than his legs. Kiahna liked to hold court with Max on dozens of adult topics. The death penalty—Max was against it; more money for public schools—he was for it. Max was fiercely patriotic, and at school he sometimes organized red, white, and blue days in honor of the U.S. troops in the Middle East.

But this morning he'd been quiet.

"When do you finish working?" They lived in a two-bedroom apartment, and he slipped into her room while she was still pressing her standard-issue airline navy blazer.

Kiahna studied him. "Dinnertime tomorrow, same as always."

"No, not that way." He hopped up on her bed and sat cross-legged. "When will you stay home in the daytime? Like Devon's mom or Kody's mom?"

"Max." She turned from the ironing board and leveled her gaze at him. "You know I can't do that."

"Why?" He anchored his elbows on his knees.

"Because"—she came a few steps closer and sat on the edge of the bed—"those moms have husbands who work."

"So why can't we have a husband?"

"C'mon, Max." She cocked her head and brushed her finger against the tip of his nose. "We've been through this, sport."

Buddy padded into the room and sank in a heap near Max's feet. "Yeah, but . . ." Max brought his fists together and rested his chin on them. His green eyes caught a ray of morning light. "Forever?"

"For now." She crooked her arm around his neck, pulled him close, and kissed the top of his head. His dark hair felt soft and damp against her cheek, still fresh from his morning shower. "Until something better comes along."

"Like a husband?" Max lifted his face to hers. He was teasing, but beyond the sparkles in his eyes was a river of hope, a hope that ebbed and flowed, but never went away.

Kiahna smiled. She tousled the hair at the back of his head and returned to the ironing board. Max knew better than to push. A husband had never been in the picture. Not a husband and not a daddy. Kiahna couldn't trust a man with her own heart, let alone her son's. Besides, it wasn't God's plan for her to have a husband. At least that's the way she'd always felt.

Max slid onto the floor and looped his arms around Buddy's neck. The dog rewarded him with a solid swipe of his tongue across Max's cheek. "Buddy understands."

"Yes." Kiahna smiled. "Buddy always does."

⌒

A soft bell sounded, and Kiahna sucked in a quick breath. They were at ten thousand feet—time to prepare the beverage cart and make the first pass through the cabin. Steph approached her from the other side of the aisle.

"You okay?" She had one hand on her hip, her eyebrows lowered into a *V*. "What was the trip about the announcement? Never seen you freeze like that."

Kiahna stood and smoothed out the wrinkles in her navy cotton skirt. "I don't know." She gave her partner a smile. The feeling, the strange restlessness, had plagued her ever since her talk with Max. "Busy morning, I guess."

"Yeah, well"—she rolled her eyes—"you wanna talk busy? It's four o'clock, and Ron . . . you know Ron, right?"

"He moved in last month?"

"Right." Steph grabbed a piece of gum from her skirt pocket, slipped the wrapper off in a single move, and popped it into her mouth. "Anyway, he gets this call at four this morning, and it's the—"

A sudden jolt rocked the aircraft so hard Steph fell to her knees. Gasps sounded throughout the cabin, and somewhere near the wing one of the children began to cry. Kiahna fell back against the service counter and reached for a handful of soda cans that had fallen to the floor.

"What the . . ." Steph was struggling to her feet when the plane tilted hard in the other direction. The motion knocked her back to the floor. In the tenth row, a handful of screams and shouts rang out from a group of college kids, journalism students heading back home from a convention.

Turbulence.

Kiahna grabbed hold of the nearest wall and felt the blood drain from her face. The air was always choppy over the islands, especially in spring. She was about to help Steph to her feet when the copilot leaned out from the cockpit.

"We're going back." The man's upper lip was twitching. His whispered words came fast. "Something's wrong with the tail." He swallowed hard. "The whole bloody aircraft wants to nosedive."

Nosedive? Kiahna stared at him. This wasn't happening, not this morning. Not when every fiber in her being had warned her something wasn't right. The copilot was gone again, and Kiahna shifted her gaze to Steph. The girl was a New Yorker, twenty-two, twenty-three tops. She was cocky and brash and had a quick tongue, but now her face was gray-white. "What . . . what do we do?"

Kiahna reached for her partner's hand and helped her to her feet. "We work the cabin. I've done an emergency before." Her voice sounded familiar, but only remotely so. "We stay calm and everything will work out fine."

"But what if we—"

"No *what-ifs.*" She took the lead and headed down the aisle. "We have to work."

They weren't through first class when a strange popping sound shook the plane and propelled it downward. *It's the descent,* Kiahna said to herself. And then again for the benefit of the passengers. "We're making our descent. Cover your heads and assume a forward roll position."

Kiahna didn't dare turn around, couldn't bear to meet Steph's questioning eyes. The truth had to be written across her face: the sharp angle of the aircraft didn't feel like a normal descent pattern.

It felt like a nosedive.

Panic worked its way through the rows in a sort of sickening wave.

"Jesus, help us!" a lady shouted from row eight. She had an arm around each of her children.

"Someone *do* something!" The scream came from an area near the back of the plane, and it set off a chain reaction of loud words and frantic cries for help. No one had any doubt they were in trouble.

Still Kiahna moved forward. At each row she demonstrated the crash-landing position. Hands clasped at the back of the neck, body tucked as far forward as possible. "Assume the emergency position," she said over and over again. "Assume the emergency position."

"What happening?" An Oriental man grabbed her arm; his eyes locked on hers. "What, lady? What?"

Kiahna jerked herself free as the nose of the plane dropped again. The aircraft was almost entirely vertical.

The captain's voice—tense, but steady—filled the cabin. "Prepare for an emergency landing. I repeat, prepare for an emergency landing!"

Babies were wailing now; parents grabbed their children to keep them from falling toward the front of the plane.

"Lord, have mercy on us," a woman screamed.

The voices mingled and became a single noise, a backdrop that grew louder and then faded as Kiahna caught a glimpse of the ocean out one of the windows. In that instant time froze.

Kiahna was back at home again.

* * *

"Come on, Max. Get your backpack. We're running late!"

Max rounded the corner, Buddy at his side. "I can't find it."

"Check the coat closet."

He darted across the kitchen and toward the front door. She heard him yank the closet open. "Here it is!"

"Grab it; let's go."

The whole scene took a fraction of a second to flash across her mind, all of it routine, mundane. No subtle nuances or hesitations, nothing to indicate that this morning could be their last. Nothing but the strange pit in her stomach.

She closed her eyes . . . where was Max right now? He stayed with Ramey Aialea mornings until the school bus came, and again in the afternoon and through the night when she had a layover. The woman would see him off to school the next day and take care of him for an hour or so when school got out. Ramey was in her late sixties, a weathered grandmother in poor health who took in Max as a way of staying young. She lived just a block away and felt like family to Kiahna.

Max had been with Ramey since he was born.

That morning, as happened so often, Kiahna and Max had piled into Kiahna's old Audi and made time to Ramey's first-floor unit. Ramey and Kiahna both lived in the same modest residential section of the island, the place where apartments filled every available square inch, leaving room for only an occasional palm tree. The place where the island's food servers and hotel maids and resort staff lived.

The apartments weren't much, really. But Kiahna's complex had a fairly clean pool and a patch of gravel with a swing set. More amenities than some. That, and paradise every day of the year. It wasn't a bad place to raise a boy. A native to Honolulu, Kiahna wouldn't have lived anywhere else.

By the time she and Max arrived at Ramey's apartment, Kiahna's strange feeling had set in. She didn't want to waste time making idle talk with her old friend. Instead she stepped out of the car and met Max near the front bumper. "Have a great day, sport."

He squinted into the sun. "Do you have to go?"

"Yes." She pecked him on the cheek. "We'll play Scrabble tomorrow night, okay?"

"It's too sunny for Scrabble."

"Okay, then basketball? Give and go, all right?" Kiahna rested her hands on her knees and kept her face at his level.

"Really?" Max's eyes held a hint of doubt. "Give and go?"

She winked at him. "As long as it's light out."

Max bit his lip. "Japan's a long way from here."

"Yes." Kiahna angled her face. Why was he talking like this? She'd flown since before he was born. "But not so bad when you go all the time."

"Yeah." He lifted one shoulder and let his gaze fall to the ground. "Sorry about this morning."

"For what?" She fell back on her heels.

"The husband stuff." He lifted his eyes to hers. "I just get sad when you're so far away all day." A few seconds passed. "What if I break my arm? Who'll help me?"

"Ramey, silly."

"She's my 'mergency contact." He pushed the toe of his tennis shoe against her leather loafers. "But I mean the hug part and the singing part. Who'd do that?"

Kiahna hesitated only a moment. This was the part of being a single mom that always made her throat swell—the idea that she couldn't be all things to Max, not while she had a full-time job.

"Well"—she framed his small face with her fingers—"*I* would."

"You'd be somewhere over the ocean." He wasn't arguing with her, only making a point. Sharing a fear she hadn't known he'd had until now.

"Even if we're oceans apart I'll always be right here." She lowered one hand and let her fingers rest on the spot just above his heart. "You know that, right, sport? Remember our song?"

A breath that was more sad than frustrated slipped from him. In a rush of arms and hands and fingers he threw himself into her embrace.

Her voice was a whisper, and she breathed it against his face as she stroked the back of his head. "Come on, sport, right?"

"Right." The word was a defeated huff, but it would have to do.

"Taco Bell tomorrow?"

"Sure."

"You can do better than that." She straightened and made a silly face, hoping she could coax a smile from him before she left. She did an exaggerated pout and mimicked him. "*Sure . . .*"

The hint of a grin broke Max's expression, and before he could stop himself, a giggle followed. "Okay, fine. Taco Bell!" He burst out the word and laughed at his own humor. "Better?"

"Much." She stooped down and kissed his cheek again. "Keep your chin up." When her face was still at his level, she looked straight through to his soul. "I love you, Max. See you tomorrow."

❦

A faint whistling sound was coming from outside the airplane, and it snapped Kiahna from her memories. They were headed straight for the Pacific Ocean, the pilots unable to pull out of the dive. They had half a minute at best, and Kiahna was using all her strength to keep from tumbling down the aisle and slamming into the cockpit doors.

The news would have to come from Ramey . . . the news and the details that would follow. She'd written out her last wishes seven years ago, days after Max's birth. And there was the letter, of course. A different one every year on Max's birthday. But even with all her preparations, she never thought it would come to this.

Don't forget what I told you, sport . . . I'm with you . . . always with you . . . as close as your heart.

For an instant she turned her thoughts toward God. She had loved the Lord all her life, loved Him even when she didn't always understand Him. If this was the end, then she would be with Him in a matter of minutes. *God . . . give us a miracle . . . or give one to Max. Please, God.*

The screaming and crying around her grew louder, then in the final moments it faded. Kiahna made a desperate attempt to right herself, to stand up so she could calm the craziness in the cabin.

They could still make it, couldn't they? The aircraft could straighten out before impact and settle safely on the surface of the ocean. The Coast Guard would be called out and they'd inflate the emergency slides and rafts. Everything would be okay and she'd tell Max all about it that night. Each seat cushion was a flotation device, right? Wasn't that what they told people every day on this flight?

I love you, Max . . . don't forget me.

Her mind jumbled, and then cleared just as quickly, until finally two thoughts remained. As the plane made impact with the water, as the fuselage splintered apart and ocean water gushed into the cabin, it was those two thoughts that became her last.

The thought of Max, and what would become of him after today.

TWO

The frantic race of another busy weekend was on from the moment Connor Evans woke up.

It was the first Saturday in April, and the girls had two birthday parties to attend. Michele put him in charge of wrapping presents and dropping their daughters off at the first party. The second was immediately after, and a neighbor would ferry the girls across town, after which Connor would pick them up.

Michele was redoing the kitchen, and sometime between drop-offs and pickups, Connor wanted to stop by Home Depot and find a riding mower for the backyard. His fall fertilizing had paid off, but now the acre of grass out back was halfway to his knee, typical of what was happening throughout Florida.

His neighbor liked to pause and hold his hand to his ear.

"Hear that, Evans?"

"What?"

"That whooshing sound." He'd point to his yard. "That's the sound of our Florida grass growing."

It seemed almost true. After West Palm Beach's record-breaking March rain, the grass was growing even faster than usual. Connor could pay someone to cut it; lots of pilots did. But what fun was that? Besides, he liked spending time in the yard. Easy, monotonous downtime. Quiet enough to give his mind the rest it needed after a week of flying commercial aircrafts.

It was 10:50 when he climbed into his silver Tundra and tapped the horn. He leaned his head out the window. "Come on, girls"—his fingers tapped out a rhythm on the steering wheel—"party starts in five minutes."

Elizabeth and Susan were ten and eight that spring, as different from each other as he and Michele had been when they first met. Elizabeth, their firstborn, was sweet-spoken and demure, a child whose favorite activities included playing tea party with her three baby dolls. Elizabeth lived in dresses and ribbons and lace, and wanted her hair curled even on play days.

Susan was supposed to be a boy from the beginning. The ultrasound technician told them so halfway through Michele's pregnancy. "Yes sir"—the man grinned across the room at Connor—"looks like you got yourself a healthy little boy."

The boy part turned out to be Susan's umbilical cord. She was born with a lusty scream and hadn't quieted down since. Keeping Susan's hair brushed and her clothes clean was a full-time job, and with Michele already busy running a home hair salon, she had long since stopped trying.

Connor was secretly glad. If he couldn't have the son he'd always dreamed of—and Michele was adamant about not having more children—at least he had Susan. Pigtailed Susan to toss a ball with or play Ping-Pong with or take to spring training games when the major league baseball teams flocked to Florida.

Connor had been an only boy growing up. He had sisters who were younger than him, but his days were spent playing football and basketball, hanging with his teammates, and surrounding himself with guy things. College had been more of the same. Guy games and guy talk and guy silliness on evenings and weekends— right up until graduation, when he met Michele.

He cupped his hands around his mouth. "Girls! I'm *leaving*." He sat back and released a burst of air. Nice threat, but it meant nothing. He couldn't go to the party without the girls, and he'd never been able to keep them from running late. They were Michele's daughters, after all.

Then, in a sudden blur, they flew out the door. Susan led the way, leggy and grinning, a present tucked under her arm. *Crazy girl.* Connor grinned. *She looks like a pee-wee running back, bent for the end zone.*

Elizabeth was behind her, skipping with dainty steps, a present clutched to her chest. Her hair was curled, and she smiled at him, mouthing a quick apology as they made their way to the truck. First one, then the other piled into the backseat, and the air filled with breathless giggles.

"Sorry, Daddy."

"Yeah, sorry." Susan followed Elizabeth's lead. "It's okay if we're a few minutes late."

"Let me guess." Connor stifled another smile. "Mom told you that."

"She said something else." Elizabeth dropped her chin. Her voice had that sing-song sound girls could turn on at will, and her eyes grew big—clear warning that some serious teasing was at hand.

"Yeah." Susan let loose another giggle. She covered her face with both hands. "She said to tell you she has a *crush* on you."

More laughter, and the girls began talking at the same time. Who would be at the party? What games would they play? What presents did the birthday girl really want?

Connor let his mind drift.

Michele had a crush on him, huh? A slow smile lifted the corners of his mouth and traveled up his cheeks. His heart filled with thoughts of her, his precious Michele. Her shoulder-length dark hair piled loose on top of her head, work smock smudged and smeared, a paintbrush in her hand, telling their girls she had a crush on him.

The picture took his breath away.

He backed out of the drive and headed down Oak Street toward the parkway. At the first light he gazed at the sky, the place where he spent so much of his time. Just God and him taking one planeload of people after another into the vast open sky, and bringing them safely down. Over and over and over again.

Life on earth and life above it, everything was good. No, it was better than good. These days it was more than he'd dreamed. He had a family that played together and laughed together—a family where they actually liked each other—and a relationship with his wife that made other men openly jealous.

He turned again and pulled into the left lane.

Michele wasn't rail thin the way a lot of pilots' wives were. She wasn't heavy, either. Medium, she liked to say, with enough extra to give her a few curves. Once in a while she'd go on a diet or exercise kick, determined to lose twenty pounds. But she'd been the same size since Elizabeth was born. Most of the time she seemed content to stay that way.

Connor didn't care. He wouldn't change a thing about her. Besides, overly thin women didn't age well. Michele was vibrant and full of life, with a beauty that went beyond her pretty looks. Without question she was the brightest spot in his life.

Six years ago he'd paid a contractor to build an addition on the back of their house, a place where Michele could work magic on the hairstyles of church friends and neighbor women. The idea had paid off in every way. She was home each day for the girls and had enough energy and desire to love him long after the girls were in bed.

"We're almost there, Daddy!" Susan clapped her hands.

"Yep, two blocks." Connor glanced over his shoulder and smiled at her.

Though more rough-and-tumble than her sister, Susan was the mirror image of Michele. Michele, the woman who had made him forget his plan to not fall in love until he was twenty-five, the woman who walked into his life and in two weeks showed him more about love than he'd understood in a lifetime.

She was bright and witty, charming and sensuous. A woman who cared for him and the girls ahead of any part of her career. And running her in-house salon was definitely a career. A quiet chuckle made its way up and past his lips. He shook his head as he saw a driveway ahead anchored by pink balloons. Michele would debate anyone who thought hairstyling less than a career.

She was feisty that way. Feisty and funny and his best friend. The past few years she'd made a decent income, as well. Enough to pay for twice-a-year vacations: exotic Disney cruises with the girls or visits to exclusive dude ranches, and intimate vacations for just the two of them to places like Bora Bora and Tahiti and the South of France.

Yes, he had a crush on Michele, too. He'd have to tell her so later that evening.

"Okay, girls. Mrs. Reed will take you to the next party."

"And you'll get us after that." Elizabeth gave him a coy smile. "Right?"

"Right."

Connor pulled into a familiar driveway, the house where the party girl lived. A cluster of little girls poured from the front door of the house, jumping and waving and squealing. Elizabeth and Susan blew Connor kisses and scrambled out of the car.

He was five minutes down the road when it happened.

Stopped at a red light, he watched a burgundy sedan come up behind him in the adjacent lane. The car wasn't speeding, but it wasn't slowing down, either. Without stopping, without giving Connor any chance to intervene, the car careened through the red light and straight into the side of a white minivan.

"God ... no ..." His prayer came an instant too late.

The crash was horrific, louder than anything Connor could remember. A cloud of glass and metal and car pieces filled the air above the intersection and then settled across the roadway like fallout from a bomb. Connor was out of his car before the mini-van came to a stop.

His assessment of the scene was second nature, the kind of thing he'd learned in the military. *Okay, Evans, locate the victims . . . iden-tify the serious injuries . . . figure out the level of help needed.* He raced up to the burgundy sedan and peered inside. Just one person, the driver, and he looked unconscious.

But what about the minivan? Minivans held children, didn't they?

He tore across the intersection, squinting to see through the tinted windows. The impact was on the driver's side, so he went around and flung open the sliding passenger's door. Only then did he see that the woman and teenage boy inside were alive and mov-ing around. Side-door airbags had inflated upon impact and prob-ably saved their lives.

"You okay?" Connor had his cell phone open. He dialed 9-1-1 before the woman could answer.

"I . . . I think so." The woman rubbed her neck and began to cry. "Did he run the red?"

"Yes. Never even slowed down." He held the phone to his ear and waited while it rang. "I'll check on him."

Other cars were stopping now, people getting out and milling about. As the emergency operator answered, he heard a woman behind him scream. "He's not breathing! Someone help!"

"Nine-one-one, what's your emergency?"

Connor explained the situation as he jogged toward the bur-gundy sedan. "One of the victims isn't breathing. Please hurry."

He snapped the phone shut and worked his way past the few people standing near the driver's door. Being a pilot didn't make him a paramedic, but he knew CPR. If the man wasn't breathing . . .

"He's dying," the woman shouted. "His chest isn't moving!"

"Excuse me!" Connor made a final shove toward the car. "Please . . ."

The screaming woman stepped back, and for the first time Connor got a clear view of the old man's face. As he did, he felt his blood drain from his face. "Dear God . . ." His voice was a whisper, and he froze. "It can't be . . ."

His father lived on the other side of the country, but for a fraction of a second he was certain the man lying motionless behind the wheel was his dad. The woman behind him yelled something again, and it snapped Connor into motion.

The man wasn't his father; it wasn't possible.

Connor grabbed the man's limp wrist and felt for his pulse. Nothing. A fine layer of sweat broke out across the top of his forehead. The man's face was already turning gray, but still the resemblance to Connor's father was striking. In quick, jerky movements Connor slid his thumb from one spot on the man's arm to another, and finally to his neck. Still no pulse.

He placed the back of his hand near the man's mouth and nose, but felt no movement of air. Everything he knew about emergency treatment at an accident scene told him not to move a victim. But this man was either dying or dead. Connor spun around and brushed back the crowd. "We need space." Then he hoisted the man into his arms and moved toward the sidewalk.

A few yards away an ambulance pulled up and behind it a fire truck. The sirens must've been sounding for a while but Connor hadn't noticed anything but the face of the man in his arms. A face he'd been running from for—

"Step back, please." A paramedic set down his bag, and Connor did as he was told.

Three steps away, he stood mesmerized by the scene, watching the team of paramedics work on the old man, pounding on his chest, forcing oxygen into his lungs. Ten minutes passed, then fifteen. Finally they gave up.

"Heart attack," one of them said. "Dead before the impact."

They pulled a sheet over the man's body, and everything seemed to slow down. The branches in the trees lining the streets stirred in the early afternoon breeze; one by one the onlookers returned to their cars. The drama was over; the guy was dead.

A police officer tapped Connor on the shoulder. "Move along."

Connor nodded, but his eyes were glued to the lifeless form beneath the tarp. Was this how the scene would look when his father died, some not-so-far-off day? Gone without warning, no family around even to identify his body?

He took his time heading back, and skipped Home Depot. Michele was on a stool working an off-shade of yellow onto the kitchen wall. The cordless phone was tucked between her shoulder and her cheek, and she was saying something about the school carnival in May.

"That's why we buy the tickets early, the savings is unbelievable." Pause. "Yes, I'm telling you, have her call the school office and . . ."

Connor stopped listening.

Pungent paint fumes filled the room. He took the seat at the kitchen table closest to Michele's stool and locked eyes on the back of her head. She hadn't heard him come in, but at the sound of the chair she spun around and waved her paintbrush at him. She gave him a crooked grin, rolled her eyes, and pointed to the phone.

Normally at this sort of moment, he'd find a way to rescue her, yell that he needed her or that someone was at the door. But he couldn't bring himself to do it. He smiled at her with his eyes as he sat back and waited.

"Okay, Sally, right . . . yes . . ." She glanced at him over her shoulder again. "Mm-hm, Connor's home. Okay, gotta go."

She hung up, balanced the paintbrush on the can, and took a slow step down from the stool. "Connor . . ."

"Hi." He met her eyes and saw her concern. He dropped his gaze to the floor. If only he could shake the image of the man's face, but he couldn't. Not when the resemblance was so striking.

"What is it, baby?" She came to him, touching his face as she pulled up a chair. "You look awful."

He lifted his eyes to hers again. "I just watched a guy die."

"*What?*" Her eyes grew wide and she took hold of his arm.

A slow breath filled Connor's lungs and the story spilled out. He told her about the burgundy sedan, about the deafening impact.

"The people in the minivan were fine." He lifted one shoulder and tried to sound unaffected. "But the old guy in the sedan . . . he was dead before they hit. Heart attack."

Michele searched his face, clearly looking for more.

"It wasn't the accident." Connor let his head hang, and with his free hand he massaged the muscles at the base of his neck. Not even international flights left him this tense.

"Okay." Michele slid her hand down his arm and wove her fingers between his. "What is it?"

He looked up once more. "The guy was a ringer for my dad, Michele. He looked just like him."

She ran her tongue over her lower lip. "He wouldn't be here, would he?"

"No." Connor rested his forearms on the table. "It wasn't him. But for a minute . . ."

Silence joined them at the table and dominated the conversation. Michele released his hand and stood, studying him, an odd sadness in her gaze. Connor knew what she was going to say before she said it.

"Maybe this is God's way, a reason to call him and—"

"Don't!" He regretted the sharp word as soon as it left his mouth. A low moan escaped him, and he felt like an eighty-year-old man as he struggled to his feet. For a long time he faced her, hating himself for the fresh pain in her eyes.

She took the slightest step backwards. "You never even hear me, Connor." Tears glistened in her lower lashes. "The man's your father."

"The man's a stranger."

"Because you let him be."

"No." His voice rose a notch. "Because he wants to be."

She pressed the palm of her hand against her forehead and grabbed at her hair with her other hand. Her words were a desperate hiss. "I *hate* this."

He hated it, too. He watched her and wanted to say so, wanted to tell her how awful the whole mess made him feel. How he hated the silence and bitterness and empty, wasted years. Hated the way his own father hadn't cared enough to call any of them, not even the girls. But he could say nothing, really. He knew better than to involve Michele. Her thoughts on the issue were too simple. *He's your father,* she'd told him a hundred times in the past eight years. *Call him and tell him you love him.*

But he couldn't; and after this long, he simply wouldn't. Even if the image of the dead man in the burgundy sedan stayed with him all month.

Michele wiped her hands on her smock and used her shoulder to dab away a tear. She narrowed her eyes and stared at him, straight to the most dank, dark places of his soul. "Life is short; one of these days it'll be too late."

He worked the muscles in his jaw, then let it go. Holding out his hands, he took slow, tentative steps toward her. "Ah, baby, I'm sorry." They came together in an embrace, and Connor breathed in the fragrance of her shampoo. "It's not your fault."

"But you won't call, right?"

"We've been through this." His voice fell flat. He shouldn't have told her about the accident; no matter what the dead man looked like, there would be no phone call to the West Coast. "Let it go, okay?"

Discouragement filled her eyes, but she held his gaze. "Okay."

He could hear that it wasn't, but he wouldn't push the issue. It was one thing to have no relationship with his father, but Michele … ? She was everything to him. He drew back and glanced at his watch.

"Errands?" The question, though it rang with sadness, was her way of saying she wouldn't dwell on the topic. They'd learned at least that much in the past eight years.

"Yep." He grabbed his truck keys from the kitchen table.

She stepped back onto the stool and faced him. "Don't be long."

"I won't." Connor grabbed a glass of water, downed it, and made his way across the kitchen. "I still need the mower."

For an instant she only looked at him, her eyes deep and thoughtful. As she turned away she said, "You need a father, too."

Her words were so soft, Connor almost didn't hear them. A hundred replies flashed in his mind, but he chose the safest one. "I love you, Michele."

With that he was out the door.

Not until he got in his truck did he realize he'd been shaking. He started the ignition. What a way to kill a Saturday. Even buying a riding mower wouldn't make him happy in light of the skeletons that had come to life that day.

As he was pulling out of the driveway he turned on the radio. Country music. That's what he needed. Garth Brooks or Kenny Chesney or Tim McGraw. Something to wash away the grimy residue of his past, to remind him his yesterdays counted for nothing. All that mattered was today. Today and tomorrow and every minute of the future he and Michele and the girls had ahead of them. It was still a brilliant spring day. Maybe an hour or two on a riding mower would right his world, after all. A song ended and the deejay came on.

"Investigation continues into yesterday's plane crash in the Pacific. Today the FAA released a—"

Connor turned up the volume. What had the man said? A plane had crashed into the ocean?

"—report that the fuselage was found broken apart in relatively shallow ocean waters. A team of divers is looking for the cockpit's black box to determine whether pilot error was to blame. Western Island Air Flight No. 45 from Honolulu to Tokyo crashed minutes after takeoff. Witnesses said the aircraft lost speed and then nose-dived into the Pacific. One hundred eighty-eight passengers and crew were aboard the flight. Search and rescue officials fear there are no survivors."

He jerked the wheel and pulled off to the side of the road. What was *with* this day? First the guy in the burgundy sedan, and now this? A plane crash? Nearly two hundred people lost somewhere in the Pacific?

He'd never worked Western Island Airlines, so he wouldn't have known any of the crew. Even so . . . he pictured a 747 plummeting to the ground, nose first, and he shuddered. Pilot error. It had to be pilot error. Birds that big didn't fall from the sky.

His heart raced and he gritted his teeth. *Get a grip, Evans. These things happen.*

A constant stream of scenarios raced through his mind. A missed switch or an incorrect setting. Yes, it had to be pilot error. He gripped the steering wheel and studied his knuckles, his hands. How horrible would it be for those same hands to be at the controls of a nose-diving aircraft? How awful not to be able to pull out of it?

Almost at the same time the statistics began shouting the truth through the hallways of his subconscious.

Come on, Evans, thirty thousand Americans fly every day . . .

Connor relaxed his grip on the steering wheel. Of course they did. Hundreds of flights took off each hour across the world without incident, day after day, week after week, month after month, and most of the time, year after year. Flying wasn't only safer than driving, it was safer than riding a bike. Safer than swimming or football or rock climbing. A person was more likely to choke to death on airline food than to die in a plane crash.

"Have mercy on them, God." As he whispered the words, his heartbeat settled into a normal rhythm. Tomorrow at the airport he would find the list of missing crew members, just in case he recognized any names, guys he'd known at West Point, maybe. But even then, he couldn't dwell on the crash.

It was one aircraft, one mistake.

At least it wasn't his airline. After so many years of flying, he knew many of the pilots and flight attendants. A loss like yesterday's crash within his own airline would definitely cost him a few friends.

As he pulled into Home Depot he dismissed thoughts about the crash and set his mind to the task at hand. Picking out a decent riding mower.

Over the next few hours he found his machine, brought it home, and took down the grass in the backyard; then he picked up the girls from the party and listened to a thirty-minute replay of the birthday girls' reactions to Elizabeth and Susan's gifts. By then Connor had forgotten everything bad about the day.

The car accident, the old man. Even the plane crash.

All he could think about was how wonderful his life was, and how much he hoped it would go on this way forever.

THREE

Something was wrong. Max knew it as soon as he came home from school.

Ramey was waiting for him at the bus stop and she had Buddy with her. At first he felt his heart get extra happy at the sight of that old dog because the two of them were bestest friends. He ran off the bus and wrapped his arm around Buddy's neck.

But halfway home from the bus stop, Max noticed a funny feeling in his stomach, the same kind of feeling he had when one time he ate an old cheese stick from his backpack. Sort of mixed up and jumpy and sickish all at once. And he knew why he felt that way.

Ramey never brought Buddy with her to the bus stop.

Buddy stayed home in his own backyard with lots of food and water, waiting for Max and his mom to come home.

"Can't he stay with me at Ramey's?" Max asked his mom over and over.

"No! You ask a hundred times each month and the answer's still no, Max. Ramey can't have dogs at her apartment."

Max wasn't sure about the hundred times. More like eighteen or nineteen. But ... if Ramey wasn't allowed to have dogs in her apartment, how come Buddy came to the bus stop with her today? And how come he stayed for dinner and had his food bowl in the backyard?

Those were questions he thought about all evening while Ramey talked on the phone.

"Here," she told him. "Watch a movie. I'll be right in."

"Can I watch TV? TV's better than a movie because it's educational. Mommy told me that."

Ramey made a face he hadn't seen before. "No, Max. No TV. Not today. We'll watch a movie together."

"Okay."

Ramey looked strange in her eyes, the way his friend Wilton looked when he forgot his bike at the pool and someone stoled it. Scared and mad and not sure what to do. Ramey grabbed the top video from the stack and pushed it into the VCR. There was no school tomorrow, so staying up late was okay. Max found his favorite spot on the fluffy purple couch, and when Buddy climbed up beside him, Ramey didn't say a thing.

She didn't join them, either.

Instead she kept her voice in a whisper and sometimes her cheeks looked wet. Was she crying? Max tried to listen to what she was saying, but most of the time the video was too loud.

He did hear a couple of things, though. "What am I supposed to do?" And "I won't say anything until there's proof."

The movie was *All Dogs Go to Heaven*, and Max watched it with the side of his face against Buddy's. Every few minutes Max checked to make sure Buddy was watching it, but halfway through the movie the dog fell asleep. And Ramey stayed on the phone the whole time.

When the movie was over, Ramey put on another show. *Peter Pan, Part II*. She brought Max a meat sandwich and milk to eat in the TV room. Max's funny feeling got worse. Ramey *never* let him eat in the TV room.

Finally, when the second movie was over, Max walked up to Ramey and tapped her on the shoulder. She was still on the phone. Her eyes had little black lines running under them.

"Yes, Max? Do you need another movie?" She used her whisper voice.

"No." Max whispered back. "I need my mom. See?" He pointed out the window. "See how it's dark out there, Ramey? That's when my mommy's supposed to call, only what if she can't call because you're on the phone?"

Ramey stared at him, and little bits of water spilled into her eyes. She did a big sniff. "Max, we'll talk about that in a minute."

He pushed out his bottom lip and walked with slow feet back to Buddy. "Hey, Buddy, wake up." Max gave him a light shake near his old red collar. "Wake up, boy."

Buddy lifted one eyelid, then the other. Max put his face up close against Buddy's nose and waited until the dog licked his cheek. Then Max put his fingers on either side of Buddy's wet nose. "I'm telling you, Buddy . . . something's funny here."

The dog tilted his head to the side and gave Max another lick.

Just then Ramey came up to him. She looked old and tired, and her face was reddish. "Max, your mom can't call you tonight."

A scared feeling came into Max. A goldfish feeling. One time he and his mom watched a show about people who ate live goldfish.

"I bet they wiggle around in those tummies for a long time," Max had told her.

That's how he felt now. Like maybe ten or eleven goldfish were wiggling in his stomach. He let go of Buddy and stood up straight and tall. The way his mommy liked him to stand. "How come?"

"Because something's come up, and she can't call, that's why."

The goldfish wriggled around some more. "Why?"

"I don't know, Max. We just have to wait." Ramey came and sat down on the edge of the sofa in front of where he was standing. Then she hugged him the way she did once when his turtle died.

Max stood stiff and scared. "Is she going to call me tomorrow? Before she flies?"

"I hope so." Ramey's voice sounded disappointed. Like she didn't really think his mom would call then, either.

Max pulled back and sat down. All of a sudden he didn't want to think about getting a phone call from his mom. Buddy jumped off the couch and lay down on the floor in front of him. Max patted his head. "Good boy, Buddy. It's okay."

Ramey let Max sleep on the couch that night, him on the top and Buddy on the floor beneath. But no TV; definitely no TV. In the morning Ramey came to him and reached out for his hand. He liked Ramey a lot because she was sort of like family. But he didn't like holding hands with her. Her hands were roughish. Plus, she wasn't his mom.

"Max, I have something to tell you."

He sat up and rubbed his eyes because sleep was still in him. Ramey sat next to him, and he noticed her eyelids were thick. The way his teacher's eyelids looked when kids in Room 8 gave her flowers. *Allergy*, teacher called it. Maybe Ramey had allergy, too.

A long breath came out of Ramey. "Your mom isn't coming home, Max."

He sat up a little straighter. "What?" Why would she say that? Ramey was wrong. "Only two days away. She promised."

Ramey moved her head with little shakes. "No, Max. Something happened. Your mommy isn't coming home ever again. Not ever."

The goldfish feeling was back, but this time he was mad, too. Very mad. "*No*, Ramey!" Next to him Buddy did a little bark. "Don't say that. She's coming home today. Before dinner!"

Teardrops started coming down Ramey's cheeks. She sat on the couch and put her hands over her face. "Help me do this!"

Max wasn't sure what to say. Buddy was sitting up now, watching Ramey the same way Max was. Max didn't want to be angry, but every time he let go of the mad, a scared feeling came. A big scared feeling that made him want to run out the door and straight home.

Finally Ramey lowered her hands. "Come here, Max."

He didn't want to do it, but he had to. Gentlemen obeyed grown-ups. His mother taught him that. His feet dragged across the carpet until he was standing near Ramey's knees.

She took hold of his shoulders and looked straight at his eyes. "Max . . . your mom is dead." A crying sound came from Ramey. "Jesus . . . Jesus took her to heaven to live with him."

Max jerked back hard and fast and shook his head. Ramey never lied to him before, never. But his mom wasn't dead. She kissed him good-bye yesterday morning and he saw for himself. She wasn't dead; she was alive. Very, very alive. "No, Ramey . . . you're wrong." He backed up and ran quick into the bathroom and shut the door. Then he pressed his back against it so no one could get inside.

His breathing was fast and hard like when he raced Jimmy Jackson at recess. He squeezed his eyes shut and told his brain to think fast. Why would Ramey say that thing? His mommy was fine, she wasn't sick or old or anything. Jesus didn't take her to heaven. She was in Tokyo, that's all. Same as always.

His breathing got slower. She would call any minute.

Then a very awful idea popped into his heart and made his eyes sting. What if something bad happened to her airplane? Like maybe the wings fell off, or a door blew open? Or the pilot landed in the water? One time he asked her about airplane doors. "If someone opens the door, what happens?"

"You can't open the door when the plane's flying, Max. It isn't possible."

"But if someone did, couldn't you fall out?"

"I guess." She did a little laugh at him. "But that won't happen. Airplanes are super safe, okay?"

He asked her a few more times, but she always told him the same thing. Planes were safe. Wings didn't fall off, doors didn't blow open, and pilots never landed in the water. Never.

A knock came against the door and Max felt it push against his back.

"Max . . . open up. Please." Ramey wasn't crying anymore, but scared was in her voice. Scared and nervous and not sure what to do.

Now that the idea was in his head, he couldn't make it go away. What if something bad *did* happen to his mom's airplane? What if she didn't know it could happen, but it could? He stepped away from the door and opened it slow and careful. Then he peeked out at Ramey and he was all of a sudden afraid to ask.

His mom's words whispered in his heart. *Be brave, Max ... whenever you're afraid be brave.* He did a swallow and straightened his shoulders. "Ramey, did ... did something bad happen to her airplane?"

She did a little nod with her head. "Yes, Max. Something real bad."

His eyes got stingers in them again, and his throat stuck together the way it did when he ate pancakes too fast. "Did the wings fall off?"

"No." Ramey opened the door a little bit more, and Buddy stuck his nose through the space. "It landed in the water, Max." Ramey's cheeks had wet on them again. "It never made it to Tokyo."

It never made it? A broken feeling grabbed Max's heart, and his knees felt rubbery. "They landed in water?"

"Yes, Max." Ramey made a crying sound again. She pulled him close and hugged him to her big, gray dress. "I'm so sorry, honey."

"Mommy said airplanes never land in water." He pushed back and looked at her again.

"They usually don't. But this time, well ... something must've happened. Max ... she didn't make it, honey."

"But Mommy knows how to swim, Ramey. Maybe she's swimming back to the island."

Ramey looked up and made her eyes shut tight. Then she said, "Please ... I can't do this."

Max tugged on her sleeve. "Is she swimming, Ramey? Is she?" Max couldn't take a breath until Ramey answered him. "We could help her; it's not too late."

"No." Ramey's body made a shaking move and for a long time she didn't talk. "She's dead, Max. Everyone on the plane died."

"But maybe she isn't dead . . . maybe she's in there and she needs someone to help her out." He started to run for the front door, but Ramey caught him.

"She's not in the ocean anymore, Max." Her face was wet, and the skin around her eyes was even thicker than before. "She's in heaven. With Jesus."

Max couldn't run or move or even breathe. His mom was dead? Her plane landed in the ocean, and now she was in heaven? His legs crumpled under, and he fell to his hands and knees. "No, Ramey! She can't go. Not without me . . ."

His eyes got blurry and tears started coming down his face. More tears than he'd ever had in all his life. How could Mommy be gone? Who would read to him and hug him and love him now? Who would make him blueberry pancakes for breakfast and get him dressed in the morning and take him to the park for roller-skate lessons? Who would sing him his special song about *I love you, Max, the most, I love to make you toast*?

Buddy came up beside him and licked his face.

"Go away, Buddy."

The dog stepped back and lay down. He had sad in his eyes, and Max felt bad for yelling at him. Buddy must've known about Mommy's plane landing in the water. But why couldn't someone get her out of the plane and bring her home? "Mom!" His voice was loud and scared, so wherever she was she might hear it. Even all the way to heaven.

Ramey put her arm around him and sat him on the couch. She sat beside him and hugged him for a long time. They cried and cried together, and the more Max thought about it, the more true it felt.

His mommy was dead. She really was.

He knew, because a hole was in his heart now. A big hole where his mommy used to be. His whole self must've been filled with tears because they spilled out from his eyes without stopping. For Ramey, too. And he couldn't understand that, because it was *his* mom who died, that's why. After a long time, Ramey told him, "Let's pray."

Pray wasn't something Ramey did, but he and Mommy did it all the time. Ramey prayed before they ate sometimes, but that was all. She didn't know the other things about God, like that He lived in heaven, Max was pretty sure about that. But now God wasn't the only one there, because his mommy had joined Him. Max wiped his hands across his cheeks.

All he needed was a map and he could go there, too. Maybe Ramey could look it up on the Internet. But until then, God would have to tell his mommy how he was feeling. He knew about praying, but he wasn't sure about messages. "Could God give Mommy a message for me?"

"Yes, Max." Ramey bit her lip and her chin got jiggly. "If there's a God, somehow He'll tell your mom."

"Is there a God?" Max wanted to be sure. He always thought so; Mommy always told him so. But he didn't want to give Him a message if He wasn't real.

"God . . ." Ramey's eyes were closed again. Her voice was extra quiet. "Where are you?" Ramey's head bent down. Crying came over her for a minute and then she looked up and did a couple nods. "Yes, Max. There is a God. Even on a day like this."

"Okay, then." Max folded his hands together the way he and his mommy always did. But sad filled his mouth and he couldn't talk. *Mommy . . . Mommy, where are you? Come back to me, please . . .* The words stayed in his mouth. A missing feeling came all through him. He didn't just miss her in his heart and in his head, but his arms missed her and his hands and his feet. Because after today he wouldn't hug her or swing hands with her or walk beside her. Not ever again.

"Max?" Ramey put her hand over his two smaller ones. "Want me to say it?"

"No, thank you." He wanted God to hear the message straight from him. He did a little sniff. "God, hi, it's Max." He moved a little in his seat because he had never asked God to give a message before. "Ramey says my mommy's with You now, so can You tell her something for me?" He waited, in case God wanted to say something back. When he heard no words, he started again. "Tell her I'm sorry I wasn't there when her plane landed in the water, because I would've helped her out. Me and her coulda swimmed to the island, and she wouldn't have to live in heaven."

The missing feeling got worse, and he remembered his mom's face.

Be brave, Max . . . be brave.

Max sat a little straighter. "But I guess now it's too late, so will You tell her something else, God, please? Tell her I'm being good for Ramey and that Buddy says hi." Buddy made a little whiny sound. "And tell her to sing me our special song, 'I Love You, Max, the Most,' tonight before she goes to bed." He wasn't sure how to finish. "Thank You, God. I'll think of more stuff later."

It wasn't until that night when he and Buddy were in bed that Max realized something. If the plane would've landed on the ground like it was supposed to, his mom would've been home by now. She'd be in his room, sitting on his bed and singing him his song.

But if God gave her the message, then maybe she was singing it right now. He thought about that for a minute. Maybe she was waiting for him to sing it with her. His throat felt like a frog was in it, so he did a loud cough.

Buddy looked up, and his ears got pointy.

"It's okay, boy." Max patted Buddy's head and gave it a light push back down toward the bed. "Go to sleep."

Buddy made a soft breath on Max's arm, and a tired sound rattled in his neck. Then he dropped down his head like a good dog. That's when Max began to hum just a little. Finally the words came, too. The words to their special song. He circled his arm around Buddy's neck and sang them soft as a buzzing fly.

"I love you, Max, the most, I love to make you toast. When oceans we're apart . . . you're always in my heart."

The humming part didn't sound the same without his mom, but it made the hole in Max's heart feel smaller. Even if his hum was in a whisper voice. Because if his mom was singing their song somewhere in heaven, then they were together sort of. The song had hand motions, which meant he could sing it with his voice and his words and his hands, the way he and Mommy always sang it.

First his hands over his heart, then one hand open like a pretend bread, and one hand brushing back and forth like a pretend butter knife, the way his mom made him toast each morning. Then big arms for the ocean, and last, hands back over his heart.

He started again, but his eyes felt watery, so he didn't do the hand motions. They were only fun when he and his mommy were in the same room. It wasn't the same if she was in heaven.

"I love you, Max, the most . . . I love to make you toast. When oceans we're apart—"

Just then he stopped because he remembered a P.S. for God. Mommy told him about P.S. It's when you write a note and add something at the very end, something 'portant you forgot.

"God?" He whispered. His throat was sticky, and the hole in his heart was big again. Bigger than before. "God, if You're there, it's me, Max."

Buddy stretched out against him and did a huffy sound. His nose was cold and wet against Max's arm.

"God, I forgot a P.S." Max blinked in the dark room and ran his fingers into Buddy's warm fur. Buddy had been next to him all day because Buddy missed Mommy, too, that's why. Ramey was nice, but Buddy was all the family Max had left now. He heard Ramey say that to someone on the phone during lunch. "Please, God, tell my mom I'm going to talk to Ramey tomorrow about heaven. Because I'm not sure how to get there, God. But if Mommy's going to live there, I want to live there, too. Really soon, okay?"

When Max finally fell asleep with his arm around Buddy, he dreamed about airplanes landing in water and a place called heaven where they could all be together. Him and Mommy and Buddy. The way a family should be.

Forever and ever and ever.

FOUR

Ramey couldn't stop the flow of memories. They came to her constantly, bits and pieces of Kiahna's life, information that Ramey had to rely on now that Kiahna was gone.

Just weeks before Max was born, Kiahna sat Ramey down and told her what to do if one day she didn't come home.

"Let's talk about death." Kiahna rested her hands on her extended abdomen and leveled her gaze at Ramey.

"Stop." Ramey had brushed her off, not sure Kiahna was serious. "This is your season of life. Don't talk like that; you scare me."

But Kiahna didn't let up. "Ramey, I mean it. If anything ever happens to me, you need to know what to do."

Ramey looked at the young woman for a moment and finally nodded. "Okay. Tell me."

The plan was simple. Kiahna had written a brief will and a note for her unborn son. The two documents were being kept by an attorney on the island, someone Kiahna had paid to handle things in an emergency.

"What about the boy's father?"

Kiahna's expression shut down like a bank at closing time. "No. You must not ask about him."

Ramey never asked again. Whoever the man was, he'd hurt Kiahna deeply. The girl was beautiful inside and out, half Irish, half Hawaiian, leggy with tan skin, pale green eyes, and a heart deeper than the waters off Honolulu. But the only men allowed access to that heart were God and Max. Always Max.

Ramey used to dream about finding Max's father and shaking him, asking him if he knew what he was missing by leaving Kiahna pregnant and alone. Max was an amazing boy, a child filled with awe and wonder, very much in need of a father.

At first, when Max was a baby, Ramey would ask Kiahna whether she was meeting anyone worth dating. "Every time I think of that boy I see a father in his future," Ramey would say. "With all those businessmen and pilots you work with, one of them must be worth smiling at."

Kiahna's features would take on a faraway look. She would give a few subtle shakes of her head, and that was as far as the conversation went. By the time Max was three, Kiahna told her it wasn't a daddy the boy needed. It was a Father. A heavenly Father. Kiahna grew up in a church, but that year her faith became doubly important because of Max. She wanted him to know everything about living a life for God.

But when Kiahna tried to share her faith, Ramey bristled. "It's all a fantasy, Kiahna. It's okay for you, but keep it to yourself."

"I won't ask you about God, if you don't ask me about men."

Ramey planted her hands on her hips. "Deal."

Every now and then, though, Ramey found a way to bring the forbidden subject up to Kiahna.

"Look, I have God and Max." She'd give Ramey a shrug and a sweet smile. "That's enough for now."

Ramey got the point, but that didn't stop her from mentioning a single man down at the grocery store, or another one out by the pool. Kiahna's response was always the same. There would be no men in her life except for her son.

A handful of years passed, and Ramey's own two children moved to the mainland and rarely made it back for visits. Ramey still had a heart full of love, so she opened a day care in her home. Six children came every day after school, but Max was the only one who sometimes spent the night. When he turned five, Ramey was too ill and too tired to care for so many children. She kept only Max, and she realized something about the boy.

He felt like her own.

Now she was sixty-eight with heart disease, diabetes, poor circulation, and failing eyesight. With Kiahna gone, whatever Max's future held Ramey wanted very much to be part of it. But she couldn't be the only part. Max was an active child, a boy who learned from Kiahna on the sidewalk outside their apartment how to throw a spiral pass, one who raced his mother down the beach and took bike rides with her on lesser-known island trails.

Ramey's body simply didn't have that much left to give.

So it was, first thing Monday morning, three days after the tragedy, Ramey was on the phone with Kiahna's attorney, hoping against hope that whatever financial plan the documents held for Max, they also contained some type of physical plan.

Ramey wasn't sure what she was hoping for. That Kiahna had a long-lost sister maybe, or an aunt or uncle. Someone who cared enough to step in and be a family for Max. The receptionist at the attorney's office had her on hold, but that didn't bother Ramey. She would've waited all day if it meant helping Max. Poor baby. He and Buddy had been practically attached at the ankle since Saturday morning, and several times she'd found Max sitting at the foot of his bed, knees drawn up, face buried in his arms.

Sobbing and calling in quiet desperation for his mama.

Today was the first morning Ramey woke up dry-eyed, but she had no doubt there'd be more sadness before the day was done. She held the receiver close to her ear.

"Hello, this is Marv Ogle."

Ramey steadied herself. Never . . . never had she thought she'd have to make this call. Back when Max was born it had seemed impossible that Kiahna would ever be anything but the boy's mom, young and alive and driven by faith. "Hello, Mr. Ogle. Kiahna Seifert is a client of yours, I believe."

"Kiahna?" The man's voice softened. "Yes . . . she's a client."

"Well . . ." Ramey swallowed. She had the feeling Kiahna had been more than a client to this man. Perhaps she had even been a friend. "I have some bad news, Mr. Ogle." She closed her eyes for a moment. "Kiahna was killed in Friday's plane crash. She . . . she was a flight attendant."

A moment passed while the man recovered. "Are you sure?"

"Yes."

The attorney moaned, and his voice cracked when he spoke again. "I was worried. I heard about the crash and looked for a victim list, but the papers haven't printed it yet."

"No." Ramey blinked back a fresh wetness in her eyes. "They're still notifying next of kin."

"You're absolutely sure?" He sighed long and slow, the way people did in hospitals and funeral parlors. "I thought she flew the Los Angeles route."

"Before Max was born." Ramey stared at her hands and saw they were shaking. "It's been Honolulu to Tokyo ever since."

Another quiet moan. "My dear Kiahna." The attorney said her name as though by itself it might have contained a thousand memories. "This was her worst fear."

"Yes, sir."

"Kiahna was like a second daughter to me."

"Oh." Ramey understood. She felt the same way. "I didn't know."

The man's voice drifted. "She and my daughter were best friends through junior high, closer than sisters. Marlee . . . she fell in with a bad crowd and when high school came around, she and Kiahna didn't spend much time together. Even then Kiahna was a friend. A sweet girl who lived out her faith every day. She . . . she would drive to parties and pull my daughter out. Then she'd come by the next morning to talk a little sense into her. She did everything possible to save my daughter from the life she'd fallen into."

The man grunted as though he was trying to gain composure. "Marlee died of alcohol poisoning the summer before her senior year. At the funeral, Kiahna hugged my wife and me and told us we were like parents to her. That if we ever wanted time with our second daughter, she'd be there."

A single teardrop pushed its way from the corner of Ramey's right eye and a warm stream of tears followed. She couldn't think of a response.

The man sucked in a quick breath. "We hadn't seen her in a while, but she came by a few months ago. Brought my wife flowers and chatted while Max ran around out back." He paused. "She loved that boy more than life."

"Yes. Yes, she did." Ramey wanted to keep sharing lovely memories of Kiahna, but the matter at hand was pressing. "Mr. Ogle, you have Kiahna's will, is that right?"

"It is." He sounded suddenly tired in light of the obvious reason for the phone call. "Two envelopes—one with her last will and testament. One with a letter for Max."

"The one she wrote before he was born?" Ramey gripped the phone a bit tighter. "She told me about it."

"No. She brought by a new one every year around Max's birthday. So the file would be current."

Ramey's heart sank a bit in her chest. The physical ache within her doubled. Why . . . why would God—if there was a God—take Kiahna when she loved her little boy so? When she was all the child had? She squeezed her eyes shut. "Mr. Ogle, Max is in my care. We need to know Kiahna's intentions." A lump formed in Ramey's throat. "The sooner the better."

Ramey heard the sound of pages flipping. "This afternoon at two o'clock, how does that look for you?"

She glanced through her sliding glass door. Max was on the small back patio, lying on the cement, his head resting on Buddy. He was in no condition to go to school, and depending on what Kiahna's letter told them, he might not return. Whatever Max's future held, a resolution was needed. She brought her thumb and forefinger to her face and massaged her temples. "Two is perfect."

The attorney hesitated. "Will Max be there?"

"Yes. He . . . he has nowhere else to go, Mr. Ogle."

"I understand." Again the man's pain resonated across the phone lines. "But some of what I'll be reading to you is very sensitive. We'll need at least some time alone. Without the boy."

A dozen thoughts competed for Ramey's attention. Kiahna's documents held something sensitive? What was it, and why hadn't she shared the information earlier? Ramey's throat grew tight again, and she heard herself begin to wheeze. An asthma attack. She'd need her inhaler within a few minutes or she'd be in trouble. She gave the attorney directions to her apartment. "Mr. Ogle"—she coughed twice—"I'll have Max play inside. We can talk on the patio."

They hung up, and Ramey found her medication. Three puffs and her airways were clear again. For now, anyway. Her doctors had told her that her health was deteriorating, succumbing to the many ailments that plagued her. Asthma was only one of them, and each was a reminder that Max had no one.

Short of becoming a ward of the state, whatever plan Kiahna spelled out in her will wouldn't be one of many options for the child.

It would be his only hope.

FIVE

Tuesday was Michele Evans's favorite day.

Though a new schedule came out each month, the airline had been giving Connor a series of short flights that started Tuesday at two o'clock in the afternoon, home again Wednesday night, out Thursday by seven in the morning, and home late Friday. The schedule allowed him weekends at home—time for yard work and backyard projects and outings with the girls.

But most of all it gave him his Tuesday mornings with Michele.

A routine had developed, one she looked forward to all week. Each Tuesday they'd get up with the girls, share hot pancakes and sausage, take Elizabeth and Susan to Lakewood Elementary School, and return home by eight-thirty. At that point they'd unplug the telephone, climb back into bed, and share the next three hours pretending time didn't matter.

A mini-vacation in the midst of a mundane week.

On Tuesdays they could be intimate without fear of the girls needing them, they could talk about the past week without interruption, and once in a while they even had time for a dip in the hot tub.

Already this Tuesday morning had been fantastic. Sunshine warm enough to leave the windows open, lovemaking that would keep a smile on both their faces at least until Connor came home Wednesday night, and a conversation that was only just getting started.

"So what exactly happened at the fair? Tell me about Elizabeth's science project." Connor rolled onto his side and studied Michele. She was propped up on two pillows, flat on her back and still beneath the covers. Her knees were pulled up, and as she grinned at him she felt a decade younger than her thirty-nine years.

"Okay"—she angled herself onto her side so they were facing each other—"remember the idea? Prove which kind of junk food ants liked best?"

"Right." He slid a few inches closer and ran his fingertips through her bangs.

"We put out ant-size piles of Oreo cookies and Butterfingers, chocolate cake and marshmallows." She raised her eyebrow at him. "Guess what happened?"

"Butterfingers?" His voice was low, soothing. The way it often was hours into their Tuesday mornings.

"Nope. They hated all of it. Elizabeth brushed strawberry jam on the cardboard so the ants would get stuck, but as of yesterday, she didn't have a single ant."

"Maybe they don't like strawberry jam?"

She grabbed a pillow and gave him a soft whack across the face. "Stop."

This was her favorite part, the moments of laughter and silliness. In some way, these times made their marriage strong, kept her more in love with Connor Evans every year. If they could play together this way, they would always be okay.

The conversation drifted from the kids to the house and finally to her hair clients.

"Renee Wagner came in yesterday."

Renee was married to a pilot who worked for Connor's airline. The two couples had been close five years ago, but over time the men took on different schedules. Renee's husband, Joe, worked international flights, so his hours almost never coincided with Connor's. Renee spent most of her hair appointment crying.

Connor stroked the day-old growth on his chin. "I haven't seen Joe in months."

Michele sat up and leaned against the headboard. "Then you don't know?"

"Know what?" Connor's eyes told her he had no idea.

A sigh slipped from Michele's throat. "They separated two weeks ago."

Connor pushed himself into a sitting position, never taking his eyes from hers. "You're kidding? Renee and Joe?"

"She was pretty broken up. I figured you would have heard at work."

He raked his fingers through his hair and shook his head. "Guys don't talk about that stuff. Not unless you're sharing a cockpit, and even then . . ."

"I guess he met someone overseas. Europe somewhere."

"Oh, man."

For the slightest instant, Michele thought she saw something in Connor's eyes. An odd flicker that was there, then gone. She didn't dwell on it. Both of them knew the score. Affairs weren't uncommon for pilots.

"I don't get it." Michele drew her legs closer to her chest. "Renee's one of the most beautiful women I know. Two little boys, and a house in the Heights." Her voice dropped some, and she searched her husband's eyes. "How could he, Connor?"

A tired sound came from him. "Simple." Connor held her eyes. "Too much time on the road."

"You're on the road and you're faithful."

"That's different." A smile filled out Connor's face once more. He caught her face in his hands and drew her close for a lingering kiss. "I've got the best marriage in the world, and the best wife, too."

Michele rubbed her nose against his—but the mood wasn't quite what it had been. "You have, right?"

Connor drew back and studied her eyes. "Have what?"

"Been faithful?" She'd never asked before, never needed to. She had no reason to ask it now, but after what happened to Renee, her heart wanted reassurance.

"Ah, Michele." He brought his hand up alongside her face and brushed her cheekbone with his thumb. "Do you have to ask?"

"No, it's just . . ."

"Baby, listen." His expression changed and suddenly she felt he was looking straight to the deepest part of her soul. "I've never loved anyone but you. Not ever."

Something in her heart relaxed, a part that for some reason had been holding its breath. "I just thought . . ." She gave him a sad smile. "After talking to Renee, I don't know. She thought everything was okay, too. I guess every now and then it's good to hear it from you."

"Michele." He let his forehead fall against hers. "You have nothing to worry about. Not now . . . not ever."

"Good." She framed his jaw with her fingertips. "Sorry for asking."

Connor glanced at the alarm clock on her bedside table. "Almost noon. I better shower." He leaned in and planted one last kiss on her cheek. Then in a single fluid movement he pushed himself off the bed and headed for the bathroom.

"Wait . . ." Michele slid to the edge of the mattress.

Connor stopped and looked back at her. "What?"

"What about the Bible? Every Tuesday, remember?"

"Right." Connor frowned. "I completely forgot."

"Me, too."

He glanced at the clock on their bedside table. "Can we start next week?"

"Sure." Michele hid her disappointment. For months they'd been meaning to get back to reading Scripture, praying together. But always time seemed to get away from them.

Connor stretched and flashed her a crooked grin. "We'll do it next week for sure . . . I promise, okay?"

"Okay." The disappointment faded. Michele studied Connor, dressed only in a pair of shorts, and was struck again by the strength of his body, the way he cared for himself. Connor Evans was a man who had once single-handedly pulled his plane out of a death spin. He liked to say he appreciated his wingmen as much as his copilots, but he never allowed himself to rely on either. And when it came to his workouts, they were an hour a day, three days a week, whatever city or hotel he happened to be in.

"My body's a tool," he'd said a hundred times. "I'm only as good as my level of physical fitness."

Michele smiled. Every aspect of her husband's life involved some type of perfection. Perfection in the cockpit, perfection at the gym, perfection in the way he doted on their girls. Even perfection in their marriage.

Michele watched him walk away until he closed the bathroom door. Only then did she realize how quickly he'd changed subjects. One minute they'd been talking about affairs and faithfulness. The next he was heading for the shower. She froze, replaying their conversation in her mind. Maybe the switch hadn't been so sudden. After all, he showered at this time every Tuesday morning, and he was nothing if not punctual. And praying and reading the Bible together would become routine too—if they could find a way to get back to it.

From inside the bathroom, she heard Connor turn on the shower, but instead of heading downstairs to make him a sandwich, she sat there, unmoving. At the center of her heart, something didn't feel right. Was it something Connor had said, the tone of his voice, maybe? Or was it simply her sorrow for Renee? A chill made its way down her arms. How would it feel to be Renee Wagner? Michele remembered something Renee said once, a year ago.

"I don't have to worry about Joe." She gave Michele an easy smile. "Some guys have cheating in their blood, but not Joe. He can't even tell when a woman's hitting on him. The last thing he'd do is have an affair."

Michele let the words play again in her mind. She could see herself nodding along, agreeing with her friend. Yes, Connor was the same type of man. The kind who could turn heads as he strode down an airport hallway, and never look anywhere but straight ahead. Good guys, safe guys. The kind that didn't cheat on their wives.

But one lonely night across the ocean in Rome, Joe tossed the rulebook out the window. An affair, one lousy affair, and now what? Eighteen years of marriage ... the family they'd spent a lifetime building ... all of it gone.

So why were Joe and Renee's troubles bothering her now? Joe and Connor were different men, weren't they? For one thing, Joe didn't have Connor's faith. Even though they didn't attend church as often as they once had, even though they couldn't make time to pray together, God was the staying power in her husband's life.

Right?

Michele stared at the closed bathroom door and a strong breeze rattled the blinds. She jumped at the sound and rose to her feet.

Enough.

She needed to get downstairs and make Connor lunch before he left. Worrying was nothing but a waste of time. What had happened to Renee would never happen to her, never. Connor was not a man given to impulsive moments, unplanned emotion. He was far too self-controlled, too sure of what he wanted from life and his future and his relationship with her and the girls. Too perfect to let himself make a mistake like that.

Not even overseas on the loneliest night of his life.

⌒

The shower had been running for five minutes before Connor's heart settled into a normal beat. What would have made Michele ask a question like that?

Had he always been faithful?

She'd never brought that up before. Never.

Water streamed down Connor's chest and arms. Had she seen anything in his reaction? A hesitation or twitch of some kind? His face must've gone pale as he scrambled for the right words. Even now he had no idea how he'd come up with a cool, quick answer.

Connor worked the shampoo through his hair and nudged the hot water knob higher, hotter. Space. That's what he needed now, space between the troubles with Joe and Renee—and the conversation with Michele. By the time he was out of the shower and dressed, Michele would forget the whole thing, and the topic of his faithfulness wouldn't come up again. Not ever. Michele was everything to him now, and never . . . never would he let himself do the thing Joe had done.

That was a lesson he'd already learned.

Suds ran down his face and chest, and the clean smell of bar soap filled the warm wet air. He loved Michele more than ever. Or maybe he'd always loved her this much. That awful night eight years ago was so far back down the road, most of the time Connor could convince himself he'd never been there at all. He was a good guy. Out of a hundred opportunities to fall, he'd been almost perfect.

Ninety-nine times perfect.

And that one time had been nothing more than crazy circumstances and strange twists of fate. Even then he hadn't been bored with Michele or wanted another woman. Michele was everything to him. As the hot water pounded his shoulder blades, Connor let the shower fill his senses and take him back, back to the days when he and Michele first met.

Six

High school romances didn't mean a thing to Connor. He was a decent football player and a starter on the basketball team, one of the socially elite who had no trouble finding a date. But Connor rarely let things get serious with any of them, not in a physical or emotional way. He dated girls one weekend and forgot about them the next. His father drilled into him the importance of studying, of setting a goal and going after it. From the beginning his goal was clear.

He would be a pilot.

After graduating he earned an appointment to West Point. In his senior year, months away from being made an officer and earning his wings, he made time for some relaxation. That's why he agreed to go to a barbecue with a group of guys from school. Connor wasn't given to reckless drinking or drug use, not so much because he was afraid of how it would make him feel, but because he was afraid of his father.

"Always be on top of your game, Son," he would say. "Keep away from the stupid things other boys do. That goes for women, too. Don't let anything take away your edge."

And Connor hadn't. Not drugs or drinking, and especially not women. Not that there had ever been a shortage. Women liked West Point students, especially seniors, and they'd made themselves available to Connor since his freshman year. His lanky, muscled body and clean-cut dark hair always turned heads, though Connor had come to think of his looks as something of a curse. Because his father was right. If he got mixed up with a girl too soon, his dedication toward becoming an officer, earning his wings, and getting in the skies would be compromised. And he wasn't about to let that happen.

But by his senior year, a barbecue seemed harmless enough.

It was at Paul Overgaard's house. Paul was also a senior, probably Connor's best friend at West Point. The two had rooms across the hall from each other, and despite the gravity of their classload, and the goal of making officer, they shared an easy sense of humor.

Paul's family lived close by, but Connor had never been to his friend's house until now. From the beginning of the party, he was certain he'd made the right choice by coming. Paul's parents' house was a palace. The backyard was spacious with a massive swimming pool and in the distance, a sand volleyball court.

He was glad he'd worn his swim shorts and a T-shirt, and as soon as introductions were over, the guys headed out to the sand pit for a three-game volleyball tournament. The competition felt wonderful—it was good to do something other than flight training and class work.

At the end of the set, his team came up losers, but Connor didn't care. The stress of upcoming finals was gone, and he ambled with the guys toward the smell of fresh-cooked hamburgers. He made up his plate, grabbed a seat with Paul and a few of his buddies, and took his first bite.

That's when he saw her.

Like a vision, she strolled out through the sliding doors. She was long legged, with a figure that made him set the burger back down on the plate. She had pale brown eyes and dark hair that fell in waves around her face and shoulders. Her laughter rang out across the patio, and when she smiled, the sun looked dim in comparison.

"What's the matter?" Paul poked him in the shoulder and followed his gaze toward the group that had just entered the backyard area. "Connor, come on. Don't be stupid."

He swallowed his bite and shook his head. "Man, she's the most beautiful girl I've ever seen."

"Don't you know?" Paul laughed and leaned back in his chair. "That's my kid sister. I've got two of them. That one's a junior at the state school an hour away." He shot her a look over his shoulder. "They're already out on break."

"Why didn't you tell me about her?"

"You never asked."

"Okay." Connor nodded, but he was in a trance. "That's fair enough." He paused, studying her. "She's home for the summer?"

"Yes." Paul chuckled. "You can go back to eating."

"Does she have a boyfriend?" Connor's eyes were still locked on Paul's sister. "Tell me she doesn't have a boyfriend."

"You have a month left, remember?" Paul gave him a kick under the table. "You told me to remind you if you ever got like this."

"That was different." He grabbed a napkin and wiped his mouth. "Introduce me."

At that moment, the girl turned and found Paul. Still talking to the friends around her, she made her way to their table and gripped her brother's shoulders from behind. But already her eyes had found Connor's. "Hey, big brother, how's school?"

Paul looked up and grinned at her. "One month left."

"What about your friend?" She motioned at Connor with her chin. Her eyes held a teasing that made it clear she was intrigued.

"Connor?"

"Okay, yes." She angled her face and her smile looked more shy than before. "What's Connor's story?"

"I've got it." Connor shot a look at Paul. Then he stood and held out his hand. "I don't think we've met. I'm Connor Evans." He could feel his eyes dancing, teasing her the way she'd been teasing him. "My story is the same as your brother's. Senior at West Point, graduating officer in a month."

"I see." She took his hand and gave it the slightest squeeze. "Nice to meet you, Connor. I'm Michele."

They were together the rest of the evening. Over the next four weeks, Connor drew on all his discipline and saw her only twice. The evening of their graduation and wing ceremony, Connor and his family joined Paul's family at the reception.

When the commotion died down some, Connor found Michele. "It's stuffy in here."

She smiled. "Yeah, all those pilot egos crammed into one room."

"Touché." He grinned at her. "Let's take a walk outside. The pond's just a few minutes away."

She took his hand and when they reached the pond, he turned and drew her close. "Michele, I've thought about you every day since we met."

Her eyes fell to the ground, and a blush spread across her cheeks. "I wasn't sure."

"I would've called you every day, but I had finals and graduation and . . ." He searched her face. "Well, now I have the whole summer ahead of me." His voice fell a notch. "Let me take you out, Michele. Please."

Connor realized as he stood there, brush and tree groves surrounding them, that she was the first girl he'd sought after. Every other time the girl had done the seeking. He held his breath, waiting for her answer.

"Okay, but don't fall in love with me."

She was grinning, teasing him the way she'd done back at the barbecue. He took a step back, his hands on her shoulders. "How come?"

"Because I could never be with a pilot."

"Really?" He raised a single eyebrow. "Too much like your brother, huh?"

"No." Her smile fell away. "Because I'm scared to death to fly. I couldn't stand to fall in love with someone who spent half his life in the skies."

With feather-soft care, Connor eased his hands up her neck and on either side of her face. "Well, then ..." He wanted to kiss her with everything in him, but he held back. "We'll have to change that, won't we?"

For the next two months they were rarely apart. The attraction was there for both of them, but Connor didn't let her see how intense his feelings for her had become. Before the summer was up, he got permission to borrow a friend's Cessna. He got her to the airfield by telling her he was taking her out to eat, giving her a chance to watch takeoffs and landings and see that they weren't so frightening.

Instead, when they climbed out of his jeep, he reached into the back and pulled out two helmets, one for him and one for her.

"Connor ..." Her face went slack, and her mouth hung open. "What are you doing?"

"Helping you conquer your fears." He smiled and took her hand. And to his surprise, she took his in return.

They flew for an hour that night, circling over the area and doing basic maneuvers that caused Michele to gasp out loud. She was seated behind him, and several times she reached out and grabbed his shoulders. "Connor!"

Her voice was muffled in the helmet, but even from the front seat he could hear the panic in her voice fade. A minute later, she'd laugh, her hold on him looser than before. When they were back on the ground, he waited until they were in the parking lot near his jeep again before he asked her what she thought.

"You won't believe it." She giggled, her cheeks ruddy from the exhilaration of the flight. "It was amazing, Connor. I'd go up again in a minute." She gave him an impulsive hug. "You took away my greatest fear."

"Good." He leaned his back against the door of his car and eased her close to him. Then, for the first time, he kissed her. The slow, lingering sort of kiss that bared everything he felt for her, the kind he'd never given any woman before or since.

"Why?" When she pulled away, she was breathless, her eyes colored with passion. "Why good?"

"Because I broke your rule, Michele." He framed her face with tender hands and kissed her again. This time he looked straight to her soul and said the words he remembered clearly to this day. "I fell in love with you. And I know I'll spend half my time in the air, so I had no choice—"

She kissed him this time, grinning all the while. "No choice but to teach me to love being up there, just like you do."

The memories stayed with Connor long after his shower. As he made his way to the airport, they played in his mind, keeping him company and assuring him that Michele's question was innocent enough.

Married people asked that of each other now and then, didn't they? *Honey, have you been faithful? Have you ever cheated on me? Am I the only one you've ever loved?* His answer had satisfied her. And, thankfully, he'd been right—she hadn't brought it up again.

Still . . .

Connor shuddered. He pulled his suitcase and flight kit behind him, a sleek black unit emblazoned near the top with the airline's fashionable insignia. He'd been briefed on the upcoming flight, a two-hour hop from West Palm Beach to Atlanta, followed by three short flights across the Midwest, and an overnight in Dallas. His copilot that day was a man he'd flown with before, a young guy hired a year ago.

Young and idealistic and dedicated to his family.

The way Connor was when he first started flying. The way he still felt.

He checked his watch and stepped into a men's room three gates from his own. He had an extra fifteen minutes, time to make sure his uniform was pressed the way he liked it. The conversation with Michele had gone longer than usual, and he'd been in a rush since he left the house.

Three men were washing their hands, and Connor waited until they were gone before stepping in front of the mirror.

He already missed her, missed the proud way she held her chin, and the teasing sparkle in her brown eyes. Michele was not one of the needy, insecure housewives so many pilot friends married. She was a free spirit, a woman who carried a sense of independence that drove him crazy with desire. No matter how long they lived he would never quite catch her, never see her without seeing the challenge she'd been to him back when they first met.

No, he couldn't get enough of her, even after nearly fourteen years. Their Tuesday mornings were constant proof. He loved that time each week with his wife. Loved the way she often initiated their lovemaking, and the way their arms and legs tangled together, making it impossible to tell where one of them ended and the other began. If that morning he'd missed some of his usual routine, he'd live with the fact.

Alone time with Michele was worth every minute.

The bathroom was filling up with passengers again, and Connor made one last tuck of his uniform. He had ten minutes before he had to be at the gate, and halfway through the door he remembered something.

The plane crash.

He'd never seen a passenger list, and though this was his first day back since the accident, he'd heard none of the other pilots or staff talking about it. He probably didn't know anyone on the plane. But he never read about an aircraft going down without wondering who was on board. Too many years in the air to not at least check.

The nearest counter had a woman working it and no one in line. He went to her and gave her a polite nod. "Hey."

"Hello, Captain."

Connor didn't know her, but she had a familiar face. "Have you seen the passenger list from the Western plane crash this past weekend?"

"Yes." The woman thought for a moment. She was older, fifty-two, fifty-three, a former flight attendant, no doubt. "Over at Gate Eleven."

Connor nodded his thanks and worked his way back into the flow of traffic along the concourse. Eleven was two gates past the one where his plane was parked. He grinned at himself. His plane. Michele liked to tease him about the way he took ownership of every aircraft he ever flew.

The thing was, he had to take ownership. It was why he flew so well, not by mere instrumentation and formulated turns, but safer and more instinctively. By the seat of his pants, she liked to say. And she was right. But that same flying was why he'd always come home to Michele—especially after the Gulf War.

He picked up his pace and focused hard on the action at Gate Eleven. The attendants were intently working two lines for a flight due out in twenty-five minutes. He came up alongside the counter and waited until one of them noticed him.

"Captain, what can we do for you?"

"I understand you have the passenger list?" He kept his voice low, so the passengers wouldn't hear him. "The one from this past weekend's Western crash?"

The attendant returned her eyes to the customer at her counter, reached into a drawer, and pulled out a folded newspaper. With only a quick glance, she handed it to him and flashed him a sad smile. "You can keep it. None of us knew the pilots or crew."

He took the paper from her. "I'm checking the same thing."

She returned to her line of passengers, and Connor moved to a spot near the windows, removed from the crowds. There he unrolled the newspaper. It was already opened to the passenger list.

Jared Browning, pilot; Steve McCauffey, copilot; Angela Wielding, flight attendant; Kiahna Siefert—

Kiahna Siefert?

His heart thudded hard, then stopped. He stared at her name, taking it in one letter at a time. That was her last name, wasn't it? Siefert? The Kiahna part he was sure about. No matter how hard he'd tried to forget it, every now and then, in the early morning hours before dawn, her name would come.

Kiahna.

With a jolt, his heartbeat resumed, twice as fast as before. How many years had it been? Almost eight, right? He'd met her that awful summer, back in 1996 when his entire world was upside down. And even then they'd known each other only a few hours, the time it took for a massive storm to make its way across Hawaii and farther out into the Pacific.

Just long enough for her face to be indelibly written across the canvas of his mind, his heart. She was breathtaking. A Hawaiian girl with deep green eyes, light skin, and a hundred dreams about her future. For an hour she had seemed the answer to every problem that stood against him.

And now she was dead.

Passengers came and went a few feet from him, but Connor was frozen in place, his heart still pounding. His eyes remained locked on her name, willing it to disappear from the awful list. But no matter how hard he stared at it, the words wouldn't go away.

Kiahna Siefert.

Yes, it was her. Of course it was. She'd switched airlines, but she'd stayed in Honolulu, where she was raised. And what else? Had she married or studied medicine the way she'd dreamed? Had she raised the family she'd spoken so openly about?

A dark and buried memory flashed in his mind: him and Kiahna early on the evening they'd met. Because of the storm, hotel space was limited, and somehow their paths had crossed. A few hours in the lobby and then ...

He closed his eyes, willing the memory to disappear. Instead it grew more vivid, her words as clear as they'd been that night. She talked about her hopes and dreams, and he shared his frustration over being stationed in Los Angeles, his fears about the FAA investigation. He even told her about his father.

The only thing he didn't tell her was—

"This is the first boarding call for Flight 1205 to Atlanta."

Even two gates away he heard the announcement. They were waiting for him. He blinked and in a sudden, swift movement rolled the paper, tucked it beneath his arm, and headed for his plane. Before he reached the Jetway he crushed the newspaper into a tight wad and popped it into the first trash can. As he boarded the aircraft and took his place in the cockpit, he had a sudden awful thought. One so bad he would never have admitted it to anyone.

If the article was correct, then the single darkest secret in his life was no longer a threat. Never again would he wake up breathless at three in the morning as he'd done four or five times a year, every year since. No longer would he backtrack through the alleys of his mind, desperate for a way to cover his bases, to make sure Michele and the girls never, never learned about his layover in Honolulu the summer of 1996.

Connor had kept the information to himself, never told another soul about it. But the possibility always existed, as long as Kiahna was alive, that somehow the truth would get to Michele.

Now . . . that possibility had drowned right there in the ocean. Kiahna was dead; his wife would never find out.

Connor felt himself relax. He adjusted his tie and tugged on the brim of his hat. It wasn't his fault her plane had gone down. Rather it was one of those strange and rare occurrences, the freak one-in-a-million air disaster that hit the industry every few years. His copilot was saying something, running through some of the checks on gauges and computerized systems.

He exhaled and realized he'd been holding his breath. Once more he read over the flight plan, but he couldn't concentrate. He was too busy hating himself. Because at a time when he should have felt sorrow and remorse for the green-eyed island girl who'd lost her life, he felt only one thing.

Complete and utter relief.

SEVEN

The doorbell rang at five minutes before two.

Ramey watched Max, how his eyebrows lifted and a spark came to life in his expression as though maybe, just maybe, his mother had come home. Maybe she'd found a way to swim off the doomed airplane and make her way back to the island, after all.

But even with his little-boy hopes, the glimmer lasted only a moment. "Who is it, Ramey?"

She considered lying to him, telling him it was a passing salesperson or a personal friend. Anything to keep Max from knowing that days after his mother's death he was about to be dealt a hand that would decide his future. But in the end she decided against it. The boy knew the attorney. No point raising his suspicions about the visit.

Once more, the doorbell rang.

"Ramey?"

The boy's voice brought her back to the moment. She said, "It's Mr. Ogle, you remember him, right?"

Max's eyes were wide and vacant. "Yes."

She headed for the apartment's small foyer, watching Max the entire time. "He wanted to make sure you were okay."

Max nodded, and his chin quivered. He stood straight and still, waiting.

Ramey opened the door and stepped back. The attorney was a man in his fifties, pleasant and distinguished with black slacks and a white short-sleeve dress shirt. Standard island business fare. He introduced himself and then stepped past Ramey toward Max.

The moment their eyes met, the attorney dropped to one knee and held out his arms. "Max . . ."

The child hesitated. Then in a rush he ran to the man and clung to him. His back shook and his words were short and choppy, almost impossible to understand in light of his sudden wave of emotion. "Mommy's . . . plane . . . landed in the water."

Mr. Ogle stroked Max's back. "I know, pal. I know."

"She couldn't get out."

"I'm sorry." The attorney held Max for a long time, until the boy's sobs subsided. Then he drew back and studied Max's face. "I need to talk to Ramey, okay?"

"Okay."

Max looked at Buddy and that was sign enough. The dog was on his feet at Max's side, and the two went outside.

When Ramey and the attorney were alone, she struggled to find her voice. "Should we sit down?"

"I think so." His eyes held hers, unwavering. He nodded to the sofa. "It won't take long."

Ramey glanced at Max as she followed Mr. Ogle. The boy had dropped to the cement patio and had his arm around Buddy's neck again. Her eyes stung, and she blinked hard to stop the tears. At least the boy had Buddy. She took the spot at the other end of the sofa so that one seat cushion separated them.

"Kiahna's instructions were very clear." Mr. Ogle pulled out a two-page document and a white sealed envelope from a file and spread them on the space between them. Less writing covered the top page, and the attorney held it up. "This one is a will, Kiahna's last testament. The first part is fairly straightforward. It leaves Max all her worldly belongings—a few thousand dollars in savings and whatever material goods she's collected. And her life insurance, of course.

"The second part is somewhat unusual." He leaned back and exhaled. The tension in the room doubled. "It's a request, something that wouldn't be legally binding, really. But it was her wish all the same."

Ramey folded her hands, waiting.

"I'll read it." Mr. Ogle held the paper closer and did a small cough. "'In the event of my death prior to Max's eighteenth birthday, it is my desire that before he is turned over to state custody, he spend two weeks with his father.'"

"His *father?*" Ramey's breath caught in her throat. The man Kiahna had refused to talk about, the one whose identity and whereabouts remained a complete mystery? She forced herself to listen.

"Yes." His eyes found his place on the document. "The letter goes on, 'The man is a married pilot who was living in Los Angeles eight years ago. I am providing you with all the information I have; it should be enough to find him.'"

A knowing filled Ramey's heart. No wonder Kiahna hadn't wanted to talk about him. Max's father was a married man, which meant . . . what? That his time with Kiahna had been only a one-night stand? Or worse, that he had led her on, made promises to her, and then left her alone with Max?

Either way the situation was sad, and somewhere in the center of her being, Ramey's heart began to hurt.

Mr. Ogle kept reading. "'If you find him, and if he's willing to agree to the two-week visit, tell him that at the end of that time he'll have to make a decision about Max.' As you know, Kiahna didn't list the father on Max's birth certificate, so the man will have to decide whether to adopt Max and tell him the truth, or send him home to be placed for adoption by the state."

Ramey tried to imagine the reaction the man might have to the news. For that matter, whether he'd even consider such a request after so many years.

The attorney was almost finished. Kiahna's letter went on to provide the man's name, the name of the airline he flew for, and two phone numbers. One for the airline where the man worked, the other for the apartment where he had lived back when they spent their one night together.

"That's it? One night?"

"Apparently." The attorney pursed his lips. "Makes me wonder if he even knows about Max."

Ramey thought about that. Kiahna had been pregnant when she made the will, and since part of her request included telling the man about Max, chances were he had no idea he'd fathered a son with Kiahna. None at all.

Mr. Ogle set the paper down and looked at Ramey. "The apartment will be useless. Too long ago." He narrowed his eyes. "The airline's our best chance."

For a moment neither of them said anything. Then, for the first time since the attorney began speaking, Ramey thought of something other than the information in Kiahna's will.

"What about Max?"

The attorney reached for the sealed white envelope and held it up. "She wrote him a letter. The directions on the envelope say that it can't be opened until Max is present." He paused. "She wanted him to hear it first."

For a crazy instant, Ramey wanted to tell the attorney to take the letter and leave. Kiahna couldn't possibly have wanted Max, just days after her death, to travel from the island and spend time with a stranger! But she waited only a heartbeat before she stood. Kiahna and Max were as close as any mother and son Ramey had ever seen. Whatever the letter held, it was exactly what Kiahna wanted to say. She sniffed and looked at Mr. Ogle. "I'll get him."

⌒

Max was remembering a special butterfly day between him and his mom.

Butterfly days happened once a month because butterflies helped you remember that life was good. At least that's what Mommy always told him. She would pack him a peanut butter banana sandwich and a juice pack and they would set out.

You had to get in your car and drive a long time, more than just the time it took to go to the store for milk or hot dog relish or marshmallows. Usually they sang songs, and after five songs or six if they were quick ones, the street would end and become bumpy and slippery. That's when his mom would reach her hand back through the seats and hold his fingers.

The bushes and trees were thick back there, and after another song the trees made a wall along the road so that it didn't feel like a road at all. More like a secret path. Then, after he counted three coconut trees and two mailboxes, they would stop. Through the trees was a grass place and a bench.

"Okay, Max," Mommy would tell him. "We're here."

That's when she'd grab hold of the lunch bag, and they'd climb out of the car, careful not to get scratched by the trees and bushes. His mom would smile at him and they'd hold hands over to the bench. Max would move his feet very quiet because the butterflies didn't like a lot of loud shuffling feet, that's why.

Once they reached the bench, his mommy would turn to him and do a wink. Then she'd shush him real quiet, just in case he forgot about the butterflies.

They would sit down and his mommy would put her arm around him and hug him close. "Now we wait."

After about as long as two TV commercials, the butterflies would come. Two or three butterfly friends, and then whole entire butterfly families. Their wings were sunny yellow and pumpkin orange and chocolate brown and darkest black, and every time Max saw them come and bounce around in the close sky above them he thought the same thing.

Butterflies were God's bestest artwork.

His teacher told him once that artwork was when little boys colored inside the lines. God definitely colored inside the lines with butterflies. Pretty soon the butterfly families would become a butterfly village all bouncing and lifting and falling over him and his mommy.

She would lean close to his ear and whisper, "Know what I love about butterflies, Max?"

"What?"

"They prove that God gives second chances."

"Why?" Max knew the answer, but he liked to hear her say the words.

"Because a butterfly spends most of its life as a caterpillar, scooting along on the ground, barely getting by. When a caterpillar sees a butterfly he thinks how wonderful it would be to fly."

"And then one day he gets tired."

"Very tired. He builds a little room, curls up inside, and takes a nap. Deep in his heart he wonders if maybe that's all. Maybe life is over."

"But one day . . ." Max always smiled here, because this was his favoritest part of the story.

"One day the caterpillar wakes up, and God has done an amazing thing. The caterpillar shakes off the little room and feels something on his back. This time when he goes a bit down the tree branch he doesn't scoot like before."

"He flies!" Max would look back at the butterflies.

"That's right." His mommy's voice would get sort of scratchy at this part of the story. "And one day, Max, you and I aren't going to scoot anymore, either. Because God loves us even more than He loves the butterflies."

"Right."

"So butterflies make us remember, don't they, Max?"

"Yep."

"That life is good no matter what. Because just like the cater-pillar, the best days are ahead of us, and then . . ."

"And then we'll have wings just like the butterflies."

That's when they'd wait a little bit with no words. And after that Mommy would pick up the lunch bag and give them each a sand-wich. Some of the butterflies would go away because of the crinkly bag, but it didn't matter because Max understood. Butterflies couldn't stay in just one place.

That's why they had wings.

⁓

Max stopped remembering and looked at Buddy. He was asleep, his furry legs stretched out both ways. Max looked up to the sky and wondered. Maybe this was what Mommy meant by one day they'd have wings. Maybe this was the part of her life where God was giving her a second chance, just like the butterfly.

If that was true, then maybe she could bounce and rise and fall over to Ramey's back patio. Because the hurting feeling inside him was worse than before. But then . . . he didn't want her to be a butterfly, not really. Because butterflies couldn't laugh or hug or sit next to you and hold your hand. They couldn't sing you a special song.

Behind him, a door made a noise and he did a fast breath. Because all of a sudden he remembered about the talking inside. And the special meeting with Mr. Ogle.

"Max." It was Ramey. "We need you to come in for a minute."

He turned around and stood up at the same time. Ramey's voice was tired, the way it had been that day when Mommy's plane landed in the water. "Why?"

"Because Mr. Ogle has to read you something."

She held her hands out to him and he came to her, hugging her big legs close because sadness was so strong it wanted to make him fall on the floor. "What's he going to read?"

"A letter from your mom."

Max raised his eyes at Ramey. "From my mom? From heaven?"

Water came across Ramey's eyes. "No, Max. A special letter she wrote you earlier this year."

"How come . . ." Max rubbed his eyes because he didn't want to cry again. "How come she didn't give it to me before?"

"Because she wrote this in case . . . in case . . ."

"In case her plane landed in the water one day?"

"Yes." Ramey did a long breath. "In case of that."

Max couldn't figure out the feeling in his tummy. It was sad because his mommy was gone, but happy, too. Because the letter was a piece of her she left behind. A piece just for him. And that made him feel special.

He took Ramey's hand and led the way into the apartment. Mr. Ogle told him to sit in the middle between him and Ramey. Then he said the same thing Ramey had said about his mommy leaving him a letter. Max nodded and tried to have patience. His mommy always said patience was good.

Finally Mr. Ogle opened a piece of paper and began reading.

"'Dear Max, if you're hearing this, then . . . I've already gone home to be with Jesus.'" Mr. Ogle stopped and bit his lip. "'Before I go on, you need to know something: I'm safe in heaven now. No matter what else, I want you to know that; I'm okay. And, Max, you're going to be okay, too.'"

Max sucked in his cheeks so he could stay strong on the inside. But two tears spilled onto his face before he could stop them. He rubbed his cheeks hard and looked at Mr. Ogle so he'd keep reading.

"'Deep in your heart I'm certain you wonder about your father. If you're old enough, then you know that even though you don't have a daddy, Jesus is your Father. But, Max, I want you to know you have a human father somewhere out there. He is a man I loved very much, but only for a short time. He couldn't stay here on the island, Max, because he had to go home.'"

Mr. Ogle looked at Ramey. That gave Max a chance to put his hand over his heart and feel how the beat there had gotten fast and jumpy. Very jumpy. His father was out there somewhere? Why hadn't his mom told him that before? Mr. Ogle did a choking sound and looked back at the piece of paper.

"'Home was so important to your father, Max, that when God gave you to me, I never told him. Never once. Because he had his home across the ocean, and we had our home here, on the island. I don't know if you'll ever find your father, Max. But I wanted you to know he was somewhere out there, and that he doesn't know about you.

"'Also, Ramey is going to help you find a special friend of mine, a man who lives on the mainland. If Jesus takes me to heaven, and if Ramey can find my special friend, I want you to spend a few weeks with him. This might be hard, Max, but it means a lot to me. It's what I want you to do. Really and truly.

"'I know you love the island where we live, and our special places where we go for talks. But this trip will be good for you; I believe that with all my heart. My friend has a nice wife and two little girls about your age. If it happens, then God wanted it to happen, Max. If it doesn't, then God didn't plan for you to meet my friend.

"'It's funny, Max, as I write this I feel sure that you'll never hear it. Because I want to be here with you forever and always. But if not, if something happens, and Jesus brings me home to live with Him, then the things I'm telling you in this letter are very important.

"'Be a good boy, Max. Whatever you do, remember to be strong and brave, and to love Jesus. When you're sad, remember our song, because it will always be the truest thing I could tell you. And remember that even if you never find your father on earth, your

Father in heaven is watching over you. And if God lets me, I'll be watching you, too. Cheering you on when you're up to bat in baseball, pulling for you when you have a spelling test, and believing in you always. Believing that you'll do your best to grow into a young man who will make me proud of you. Even from as far away as heaven.'"

That part stuck in Max's heart like peanut butter. His shoulders began to shake and more tears came. It wasn't right to hear his mommy's words with Mr. Ogle's voice, that's why. And because if she were only here one more day he could hug her and tell her yes. Yes, he would always do his bestest work for her even when he was a grown-up man.

Ramey patted his knee. "You okay?"

He wanted to say no, but then he wouldn't hear the rest of the letter. So he quick moved his head up and down and used his shirtsleeve to wipe the wet on his cheeks. He looked at Mr. Ogle. "Finish, please."

"Okay." That's when he noticed Mr. Ogle had wet eyes, too. The man took a slow breath and looked at the paper once more. "'And here's the best part, Max. Remember our special butterfly days? I'm finally getting my second chance, sport. And one day not so far from now we'll be together again, and we won't scoot around like caterpillars on the ground. We'll fly. Well, that's all. I love you, Max, the most. Forever and ever, Mommy.'"

EIGHT

Connor was coming home.

That thought kept Michele moving through the day, and now that she was almost finished with her last client, she could hardly wait to see him. At just past four o'clock she grabbed her tallest can of Shaper hairspray and applied it in short bursts around the woman's hair. Five minutes later the client was on her way.

Michele was just catching her breath when she heard the door behind her creak open. Before she could turn around she felt his hands on her waist, his breath against her skin. "Hi."

A warmth radiated out from her heart, the way it always did when he came home. She turned in his arms so that they were facing each other and slid her hands up around his neck. "Hi, yourself."

"I have an idea." He grinned and searched her eyes, but before he could say anything more, she brought her lips to his and kissed him. The kind of slow kiss they hadn't ever stopped sharing.

When they pulled apart to catch their breath, she brushed her nose against his. "You always have an idea."

"Yes"—he gave her another brief kiss—"but that's why you married me."

She leaned back and lowered her chin, flirting with him the way she'd done since the first time he took her flying the summer after his college graduation. "Is that what you think?"

"Well . . ." His eyes told her how much he'd missed her. "That and a few other reasons."

They came together again and she rested her head on his shoulder. "Maybe we should hear about your *idea* later." Once more she drew back and this time she could feel the way her eyes danced.

"You have four phone messages, a broken window in Susan's room, and the girls will be starving in an hour." She poked a finger into first one of his sides, then the other. He'd been ticklish as long as she'd known him, and her playing always seemed to strip him of the strain of his job.

"Not *that* kind of idea." He chuckled as he squirmed in her arms and caught her hands with his own. "Let's have a picnic. Over at Langley Park by the beach."

"A picnic?" Michele tilted her head. "Hmmm. Not bad. We could pick up some chicken and skip the cleanup."

"Exactly." He was moving closer to her again, working his hands up her back and drawing her into his arms. "Of course the other idea could be even better . . ."

Connor wiped his hands on his napkin, and eased his legs out from beneath the table. Then he turned to face Elizabeth and Susan. The girls were staging races on the beach, and Michele was acting as the official. He crossed his arms and felt the corners of his mouth work their way up his face.

The picnic had been a hit.

It was warm, not quite eighty, and this April was one of the nicest he could remember. He let his eyes wander from the girls to the expanse of ocean beyond them. Beautiful, blue water that could have been a beach in Cancun or somewhere on the Mediterranean. How was it possible that everything had worked out so well? Back during those awful days in Los Angeles he'd been convinced life could never be good again.

But nothing about that time had been his fault. Life had simply formed a conspiracy against him, and in the course of a few months he figured out a way to deal with it.

But here . . . now . . . he was one of the lucky ones. He had it all, and life was bound to keep getting better.

He stood and stretched. Then without waiting another moment he loped over to the place where Michele was about to signal the start of another race. "Wait a minute, count me in."

Susan and Elizabeth ran to him and grabbed his hands. "Race us, Daddy . . . come on, race us." Their voices sounded almost the same as they pulled at him and jumped up and down on the sugary white sand.

"Okay." He winked at Michele. "But be easy on me. Your old man isn't what he used to be."

The girls giggled and lined up on either side of him.

Michele lowered her voice and leaned first toward Susan, and then Elizabeth. "Beat him good, girls." Then she grinned at Connor. "On your mark, get set . . . go!"

Connor intended to let the girls win, but he ran anyway, so they'd think he was trying. He was fifteen feet out when his left foot caught on a string of seaweed. He reached down to free himself, but before he could, he fell smack onto the ground. Without his hands free, his face planted flat against the sand.

Michele was laughing before he had a chance to sit up.

"Daddy!" The girls were at his side. Elizabeth knelt near him, her curls falling in a cascade over her shoulder. She helped him to a sitting position. "Are you okay?"

Susan stayed on her feet, covering her mouth so he wouldn't see her laughing. "Daddy . . ." A few short bursts of laughter broke free. "You look like a sea creature."

"I feel like one." Connor chuckled as he reached down and pulled the wrap of seaweed from his foot. Sand was in his mouth and he leaned over and spit some of it out. His arms and legs were also covered with sand, and his knees were skinned where they'd taken the brunt of his fall. The picture of competence and dignity.

Michele was at his side now. Her entire body shook from the quiet laughter simmering inside her. "Susan's right." She laughed out loud this time. "Your face ..."

Connor felt his cheeks and chin and forehead. Sure enough. He'd picked up an entire mask of sand. His chuckle joined those of his family, and all four of them fell to the ground laughing.

Almost a minute passed, when Connor gave a flick to Susan's ponytail. "You still didn't win the race, you know."

Elizabeth and Susan looked at each other, and in a flash they were up and tearing down the beach to the makeshift finish line— a trash can twenty-five yards away. Connor brought his legs up and leaned forward. He could feel Michele near his side as they watched Susan raise a victory hand.

"I won!" Her voice mixed with the sound of the distant surf and faded in the wind.

They watched Elizabeth give her sister a high five. The two girls wandered toward the shore and began looking for seashells. The tide was out, and the sand was covered with a hundred different types.

"We have the best kids in the world." He leaned against Michele, his eyes still on the girls.

"Yes." Michele let her head fall against his. "And they have the best daddy." She gave him a light elbow in the ribs. "Even if he does look like a sea creature."

They laughed and the ring of it mingled with the hush of the gentle waves. A breeze had picked up and the air smelled of early summer and salt water. Connor reached out and took Michele's hand in his. "Okay ... so tell me about my phone messages."

Her voice was relaxed and easy, content after their evening together. "The dentist had a cancellation and wants to see you at nine tomorrow for your checkup."

"On a Saturday?"

"It's new. The guy puts in four hours every Saturday."

"Wow. Okay . . . got that. What else?"

A flock of seagulls swooped low over the water just beyond them and their cries competed with the sound of the waves. Michele ran her thumb along the side of his hand. "The guy from the bank wants to set up a meeting, something about rates and refinancing. And the lawn mower part you ordered is in."

Connor nodded. "Very serious messages." He turned and kissed her cheek, then locked his eyes on the girls once more. They were moving closer, working their way up the beach, their hands full of sand dollars and clamshells. This close to the water, he liked keeping them in his view. His tone was a teasing one when he continued. "Yes, those are major messages, all right. I can see where the world might've stopped if I didn't hear about those."

"Now . . . the dentist was pretty important, you have to admit."

He glanced at Michele again and remembered something. "Didn't you say I had four of them?"

She nodded. "Wasn't that four?"

"Three. The dentist, the bank, and the hardware store."

Michele thought for a moment, and then her face lit up. "I remember." Her smile faded some. "It was a strange one. I have no idea what they want or why they called."

"Who was it?" Connor's eyes were still on the girls. The sun was setting behind them, spraying pink and blue across the eastern sky.

"An attorney." She hesitated. "Marv somebody. Said he was from Honolulu."

Connor felt his body go stiff. He pulled away from Michele so she wouldn't notice. *Calm, Connor . . . be calm.* He couldn't draw a deep breath. "Honolulu?"

"Strange, huh?" Michele slipped her legs beneath her and doodled a series of circles in the sand. "Probably one of the lawsuits you have to testify for."

"Yes. Probably." Connor took a long breath and held it. That had to be it. What other explanation was there? He had no connection to anyone in Honolulu, not now. Not since the plane crash. But attorneys . . . they held offices all around the country, didn't they? Of course they'd be stationed in Honolulu. Why not?

"What do you think it's about?" Michele looked at him and he caught the innocence in her eyes. She had no doubts, no suspicions. Only a passing interest at why an attorney from Hawaii would call him at home.

Like lightning, Connor's mind began to flash with possibilities. It wasn't uncommon for pilots to be called into court. And over the years he'd been used by the airline as a professional witness, someone who would articulate the company's policies and standards if a passenger sued for one reason or another. Too much turbulence, too rough a landing, too much pepper in the onboard meal. It could have been a hundred reasons.

He swallowed hard and uttered a dry laugh. "Who knows. These days people sue over anything."

"And you're the expert because you've testified a dozen times on these cases."

"I guess." His voice no longer sounded like his own. With everything in him, he wanted to believe that the reason for the call had something to do with a lawsuit. But the timing was too strange, too close, to the recent crash. He stopped himself from saying anything more.

Michele gave a soft huff. "Why you, Connor? Couldn't they use someone current, someone who flies into Hawaii now? You haven't been there in years."

"Right." Connor massaged his throat and managed a smile. "But once you're on the list of expert witnesses for the company, they keep using you."

It was true. Attorneys working for the airline called Connor three or four times a year looking for him to testify on its behalf. But never had they called from Hawaii. In fact, other than once when a Chicago attorney had contacted him, they consistently called out of Atlanta, the airline's home base.

Chills flashed down Connor's arms and the length of his spine. If the attorney in Honolulu wasn't with the airline, then who was he? And why, just days after the air disaster, was he calling him at home?

The thought kept him distracted throughout the night, and regardless of the ideas he'd had when he first came home that afternoon, Connor let Michele head off to bed alone. When the house was quiet he crept into the office and signed onto the Internet. There, for the next three hours, he searched the Web for every detail he could find about the crash. Who was Kiahna Siefert, anyway, and what connection could he, Connor Evans, possibly have had to the tragedy?

By three o'clock that morning, Connor was convinced that the answer was simple. There was no connection. He hadn't spoken to Kiahna since that long-ago summer night, and he knew nothing about either the airline or the flight in question. The fear he felt was nothing more than an overactive imagination and a forgotten bit of guilt, resurrected by the crash.

First thing Monday at work, he would call the attorney back. Until then he would put the entire matter out of his mind. Obviously his fears were unfounded. Once he was convinced of these things, once he was certain no connection existed between the phone call and his time with Kiahna, Connor climbed into bed next to Michele.

The strange message all but forgotten, he was asleep instantly.

NINE

Connor had fifteen minutes before he had to report to the gate.

He moved at a snappy pace, his single piece of luggage rolling along behind him, smooth and efficient. The pilot's lounge was a few gates from the one he'd be flying out of, but he didn't want to make the call from there. He strode across the concourse to an empty gate across from his.

The area was quiet, and he took a seat next to the sheet of glass windows. He flipped out his cell phone and reached into his pocket for the long-distance number. He studied the scrap of paper and felt his stomach tighten.

Marv Ogle.

The attorney's name meant nothing to him, and neither did the phone number. But here, in the light of day, the reasons he'd dreamed up to explain the message no longer seemed airtight. For half a second, he thought about praying, but he changed his mind.

Prayer was for difficult situations, right? Trials or emergencies or major life decisions. No need to bother God with something like this. He clenched his jaw and tapped out the number sequence. Even with the typically poor airport reception, the call went through without hesitation.

"Ogle and Browning," a voice on the other end said.

"Marv Ogle, please."

"Who's calling?"

Connor felt his heart skip a beat. "Connor Evans. Returning his call."

"Just a moment."

A tinny version of something slow and instrumental played in the background, and Connor glanced at his watch. Thirteen minutes before he had to report. He was about to hang up and try again after he landed in Atlanta, when he heard a click.

"Hello ... Marv Ogle, can I help you?"

"Yes." His throat was suddenly tight. "Mr. Ogle, I'm Connor Evans. You left me a message a few days ago."

The pause that followed lasted a lifetime and an instant all at once. When the man on the other end finally spoke, Connor's shoulders relaxed. At least after this he wouldn't have to wonder.

"Mr. Evans, I'm afraid I have some very sad news for you."

Connor held his breath.

The attorney continued, his voice a notch more somber than before. "As you're probably aware, Western Island Air Flight 45 crashed last week and left no survivors." He hesitated. "I represent the estate of Kiahna Siefert, a friend of yours, I believe. I'm afraid she was on the flight."

A pounding started in Connor's head. How could Kiahna's death involve him in any way? Had she left a list for him to contact everyone she'd ever known? He closed his eyes and found his voice. "Yes, I ... well, we hadn't spoken in several years."

"I'm aware of that."

Connor wanted to shout at the man. *Get to the point!* He could do nothing for Kiahna or her estate now. He pinched the bridge of his nose and forced himself to sound appropriately saddened. "I saw her name on a passenger list. I'm ... sorry about what happened to her."

"Yes ... well, that's only part of the reason why I called."

He wanted to exhale, but his airways were paralyzed. "I don't understand. Kiahna and I ... we had no ties at the time of her death."

"Actually, you have one, Mr. Evans. A seven-year-old boy named Max Riley."

Connor's eyes flew open. What? A boy named Max Riley? He stared out at a handful of aircraft parked at various angles across the airport's apron. A seven-year-old boy? How would a child involve him and Kiahna? She had no children that he'd known about.

Unless the boy wasn't only Kiahna's, but . . .

His brain swirled and in less time than it took his heart rate to double, everything around him stood still. He considered snapping the phone shut. Walking away and pretending he'd never heard the man's last words.

But he'd heard them. He'd heard them and with everything in him he knew he was neither dreaming nor the victim of some sort of prank.

A seven-year-old boy?

The floor dropped away, and Connor felt himself begin to freefall. Faster and faster into an abyss that couldn't possibly have a bottom. The math was not difficult. Seven years old? He'd been with Kiahna the summer of 1996.

There could be only one reason attorney Marv Ogle was calling him now.

"Mr. Evans, are you there?"

He squeezed his eyes shut and shielded them with his hand. "Yes . . . I'm sorry. How . . . how does this involve me, Mr. Ogle?"

Another pause. "The boy is your son."

So there it was. With five short words, the man threw a spear at Connor that caught him in the chest and tore open his heart. A spear that burst his nicely fashioned reality and ripped a hole in all the justifications he'd ever made about that long-ago night. He had a son? A son he'd never known about nor heard of until this moment?

"Mr. Evans," the attorney went on, "Kiahna left very specific instructions for the boy, and part of those included contacting you."

The attorney paused again. "The child has no one. Kiahna wanted you to consider taking him for two weeks, getting to know him before he was made a ward of the court."

His head pounded harder with every word. He had a son? A seven-year-old boy named Max Riley? If he was the child's father, why hadn't Kiahna told him sooner, as soon as she'd found out she was pregnant? And now . . . now she wanted the boy to stay with him for two weeks? What about Michele and Elizabeth and Susan? What about the way their lives were going so well, exactly as he'd planned for them to go?

But with every question fighting for position in his mind, only one demanded his immediate attention.

He had a son?

After all these years, there was a boy in Honolulu who was his very own?

The truth twisted his heart and made a logjam of his words. He knit his brow together, concentrating until the clog broke apart and his words began to come again. "How . . . how do you know, Mr. Ogle? She never told me."

"I've known Kiahna since she was in high school, Mr. Evans." The attorney sighed in a way that rattled Connor's nerves even further. "She was a good girl; she didn't sleep around. After . . . after she found out she was pregnant, she told my wife and me what happened. The whole story."

Nausea welled up in Connor. With every sentence the weight of the millstone around his neck grew.

"We told her to contact you, but she wouldn't. Never told a single person your name or how she'd met you. Just that you'd been together."

"How . . ." Connor didn't recognize his voice. He had five minutes to report to the gate, and he was barely able to think, let alone move. "How did you find me?"

"When Max was born, she brought me an envelope. Inside were two documents—a will, and a letter for Max. She replaced the letter every year on Max's birthday. But the will stayed the same. In it she named you and the airline you work for. She asked that we do everything we could to find you . . . before her son be given over to the state."

"Is he mine? Legally?"

"No. Your name isn't on his birth certificate."

"Oh." Connor was buying time, trying to fit this new information into his framework of reality. "She wanted me to adopt the boy?"

"Not that either. At least not at first." The man's tone was kind, not accusing. "She wants him to visit you for two weeks. During that time he would be told only that you were a friend of his mother's. When the trial period is over, you would have a choice."

"A choice?" Connor's hands shook. Sweat drops rolled down either side of his face.

"Yes. You could send him back and never contact him again. Or tell him the truth and keep him forever."

The nausea grew worse. All his life he'd prided himself for his quick reactions, his ability to confidently tackle any problem he'd ever faced. He had run bombing missions in the Gulf War and pulled himself out of a death spin when his tail was hit by enemy fire. Twice he'd made emergency landings that had caused the airline to rewrite that part of the handbook. Connor could count his mistakes on one hand.

But this?

This was so far out of his league he couldn't remember how to breathe, let alone think up a way to unravel the ball of knots he'd just been tossed. For the first time in his life, he had no idea what to do next, no clue what to say. The news was still detonating in his soul, taking no prisoners as it worked its way through his consciousness and into the reality of his world.

"Mr. Evans . . . I realize this is probably somewhat of a shock. Do you have any thoughts on Kiahna's request?"

Thoughts? Yes . . . he had thoughts, but what were they? Across the concourse he heard the first boarding announcement for his flight. He opened his eyes and let them dart around the empty gate area that surrounded him. As though maybe the answer lay somewhere out in the open.

"I . . ."—he chewed on the inside of his lip—"can I have a week to . . . to talk to my wife?"

"Of course." The man's voice was sympathetic. "But I'll need to know, Mr. Evans." He made another loud exhale. "Max is staying with his baby-sitter, but she's not well. If he's going to be put up for adoption, we should set the procedure in motion as soon as possible. Homes for seven-year-old boys are not easily found."

At mention of the child, anxiety tightened the knots even more. He still seemed to be falling, still couldn't stop the spinning in his head, but even so he couldn't hang up without asking one last question. "What's the boy like?"

"He's . . ." The attorney's voice cracked.

In that instant Connor knew. Everything the man had said was true. He'd known Kiahna all her life, and he knew the boy, as well. This phone call was probably as difficult for him as it had been for Connor.

"I'm sorry." The man coughed. "He's . . . he's a very special boy, Mr. Evans. He's striking looking, tall and well built for his age. He loves baseball and football. He has his mother's tanned skin and green eyes, and a face that must come from someone in your family. He laughs and loves easily. He and Kiahna seemed to . . . well, they seemed to share one heart, really."

Connor closed his eyes. He could almost see the boy, the way he must've looked throwing a ball or walking alongside Kiahna. Because after all these years, he still had not forgotten what she looked like. If he had his mother's eyes, the boy would stand out in a crowd of a thousand seven-year-olds.

The second announcement came over the PA system.

"Look ..." Connor glanced at his watch. He needed to switch gears, become the professional pilot once more. Not the broken man he'd been that awful summer. "Give me a week. I'll call you as soon as I know."

They ended the call, and Connor blocked everything he'd just learned from his mind. As he jogged to the gate, not one detail was allowed time in the foreground of his mind. Not one.

He checked in, took his place in the cockpit, and went through the motions of preparing for the flight. Concentration was a must in any piloting situation, and this one would be no different. Connor gave the matter at hand his full attention, making appropriate conversation with his copilot, and taking the plane full of passengers through a textbook takeoff.

Not until he was up at thirty-three thousand feet, disconnected from everything that awaited him on the ground below, did he let down his guard and then, like the rush of airspace that surrounded his plane, the memories came. Vivid and in full color, they came, and in light of the news the attorney had shared with him that morning, he could do nothing but let them.

TEN

There'd been reasons for his fall.

But they had little to do with the bizarre circumstances of that stormy August night when all Hawaiian air traffic was grounded for three full days. Rather, they involved the five months prior, at least that's how Connor saw it.

He pressed back into the seat of his cockpit and stared at the vast stretch of blue before him. No, if he was honest, the problems started a year before that, in the days after Michele's mother woke up one morning vomiting, and wound up dead two hours later of a brain aneurysm.

Connor had been flying a little more than three years by then, and competition for schedules and hours was tight. But after her mother died, Michele—who was five months pregnant with Susan—slipped into a depression that frightened him. She spent entire days in bed, doing nothing more than feeding and clothing Elizabeth, who was almost two at the time.

One afternoon when he came home from work, he found Michele asleep on the sofa, their daughter toddling around the kitchen alone. He knelt near his wife, frightened that somehow she, too, had died.

"Michele!" He shook her, and when she stirred, relief flooded his heart. "Michele . . . how long have you been sleeping?"

The scene happened again three times in the next two weeks, until finally Connor was forced to make a decision. His wife wasn't dead, but she might as well have been. She was no longer capable of taking care of herself, let alone little Elizabeth. He contacted the airline the next morning and requested two weeks off, with a shortened schedule after that.

Michele's improvements were immediate.

They found a baby-sitter who could come in while they attended counseling together. And after a two-month dose of antidepressants, and the prayers of their friends at church, Michele was herself again.

But by then the damage at work was done. Connor had fallen to the bottom of the seniority chart, and after Susan was born in November, he was assigned a temporary move to Los Angeles.

The memory broke apart and he tightened his grip on the controls. He'd thought about that assignment a thousand times since the night with Kiahna. If only it hadn't been temporary. If the airline had been willing to move his entire family to Los Angeles, then at least he would've had more time with Michele.

The transfer was effective in March, but from the beginning they both knew it could last months. Which meant Michele and the girls would stay in Florida, while he set up a company-funded, furnished apartment in Los Angeles.

"I'll be home at least once every week," he told Michele.

And he was at first. But after a while, the commute was hardly practical. Twice-a-week flights from Los Angeles to Hawaii with a layover in Honolulu left him exhausted, struggling to find the energy to go on.

Michele became friends with Renee Wagner, and since both of them were often home alone, they helped each other. Knowing that Michele had a friend made it easier to sometimes let as many as three weeks go by without a visit home.

Then in May, the unthinkable happened.

Connor was bringing a 737 into Los Angeles International Airport when the tower gave him orders to land on one of the western runways. The request was unusual—every other time he'd been instructed to land from the east. But something else made it strange. As far as Connor could tell, another jet a few miles south of him was headed for the same runway.

Even now, Connor remembered the fear. LAX was one of the busiest airports in the world. Every pilot knew how possible it was for an air traffic controller to make a mistake.

He made the request without giving it further thought. "Flight Four Zero Three requesting change of runways, over."

Silence filled the airways, and Connor glanced out the right side of his cockpit. The neighboring aircraft was closer now, narrowing the distance that separated them. Normally, he would've made a second attempt at the request, but time had run out. If he was going to avoid a possible collision, he needed to make a northern angle and land on one of the adjacent runways.

"Hey." It was his copilot. The man sat straighter in his seat, his voice tense. "What're you doing?"

Connor felt sweat on his brow. He snapped at the man, "We've got company." He nodded his head toward the first runway. "Another aircraft coming in." His eyes narrowed. "I had to make the change."

"But you didn't get—"

"I did what I had to." He glared at the man. "I know what I'm doing."

He was partway through making the move when he tried again. "Flight Four Zero Three, requesting change of runways, over."

"Name your reason, Four Zero Three."

"Congestion coming in on the assigned runway, over."

The pause that followed was Connor's first sign that something was wrong. When the controller's voice came over the air again, his tone was frustrated, almost panicked. "We're picking you up moving away from the designated runway, is that correct?"

"Yes. My first request went unanswered, so I made the decision to avoid a ground collision."

"That decision isn't yours to make, Captain." The controller gave a huff loud enough for any incoming flight to hear it over the radio. Then he cleared Connor's flight for a landing on the other runway.

Long before he landed the plane that day, Connor knew he was in trouble. Representatives from the FAA ushered him into an initial inquiry the moment he was at the gate. At the end of the brief meeting, a red-faced man in his fifties stared at Connor and shook his head.

"This type of defiance is unacceptable, Captain Evans." He tapped his pencil on the sheet of notes he'd taken. "I'll be recommending a formal FAA investigation first thing in the morning."

The demotion came before his next flight.

He was informed that until the investigation was completed, he would fly as a copilot only. Michele was frightened by the change, worried Connor would be stationed in LA longer. For the next month, every time he and Michele spoke, things felt strained between them. Tense. As though they'd become strangers.

Finally, in June that year, Connor made a decision. He would purchase a small regional airport near their home in West Palm Beach and he'd forget commercial aviation for good. The FAA could figure out their investigation without him.

The airport had been on the market for nearly a year, and after his transfer to Los Angeles, Connor checked on the price every month or so. It had dropped from nearly a million dollars to $550,000. With a hundred thousand down, he could have payments that would easily be covered by the small plane owners who used the airfield.

Finding the hundred down was the problem, but not one Connor couldn't see past.

Connor's father, Loren Herman Evans, had been more than an ace pilot in his day. Long before he hung up his wings, he and Connor's mother invested heavily in real estate. It wasn't so much what they bought, as where. They purchased open land and rental houses in an area of New Jersey thirty minutes outside of Manhattan.

By the time his father retired and sold their real estate holdings, the value of each piece had gone from tens of thousands to hundreds of thousands. When it was all sold and counted out, his parents netted nearly two million dollars.

Pilots were a different breed, and though Connor had never had an intimate relationship with his father, they shared a mutual respect and admiration for each other. There was no one Connor would rather shoot a round of golf with, but hugs were stiff and rare, declarations of love all but nonexistent.

His parents settled on a ranch in Cambria, California, not far from San Luis Obispo and the Pacific coast. His dad was healthy and hearty, a man whose gray hair and piercing blue eyes only made him more attractive as the years passed. For a while he dabbled in stocks, but he showed a continual penchant for buying high and selling low. Finally Loren Evans relaxed and left his money alone.

Once a year in the spring he organized a family vacation for Connor and Connor's three sisters and their families, and over time the lot of them came to expect glitches in the itinerary. One year their hotel reservation ran out three days before their outbound flights. Another time they were forced to bring cots into each of the rooms to make up for his booking three rooms instead of six.

In the summer, Connor and Michele would meet up with his father at the Cambria ranch, where he cranked up a bucket of homemade strawberry ice cream and convinced the group to play a round of croquet. At some point in the visit the conversation would turn to the paperwork towers in his father's office.

"Hire someone, Dad," Connor would say. "You shouldn't have to live like that."

But always his father's answer was the same. "I like it this way. I know exactly where everything is."

His answer was typical pilot speak. Always in control; never admitting error or defeat. It took utter confidence to take hundreds of people into the air every day, so Connor understood. He was the same way, after all. Still, sometimes Connor wondered how his father had ever been organized enough to fly commercial airplanes.

In the end, their visits were pleasant enough, and Connor did more than respect his father when they were together. He enjoyed him.

So when the idea for the regional airport came up, Connor used his two-day break to drive north to Cambria and talk to his father. He felt certain of the outcome. What would a hundred thousand dollars be to his father? Besides, the man had always been generous, giving to charities and scholarship funds. Why would this time be any different? By then, Connor's mother was dead and his father had already suffered one heart attack. It wouldn't be long before at least part of the money was his anyway.

Connor waited until they were seated at a table on his father's back veranda, overlooking acres of rolling green hills and oak trees.

"Dad, I'm thinking about leaving commercial aviation."

His father looked up, but said nothing. The lines on his forehead froze, and his expression turned to stone.

Connor gulped back his sudden doubts and launched into an explanation of the airport and his ideas about running it. "The place could handle twice the air traffic it has now. With a little advertising and promotion, profits could double in two years."

Silence hung in the air for a beat. "You know my feelings on finishing a job. Work now, invest now. Make a hobby out of a regional airfield later, when everything else is finished."

"Dad." Tension sprouted between them. "I'm a man, and if I don't want to wait for retirement to change careers, I don't have to."

"Fine." His father's gaze was unwavering. "Why are you here, then?"

Connor was convinced his father already knew the answer, but he plodded ahead. At that point, only a confident request would earn his father's favor. "I'd like a loan against my inheritance, Dad. Either that, or I'd like you to consider going in on the airport with me."

His father looked hard at him for a moment and then chuckled. "You're kidding, right?"

A rush of heat filled Connor's cheeks. "No, Dad. I need the money. I've already made up my mind. The airline has me stationed across the country from Michele, and the FAA investigation is—" Suddenly he stopped short.

He watched his father's eyes narrow and grow angry, disapproving. "What investigation?"

Connor gave his father a short version of the story, heavily weighted in his favor. But still the old man sat unmoving, his arms crossed. Connor finished with, "So that's why I want out. It isn't worth it. Michele and I are fighting all the time, and the girls won't even know me. I need to get back to Florida."

"You need to obey the rules." He gave an abrupt shake of his head and smacked his lips. As if Connor had buzzed the control tower or done a 360 loop with a plane full of passengers. "That's always been your trouble, Son. You think your opinion is all that counts." He hesitated. "Stay in the air and you'll never be sorry."

Connor's control dissipated like early morning clouds over Phoenix. For the next hour, he and his father debated—sometimes in loud voices—Connor's request for the money and his father's staunch refusal to write Connor a check.

The last thing Connor said before he left was this: "If you won't help me, I can't possibly call you my father."

His dad stood up and followed him to the door. He wasn't ready to give in, but he was clearly concerned by Connor's statement. The elevation of his tone made that much clear. "Don't be childish."

"Look, Dad . . ." Connor spun around and met his dad's gaze head-on. Anger filled his heart, anger that had been building toward the man for decades, anger about his expectations and lack of expressed love. All of it came to a head. "I always wondered how you really felt about me." Connor bit the inside of his lip. "Now I know. You think I'm cocky and arrogant, irresponsible." A chuckle that was more angry than funny came up from him. "I'll tell you what. Until you change your mind about the money, our relationship is over." He took another few steps toward the door. "I'll be waiting."

He hoped his father would reach out and grab his shoulder, tell him not to be crazy, that it was all a misunderstanding and yes, they could talk about the loan, or at least they could talk about their relationship. After analyzing that moment for so many years, Connor was convinced the argument that day wasn't about the money. At least not on his part.

It was about seeking his father's approval. The airport and the loan to fund the purchase was only the means by which Connor sought it. But the combination of the man's attitude and his callous statements convinced Connor that the relationship had suffered a heart attack that afternoon.

After that confrontation, Connor felt like a lost boy, confused and out of sorts. At times that week, he wondered if he'd become a different person altogether. He was no longer satisfied with being a commercial pilot. He suddenly no longer had a father—or a passionate interest in his wife.

And whatever his waning feelings toward Michele, she felt even less excited about him. The loss of her mother and her frustration with his living in Los Angeles had brought back her depression.

The few times they were together each month, Connor found himself afraid the wife he loved might never return. Gone was the woman who looked into his eyes, hearing not only his words but his heart. Instead Michele's expression seemed distant. Dead.

Often she handed Susan to him the moment he walked in the door. "Here, she needs a new diaper. I'm going back to bed." Then without another word, she'd turn and head for their bedroom.

Their bond badly frayed, Connor avoided coming home.

All of these feelings weighed on him that fateful Thursday in August 1996. He'd already had a one-night layover in Honolulu, and that morning he checked out of his hotel. But because of the storm, his early afternoon flight was delayed first one hour, then two. By the afternoon the tropical storm grew to hurricane levels and took up residence just off the islands.

Winds were too strong to fly in, so while Tropical Storm Henry did its slow dance around the Hawaiian Islands, Connor and hundreds of pilots, flight attendants, and passengers sat grounded. Hotel rooms were gone in less than an hour, full with both the outgoing and incoming tourists. Some people gladly roomed with strangers. Whatever it took to find a safe place to stay.

He saw Kiahna for the first time Thursday night, when the storm was building at a rapid rate. From the beginning, something about the young woman reminded Connor of Michele. The way she angled her head, or the light in her eyes when she talked to the waiter. Not the flirty, forced look some flight attendants had with men, but something deeper. A sensitivity, maybe.

She was pretty enough—light tan island skin, and vivid green eyes. But even so he wasn't interested. Intrigued, yes. Curious about the way she reminded him of Michele, but nothing more. Their tables were adjacent, close enough that he was aware they had ordered the same thing. When the waiter returned to the kitchen, her eyes met his and held. What would it hurt? He had plenty of time to kill. Besides, he wanted to know exactly how much like Michele the woman was. So Connor spoke first.

"You live here?"

"Yes." An odd sadness haunted her eyes, but she smiled. "My flight's delayed. And with the storm, we might not fly at all." She leaned back and studied him. "You're a pilot?"

Connor nodded. "Finished my layover. Supposed to fly out a few hours ago. The new time is in two hours."

"Me, too." She glanced out the nearest window. "But I'm not counting on it. This one could hit pretty hard."

Their conversation continued. Questions from Connor about the island, and questions from her about the airline he worked for. Before their meals were delivered, they joined tables, and he told her about his plans to own a regional airport. When dinner was over, she anchored her slim elbows on the table, linked her fingers, and rested her chin.

"You know what I like about you?"

The candid way she spoke caught him by surprise. She was so like Michele. The Michele he'd fallen in love with. "What?"

"You're a doer; I can tell. You'll do whatever you set your mind to, and somehow you'll make it work out."

In the hundred times since, whenever Connor would analyze that scene looking for escape routes, he was certain that comment was the turning point. Back then, Michele was forever telling him he wasn't doing enough. Not enough to find a way out of Los Angeles, not enough to help with the kids, and not enough to keep her happy. But without knowing him, the island girl saw something in him Michele no longer saw.

He was a doer.

The rest of the memory was smudged black and charcoal, streaked with dirty oranges and yellows. He'd tried to get away from her, hadn't he? Hotels and bed-and-breakfasts, even the airport pilot lounge, none of them had been open. And he tried at least what, three times to tell her he was married? Tried to find a way out of the strange circumstances that somehow conspired to bring them together.

But it was no use. His convictions about faith and morality and marriage were no match for the way things played out that night, or the temptations that presented themselves in the next twenty-four hours.

Not in light of her comment.

As time passed, the FAA investigation ended in Connor's favor, with a warning for him to follow control tower instructions. Flying became fun again, and with the help of prayer and medication, Michele found her way out of depression. Before the end of that awful year, he was even stationed back in Florida.

But he would never be the same again.

Because his feelings for his father had all but died. And the secret of what happened that stormy night was locked permanently in the darkest closet of his heart.

In a place where Michele would never find it.

Next to him, his copilot mumbled something, and the sound of it caught Connor's attention.

He let the memory go. Besides, who had time for remembering? He had a plane to land, and a future that suddenly demanded his every waking minute. Somewhere in Honolulu he had a son, a boy who maybe even looked like him, a child who needed a home.

He realized something then, something as painful as it was stark and true. He could call Marv Ogle back and tell him no, and none of them would ever be the wiser. Max would never know his father rejected him, and Michele … Michele would never know a thing about that awful summer night.

The muscles in his jaw tightened. How could he tell her a thing like this, that nearly eight years ago he'd had an affair and never found a way to tell her? He sighed and the sound of it filled the cockpit. Beside him, his copilot glanced over.

"You okay?"

"Yeah." Connor's answer was quick. "Fine."

The words tasted bitter and deceitful, because the truth was only just starting to work its way through him. No matter what pain his decision would cost Michele and the girls, he could think of no way around it. He hated himself for what he was about to do, what was about to happen to his life, his home, his family. But now that he knew about Max, now that he understood that somewhere in Honolulu lived a boy that was his own flesh and blood, his mind was already made up.

Regardless of Michele's response, or the lies they'd have to tell the girls at first, the answer was obvious. He could argue with himself, refuse the possibility, even deny it existed. But still the boy would come. No matter what he might want to tell himself about putting Michele's feelings first, or leaving well enough alone, the boy would come.

Connor couldn't live with his curiosity otherwise.

The visit would last only two weeks, a trial run, to satisfy Connor's questions even though the very act of doing so would scar Michele and the girls for life. But if he was honest with himself, Connor would admit he was already looking past the trial run with Max, and on into the slightest hint of a possibility. The possibility of a future with the boy.

A future that in the past few hours had changed to include a son he'd not yet met.

Which was why his throat felt thick, and he had to work to fight the overwhelming urge to hate himself. Because no matter how much pain he was about to inflict on his family, he would do it willingly, all so he could take a chance at being the boy's father. All so maybe, just maybe, he might have the one thing he'd wanted all his life.

A son to call his own.

ELEVEN

The date was Connor's idea, and it improved everything about Michele's day.

He called her before his last flight and asked her to find a sitter for the girls. "Meet me at the beach, at our spot."

She was finishing a haircut, and the sound of his voice was a balm to her soul. She sank into her desk chair and dropped her voice to a whisper. "What's the occasion?"

"I miss you; we need time alone."

His answer kept Michele guessing for the rest of the afternoon. Nothing in his tone suggested the talk would be anything serious, but maybe he'd decided to contact his father. Maybe after seeing the car accident the other day he'd realized that life was too short. His father couldn't possibly have long to live, his heart being damaged as it was.

Or maybe it was something else.

Maybe he'd gotten a promotion at work and now he'd be flying international flights again. International flights brought a pilot more hours, which in turn meant more money. Only the most senior pilots had the option of flying international. Though Connor had flown them when he was younger, after the FAA investigation he'd had to work his way back to the place where he was now.

By the time Michele handed off instructions to the sitter, kissed Elizabeth and Susan, and headed for the car, she was almost certain that was it. It had to be. And knowing Connor, he was probably wondering if that type of promotion would actually be good for his family.

Of course he wanted to talk.

She pulled onto the main highway and pictured their spot.

The place was three miles north of the beach where they liked to take the girls. It had more grass, with a beach too narrow for most tourists. A fallen log not far from the sand worked as a bench, and every few months she and Connor made their way to the spot for time alone.

Michele turned her car onto the frontage road. She was almost there now, and her heart beat harder at the thought of his news. Whatever it was. Yes, he'd left only the day before, but life at home had been crazier than usual—missed hair appointments, late clients, and a permanent wave that practically burned the hair off the head of a seventy-two-year-old woman from the school's volunteer library staff.

All morning Elizabeth and Susan fought over which of them owned a certain blouse, each certain that it belonged to her. When Michele told them to work it out, they ripped the shirt in two, and were relegated to their bedrooms as soon as they returned from school.

An hour of quiet intimacy with Connor was just what she needed.

The talks they had at their beach spot were crucial for her, maybe even more than for Connor. It was at their quiet spot that they used to pray together, back before life grew so full and busy. But even without prayer, here she didn't bury her emotions the way she so often did. Passion and depth were a part of her, the same way they were a part of Connor. But it was easier to breeze through the day confident in her work and her time with the girls, listening to her clients pour their hearts out while she did little but interject an occasional yes or no.

Her heart took time to draw out, and Connor was excellent at doing that. He'd start with lighthearted, silly one-liners, and like a therapist or a magician, he'd pull from her a detailed report of her innermost feelings. Whether she'd wanted to share them or not. The thing of it was, she'd spent her life before Connor being independent, not needing anyone but herself and her God.

But Connor . . . Connor she needed. It had been that way from the beginning, and every year she relied on him more, found herself more in love with him. It wasn't the same crazy, starry-eyed love they'd shared after college. Rather it was something deeper, something that blended love and friendship and complete, utter vulnerability.

The combination was intoxicating. Michele rarely let her mind wander, as she had a few days ago, down the path of what-ifs. Because deep within her, in a place only he was allowed to see, she didn't think she'd survive if anything ever happened to him.

She pulled into the parking lot and headed for their familiar spot. Connor's car was there, and already she could feel the layers slipping away. From the place where she parked she saw him, saw his back to her as he stared out at the Atlantic Ocean.

For a fraction of an instant she wondered if something was wrong. His posture wasn't quite right, not as tall and proud. More defeated, somehow. But she dismissed the thought as soon as it came. Connor didn't call her out here to tell her bad news. What bad news could he possibly have?

She took light steps, and managed to sneak up behind him without gaining his attention. When she was a few inches away, she eased her fingers over his shoulders and loosely around his neck. "Hey . . ."

He turned just enough to see her. "Hi." His smile looked forced, and again she swallowed back a surge of doubt. "Thanks for coming."

"I needed it."

"Rough day?"

"Very." She walked around the log and took her place beside him. "Bad hair for Thelma Lynn, a torn blouse for Elizabeth and Susan." She angled her face and caught his gaze. "But this was a good idea."

Connor searched her face, then looked back out to sea and a sad sort of moan came from deep within him. Michele could barely hear it above the sound of the surf, but it touched a nerve in her soul all the same.

"Michele, we need to talk."

"Okay." She ignored his tone and kept hers light. "I'm here."

He hung his head and with his right hand, he rubbed the base of his neck. When he looked up, he sucked in a full breath and found her eyes again. "Remember that call the other day, the one from the attorney in Hawaii?"

"Yes." Michele reminded herself to smile. "They want you in Honolulu for a week to testify, and you're taking me along." She let loose a bit of stiff laughter. "Right?"

"I wish." Not even a hint of humor shone back at her from his eyes. He took her hand in his and worked his fingers between hers. Without looking away, he exhaled through his nose and gave a single shake of his head. "What I'm about to say is the hardest thing I've ever told you. I want you to know that."

A lightheaded feeling came over Michele and made her dizzy. She gripped the edge of the log with her right hand and felt her guard go up. What was he talking about, the hardest thing he'd ever told her? She gave a slight nod of her head. "The hardest thing, Connor . . . what do you mean?"

He turned so that he was facing her and brought his other hand to circle around the one he was still holding. "The attorney was representing the estate of a woman named Kiahna Siefert. She was a flight attendant killed in the Western Island Air crash the other day in Honolulu."

Michele felt a twinge in her feet—she had the sudden urge to run. Why would an attorney for a dead flight attendant want anything to do with her husband? Did Connor know the woman? If so, why hadn't he ever mentioned her?

And why was this the hardest thing he'd ever told her?

She stared at the path to the beach and wondered how long it would take her to jerk her hand free and run to the surf. She could jump into the waves and swim until she was too tired to move another inch, and when she looked back at the beach Connor would be gone. It would all be a dream, and she would wake up beside him, free from worry or concerns about an attorney or a dead flight attendant or anything that might even remotely involve her and Connor.

Instead she tightened her grip on the edge of the log and found the strength to speak the single question burning a hole in her heart. "Did . . . did you know her?"

"Yes." Again Connor held her gaze, but this time she was sure she saw regret layered across his expression. "For a short time."

She dug her nails into the wood and made a weak attempt to pull her other hand free from his. He didn't let go. Anger joined the host of emotions wreaking havoc on her insides. "Get to the point, Connor."

"I'm sorry." He looked at the water once more and gave a slow shake of his head. "The attorney tells me Kiahna left behind a son, a seven-year-old boy." Connor's voice fell, and Michele had to strain to hear it above her pounding heart. He turned to her again, and this time his eyes were colored with an even deeper regret, a regret she hadn't known he was capable of.

He looked straight up for a moment, and then back at her. "The boy is mine, Michele. I didn't know about him until yesterday."

"Y–yours?" She stared at him, her throat so tight the word barely squeezed through. She pulled her hand from his and crossed her arms hard against her stomach. Shock slapped her around and left her speechless, unable to even imagine what might come next.

If the child was Connor's, then . . .

He'd had an affair.

He'd been with another woman and never told her about it. Even when she'd thought everything was perfect between them. Pain seized her chest and she knew instinctively what it was. A piece of her was dying. The part that had trusted Connor without hesitation was suddenly gasping for air, losing its heartbeat, unable to exist in light of the news.

What had she done wrong? She grabbed at the details floating in her mind and ordered them to line up. If the boy was seven, then Connor was with his mother what . . . eight years ago? So what was it, her depression? The trouble she'd had with losing her mother? She could hardly help those things.

She'd been pregnant back then, hadn't she? Pregnant with Susan. So, maybe he hadn't been attracted to her. Maybe she wasn't thin enough for him.

And who could blame him?

"It was my weight, right? I wasn't thin enough."

"No!" He shot her a look that mixed shock with growing shades of desperation. "Of course not." He rested his forearms on his knees and stared at the sand and grass beneath them. "It was one time, Michele, I swear. One night when we were grounded in Honolulu during a storm."

Michele closed her eyes and in a rush the things he was saying became real. It was true; he'd had an affair with a flight attendant. Michele held her breath and in the devastated places of her soul, a desperate prayer began to form.

God . . . I'm dying. I can't breathe . . . help me.

Daughter, I am here with you . . . I will never leave you nor forsake you. Never . . .

She sat up a bit straighter. Where had the voice come from? It was the faintest whisper, but then … it wasn't a whisper at all. More of a soft breath inside her soul. She had believed in God all her life, but never had she felt anything like this, this certainty that God Himself had spoken to her.

He would never leave her nor forsake her? Weren't those words in the Bible somewhere? The thought gave her the strength to open her eyes and consider once more the things Connor had said.

In the distance a couple walked by, hand in hand, their voices blending with the breeze and the sound of the water on the sand. Michele turned to Connor and stared at him. He had his hands over his face, but he was still staring at the ground through the cracks in his fingers.

Michele gritted her teeth, hating him for doing this to her, to both of them. Hating him and desperate not to lose him all at the same time. How *dare* he call her out here to say something so devastating? She wanted to slap him and scream at him, fall into his arms and run for her life, but she was frozen, unable to do anything but focus on breathing. Black dots danced before her eyes, and she held her breath, determined not to give in to them, not to pass out from the blow.

It struck her that while Connor was staring at the ground, she couldn't think of anything to do but look at him. She couldn't scream or laugh or run or cry. That type of pain would come later, for sure. But now it was all she could do to navigate the broken pieces of her life. She whispered the words that wouldn't go away. "How could you?"

Without looking up, Connor opened his mouth. "Everything was so crazy that summer, Michele … I never meant for it to happen."

She had to keep from covering her ears and spewing something awful at him. Instead she forced herself to analyze the situation. If the boy was seven, then yes, the affair had happened in the summer of 1996, the year Connor was stationed in Los Angeles and every-thing about their lives seemed to be falling apart. She'd always believed that she was the reason he'd found his way back, the rea-son he'd been able to continue on as a pilot and put the mess with the FAA investigation behind him.

Now, in a single moment, all of that certainty was gone.

"Connor . . ." She had no strength for the questions that lined up and demanded her attention. But first—no matter what it cost her—she needed the rest of the story, the part about the boy. "What did the attorney say?"

Her husband made a slow move to straighten himself. The con-fident, cocksure man who never let life get the better of him was defeated for the first time as far back as she could remember. His shoulders looked small, his face drawn and wrinkled around the eyes, as though exposing the secrets of his past had aged him ten years in as many minutes.

He dragged his fists hard and rough across his cheeks, and gave another brief look at the sky before turning to her. The air eased from his lungs and he seemed to shrink some more. "His mother left instructions that if anything ever happened to her, the attorney was supposed to find me."

"Why?" How dare this other woman want her son to meet Con-nor . . . after so many years. "Why would she want him to call you?"

His eyes searched hers. "She wanted Max to spend two weeks with me . . . with us. He wouldn't know I was his father, Michele. It would only be a chance to connect. Then . . ." He paused and pursed his lips. "Then if things worked out, maybe he would come here."

She was on her feet. "Here? With us?"

"Yes." The word was so soft, so hesitant, Michele almost missed it.

Her mind raced, and she took two steps toward the water, spun, and walked back to Connor. "You told him no, right? We couldn't do that, Connor, none of us. Not me or you or the girls. Tell me you told him no."

Connor only looked at her, his eyes begging her to understand. When he said nothing, she knew. Not only had her husband had an affair and fathered a child, but now, instead of moving on, he wanted the boy to become part of their family. The idea was unthinkable, the information more than she could process.

Without saying another word, she turned and headed down the beach.

"Michele!"

His tone sounded weak, hopeless, and she neither stopped nor turned around. She walked to the place where the surf lapped against the shore and veered right. Then she ran as hard and fast as she could, harder than she'd ever run in her life until she was certain she'd placed a mile between her and Connor.

There, alone on the beach, she dropped to the sand and let the flood of hurt come.

How *could* he? How could he destroy her with not one, but two bombs in a single conversation? She was still trying to believe he'd cheated on her, still trying to reckon with the idea that all those years ago he'd slept with another woman. But the idea of bringing that woman's child into their home?

Connor had to be crazy to consider it.

What would the girls think? Daddy had a *special friend*, and now her son was going to move in with them? They'd see through that story before they were in middle school, and then what? Would they hate him for being unfaithful, hate him for taking them to church all those years, all the while living a lie?

She didn't know how long she sat there, letting the ocean breeze play against her wet cheeks. With every passing minute, her options became more painful, if less complicated. Connor had given her no choice, really. He wasn't looking for her approval in the matter. He was telling her what he wanted to do.

Otherwise he never would've brought it up.

He'd kept the news of his affair silent for nearly a decade. Surely he could've taken the details of it to his grave without her knowing the truth. Here, now, only one reason existed for his saying anything.

He wanted the boy, wanted a chance to have the son she'd never given him.

"*Why*, God?" She shouted the words at the ocean. "Why weren't we enough?"

Connor would force her to agree to the plan, because what were her options? Tell him no, and have him quietly resent her forever? That would never do, but then neither would bringing that child into their home. How long could he live with them before she went crazy from the constant reminder of Connor's unfaithfulness?

The truth of that burned within her, but it left her no choice. Whatever happened from here, the boy would have to come. If she refused Connor the chance to see the child, he'd hold it against her for the rest of her life.

And if he came . . .

Michele stood and walked back to Connor. She felt like a zombie, a member of the walking dead. He was still there, sitting on the log, waiting for her. When she was close enough for him to hear her, she crossed her arms and locked eyes with him. "Bring him, Connor."

She hated the momentary flicker of hope that flashed in his eyes. The look was gone as quickly as it had come, replaced with a more appropriate guilt and regret. "Michele . . ."

"I'm serious. Bring him."

For a long while Connor said nothing. Then he looked at her, searching her eyes. "Really?"

"Yes. Bring him here for two weeks." Her voice had taken on a different quality in the past hour, though she couldn't quite figure what it was. Before she changed her mind, she continued. "We'll tell the girls he's the son of one of your friends."

She held his eyes a moment longer, then turned and made her way to the car. She pulled out of the parking spot and left him sitting on the log, still facing the ocean. That was fine with her. He could drive home by himself and think about how he'd been willing to destroy her, ruin all they shared, for a boy he'd never even met.

She was halfway home when she found a way to define the difference in her voice. Whereas before it sang with joy and hope and possibility whenever she was with Connor, now it sounded dry, mechanical. It was a tone that was bound to get worse as time went on, as the boy came to stay with them, and she was forced to see in his face a woman who had lured Connor into sleeping with her.

She felt sick at the thought of seeing him.

"God . . . I can't do this."

No reassuring thoughts flitted through her head this time, and again she was struck by her voice. Because she recognized the sound. She'd heard it that long-ago morning when her mother called to report that she was feeling sick.

"Honey, I think I need a doctor," her mother had said. And the sound of her voice was almost exactly the same as the sound in her own voice now. Dry and broken and terrified.

The sound of someone dying.

TWELVE

Again, Connor made the call from a quiet chair at a deserted air-port gate.

He was transferred to Mr. Ogle's office, and when the man didn't answer, Connor left him a message. "Call me as soon as possible."

An hour remained before he needed to report to his gate, and he had nothing else to do. So he sat back, clutched his cell phone, and thought about his life. In less than twelve hours it had become a nightmare.

Michele hadn't said anything more than necessary, functional things since hearing the news. "Pass the salt, please," or "Here's your laundry." Their Tuesday morning time was spent with her in the utility room organizing the cupboards. It felt like a lifetime ago that he'd promised they would pray together, read the Bible together. The girls had noticed last night, of course. Each of them came to him several times with their concerns.

"What's wrong with Mommy?"

And from Elizabeth, their oldest, "Are you and Mommy in a fight?"

He did his best to calm their fears, explaining that Mommy and Daddy had a lot on their minds, but no, they weren't in a fight. It was true. Michele didn't seem up for a fight. She hadn't asked about Kiahna or how he'd met her or how important their time together had been. Almost as if she'd rather let their relationship die a sudden death than know the details of that August night, and fight him over what had happened.

Connor tightened the grip on his phone. No matter what direction things went from here, he would never forget the look on

Michele's face when he told her the news. She'd always talked about how much she trusted him, and recently how what had happened to Renee and Joe would never happen to the two of them.

But he hadn't known until that evening on the beach exactly how much she'd believed in him. He watched the truth become clear in her heart as the initial shock wore off and the facts became part of her. The doubt in her eyes since then was enough to bring him to his knees.

Not literally, of course.

This wasn't the type of thing he was going to run to their pastor over, not the type of thing he'd go to the men's minister to confess. It happened eight years ago, after all. Eight years. He'd been perfect since then, faithful, honest, everything Michele and the girls needed. Even now, in the wake of the trauma his announcement had caused Michele, they had no issues to resolve, no conflict to work through. Her heart was bruised, yes, but as long as she could separate the past from the present, Michele would eventually forgive him for something that had happened so long ago.

Counseling would be a waste of time at this point. Unless Michele couldn't learn to trust him again. Then he'd call the pastor for sure.

But not yet. For now, the situation was simple. They would take the boy in for two weeks and make a decision after that.

He hated how the truth had hurt Michele, regretted the confusion it was causing his girls, but the affair hadn't been his fault. He hadn't planned it, after all. It simply happened. The result of a kind of accumulated pressure unlike anything he'd ever experienced. He'd never loved Kiahna. Never even fallen for her. It had just been one of those things, one of those awful situations that happen.

Yes, he'd made a wrong choice, but that was in the past. Too far in the past for Michele to doubt him today.

But she did. No question about it. Doubt filled her eyes the way hope and joy and love had filled them just a few days earlier.

The phone in his hands vibrated and he jumped. In one motion, he flipped it open and pulled up the antenna. "Hello?"

"Mr. Evans, this is Marv Ogle, the attorney in Honolulu."

"Yes, Mr. Ogle." Connor felt his chest tighten. "My wife and I have made a decision about Kiahna's boy." He paused. After his next statement, there would be no turning back. "We'd like Max to come visit for two weeks, the way Kiahna requested in her will."

"Very well." The man's voice filled with a kind of uncertain relief. "Today is Tuesday. When shall we fly him out?"

Connor already had an answer, not that he'd discussed it with Michele. When he'd tried the night before, she held up one hand and shook her head. "This is your thing, Connor. Do what you want."

Now he slid to the edge of his seat and clenched his jaw. "How 'bout Friday evening?"

"Friday evening." The attorney paused and the sound of shuffling papers filtered through the phone lines. "Very well, that should work."

"Can we . . . talk about the guidelines, the story we'll tell him?"

"Certainly. Kiahna assumed you wouldn't want to tell the boy you were his father. Not at first, anyway."

"Right." Connor felt his heart beat harder against his uniform. It was really going to happen; in a few days he would meet his son for the first time, come face to face with the sins of his past. Shame colored his tone. "What will you tell him?"

"Just what Kiahna said in her letter, that you were a friend of hers, and that it meant a lot to her that Max spend a few weeks with you."

"Okay." Connor swallowed. His palms were sweaty, and the list of questions he'd prepared suddenly slipped his mind.

"Max knows he has a father, Mr. Evans. Kiahna told him in her letter that perhaps one day he would find his biological dad and have a relationship with him. Then again, perhaps not. Either way, he believes he has a father in God." The attorney paused. "Faith is very important to Max."

Faith?

Guilt washed over Connor as he considered that. He was supposed to be a man of faith. But since 1996 his relationship with God hadn't amounted to much more than a few appearances at church each month and the constant intention to get back to praying, back to reading the Bible. Back to connecting with God. Instead he'd rarely found time, and in the absence of a relationship with the Lord, Connor had done his best to work things out on his own.

But Max . . .

Apparently Max believed in a way that made people notice.

"What . . . what else?" Connor was stalling, buying time until his thoughts cleared.

"He loves a cold can of Coke, especially the little bit that gets stuck on the inside rim of the can. His favorite food is whipped cream and blueberry pancakes, and on stormy nights he's afraid of the dark. He likes trees because they point up to heaven, snowmen because they seem real, and any kind of animal. He's the fastest boy on his baseball team, and he loves listening to Jana Alayra's music."

"Jana Alayra?"

"She sings Christian songs, stuff for kids. When her CD's playing in the house, he sings along at the top of his lungs."

"He's a singer, too, huh?"

"Not really." The attorney chuckled. "He's tone deaf, but he loves it all the same. And seeing him sing songs about not veering from the path that's right is as beautiful as anything I've ever heard."

An idea struck Connor. Mr. Ogle loved Kiahna's son like his own. It was something he hadn't asked the man, but better that he do so now, before the boy came for the visit. "Mr. Ogle, have you and your wife considered adopting Max?"

The pause at the other end frightened Connor in a way that was irrational. "We've known Max all his life, Mr. Evans, but we're old enough to be his grandparents. I'm afraid we wouldn't be much good to a boy as active as Max. The same is true for Ramey."

"Ramey. The baby-sitter?"

"Yes. Ramey would take him, but the doctors have said she has a year or two at best. Heart disease is winning the battle for her energy, and caring for Max would only make her disease less manageable."

"I see." So there it was. He alone was the answer for the boy. The responsibility was almost as overwhelming as the possibility. "Anything else?"

"Hmmm ..." The attorney thought for a moment. "Oh, yes. I almost forgot about Buddy. Max's best friend is his Labrador retriever, Buddy. The two were inseparable before Kiahna's death, and now ... well, the dog hasn't left his side ever since."

"Meaning ..."

"Meaning would you mind if Buddy came with him for the visit? He's completely house-trained, and in warm weather you can keep him outside around the clock. I think it would be helpful for Max."

Connor didn't doubt it. But he and Michele had long since agreed that dogs belonged on wide open farms. Fencing one up in a neighborhood lot was cruel, and often resulted in the kind of incessant barking that turned neighbors into enemies. Besides, Michele had never liked the idea of owning pets. Too much mess and upkeep. The girls were content with their Barbies and goldfish.

He took a moment to imagine what Michele would say if he came home and told her that Max was coming with his dog. A shudder worked its way down his spine, and he cleared his throat. "Uh, no. I'm afraid we can't have the dog. Is there anywhere he can stay?"

Disappointment rang from the attorney's voice. "I discussed that with Ramey, the boy's baby-sitter. She offered to keep Buddy if you were unwilling."

Unwilling. The word poked darts at his conscience, but he could do nothing about it. Bringing Max home would be shock enough, without bringing the dog, too. "I'm sorry, Mr. Ogle. The news has been hard enough on my wife."

"Of course."

"It's only two weeks."

"I understand."

But would Max? How was the boy supposed to feel, yanked from his home and his dog and everything he knew about life and sent to live with a family he'd never met? The question sent an undercurrent of doubt across Connor's resolve.

The attorney launched into some of the details. He was online now, surfing the Internet and finding flights that would work. The most likely one was outbound on the airline Connor flew for. He promised to take care of the reservation, and the conversation stalled.

Mr. Ogle changed directions. "You understand Kiahna's intentions in requesting this visit, is that correct, Mr. Evans?"

"Yes." Connor's stomach tightened. "It's a trial. If we . . . if it works out, we would keep him."

"Exactly. Kiahna didn't list you on the boy's birth certificate. So even though you're his biological father, you and your wife would need to go through the courts to make his adoption legal." The man paused. "And if you don't want him, Kiahna wishes for you never to contact the boy again."

Connor had assumed as much, but he hadn't been sure until now. He felt the stakes of the boy's visit triple. "I'm not sure which way it will go. Not yet anyway."

"Would you like to know my thoughts?" The hint of a smile sounded in the attorney's voice.

"Okay . . ."

"You'll keep him."

Connor tightened his grip on the phone. The idea seemed impossible at this point. "How can you be so sure?"

"Because I know Max, Mr. Evans. It's simple, really. Max is an easy boy to love."

The conversation ended, but Connor sat stone still, replaying the attorney's words in his head. His son sounded like a fantastic kid, but what if he came to visit and hated Florida? What if all he wanted was to catch the next plane back to Hawaii so he could be with this Ramey woman and the Ogles and his best friend, Buddy?

Of course that was only half the battle they faced.

The real issue was how Michele and the girls would take to his presence in their family. Timing for Max's visit would be perfect. The boy would arrive Friday, just in time for the family's annual camping trip, a time when the kids took a few days off school and they enjoyed their favorite lake without the usual crowds. Connor had asked Michele if she wanted him to wait and have the boy visit the following week, when the vacation was over, but she said no.

"We might as well get used to him, Connor. Whether he comes on the vacation or not, he'll be with us. There's no getting around it."

While her answer wasn't exactly positive, she hadn't refused.

The more Connor thought about the plan, the better it seemed. They'd made reservations almost a year earlier for their favorite spot, a shady campground just off Lake Okeechobee. The boat docks were fifty yards away in one direction, the beach fifty yards the other way. Connor had serviced the jet skis and gone over the camping equipment days ago.

He had no doubt that once the boy got past feeling homesick, he would like their family. And if he was as lovable as Mr. Ogle thought him to be, then they would all love him in return.

Even Michele.

THIRTEEN

The phone call came later that day.

Max was at school, and Ramey learned the news just before lunchtime. Max was going to Florida to spend two weeks with the man who had fathered him. Not that Max would know. The man was only willing to take the boy for two weeks, and Buddy wasn't welcome for even that long.

Ramey settled into her chair near the television.

No question, it wasn't fair. But then that was the way of life, wasn't it? How fair was it that she was sick, that even if she wanted Max she couldn't care for him in her condition? She glanced down at the floor near her chair, where Buddy lay curled in a ball. At least she could take care of Buddy. He was a good dog, and she would be there for him when he missed Max.

Earlier that day she'd gone to Kiahna's apartment and sorted through some of her belongings. A moving company was coming to take her furniture to storage until Marv Ogle could decide what to do with it. Ramey had offered to pull together a few bags of clothes for Max and whatever items might be too precious to place in storage.

She found the journal in a nightstand beside Kiahna's bed.

Inside was a detailed accounting of her time with Max's father, as well as her reasons for standing by her faith in the years since. Dozens of entries were devoted to Max, and Ramey's eyes were blurred before she placed the clothbound book in a bag and moved on.

An hour later she had packed everything of any sentimental value. Max's baby book, two photo albums, a box of his schoolwork, and Kiahna's Bible. Mr. Ogle had offered to come by and collect the heavy clothes bags when he was finished with work. But the other items, Ramey brought home herself.

The small bag sat near the patio door, and Ramey struggled to her feet. Maybe something in Kiahna's journal would help her know how to break the news about the trip to Max. She opened the book and thumbed through it.

Her eye connected with an entry dated November 12, 1996. Ramey worked the numbers in her mind and realized Kiahna would've been maybe three months pregnant. A twinge of guilt hit her as she stared at the date. Maybe Kiahna wouldn't have wanted anyone but Max to see her journal. But then, this was different. Kiahna would've wanted her to read the journal if it could shed any light on the way she'd felt about Max's father.

She took a deep breath and found the beginning of the entry.

The doctor says the baby is growing fine, but he knows nothing of my heart, how much I wish I could call Connor and tell him the truth. But I won't, not now or ever. I promised God and myself. If things had been different, Connor and I would've fallen in love slow and proper, married and lived a hundred years together. But he was already spoken for, already committed to a family he loved.

God's ways were clearer to me after Connor. Of course God didn't want us to be together that night because, despite the way we shared our hearts, we should have waited. Then I would've known about his wife, his family. Instead I gave in to my emotions, and now the shame of what we did will stay with me a lifetime.

No, nothing will change my mind about calling him, not even the precious baby growing within me.

When this child is older, maybe he'll seek Connor out for himself. I'll explain that yes, I loved his father—if only for a short time. But what we did by coming together that August was wrong, and I will beg God's forgiveness every day of my life as long as I live. Even so, that doesn't change the way I felt about Connor. Or how determined I am to keep the truth about our baby to myself.

One day, though, one day it could happen. If my God and Father takes me home before my child is full grown, it'll be up to Connor. Because if that happens I'll want my baby to find him.

I pray that if that happens, that God will be merciful in bringing forgiveness to Connor's family. Forgiveness for me and Connor and anyone else who was hurt by what happened that stormy night.

Ramey blinked and a single tear fell on the page just beneath where Kiahna's entry ended. So she had loved the man, after all. The young woman's words were exactly what Ramey had hoped to find. Connor wasn't a man she hated, or someone who had hurt her. He was a man already spoken for.

No wonder Kiahna had never fallen in love again. She took her love for Max's father with her to the grave, as determined to leave him alone as she'd been the day she'd written that journal entry.

Ramey closed the book and stared out at the simple patio beyond her sliding glass door. Nearly all her life she'd shied away from prayer and talk of God. But now, in light of Kiahna's journal entry, she felt obligated to ask Him for a little help. Just in case He was real and actually could hear her.

"God . . ." At the whispered word, she glanced around the room, as though perhaps a flash of light might race through it. She let her eyes settle on the ceiling. After a moment of silence she felt safe enough to continue. "God, if You're up there, then You've got Kiahna now, and . . . well . . ." Her words stuck in her throat and she brought her fingertips to her eyebrows. This wasn't a time to cry, not when she had business with God.

She waited for the lump in her throat to ease some. "If You've got Kiahna, then You know how much we miss her. And You know how hard things are for Max." She did a short cough and swallowed back the sadness in her voice. "From the sounds of it, Kiahna made a mistake with Max's father. But, God . . . I know how sorry she was. She died sorry, I'm sure of it. And now, well, now Max is in a heap of trouble, because what man would want to find out about a son he never knew he had, a son who might ruin his marriage or his whole family."

Her hands fell back to her lap and she soothed her thumb over the worn cloth cover of Kiahna's journal. "What I'm saying, God, is Max needs a little help here. If You want the boy to live with this . . . this Connor man, then You're going to need to work a miracle. A forgiveness miracle, God. Otherwise none of this will work out, and Max will wind up—"

The sadness came then, and Ramey could do nothing to stop it. Because if God didn't work a forgiveness miracle for all of them, then Max would become a ward of the state. And there was no telling what would happen to him after that.

Ramey leaned over and snatched a tissue from the box on the coffee table. She dabbed her eyes and blew her nose and ordered herself to get a grip. If God was still listening, she needed to finish her prayer. For Max's sake.

"So, God, please . . . do this thing for Max. And if You do, I promise You something . . ." Ramey hesitated. She hadn't planned on making any promises to God, but her words were flowing without a filter. "I promise I'll believe in You, God. If You let Connor and his family forgive each other, if You let Max find a place with them, I'll believe in You for the rest of my life."

When Max came home from school, Ramey piled him and Buddy and a picnic dinner into her beat-up station wagon.

"What about my homework?" Max bit his lip. He seemed unsure about the trip. But then he'd been unsure about most of life since his mother's death. The only time he looked at peace was when he was reading the Bible his mother gave him the year before, or when he sat with Buddy out on the patio.

Ramey sighed and motioned Max to come closer. "Buddy loves the beach, right?"

"Right."

"So let's do homework later. Let's spend a few hours on the sand. You can play with Buddy, and then we'll have a picnic and talk a little."

Red flags flashed in Max's eyes. "Talk about what?"

"About life, Max, okay? About life." Ramey turned for the door. "Come on. Buddy needs to get out."

Max set his backpack down and followed her.

They were set up at the beach half an hour later with an early picnic dinner of peanut butter and banana sandwiches and red fruit punch. When they were finished eating, Max and Buddy ran down the beach to chase seagulls.

Ramey brought a bag with her and pulled out a notebook. The idea had been forming in her mind since earlier, after reading Kiahna's journal. If Max was going to spend two weeks with this Connor Evans man and his wife, then several things seemed certain. First, if Kiahna had loved the man in so short a time, Ramey had no doubt that he'd cared for her in return. That meant that no matter what grief the news about Max caused him, Connor would feel for the boy. Max had that effect on people; his father would be no exception.

The problem was bound to be with Connor's wife.

Ramey thought back to the days before her own husband died. How badly would her world have been shaken if he'd come home one day with that kind of news? That he had a son in another state, with a woman he'd slept with while they were married?

She watched Max run through the surf, Buddy close at his heels. It wouldn't matter if the child was wonderful. The blow would've been enough to knock her off her foundation. Maybe even tear their marriage apart.

The idea came to her after the prayer, after she begged God— if He was listening—to make a forgiveness miracle for Connor's family. Maybe she could do something to help, give a message to the man's wife about what God might want in this situation.

She opened the notebook and found a clean sheet of lined paper. Then, with another glance at Max, she began to write.

> *To Mrs. Evans:*
>
> *Hello. My name is Ramey, and you don't know me. I've been Max's baby-sitter for all of his life. Whenever his mother was out of town on a flight, the boy was with me. During that time I haven't been much of a believer. In fact, I haven't believed in God at all, really.*
>
> *But now as I watch Max, as I think about the months and years he has ahead, I want to believe, ma'am. With all my heart I want to believe.*
>
> *Marv Ogle tells me that you and your husband are Christians, the same way Kiahna was a Christian. I've read through some of Kiahna's journal so I might understand Max's situation better, and what I found has given me the beginning of belief. Enough so that I've asked God for a forgiveness miracle for Max.*
>
> *You see, ma'am, I might not be very educated, but I know it will take a forgiveness miracle for life to work out the way Kiahna and even, I think, God wants it to work out.*

She kept writing, detailing for the woman a Scripture she'd found on the inside cover of Kiahna's journal. It was a verse that seemed strong, somehow, in a way Ramey had never felt before. She ended the letter as best she could. Then she folded it and placed it in an envelope. Across the front she wrote, *For Mrs. Evans.* Before Max left she would stick it in his Bible and remind him to give it to the woman. Then she wrote Max a short note. She would stick both letters and a picture of Kiahna and Buddy in Max's Bible. That way he'd remember what was in his heart even when he was so far away from home.

She looked up and scanned the beach for the boy and his dog. The sun was dropping in the sky, and Max and Buddy had tired out. They sat together near the shore, Max digging his toes into the sand, looking out at the ocean, one arm flung around Buddy's neck.

What could he be thinking? Ramey bit her lip. If she did nothing else for Max in all her life, she would stay happy that night. Sadness would only tell Max that whatever lay ahead could be even more painful than the days he'd already survived.

She cupped her hands around her mouth. "Max . . ."

He turned his head in her direction. His eyes looked more at peace than they had earlier. "Yes, Ramey?"

She swallowed hard. After this conversation his future would be set in motion, one way or another. "Can I talk to you, bucko?"

His mouth hung open, as if her question scared him. But he stood and began walking, Buddy beside him. When they reached Ramey, they both dropped to the ground in front of her. Max looked up, his eyes searching hers. "Is this about Mommy's friend?"

So the boy remembered. He'd probably been thinking about spending two weeks with a stranger ever since hearing his mother's letter. Ramey lifted her chin. *No tears . . . no tears . . .* "Yes, Max. It's about that." She reached out and used her thumb to brush a lock of hair off from Max's forehead.

The boy's eyes grew wide. "What about it?"

"Well"—Ramey looked to the deep places of the child's heart— "Mr. Ogle found your mom's friend, and he wants to see you. He lives in Florida with his family. You'll be gone for two weeks." She hesitated. "I wanted you to know."

Max's chin quivered some and anger flashed in his eyes. He put his arm around Buddy. "I don't want to go. I want to stay here with you."

Ramey had never been overly affectionate with the boy. She had never needed to be; Kiahna had showered him with more than enough love. But Kiahna was gone forever, and as Max's shoulders began to shake, she reached out to him. He stood and came to her, falling against her and burying his tan, little-boy face in the soft part of her shoulder. "Don't make me go, please, Ramey."

"Max . . . shhh. It's okay." She soothed her hand against his back, and beside them Buddy rose to his feet and whimpered. "Your mom wants you to do this, remember?"

He drew back, his eyes searching hers. "But she was wrong, Ramey. She thought I would want to go, but I don't. Not ever." He took three quick breaths and rubbed his cheeks. "Do I have to, even if I don't want to?"

Ramey's heart hurt and she made a mental note to take additional nitroglycerin that night before going to bed. Stress like this wasn't good for her. She cocked her head to the side and managed a sad smile. "Yes, Max. You have to go. You leave Friday."

His mouth hung open, and his eyes filled with hurt, as though somehow she'd betrayed him by letting Mr. Ogle and his mother's friend make plans without his approval. He gave a few slow shakes of his head and then he gulped back another wave of sobs. "Is . . . is Buddy coming with me?"

Ramey moved her hands to his shoulders and hoped with everything in her that Max would understand, that he would move past the pain he was feeling to a point where he would be open to whatever God might do in the coming weeks. If God had heard her prayer.

"No, Max." She chewed on her lip for a few seconds. "Buddy will stay with me."

For a moment, Max didn't move. He stared first at Ramey, then at Buddy. "No . . . that isn't *fair*, Ramey." His voice rose and he pulled away from her. "No!" Then he turned and ran, hard and fast, toward the surf.

Buddy seemed confused by the boy's outburst. He stood, looked at Ramey, and wagged his tail. Then he followed after Max. Ramey watched the boy reach the water and shade his eyes.

"No, Mommy!" He shouted the words out over the water. "Don't make me go, not without Buddy!"

This time Ramey could do nothing to stop her tears. They escaped from her heart and made a silent stream down her face. It dawned on her that she needed to ask God for one more part to the forgiveness miracle. Because before Max could ever learn to like the man in Florida—or any part of his family for that matter—he would have to do something he'd never had to do before.

He would have to forgive the mother he loved more than life.

FOURTEEN

Ocean water was getting Max's shorts wet, but he was too mad to care.

He lowered his voice, and this time the words he spoke to his mommy were whispered. From his heart to hers. "Why . . . why should I go?"

The ocean made a *whooshing* sound, and Max had the strongest feeling. If only he could swim across the ocean and find her plane, maybe she wasn't really dead at all. Maybe she was sitting on top of it, waiting for someone to find her. He could be the one, couldn't he? He could find her and sit up there beside her and ask her why she wanted him to take a trip to Florida, wherever that was. Especially when all he wanted to do was stay with Buddy and Ramey.

He dropped to the sand and felt a little bit of wave fill into his shorts pockets. Buddy leaned close to him and licked his face. "She could be alive, don't you think, Buddy?" Max turned his nose to the dog and accepted another swipe across his cheek. "Yeah. Me, too."

A long huff came from inside him, from his heart, maybe. He looked back out at the water, and all of a sudden he remembered what Ramey had told him the day he found out about his mother's plane.

She's dead, Max. No one on the plane lived . . . no one on the plane lived . . . no one on the plane lived.

New tears covered over his eyes and made the ocean blurry. His whispery words were more scratchy than before. "But . . . what if she was the onlyest one?" Buddy made a little whining sound, and Max rubbed him behind his ear.

This time he looked up to the sky, the place where God lived. "Is she really gone, Jesus? Is she with You? Or is she on the plane, waiting for me to help her?"

Most of the time God didn't actually talk back to him. Not with words. But once in a while he could sort of feel what God was saying. He shut his eyes and waited. And just then it came. A feeling that was happy and sad all at the same time, because Ramey was right, that's why. His mommy wasn't on the plane at all, not anymore. She was up in heaven with Jesus.

But what was he supposed to do with the mad in his heart? Mommy should've known he wouldn't want to leave the island to stay with some friend of hers. He wanted to be here, near the water where the two of them had played as far back as remembering could go. Near their apartment and Ramey's apartment and Buddy.

He stretched out his legs, opened his eyes, and let the water come over him. The ocean had a thing called tides; that's what his mommy taught him. When the tide was out, the sand was extra big. But when it came in, it moved real slow up the beach until most of the sand was underwater.

The tide was coming in now, but Max didn't care. Waves could come to his waist and he wouldn't move, because he needed to understand. He squinted his eyes up at the sky again. "God ... I don't want to go to Florida." He lifted his arm and wiped at his cheek with his shoulder. "But I don't want to be mad at Mommy either."

A sense came in him then. A sense was when you knew something even though no one had said it. Mommy told him that good senses came from God, and that when they happened, Max better listen to them in case God was trying to tell him something. This time the sense was that Mommy had a reason for asking him to see her friend.

A reason?

Max had never thought of it that way. But when he turned it around in his brain, the sense seemed pretty smart. His mommy always had a reason for telling him something. She wanted him to wipe his shoes on the mat after playing at the beach, but that had a reason. So he wouldn't make the carpet dirty. He had to wash his hands before he ate, and that had a reason, too. So he wouldn't eat germs with his food.

Yes, maybe the sense inside him was right. Mommy had a reason for the Florida trip. All he had to do was not be mad at her so he could pay attention to what the reason was. The sense got stronger. If he went to Florida, if he used his best manners and didn't complain too much, he would know the reason why his mommy wanted him to go. One day God would make the reason extra clear to him.

Max ran his hand along Buddy's back and leaned against him. "I'm gonna miss you, Buddy."

A comfortable sound came from Buddy's nose. He brushed his head up against Max's and then lowered his furry chin down on top of his paws.

"Listen, Buddy." Max sat up and stared at his dog. "Don't get sad, because I'm coming back, okay? I'll come back just like Ramey said, and after that you and me will be together forever, okay? Okay, Buddy?"

The dog lifted his eyes and then let them fall back again. That's what Buddy always did when he was sad. Max leaned over and hugged the dog, held him close the way his mommy used to hold him when he had a hurt knee or a bad day at school. "That's okay, Buddy. I'm sad, too. But I have a sense. Everything's going to be okay, Buddy. You'll see."

One more time Max sat up, and this time he stood up. Warm ocean water ran down his legs, but he didn't think about it too much. He looked up at the sky one last time and smiled. Smiles could happen even if tears happened at the same time. Max had found that out ever since his mommy went away. He sucked in a breath and whispered one more thing to God.

"Thanks for the sense, God. I felt it." He wiggled his toes until his feet sank a little in the sand. "I'm sorry for getting mad. And could You tell my mom something, please? Tell her I'm not mad at her for making the part in the letter about going away for two weeks. I forgive her, okay? Could You tell her that, God?"

Max didn't need a sense this time. His mommy taught him a long time ago that God was good at passing on messages to people, and God 'specially liked it when people forgave each other.

"Know what love is, Max?" his mom used to ask him sometimes. "Love is what happens when people forgive."

Max was glad he thought of that. He loved his mommy very much and he couldn't stay mad at her.

He looked over his shoulder at Ramey. She looked old and tired and a little bit cold. He didn't want to stay mad at Ramey, either. The trip to Florida wasn't her fault. Max brushed the sand off his shorts and looked real quick at his dog. "Come on, Buddy. Let's go home."

Buddy followed him again, and as soon as he was close enough to Ramey, he said the things in his heart. "I thought about it, Ramey. I'll go to Florida."

Her forehead got bunchy lines on it and surprise showed in her eyes. "Really? You're not mad anymore?"

Max shrugged and felt the corners of his lips lift up. "I'm scared a little, but I'm not mad. God gave me a sense."

Ramey leaned closer. "A sense?"

"Yes. Sense is when God tells you something. But you have to be very still to hear it."

"Oh." Ramey reached for his hand and wrapped her fingers around his. "What sense did you get?"

"That one day I'll know why."

Ramey's mouth stayed open and at first no words came out. Then she said, "Why what?"

"Why Mommy wanted me to go on the trip."

"Oh, right."

One more thing was in his heart to tell her. He took a step closer and looked at her eyes. "I'm sorry, Ramey. I didn't mean to be mad at you. "

Then Ramey said the thing that his mother said meant love. In a happy sort of sad voice she said, "I forgive you, bucko."

And right then, as she said those words, Ramey got something happy in her eyes. Something happier than she'd had for a long, long time.

FIFTEEN

All week, conversation between Connor and Michele came in fits and starts, and the trip to the airport that Friday evening was no different.

Michele wanted to come, wanted to be there to see her husband's reaction when his only son walked off the Jetway. Other people might have to wait at the security staging area, but not Connor and Michele. Pilots had privileges, even with the changes in travel since September 11.

They rode in silence, and a Martina McBride song came on the radio. Michele wasn't really listening, but the point of the song seemed clear enough. "You'll get through this . . . you'll break new ground . . ."

She leaned over and changed the station. Martina had no idea what Michele Evans could survive or what type of ground she was capable of breaking.

Connor drove, his eyes locked on the road ahead. She didn't have to see his expression to know what he was feeling, that mix of fear and excitement over what lay ahead, the fact that he would finally get to see the boy whose existence had so thoroughly changed their lives in a matter of days.

He was driving sixty-five, seventy. Fifteen miles over the speed limit. She rolled her eyes and gazed at the traffic ahead of them. "Speeding won't get him here any sooner."

He shot her a confused look. "I'm not speeding."

"You are."

"No." He looked at the speedometer. "I always drive like this."

"Right." She hated the sarcasm in her voice, hated how it seemed part of her persona now. The bitter wife, still in the dark about why she hadn't been enough for her husband. The angry spouse, bent on punishing Connor for finding her less than perfect.

Connor exhaled and it sounded like steam releasing from the darkest places inside of him. "I'm not in a hurry, Michele. His plane doesn't come in for another hour."

She said nothing. These days if his statements didn't demand a response, she didn't give one. Twice he'd tried to sit her down and explain what had happened with the boy's mother. But always she stopped him before he got started.

"Spare me the details, will you, Connor? I'm not interested." She flashed angry eyes at him. "Besides, I can use my imagination. Long layover, planes grounded in a storm, some smart-looking flight attendant wants your attention and you think, *She looks a lot better than the one I have back home.*" She uttered a poisonous laugh. "Believe me, Connor. I don't need the details."

Each time her response seemed to paralyze him. He'd stand there in front of her, his mouth open. As though he truly wanted to tell her more about what happened, wanted to explain his actions in some way. But then his mouth would close. He'd drop his shoulders and turn away. What could he say? That Michele had nothing to worry about because he'd never so much as called Kiahna after their time together? That he'd never loved the girl?

Michele turned away from Connor. She already knew that much.

Lust. That's what happened to Connor. And now the product of his lust was about to walk into their lives. She hated that, too. The boy had nowhere to go, but still she felt nothing but spite for him. What had happened to the kinder, confident person she'd been two weeks earlier? How could she dream of holding anything against an orphaned little boy?

She had no answers for herself.

Connor took the next exit and the road veered in a semicircle. The sensation made Michele dizzy, not that it took much these days to do that. Her eating habits were completely out of whack. An entire pack of Oreos one day, nothing but water and herbal tea the next. She wanted to starve, never eat another bite of food again. But sometimes her feelings were so jumbled up she couldn't do anything but eat herself into a bloated state of oblivion.

She hadn't told Connor, of course. He didn't need to know about her binge eating. It wasn't something she did all the time. Only when her emotions were more than she could handle. He'd tell her the same thing Renee would tell her, the same thing her sister, Margie, would tell her. Get a grip. Get some help. Grab onto God and don't let go. Eating wasn't the answer; prayer and Scripture and counseling were.

But so far, she hadn't felt like doing anything but eating. Eating and crying and hiding in her craft room so the girls wouldn't see her tears. So Connor wouldn't see the cookie wrappers. She kept a role of paper towels in her bottom desk drawer. Any food trash was squished into a ball, wrapped inside a paper towel, and tossed in her trash can. That way no one would be the wiser.

Besides, what did it matter? Connor could say he was sorry, he could tell her that he still loved her, still found her beautiful. But he'd been saying that back in 1996, hadn't he? Why should she believe him now?

"What are you thinking?" Connor kept his eyes on the road ahead of them.

"Don't ask."

"Michele . . ."

The pain in his voice made her cringe. She was new at hating, and sometimes when his voice sounded the way it did now, she longed to lean over and hug him. Cry with him and scream at him and hold onto him for dear life. Instead she looked out the side window and said nothing.

"Michele, don't do this. What's Max going to think if this is how we are?"

She turned to him. "Max?" Her voice rose a level. "Is *that* what's worrying you, Connor? What *Max* will think when he comes home to a family that's falling apart?" Another bitter laugh. "Well, don't be surprised when I tell you I don't exactly *care* what Max thinks." She clenched her fists and made a sound that was part moan, part yell.

"I'm just saying it'll be awkward." Connor's tone had lost all of its previous sureness. He sounded more like a nervous child dealing with an abusive parent than the conquer-anything pilot.

She lowered her voice. "You want awkward, Connor? Look at the faces of our girls when we get home. See the subtle knowing in Elizabeth's expression and the fear in Susan's. You think those girls don't know something's wrong?"

"Of *course* they do." For the first time that day, he raised his voice at her. She watched him make a straight line of his lips. "I'm sorry. I didn't mean to yell. What I'm saying is, nothing will be right as long as you stay mad at me."

He might as well have kicked her in the gut. Did he really think that's all this was? A case of her being mad at him? "You had an affair, Connor. You slept with some woman in Honolulu, and a few weeks later you came home and acted like nothing ever happened. Every year since then you lived with the truth, but never, not once, did you come clean with me." She dug her fingernails into her thighs. "As long as I'm *mad* at you?"

"Okay, I get it, but at some point you need to listen to me, Michele. Let me explain what happened." He worked the muscles in his jaw, checked the traffic, and changed lanes. The West Palm Beach airport was two miles up the highway. "It was years ago." He clenched his teeth for a moment. "Yes, you just found out about it, but that doesn't change the fact that I've been faithful for almost eight years. It doesn't change the way I feel about you." He reached for her hand but she pulled away. He hesitated but only for a moment. "I love you, Michele."

Deep within her a voice echoed in her soul. *Don't say it ... don't say it, Michele.*

"Yes." She closed her eyes and ignored the warning. "But right now you love that little boy more."

Connor said nothing after that. Michele stared out the window, but in the corner of her eye she could see her husband's expression harden. Again, she wanted to hug him, tell him she was sorry for being so mean. But the wall between them was cement block and razor wire.

She couldn't imagine a way over it, even if she wanted to.

They parked and headed into the airport, side by side. It struck Michele that they finally looked the way she'd seen other couples look in crowded places. Back before her world stopped turning, she and Connor would be walking together, holding hands and leaning in for an occasional whispered one-liner, when they'd pass a couple with dead eyes and three feet of space between them.

"Let's never be like that," she'd whispered to him more than once.

"Never."

But now here they were, just like that. Part of the community of walking dead, together but as cold and alone as if they were in separate parts of Alaska. They reached the gate as the boy's plane rounded the corner and pulled up. Michele crossed her arms and held herself tight as she watched the Jetway accordion out to meet the aircraft.

Fitting ... that Connor's world would connect with the Hawaiian flight attendant here, in an airport. The same way they'd first connected that summer night in Honolulu.

Connor moved a step closer and focused on the tunnel leading from the plane. "He should be one of the first ones off."

Again she said nothing. What could she say? Good? Great, that they'd be seeing him sooner than later? She clenched her jaw and followed Connor's gaze. Two flight attendants came through first. They each took a waiting wheelchair and disappeared down the tunnel again.

Ten seconds passed. Fifteen. Twenty.

She was just about to turn away, to look across the concourse and wonder whether anyone else was waiting for a person who would forever alter their lives by merely getting off a plane. But before she could turn, she saw a blur of motion near the tunnel entrance. And suddenly a male flight attendant exited next to a brown-haired boy with green eyes and honey-colored skin. He was smaller than she'd pictured him, but he was only seven, after all. In the days leading up to his visit, the boy had taken on a larger-than-life image in her mind.

But the most striking thing about him was his face: There was no question he was Connor's son.

Michele wasn't sure where to look. At the boy and his uncanny resemblance to Connor, the boy who was absolutely her husband's, or at Connor and the reaction he had to be feeling. In the end she tore her eyes from the child and watched her husband, watched the way he took a quick step forward, then stopped himself.

He wants to run to the boy. If I wasn't here he'd have the child in his arms in less than a minute. She turned back to the boy and saw the flight attendant notice them.

"Is he with you?"

"Yes," she heard Connor say. "We're here for him."

The words felt like daggers in Michele's soul.

The attendant walked the boy to them. Connor showed his pilot's identification and signed a release form. This time Michele looked at the boy, and a soft gasp filled her throat.

He didn't only look like Connor; he looked like Connor's father. She had expected that, when she saw the boy, she would find herself looking into the face of the woman who'd lured Connor into a one-night stand. Instead, the face was as familiar as it was beautiful. The same face she'd smiled at a million times, the one she woke up next to and looked at across the dining room table.

The only possible resemblance to his mother was his eyes. Piercing green eyes lit up his face and made a stark contrast against his tanned skin and dark hair. His mother must've been breathtaking.

The flight attendant finished his work and left them alone.

"Max?" Connor stooped down and held out his hand. "I'm Mr. Evans, your mom's friend."

The boy reached out and shook Connor's hand. "Nice to meet you, sir."

Something about hearing the boy's voice shot a crack through Michele's tough exterior. He sounded sweeter than an angel, and it took everything in her to remember that he wasn't just any other boy. He was her husband's illegitimate child. She stiffened and cleared her voice. "I'm Mrs. Evans." She nodded at the boy but stopped short of holding out her hand.

"Nice to meet you, ma'am."

Connor's voice was tight, pinched with a kind of glad emotion that only made Michele more angry. "Did you eat dinner yet?"

"Yes, sir. On the plane."

"Well"—Connor straightened—"we're happy you could come, Max."

Michele shifted her attention back to her husband. His face was masked in nonchalance, but beneath that mask she saw a sort of awe, a light he couldn't hide. Hatred flooded her soul again. She had seen Connor look that way only three other times in her life. When they faced each other at the front of a church fourteen years earlier, when Elizabeth was born, and when Susan entered the world.

The fact that he felt that way now knocked the wind from her and nearly dropped her to the airport floor, even as passengers streamed by them. How *dare* he give a look like that to a boy he'd only just met? As if his arrival was packed with as much emotional meaning as any of those previous events? She leaned back on her heels to keep from falling.

As she did, Connor reached out his hand to the child and smiled at him. "Come on, Max. Let's get your suitcase."

Her body moved despite the fact that her heart had crashed to the ground somewhere back at the gate. The concourse was crowded, and though Michele tried to stay even with Connor and the boy, several times the foot traffic kept her a few feet behind, as though there wasn't room for all of them to walk the path together.

The irony slapped her in the face. Of course there wasn't room for all three of them. Not on the concourse, and not in life. And sometime in the very near future Connor would have to decide who was going to stay.

Her or the boy.

They reached the luggage carousel and Connor leaned close to the boy again. "You remember what your bag looks like?"

"Yes, sir." The boy looked up at Connor and blinked. "Long and blue with a zipper on the middle. A ruffle bag, I think."

Michele watched Connor stifle a grin. "A duffel bag?"

"Right. That's it. That's the name Ramey called it."

Michele dropped her arms to her side and stared at them. Connor was in another world, as if he and the boy were the only two people on earth. Already he was bonding with the boy, becoming friends, finding humor in the things he said.

Connor looked at her and motioned her closer. "Help us find Max's bag, okay?"

The boy looked up, and for the first time his eyes held hers. It didn't matter that he looked like Connor; his eyes were his mother's.

She had no doubt. Looking into them now made her feel like the woman was standing next to her, linking arms with Connor and laughing at her for ever trusting him.

She blinked and managed the slightest smile in the boy's direction. "Yes, of course." Her eyes darted from the boy's face to the moving belt and the luggage that was just starting to spill onto it. "A blue duffel bag."

The boy looked, too, and after a few minutes he pointed. "There it is! I see it!" He took a step closer, but Connor took gentle hold of his shoulder and stopped him.

"I'll get it." He reached over and pulled the bag easily up and onto his shoulder.

As he did, Michele caught sight of the tag fastened to the black nylon handle. In big, black letters it said simply, *Kiahna Siefert, Western Island Air.*

The label was the last and greatest blow . . . the surefire explosion that ripped through her soul and told her the truth. Her husband had fathered a child with another woman.

Connor caught Max's hand in his once more, and Michele knew.

Whatever decision was yet to come, for the most part it had already been made. If the future held room for only two of them, then she would need to start thinking about where she was going to live. Because she knew Connor Evans better than she knew herself.

And the way he held that little boy's hand, he wasn't ever going to let go.

Sixteen

Connor's heart was killing him.

Wracked with a series of wildly varying emotions in a way he'd never experienced before, he was beyond exhausted long before the three of them pulled out of the airport and back onto the highway.

The scene that had just played out was destroying his wife; it had to be. And because of that, he was desperate with grief. But at the same time . . . at the same time a myriad of brilliant colors was going off in his mind. Colors he'd never even imagined before this day. The reason for them was simple.

He had a son.

All he could do as they headed home was replay the way he'd felt back at the airport, again and again and again.

From the moment he laid eyes on Max, he knew the boy was his. The child was strong and healthy and striking, just the way Marv Ogle had said he would be. And the resemblance to Connor was amazing. Same strong jaw, same dimpled chin, same forehead.

As Max came closer, Connor felt himself falling hard for the boy, allowing the child entrance into a very select place in his heart. A place from which there would be no return, whether Max stayed with them or not.

But it wasn't until he took his son's hand in his that he felt it. A connection different than anything he'd ever known. It was part remorse, part rejoicing. For here was a son he'd missed without knowing it. Missed Max's birth and his first smile, his first steps and early days of preschool. Connor hadn't been there to marvel over his son's first attempt at writing his name, nor had he been there to watch him take his first at-bat in baseball.

Those moments, all of them, were gone forever.

But the rejoicing came in knowing that, because of some twist of fate, they'd found each other. Now, if Connor had any influence on Michele, he would never let his son go.

Connor checked the rearview mirror and met Max's eyes. The boy gave him a shy smile. "Florida looks like Hawaii."

"Yes, I guess it does." Connor grinned back at him and cast a quick look at Michele. The comment hit its mark. She turned and looked out her window, refusing to take part in the conversation.

Five minutes passed, and the tension in the car felt thicker than glue. He turned on the radio and punched a series of buttons and zipped past one commercial after another until Lee Greenwood's "God Bless the USA" filled the car.

Max didn't say anything, but Connor watched him in the mirror, checking on him every few seconds. It occurred to Connor what a good job Kiahna had done with their son. He was painfully polite, and more than a little shy. Connor figured the shy thing had more to do with the situation than Max's real personality. If Max and Michele didn't want to talk, Connor would. He rambled on about the girls and their camping trip, trying to sound as normal as possible. Still, the tension remained.

They arrived home in thirty minutes, and Connor hesitated before getting out of the car. It was only seven o'clock. The girls would be up, anxious to meet the son of Daddy's friend. He'd sat them down earlier in the week and told them about Max, that he was coming for two weeks and that he'd join them on their vacation.

Neither of the girls seemed bothered by the idea, though they wondered if he'd have his own sleeping bag for the trip. Susan wanted to know if he liked climbing trees, and Elizabeth wondered if he was old enough to ride a bike in the street. He still hadn't seen the fear and doubt Michele was certain they were feeling.

Either way the moment at hand was a big one.

Michele climbed out in silence and went inside without saying a word. That left Connor and Max in the garage, making sure he had his blue duffel bag. Before they went inside, Max looked at him, his eyes wide. "Is this house all yours?"

Connor wasn't sure what the boy meant. "Well, not really. It belongs to my wife and daughters, too."

"Yes, but . . ." He looked over his shoulder at the garage and back at the entrance to the house. "It's so big. I thought maybe . . . maybe other families lived here, too."

"Nope." Connor kept his tone even. The boy had probably lived most of his life in near poverty, all because he hadn't had a father to help out. He smiled at Max and took his hand again. "Just us." They stepped inside and walked through the utility room toward the main living room. "Ready to meet the girls?"

Max nodded. "Ready."

They were waiting on the sofa together. Connor had hoped Michele would be with them, but she was nowhere around. When the girls spotted them, they stood and took a few steps forward.

Elizabeth dropped her eyes to the place where Connor held Max's hand, and instantly he let go. As he did, her expression changed and the sweet smile that was so typical of her personality flashed on her face. "Hi . . . you must be Max."

He nodded. "Hi."

Susan skipped the formalities. She took a few quick steps in his direction and then motioned toward the stairs. "Wanna see my new Lego set?"

Max's eyes grew wide. "You have Legos?"

"Sure. Not all girls play with dolls, you know." Her lighthearted laughter broke the tension, and the threesome started to move away.

Then, as though he'd only just remembered where he was, Max stopped and looked at Connor. "Is it okay? If I go up and play with them?"

Warmth beyond description filled the center of Connor's being. These were his three children. Playing together for the first time. He struggled to find his voice. "Yes, Max. Go play."

He listened to their silly chatter as they headed up the stairs.

"How was your plane ride?" The voice was Elizabeth's, less childlike, and more to the point. "I hate the turbulence."

"Yeah. Me, too. But this one was great. Not too bumpy."

"Hey, guess what?" Susan wasn't about to let Elizabeth have the upper hand in the conversation.

Connor felt a pang at his daughters' determination to make Max feel welcome. How would they feel if they knew the truth?

Susan was rambling. "And then I also have Lego sets that make a plane and a spaceship." Her voice faded as she must've run ahead of the others, intent on showing Max her entire Lego collection.

"Wow, could I play with it?"

Their voices grew too distant for him to make out. Only then did he remember to exhale. He needed to find Michele, needed to talk to her and see what she was feeling, why she left the family and went up to her room. Why couldn't she have made even a little effort that night?

But first he had something to do.

He crept into his office and opened the top drawer of his filing cabinet. Tucked behind a dozen manila files was a small stack of three picture frames he'd hidden years ago. He pulled them out, careful not to bump them on the cabinet. Then he looked at the one on top. It was a picture of him and his father, taken at his graduation from West Point. The photo was always one of his favorites because his father looked so proud of him.

He studied it now, studied the way his arm hung loosely around his father's shoulders. The way his other hand was linked to his dad's in a handshake to mark the moment. He pulled the frame closer, looked intently at his father's eyes. There had been no sign back then, no hint that one day the two of them would walk away from each other forever.

No sign except the obvious.

His father had often been proud of Connor's accomplishments, but he couldn't remember once when the man had been proud of him as a person. Proud just to call him his son. A memory began to take shape, one from the year before their falling out. Connor had been helping Elizabeth walk along a gravel path through his parents' backyard garden at the ranch in Cambria.

"What are you doing out there?" His father had barked the words from a distance, his hands on his hips.

Connor remembered smiling, wishing his father would smile back. When the man's mouth remained slack, Connor spoke up. "Helping my little girl take a walk, Dad. Wanna join us?"

"You'll spoil her, Connor. She's two years old; she can walk by herself." He walked away, shaking his head and muttering something about independence and knowing when to let go.

The thoughts that ran through Connor's head that afternoon were the same ones that ran through his head now. How could it be right to build independence in a relationship with a two-year-old? Didn't love factor into the formula anywhere? And wasn't that why he hadn't ever felt close to his father? Independent, yes. But close ... definitely not.

Connor pushed the memory aside and set the picture back in his filing cabinet. Next was a photo of his entire family, taken either his sophomore or junior year in high school. His mother was in the center, the way she'd been when she was alive. Her smile was vibrant and alive, reaching his heart even through the grainy finish of a yellowed photograph. On either side of her sat his three sisters, each of them younger than he and only a year or so apart. In the back, tall and proud, stood his father and him.

The photographer that day had suggested that Connor sit beside his oldest sister. Two children on one side of their mother, two on the other. But Connor's father wouldn't hear of it.

"Connor's a man, not a child," he snapped. "He'll be in the back with me."

The words seemed as strange now as they had back then. Connor's a man, not a child? How old could he have been, sixteen? Seventeen at the most? What was wrong with being a kid, anyway? And maybe that was another problem with him and his father. The man had never looked at Connor the way Connor had looked at Max an hour earlier.

That look of love and adoration and awe all mixed up and shining from his father's eyes was something Connor had never known, even in the best of times. Pride, yes, but love and adoration and awe, no.

He studied the eyes again, looked at the way his sisters seemed somewhat stiff and uptight. They were happy girls, all of them. And they'd grown up to have nice families, sweet children. But back then they had feared their father, no doubt. Yes, he could be the life of the party, whipping up a batch of ice cream, organizing a game of croquet. But he was the sergeant, the one in control at every gathering. For the picture, he had ordered everyone to do exactly as the photographer said, and in minutes he turned their normally cheerful dispositions into a front of fear and high expectation.

How different might the portrait have looked if he'd simply taken his place and let the natural light in the eyes of his children shine through?

Connor looked more closely. Of all the eyes in the photo, his own were the hardest to read. If he was remembering right, that day had been difficult for him. Right before the portrait sitting, Connor's best friend had moved across town with his family.

He might've been sixteen, but he remembered how his heart had broken in two when Mike Estes pulled away in his family's van. All he'd wanted was to find a quiet place in the woods, somewhere to sit and think for a few hours. Instead, they had to get ready for the picture.

His father pulled him aside before the family gathered outside on the lawn and warned him about his attitude. "I'll have none of this moping around stuff." He straightened his jacket and dusted a bit of white fuzz off Connor's sleeve. "You'll be happy for the picture, and afterwards we'll change out of our clothes and make some ice cream." He hesitated. "Friends come and go in life, Connor. Get over it."

Connor stared at the photo, searching his old man's eyes. *Is that how you feel now, Dad? People come and go in life, and get over it?*

Sadness flooded his heart, because the answer was obvious. Of course that's how his father felt. Otherwise he would've found a reason to call by now, whether he'd changed his mind about the money or not. His silence over the years was further proof that he had never really connected with Connor in the first place.

Connor set the photograph with the other one in the back of the drawer, and closed his eyes for a moment. He could never feel that way about his own children, not his daughters nor his son. Now that he'd met Max, if things didn't work out and the boy had to be sent back to Hawaii, he would hurt forever from the loss.

Get over it? Connor couldn't begin to imagine how.

He opened his eyes and looked at the third and final photograph. The moment his eyes connected with the image, he felt his heart skip a beat. This was the picture he'd been looking for, the reason he'd come into the office in the first place. It was a photo of his father as a boy, maybe eight or nine years old. What he saw in the frame told him what he had only suspected before.

Max was a mirror image of the man.

Yes, the boy looked like Connor, but the resemblance to his father was breathtaking. Connor stared at the image, at the young boy so fresh and untainted by the views he would later take on.

"If only you'd kept a little of what you were as a boy, Dad." Connor's words were barely audible, and he narrowed his eyes. "You should see him; his name is Max, and Dad . . . he looks just like you."

The longer he stared at the image, the more his heart filled with sorrow. Sorrow and anger and frustration over everything in his life that hadn't worked out. Not just the affair, or the way Michele had changed, or the idea that he'd fathered a child without ever knowing it. But the fact that his dad would never know he had a grandson.

And the pain that caused him as he stood there in his office, looking at pictures of his father, was one more thing Connor was sure he'd never get over. And it was then, standing there in a sea of realizations, that Connor made up his mind. He would call the pastor, after all. Not because he'd done anything wrong in the past eight years, but because he needed help figuring something out. Something that, between his pain and Michele's, he couldn't sort through on his own.

How in the world to move forward.

SEVENTEEN

Max wasn't afraid of the dark, at least not at home.

But this was his first night at his mother's friend's house, and nothing seemed right. Mr. Evans told all the kids to brush their teeth and go to bed, but he was pretty sure the girls were still up because he could hear girl voices down the hall.

Everyone had their own bedroom at the Evans's house. Even him. Mr. Evans showed it to him after he finished playing Legos. The bed was bigger than his whole room at home. If Buddy was here they both could've stretched out in it and still had room for Mommy to cuddle with him. Of course Mommy was gone now. She wasn't ever going to cuddle with him again.

He rolled over in the big bed and blinked. Light from the stars was bright in his window, and he squinted his eyes real small so he could see them. Was heaven out there somewhere? Just past the stars and the moon? It must be, because whenever people talked about heaven they looked up. And up had to be higher than the stars and moon.

But that meant there was another problem, because the stars and moon were very far away. His teacher told him so in class before he left for Florida. And if the stars and moon were very far away, that meant his mommy in heaven was even more far away. The thinking of it made his eyes get wet again. His eyes were always wet, because it wasn't fair, that's why.

He turned over again and thought about the Evans family.

They were nice to him. Susan's Legos were better than Kody's or Carl's or any of the guys in Mrs. Watson's second grade class. It was the best collection in the world probably.

But something wasn't okay with Mrs. Evans. She was more quiet than most mommies, and he wondered if she had a hurt tummy or a head pain. His mommy got head pains sometimes, and when that happened she didn't smile very much. Of course not anymore, though. Because Ramey said in heaven you had no more pains or tears.

He smiled a little at that thought, because he was glad his mommy wouldn't have head pains ever again.

The voices down the hall got louder than before, and Max had an idea. Maybe he could walk sneaky quiet out of the room and listen to what they were saying. He liked to do that sometimes when his mommy was on the phone, or when Christmas was coming and she had a friend over to help her wrap stuff.

But this was different. This was someone else's house and maybe they wouldn't like seeing him in the hall sneaky quiet, listening to what they were saying. But he really wanted to hear. Because maybe they were talking about him, and how he was feeling, and maybe if he heard their words, he could pop his head into the room for a minute and tell them himself.

The more he thought about the idea, the better it seemed. Finally, he slipped his feet out of the giant bed and lifted them one at a time, as sneaky quiet as he could go. He opened the door with careful hands and pushed his head into the hallway. It was dark except for a light at the end.

Max was pretty sure that was Elizabeth's room down there.

He took more quiet steps until he was only a very little bit from Elizabeth's door. Then he stopped and leaned against the wall. His breathing was loud and so was his heartbeep. He waited for both of them to quiet down, then he started listening.

"I still don't understand."

Max did a big nod from his spot out in the hallway. Yep, that was Elizabeth. She had an older voice than Susan, plus also she was more serious. Serious meant you had a little trouble laughing about things.

Mrs. Evans made a sort of hurt sound. "Elizabeth, I've explained it the best way I know how. Daddy was friends with Max's mother. She was killed in a plane crash two weeks ago, and in her will she asked that Max be given a chance to spend a few weeks with us."

"In her will? Doesn't that seem a little strange to you, Mother?"

Max's heart started beeping louder. Were they fighting? About him? He looked down at his chest. *Okay, listen, heart . . . be quiet down there.* He said the words in his head, and he breathed out hard, the way he'd seen Ramey do when she was upset. It worked, too, because his heartbeep got a little more quiet.

"Yes, Elizabeth, it seems strange to me. But it's the truth. Max's mother wrote a letter and asked her attorney to find Daddy. She wanted Max to spend two weeks here before he goes on with his life in Hawaii."

Silent sounds came for a minute. "Did Daddy like Max's mother?"

"Of course he liked her, honey. They were friends."

"Not that kind of like, Mommy. You know . . . did he *like* her? Like a girlfriend?"

Outside in the hallway, Max held his breath. He had wondered the same thing. His mommy never seemed to have a boyfriend, but maybe Mr. Evans had been that for her. He made his breathing as quiet as he could.

"Look, Elizabeth, it's late. You need to go to bed."

"Okay, but I don't like it. What if Daddy did love Max's mother? What if he wishes he was with her?"

"The woman's dead, Elizabeth. There's no need to worry about Daddy wanting to be with her now."

"Not now, but before."

"Elizabeth, stop. Go to bed before I lose my patience."

The tears were back, and Max felt them hot against his cheek. He didn't want either Elizabeth or Mrs. Evans to see him crying, so he made fast, quiet steps down the hall and back to the big bed. Elizabeth and Mrs. Evans had been fighting about him. He knew it.

What he didn't understand was why? Why did they sound like they were mad at his mommy? If she and Mr. Evans were friends, then that should mean they would like her better, not worse.

The light from outside was still bright, so he reached under his pillow and pulled out his Bible. Ramey had tucked four things between the pages. A letter for Mrs. Evans, a letter for him, a picture of Buddy, and a picture of his mom. He set down the letter for Mrs. Evans on the edge of the pillow. Then he took the other letter and opened it. Ramey wrote it in big words so he could read it all by himself.

Dear Max,

Read this when you are sad and then you will feel glad. I love you and your mom loves you and Jesus loves you. Your mom used to tell you a little song. You can sing it now if you like. You are not alone, Max.

Love, Ramey

Max dried his tears on his pajama sleeve and gave a little nod at the letter. Ramey was right. He should sing his special song from his mommy. With quiet words, he did a small throat clear and began to sing.

"I love you, Max, the most, I love to make you toast . . ."

He wanted to finish, but a ball was in his singing throat. Because he missed Mommy so much, that's why. Not just his heart and his hands and his feet missed her, but his eyes missed her, too. Because every time he wanted to see her, she was never there. He missed her so much he could almost feel her there beside him. That's when he remembered the last part of the song.

When oceans we're apart, I'm right here in your heart.

That's right! He sniffed some and dried his tears again. She used to tell him that all the time. And heaven was at least oceans apart. He did four fast breaths and folded Ramey's letter back into the envelope. As long as his mommy was in his heart, he could look at the next special thing.

He pulled out the picture of Buddy. The dog's eyes seemed to say, "Hi, Max, I miss you."

"Hey, Buddy . . . I miss you, too. Hope you're being good for Ramey."

He counted in his mind for a minute. "Thirteen more days and I'll see you again, Buddy. I'll be there as soon as I can." He gave the picture a little pat and returned it to the right page in his Bible.

Finally, he took out the picture of his mother.

She was the most beautiful mommy in the whole world. She had hugging hands, and a happy face, and eyes that laughed when he did something silly. She had strong arms for throwing a ball with him, and good legs for running on the beach.

No one would ever be prettier than his mommy.

He studied the picture for a long time, then he remembered the last part of his song one more time. *When oceans we're apart, I'm right here in your heart.*

A little yawn slipped from his mouth, and he snuggled back down into the covers. He put the Bible with his other special things back up on the shelf, and accidentally knocked the letter for Mrs. Evans onto the floor. But that was okay. He could get it in the morning.

The only thing he kept out was the picture of his mother. Before he fell asleep, he kissed his mommy on the face, and smiled at her. "I love you. I hope God tells you I said hi."

Then he held the picture against his heart and tried to imagine her there, right inside him, telling him everything was going to be okay. *Be brave and strong, Max*, he could hear her saying. *Brave and strong. Everything's going to be okay.*

Max closed his eyes with the picture still up against him and his mother's face and words in his head. His mother's special song in his heart. By the time he fell asleep, he had almost forgotten about Mrs. Evans and her daughter, Elizabeth, and the fact that maybe they didn't like him or his mom. Instead he slept with just one thought in his head.

Mommy wasn't far away at all. Because the thing she'd always told him was true. Whenever he wanted her to be with him, she was. Right there in his heart where she would always be.

EIGHTEEN

The trying conversation with Elizabeth over, Michele tucked her into bed. But the moment her daughter lay down, the questions came again.

"So you think they were just good friends? Max's mother and Daddy?"

Michele dropped to the side of her bed. "It was a long time ago, honey. All I know is she and Daddy were friends."

The lie grated against her tongue and brought up a host of questions in Michele's own mind. What would the girls think if they ever found out? Would understanding how their father fell be more difficult knowing that they were lied to? That the boy sleeping in the room down the hall wasn't only the son of their daddy's friend, but their daddy's son, too?

And how was she supposed to go camping on Monday morning? An entire week at the lake, pretending her life wasn't falling apart? Michele couldn't think of a single reason why she should go. She reached out and massaged Elizabeth's shoulders. The girl felt stiff and tense, further proof of everything she'd guessed to be true about the boy's arrival. The girls were confused, of course. Elizabeth the most because she was older, old enough to wonder why, if the boy's mother and her father were such good friends, hadn't she been to the house once?

"Lie down with me, Mommy. Please." Elizabeth caught Michele's hand and cuddled it close to her face. "I can't sleep."

Of the many changing patterns that had come about since she'd had knowledge of the boy, this was one of them. Sleeping next to

Elizabeth or Susan in their double beds, instead of spending a night awake and restless lying next to Connor.

"Okay." Michele squeezed her daughter's hand. "Move over."

Elizabeth slid to the other side of the bed, and Michele lay on the comforter beside her. When she was settled, she rubbed Elizabeth's back until the muscles along her spine began to relax. Michele turned off the bedside light and let her eyes adjust to the darkness.

"How come no one ever told us about her?" Elizabeth lifted her head off the pillow high enough to make eye contact.

Michele's heart felt limp and drained, too weary to respond. She sucked in a quiet breath and tried to stall. "About who?"

"The woman." Impatience stirred in Elizabeth's voice. "Daddy's friend, the one who died. How come no one ever told us about her before?"

"Because." Michele gazed at the darkened ceiling. "They were friends when you were just a baby."

"But friends stay that way forever, right? How come they were friends back then and not now?"

Michele leaned up on one elbow. "Elizabeth." She couldn't answer another question if it involved the spelling of her own name. "I found out about your dad's friend the day before you did." She made an effort to keep her voice gentle. "Now, let's get some sleep. We can talk tomorrow."

"Okay." Elizabeth allowed her head to fall back to the pillow. She yawned and her voice was tired. "Sweet dreams."

"You, too, honey."

"I love you, Mom."

"Love you, Elizabeth."

With so many aspects of life suddenly foreign and uncomfortable, the familiar back-and-forth exchange with her oldest daughter was the only part of the night that felt right.

Connor was home, but last she'd seen him he was on the back porch. The place where he sat for hours lately, staring across their backyard, ignoring the way she was dying as she roamed around their house alone. Michele's heart skipped into an irregular beat, as though even her body couldn't remember how to act, in light of what had happened.

What was he thinking, sitting out there all that time? Was he asking himself if it had been worth it, passing the time in a stranger's bed when he had a family back home? Was he wondering how she was handling the news, whether their relationship would ever be the same again?

Maybe he was thinking about the boy, how strong the resemblance was between him and his father and himself. Or was it worse? Was he relishing the idea of finally having a son, masterminding a way to keep him longer than two weeks?

She could hardly be upset with Elizabeth. A dozen questions flashed in her own mind at least every few minutes. And the fact was, she and Connor weren't speaking enough for her to know the answers to any of them. A few times he'd pulled her aside and tried to talk to her. "Quit it, will you, Michele?" He took her hand and led her into the laundry room earlier that day, his face tight, etched with a kind of concern he'd never shown in all the years they'd been married. "You're treating me like a stranger."

She worked her hand free from his. "You are, Connor. Until a week ago, the man I've known and loved had been nothing but faithful and honest and true." She lowered her voice and gestured in his direction. "So give me time, okay? This . . . this man you really are is someone I don't know, not even a little."

"I haven't changed." His words held a quiet desperation. "It was one mistake, Michele. One mistake."

"Well, excuse me for not jumping right into my new reality and knowing how to swim in it." Her tone was callous and filled with hate. "I'm drowning, Connor. Give me a little space so I can figure out how to get to shore."

She'd walked out then, unable, unwilling, to look at him another moment. The rest of the day they'd avoided each other, and now that it was so late, she doubted they'd speak until tomorrow. And then what? Were they supposed to get up early and get ready for church, as though this Sunday wasn't entirely different from any other they'd faced as a family? Was she supposed to help the girls pick out nice clothes, and curl Elizabeth's hair? Get herself into something that didn't make her look too heavy, and then head off to the ten o'clock service pretending that the boy with them was nothing more than a cute little visitor, a family friend?

The idea made her tired, but not quite tired enough to fall asleep. She directed her attention to Elizabeth, and heard the tender rhythmic breathing sound the child had always made whenever she slept. Careful not to disturb her, Michele slid her feet onto the floor and tiptoed from the room.

Being tired was one thing; finding the sort of sleep she'd known before the news was another. She closed Elizabeth's door behind her and peeked in through an adjacent one at Susan. Her youngest girl was sprawled out across her bed, legs and arms widespread in varying directions. Susan had always been a restless sleeper, and having the boy in their home had done nothing to alter her normal routine.

The fact allowed a single ray of peace to shine a dim light across Michele's soul.

She took a few more steps and stopped at the door of the guest room. Without really wanting to, she went partway in, far enough to see the boy curled up and sleeping. He looked lost on the oversized bed, and for the first time since he'd arrived, Michele felt a twinge of pity for him. The thing she'd been telling herself since finding out about him was true, after all.

The mess they were in wasn't his fault.

She took a step closer. He was holding something to his chest, something Michele couldn't make out in the shadows. Probably a favorite toy, or stuffed bear. A special blanket even. Something to remind him of home. She let her eyes adjust to the light in the room and imagined how the boy must feel.

His mother had been taken from him without warning. In the days since, he'd been forced to live full-time with a baby-sitter, and then hop on a plane—the same kind of plane that had taken his mother's life—and travel across the ocean for a visit with a family he'd never known existed. Perfect strangers, really.

Yet if she was honest with herself, he was handling the situation better than she was. She stared at him a moment longer. Something made her want to go to him, brush the lock of hair out of his eyes, and whisper to him that everything would be okay one day. That no one blamed him for the strange circumstances they were in.

But she stopped herself.

Nothing good could come from letting herself feel for the boy. Merely looking at him, connecting with those green eyes and that beautiful complexion, was enough to make her sick to her stomach. Not because of anything he'd done, obviously, but because his mother had managed to seduce the only man she'd ever loved.

Michele swallowed a lump in her throat. The woman she detested was the same one the boy cherished every waking moment.

She turned and left the room. What good could she ever do the boy when she felt that way about his mother? She padded down the hallway and into her bedroom. It was dark, but light from the hallway spilled halfway across the floor. Enough to see her way around, and with silent steps she went to the mirrored sliding doors that hid the closet she shared with Connor.

The mirrors were kind, the way only a few mirrors were.

When she needed to feel good about the way she looked she avoided the bathroom mirror and the one standing in an oak frame at the corner of their room. The mirrors in their foyer were no better. But the sliders . . . the sliders were far more friendly, making the too-curvy parts of her body look long and slender and almost beautiful.

She went there now and scrutinized her image in the semidarkness, first the side view, then the full front image her body made. Her pants stopped short above the ankle, Capri pants, they were called, a way to dress for the increasingly warmer weather without showing her legs. She angled her head and took in the way they made her legs look. The effect was supposed to be slimming, but was it? Really?

And what had happened to her plans to lose weight before the camping trip? Back in February she'd written out yet another eating plan, one she'd put together from the dozens of diet books she'd read over the years. Eggs in the morning, tuna salad and an apple at lunch, chicken and vegetables for dinner. She'd written it all out, calculated that if she followed that type of a plan and ate only a handful of raw almonds or a piece of string cheese when she was hungry between meals, she should lose at least two pounds a week. Maybe five pounds early on, since the first week always showed the most impressive loss.

Michele smoothed the material where it covered her hips. The fleshy feel of her body beneath her fingers actually turned her stomach. What had gone wrong? She hadn't only planned out the meals and written a list of the things she wouldn't go near—Oreo cookies in the afternoon and ice cream after dinner—she'd made a schedule about what to eat and when to pray for strength, and what she'd weigh week by week in the time leading up to the camping trip. If she'd stayed with it, if she'd eaten no sugar and no white flour, and kept her calories at roughly twelve hundred or less each day, then by now she'd be back to her wedding weight.

Thirty pounds lighter.

She thought back to the days after she'd made the plan. Days one and two were strong, doable, the way they often were. But by the third day she'd felt a strange sense of confidence, as if somehow handling the rest of the scheduled diet days would be a breeze now that she'd gone forty-eight hours without sugar.

The memory became clearer in her mind. They'd been at an open house for Elizabeth's class. One of the parents had made oversized chocolate chip cookies, and the entire room pulsed with the smell.

"Be sure to try Mrs. Edwards's cookies," the teacher advised them. "Her recipe won first place at the Palm Beach County Fair last year."

And there it was. A reason to try the cookies—just a taste. She joined the others gathered around the tray of baked goods and slipped three cookies into her napkin. One for Susan, one for Elizabeth, and one for Connor. She took a piece off Connor's cookie just to say she'd tried it, then offered him the rest.

But he only shook his head and flashed her a smile. "Thanks, hon, but I'm okay. Too much dinner."

Michele gave a light shrug and turned to the girls. Only Susan accepted a cookie. The other two Michele folded into a napkin and set in her purse. But throughout the night she broke off and ate small pieces, and by the end of the evening, she'd eaten both cookies.

After that she noticed that the tray still held more, so when Connor was busy talking to one of the other parents, she worked her way back to the table, took two more cookies, and wrapped them in the napkin in her purse same as before. That way if Connor or the girls saw her, they'd think the cookies were the same ones they'd turned down. Not Michele's third and fourth cookie for the evening.

By the time she went home that night, she'd eaten six cookies, and was suffering from indigestion and a bad case of regret. So bad that she'd beaten herself into the wee morning hours, confirming everything that had ever been true about her and her struggle with weight. She was a wretch for not being strong enough, a weak-willed carbohydrate addict who would easily trade a thin future for a handful of chocolate chip cookies. She would never be thin, never lose the extra weight, never wear the clothes she wanted to wear.

The tape in her head played for hours, and the next day she simply hadn't had the strength to try again. Forget diets, she'd told herself in the morning. Eat healthy food, healthy amounts, and eventually the weight would come off. By that evening when she was eating ice cream with Connor and the girls, the critical voice in her head was little more than a distant memory.

Michele turned sideways and stared at herself again. How many years had she wasted worrying about her weight? And why had she let a handful of cookies stop her from meeting her goal? Up a few pounds, down a few. The same rut she'd been caught in since being pregnant with Elizabeth.

Back then, Connor offered to help her, work out with her, or help make sure the house held only nutritious foods. But his offers only made her feel unattractive and self-conscious, as though he was watching every bite she ate. Finally one day after she'd gone shopping for clothes four sizes larger than before, Connor pulled her aside.

"What can I do, Michele?" The concern in his eyes had been genuine. "You're still beautiful to me, but I can see how miserable you feel. Tell me how to help and I'll do whatever you need."

Michele had leveled her gaze at him, hoping he would see that her anger wasn't directed at him, but at herself. "Stop talking about it."

His expression went blank. "Stop talking about it?"

"Yes." She reached out and took his hand. "I have to figure it out, okay? Every time you say something I think I'm ... I don't know, ugly in your eyes."

He lowered his eyebrows and came to her, taking her in his arms and holding her for a long while. "I've never thought that a day in my life, Michele. You're the most beautiful woman I know." He kissed her. "So what if you've gained a little weight? No one would ever call you heavy or think you had a problem."

"Well, *I* do." Tears filled her eyes. "Obviously, I do. You know how I used to look." She sniffed hard and pulled back enough to look into his eyes. "I'm just saying it would be better if the changes came from me, without you talking about it."

"At all?"

"At all. It'll be my thing."

The memory broke into fragments and disappeared.

That had been nine years ago. Nine years and not once had she made good on her promise to Connor. Every plan she'd ever tried had ended in failure, while she survived by justifying her eating habits.

She would tell herself that she didn't need to diet because she'd stayed about the same weight since having the girls, or she'd remind herself that occasionally she'd still pass some man on the street and feel him smile appreciatively at her. She was still nice looking, still knew how to dress to make the most of her strong points, her long legs and thick, dark hair. As long as she wasn't gaining ten pounds a year, why fret over it?

But nothing she told herself changed the overwhelming truth.

She hated being overweight, hated having a closet of clothes that didn't fit her. She frowned at her reflection again and felt her stomach turn. In nine years she hadn't once been successful in her battle to lose weight.

No wonder Connor had slept with another woman.

A thought flashed in her mind. Maybe it wasn't her weight; maybe it was something more, something deeper. Something she had done that might have pushed Connor away.

But the thought was gone before it could take root. She'd done nothing more than eat too much. And that was damage enough.

Michele slid the door open, flipped on the closet light, and walked to her section of summer clothes. Four pairs of Capri pants, three pairs of shorts, and a handful of short-sleeve blouses. Tomorrow she'd have to draw from that collection in order to pack for the camping trip.

She pictured how the scene would probably play out.

Connor would be glued to Max, teaching him how to bait a hook or ride a jet ski, all the while no doubt seeing the boy's mother every time their eyes met. Whoever she was, Michele was certain she'd been thin and striking. Otherwise her husband wouldn't have been tempted to sleep with her.

Michele stared at her reflection again. And what about her?

She was about to spend a week with Connor, knowing that every time he looked at her he was likely wondering why she was still wearing bigger sizes, not the petite sizes worn by the flight attendant. The thought of that left her trembling with fury.

The clothes hanging before her looked like prison issue outfits she'd be forced to wear as punishment for not taking matters into her own hands and doing what she'd said she would do. She backed away, stepped out, and turned the light off. In the time it took her to do that, she made up her mind.

They could go without her.

Elizabeth and Susan had been looking forward to the trip for months, so they could still go. But certainly it didn't matter if she didn't come along this time. She could go to her sister's house, sort through the remains of what once was a wonderful life, and see if any sort of salvage was possible.

God would be okay with that, wouldn't He?

She would take time to herself at her sister's, read the Bible the way she'd been meaning to since hearing the news about Connor's affair. Maybe if she was away from Connor she'd be able to hear God's voice above the skirmishes in her heart.

She headed out of her room and down the hallway again. Yes, a little time away from each other would be good for all of them. After all, she wasn't the one who'd been unfaithful. Let Connor sweat a little, let him wonder whether she was leaving him for a week or forever. Connor could handle all three children by himself.

The girls were wonderful campers, fully capable of putting up the tent, rolling out their sleeping bags, and fishing on the edge of the lake. They'd been able to swim and jet ski since they were kindergartners, and they weren't adventurous enough to stray from Connor.

The boy? Well, he was Connor's problem. Single parents took kids camping by themselves all the time. With every passing second the idea looked better. Why walk around camp feeling self-conscious all week, worrying if Connor was dreaming of a woman he'd been with some long-ago August? She'd rather not go and avoid the comparison.

Once her mind was made up, she expected to feel better, expected the ache in her heart to ease some. Instead it felt worse, and that left Michele disoriented and nauseous, able to see something she hadn't seen until that instant.

There would be no shortcuts climbing free of the tangled web her life had become, because the idea of spending a week away from Connor hurt just as much as spending a week with him. All of which meant that even if she hated herself for it, even if it made her feel desperate and trapped and hopeless, at least for now one truth remained. It was a truth that surprised her.

She was still in love with her husband.

NINETEEN

In the end, Connor did everything he could to talk her into going on the trip.

Though they missed the service, he met with the pastor Sunday afternoon. He explained the situation and how his night with Kiahna had been a mistake. "The thing is"—Connor leaned forward in the chair opposite the pastor and took hold of the armrests—"it could've happened to anyone. It was a series of bad choices, and it's in the past."

"Not for Michele." The pastor was in his early seventies. He preached only once a month, handing over the pulpit most weeks to his younger associate. His voice was scratchy and unhurried. "For Michele it happened two weeks ago."

"I realize that, but I messed up just once. Now she's questioning everything, our entire marriage."

The pastor stared at him for a while. "Why are you here, Mr. Evans?"

"I need help." Connor raked his fingers through his hair. "We leave for vacation tomorrow, and she doesn't want to go with us. All because of Max."

"I suspect she's troubled by more than Max."

"Look." Connor glanced at his watch. He'd come to the man for a quick fix, advice that might clear the fog of confusion and make everything right again. "I can't do anything about the past. And she doesn't want to talk about it, anyway." He exhaled in a short burst through his teeth. "Her attitude's bringing all of us down. I know she's hurt, but that woman meant nothing to me. It was an accident and it's long over. Everything's been fine for years. How can I make Michele forgive?"

"Only God can do that, but I can give you a hint . . ." He settled back in his chair, his gnarled hands folded across his lap the way he might look if he were praying. "It'll start with you."

With me? Anger filled Connor's senses. He clenched his jaw and then in sudden defeat he gave up and released a soft chuckle. The pastor obviously hadn't heard a word he'd said. "With me?"

The man gave a slow nod. "Yes. With you."

"Okay." Connor chuckled again. "Whatever."

They exchanged a few more words, but the conversation was over. Michele didn't understand him, and neither did the pastor. He'd have to figure a way out of the mess he was in without anyone's help.

As he left the church office, Connor shot a look at the scattered clouds above him. "God . . . looks like it's You and me on this one."

The statement was only half serious, and Connor heard no audible answer, no strong sense of knowing deep within him. If God had been listening to his prayers, he never would have run across Kiahna in the first place. Connor climbed in his car and strapped on his determination.

He would get home and do what he could to convince Michele to come with them.

When he found her in their bedroom half an hour later, he reminded her that their time with Max wouldn't be an actual trial run if she wasn't there; and he added that Elizabeth and Susan would certainly find it strange that their mother had taken a private vacation instead of joining the family at the lake.

By Sunday night, he resorted to begging.

"Please, Michele. Come with us." He found her standing at the rail on the balcony off their second-story bedroom, but still she kept her back to him. "I need you there."

She lifted her chin and stared at the dusky horizon, beyond the row of houses that made up their neighborhood. "I can't."

Anger splashed itself against the moment. "I've never asked much of you, Michele. But just this once—"

"*What?*" She spun around and faced him, her eyes wide. "*You've* never asked much of *me?*" She laughed in that new, acid way he'd come to expect. "You asked me to wait at home for weeks on end while you flew from Los Angeles to Honolulu . . . nine months of that, Connor. You asked me to care for our girls, keep up our home, and never stop praying that you'd get reassigned back in Florida. On top of all that you asked me to be faithful, and guess what? I was, Connor. Sure, it was lonely, but always I knew that someday you'd be coming home for good." She lowered her voice. "Let's talk about what I've asked of you."

He took a step backwards, knowing what was coming, knowing that listening to her spell it out was part of his punishment.

"Just be true to me, Connor. That's all I asked. Go to work and come home still in love with only me, forever and ever." She hesitated, seeming to gain some sort of control over her anger and hurt. When she spoke again, her voice was a quiet kind of steel. Gentle, but utterly unbendable. "Don't ask me to go, Connor. I can't." Her eyebrows relaxed some, and she turned once more toward the railing. "I won't."

She spent the night with one of the girls again, and made sure they were packed. He took care of himself and Max, and when it came time for bed, he tucked the boy in with a smile that took every ounce of his effort. "Excited about the trip?"

"Yes, sir." The boy pulled the covers up to his chin. Neither his tone nor his expression gave away any of what he might be feeling.

Connor sat on the edge of the boy's bed and pursed his lips. "Max . . ."

"Yes, sir?"

"You don't have to call me *sir* anymore."

A layer of formality faded from Max's eyes, but he said nothing.

"*Sir* is for strangers, and the two of us . . . well"—Connor cocked his head to the side and grinned at the boy—"we're more like good friends who never got to meet until this week. Okay?"

Max made a little gulping sound. He nodded his head a few times. "Okay."

In the moonlight, the boy's face, the angles and curves of it, were so like his own, so like his father's. He'd been too busy handling Michele to take time simply to study the child and marvel at the fact that the boy was his.

"Mr. Evans?"

"Yes, Max." He gave himself permission to run his fingertips along the boy's forehead, the side of his face, the way he had always done with Elizabeth and Susan.

"Could you give me my Bible? I forgot to look at it before bedtime."

His Bible? Hearing that sent a ray of guilt through Connor's heart. His son had a Bible? One he read every night? He blinked, for the moment unable to do anything but let that single fact work its way through him. What about his own Bible, lying dusty and unread upstairs in the bookcase near his bed? How long had it been since reading it was a priority? And how many hundreds of other little details did he not know about his own son?

"Mr. Evans?"

Connor jumped a little and scanned the bureau near Max's bed. There, on top, was a white book with the words *My First Bible* written in yellow, kidlike lettering across the top. Even before he picked it up, he could see that letters or photographs were stuck between the pages. He was careful as he moved it from the bureau to Max.

"Thanks."

"You're welcome."

Max held the Bible to his chest and gave Connor a look. Though he had only known the boy for a few days, Connor could sense that he was asking him to be a part of this nighttime routine. At least for tonight.

Connor twisted the button on the small bedside lamp so Max could see the words. "What part are you at?"

The corners of Max's mouth rose a bit. He sat up and leaned against the headboard, then he opened the book, took a handful of things from it, and set them on his lap. "I already read about John the Baptist." He kept his eyes on the book, studying the pages with an intensity that reminded Connor of himself.

After flipping through most of the Bible, Max stopped and pointed to one of the pages. "I'm here." He looked up at Connor. "The Sermon on the Mount."

"Could you read it to me?"

"Sure." Max pulled himself up a little straighter and brought the book closer so he could see the words. "'Jesus knew that the people needed Him. They needed His words so that their hearts would be right. One day He went to a place in the mountains and began to talk to the people …'"

Max kept reading, but Connor was no longer listening. His heart was stuck back on the first part, where Jesus knew that the people needed His words so that their hearts would be right. How simple was that? Simple and sound and true beyond anything Connor had told himself in the past ten years.

When was the last time he'd had those profound truths in the forefront of his mind? Back when he met Michele and the two of them began dating, definitely. But when had he stopped? When had he chosen to get through a week or even a day without God's words to guide him? And how come bells hadn't gone off, alarms to signal the fact that without the wisdom Jesus gave, he was bound to fall?

If his heart had been right that summer eight years ago, he never would've been unfaithful, never. Tempted, maybe, but he would have seen the way out, the way promised by God Himself. But then, he wouldn't have this wonder child sitting before him to remind him of everything he'd forgotten.

Connor let the thought pass. It was a little late to be thinking about where he'd gone wrong with God. Even if he could figure it out, he wasn't sure where that would leave him now. He'd lied to Michele for nearly eight years. It was hardly time to pretend he could be counted among the godly.

Max was finishing up, talking about love and how it was the greatest command of all. Connor studied the boy, the way he read quickly and with voice inflection. Whatever Max had lacked growing up without a father, Kiahna had obviously done her best to make up for it.

"'... And this is what I want you to do.'" Max turned the page and looked up at Connor. "This isn't from the Sermon on the Mount, but it's my favorite part." His eyes fell to the book again. "'I want you to love Me and love each other. This is the most important thing, that you love each other.'" He let his eyes fall to the bottom of the page, then he looked up at Connor. "Then there's a question time, but I'll read them in the morning."

"You read in the morning, too?" Connor shifted some. God might as well have shone a spotlight at him, searching his heart for a reaction to his son's faithfulness. Connor crossed his arms and bit the inside of his lip. The boy's example was more than Connor could absorb.

"Yes." Max closed the Bible. His expression was as open and earnest as an angel's. "Mommy says the days are better when you start them with Jesus." A shadow fell over his face and his eyes grew damp. "She used to say that, I mean."

The words caught Connor by surprise. His heart scraped along the ground for a few seconds and he reached for Max's hand. He needed to take things slow with the boy, build a friendship with care, especially since chances were he was going home in two weeks. Connor searched his face, the well of sorrow and fear there, and with everything in him he wanted to take the boy in his arms and rock away the pain.

But he forced himself to hold back. Neither of them would benefit by making that kind of connection, only to lose it.

Instead he nodded to the few things on Max's lap. "What do you have there?"

The sorrow faded and the boy's eyes held a sparkle Connor hadn't seen yet. "My special things."

"I see." Connor resisted the urge to stare at them, figure out what might be so special to his son. "Special things are good."

Max picked them up and held them with a care that went beyond his seven years. "Want to see?"

"Really?"

"Sure." Max shrugged. "Special things are okay to share." He picked up the first item, a dog-eared Polaroid photo, and held it out for Connor to see. "This is my bestest friend, Buddy."

Again the child's words were like a sucker punch to the center of his conscience. His friend, Buddy. The dog Connor had refused to allow to come. One more reason for the sorrow that came and went in Max's eyes. Connor exhaled through his teeth. "He looks like a great dog."

"He is." Max gave the photo a sad smile. "The best."

Connor's throat was too tight to speak. Seeing Max's special things was going to be more difficult than he'd thought. Because with each one, Max was giving him a glimpse of his heart, his little world. A part that would stay with Connor forever, even if the child sitting across from him had to go.

Max placed the photo of Buddy at the bottom of the small stack and picked up the next item. "This is from Ramey. It's a letter telling me to be good and remember the things my mommy told me. Especially our song."

Connor couldn't stop himself from asking. "Your song?"

"Yes." Max looked up again.

This time the protective layers he'd come with were gone, and Connor could see straight to the boy's soul. "Did your mom make it up?" Connor's voice fell some, respectful in a way that seemed appropriate given the level of importance Max's special song clearly held for him.

"Mm-hmm." Max looked back at the envelope from Ramey. For a moment he seemed to consider whether he might sing the song for Connor, but then he sifted the smudged white envelope to the bottom and took hold of the third and final item. "This is a picture of my mommy." He studied it before lifting it up to Connor. "You're her friend, so you already know what she looks like, but you can see it anyway."

Connor wanted to close his eyes, but it was too late. It hadn't occurred to him that one of the special things would be a picture of Kiahna. And now ... now his eyes fell on her image and in a rush every memory of her came back. She looked the way he remembered her. But the picture brought into focus the tiny details he'd forgotten over time. The way her green eyes took up half her face, and her striking figure.

The picture showed her sitting on a log in some kind of forest setting, but as Connor looked at it he could see her at the airport restaurant, the way she'd looked when the two of them first met, the way she'd looked when they left together looking for a place to talk and—

He swallowed and directed his gaze back at Max. "She's very pretty."

"I know." Max looked at the photo again. "I think she'll be pretty in heaven, too." He lifted his eyes to Connor. "Don't you?"

Connor was grateful Michele was nowhere nearby. "Yes, Max." He patted the boy's hand. "I'm sure she'll be very pretty in heaven."

Max made a neat stack of his three special things and stuck them back in his Bible. Then he handed the book back to Connor. "Thanks for letting me look at it. I know it's late."

A Bible from his mother, two photos, and a letter reminding him what was important. The most precious things his son owned. Again Connor couldn't make his throat squeeze out the words. He took the book, set it back, and turned off the light.

Max yawned as he slid back beneath the covers. "When do we leave tomorrow?"

"Early." Connor took Max's hand and gave it a gentle squeeze. "I'll wake you and the girls in time to eat breakfast." He gave the boy another smile. "A good breakfast is the first part of taking a camping trip to the lake."

"Then what?"

"You mean, what happens after we get to camp?"

"Yeah, do we build a tent?"

Connor searched the boy's face. "You've never camped before, have you?"

"No." His eyes fell. "Mommy said we'd go, but we . . . we ran out of time." He looked up again. "What do we do when we get there?"

"First . . ." Connor coughed to clear the emotions from his throat. "We'll set up camp. The tents are already made, but they need poles so they can stand up. Then we'll make up our beds, and put the food away, and probably do some fishing."

"Wow." Max's mouth hung open.

"I know, it's a lot." Connor smoothed out the wrinkles in the bedspread. "That's why we have to get up early."

Max was quiet for a beat. When he spoke, his voice was a mix of fear and concern. "What about Mrs. Evans? Isn't she getting up early, too?"

"Well . . ." Connor took in a sharp breath through his nose. "Mrs. Evans isn't going with us this year."

"That's what I thought." Max's eyebrows bunched together. "It's 'cause of me. She doesn't like me, right?"

Connor closed his eyes just long enough to gather his thoughts. When he opened them, he looked through the dark shadows of the room, straight to Max's soul. "No. It's not because of you, Max." Anger flashed inside him, but Connor ignored it. He could be mad at Michele later. "Mrs. Evans doesn't like to fish all that much, see. And this week her sister wanted her to come for a visit." Again Connor forced a smile for the boy. "So it worked out just fine. You and the girls and I will go camping, and Mrs. Evans can go see her sister."

Max's eyebrows stayed low and together. "Really?"

"Really."

"Okay." The frown eased some. "I wish she was coming with us."

"Me, too, Max." This time, Connor spoke despite the lump in his throat, but his voice was little more than a whisper. "Me, too."

TWENTY

The plans for Michele's trip to see her sister came together by Sunday night.

Once Elizabeth and Susan were packed and in bed, she worked from their home office. Connor was helping Max, no doubt. Earlier that day Connor finally gave up on changing her mind, and now he seemed content to keep his distance.

Convincing the girls hadn't been as easy.

"If you're not going, I'm not, either." Elizabeth had dug her fists into her waist, her eyes angry and narrowed. "You can't do this, Mom! We've been planning it for a year."

"I'll go next time." Michele kept her voice calm, hoping the girls would see her resolve and give up.

"But it won't be right without you." Susan sat on the edge of Elizabeth's bed for the discussion. "You're a better jet ski driver than Dad."

"Yeah, and plus he'll be busy with that Max kid." Other than the first hour or so, Elizabeth still hadn't warmed up to the stranger in their house.

"He'll be with all three of you." Michele remembered to smile. She flipped the lid of the girls' suitcase open. "The important thing is that you have a good time. You don't need me for that."

"But you *never* do this." Elizabeth was bent almost in half, her cheeks red. She raised her hands and dropped them again. "It's just wrong, Mom. We're not a family without you."

"Okay." Michele set a pile of shorts into the suitcase, stood, and faced the girls. "You want the truth?"

"Yes!" Their voices came in stereo, equally hurt and frustrated.

"I want Daddy to have a chance to get to know Max." Michele didn't blink. She left out the part about not being able to stomach the idea of having to live up to the memory of an island affair, or not wanting to watch Connor fall in love with the woman's son.

Susan was on her feet. "He can get to know Max if you're there, Mommy."

"No." Michele crossed the room and set her hand on Susan's shoulder. "It'll go better without me. Besides, I haven't seen Aunt Margie in almost a year. I need this time with her." She looked from Susan to Elizabeth and back again. "Okay?"

"Are we still going to Wisconsin this summer?" Resignation rang in Elizabeth's voice.

"Of course." She stretched out her arms, inviting the girls to come close for a group hug. "That vacation will just be our family, no friends along."

The girls exchanged a look, and Elizabeth took the lead. "Okay." She huffed a drawn-out, exaggerated sigh. "I still don't think it's right, but if that's what you want to do . . ."

"Besides, you know how Dad is . . ." Michele gave first Susan a kiss on her cheek, and then did the same for Elizabeth. "You'll be able to stay up later and eat twice as many s'mores as usual."

Susan allowed a grin. "Yeah."

"And we'll all be together again in a week."

A scowl still shadowed Elizabeth's face, but she lifted one shoulder. "We'll miss you."

"I'll miss you, too." Michele returned to the suitcase. "But think of all we'll have to talk about when we get back."

Michele slept very little that night, but made up for it on the flight out west. She arrived in LA before three that afternoon, and two hours later she was northbound on the Ventura Freeway, the ocean on her left, mountains on her right, and Santa Barbara just five minutes away.

Margie Bailey and her husband, Sean, lived in Santa Barbara on a craggy plateau overlooking the Pacific Ocean on one side, and the hilly entrance to the Santa Ynez Valley on the other. The house was more of an estate, situated behind gated walls and giving Margie and Sean the privacy they wanted, despite the congestion that had come to mark most of the city.

Sean was a plastic surgeon. Margie met him at Westmont, a small, private Christian college on the south side of Santa Barbara. Sean's hours allowed him ample downtime to hike and bicycle and vacation with Margie. The two were content with having no children, and together they planned to spend the rest of their lives on California's central coast.

Despite their different lifestyles, Michele and Margie shared the faith they'd been raised with and a relationship stronger than time. They were also close to their brother, Paul, but the two sisters shared a bond so strong that they liked to say when Margie was sick, Michele came down with a fever, or if Michele was having a hard day, Margie got a headache. Michele was eighteen months older, nicknamed *Mitch* when Margie was learning to speak. Michele hadn't told Margie about Connor's affair or the plane crash or the little boy staying at their house. The sum of the information seemed too big to condense into a single telephone conversation. So when Michele decided to forgo the camping trip, a visit with Margie was the perfect alternative.

Without talking about it, neither she nor Connor had made any attempt to get up for church on Sunday. Instead, she called Margie, explaining only that she needed to get away for a week, and that she wasn't going with her family on the camping trip.

"Something happened."

"Yes." Michele massaged the bridge of her nose to keep from giving in to the tears. "We'll talk about it when I get there."

Being the wife of a pilot meant that catching a flight wasn't a problem. She booked a standby reservation on a less popular 6:00 A.M. flight from West Palm Beach to Los Angeles International Airport. In LA she rented a car and drove to her sister's house.

Margie knew better than to ask questions right away.

They hugged, and Michele joined them for lasagna. Since Michele's encounter with the mirror the other night, she'd only picked at her food, and that evening was no exception. Four bites into her lasagna she crumpled her napkin and set it on her plate. She didn't want Margie to notice her lack of appetite, otherwise she'd get a lecture on how great she looked and how she didn't have a weight problem and definitely didn't need to starve to feel good about herself.

Not that Michele believed her. Margie hadn't gained three pounds since college, so topics involving food and excessive weight were ones they rarely discussed.

On this night, Margie didn't notice the uneaten lasagna, and Michele was relieved. They made small talk throughout the meal and afterwards during dishes. When they were finished eating, Sean muttered something about having work to do in their upstairs office. Margie kissed him and whispered a quiet thank-you, and she and Michele headed into the den to talk.

Michele took the spot at one end of their leather sofa, and Margie took the other. They were barely seated when Margie met Michele's eyes and asked the question that had been coming all evening.

"Okay, big sister, what is it?"

"Connor's camping with three kids, not two."

Margie leaned back some. The subtle rise in her eyebrows made it clear she hadn't been expecting that answer. "Three?"

"Yes." Michele took hold of a nearby pillow and clutched it to her middle. Normally that was something she did to hide the fact that her stomach wasn't flat. But here with Margie it was the only way she knew to ward off the empty feeling in her gut. Her eyes met Margie's again. "He took the girls, and a seven-year-old boy named Max."

Margie wrinkled her nose. "Max?"

"Max is . . . he's Connor's son." Her voice cracked, and she hung her head. This wasn't the time to break down. She brought her back teeth together and sniffed. Then she found her sister's eyes once more. "Connor had an affair with the boy's mother back in 1996."

"No." Margie's face was three shades paler than before.

"Yes . . ." Nausea rose up and made further explanation impossible. "Yes, Margie."

"Connor's never loved anyone but you. The two of you are . . . you're the reason I believed in love enough to get married. Tell me you're making it up."

"I can't."

"Mitch . . . I can't believe it."

"It's true." Michele angled her head. She was still as confused as Margie about what had happened. "I wish it wasn't, but . . ." She gave a few quick shakes of her head and then all of it, every word of Connor's talk at the beach, every detail about his reaction to the boy and the way their lives had changed swept over her. And the flood of tears she'd held off threatened to drown her.

Margie said nothing. She slid over and put her arms around Michele's neck and held her until Michele could catch her breath and get enough of a grip to speak.

Then she explained everything she knew about what had happened. "There was a storm that weekend. All the planes were grounded. He met her at the airport in Honolulu; she was a flight attendant for Western Island Air." She sniffed and took a tissue from the box on the table. She wiped her nose. "I don't know how many days or hours they spent together, but they shared at least one night."

"That's all you know?" Margie sat facing her now, her eyes as wide with shock as they'd been when she first heard the news.

"I don't *want* to know more." Michele pulled her legs up and hugged her knees to her chest. "What good would that do?"

"Okay, so what happened? Why does she call now, why send her son off to your house after all these years?"

"She died." Michele felt herself sink an inch. "She was in the Western Island Air plane crash last week."

"Oh, Mitch." Margie's expression went slack, her voice dropped to a scratchy whisper. "No."

"Yes." Michele rocked a bit. The news was still so awful, she could hardly speak it. Even to Margie. "The woman left a will, asking that the attorney in charge of her estate contact Connor before putting the boy up for adoption." She paused. "He has no other family."

For a long while they said nothing. Then Margie took Michele's hand. "I'm so sorry, Mitch. You have no idea . . ."

"I have some idea." She uttered a sound that was more cry than laugh.

"But Connor isn't the cheating type . . ."

"I know."

"He wouldn't recognize a female who had something for him if she had the truth plastered on her forehead." Margie sat cross-legged. "He was the last one in the world who should've had an affair." She thought about that. "I mean, no one should have an affair, but Connor? Connor Evans?"

"Yeah." A sad sound escaped her. "I guess no one's safe."

"So . . ." Margie grew still, her normally bright eyes dark with the weight of the moment. "You're staying with him, right? I mean, you're going to work through it with him, aren't you?"

It was the first time anyone had asked her, and the first answer that came to mind frightened her. "I'm not sure."

"Mitch . . . what he did was wrong, but it was eight years ago, honey." Margie's eyes glistened. "You can't throw away what you have now over something that far back in the past. Unless . . ."

"No." Michele shook her head. "Connor says that was the only time." The words felt plastic, and for the hundredth time Michele let doubt have its way with her. "Of course, he's lied about the Hawaiian flight attendant all these years. I guess he could be lying about other times."

"No, Mitch. You can't think that way."

"I don't know." Michele eased her hand away and folded her arms tight against herself. "Makes me wonder if my weight had something to do with it. I kept telling him I'd lose it on my own, but . . ." She patted her thighs. "It hasn't happened yet."

Margie gave her shoulder a small shove. "Don't be crazy. Connor's nowhere near that shallow. Whatever was going on with the two of you back then, your weight wasn't the issue."

Michele thought about that. "If not my weight, then what?"

"I'm not sure. Maybe it had nothing to do with you. Or maybe it's something God has to show you."

"Yeah, well . . ." Michele worked her fingers into fists. "Maybe Connor hasn't been attracted to me for a decade, Margie. Have you thought of that?"

"Mitch, Connor's in love with you. Maybe more since he moved back to Florida than ever before."

"Oh, yeah?" Michele allowed a sad smile. "How would you know?"

"Because . . ." Margie pulled herself up a bit straighter. "You send me pictures every Christmas. I can read the man's eyes like a book, Mitch; he's crazy about you." She reached out, caught Michele's closest hand, and squeezed it. "Don't let him go. You have the girls to think about . . . your future with Connor. Please . . ."

The conversation drifted, the two sisters alternately crying and laughing over memories from Connor and Michele's marriage. Like the wake after a funeral, Michele thought. Remembering the dead—both the good and bad times.

Margie recalled the irony when Michele told her that she'd met a pilot. "You were terrified of flying."

"I know." Michele rubbed her eyes. They were still swollen from the crying she'd done earlier. "I think that's why I fell in love with him. He was the only guy who ever made me face my fears."

"And you helped him with his."

"The delivery room, yes." Michele still had hold of the pillow. She laughed and let her head fall back a bit. "I thought for sure he'd faint the minute the doctor yelled, 'Push!'"

Every ten or fifteen minutes, the conversation would fall silent, and once Margie looked at Michele and said the thing neither of them had talked about in years.

"What about Connor's father?"

Michele's heart sank another notch. "He doesn't know." At least once a year, without Connor knowing it, Michele had called the old man, given him an update on the girls and the life the four of them were living. Always she would end the call with a plea. "Call him, Loren. Please."

The old man's answer was the same every time. "When he's ready, he'll call me. Let's leave it at that."

Michele had talked about the phone calls with Margie, so it was no surprise that she would bring him up now. "I've thought about seeing him this time, taking a drive up to Cambria and telling him what happened."

"You should." Margie rested her head against the back of the sofa. "Maybe it'll help."

"With him and Connor?"

Margie made two small lifts with her shoulders. "With all of it."

"I don't know." She was running on fumes, hungry after her half-eaten meal and working on East Coast time, three hours ahead of Margie. The idea of calling Loren Evans, telling him what had happened, seemed suddenly overwhelming. She raked her fingers along the legs of her jeans. "I'll see how I feel tomorrow."

The conversation went on for another hour and ended with the two of them holding hands and praying out loud, something Michele hadn't done since the last time she'd been with Margie.

"God, please give my big sister a miracle." Margie's voice grew tight and she hesitated a moment. "Her family needs so much healing."

When they were finished praying, they talked some more until finally there was nothing left to say. The fact that Michele was there had said it all. As she brushed her teeth and turned down the bed in the guest room, she pressed her fist against her stomach, the way she often did now to ease the knots there.

But the ache wasn't as bad as before.

Was that how powerful her memories of the past were? So strong that they could ease the pain of today? She lay in bed and wondered what Connor and the kids were doing. Still eating s'mores around the fire, no doubt. Connor would let them stay up as late as they wanted, and since he was a night owl, he'd enjoy every minute.

And what about the boy?

Was he liking his camping experience? Had the girls warmed up to him? Was Connor falling for him? If she and Conner survived the affair, it would have to be without the boy. Michele couldn't begin to imagine a life with him in it, a reminder of Connor's unfaithfulness at every breakfast, every dinner, every family outing.

If only they could be sure the boy had a good home, a place where he'd be okay, then Connor would have an easier time letting him go. No doubt guilt was playing a role in Connor's thoughts and actions, guilt about what he'd done to Michele and the girls, yes. But guilt regarding the boy as well. After all, he'd done nothing to help the boy's mother, given no financial assistance, no emotional support.

Now that he was aware of the boy's existence, she was fairly sure Connor was struggling over not only his curiosity about having a son but also his obligation to the child. These thoughts played in Michele's mind for nearly an hour before she fell asleep.

When she woke the next morning, she had an idea. At first the idea felt sneaky and manipulative, the sort of thing she knew wouldn't be right. But by lunchtime, she'd made up her mind. Wrong or not, what she was about to do could give Connor the assurance he needed to let the boy go.

At one o'clock that afternoon she called information and found the number for Marv Ogle, the attorney in Honolulu. She was connected to the man after only a few minutes on hold.

"Marv Ogle." The voice was familiar, the one she'd heard on the answering machine before her current nightmare began. "How can I help you?"

"Mr. Ogle, this is Michele Evans, Connor's wife. Max is staying with us."

An instant warmth filled the man's voice. "Yes, how's it working out?"

"How is it?" Like sandpaper, guilt grated against her soul. She could hardly say she was giving it a try. She cleared her throat. "Things are fine, but . . . well, we were wondering what options Max has when he goes home."

"Options?"

"Yes." Michele closed her eyes and tried to believe she wasn't somehow manipulating the outcome of their two-week trial with the boy. "In other words, where would the boy live?"

"I see." Disappointment rang in the attorney's voice. "Like I told your husband, Max really has no one, Mrs. Evans. His baby-sitter loves him, but she's dying of heart disease, so that's not a permanent option." He paused. "My wife and I could take him until the state found a permanent home for him, but we're near retirement and we travel quite a bit. Our lifestyle isn't conducive to raising a young boy, you understand."

Mine isn't either, mister. Michele bit her tongue. "So what about adoption? Are you aware of anyone, any situation where a family might want him?"

"Not at this time." The attorney sighed. "I suppose I could put feelers out, let the private adoption attorneys know about him." Silence filled the phone line. "Are you saying that it isn't working, Mrs. Evans?"

Michele tightened her grip on the receiver. "Max is a lovely child." She covered her eyes with her free hand. "But taking him into our family, Mr. Evans . . . it's more than we can do." She clenched her teeth. "You understand?"

The attorney's hesitation lasted only a few seconds. "Of course. If this is something you and Mr. Evans agreed on, then I'll get to work on it right away."

"Yes." She opened her eyes and stared straight ahead, her resolve intact. "Both of us feel he'd be better off with an adoptive family." The lie tasted bitter, but she pressed on. "We'd like to know as soon as you receive any interest in him."

"Mrs. Evans." The attorney seemed at a loss for words. "Max is an older child. Interest in an older child can take some time. A year or more. Sometimes older children never get adopted. I hardly imagine we'll have interest in the next week or so."

"I realize that." She bit her lip and begged God that someone would come along, someone interested in a boy Max's age. "But please, if you hear anything, contact us right away."

Michele clicked the off button and sat unmoving, the receiver in her hand. What she'd told the attorney was true—the boy needed a different home. One in Honolulu, with a family who wanted him. Connor couldn't possibly expect her to agree to keeping the child, so if God was going to work a miracle the way she and Margie had prayed, then the call to Mr. Ogle was her way of helping make it happen.

That's what the miracle would be. Sometime in the next week the attorney would hear of a family simply desperate for a boy like Max. Connor would get word of the family's interest, and feel practically obligated to let the boy return home. It would be the perfect solution, the only way she could move ahead and rebuild the life she and Connor and the girls had always shared.

Michele stared out the window at the palm trees that lined her sister's courtyard. *Okay, God? Will You do that? Will You let that be the miracle, please?*

In response, something her sister said ran through her mind again. Whatever was going on with Connor and her back then, her weight wasn't the issue. But if it wasn't her weight, then what? What had she done to make Connor vulnerable to a woman like Kiahna Siefert?

Or maybe she hadn't done anything wrong at all. She closed her eyes and tried to picture the scene at the campground that afternoon. Connor, Elizabeth, Susan, and Max. Fishing and playing on the shore together. Riding jet skis and eating around the campfire, laughing at Connor's silly stories and having a great time.

The images made Michele sad in a deeper sort of way than anything else that evening. Not because of the bonding they were probably doing, the girls and Connor and the boy. But because if God didn't find a family for Max, if for some reason Connor chose to keep him, then a separate family vacation was hardly a temporary solution.

It could very easily become a way of life.

TWENTY-ONE

The girls and Mr. Evans were fishing from some chairs near the water, but Max wanted to find pretty rocks. Ramey liked pretty rocks, because whenever he found one walking home from the bus stop, he'd give it to her and she'd set it on the shelf by the TV.

He wanted to bring a whole bagful of pretty rocks home from his Florida trip.

"Mr. Evans?" He took careful steps between the folding chairs because 'Lizabeth said fish don't come if you bump someone's fishing pole. When he reached his mommy's friend, he put his hand on the man's knee. "Can I walk along the water and look for rocks?"

"Sure, Max." Mr. Evans patted his hand very nice. "Just stay close so we can see you."

"I will." Max smiled, then he took more careful steps through the chairs and walked just along the edge of the water.

Being at the lake made him remember the ocean, and the times when he and Mommy walked near the water. Sometimes they found pretty shells or sand dollars. But whenever he found a pretty rock, he gave it to Ramey. Mommy never got jealous about that. She liked the pretty shells, and Ramey liked the rocks.

Max stopped and took his tennis shoes off. Next he pulled off his socks and squished them into his shoes so they wouldn't get lost. He set them a few steps away from the water in case the tide came in. Did lakes have tides? His toes liked being free, and he pushed them into the sand. It was different than the beach sand back home, more bumpy and rough. But it felt good.

He headed back to the water.

Their camping trip was going pretty good. He wasn't afraid to sleep in a tent anymore. The first night he made a plan to sit up in case a bear or an alligator or a snake tried to climb inside. But Mr. Evans saw him and asked what the problem was.

When Max told him, Mr. Evans's eyes got soft. "Move your sleeping bag over here for tonight, by me."

The tent was big inside, with two rooms and a zipper wall in the middle, but Mr. Evans said they would leave the wall open for the trip. 'Lizabeth and Susan were sleeping together in the front part, Mr. Evans in the back, and Max in the middle. A warm feeling came into his heart when Mr. Evans asked him that thing, so he moved his sleeping bag right up next to where his mommy's friend was sleeping.

"Nothing's coming into our tent, Max, okay?" Mr. Evans rubbed his back for a minute. He used a whisper voice because the girls were already asleep. "You're safe with me."

"Okay." Max liked the sound of that. And after he lay down, it was true. He felt safe next to Mr. Evans, and that night he fell asleep holding hands with that man. Mommy's friend was tall and strong and smart. Bears and alligators and snakes wouldn't think of hurting him with Mr. Evans nearby.

Something caught Max's attention and he stopped. In front of him was the bestest rock he'd ever seen, just laying there on the ground. It was shiny black like a marble with four snowy white little stripes on it. He picked it up and turned it over in his hand. Dirt covered up the back, so he quick put it in the lake water and rolled it around in his fingers. When the dirt was off, he looked hard at it and saw a wonderful thing. The stripes went all the way around! Like white rings on a black marble. Only it wasn't a marble, it was a rock, and that was even better because God made rocks.

Wow! Ramey was going to love this one!

He took one more close look, and then stuffed the rock in the front pocket of his jeans. Pockets were a perfect place to save rocks.

Max walked a little bit more and he saw a big rock, the kind good for sitting on. He wasn't tired, but he stopped anyway. Big rocks were also good for thinking. He grabbed onto the top of it and pulled himself up. Then he sat so he could see the lake water. Mr. Evans and the girls were back some, but even if he looked straight out he could see them in the side part of his eyes.

Max did his best thinking near the water, and even though this wasn't an ocean, it was still water. And Max had a lot of thinking in his head.

The first thing he wanted to think about was Buddy. Max was pretty sure the old dog would love camping, especially the fishing part. Buddy got pretty excited whenever he smelled fish. But also the tent part, because Mommy used to say Buddy liked being a watchdog for him. He could probably even keep Mr. Evans safe.

Sunshine was out that day and it was hard to see over the water. Max made a shield with his hand and put it over the top of his eyes. Right away seeing was better, so Max kept his hand there.

The other thing in his head was something his mommy had told him in that letter, the one Mr. Ogle read him. Not the part about being brave and strong and remembering that she loved him. The part about having a daddy somewhere out there. At first he didn't want to think about that thing. He wanted his mommy back, not a daddy he didn't even know.

But now, after being with Mr. Evans, the idea of a daddy was in his head a lot. Sometimes he woke up thinking how it would feel to have a dad like Mr. Evans, someone strong and nice who would love him for always. 'Lizabeth and Susan were lucky to have Mr. Evans for a dad, but Max wasn't sure they knew they were lucky.

He remembered how he used to think that way before his mom died. But back then the thinking lasted only a minute because he didn't need a daddy, not really. His mommy was all he needed.

But now she was gone . . .

Plus she must have wanted him to find his daddy someday. Or else she wouldn't have put that part in the letter, right?

Max's hand was tired, so he let it fall back to his lap. He lifted his face to the sun and closed his eyes. How was he supposed to find his daddy when the world had so many dads all spread out everywhere? Or maybe his daddy was looking for him and one day he'd walk up to Ramey's door and knock and there he'd be. The daddy his mom had told him about. He squinted his eyes and looked up at the sky where God lived.

God . . . Hi, it's me. Max. He kept the words in his head. *I was thinking about my daddy somewhere out there. The one my mom told me about. Do You think maybe You could ask my mom where I should look for him? Because there's a lot of dads and what if I don't know what he looks like or what his voice is?* He thought for a minute. *And tell my mom I miss her. The missing doesn't make my stomach hurt as much, but well, my heart still hurts. I think it always will. A'course if I find my daddy that would help.*

Max kept his eyes closed and decided this was a good time to sing his mommy's special song. That way she would feel close again. He opened his mouth and let the words come quiet and small. "I love you, Max, the most . . . I love to make you—"

"Max?"

He opened his eyes speedy quick and turned around. It was Mr. Evans, and he had worry in his eyes. Max hopped off the big rock and looked at his mommy's friend. "Hi."

"I saw you sitting up there." Mr. Evans put his hands in his pockets. "I don't know. I thought maybe you might want to talk."

Max made a line in the sand with his big toe and then made his eyes find Mr. Evans again. "My brain had some thinking in it."

Mr. Evans nodded. "That happens to me a lot." He looked out at the water. "Especially lately."

"Me, too."

"So . . ." Mr. Evans looked at him again. "What thinking was your brain doing today?"

Max leaned back against the big rock. He didn't like talking about the thinking in his head unless it was with his mommy. But Mr. Evans was her friend, so it was probably okay this time. He put his hand over the top of his eyes again so he could see better. "About my daddy."

Surprise went across Mr. Evans's face. He turned around and rested against the rock, too. Max liked how their arms were side by side, the way he was sometimes side by side with his mommy when they had their talks. Mr. Evans made a long breathy sound. "What do you know about him?"

"Well"—Max felt his pocket to make sure the rock for Ramey was there—"Mommy said he's out there somewhere, and that one day maybe I'll find him."

Mr. Evans waited. "That's all? That's all you know?"

"Mm-hmm. Mommy just told me about him in her letter, the one Mr. Ogle read to me after . . . after she didn't come home."

"I see." Mr. Evans squinted at the sun a little. "So that's what you were doing? Thinking about your daddy?"

"Not just thinking." Max made his bottom lip wet with his tongue. It gave him a little nervous feeling talking about this, but Mr. Evans was a good listener. "I asked God about it, too."

"You did?"

"Yep. Because so many dads live out there, I don't think I'll ever know who he is unless God shows him to me. So I asked God."

For a minute it seemed like Mr. Evans might hold him close with both arms, the way he'd seen the man do with 'Lizabeth and Susan. But then instead he felt the man pat his head and watched him move away from the rock. "Max, I think God's going to answer your prayer."

"Really?" A happy feeling filled Max inside. If a smart man like Mr. Evans thought God would answer about helping him find his daddy, then maybe that's exactly what God was going to do.

Mr. Evans turned and looked at him. "Really."

Max moved his head up and down, and then he remembered the rock. "Look what I found." He used tight fingers to pull it from his pocket, because he didn't want to drop it into the lake. Then he held it up for Mr. Evans to see.

"Hey, that's a beauty." Mommy's friend leaned close and looked at it. Sometimes grown-ups looked real fast when a kid had something to show. But Mr. Evans really liked the rock because he looked at the top and bottom and even at the sides. "Who's it for?"

"For Ramey." Max put the rock back in his pocket. "I always give her special rocks."

"I see." Mr. Evans looked at him for a long time. "Ready to try some fishing?"

Max still had more thinking in his head, but he liked Mr. Evans a lot. "Would you show me how again? I messed up last time."

"Sure." Mr. Evans held out his hand. "Come on, we'll walk together."

Max reached out and took hold of Mr. Evans's fingers. On the walk back they talked about rocks and tides and what kind of worms fish like best. But Max wasn't thinking very hard about that stuff, because he kept thinking about how his hand felt in Mr. Evans's, and how he hoped one day when he found his daddy that the two of them could hold hands, too.

In fact, he hoped his daddy would be just exactly like Mr. Evans.

TWENTY-TWO

Connor knew the score from the moment they set out on the camping trip. A week with Max—teaching him to fish, taking walks along the shore, watching him play with the girls—would make it impossible not to bond with him.

But he hadn't expected it to happen so fast.

The girls had set their poles down and taken their water noodles down to the lake. He could see them floating in the roped-off swimming hole, so he directed his attention to showing Max how to bait a hook.

"You can't kill the worm, because the fish need to see it moving."

"That's how you trick 'em, right?"

Connor stifled a grin. "Right."

When Max's hook was out in the water a ways, Connor baited his own rod and cast out a few yards away. They fell into a comfortable silence, fishing side by side with the girls splashing and playing a ways off. Connor took his eyes off his bobber and let them settle on Max.

The feelings he had for Max went beyond anything he'd imagined. Marv Ogle had been right, his son was easy to love. Not just for him, but for the girls, too. Before the trip, Michele had pulled him aside one last time and warned him to be careful of the girls' feelings.

"Elizabeth is suspicious of him." She kept her voice low so the children wouldn't hear her. "You need to respect that, Connor. Don't force them to be friends."

He'd done nothing of the sort. Instead, the children had found their way all by themselves. The first night Max was struggling with his sleeping bag, an older bag Connor and Michele had kept in the storage closet. Connor was still unloading things from the car, but when he peeked in the tent, what he saw made his heart sing.

Elizabeth had stationed herself next to Max, and she was showing him how to guide the zipper.

"The cloth gets in the way sometimes," she told him. "So push it away with one hand and then it'll zip up just fine."

Max did as she said, and when it got stuck two more times, Elizabeth helped him get it back on track. When the bag was zipped up and smoothed out in the middle of the tent, Elizabeth patted Max's back. "Good job, Max. You'll be a camper before you know it."

They were midway through the trip, and that type of scene had played out dozens of times each day. The night before, Max announced he was making s'mores for each of them. Susan and Elizabeth exchanged a giggly smile, but they nodded their approval. "Okay, Max. Thanks."

Each marshmallow caught fire before Max had a chance to back it out of the heat. But he went ahead undaunted, and for each girl he placed the gooey black-and-white mess on top of a piece of chocolate, sandwiched between two graham crackers. "Here!" He handed a s'more first to Elizabeth, then to Susan.

Connor half expected them to give the boy a stiff thank-you and then dump his creation in the nearest trash can. Instead they each hugged him and remarked that his was the best s'more they'd ever seen. And they ate the entire thing. Both girls.

If only Michele could see them. If only she'd let her guard down enough to give Max a chance. Connor was convinced she'd fall in love with him, the same way he and the girls already had.

He studied Max, the intensity in his young face as he made slight movements with his fishing pole.

Max shifted his eyes to his and smiled. "Like this?"

"Perfect." Connor had told him to keep the bobber moving, because that meant the worm would move. And moving worms were the kind that attracted fish. "I'll bet every fish in the area is thinking about that worm right now."

The boy turned back to the lake and once again studied his bobber. Connor understood the reason Michele didn't want to be around the child. It was one thing for her to know he'd had an affair, but to see living proof of his betrayal . . .

So far she hadn't been able to look past that part to Max himself. In the past few days, that had become Connor's prayer. That Michele would see what she was doing, and by the time they came home, she might understand how well Max could fit in their family.

He cocked his head and watched his son's mannerisms, the look in his eyes. No wonder Michele struggled. As much as he could see the Evans family resemblance there, he was definitely Kiahna's son.

He remembered the photograph Max kept tucked in his Bible. Yes, Kiahna had been as likable as Max. Their time together had been wrong, wracked with the kind of life-strangling sin that still sucked the life from his relationship with God. Nothing about his time with her had been right. But he'd gotten a glimpse of the woman's heart that weekend. A look he remembered even after years of trying to forget.

Except on rare unguarded moments, Connor didn't go back. But here, now, he felt time slip away, felt his heart going down the old forbidden roads, following a trail to that stormy evening in Honolulu. Back to a time when he broke the most important promise he'd ever made.

⁓

The meal had been the icebreaker.

Once Connor and Kiahna combined tables to eat together, conversation moved quickly from surface talk about their similar tastes, to formal introductions, to Kiahna and the reason for the sadness in her eyes.

Most flight attendants stayed together in groups, moving across the concourse, visiting the rest room, or grabbing a bite to eat. They were easy to spot, slim and fit, sharply dressed in their pressed airline uniforms, hair pulled back, makeup just so. Each pulling a smart-looking bag behind them.

They'd laugh and talk while they walked, waving animated hands, catching up on the latest passenger story or the way one of them had stumbled over the preflight preparation talk or some irresistible tale from back home. Where pilots might never make emotional connections with each other, flight attendants quickly moved beyond the surface details of their job. They shared about family and children, broken romances and budding relationships.

Rarely did they keep to themselves the way Kiahna was, and the picture she made—sitting alone at the table—intrigued Connor.

"Where's the rest of the group?" He caught his straw between his thumb and forefinger and took a long swig of iced tea. The conversation refreshed something in his soul, something that had been gasping for air in light of the troubles in his life.

"The other attendants?" Kiahna set her fork down and smiled. "We go our own ways."

"Oh." Connor cocked his head. "How come?"

"They're too fast for me."

"Too fast?"

Kiahna gave him a sad smile. "Surely you know Western Island Air's reputation?"

Connor thought for a minute. "Maybe not."

"My crew flies nights, Captain Evans."

"Connor." His response was quick. For some reason it mattered that the girl sitting across from him drop the formalities. "Call me Connor."

"Okay." Her smile was utterly guileless. "My crew flies nights, Connor. It takes more than Diet Coke for most of them to stay awake."

The truth of what she was saying sank in. "Drugs?"

"Cocaine." She shrugged one shoulder. "Cocaine before the flight, and men after. I do better to stay by myself."

Connor sat back and studied her. "Strong convictions, huh?"

"I guess."

"Why?" He figured maybe she was married, living a quiet, conservative life in which there would never be room for the racy lifestyle her peers were living.

"Faith, I guess." She tugged on a slender chain she wore around her neck and pulled a simple cross from beneath her uniform. "I'm a Christian." She let the cross fall back in place. "My parents used to say faith wasn't something you could pretend about. It wasn't real unless it looked like faith and acted like faith." She folded her hands on the table in front of her. "I buried my mother three days ago, six months after we buried Dad."

A hundred questions fought for position, and he asked her the one that jumped out in front. "How did they die?"

"Dad died of a heart attack. He was Irish; heart attacks ran in his family." Her eyes fell and she stirred her straw in slow circles through her soda. "Woke up one morning and never made it to the breakfast table."

Connor wished he could take away the raw pain in her eyes. "I'm sorry."

"It's okay." She shrugged and gave a quiet sniff. "They're in heaven, right?"

"Right." Connor didn't want to think about heaven. "Your mom?"

Kiahna's eyes fell to her drink again. "She was Hawaiian, a strong woman who would've lived to be a hundred." She looked up. "But the cancer got her first." She hesitated. "I think her body gave up after Dad died. Her immune system shut down and cancer took over."

Connor had the strangest desire to walk around to her side of the table and hug her. He tried to guess her age, and figured she couldn't have been more than twenty-three, twenty-four at the most.

He took another sip of tea. "Are you . . . are you married?" She wore no ring, but that wasn't proof. His own wedding ring was in his bag somewhere. He'd taken it off that morning before his work-out and forgotten to put it on again.

"No. I live with a roommate, a flight attendant for another airline."

"No siblings?"

"I was an only child." Her smile warmed some. "My parents used to tell me they had just one baby because they couldn't imagine ever loving another child as much as they loved me." She lifted her eyebrows. "We were very close."

Connor was still stuck on the thing she'd said a moment earlier. She had no family? Only a roommate? A fiercely protective feeling welled up within him. How fair was it that a girl with such faith, such desire to live for God, had lost her parents and didn't have anyone more than a roommate to come home to?

She seemed to read his thoughts. "It's okay. I'm in school full-time. My roommate's a good friend."

"What are you studying?"

"Medicine. I'm going to be a doctor." She gave a sideways nod of her head. "Maybe God will use me to cure cancer. So that people like my mother would have a chance to live."

Connor stared at her, speechless. She was amazing. Faithful, true, and with a determination that was all but extinct in the self-centered society they shared. He forced himself to focus. "How far along are you?"

"A year away from my bachelor's."

Connor tried to do the math. "So you're what, twenty-two?"

"Twenty-one." She lowered her mouth and took a sip from her drink, keeping her eyes on his the whole time. "I know ... most people think I look older."

"Definitely." Connor was thirty-three that year, and the girl's age reminded him he had no business asking about the details of her life. Bad enough that he was married and having lunch with a young, single flight attendant. But a twenty-one-year-old? She was barely out of her teens.

"I'm alone by choice, Connor." She sat back. "I was in love once, a young professor at the college. But he didn't understand. He wanted to marry me and take care of me, have me drop out of school so I could be there for him." Her eyes didn't waver. "But I don't want that, not yet. I'm going to be a doctor; nothing's going to stop me. Love and marriage, raising kids, all that can come later." She softened some. "For now it's me and God and my studies. The flight attendant thing is the best way to pay the bills."

Their conversation shifted to the task of piloting a commercial aircraft, and Connor was impressed with how well she listened. He added intelligent to her list of attributes. Intelligent and driven.

When they were finished eating, she insisted on paying for her own part of the bill. Together, they moved into the concourse, intent on finding out information about the approaching storm. They each had their pull-behinds, but their pace was unhurried.

She gave him a smile that held no pretense, nothing flirtatious. "I like you, Connor. Most pilots are arrogant. But you're ... you're easy to talk to."

He felt the compliment make its way through his body. It was time to mention Michele. "That's what my w—"

"Attention, please." The voice was loud and made it impossible for Connor to finish his sentence. "Because of a storm system, the airport is closing down until further notice. Repeat, there will be no landings or takeoffs until we've been given the clear from the weather service."

Connor stopped and let his weight fall back on his heels. "Great."

"Maybe it'll be gone in an hour or so." Kiahna moved ahead toward the counter. "Let's ask."

Trailing a few feet behind her, Connor thought about how long it had been since he'd seen Michele, and how he would've visited her this weekend if it weren't for the storm. But maybe Kiahna was right, maybe it would pass in an hour or so. One thing about that moment stood out even now.

How badly he had hoped she was right.

Twenty-Three

Connor drew himself from the memory and focused on his girls. But he couldn't shake off his thoughts.

The affair hadn't been his idea any more than it had been Kiahna's. He'd forgotten how determined he'd been to leave Honolulu, to get home and make contact with Michele. As intriguing as he found Kiahna, as much as she reminded him of a younger Michele, he had no interest in spending another hour with her, let alone a night.

No, what happened next, even at the time, had felt like some sort of orchestrated drama over which he had no control. He blinked and let the images from that hot August evening continue.

⁓

A line of passengers swelled around the counter. Connor stayed close behind Kiahna as she approached the gate agent from the side. "What are they saying about the delay?"

The agent checked her computer. "Looks like nothing leaves until tomorrow morning at the soonest."

"Excuse me." Connor stepped forward. "I need to get back to Los Angeles tonight." He glanced at his watch. "Are any of the flights cleared for takeoff? Mine's supposed to leave in an hour."

The woman gave him a blank look. "We made an announcement."

"Yes." He gave a quiet huff. "But please . . . I need to get back."

"Captain, the airport is shut down." She pointed at the window. "Those are hurricane-force winds. Phones are out along the coast." She turned back to the growing crowd of passengers around her counter. "You'll have to wait with everyone else."

They found a bench not far away and sat down. Kiahna caught his eye and twisted her mouth up some. "I think it could be a few nights, actually."

She barely had the words out of her mouth when another announcement came on. "Attention, please: The Honolulu Airport is now closed for the night. Officials will review the situation with the weather at noon tomorrow. The weather service has advised us that flights might be grounded for two to three days."

The traffic in the concourse froze during the message, but the moment it was over, passengers scattered toward the doors and a bank of phones along both walls. Connor watched them, running and fighting for position. He wasn't sure whether to join the rush or sit back and wait for the crowd to pass. "Everyone needs a room."

Kiahna made a little frown. "It'll be too late for most of them."

"You think so?"

"The weather warning's been around all day. Tourists planning to leave will have changed their mind and kept their rooms. Twice as many tourists for the existing rooms? At the peak of summer?" She stared at the throng of people moving past them. "Most of them will be sleeping in an airport chair."

He looked back at the gate counter. "I'll call my supervisor and see what they want me to do."

Five minutes later he was back with the news. "I'm in the same boat as the rest of them. The pilots' club is full, no rooms any-where, and no flights until tomorrow at the earliest." He leaned back and stretched out his legs. "I better get comfortable."

Kiahna watched him, saying nothing. Now—years later—he could guess what she might've been thinking. Probably that the two of them had known each other for less than an hour, so maybe she shouldn't make the offer. Or possibly that if she invited him, he would get the wrong idea.

Whatever had gone through her mind, she made her decision and broke the quiet between them. "You could stay at my place, Connor. My roommate would be there; you could have the couch."

Instantly, two thoughts flashed in his head. First, he hadn't yet told her he was married. Without his ring, she may have assumed he had no one waiting at home for him. Second, if the phones were out, he'd have no way to call Michele and tell her what he was doing, where he was going.

After that, a series of thoughts bombarded him, one after another. Thoughts that screamed for him to get up and run the other direction, ones that reminded him he was a married man and spending the night on this single woman's sofa couldn't possibly be a good idea. But she had a roommate. Besides, he wasn't attracted to her; he merely needed a place to sleep. He sat up a bit and met her eyes. "Really?"

"Sure." She slid to the edge of the bench. "It'd be safer than any place near the water."

Safer . . . The word played in his mind for a moment. He was quiet. What would Michele think? Maybe he should stay at the airport, wait for an opening at the pilots' lounge, even find a few seats where he could stretch out at one of the gates.

"It's okay, Connor." She gave a light laugh at his obvious struggle. "You're a pilot for one of the largest airlines in the industry; I wouldn't have asked you if I didn't have a roommate. We won't be alone." She lifted her chin, and her tone held not a trace of teasing or flirtation. "A good night's sleep is important."

He made a deal with himself. He would stay, so long as he told her about Michele. Between that truth and Kiahna's roommate, there would be no room for danger.

"Okay." He stood, and she did the same. "I should probably call home and—"

Before he could finish his sentence, a teenage boy walking past and slurping something from an oversized cup, tripped, and fell flat out onto the concourse floor. As he did, his drink lid popped off and what felt like a quart of root beer shot from the cup and doused the front of Connor's uniform.

"Hey!" Connor stepped back, arms out, shocked by the sudden cold against his chest.

Kiahna helped the boy to his feet and in a flurry of red-faced apologies, the teenager was gone. Kiahna turned to him and covered her mouth with the tips of her fingers. "You're a mess."

"Thank you." Connor made a slow exhale. With a polite smile, he nodded at Kiahna and pointed toward the rest room. "Watch my bag, will you? I'll be back."

By the time he returned, Kiahna was laughing out loud. "Come on." She set off toward the airport's front door. "Let's get you to my place so you can clean up."

They were just out of the airport parking lot in her beat-up Honda Civic when Connor remembered about Michele. "Listen, I'll need to use your phone. My w—"

Kiahna's scream stopped him short.

In a heartbeat, a trash can blew into the road and an oncoming car swerved into her lane to miss it. Almost as quickly the other driver yanked his car back onto the right side of the road. Kiahna straightened out the car, breathless from the near disaster.

"Nice work." Connor's voice shook, the adrenaline rush as swift for him as it must have been for her.

"I thought we were dead." Kiahna drew a slow breath and pulled back onto the road. "Let's see if we can do this."

When they arrived at her apartment, they hurried inside as soon as Kiahna had the door unlocked. "Whew!" She fell back into an oversized chair and used her fingers to brush her hair from her face. "The wind hasn't been like this since I was a little girl."

He stood, awkward, beside his suitcase and gave her an uncertain smile. "Where's your roommate?"

"I don't know." Kiahna glanced at the kitchen and toward the hallway. "Lara?" Her voice hung in the air, but no one responded. Kiahna took a few steps into the apartment. "Lara, I'm home."

"Maybe she's sleeping." Connor hoped so. He couldn't ask Kiahna to go back out in this weather. But he'd call a cab before he'd stay the night with just the two of them.

"She should've been home hours ago." Kiahna went to a narrow table that lined the hallway a few steps away. Her answering machine was blinking, and she pushed a button. A voice came through the speaker.

"Hey, this is Lara, I'm stuck at work." Fear colored the caller's voice. "The road's blocked by trees. It could be a few days before they clear it away, so a bunch of us are staying at the house of one of the clerks here."

Kiahna clicked a button and turned off the machine. Then she lifted her shoulders twice and looked at him. "Now what?"

Connor fell against the door. "Look, Kiahna, if she's gone for the night I should call a cab."

She dropped in the nearest chair and frowned. "Sorry about this. I had no idea . . ."

"I know." Connor opened a phone book beside the phone and flipped to the taxi section. "I'll have them take me back to the airport. The floor of the pilots' lounge will work."

He lifted the receiver and hit the on button. But instead of a dial tone, it was dead. "Hmmm." He tapped on the button four times and tried again. Still dead. "Are the phones out?"

"They were out near the coast." She stood, made her way toward him, and held the receiver to her ear. She repeated the same moves Connor had made, tapping the button several times. But each time she held the receiver up she only shook her head. "Not a spark of life."

Connor took a step backwards and considered his options. He was stuck there, like it or not, about to spend the night alone with a flight attendant he'd only just met. Suddenly he couldn't draw another breath without telling her the truth. "Listen, Kiahna, I tried to tell you before. I'm married."

There. He'd said it.

Her smile was quick and uncomplicated. "That's fine. You're safe; I told you that. Besides, I figured you must be married; most pilots are." She gave him a curious look. "I could go stay with my neighbor if it'd make you more comfortable."

Suddenly he felt foolish for worrying. "No, that's okay." Neither of them had ulterior motives. She was still grieving the loss of her mother, alone in the worst storm to hit the islands in decades. Of course he could stay. He'd take the couch and make sure she was safe for the night. Then in the morning the phones would be back up, and he'd call for a cab.

The ominous clouds outside brought an early nightfall, and Kiahna put together a chicken salad and warm bread for dinner. They talked about their faith and the dreams they'd had as kids. Halfway through the meal, she narrowed her eyes and said something that made his heart skip a beat.

"How long have you and your wife lived in LA?"

"Actually . . ." He let his eyes fall to his plate. "She lives in Orlando. It works out better that way. At least for now."

"Oh . . ." Her expression changed, but not enough for Connor to comment on it. Again her mannerisms, the shine in her eyes reminded him of Michele. But the realization only made him miss his wife, the way she'd been before her depression. Either way, he felt nothing but kindness for the stranger across from him. And the certainty of that convinced him that Michele would understand his predicament. What else could he do?

They finished dinner and moved into her tiny living room for a movie. Connor took the seat farthest from her and outside the storm intensified. Halfway through the show, the electricity went out.

"Okay." Kiahna didn't sound frightened. "Now if I can remember where I put the flashlight."

"We should have thought of that earlier." He wondered if she could hear his pounding heart from across the room. "Want help?"

"No, stay there. I think it's in the cupboard by the refrigerator."

He heard her grope her way from the living room into the kitchen, and after a few seconds of shuffling sounds, there was a click, and light sprayed from the place where she was. "Found it."

He gripped the arms of his chair. "What time is it?"

She appeared in the doorway and returned to the spot where she'd been sitting. As she did, she shone the light at her wrist. "Nine-fifteen."

"No wonder I'm not tired." His words felt awkward on his tongue. Why not turn in early? Send Kiahna off to her room and crash on the couch? Before he had time to process that, she interrupted his thoughts.

"I know." She shone the light toward a cabinet at the other end of the room. "Want to play poker?"

"Poker?" He couldn't contain a chuckle. "What would your God-fearing parents say about that?"

"Dad loved a good game of poker." She headed toward a small lamp stand with a set of drawers at the base. "He used to say cards were good for the mind. But no gambling, never that." She cast him a shadowy smile over her shoulder. "He taught me to play when I was six."

"All right, then." Connor chuckled again. "Where should we play?"

She grabbed a deck of cards and a box of poker chips from the cabinet, and tossed them on the small coffee table in front of her sofa. "This works for me." She dropped to the floor cross-legged. "You can have the sofa."

After a while, she owned all the chips, and he tossed his cards on the table. "Okay, you got me. Your daddy taught you good." He grinned at her, struck by the picture she made sitting across from him, her hair still windblown, innocence shining in her eyes.

What he wouldn't give to have Michele there, looking at him like that right now.

Her smile faded. "Yes. He was a good teacher and ... and a good friend." She met his eyes and the sadness in her face lifted. "Tired yet?"

"Not really."

She bit her lip and looked around the room. A gust of wind howled outside and they heard a crash of something blowing across the road. "Wicked storm."

"I know." Connor stared at the window. Mature trees lined the apartment perimeter; he hoped the winds didn't get strong enough to topple them.

"Hey. Wanna see my scrapbook? I put it together after my parents died ... sort of a walk through my childhood."

"Think that'll put me to sleep, huh?" It was fun to tease her.

"Well"—she grinned at him—"if it does, then I guess that's a good thing. Should I get it?"

Don't do it, Evans ... tell her good night. Flee ... flee as fast as you can.

Connor immediately recognized the voice echoing on the inside of his heart. *I hear you, God ... I've got it under control. Besides, I'm not interested in her.*

She was waiting for an answer. "Sure. I'd love to see it."

They sat side by side looking at the book. Toward the end, she turned to him and tapped the open page. "That's it."

He glanced down and saw that a few pages remained. "What's on those last ones?"

She hesitated, and for the first time since he'd run into her at the restaurant, a vulnerable look flashed in her eyes. "A few poems I wrote."

He held her eyes and felt something begin to stir in his gut. "Show me."

Her eyes fell to the book, and after a few seconds she looked at him again. "Okay." She slid the book from her lap to his, and her hand grazed his leg with the slightest sensation. "No one else has ever seen them."

The poems were beautiful, deep and heartfelt, and Connor felt privileged that she was trusting him with a glimpse of her soul. As he read them, he ached for how much she still missed these two people who had been her parents. When he finished, he looked up and saw tears in her eyes.

Slowly, he shut the book and placed it on the coffee table. "Kiahna, you're a gifted writer. Those poems . . . they're beautiful." He yawned then. "Well, I think we both need some sleep."

"You're right."

They said good night, and she left for her bedroom. He was almost asleep on the couch a half hour later when he heard her scream. Even in the darkness, he was at her side in an instant. Glass glinted in the moonlight, covering the floor on the window side of the bed. He walked around it, grabbed the flashlight from her nightstand, and clicked it on.

"Something hit me." Kiahna was huddled on her bed in a nightshirt, her hand pressed to her head.

"Let me see." Connor held the light near her forehead and caught his breath. A gash ran from the end of her eyebrow toward her temple. Already a knot was swelling near the wound. "Do you have a first-aid kit?"

"Yes." She made a soft moaning sound. "I feel sick, Connor."

He shone the flashlight on the floor and saw what had happened. A tree branch had crashed through the window near her bed and hit her head. If she was nauseous she might have a concussion, and there was nothing he could do about it. "Let's get out of here."

She struggled to her feet, and he helped her into the living room and onto the couch. Once she was seated, he put a pillow beside her and covered her bare legs with a blanket. "Don't lie down yet. Where's the kit?"

"In the bathroom." Her words were slow and deliberate. "Under the sink."

Once more he aimed the light at her head. Blood was running down the side of her face. "Keep your hand against your head until I come back."

"Mmm-hmm." She swayed some.

"Let's see if the phones are back up." He grabbed a phone from a nearby nightstand and checked for a dial tone. None. He whisked his cell phone from his pocket, but the message in the window still read *No service.*

A sense of urgency filled him. He had to work fast. If she was in trouble, he'd take her in the Honda and they'd drive until he found help. He found his way to the bathroom, grabbed the kit, and soaked a washcloth. "Don't fall asleep, Kiahna," he called to her as he headed back to her side.

"Mmmm."

He cleaned the blood, dried the area around the gash, and used seven small bandages to pull the edges together. One larger bandage went over the smaller ones, and in fifteen minutes the bleeding had stopped.

"How're you feeling?" He stepped back and used the flashlight to study her look. Her face was pale, even in the dark of the room. "Still sick to your stomach?"

"A little."

"You didn't black out, did you?"

Kiahna leaned her head back against the sofa. "I don't think so. I'm not as dizzy as before."

Connor recalled a few things about first aid from his time at West Point. A blow to the temple was the worst kind, and even if she hadn't lost consciousness, she should be watched, woken every hour at least. He aimed the flashlight at her eyes, and both pupils responded to the light. He lowered it a few inches below her chin and tried to study her expression in the glow. "You feel well enough to stay here? I can take you for help if you need it."

"No . . ." She shook her head. "I can stay here. Really. I'm too tired to go anywhere."

"You can sleep here on the couch. I'll stay beside you on the floor and wake you every hour just in case."

"All right." She fell sideways and stretched out, asleep before her head hit the pillow.

As a pilot, Connor had pulled all-nighters before. He was trained to stay awake in difficult situations. But after waking Kiahna twice over the next two hours, he was overcome with exhaustion. The floor was hard, the wood damp against his pants.

He clicked on the flashlight and sized up the sofa situation. It was wider than most, easily wide enough for both of them. He shone the light on his watch and set it to wake him up in an hour. Then he stretched out alongside her and turned his back to her. He rested his head on the armrest and closed his eyes. Just an hour. He'd sleep some, and when the alarm sounded he'd wake her again and make sure she was okay.

But within minutes he was sound asleep.

To this day he could remember the dream he'd had that night. It had been of Michele and him, back when they first fell in love. Back when Michele believed in Connor the way Kiahna had said she believed in him. That he was a doer, a man of competence and confidence.

When the alarm went off, Connor heard it, but only at some deep, half-asleep place in his brain. He groped around the floor beside the sofa and pushed the button to stop the beeping. Then he turned and felt a body beside him.

Michele. He smiled and put his arm around her, pulling her to him, running his fingers along the side of her body.

She stirred, and before he knew what was happening, before he remembered that he wasn't home, and that the woman beside him wasn't Michele, but a flight attendant he'd met only that afternoon, his lips found hers. The kiss was slow and easy, but with an aching need that doubled with each second.

A minute passed before they pulled back, and in a moment he would remember forever, their eyes met. Only then did Connor realize where he was and what he was doing. That the woman in his arms was Kiahna, not Michele.

And in that moment he knew something else.

He'd been lying to himself about his attraction to her. She was young and passionate and riddled with a terrible loneliness. She needed someone . . . almost as much as he did.

"Kiahna . . ." His ragged voice gave clear evidence of his desire.

That's when he'd heard it. A warning as clear and distinct as if God was standing beside him shouting at him: *Get up and apologize, move away from her . . . Flee, Son. Flee . . .*

Connor made a subtle press of his body against hers. *Everything's okay. I'll flee later.* "I'm sorry . . ."

She swallowed, her eyes wide. "It's okay."

Flee, Son . . . move away . . .

His lips drew closer to hers, guided by a force stronger than anything he'd known before or since. And as they began to kiss he knew it was too late. He couldn't break free of the wave of longing suffocating him, moving him closer to her with every heartbeat.

Flee, Son . . .

He pulled back and studied her once more. "Kiahna, come here."

She came to him.

The warning voice grew dim. *Flee . . .*

He kissed her again. *Just a little more . . . I'll move across the room in a minute.*

It was the last lie Connor told himself that night.

After that he didn't give another thought about her concussion or the wind or the rain or whether the entire roof might come off in the storm. He was completely and utterly consumed by her, by being with her.

When he woke the next morning he wanted to throw up.

What had he done? How had he allowed things to go so bad? The storm had cleared overnight, enough for her to take him to the airport. They were silent, awkward as they made their separate ways around the apartment. Her dizziness was gone, and he was no longer worried about her head.

He was worried about his own.

What had he been thinking to kiss her like that? And how come they'd lost control so easily? At the time he had no answers. Only later would he be able to piece the nightmare together. Michele's depression, the distance that caused between them, his troubles with the FAA, his tiring commute from LA to Orlando, the troubles with his father.

All of that, combined with the way Kiahna had looked at him, the way she'd talked to him . . . the same way Michele spoke to him in their early days.

It all added up now, but back then on that awful morning after, he was too shocked to make sense of anything but the obvious. He had to get home.

The ride to the airport was even more strained, neither of them saying a word until she parked the car at the departure area, climbed out, and met him on the curb.

"I'm sorry, Connor. I've never done anything like that in my life." She could barely look at him. When she did, her eyes brimmed with tears. "I feel awful."

"Me, too." He took a step back and held the handle of his suitcase. "I'm sorry, I . . . I don't know what to say."

"You were lonely. I should've gone to the neighbor's."

Lonely? He let her word play in his mind. "Not that lonely. It's no excuse."

"But your wife?" Then she asked a question that haunted him still. "How long have you been separated?"

"Separated?" He searched her eyes, confused. "I told you, Kiahna. I'm married. Everything about last night was . . ." His eyes fell to the ground for a few seconds. "It was wrong. It never should have happened."

"But . . . you said you lived alone in Los Angeles. I thought . . ."

And in a rush, the realization hit him.

She thought he and Michele lived in separate states because they were on the verge of divorce. "No, it's . . . it's nothing like that. I live in Los Angeles because I'm stationed there. My wife and the girls, our life is in Florida. I commute back and forth." His eyes shifted to the ground again. He wanted to disappear, close his eyes, and never again have to see the island girl standing before him. He exhaled hard through pursed lips. "Los Angeles is temporary, until I get assigned back to Orlando."

"Oh. I . . . I misunderstood." Her cheeks grew red, and she took small, jerky steps back to the driver's door of her car. Then she stopped and met his eyes one last time. "Good-bye, Connor. I'm sorry . . ."

"Me, too."

That was the end of it. He never heard from her again, never heard anything about her.

Until Marv Ogle's call a week ago.

A noise caught his attention, and Connor released the memory.

"Hey! Mr. Evans, I think I got a fish!"

"Good." Connor blinked, still trying to clear his head. He turned to Max. "Hold onto him!"

"Okay." The boy was on his feet struggling with his fishing pole, eyes dancing, a grin plastered across his face. "I always dreamed I'd catch a big fish like that one."

He moved in a single fluid motion from the chair to a position behind Max, where his arms came around the boy and surrounded his smaller hands on the rod. "You're right. Feels like a big one." Connor used his wrists to jerk the pole. And a flash of silver jumped from the water twenty-five feet out. "Oooh, I think it's a trout!"

Elizabeth and Susan were still swimming, talking to a few girls and unaware of the commotion. Together, Connor and Max reeled in the fish and fought to hold it while Connor removed the hook from its mouth.

"Looks like you caught us dinner, Max." Connor gave the child a quick squeeze, then fastened the catch chain through the fish's mouth and tossed it into shallow water where it would stay fresh until later.

"Yeah." Max moved to the shoreline and stared at the fish, flopping only once in a while now. "I bet it's the biggest fish in the whole lake."

Connor helped the boy bait his hook and then returned to his chair. But all the while he couldn't stop thinking about Max's statement, how he'd always dreamed of catching a fish that big.

His eyes narrowed, and he looked out beyond the horizon. Kiahna had dreamed of something, too. Becoming a doctor and curing cancer. It hadn't occurred to him until just now, but there could only be one reason why she didn't make it to med school. She'd gotten pregnant.

From what Mr. Ogle had said about Kiahna, her son came first from the moment she found out she was carrying him. She must've made the decision to go it alone, knowing that he had a family of his own in Florida. And the decision cost her every dream she'd ever had. Kiahna raised Max in a small apartment, probably the same one where he'd stayed during that stormy August night. Mr. Ogle said they lived paycheck to paycheck from the day Max was born.

Connor let the truth settle into the barren, sandy bottom of his heart.

Then another thought hit him, the worst one of all.

Kiahna should've been a doctor by now, practicing in some medical building, making rounds at the local hospital, and finding a cure for cancer. The only reason she was on the doomed Western Flight 45 in the first place was because he'd gotten her pregnant, forcing her to keep her flight attendant job and focus entirely on raising Max.

The truth hit him like a city bus, square in the chest. And in that moment he made a decision.

Through his own selfish behavior and ignorance, he'd done enough harm to the precious boy sitting a few feet from him. It was time to step into his life, not out of it. Time to do whatever he could to make Max's life happy and warm and safe, time to shower him with the kind of love Connor was dying to give him. One day he would make up for all he'd cost Max.

Even if he spent his whole life trying.

TWENTY-FOUR

Michele was trying her best to concentrate.

Margie and Sean had invited a few friends over, two couples and Bobby Garrison, an old high school friend of Michele's whom Margie ran into at an art show a few weeks earlier.

From the beginning, the group seemed to be trying too hard to tell funny stories and keep up a light banter. Almost as though Margie had warned them Michele's marriage was on the rocks, so don't let the mood get too somber.

One of the men was talking about a trip he and his wife had taken to Sanibel Island, Florida, a few weeks ago.

"You know Sanibel Island, right, Michele?" The man gave her a quick look, his eyebrows raised, ready to tell whatever story was going to come next.

"Yes." Michele allowed a polite smile. She and Connor spent an anniversary on the Gulf Coast once and stayed a night on Captiva Island, just north of Sanibel. "I know the area."

"Anyway"—the man turned to the others—"we're flying home and we have this layover in New Jersey." He raised one eyebrow. "I know, not exactly a straight route."

His wife laughed and patted the man's knee. "So we have an hour, and John goes to the men's room with the old gray backpack, the one with the broken zipper that we've been meaning to throw away." She paused only long enough to grab a quick breath. "You know, we used it for our wallets and a bag of snacks, a few books, that kind of thing."

"How was I supposed to know Melinda had her makeup bag inside?"

"So he goes in, with all these tough New Jersey guys and New York businessmen coming and going, and the bag comes open." Melinda was already laughing.

"Makeup spills all over the floor, I mean all over. Foundation and mascara and pencil-type things." He spread his hands out in front of him and made a whooshing sound. "All over the men's room floor."

Other people joined in and were chuckling now. Melinda was gasping for air between bouts of laughter, dabbing at tears in her eyes. "So every one of the guys turns and looks, and there's John." Another burst of laughter. "Scrambling around the floor stuffing makeup into his backpack."

John rolled his eyes. He was laughing so hard his whole upper body shook. He sucked in a breath. "I look up and tell them, uh, it's not like it looks. The makeup belongs to my wife."

"And then . . ." Melinda hooted a few times. "A construction worker heads out the door, rolls his eyes, and says, 'Sure, pal, and I'm the Easter Bunny.'"

The stories continued for the next half hour.

Michele chuckled at the appropriate times, but only because she didn't want to attract attention, didn't want people feeling sorry for her. Every now and then she made eye contact with Bobby across the room, and finally he motioned for her to follow him out onto the back deck.

She waited until he closed the sliding glass door behind them before turning to him. "Thanks."

"Don't worry about it." He leaned against the railing and studied her. "You looked like you needed rescuing."

Michele took up the adjacent rail, a few feet from her old friend. A cool ocean breeze blew across the deck, and high clouds blocked out the stars. This was the first time she'd been alone with him all evening. "I wasn't in the mood."

They were quiet for a few minutes.

"So . . ." Bobby's eyes held hers. "It's been a long time."

"Twenty years at least." She took in the length of him. "You look good."

"And you."

Michele dismissed the compliment. She was thirty pounds heavier than she'd been the last time she saw him. "Margie says you're an artist."

He shrugged, his grin setting off familiar dimples in both cheeks. "I paint some."

"She says you're good." Michele still held his gaze. "I'd like to see your work."

"Okay." He stretched his legs out some and crossed them at the ankles. "Someday."

She shifted so she could see him better. "Did you and Tammy ever marry?"

"We did." He drew a slow breath. "She left me two years ago for her nursing instructor."

Michele felt her heart sink. Was no one safe? "Tammy?" She looked up and let her gaze settle on the silhouette of mountains in the distance. "You were perfect for each other."

"I thought so, too."

More comfortable silence settled over the moment, and Michele was glad for the chance to see him. She and Bobby had never dated, but they ran in the same circles through junior high and high school. She couldn't remember the number of times the two of them stayed up late talking about one teenage drama or another.

"Margie tells me you're having trouble at home." Bobby hooked his thumbs on the front pockets of his navy Dockers.

"Some." Michele met his eyes again. "Connor had an affair eight years ago. I just found out last week."

Bobby winced.

"Apparently he got the girl pregnant and didn't know it." Michele crossed her arms and willed away the pit in her stomach, the same one that came each time she thought about the situation. "She died in that plane crash in Hawaii; her attorney called Connor because he was listed in the girl's will. The boy has no one, apparently."

A knowing look filled Bobby's expression. "That's why you're here."

"Yes." Michele looked at the animated discussion still going on inside, and then back at Bobby. "Trying to figure out my life."

His smile was comfortable and easy. He held out his arms. "C'mere, friend. I think you need a hug."

Their hug stirred warm memories—but nothing more. "Thanks, Bobby. I'm glad you're here."

"Me, too." He pulled back. "What is it you want, Michele? Have you thought about it?"

"Yes." She searched his eyes, grateful for the chance to consider the question. "I want to call Connor and tell him I love him."

He did a slow nod. His expression held no disappointment. "Then go. I'll be out here if you need to talk."

For the first time in days, Michele's smile felt genuine. "You're still a great listener, Bobby."

"My pleasure." He gave her a mock bow. "Anything for an old friend."

Michele crept inside unnoticed, slipped into the guest room, and used her sister's phone to place the call. Connor had his cell phone, but she hadn't called once since the trip began. Now it was Thursday night.

She hadn't realized until now just how much she missed Connor. Funny, too, because Connor often was gone longer than three days in the course of flying. But she always knew they'd be together again soon.

This time . . . she wasn't sure.

The number came easily, and after three rings Michele heard a click. "Hello?"

It was Elizabeth. An ache spread across Michele's chest, and she closed her eyes, imagining her oldest daughter sitting with the others around a campfire. "Hi, honey. It's Mommy."

"Mommy!" Elizabeth's voice faded some. "Hey, guys, it's Mom!" She paused. "We miss you so much . . . and we're having such a good time. You should be here, Mommy, can you come? Can you?"

The rush of words left Michele speechless for a moment. She allowed a gentle laugh. "I'm a long ways away, sweetheart. But I miss you, too." Michele bit her lip, not sure she wanted to ask. "How's it going with Max?"

"Great!" Elizabeth's tone held an unreserved happiness. Nothing like the doubt that had plagued her before the trip.

"That's good." Michele hated the way her heart sank at the report. "Tell me about it."

"Well, the first day we helped him with his sleeping bag because he didn't know about the zipper and he had the middle spot and we had the room near the front door, so we helped him. And the next morning we made blueberry pancakes and you won't believe it, Mom. That's Max's favorite kind!" She barely took a breath. "And that day we showed him how to fish, only he didn't catch a big one until yesterday, and he and Daddy reeled it in together and we ate it for dinner, and everyone told him it was the best fish of the trip so far. Oh, and I forgot about yesterday when we went swimming and Max is the best swimmer, Mom. Even better than me and Susan because . . ."

Michele tuned out the rest of the report. Connor and Max caught the best fish of the trip? The image turned her stomach. Why had she called in the first place? After another minute of Elizabeth's report, Michele cut in.

"Honey, is Daddy there?"

"Oh." She made a quick giggling sound. "Sure, Mom. Here he is."

As the phone was passed, Michele heard voices in the back-ground. Susan was singing, and a boy's voice—obviously Max's—was joining her at full volume.

Connor came on. "Hey, just a minute. I'm going to move over by the tent so I can hear." A few moments passed. "Okay. There." He breathed in. "How are you?"

"Fine." She could hear the bitterness in her tone, but she was helpless to do anything about it. "Just thought I'd see how the trip was going."

"It's good." His voice was light and cheery. Didn't he feel any of the emotional turmoil that haunted her every waking moment? "I wish you were here."

She closed her eyes and rested her forehead in her free hand. The small talk was killing her. "Sounds like you're having a good time."

"We are." He hesitated. "Max is getting along great with the girls."

"That's what Elizabeth said."

"He's a great kid, Michele. If you were here, you might think so yourself."

"Connor." She wanted to scream at him. "I didn't call for a glowing report about the boy."

"His name is Max."

Something in her husband's tone—something almost steely—caught her short and made her heart skip a beat. What had happened in the past three days? Was the connection between father and son already so strong that Connor felt the need to defend the boy to her? She held her breath and waited until her heartbeat resumed. Then she gritted her teeth and found her voice. "I know his name, Connor."

"You're always calling him 'the boy,' that's all." His words were gentle again. "Maybe it would help if you called him Max."

"Help what?" Anger stirred. This wasn't at all how she'd expected the call to go.

"Help you accept him." A long silence followed. "Michele, I think we should consider keeping him. He's . . . he's a great kid, and he needs a home." He paused. "How can we turn him away?"

Her eyes flew open and she was on her feet, pacing the length of the room. "Do you *hear* yourself, Connor?" Her voice rose a level. "I thought I made myself clear before I left. I can't bring the son of some floozy flight attendant into my home. I'll think of your . . . your backstreet affair every time I see him!"

"First of all"—Connor was angry now, his words a study in controlled fury—"she wasn't a floozy. And second, it wasn't a backstreet affair. It was wrong, but until you let me explain myself you won't understand how it happened."

Michele's head was spinning, and she thought she might faint. "Connor . . ." She sat on the edge of the bed. It took all her energy to finish her sentence. "You're defending her to me?"

"Michele, you don't understand." The anger was gone, and in its place, Connor sounded defeated.

"No, I don't." She massaged her fingertips into her brow. "I need to go."

"We just started talking."

"I can't think of anything else to say."

"Michele . . . don't do this."

"Good-bye, Connor. I'll call you some other time."

"You're coming home Saturday, right?" He sounded resigned to the fact that they weren't going to get any further tonight. "Same as us?"

"Actually—" Her voice cracked. Her throat was thick, and she waited a moment to find her voice. "I think I'll stay a few more days. I don't know. I'll be in touch."

"Time away isn't going to make any of this any—"

"Connor." She was exhausted, unable to take any more of his pleading. "I'll call you later."

She hung up without saying any of the things she'd planned to say. Without asking him to tell the girls she was thinking about them, without telling him how badly she missed them, and without doing the one thing she'd set out to do.

Tell him she still loved him.

The receiver was still in her hand. She lay back on the bed and brought her arm up over her eyes. Okay, so he had feelings for the boy. Couldn't he have waited until they were together again to let her know? Did he have to take over the conversation right from the beginning, going on about how great the child was, how well he was getting along with the girls?

She sat up and looked around the room until her eyes fell on her purse, hanging from the back of the door handle. An idea hit her, and though she felt a decade older than she had an hour ago, she struggled to her feet, took the purse, and found the address book in the side pocket.

Connor would've hated the idea of her calling him. But in that moment, nothing could have made the possibility more intriguing. She thumbed through the tiny pages until she reached the *E* section, and there it was.

Loren Evans.

She sniffed and dabbed at her tears once more. Then she dialed the number. He picked up on the second ring.

"Hello?"

"Loren?" Her tone held none of the sorrow she was feeling. "Hi, it's Michele."

"Why, Michele . . ." His voice filled the phone line, rich and full. She could almost see his smile. "How are you, little girl?"

It'd been six months since she'd called the man, but years since they'd seen each other. *Don't let him guess why I'm here, God . . . please.* "Hey, I'm in Santa Barbara visiting Margie."

Her father-in-law was quiet for a moment. "Brought the whole family?"

"No." She knew her response would come as a relief. Loren would've wanted to see the girls, but certainly not Connor. "I'm by myself." She clicked her fingernails together. "I was thinking about coming by tomorrow, if you're not busy."

"No, ma'am." His chuckle stirred memories of the past. "Not too busy for my favorite daughter-in-law. What time you want to come?"

"After lunch. Say, two o'clock?"

"Great." He stopped. "Everything okay, Michele? You sound upset."

She wasn't sure whether to laugh or cry. That was the exact response she had hoped to get from Connor a few minutes ago. "I'm okay, Loren." She tightened her grip on the receiver and managed to sound believable. "We can catch up tomorrow."

"Okay then. Two o'clock it is."

They hung up, and Michele replaced the receiver on its base.

As she slipped her address book back in her purse, she shook her head. What was she doing? What good could come from spending an hour with Connor's father? It wasn't as if the man had any influence on his son, not anymore. She lay back on the bed again and analyzed her motives for several minutes.

The reason wasn't all that complicated really. Loren Evans represented a part of her past, the part that was honest and real and before her husband's affair. Maybe by spending time with the old man, she could figure out what to do next.

She thought about her sister's party a few rooms away, and Bobby, who was probably waiting for her. But she couldn't face any of them. She changed into her sweats and a T-shirt, brushed her teeth, and climbed into bed. Before she fell asleep, she thought about her faith, the faith she and Connor had always shared.

It had grown dusty in recent years, no doubt. People wanted their hair cut on Saturdays, and that left only Sundays to run errands and prepare for the coming week. Their combined schedules made church attendance a hit-and-miss event at best. Elizabeth and Susan barely knew their Sunday school teachers, and it had been years since Michele and Connor had offered to help out with one of their classes.

How much softer would the blow of Connor's affair have been if she'd been more connected with the Lord? Would forgiveness have come easier, sooner? She let her thoughts drift, and they landed on a memory from last summer. One of the secretaries at church had called and asked if they still wanted their names on the church registry.

"Of course." She'd given the woman a nervous laugh. "We've been members forever."

"Good." The woman's voice was tender. "We haven't seen you around and we thought we'd ask. I'm glad nothing's changed."

But something had changed, hadn't it?

Connor had cheated on her, and buried the truth for all those years. No wonder he chose yard work instead of church so many Sundays. The guilt probably made being in church just about unbearable.

But what about her? Had she known in the center of her being somehow that Connor had cheated on her, that what they shared wasn't as wonderful as it felt or appeared? She thought about that, and the answer came easily.

No, she hadn't known at all. Not on the surface, and not in the deepest places of her heart. She trusted Connor without reservation, holding nothing back in the way she loved and believed in him. But maybe if she'd been closer to God she would've seen the truth for what it was. Maybe she would've asked more questions about his time in LA or the stormy night when he couldn't call home because he was stuck in Honolulu.

A sigh lifted from the basement of her soul and made its way through her teeth. "Why, God . . . why did we drift?" Her voice was a whisper even she had trouble hearing. "And how are we supposed to find our way back from here?"

She waited for some type of response, but the only sound was the distant party banter.

"God . . . only one thing will save our marriage now." She spoke the words aloud again. They seemed more real that way, more heartfelt. "Please, God . . . find a home for the boy. He needs to be out of our lives, the sooner the better. Please, God."

It would take years to ease the pain of what Connor had done to her. A hundred years to forget it. And if the boy lived with them? The healing would never come, never. It wasn't just the affair, of course. It was the fact that the woman had given Connor the son he'd always wanted. And worst of all, that Connor had lied to her. His deceit had robbed her of even the sweetest memories, because everything about the past looked tainted in light of the lie Connor had carried with him.

As Michele fell asleep she thought about the extent of the damage, the sum of the disaster he'd wreaked on their lives.

Every I love you, every kind word, every happy moment.

All of it was suspect now.

Despite her talk with God, Michele was restless that night. Several times she woke up in tears, and thought about her family and the camping trip they were enjoying with the boy. No question that with him in the picture, their marriage would never work. But unless someone stepped forward to adopt him, Connor wasn't about to let him go. And that was the saddest thing of all. Because of the boy, Connor hadn't only robbed her of her past.

He'd stolen her future as well.

TWENTY-FIVE

It was Friday morning, time for Ramey to pray once more for a miracle.

She was sitting in her recliner with Buddy on the floor beside her. Dogs still weren't allowed at the apartment, but due to the circumstances with Max, she'd gotten an exception from the manager.

In her lap was Kiahna's journal.

Ramey had read all of it in the past week, desperate to better understand the relationship between Kiahna and Max's father. What she'd learned both touched and grieved her. After Connor Evans, Kiahna had never loved another man. Her entire life was devoted to Max and making a good life for him.

If Kiahna had cared about this Connor man so much, then maybe that was really where Max belonged. Maybe it was the very thing that would cause Kiahna to smile from heaven and know that things had worked out after all.

But there was a problem.

Marv Ogle called a few days earlier and told her about the Evans woman's request. Apparently things weren't working out with Max, which meant that he'd come home and be put up for adoption.

"I'm in touch with several private adoption attorneys," Mr. Ogle had told her. "Older children are usually harder to place, but I think we can find a home for him."

She was supposed to be happy with that bit of news, but she couldn't be. She'd read the rest of Kiahna's journal in the days since Max left and she knew the entire story now. The way Kiahna and Connor Evans had met at the airport and how she'd invited him home only as a way of being kind. Island hospitality, really. Or maybe it was the hospitality she drew from her faith.

In the short time that she'd known Connor, Kiahna had come to love him. One journal entry stayed with Ramey and came to mind several times each day since she'd read it.

After Max was born, Kiahna realized something was standing in the way of her and God. Unforgiveness. How dare Connor sleep with her, make her pregnant, and leave without ever looking back? Didn't she deserve more than that? His callous ability to walk out of her life after what happened was something she couldn't come back from.

Until Max was born.

At that point she realized that love had power beyond anything she'd ever known. And it occurred to her that with bitterness and hate in her heart, she never would be able to love Max the way she wanted to love him. After Max was born, she wrote in her journal that she'd finally figured out what love was.

Ramey found the entry and read it again.

Love is what happens when people forgive. I forgive Connor Evans. A part of me will always love him, but from this day on I won't hate him. Not for one minute. I forgive him because he gave me Max.

If only the Evans woman could understand that simple truth. Love happens when people forgive.

Ramey flipped a page just as the phone rang. She picked up the receiver from the table near her chair and clicked the on button. "Hello?"

"Ramey, it's Marv Ogle. How are you?"

She'd been to the doctor the day before. Heart disease was making an uncontested run at her body, but that didn't matter. Her focus was on seeing that Max had a family. "Fine. What's the news?"

"Good, I think. I got a call this morning from an attorney on the big island. He says he has a family who owns a B&B near the beach. They've decided to adopt a young boy, someone to help them keep the place up, and take over the business one day."

Ramey scrunched up her face. "Where's the good part?"

"I know." The attorney was trying to sound positive. "That's what I thought. But I called the couple and talked to the woman. They lost their boy in a drowning three years ago. She's interested in Max, Ramey."

"Sounds like she needs a hired hand." Beside her, Buddy lifted his furry head and gave a sad-sounding yawn. Ramey reached down and patted him. "Max is a little boy, Mr. Ogle."

"I know. We talked about that. She said she'd homeschool him and teach him how to make pottery and build wicker furniture and put together an authentic Hawaiian luau. It doesn't sound too bad, really. They live in a pretty remote area; sounds like they want a child to keep them company. Someone to leave their life's work to."

"What about Buddy?" Ramey heard the suspicion in her voice, but she didn't care. Kiahna had loved Max with all her heart. Placing him in a situation where he wouldn't receive that type of love would be the greatest tragedy in Ramey's life.

"Yes, well, that's a problem."

"How come?" Ramey rubbed the soft fur under Buddy's ear.

"The woman's allergic to dogs, apparently."

Ramey smacked her lips. "That would never do for Max. He needs a lot of love and he needs Buddy."

The attorney exhaled in a way that rattled Ramey's nerves. "You need to understand something, Ramey. Older children don't get adopted easily." He paused. "Mrs. Evans said she and her husband were praying for the boy to find a family in Hawaii. They aren't interested in keeping him."

"Then *you* keep him." Her voice was louder than before. Buddy sat up and rubbed his wet nose against the back of her hand.

"We've already discussed that. My wife and I are too old to be the boy's parents. We love him, of course, but we're on the road half the year traveling and neither of us are home during the day when we're on the island. Max needs a family."

Angry tears filled Ramey's eyes, and she rubbed her back teeth together to keep from crying. When she could speak, she made her voice more calm than before. "Wanna know what I think?"

"What?" The attorney sounded tired.

"I think Mr. Evans wants to keep Max. It's just a hunch, but every time I pray about it that's the picture I get." She tapped her finger on the cover of Kiahna's journal. "It's that wife of his we need to pray for."

"I'll tell you what, Ramey. You pray for the wife, and I'll pursue the couple on the big island. One way or another we'll find Max a home. Deal?"

"Deal." Ramey didn't like the sound of that, but she had no choice, really. She said good-bye and hung up the phone.

Buddy cocked his head and made a whining sound. "You miss him, huh, boy?"

The dog gave a sharp bark.

"I know, me too." She scratched Buddy beneath the chin and turned her attention back to God.

The praying had to get stronger, twice as often, twice as long as before. Because either God worked the forgiveness miracle for Max, or the boy would lose everything he had left in life. With that thought, Ramey bowed her head and began to pray for that forgiveness miracle she'd asked God about before Max left.

Only this time she prayed as if her next breath depended on the outcome.

Twenty-Six

Loren Evans had moved twelve paper towers from the living room into various other parts of his ranch house. It was one o'clock on Friday afternoon, and Michele was coming in an hour. He wanted the place to look respectable.

Now that he'd finished tidying up, he found his Bible, the one he'd purchased for himself a year ago Christmas, and sat with it at the dining room table. With gentle fingers he flipped to the back of the book, to a place where he'd made a list of the things he was asking God for.

The things he was begging Him for.

First on the list was that somehow, someday, he and his son might find a way to bridge the ocean that lay between them. And now, after years of not seeing Connor or his wife, Michele had called and wanted to visit. Loren studied his handwriting, the way he'd carefully written out the request:

Span the bridge, God. Bring me and my boy back together.

Yes, this visit from Michele had to be part of the answer, he had no doubt. The thing he wasn't sure about was exactly what part her visit would play. After all, seeing her couldn't possibly remove the thing that stood largest in the way of bringing the two of them together.

Because that thing was pride. A pilot's pride. After twenty-five years in the skies, Loren Evans knew a thing or two about pilot's pride. A pilot couldn't afford to be wrong, not ever. Not that pilots didn't make mistakes; that wasn't it. But when a pilot erred, he didn't view his actions as a mistake. He viewed it as a change in plans, something to be battled and dealt with.

Wrong was almost never admitted, at least not among the more talented pilots.

It had been that way for Loren, and he was certain it was that way for his son. That type of pride didn't always fall away when a pilot stepped out of his uniform at the end of a day.

The very thing that made Connor and him strong as pilots was the reason the two of them hadn't spoken in nearly eight years.

For most of that time, Loren had been content to wait. His decision not to give Connor the money for the airport was the right one. He stood by it even now. The boy had no idea what it took to run an airport. His only reason for wanting to buy the property was so he could run from the FAA investigation.

Loren understood. No pilot liked being scrutinized by the FAA. But Loren had followed the case from a distance, talking to pilots in the know and getting the rest of the details when Michele called each Christmas. Connor's case had been dropped, just the way Loren knew it would be. Connor was most certainly a stronger pilot for the trials he'd gone through that year.

So through the first six years, Loren waited for Connor's call.

Once, halfway through that period, Michele asked him the obvious. "Don't wait for him to call you, Loren. Call him. That would solve everything."

Ah, but that's where she was wrong. It was where she was still wrong.

A year ago Christmas, Michele called and conversation turned to Connor. "Does he forgive me yet?"

She made a tired sound. "Honestly?"

"Honestly."

"No, Loren. He's holding onto it like his life depends on it." Her voice had filled with tears. "I'm sorry. It's Christmastime, and I wish . . . I wish more than anything that he'd call you."

The brokenness of her voice that year stayed with him for days. Later that week, his doctor expressed concern about his blood pressure.

"People don't live forever, Mr. Evans," the doctor had said. "You're on as much medication as we can give you. If the pressure keeps going up, it'll only be a matter of time."

Combined with Michele's sorrow, the events of that December caused him to do something he hadn't done since his beloved Laurel was alive. He went to church and prayed for his son. But he realized a truth that stood to this day. A hundred phone calls from him wouldn't help bridge the distance between them.

Not as long as Connor thought he was right.

No, it would take a change on Connor's part. A realization that he no longer had a need to stay angry about the money Loren hadn't lent him. An understanding that he was wrong to walk out that day, wrong to make a declaration that their relationship was over. And until he could admit that much, Loren was helpless to make a move.

Still, he prayed about it.

And since that Christmas, he hadn't missed a week at church. The new awareness of God and His workings in Loren's life had caused some changes in him, made him a little less rough around the edges, a bit more quick to recognize his faults.

He saw less of Connor's sisters these days; the girls were busy with their children, caught up in their own lives. The extra time allowed him more golf games with his friends from church, more time to play croquet with a few of the guys from the local school board he'd been appointed to.

But most important, it gave him more time to pray for Connor.

And for the next thirty minutes, until he heard Michele's car pull up in the driveway, he did just that.

Michele's palms were sweaty as she headed up the walkway and knocked on Loren Evans's door. She wore a pair of beige slacks and a navy blazer, and she pressed the wrinkles out of it as she waited. Maybe he wouldn't notice the weight she'd gained.

The moment he opened the door she chided herself for worrying about her looks. Loren lit into a smile that filled his entire face. He was out on the porch hugging her before she had time even to say hello. "Michele, my girl, you look gorgeous!"

Connor's father had always been like this. Gregarious and outgoing, friendly in a way that made people want to come back soon for another visit. He'd only been reserved around one person—his son. Connor explained it was because his father expected more from him than from other people. Either way, Michele always found it sad that she could hug Loren more easily than his own son could.

Loren still had his arms around her as she leaned back and took in the sight of him. His hair was whiter than before, thinning some. But otherwise he looked the same. Tall and robust, the same way Connor would no doubt look when he was in his sixties. There was something different about his eyes, but Michele couldn't quite place it. Maybe it was just old age. She kissed his cheek. "How are you, Loren?"

"I'm good, but I've missed you." He removed one arm and pointed the way into the house. "And how about those grandbabies of mine?"

"They're not babies anymore." Michele followed him into the house and onto a sofa in the front room. Loren sat in an adjacent recliner. "Elizabeth's ten and Susan's eight. They're getting taller every day."

"I bet they're beautiful. Just like their mother."

There it was again, and this time Michele was certain. It wasn't old age or her imagination. Connor's father had a softness in his eyes that couldn't be explained by something as simple as the passing of time.

She searched his face, looking for clues. "What's new with you, Loren? You look different somehow."

He cocked his head and winked at her. "Evans men age well, that's all."

"You've been keeping busy, then?"

"Actually . . . I've been hanging out with the church crowd." He gave her a smile that warmed the room. "Going to service each week, reading the Bible, walking with the Lord." The smile faded. "Praying for Connor."

Michele was glad she was sitting down. She had always liked Connor's father. But even when his wife was alive, he'd only gone to church once in a while to please her. Before their fallout, Loren's lack of faith was one of Connor's gravest concerns.

And now—despite the season of pain and separation between father and son—God had brought Loren into a place of believing. The reality of what had happened shot a thrill through her, one she had hardly expected from their visit.

"So how is he, Michele?" Loren settled back into his recliner and lifted the footrest. "Any closer to breaking?"

Michele folded her hands and looked to the deeper places of Loren's heart. "I think he might be further than ever." She bit her lip, warding off the tears that already threatened her voice. "Things aren't so good, Loren."

He pursed his lips and gave a single nod. "I didn't think so. Something in your voice yesterday."

"He and the kids are camping this week. Our annual trip to the lake."

"And you're here with your sister?" A shadow fell across his expression. "Then it's worse than I thought."

"Yes."

Loren returned the footrest to its normal position and slid to the edge of his chair. "Tell me about it, Michele. I want to know."

She hated telling the story, hated the way it drained her and confirmed her new reality all at the same time. Her eyes held his until she found the courage to speak. "Connor had an affair."

Loren's reaction played across his eyes like one of those animated billboard signs. Shock, then hurt, then anger. Proof that Loren still had a tough attitude reserved for Connor. "Whatever was the boy thinking?"

"It was eight years ago, right after the two of you, well, after the two of you stopped talking."

Connor's father closed his eyes for a moment. When he opened them he looked as if he'd aged two years in as many seconds. "Has it happened since?"

"No. Connor says it hasn't, and I believe him, crazy as that sounds."

Loren made a fist with one hand and covered it with the other. He exhaled hard. "So, he kept it from you all these years?"

"Yes." Michele blinked so she could see through the wetness that had gathered in her eyes. "He wouldn't have told me at all, but we got a phone call a few weeks ago from an attorney in Hawaii."

"Hawaii?"

"That's where he had the affair." Michele rattled off the details as she knew them, up to and including Kiahna's death in the plane crash. After a few minutes she came to the point. "Connor has a son, Loren. A boy named Max Riley. He's seven years old, and he's with Connor and the girls right now."

Loren's face grew several shades paler. "He got the girl pregnant?"

"Yes." Michele used the sleeve of her blazer to dab at her tears. "He didn't know until now."

"Connor always wanted a son." The man's words sounded like he was in a trance, the facts not even close to settling in yet. "And now . . . is he . . . is he going to live with you?"

"Connor wants that, I know he does." Michele felt her chin quiver. "But I don't think I can do it, Loren. Every time I see the boy I think of his mother."

"He looks like her?" Connor's father was spellbound, as shocked by the news as Margie had been.

"No." She sniffed. "He looks like Connor." Her eyes held his. "Actually he looks a lot like you, Loren. But his eyes are green like hers, and . . . I don't know what to do."

"Does Connor know how you feel?"

"Of course." She lifted her hands and let them fall again. "Honestly . . . I don't know if we're going to make it."

"Hmm." He stood, crossed the room, and sat down beside her. "I'm sorry, Michele. So sorry. For all of Connor's stubborn pilot personality, I never thought he'd be unfaithful. He was never that kind of man."

"I didn't think so, either."

He patted her knee. "I guess I have something else to pray about, don't I?"

"Yes." She peered up at him through fresh tears. "Pray for Connor to change his mind about the boy. And pray for me. That I'll hear what God's trying to tell me, okay, Loren?"

For a long time he looked at her. Then he stroked his chin and his eyes grew thoughtful. "Sometimes the thing He's telling us is not what we expect."

The man's words settled like rocks in Michele's heart. If he meant that maybe God wanted her to keep the boy, she wanted to tell him he was wrong. But before she could answer back, Loren smiled and patted her knee again. "I didn't even offer you something to eat."

‿

The moment Michele pulled out of the driveway, Loren knew.

Eighteen months of praying about his relationship with Connor convinced him that what had happened in the past few weeks, the revelation of his son's affair, the reality of the little boy, were not mere random events. Rather they were part of an intricate plan God was working in Connor's life.

Perhaps in all their lives.

His first instinct was to work on Michele, wear down her bitterness, convince her that perhaps the little boy should be part of their lives after all. But after sharing a cup of coffee with her, he recognized something about that option. It was self-serving. Because deep in his heart he loved the picture of one day—before his own death—reconciling with Connor and meeting his grandson. The only boy to carry on the Evans name.

Toward the end of his visit with his daughter-in-law, he silently asked God about it. *Tell me, Lord, what do I say to make her change her mind?*

Son ... be still and know that I am God. My ways are not your ways.

Often since that amazing Christmas, Loren had sensed God putting a knowing in his spirit, his soul. Not audible words or even a direct voice, really, but an understanding that the thought currently on the stage of his mind had been sent straight from heaven.

But this time ... this time the words were so clear, Loren couldn't resist glancing over his shoulder. At almost the same time he realized what had happened. No one behind him had spoken, but rather God was determined to make His point.

Be still and know that I am God ... My ways are not your ways ...

Both Bible verses had come up in his reading over the past two months, but now, put together, they formed a message that stopped Loren in his tracks. No question what God wanted him to glean from the words. Though with all his being he wanted to be in control here, help Michele accept Connor's son and find a way to make everyone come together, God wanted him to let that idea go and instead to consider what was best.

For heaven's sake, not his own.

And so for the rest of Michele's visit, up to and including the moment when she pulled out of the driveway, Loren thought through the scenario. Michele wasn't being selfish, not really. On a practical note, she and Connor had decided long ago that two children were enough. She ran her own business and would hardly have time for one more set of homework papers, one more load of laundry.

And this wasn't any other child. It was—as Michele had said— a boy with his mother's eyes, one who would be a constant reminder of Connor's unfaithfulness. Maybe it was Connor who was being selfish in wanting to keep the child. Maybe the greatest way he could show his love for Michele and the girls would be to give the boy up.

Then there was the boy.

At first Loren thought that having him stay with Connor and Michele was the best situation for him. But was it?

The child had spent all his life in Hawaii. He had friends there, and—in the attorney and his wife, and the older baby-sitter—the boy had adults who cared a great deal for him. The sum of it made up his home, the place where he would best remember his mother and feel connected to his past.

These thoughts, all of them, came as Loren allowed God to bring them. Not as some sort of wishful thinking or attempt to manipulate the outcome, but quiet and slow and true. The way God often brought His ways into focus.

As Michele left that afternoon, Loren's understanding of what God wanted from them was not only clear, it was urgent. Urgent enough that as he caught his reflection in the entryway mirror, he felt a sureness well up inside him, a prodding of what he had to do next.

It was something drastic, something he wouldn't have considered doing earlier that day or any other time in the past eight years. He would have to wait until Monday, of course, until the camping trip was over and his son was back home with his three children. But then he would do it, because if God wanted him to, then even a pilot's pride couldn't stop him.

Come Monday afternoon he would do the one thing that—in light of the recent events—truly could change all their lives forever.

He would call his son.

TWENTY-SEVEN

Max liked fishing, but he liked sitting beside Mr. Evans even better.

It was the last day of their camping trip, and he and Mommy's friend had an idea that they wouldn't fish in their chairs. 'Lizabeth and Susan found some friends and so they were swimming. Susan said it was 'cause sometimes even tomboy girls got tired of putting worms on a hook.

But Max wasn't tired at all. His mommy always said she would teach him to fish. She said it when he was five and when he was six and later when it turned to summer. But she didn't. Mr. Evans said because she ran out of time, that's why. And now that the camping trip was almost up, Max and Mr. Evans were running out of time, too.

So that morning Mr. Evans smiled at him and roughed up his hair. "What about something different today, Max?"

Max wasn't sure what that meant, but he shrugged his shoulders very big and said, "Sure." Because he trusted Mommy's friend about everything.

The different thing was that today he and Mr. Evans took their fishing stuff down the beach to the big rock, the one he'd found a few days ago when he wanted to talk to God about his mommy. The rock was tall and warm and just enough bumpy so that they could sit on it side by side and do their fishing.

Catching fish was really cool, cooler than he ever thought it would be. But sitting beside Mr. Evans was better because they could talk about lots of things. Things like Ramey and Buddy and the stuff he would miss most about his mommy. Mr. Evans didn't treat him like a kid, because guess what? He really listened! His eyes and face told Max that he wanted to know the things Max was saying.

And that felt better than catching fish.

Another thing was that his arm was up against Mr. Evans's arm ever since they climbed up and sat on the rock. Mommy's friend had big arms with strong muscles in them. Next to him, Max felt safe.

Sometimes he even pretended Mr. Evans was his daddy.

That's the thing he was thinking about right now. Because maybe he would never find his own daddy, but if Mr. Evans would let him get Buddy and come back to Florida, maybe he could stay there and pretend forever that Mr. Evans was his daddy. 'Lizbeth and Susan liked him better now, and maybe Mrs. Evans wouldn't be mad at him when they got back from the trip. So maybe it could work out.

At breakfast that morning he made a secret plan about that idea. A secret plan was when you had a thing in your head but didn't tell anyone else, not even grown-ups.

His secret plan was to talk to Mr. Evans that day and ask him if he was really good and if Buddy didn't bark very much, could they come and live there forever.

Now, sitting on the rock with their arms touching, Max swallowed hard. It was time. The secret plan had to happen now, because there might not be another chance.

"Mr. Evans?" Max had on one of the man's baseball caps so he didn't have to use his hand as a shield. He squinted up at his mommy's friend. "I have a question."

"Okay, Max." Mr. Evans moved his fishing rod to his other hand, and then Max felt the man's strong arm come around his shoulders. He hoped his question wouldn't make Mr. Evans mad because he didn't want him to take his arm away. Not for a long time. Relaxed was in the man's eyes, plus also a smile. "What's your question?"

"Well ..." He was about to do the secret plan, but all of a sudden a butterfly landed on his fishing pole, just a little space up from his hands. He made his voice into a hushing sound. "Look!"

"Hey, how about that." Mr. Evans leaned in and looked close at the butterfly. "It's a monarch."

"That's the same kind we have!" Max still used his best whisper voice. Only now his throat felt funny, because this was sort of like a special butterfly day, but his mommy wasn't here to see it.

Before he could say anything, a couple of tears slipped from his eyes and landed on his dirty jeans.

"Max?" Mr. Evans looked at him. "What is it, pal? Why the tears?"

Max did a quiet sniff because the butterfly was still there, but it was moving its wings very slow. Butterflies did that when they were thinking about flying away. He wiped his cheek on the shoulder part of his T-shirt and told the tears to go away. When they left a little, he looked at Mr. Evans. "Butterflies were special for me and my mommy."

"Oh." Mr. Evans's face made a sad, thinking sort of look. "I didn't know that."

Max felt his mommy's friend scratch his arm a little, the way grown-ups did when they felt sorry for you. "Yeah." He stared at the butterfly again. "We used to have special butterfly days, where we'd see tons of 'em." He looked at Mr. Evans again. "A whole butterfly village."

Mr. Evans bit his lip and studied the wings of the butterfly. "I'd like to see that, a whole village of butterflies. They're very pretty."

"God's bestest artwork."

"Yes."

The butterfly took a few tiny bug steps toward Max's hand, and he remembered some of the things Mommy always said on their special butterfly days. "Know what Mommy says about butterflies?" He felt his smile fall. "What she used to say?"

The sad in Mr. Evans's face got worse. "What, Max?"

"She said they prove that God gives second chances."

"Butterflies prove that?" Mommy's friend tilted his head.

"Yeah, because a butterfly spends all those days as a callipillar, scooting on the ground. Did you know that?"

"I did." Mr. Evans eyes were serious. Max figured it was because he liked this story.

"Then one day"—Max stared at the butterfly—"one day he gets tired of scooting around, so he builds a little room and takes a nap there." Max made his voice quiet again because sometimes it would get loud when he told a good story. And the story of his special butterfly days was a very good one. "But know what the bestest part is, Mr. Evans?"

"What?" His face was closer now, because they both had shushed their words so the butterfly wouldn't leave.

"One day the callipillar wakes up and God has done an amazing thing. The callipillar shakes his shoulders a little, and what do you know? There's something on his back!" Max shook his back a very little to show Mr. Evans what he meant. The butterfly gave a big flap of his wings, but still he stayed on the fishing pole. "That thing is wings, Mr. Evans. And now the callipillar doesn't have to scoot around on the ground because—"

"Because he can fly." A smile came on Mr. Evans face. "And that's his second chance, right?"

"Right! And Mommy always said one day me and her aren't going to scoot anymore, either, because God loves us more than He loves the butterflies."

The butterfly started taking small steps again, only this time Max felt him walk his scratchy little feet right up onto his fingers. "Wow." Max made the word as hushed as he could. "I never felt a butterfly walk on me before."

Mr. Evans set his fishing pole down and did a closer look. "How does it feel?"

In that second Max had tears in his heart because of something he remembered. Something from his mommy's letter. The tears spilled out again, quiet and slow, and even when he tried he couldn't make them stop.

"Max? You okay?" Mr. Evans got worry in his lips where the smile used to be.

"I remembered something my mommy said in the letter. The one Mr. Ogle read after she was gone."

Little bumps came in Mr. Evans's chin. Maybe he didn't want to know what his mommy's letter said. Plus also his eyes had some new wet in them. But then he said, "Would you like to tell me what she wrote in the letter?"

"Yes." Max nodded very slow because the butterfly was still moving its little feet on his hand. "I would like that very much." Max tried to remember his mommy's words from the letter. "She told me that she was in heaven now and that . . . finally she was getting her second chance."

"Like the butterfly?" A teardrop rolled down the side of Mr. Evans's face, but his words were clear. Not stuck in his throat like Max's sometimes got.

"Yes." He blinked so he could see the butterfly better. "She said that one day soon we'd be together again and we'd never scoot around on the ground. Instead we would fly. Forever and ever we would fly."

The butterfly did a tickly dance step on his hand, first one way, then the other. Then he flapped his soft wings faster than before.

So fast it was hard to see the lines of brown and orange and black because they mixed all together.

In a quick rush, the butterfly lifted up and stayed above the big rock, bouncing and lifting and falling until finally it moved up over the beach and toward a faraway tree.

Max watched him go and the whole time he wished he could have real wings, so he could chase the butterfly and catch him again, keep him so he would never forget about special butterfly days. When the butterfly was gone, the hole in his heart felt the same big as it did when he first found out about his mommy being dead.

"Max . . ." Mr. Evans hugged him close. Then he looked at him so their eyes were hooked together. "Thanks for telling me that story. I know how special it is for you."

"Yes." He sniffed again, but not as soft as before. He wanted to cover up his face and cry, but he wanted to talk to Mr. Evans even more. And you couldn't talk very much when you were crying. Plus, his mommy told him whenever he was sad or afraid to be extra brave. "Mommy had something else special for me, too."

"You can tell me if you want, Max." Mr. Evans voice was soft like the wind from the lake. He began to turn the little handle on his fishing pole.

"She had a special song for me." He tugged the hat on his head to make sure it was still there. It belonged to Mr. Evans and it was too big, so he was extra careful not to lose it. "Me and her sang it all the time."

Mr. Evans said nothing at first. He kept turning the little handle, and now the bobber and hook came out of the water and right back to Mr. Evans. The worm was gone, so he reached into a little box of dirt and took out a long squiggly one. Then he bunched it up, put it on the hook, and stood up. Next he jerked his pole real hard to the side and the hook and worm and bobber went flying out over the lake. Then he sat down and said, "Do you remember it?"

"O' course." Max smiled at Mr. Evans, but inside his heart felt sad at that thing. He looked at his bobber and decided it was time to check his worm, too. He began to turn the handle and he watched the bobber come bouncing closer on the water.

Mr. Evans brought his legs up high and rested his fishing pole on his knee. "Could you sing it for me, Max?"

Max kept turning the handle on his fishing pole, but inside his head he was thinking very hard. Because this was a big thing. He never sang his special song with anyone but his mommy. After she died he sang it to Buddy, because Buddy was his best friend. But no one else in the world ever heard it. Still . . . He looked at Mr. Evans and tried to tell if he just asked about the song to be nice or if he really wanted to hear it.

And right then he knew. Because Mr. Evans's eyes had a serious look that grown-ups got when they really meant something. He took a break from the handle on his fishing pole and set it on the big rock, the way Mr. Evans had done before. Then he folded his arms tight and looked at Mr. Evans again. "It has hand motions."

"Okay."

Max nodded. Then he put his hands over his heart and started to sing. "I love you, Max, the most . . ." He brushed one hand against the other. "I love to make you toast . . ." Wide open arms. "When oceans we're apart . . ." Hands back over his chest. "You're always in my heart."

"That's beautiful." Mr. Evans eyes were shiny.

"My mommy had to stay in Japan some nights because of her plane didn't come home at night. It came home in the morning time." The peanut-butter feeling in his throat was back, but he pushed the words out anyway. "She made up that song so I would know she was always with me. Even if the ocean stood in the way."

This time he was sure Mr. Evans looked sad, and he put his hand over his eyes and pinched his nose. The same way Mommy used to do when she was feeling extra much like a callipillar. After a minute he made a hard breathing sound and wiped his hands across his cheeks. "Could you sing it one more time, Max?"

So he did. This time he looked out across the lake and sang it with no hand motions. Just his hands on his heart so he would remember that she was there still.

"I love you, Max, the most . . . I love to make you toast. When oceans we're apart, you're always in my heart."

After that, they didn't talk for a long time. Max's head was busy thinking about his mommy and whether he had a worm on his hook still or not. He turned the handle until the bobber and hook came flying out of the water. Only they didn't come in nice and slow like when Mr. Evans did it. So Mommy's friend leaned close again, caught his pole, and helped him catch the hook.

"Can I pick the worm?" Picking the worm was the best part of fishing. Unless you caught a fish, o' course.

Mr. Evans made a little laugh. "Go ahead." He held the worm box over, and Max picked the biggest, fattest one he could find.

"The fish will love you, Mr. Worm."

It was extra strong, though, so Mr. Evans helped him put it on the hook and shoot it back out across the water. They sat like that for another long time, and then Mr. Evans turned to him. A little sad still stayed in his eyes.

"Okay, Max. Now what were you going to ask me, remember?" Mr. Evans took his arm away and picked up his fishing pole again. "Before the butterfly came?"

Max sat a little straighter. He almost forgot about the secret plan. He did a little cough so his voice would be extra strong. "Well, this week has been a lot of fun for me."

"Yes." A smile came into Mr. Evans's face and moved all the way up to his eyes. "It's been fun for me, too."

"Okay, so remember I told you about my prayer, that I would find my daddy out there somewhere?"

"Yes." More sad colored Mr. Evans's smile. "I remember."

Max tugged on the front of his cap and squinted up at Mr. Evans. "I did some thinking in my head about that, and what if I never find that daddy?" Max leaned back a little so he could see Mr. Evans better. "And so the thinking in my head told me what if I could pretend *you* were my daddy, Mr. Evans. I could go home and get Buddy and the two of us could live here with you and Mrs. Evans and 'Lizabeth and Susan forever."

Little muscles came out on the sides of Mr. Evans's mouth and he looked out at the lake. After a minute he made a sound in his throat and said, "That would be wonderful, Max."

"Do you think maybe I could do that? Because Ramey said she's too old to keep me and Mr. Ogle and his wife are never home and the manager is giving my apartment to another family, so I'm not even sure where my home is right now." Max told himself to stop talking. His mommy told him he talked too fast when he was excited, and he wanted Mr. Evans to understand every word he said.

"You want to stay with us, is that what you're saying?"

"Yes, sir. Mr. Evans, I mean. If that would be okay with you then I could get Buddy and pretend you were my daddy. If you don't mind too much."

"Max . . ." One more time Mr. Evans put his fishing pole down against the big rock, and this time he hugged him with both hands, the way he always did with 'Lizabeth and Susan. "I want that, too. I do." He pulled himself back some so they could see each other. "We both need to pray that God will help us work that out."

Something inside him said that maybe there was a problem with his plan. "Because Mrs. Evans might not want me to stay, is that why we should pray?"

"Mrs. Evans likes you, Max."

Max felt Mr. Evans move his fingers along his forehead. Then the man looked straight into his heart. Max did a little gulp. "Really?"

"Really. But still I think we should pray about it."

And so all that afternoon, even when they each caught the two biggest fishes in the lake, Max prayed. He prayed during dinner and while they built the campfire, and he prayed that night when he fell asleep in the tent next to Mr. Evans.

He prayed that maybe he wouldn't have to wait until heaven for his wings. Because if he could live with Mr. Evans and Mrs. Evans and 'Lizabeth and Susan, then they could be his own family forever. Then he would be sure his mommy was right, that God really did give people second chances. And so he prayed that if it was okay with God, Mr. Evans could be his pretend daddy. That way he wouldn't have to scoot around on the ground anymore, and he wouldn't have to wait till heaven for his wings.

Instead, he would fly right here in Florida.

TWENTY-EIGHT

Connor and the kids were home less than an hour when the call came in.

They'd been busy since pulling into the garage, unloading the camping gear, and cleaning it for next time. Max and the girls were so at ease with each other it was hard to tell they hadn't known each other forever.

Something in the genes, Connor told himself. *They're related, after all, even if they don't know it.*

The only sobering part of the afternoon was the obvious. Michele wasn't home. He hadn't heard from her since her cell phone call midway through the week. Her silence angered him. How was he supposed to help her understand the situation when she kept her distance in every way?

He planned to call her after everything was put away and the kids were busy in the backyard, but not until then. It would take that much time to let his anger cool, to remember that even if she was making things more difficult, the mess they were in wasn't her fault.

At just after four, he was helping Max put away the fishing gear when the phone rang. "Be right back." He set down the tackle box and jogged into the house. He clicked the on button just before the answering machine picked up. "Hello?"

"Mr. Evans?"

"Yes." The voice was familiar in a vague sort of way. Connor leaned against the kitchen island and forced himself to concentrate. "Can I help you?"

"This is Mr. Ogle, the attorney in Honolulu."

"Mr. Ogle, hello." Connor glanced at the calendar. It was Monday. They still had five days before the two weeks were up. "Things are going very well with Max."

"Oh." Surprise filled the man's tone. "I'm glad. A good two weeks together has to be better than the alternative." He paused. "Anyway, I went ahead and did as you asked. I put out feelers with the attorneys I know, and late last week I found a couple that's very interested."

Connor's chest felt suddenly tight, and he couldn't take a deep breath. What was the attorney talking about? "Mr. Ogle, I never asked you to . . . I've been camping all week with the children."

"But your wife said . . ."

Heat filled Connor's cheeks. A picture was taking shape, one he couldn't fathom. Because the Michele he knew and loved would never have done such a thing. He gave a shake of his head, as if maybe that could clear up the situation and make sense of it. "My wife said what?"

"So you don't know?"

"Mr. Ogle"—Connor massaged his brow with his thumb and forefinger—"I have no idea what you're talking about."

"I see." The weight of the predicament sounded heavy in the attorney's voice. "I should explain, then." He gave a tired-out breath. "Your wife contacted me last week and said you'd made a decision. Max needed to come home at the end of the two weeks. She asked me to start looking for an adoptive family for the boy, the sooner the better."

Connor could feel the blood draining from his face. She couldn't have done that, not without talking to him. When he remained silent, Mr. Ogle continued.

"I explained that finding adoptive parents for an older child could take months, years even, but she told me she was praying it would happen sooner. She told me the two of you wanted a phone call if I found anyone."

Connor's heart was pounding so close to the surface, he could feel the beat in his neck and temple. "And now ... now you've found a family?"

"Yes." He hesitated. "They've already started the process."

"But they've never even *met* Max." How had he lost control so quickly? His son was all but gone from his life, and they'd never had a chance to see that things turned out different.

"They run a bed-and-breakfast on the big island, Mr. Evans. Apparently they lost their son in a drowning accident a few years back. They want a boy about Max's age, someone to keep them company and learn the family business so he can take it over when they're too old to run it."

Connor couldn't believe any of it. He groped his way along the counter and dropped to the nearest kitchen stool. Not only had the attorney found adoptive parents for Max, but he had the boy's entire life planned out. All because of Michele's phone call. He wanted to scream that none of this was fair, that Max didn't want to live at a bed-and-breakfast or keep some older couple company all his life.

God ... help me, here. This can't be happening.

"Mr. Evans?" The attorney sounded tentative, as though he understood the dilemma even before it was spelled out to him. "I'm sorry all of this comes as a surprise to you."

"Yes." Connor squeezed his eyes and tried to think of what to do next.

"Daddy ... can we go out and play?" The girls ran into the house, with Max on their heels. "Please, can we? The car's cleaned out."

"Sure" He forced himself to smile. "I'll be out there in a bit."

When the blur of noise and motion was out in the backyard, Connor felt a lump choking his throat, cutting off every important thing he wanted to say. He massaged his neck for a moment, then did two short coughs. "Mr. Ogle, my wife and I never discussed this."

"So there's a chance you might want to adopt the boy after the two weeks are up?"

"Yes, there's a big chance." Connor didn't need even a moment to think about his answer. "The girls and I, we've connected very . . . very strongly to Max."

"And Mrs. Evans?"

"She didn't go with us on the camping trip." He gritted his teeth. "I'm expecting her home anytime, though. After that, I'm sure she'll feel the same way."

The attorney paused. "And if she doesn't?"

If she doesn't?

If Michele didn't fall in love with Max the way he had, was that what the man meant? For the past week he'd convinced himself that such a possibility didn't exist, that of course his wife would go along with the most obvious, most loving solution for Max. But now the attorney's question caused his heart to beat faster and harder than he could ever remember.

If Michele didn't love Max, if she didn't want him to stay, then he would have to choose, wouldn't he? The very idea made his head spin, and dropped his heart to his knees. God wouldn't let that happen, would He? Michele would come to her senses, surely she would.

But what if she didn't . . .

"Mr. Evans, I need to know what to do. The couple is very interested in Max. They want me to give them pictures and move ahead with the process." Kindness filled his tone, but clearly he needed an answer. "What should I tell them?"

Connor drew in a long, slow breath and straightened himself. "Could you hold off for a few days, Mr. Ogle?" He moved to the patio door and stared at the children—his children—playing together on the backyard swing set. "You told us we had two weeks before we had to make a decision. Give us that at least. Please."

The attorney considered that for a beat. "Okay. I can put off moving ahead with their application until Thursday afternoon. I'll need to know by then."

Relief like a drug flooded Connor's veins and made his knees weak. He hadn't lost the boy yet. "Thank you, Mr. Ogle. I'll be in touch."

He was just hanging up the phone when he heard the patio door behind him. A quick look over his shoulder and he saw Max, a tired grin stretched across his face. The resemblance to himself, to his father, was striking. "I think I'm tuckered out."

Connor set the receiver down and tried to ignore the heaviness in his heart. He turned and gave Max his full attention. "Are the girls tuckered, too?"

"No, they're playing house."

"And they let you get away?" He raised his eyebrows.

"They wanted me to be the little brother, but I told them little brothers sometimes take rests."

"I see." Connor grinned but contained a chuckle. He motioned for Max to come closer. "Good call."

"Yeah." Max stretched his arms over his head and yawned.

"You really are tired." Connor put his hand on Max's shoulder and gave it a soft squeeze. "Wanna rest with me for a minute?"

"Okay." Max looked straight up and smiled with his eyes.

They walked side by side into the family room. Connor sat in the oversized leather recliner and patted his knee. As if he'd done so all his life, Connor watched Max crawl up into his lap and snuggle against his chest. "Is it okay if I fall sleep?"

Connor pictured Michele coming home to the scene of Max and him in the chair. He looked down at his son and the thought vanished. "Of course." He wrapped his arm around Max and stroked his back. "Fishing can tire out a man real good."

"Mmm-hmm."

It was all Max got out before his breathing changed and became slower, more even. His body went limp against Connor's, and the feeling was exhilarating. All week he'd fought against this very feeling, the sense that he and his son had bonded beyond anything time or distance could tear apart.

Gentle snoring sounds came from Max's nose, and Connor tightened his hold on him. The poor kid must've been more tired than he thought. Not only the fishing and camping and unloading the car, but the mental exhaustion of wondering about his future.

How could Michele send him away? How could she have made the phone call to the attorney without even talking to him? It was completely unlike her. Michele—of the two of them—had always had the bigger heart, the kinder spirit. She was the fun parent, the one always suggesting a picnic at the beach or a walk through the park.

Couldn't she set aside the past long enough to imagine what Max might be going through this week? Couldn't she have asked, before making the call?

He hesitated. She did ask; she asked Elizabeth when the two of them were on the phone early in her midweek call. He hadn't heard Michele's part of the conversation, but he heard Elizabeth's. The child was effusive, going on about what a good time they were having and how he'd taught the boy how to fish, and how well Max was fitting in.

So she knew, after all.

She knew how he felt, how Max felt, and she'd called the attorney anyway. He looked down and gave the boy a light kiss on the top of his head. Then something caught his eye and he looked up.

It was their wedding portrait, a canvas oil painting of Michele and him on the day they married. He narrowed his eyes, studying the look on her face, the openhearted love that shone for anyone to see. Her beauty had been breathtaking back then, and not only because of her dark looks. There was that certain intangible quality of her heart, her ability to soar within him, even when he was in the air and she was on the ground.

Had his affair caused her such grief that she'd lost that look, lost her ability to love, in so short a time?

He breathed in the fragrance that was Max, warm and dirty from the camping trip, and let the question simmer in his heart. The answer, of course, was obvious. Michele couldn't possibly have lost her ability to love. No, she was only anxious and afraid and paralyzed with anger.

And in that instant something the old pastor had said to him a week earlier, the day he'd gone in for some quick advice, came back. He had asked the man how he could get Michele to forgive. The pastor had given him a hint.

It'll start with you.

Suddenly, for the first time, he understood what that meant.

The affair hadn't simply happened. It hadn't been a mistake or an accident or the result of a terribly tempting set of circumstances. He couldn't blame the FAA or his father or the distance he'd felt with Michele. No, fault couldn't be placed there or on Kiahna. She was only a girl, an idealistic faith-driven girl, who had trusted him one stormy night.

The affair didn't happen because of any of them.

It happened because he made a choice to break the most important promise he'd ever given Michele and his family. The promise of faithfulness. Because of that, this mess—the one that involved Kiahna and Max and Michele and Elizabeth and Susan, the one that even involved some Hawaiian couple with a bed-and-breakfast and a hole in their hearts where a little boy used to live—all of it was his fault.

His fault alone.

The truth came at him like a battering ram and planted a mountain of sorrow squarely on his chest. How come he hadn't seen that before, hadn't owned the fact that he didn't merely play a role in what had happened? *He* caused it. Pure and simple. It was his fault Kiahna had gotten pregnant, his fault she'd been forced to give up her dream of becoming a doctor, his fault she was on Western Flight 45 that fateful morning.

The truth grew heavier still.

It was his fault that, after leaving Kiahna, he hadn't found the courage to tell Michele, the courage to go home, look her in the eye, and tell her the truth so they could start rebuilding their lives. It was his fault the boy was without a father, and his fault Michele was on the other side of the country, sinking in the quicksand of anger and unforgiveness.

The sorrow—thick and oppressive—came then, and he let his head rest against Max. At the same instant another thought made its way into his conscience.

He hadn't even apologized.

Not to Kiahna, or to Mr. Ogle, and especially not to Michele.

Every time he talked about the affair, all he did was try to excuse it, rationalize it, explain it somehow. But he'd never looked Michele in the eyes and told her he was sorry.

This was the truth he couldn't stomach, couldn't figure out no matter how long he sat there. Why hadn't he taken the blame?

Max stirred and made a slight shift of his position. Again, Connor soothed his hand along the boy's back. His voice came in the gentlest whisper. "Max . . . what have I done?"

He closed his eyes and thought of where his choices had left him. *God, what sort of hypocrite am I? I've been running from all of it . . . from Michele, from the truth. Most of all from You.*

Connor tried to imagine God Almighty—how would such a holy God view him, Connor Evans, after all the mistakes he'd made? *I wouldn't blame You if You walked away from me for good, God.*

Son, I will never leave you nor forsake you . . . Return to Me.

Return to Me? The call blew across his soul like a whispery summer breeze. The response to his misery hadn't been his imagination. After all this time, after all he'd done wrong, God still cared. He was still just a prayer away, waiting to make peace with Connor the moment Connor asked. A flashlight of joy shone into the moment's dark despair. He blinked his eyes open and looked at Max. *God, he's my own son; I love him. But if I lose him, it's my fault.*

He had a choice to make now, one that would mean keeping Max or keeping Michele. And even that choice could be blamed on no one but him. The quiet sobs simmering deep in his soul tried to get the better of him, but he pushed them back.

On the surface, the choice wasn't difficult. He opened his eyes and looked at their wedding portrait once more. No, he'd made his choice a long time ago in a central California church before a hundred of their friends and families.

He would do whatever Michele wanted him to do, because he owed her that much. Without meaning to, he held Max a little tighter. He owed something to the son on his lap. But he owed Michele first. First and always.

He and Michele shared something rare and wonderful, something few couples ever know. It had been that way most of their lives together, even after his affair. It was the reason he never considered telling her the truth. Because after he was stationed in Florida again, after he came home from Los Angeles for good, things between Michele and him became better than they'd ever been.

He couldn't imagine jeopardizing that by telling her what had happened. Besides, back then it had been easy to justify his actions, easy to tell himself he'd had no control over the situation, no other way to handle his frustrations than to give in to the temptation that stormy night.

Now he knew he'd been wrong. The bond between them would've been stronger if he'd told the truth. Of course, they still would've faced the dilemma with Max, and his sudden arrival in their lives.

He kissed the boy's head again, felt the soft dark hair against his cheek. No question he could keep the boy, love him and raise him, and revel the rest of his days in the fact that he had not only two wonderful daughters but a son. A boy to carry on his name.

But if losing Michele was the price he would pay, then he'd been right when he first sat down with Max. The decision was already made. He loved Michele with all his heart, all his being. His life was with her, and when she came home he would tell her how sorry he was, tell her he'd been wrong about everything involving that awful summer.

Then he would wait until Thursday, in case she had a change of mind. If not . . . he would call the attorney and tell him to contact the Hawaiian couple. Max would spend his days working in a bed-and-breakfast, keeping company with a couple he knew nothing about. And one day he'd be the operator of a bed-and-breakfast on the big island.

Pain sliced through Connor's chest at the thought, and he knew why. The idea of Max growing up that way, of his son never knowing of his love, ripped Connor's heart in half. Taking Max away from Connor now would be like cutting off his right arm. No, it would be worse.

But it would be nothing to losing Michele.

He thought about Max's future again. By then, by the time he was grown and running the bed-and-breakfast, the memory of his mother's friend in Florida, and the camping trip on the lake, and the fish, and the butterfly, would be but a distant fleeting thought.

And his desire to be part of the Evans family, his desire to call Connor his daddy, would have long since disappeared.

Twenty-Nine

Michele flew home the next day, more because she missed the girls than because she'd figured out a solution for her life. Throughout two plane trips and the cab ride back home from the airport, she sorted out the details every way she knew how. By the time she walked through the front door, she was beyond drained.

The weather was more humid than when she'd left, and though she'd lost a few pounds at her sister's house, she felt hot and frumpy and more than a little grouchy. She should have stayed at Margie's until the boy was gone. That way she could come home with at least a good attitude, a sliver of hope that somehow she and Connor could find common ground again.

But of course she had to come home before the boy left. Because she had to see what had happened between him and Connor since she'd been gone. Not that it mattered; her decision was made, and if Connor wanted to make an attempt at their marriage, the boy would have to go home. But even after the child was gone, Connor would carry him in his heart. At least to the extent he carried him now.

And Michele had to see for herself just to what extent that was.

She set her bags down in the hallway and straightened out the wrinkles in her Capri pants. A quick glance in the mirror told her she'd picked the wrong shirt. This one showed the hint of a bulge on either side of her waist. She huffed and lifted the shirt enough to create a few bunches. Bunches hid bulges, any woman battling her weight knew that.

"Hello?" She called out and waited, but there was no response. Then as her ears adjusted to the quiet of the house, she heard the sound of distant voices coming from the backyard.

Dreading whatever she might see, she made her way to the glass door and stared outside. Connor was giving Susan a piggyback ride around the yard, while Elizabeth and the boy stood not far off, giggling and talking together. When Susan's ride was finished, she jumped off and Elizabeth climbed on. Susan gave Max a quick hug and held his hands as they jumped up and down.

"Go, Daddy!" she yelled as she turned back to her father and sister. "Go faster!"

Michele watched, hidden in the shadows of the china cabinet, as Connor picked up speed and went twice more around the yard. Then he dropped her off where the other two were standing and collapsed in a heap of laughter and weary legs. The kids piled onto him, poking him and tickling him, but after a few minutes, Elizabeth and Susan headed off toward the swings and seemed to forget about the piggyback rides.

Back with Connor, Max laid his head on the left side of Connor's heart. Then just as fast, he lifted it and made a rhythmic motion with his head, all the while grinning the same grin she'd seen a thousand times on Connor's face.

Michele felt her blood run cold. What was the boy doing? Listening to Connor's heartbeat? And what had happened to the formalities, the distance the boy had kept even from Connor before she left?

Suddenly she realized the truth. She should've gone on the camping trip. She could've kept Connor busy, and Max would've had no choice but to spend his time with the girls. Instead, the girls must've spent much of their time playing together, and whenever that was the case, Max must've spent his time with Connor.

Of course they'd gotten close.

She kept her eyes trained on her husband and his son. Connor struggled to his feet, his motions exaggerated as though he was too weary to go another round. Max flung his arms around

Connor's waist, looked up at him, and said something Michele couldn't make out.

Then Connor lifted the boy into the air and spun him around. When he set him back down, his arms came around Max's shoulders and held the boy in an embrace that was no different from one Connor would've given to Elizabeth or Susan. Or maybe it was different. Maybe Connor held on a little bit longer to Max, aware of the fact that their time together was short.

Connor stooped down and kissed the boy on the top of his head, and just at that moment he caught Michele watching them. He said something to Max, and the boy nodded and ran off to join the girls. Connor stood and faced her with a hopeful smile. His mouth opened and she could read the word "Hi" as he came closer.

She stepped back. Could she run away? The last thing she wanted was to talk to Connor now that she'd seen firsthand the love he felt for his son, the way the two of them—the way *all* of them—had connected. Anything she said was bound to sound cold and bitter and thoughtless.

But she had nowhere to run.

Connor slid the door opened, stepped inside, and closed it again. "Hey, when did you get home?"

"Just now." She took another small step backward, tried a smile, and let it die on her lips. "I missed the girls."

"Oh." The excitement in Connor's eyes dimmed. He didn't try to close the gap between them. "What about me?"

She let her gaze fall to her feet for a moment before finding his eyes again. "Of course. I missed you, too."

He brought his lips together and exhaled in a sharp burst. "Michele . . ." His eyes stared at something on the ceiling, and he ran his fingers through his short hair. When he looked at her, his eyes were deeper, more honest, than she'd ever seen them. "We need to talk."

"Okay." She crossed her arms, her heart tense and unmoved within her. No matter how he looked, she knew what he was doing. This was his attempt to change her mind, to convince her they could take the boy, after all. That she would grow to love him. But nothing he could say would make her see the boy as anything other than what he was.

The son of a woman who had slept with her husband.

Connor walked past her, and she followed him into the living room. He sat on one side of the sofa and motioned for her to sit beside him.

Every ounce of her wanted to refuse him, to take a chair on the other side of the room, but she wanted to be near him, wanted to hear what outlandish argument he was going to make about the boy. Because of that she sat down next to him and turned to face him.

He watched her, and the look in his eyes told her that she seemed more a stranger than the wife he'd married. The look fell away, and he knit his brow together. He looked even more handsome than she remembered.

"Michele, there's something I have to tell you. Something I should've said a long time ago."

A war was taking place in her heart, half of her wanting to throw her arms around his neck and tell him whatever it was, they'd work through it, they'd find a way to survive and come out stronger on the other end.

But the other half was winning, the part that hated him for what he'd done to her and the girls.

"All right." She kept her face free of expression. "What is it?"

The lack of love in her voice took even her by surprise. Why was she talking to him like this? Hadn't she missed him, hadn't that been at least part of the reason why she had to get home? And couldn't she simply have hugged him when he walked in from the yard, his face lit up at the sight of her?

The answer to every question was a resounding no, because Connor didn't even understand what he'd done. Couldn't see past his desire for the boy long enough to realize what his unfaithfulness had cost her.

"You're not making this easy."

"You haven't made it easy, either."

He looked down for a moment, and she watched him work the muscles in his jaw. When he lifted his head again, the remorse was back. "Michele, what happened in Honolulu that August was my fault." He rushed ahead as if she might stop him. "It was my fault that I wasn't seeing you as often as I should, and my fault that I was in trouble with the FAA, my fault that I agreed to spend a stormy summer night at the house of a flight attendant I didn't even know, and my fault the situation resulted in an affair."

Michele stared at her husband and felt her mouth fall open a bit. She couldn't remember Connor ever saying those words, "It's my fault." She bit the inside of her cheek and waited.

"It's all my fault, and I want to ask your forgiveness." He ran his tongue along his lower lip and searched her face, desperate for some kind of response. "I should've told you the truth when I came home from Los Angeles, but I told myself it was one of those things, something I couldn't have helped. I thought it would be easier on both of us if you never knew."

"Yeah, well, you thought wrong." The acid reply was out before Michele could stop it.

Connor jerked back the slightest bit and stared at her. "I know." His face was a study in control, his tone less desperate than before. "That's why I'm telling you this." He sat back. "What I'm trying to say is, everything that happened is because of me. But since I found out about Max, all I've done is think about myself and how much I owe that child, how much I owe—"

"*What?*" The word was a shriek, a cry that came from the most wounded part of her heart. She pointed toward the backyard. "How much you owe *him?*"

An exasperated huff slid through Connor's clenched teeth. "Not just him, you didn't let me finish." He shielded his eyes with his right hand for a moment, and then snapped it back to his side. "Michele, you're not hearing me."

"I hear you loud and clear. I knew what this was as soon as you told me you wanted to talk. It's some sort of build-up ... tell the wife you're sorry so you can convince her to keep the boy." She stood up and glared at him. "Can't you just say you're sorry, Connor? For once can't you just leave it at that?"

Without waiting for a response, she rushed out of the room. She grabbed her bags and made her way up the stairs before she heard him get up, stride across the kitchen floor, and return outside to the backyard where the kids were waiting for him.

The hurt came the moment she slammed the bedroom door behind her. Up until the point where he talked about what he owed the boy, she was tracking with him, believing that this time maybe he understood the gravity of what he'd done.

She wanted to forgive him, really she did.

But not when he was only using it to convince her of his ultimate goal—his desire to keep Max, and never send him home again.

She yanked shirts and shorts and pants and underwear from her suitcase, tossing them either in the dirty clothes hamper, or putting them away where they belonged. When she was finished, she stared out their bedroom window, then took slow steps toward it.

The window overlooked the backyard, and from her position she could see all of them. Connor and Max and the girls were playing Frisbee now, jumping into the air to snag the disc, and high-fiving each other after a particularly difficult catch. Angry sorrow choked her throat and her heart and her ability to see straight.

So much for his apology.

Their argument hadn't meant a thing to Connor, hadn't made him lose a step. She'd been right all the time, his reason for talking to her had been clear-cut from the beginning. He wanted the boy. And the longer she stood there watching the two of them laughing and playing together, the more she felt inclined to let him have what he wanted. To put her things back in the suitcase and head back out the door.

Not just a few things to get her through a week or two, but every single thing she owned.

Connor was more confused than ever.

He'd worked on his plan ever since Max fell asleep on his chest in the hours after the camping trip. As soon as he saw Michele, he would smile at her, welcome her home, and then ask her if they could talk. Once he had her alone, he would take responsibility for every awful thing he'd done by having the affair. He would take the blame for all of it, and do his best to explain his feelings about Max.

Michele was wrong about his intentions.

Not for a minute had he planned to use that talk to convince her to keep Max. Oh, he wanted that, sure. Wanted it more than he wanted his next breath. But he'd already made a deal with God that if she was going to change her mind about the boy, she'd have to do it on her own. If he convinced her, she'd be tempted to hold the decision against him for the rest of their days.

And neither of them could live with that.

But right from the beginning, his plan went terribly awry. Like a perfectly sound flight plan that somehow falls apart in the air and ends up with an emergency landing. Only this time they didn't even get that. The conversation crashed and burned long before Connor had time to say even half of what he'd wanted to tell her.

Now here it was, ten o'clock Tuesday night, and Connor sat alone in the family room, staring into the darkness and wondering what was going to happen next, how either of them could salvage their relationship.

Maybe he'd been wrong about Michele. Maybe it was too late to save their marriage. If he was going to lose her anyway, then he might as well keep Max. That way when he and Michele had to share the girls, at least he'd always have his son. The boy would never have to grow up with a couple he didn't know, his future as predictable as the seasons.

He thought back over the night, and the tension that filled the house like a poisonous fog. Michele finally came down from her room, stood at the patio door, and called out a hello to the kids. Elizabeth and Susan came running, of course, but Max hung back. Poor guy, of course he didn't come running. Even in those first welcoming moments, she made her feelings for him clear. Her eyes never even looked for him in the yard, and once she hugged the girls, she put an arm around each of them and headed back into the house.

Connor went outside then, found the boy, and played catch with him. But Max wasn't fooled.

"Mrs. Evans is still mad, isn't she?"

"Not at you, Max. At me . . . at something I did."

"You?" He flipped the ball across the yard, and Connor couldn't help but notice that he had a great throwing arm. "I don't think so . . . I think it's me."

After a quiet dinner, they spent the rest of the evening apart, he and Max watching a movie together; Michele with the girls upstairs, getting them ready for bed, reading to them, and brushing their hair. She was asleep in one of their rooms now. At least that's what he guessed. She hadn't been down since dinnertime.

Meanwhile, Max fell asleep against his side, and when the movie was over, he carried his son upstairs to the guest room. As he tucked him into bed, he hovered over him a few minutes longer than necessary. Max had carried his Bible with him on the camping trip, looking over it, reading small passages, and checking the special things he kept inside.

The Bible was back on the nightstand next to his bed now. A reminder of all he held dear. But after the past week, it wasn't all he held dear, was it? That night as Max read him a book and prayed with him, he hadn't even reached for the special things in his small white book. The reason was as clear as the stars outside his window.

Max was growing to love Connor as much as Connor already loved him.

Connor leaned down and kissed Max's cheek, just as the phone rang. He crept out of the room with quiet steps and headed for his bedroom. There he grabbed the phone on the third ring and clicked the on button.

"Hello?"

The silence on the other end was long enough that Connor almost hung up. But just as he moved the receiver from his ear he heard a familiar voice. "Connor . . ."

He brought the phone back. "Yes?"

"Connor, this is your father."

A hundred other times in that instant he would have been first shocked, and then angry. He'd told his father not to call, that the relationship they'd once shared was over. But now, with his own son's sweet smell still fresh on his sweatshirt, his knees grew weak and he could do nothing but drop to the bed.

The word that came from his mouth was small and filled with sadness, a sadness Connor hadn't fully understood until just now. "Dad?"

His father's voice was thick. "How . . . how are you, Son?"

Connor had never cried over losing his father, but now his heart was strangled by sorrow. He pictured Max, then pictured the way his own father must've felt about him, regardless of how he'd chosen to show it. And out of the ashes of eight years of silence, a sprig of hope began to grow.

Connor's words were shaky. "I'm . . . not too good, Dad. Not too good."

"I heard." He paused. "Michele came by a few days ago."

He wanted to be angry with her, but he couldn't be. Couldn't do anything but grip the phone and realize how good it felt to have his dad on the other end. "I messed up."

"Yes. We all mess up once or twice."

What was his father saying? That he himself had made a mistake by turning his only son away all those years ago? Connor fell back on the bed, and tears blurred his view of the ceiling. "I never thought the affair was my fault." He pulled his arm across his wet eyes. "Until the other day."

"You know why, right?" The man's words were gentler than they'd been before. Gentle and kind and wise.

"Not really."

"Pilot's pride, Son. You and I both have it."

"Pilot's pride?" Connor twisted his face and gave a shake of his head. "What's my job have to do with it?"

"Everything." His father took a long breath. "Pilots—good pilots—carry with them a certain kind of pride, an ability to see everything that goes wrong as a problem he can fix and move away from. If a pilot thought himself capable of error, he wouldn't be much good with a plane full of passengers. See, it's a confidence thing that works wonderfully in the cockpit." His voice fell a notch. "But not so well on the ground."

Pilot's pride? Was that his problem? If so, he'd been crazy to let it go this far, to let it get in the way of every person he'd ever loved. "What made you call?"

"I have a few things to say." A smile sounded in his tone. "And God gave me the go-ahead."

"God?" Maybe this wasn't his father after all. The man had never owned the faith they'd been raised with. That had been his mother's area.

"Yes. My pilot's pride has faded since our last meeting. God wanted me to wait until the time was right, and after Michele came by I knew. This was my time." The humor was gone. "Our time."

"Is that what you wanted to say?" Connor wanted to keep the conversation going, hold onto whatever chance this was before it slipped away.

"There's more." He hesitated. "I want you to know I'm sorry about what happened between us, Son." His father sniffed, and his voice cracked. "I've regretted it every day since."

Connor had to remind himself to breathe. "You have?"

"Yes." He seemed to think for a moment. "I still don't think buy-ing the airport would've been a good thing for you, but I could've handled it differently. Spent more time talking to you about it, researched it with you. Anyway . . ." He took a slow breath, and a lifetime of pain sounded in his tone. "I'm sorry."

It was his turn, but after so many years, Connor wasn't sure how to voice his feelings. Instead of apologizing, he sat up and pressed the receiver closer to his ear. "I missed you, Dad. Missed you a lot."

"Me, too." Nothing in his father's voice suggested he was upset that the apology hadn't gone both ways. "I hear I have a grandson."

Mention of Max doubled the sorrow welling within him. "Yes. He . . . he looks just like you, Dad. Exactly like you looked when you were a boy."

"Then he must look like you, also."

"He does." Connor stared out the window. "I love him, Dad. I've fallen head over heels for the boy."

His father waited for a bit. "That's the other thing I wanted to talk about."

"Max?" Connor was surprised.

"Yes, Son. When Michele first told me about the boy, I thought you needed to find whatever way possible to keep him. I was ready to pray for Michele to welcome him the way you already had. But then God talked to me and told me something I needed to remember, something He wanted me to tell you, too."

"Okay ..." God wanted him to? Connor stood and paced the room, taking slow steps from one side to the other, trying to take it all in. The changes in his father were almost enough to distract him from what the man was saying. "What's that, Dad?"

"God's ways are not our ways, Son. That's the message." His father paused. When he spoke again, his voice was sadder than it had ever been. "You need to send the boy home."

Connor stopped and hung his head. He could still feel Max's arms around his waist, still see him looking concerned as they played catch and talked about Michele. Still feel the way he'd all but taken over his broken heart.

He pinched the bridge of his nose. "I thought that, too, Dad. Until Michele came home today."

"Ah ... it didn't go well?"

"She's become this ... this awful person. I don't even recognize her." He looked up and finished his path to the bedroom window. "I think she's going to leave me."

"So you've already made up your mind."

A flicker of anger sparked in Connor's soul, and then died. He'd lost too many years with his father to be angry with him now. "Michele made it up for me."

"Now, Son. What you and Michele have is deeper, stronger, than this type of a test. But there's a problem. You're more willing to let her go because if she leaves, you'll have a reason to keep the boy."

Connor placed his arm against the window and leaned against the cool glass. That was it exactly, wasn't it? He'd given it a try with Michele, and since she'd rejected him, he was ready to move on to Max, right?

"Okay." Defeat rang in his voice. "What am I supposed to do?"

"Believe that God's ways are the best. And that means standing by Michele, standing by her and loving her and helping her through this time. It means sending Max home, Son. As soon as the two weeks are up."

His father was right. He was right and if he followed the man's advice, if he did what God wanted him to do, that meant Max would be gone from their lives in three short days. Three days to love him and bond with him and make enough memories to last a lifetime without him.

It was the only thing he could do, and at that moment he was sure he would do it. Michele would come around eventually, and one day they could find what they'd lost these past weeks. But only if he sent Max away.

"Okay, Dad." He couldn't stay on the phone another minute. "Okay."

"So you'll do it?"

"Yes. He'll go home Friday morning."

"You'll never be sorry."

Connor didn't know about that. But it wasn't the time to say so. "Thanks, Dad. For calling. It's been too long."

"We'll talk again in a few weeks. I want to know how it goes."

"Okay." The irony rattled the walls of Connor's heart. That he would find his father and lose his son all in one week.

"Oh, and Connor?"

"Yes?"

"I wish I could see him. Max, I mean."

"Yeah, Dad." Connor worked his fingertips into his neck, trying to knead out the tightness in his throat. No matter what his father had said about sending Max home, the old man cared. He cared, and in some ways he would carry a permanent ache over losing Max—just as Connor would.

Connor clenched his jaw and then released it. "I wish you could, too."

"Listen." His father's voice cracked. "I may not ever meet Max, but could you do me a favor?" He paused, and Connor could feel the man's sadness through the phone line. "Before you send him home, could you take a picture of him for me?"

"Sure, Dad." Connor bit the inside of his lip. "I'll take one for both of us."

THIRTY

The goldfish feeling in Max's tummy was back.

It was Thursday, and Mr. Evans said after dinner they had to talk. But it wasn't the nice kind of talk they sometimes did about fishing or butterflies or throwing a ball. No, because this time, Mr. Evans only did a small sad smile when he said that.

Tomorrow was two weeks; he heard Mrs. Evans say so, and that meant that maybe the thing Mr. Evans wanted to talk about was him going back home. Max missed Buddy, and so going home was a good thing, except he didn't want to stay there. He wanted to get his bestest dog and get back on a plane to Florida so he could live with the Evans family forever.

Plus for two days Mrs. Evans had been nicer to him. She asked him what his favorite thing to eat was, and he told her blueberry pancakes and whipped cream, or buttered toast. Either one. And yesterday she made him blueberry pancakes for breakfast and today, buttered toast.

And when he couldn't untie the knot in his shoe after the kick-ball game with 'Lizabeth and Susan, she called him over and put him on her lap while she untangled it all the way. Afterward he told her thank you very much, ma'am, the way his mommy taught him.

And the greatest thing happened. Mrs. Evans smiled at him and said, "Max, you're a very nice boy."

So maybe the Evans family had made a choice to keep him. Because everything was going so good. But when Mr. Evans said after dinner they had to have a talk, his voice didn't sound happy, like he could stay. It sounded sorry but he had to go.

Dinnertime was quiet, except for 'Lizabeth said, "Do you leave tomorrow, Max?" She sounded not happy about the idea.

Then Mrs. Evans gave her a strong look and said, "We'll talk about that later."

That's when Max knew that whatever the talk was about, it wouldn't be good news.

When dinner was over, Mr. Evans took him upstairs to his room and sat next to him on the end of the bed. "Max, I have some news for you."

The goldfish jumped around a little. "Yes?"

"You have to go home tomorrow, Max." His eyes had shiny wet in them, and his voice sounded broken. "Mr. Ogle has found a very nice couple who want to adopt you. They want you to live with them forever."

Angry and scared and wanting to run all mixed together in Max's heart. "But . . . I thought . . ."

"Yes." Mr. Evans closed his mouth very tight and his lips made a straight line. "We wanted you to live here, too. But . . . but God told us it would be better for you to go back to the island."

"Only to get Buddy." Max's throat felt dry, the way it did after a long walk home from the bus stop. "Then I want to come back here." He took Mr. Evans's hand. "I don't want to live with anyone else."

Mr. Evans was quiet for a long time. "I'm sorry, Max. The decision's already been made."

Questions were coming into his mind faster than Max could think. Who was the couple and how did they know about him? How come Mr. Evans let someone else adopt him? And how would he ever find his daddy somewhere out there if he was living with a new couple?

And the biggest question of all. "Mrs. Evans is still mad at me, right?"

"I told you, Max . . . it's because this is what God wants." He dropped his head down some. When he looked up, the water in his eyes was almost spilling over. "But I want you to know that I'll always remember our time together, okay?"

Be strong and brave . . . be strong and brave . . . be strong and brave . . .

"Okay." Max squeezed Mr. Evans's hand. "I'll remember, too."

The talk was over because Mr. Evans said that was all. Then he held out his arms and Max jumped down onto his feet and quick ran up to him for a long hug. After a while, Max pulled back a little. "I have a question."

"Okay." Mr. Evans looked at him. Hurt was in his voice. Hurt and sorry and too bad it didn't work out.

Max could feel his heart beeping hard beneath his shirt. Because this was the question he had all the time he was at the Evans's house, only he didn't know how to ask. And now . . . now he was leaving tomorrow so if he didn't ask, he never would. "Did you love my mommy, Mr. Evans?"

For a long time, Mr. Evans looked away, out the window probably, but Max couldn't tell. Then he looked back and said, "Your mommy and I were friends for a short time, Max."

"But did you love her?"

This time Max felt him put his hand against the side of his face. "Not as much as I love you."

Max's heart did a somersault inside him, because of two things. First, yes, Mr. Evans had loved his mommy. Not the married kind of love, but at least he loved her. That meant he knew how sad it was that she was gone. And two, Mr. Evans loved him even more!

They hugged again, and then they went back downstairs with the rest of the family. The night was fun with Uno and real actual theater popcorn in the microwave, and a Peter Pan movie. Everything was just perfect, except one thing.

Tomorrow he was going home.

Michele was glad Max was leaving, but she still wasn't ready to sleep in the same bed as Connor.

That night she stayed in Susan's room, and it was after midnight when she heard someone crying. At first she thought it was Elizabeth, because the girl had suffered nightmares the past two nights. She slipped out of bed and padded the few steps to Elizabeth's room, but she was sound asleep. That could mean only one thing, of course.

The crying was coming from Max.

No matter what her feelings about her husband's affair, or the woman who had been Max's mother, her heart broke at the sound of the child's muffled cries. In fact, he had been much easier to be around the past few days. Ever since she'd known for sure that he was going home.

She'd realized something early Wednesday. Connor was right. Max was a very nice boy, well-mannered and kind to the girls, polite and thankful with an easy grin and an adorable face. With no reason to keep her guard up around the boy, Michele found herself actually liking him.

Her cold treatment toward him had been shameful and wrong, and she wished there was a way she could make it up to him. The situation was hardly his fault, not the affair or the interruption his arrival had made in their lives, or the fact that he had his mother's green eyes. He was simply a little boy who had lost his mom, a boy who'd had no say whatsoever in coming to Florida to visit their family.

Earlier that day she had wondered about the boy's grieving process, when he cried for the loss of his mother. Now she knew.

She crept down the hall toward the guest room and pushed the door open. "Max?"

His face was buried in his pillow, but he lifted it a few inches and looked at her. "Yes?"

"Max, honey, why are you crying?" She crossed the room and sat on the edge of his bed. "It's very late."

He rolled over and tucked the covers up to his chin. His eyes were swollen, and in the moonlight she could see tearstains on his cheeks. "I can't sleep."

In that instant, gone were her thoughts about whose son he was or what he represented. All that mattered was that the heart of the boy before her was breaking. Breaking badly. Without giving her actions a second thought, she reached out and ran her fingers along Max's arm. "Are you missing your mom?"

Max nodded and made another couple sobs. "Y–y–yes." He pulled something out from beneath the covers and held it up. "This is my mommy. Sometimes . . . sometimes at night I hold her picture against my heart."

Michele's breath caught in her throat.

She kept her eyes from the photograph. She couldn't have made it out in the shadowy light anyway, but just in case . . . This wasn't about Kiahna; it was about Max missing his mommy. Michele's jealousy and her feelings of inadequacy had no place in this conversation.

Max took several quick breaths, his small body still convulsing from the sadness. "She . . . she told me that she'd always be in my heart." He pulled the picture back down under the covers and held it there with one hand. "Do you think that's true, Mrs. Evans? Do you think she's still in my heart?"

"Yes." Michele ached for the boy, ached to pull the child into her arms and hug away the mountain of pain he was under. Instead she caught Max's free hand and held it, the same way she would've held Elizabeth or Susan's hands. "Yes, Max, I'm sure she's in your heart."

Gradually, in lessening sobs and waves of sorrow, Max began to calm down. Michele watched him leave his mother's picture beneath the sheets and blankets. Then he pulled his arm out and dragged it across his face. He kept his other hand tucked safe and small inside hers.

After a minute he peered at her again. "Mrs. Evans?"

"Yes, Max."

"You didn't know my mommy, did you?"

Michele refused to give in to the jealousy that rose up in her heart. *He's a little boy . . . he doesn't have any idea . . .* "No, Max. I didn't know her." She squeezed the boy's hand. "But I'm sure she was very nice."

"She was." He made a few sniffing sounds. "I wanted her to get a husband so we could have a daddy, but she never did. She said I was the only man she needed."

Michele had to keep from letting her mouth hang open. What did he mean she never did? Certainly a woman like Kiahna would've had different men every few months. Casual sex and instability in the home. At least that was the picture she'd had since she learned about her husband's affair.

Twice she ran the boy's words through her head, and the picture still wouldn't come into focus. Max was waiting for an answer, and she kept her voice even. "I'm sure she was telling the truth, that you were all she needed."

"But I still wanted a daddy." Max put his free hand beneath his head so he could see her better. "My mommy loves Jesus very much, did you know that, Mrs. Evans?"

"Really?" Michele's head was spinning. Again, the picture Max was giving her was nothing like the one in her head. Kiahna didn't have men in her life? She loved Jesus? Suddenly something Connor had said came back to her. Kiahna was a nice girl . . . a nice girl . . .

She hadn't believed a word of it. What sort of flight attendant would bring a married pilot home to her apartment? The answer had always seemed obvious—until now. She studied the small boy and bit the inside of her cheek. How important it must be for Max to have times like these, when he could talk about his mother as though she were still alive.

"You believe in Jesus, right?" He gave her a sad smile.

"Yes, Max. I believe very much." But even as she said the words, they sounded tinny, phony. Coated in plastic. She'd been downright mean to a seven-year-old boy who was just weeks from losing his mother . . . she'd spewed bitter words at her husband, never giving him a chance to explain himself or even apologize . . . and when she had a chance to work things out, she'd run to her sister's house.

But she believed in Jesus.

A Scripture came to mind, one that had always haunted her whenever she read the book of James: "You believe that there is one God. Good! Even the demons believe that—and shudder." The point of the Scripture was obvious. Faith without works was a dead faith. Since the news of Connor's infidelity, what had she done to show her love for anyone but herself?

"My mommy gave me a Bible last year." He sat up some and took a white book from his nightstand. "See . . . I read it every day."

The picture continued to grow and fill in. Kiahna had been a believer. Which meant, if nothing else, Michele would be with her in heaven one day. Also, she stayed away from men and taught Max to read the Bible. Suddenly Michele wanted more information about the woman. "Tell me more, Max."

"Really?"

"Yes." She leaned in and with her free hand, she brushed his bangs off his forehead. "Talking about people we love helps keep them alive a little longer."

This time Max's smile was genuine. "I think that, too." Then he took another few breaths, the remains of his sobbing episode, and he told Michele everything he could think of about his mother.

Michele had expected him to say that she was beautiful and thin and well-dressed, that she had a pretty face and that he'd never seen a nicer-looking mommy anywhere. Instead he talked about the fact that she had a special song for him, and about their butterfly days, and how they liked to play at the beach sometimes.

Not once did he mention anything about his mother's looks.

Had Kiahna fretted about her weight, a few pounds one way or another? If she had, did she know now that Max hadn't cared one way or the other?

Suddenly Michele's obsession with her looks, her weight, and the foods she was and wasn't eating, seemed like a silly waste of time. A smoke screen. The truth presented itself, and for the first time she didn't turn away. The real problem back when Connor had his affair was that she'd been absorbed in depression, oblivious to Connor's trouble at work and with his father, unable to encourage him or love him or do anything but pull him down.

Yes, she'd had her reasons. But the way she'd cut herself off from Connor had been wrong. She finally saw the truth for what it was. Her food binges had always been nothing more than a way to hide from her emotional struggles.

The knowledge of Connor's affair had been no different.

Connor never would've left her because of her weight. Love wasn't based on how a person looked. It was how the person talked and played and spent time that mattered. How they lived and loved; that's what people remembered.

Max was saying something, and Michele focused on him once more.

"Know something else, Mrs. Evans?" Max's words were slower than before. He yawned and found her eyes again. "That wasn't all the reason I was crying."

"It wasn't?" Michele still had hold of his hand. "What else was it?"

"Because ..." This time Max looked straight into her soul. "Because I don't want to say good-bye tomorrow."

Michele reached for Max then, lifting him off the pillow and taking him in her arms. "Oh, Max ... it'll be okay."

His small body started shaking again. "I wanted ... I wanted Mr. Evans to be my pretend daddy."

"Your pretend daddy?" Michele's heart was racing now, the knowledge of what the child was going through almost more than she could bear.

"My mommy told me in a letter that I have a daddy somewhere out there. Only ... only I think it might be too hard to find him because of so many dads in the world. So I asked Jesus if ... if Mr. Evans could be my pretend daddy."

Michele couldn't contain her tears another minute. They flooded her eyes and she blinked them back so Max wouldn't see them. It took every bit of her resolve to remind herself that sending Max home was the best thing not just for their family but for Max. His school was there, and his friends. And a couple who wanted to love and care for Max forever.

"Max, it'll all work out one day. I promise you that. Jesus has plans for you that are all good."

"But I want to get Buddy and come back h–h–here." He buried his head in her shoulder and wept so hard he could barely breathe. They stayed that way until he grew calm once more. Then he pulled back some. "I wish you would've come camping with us, Mrs. Evans."

They were the most pointed words he could've said to her. Almost as if he knew that, had she come on the trip, she would've fallen in love with him, too.

With her fingertips, she wiped away his tears and said the only thing she could think to say. "I'm sorry I didn't go, Max. I'm so sorry."

"I forgive you." He caught her gaze once more. "And know what?"

"What?" Michele could barely speak, still strangled by the truth of how wrong she'd been that week. Wrong in every possible way.

"Love happens when people forgive." He gave her one more sad, knowing smile. "So that means I love you."

"I love you, too, Max." The moment she said the words, she realized they were true. What was there not to love about this child? He was so much like Connor, and so much his own person at the same time. As she held him and stroked his back, convincing him that life would turn out okay, that Jesus had a plan for his life, she thought about it again. In a just-beginning kind of way, she did love the boy.

If only she'd figured that out sooner.

Because the plan was already in motion, and deep in her soul she knew it was the right one. It had to be. Because by tomorrow at this same time, Max Riley Siefert would be back in Honolulu.

Gone from their lives forever.

THIRTY-ONE

Ramey sat on the sofa and stared at Max and Buddy, standing together a few feet from her. Max had been home three days, and now it was Monday. The Mollers would be there in fifteen minutes for their first meeting with Max and Buddy.

"Well, Ramey, do I look good?"

Buddy lifted his chin and made a soft whining sound.

"Not you, Buddy." Max bent down and patted the dog's head. "I need Ramey to tell me."

"Yes, Max. You look very handsome."

"What about Buddy?" Max had tied a blue scarf around the dog's neck.

"Buddy looks handsome, too."

The dog barked once, and Max dropped to one knee. "No barking, Buddy. The Mollers might not like dogs." He placed his hands on either side of Buddy's face. "Be quiet, okay?"

Ramey hated that they had to do this, hated the idea of parading Max and Buddy before some strange couple, almost as if they were a set of used appliances. She was still praying for a forgiveness miracle for the boy, but it was looking less likely with every day.

No one from the Evans family had called since Max returned home.

She'd talked to Mr. Ogle and agreed to keep Max and Buddy at her apartment until the Mollers's paperwork was completed, if they did, indeed, decide to adopt Max. If not, Max would go to live with the Ogles. But that would mean changing schools, and being fifteen miles from his old neighborhood. Better to make that type of change only once, she and Mr. Ogle had agreed.

And so for now Max was hers.

She was glad, though she would've liked it best if Max had been able to stay with the Evanses. Maybe Kiahna hadn't known the man that well, after all. From her journals, and the letter she'd written in her will, it was clear that she thought Connor Evans was the type of man who would make a good father for Max. But if the man could spend two weeks with the boy and still send him home, then maybe Kiahna was wrong.

Either way, it felt wonderful having Max back in the apartment with her. She'd missed him, and when he left—whether to the Mollers or to Mr. Ogle and his wife—she would feel his loss far more than she'd realized. The two weeks he'd been gone were the longest she'd been away from him since he was born.

Yes, having him around was more work for her. Sometimes she would get out of breath, and Max would have to get her oxygen tank before she could get up again. But Max was used to that; they made a good team. She would've hated to die without having this last bit of time with him.

"How much longer, Ramey?" Max was finished scolding Buddy. He stood and faced her, shifting his weight from one foot to the other. "I want to get this over with."

Ramey stifled a smile. He'd picked up that line from her, because that's what she'd told Mr. Ogle: "Send them by. I want to get this over with." A needle of guilt pricked her conscience. "Max, that's the wrong attitude, pal. Wrong for me and wrong for you."

"But I told you, Ramey." He dropped to the ground in a heap beside Buddy. The dog immediately lay down and rested his head on Max's knee. "I don't wanna be adopted. If I can't live with the Evanses then I wanna live here with you." He grabbed a fast breath. "And if you get old and die, I wanna live in heaven with Mommy and you." He paused. "Okay, Ramey? Okay?"

"What's wrong is that the Mollers are nice people. They've heard all about you and they think they want you to be their son. That would be a good thing, Max. Try to see it that way."

"Yeah, but—"

A knock sounded at the front door, and the room fell silent. Ramey struggled to her feet. "I'll be right back."

She guessed it was a full thirty seconds before she reached the door. And it was only twenty steps away. She opened it and sized up the people standing before her. "Hello . . . please come in."

"Thank you." The man spoke, and the woman offered a shy smile.

"You must be the Mollers."

"We are." This time the woman took a step forward and looked past Ramey. "Is Max here?"

Ramey studied them for a moment, then turned and led them into the TV room. They were older than she'd expected, in their early fifties, at least. They both had warm smiles and an anxious look, a mix of nervousness and excitement.

Ramey was enough ahead of them that when she entered the room where Max and Buddy were waiting, she turned around to see the reaction from the Mollers. The woman smiled and gave Max a little wave; the man stood a foot behind her, his eyes kind and glistening. "Hello, Max. We're the Mollers."

The woman took a few steps toward Max and held out her hand. "We're so glad to meet you, Max."

Max pulled himself up to his feet. "Hello." His chin stayed tucked close to his chest, but his eyes met the woman's.

Ramey leaned against the nearest wall and took in the scene. *It seems okay, God . . . I guess.* She narrowed her eyes and waited.

Mr. Moller came up alongside Max and pointed to Buddy. "Is this your dog?"

"Yes, sir." Max pulled himself up some. "That's my dog, Buddy. He wants to come, too."

"Uh ..." The man looked up at Ramey and gave a slight shake of his head. "Well, Max ..."

Ramey shrugged at Mr. Moller's distressed look and mouthed the words to him, "Good luck."

Mr. Moller patted Buddy's head. "Max, we can't have dogs." He put his arm on his wife's shoulder. "Mrs. Moller is allergic."

Max's eyes got wide. "But, sir, Buddy's ... he's my bestest friend."

Mrs. Moller stooped down to Max's level. "Maybe we can get a goldfish, or a turtle. Something in an aquarium." She put her hand along the side of Max's face. "How would that be?"

Ramey winced at what was bound to come next.

"Buddy stays with me." The utter defiance in Max's tone was underlined by his loud, panic-stricken voice. His breathing was hard and fast, causing his small chest to jump as if he'd just run up a flight of stairs. He took hold of the pretty blue scarf on his dog's neck. "Come on, Buddy. They don't want us." Before he pulled Buddy out onto the patio, he turned and shot one more line at the Mollers. "If he stays, I stay."

When the glass door was shut, Mr. Moller looked at Ramey and gave a polite nod. "Thank you for your time."

"I take it you're no longer interested." Ramey settled back on her heels.

"Oh, no. We're very interested. Children can deal with loss better than adults. He'll miss the dog for a while, but he'll be okay eventually." Mrs. Moller cast a sad look back at Max. "He's probably upset about the whole situation."

"That's exactly it." Ramey liked the woman.

The man held his hand out to Ramey and gave her another smile. "We'll let him take a few days to get used to the idea, and then we'll contact Mr. Ogle."

"Yes." The woman clutched her purse to her midsection. "We're hoping to bring him home soon." She tilted her head. "He's a beautiful child. I'm sorry he's hurting."

Her husband put his hand at the small of Mrs. Moller's back and gave her a slight hug. Over his shoulder he gave Ramey one final look. "We'll be in touch."

For ten minutes after they left, Ramey was still exhaling hard, coaxing her heartbeat back to some kind of normal. Pain radiated from her chest, and for a moment she thought maybe this was it. The heart attack her doctors had been saying could happen at any time.

She shuffled into the kitchen, snatched her nitroglycerin pills from the cupboard next to the sink, and put two of them under her tongue. There. That would help. With slow steps, determined not to die with Max and Buddy on the back patio, Ramey crossed the apartment and sat in her favorite chair.

The couple was nice, kind. But how could she let her Max live with anyone who couldn't take Buddy?

Her heartbeat slowed some, and the pain in her chest eased. She huffed hard through her nose and glanced at Kiahna's journal, still on the lamp stand table beside her chair. Kiahna believed in second chances and forgiveness, hadn't she? Wasn't that what she'd prayed for all her life?

Okay, God, so I prayed for it, too. She looked up at the ceiling, because God had to be somewhere beyond the plaster and wood boards. *I asked You specifically for a forgiveness miracle, and* this *is what You give me?* She pursed her lips. *I have to be honest, God, I'm thinking about forgetting the whole prayer thing altogether. If You're there, I'm not sure You like me enough to listen. Because as nice as they are, let me tell You, God, the Mollers aren't the answer I was expecting.*

She crossed her arms over her round abdomen.

Then she remembered something else Kiahna had written in her journal. Though her life hadn't turned out anything like she'd planned, she knew that in the darkest times God was always working. Always.

Ramey stared out the patio door at Max, lying on the ground alongside Buddy and probably crying his eyes out. She shot another quick look at the ceiling. *Times don't get much darker than this, God.* Her gaze shifted to Max again. But what if Kiahna was right? What if somehow God was working out His best miracles even now, when life looked beyond hopeless?

All right, then, I'll keep on praying, God. I'm begging You here, just begging You, God, please . . . give Max a miracle in his life. Just this once. The kid can't catch a break, Lord. I still think the miracle will be wrapped up in forgiveness, somehow. So that's what I'm asking You for. Okay? A sheepish feeling filled her heart. *Oh . . . and one more thing. I'm sorry if I sounded rude a minute ago. My dander was up, that's all. I really do think You can do this, or I wouldn't ask.*

She was still too new at talking to God to know how to end the conversation, so she looked at the ceiling one last time and whispered, "Thanks, God. I'll be right here waiting."

⌒

Max felt more scared than ever in all his life put together.

Everything in his brain and heart was spinning in circles and landing in a big mixed-up pile. His mommy had told him to always use his manners with strangers, but just now he used his mean voice on the Mollers. So somewhere in heaven she must be disappointed with him. Disappointed was worse than being in trouble, because it meant your mommy was sad inside.

"Don't be sad, Mommy." Max said the words near Buddy's ear, and his dog did a loud huffy breath. "I'm sorry . . . I'm so sorry."

But that wasn't even the only thing mixed up. Also he looked at Mr. Moller's eyes, and he saw a grown-up look that meant he wasn't changing his mind. Max thought about kicking and screaming and throwing himself on the floor. He never did that before, because his mommy would give him that serious look even if he got a whining voice. But once he saw a boy in first grade do that kicking thing, and it worked, sort of. The principal came to first grade and helped take that boy away. So if the boy didn't want to be in class, then it worked, right?

He thought about that. But just when he was maybe going to throw his own fit, Mr. Moller looked at him that way. Smiling, but very serious. Max knew it didn't matter what he did, they were still going to adopt him. But not Buddy . . .

And so here was the confusing thing. What about God? His mommy always told him God had a plan for him. Max wasn't sure if it was a written-out plan somewhere in a desk in heaven, or something God was working on a little more every day. But He had a plan, because that's what his mommy told him, and she never, ever lied.

Plus also, Mr. Evans at the airport hugged him hard and said he loved him and told him the same thing, that God had a plan for him. Even Mrs. Evans told him that. But why would God leave Buddy out of the plan?

He gulped hard and slipped his hand beneath Buddy's new blue scarf. Ramey took him shopping on the weekend for it because sometimes people liked dogs that were pretty. Buddy was always pretty, o' course, but maybe the Mollers wouldn't think so unless he had a nice scarf.

Max also thought maybe they should buy a toenail cutter thing because Buddy's toenails were too long. Even for a dog. Also Mommy used to say it was 'portant to have clean-cut toes. But Ramey said the Mollers probably wouldn't look at Buddy's toes. At least not on the first visit. And plus the cutter was four dollars and ninety-seven cents.

And the most mixed-up thing was that Max didn't care what the Mollers thought of him and Buddy, because he didn't want the Mollers to adopt him. But Ramey said maybe this was his only chance, and that only made him more sad because it wasn't his only chance at all. It was his second chance.

The Evans family was his first chance.

He sank his face against his arm, in the quiet part by his elbow. *God . . . I'm very scared, God. Please help me know what to do next. If I need to cut Buddy's toenails, I will, but please . . . please don't send me to live with the Mollers.*

Another bit of scared came in his heart. He squished himself against Buddy and prayed some more. *Mommy told me that You give people second chances, God. I believe You because Mommy has a second chance right now, with You in heaven.*

He opened his mouth because he really wanted God to hear this part. "But what about me? Please, God . . . could I have a second chance with the Evans family? Or if not, could you show me where to find my daddy somewhere out there?"

Most times when he finished praying, Max would have a slow, warm feeling in his tummy. Peace, his mommy called it. But this time his heart still felt extra thumpy, and he wasn't sure at all about the big pile of things inside him.

He could still hear his mommy's voice, still smell her and feel her skin soft against his. *Be brave, Max . . . whenever you're afraid, be brave . . .*

And that was the worst part of all.

For the first time ever, he couldn't be brave for his mommy. He couldn't even remember how.

Thirty-Two

It was Tuesday morning, and Michele was doing everything she could to get their lives back to normal.

She'd let Connor and Max go by themselves to the airport on Friday, and when Connor returned, she met him at the door with a hug. "I'm sorry, Connor." She let her forehead fall against his chest. "I've been terrible."

His eyes were bloodshot, but they filled with a tired kind of hope. "We both have."

"But your affair . . . it was my fault, too. I was . . ." She hung her head for a moment. "I was so caught up in myself I didn't remember to love you."

Connor tightened his hold on her and rested his forehead on her shoulder. "That's okay. You were sick; you couldn't help it. It was me, Michele. All me."

"No." She pulled back and searched his eyes. "I was wrong back then, even if I was sick. And I'm sorry." A moment passed before she could speak. "You needed to know."

For a long while they only looked at each other. Then he nodded, his own eyes damp. "Thank you."

She gave him a single kiss and studied his eyes once more. "And something else. I wasn't ready to hear about Max's mother before. But if . . . if you want to tell me sometime, I'm ready now."

"No." He wore defeat like a mask, as he kissed her forehead. "That's okay. It doesn't matter anymore."

That night they shared a bed but nothing more. The fact that they were together was a start, but Michele wondered if the damage she'd inflicted on Connor's heart was something they'd live

307

with forever. He was still dedicated to her, clearly. Otherwise he would never have sent Max home. But would he ever be in love with her the way he'd been before? In the days since Max left, Michele caught her husband sitting on the front porch the way he had after he first found out about Max. She'd go to him, put her hands on his shoulders, or loop an arm around his neck and try to get a glimpse of what he was feeling.

"Hey . . . pretty night?"

He'd look up, a distant smile tugging at the corners of his lips. "Yes. It's nice out here."

"So"—she'd pull up a chair and search his eyes—"what are you thinking?"

"About life. How strange it is, how one decision can affect so many people for all of time."

Other times his answer was more to the point: "Max. What he's thinking right now."

His words always made her sit back, shocked at what he had become in a matter of days. The old Connor would've given her a standard, "Nothing, dear," and then turned the conversation to her. But not anymore. Now he was an open book, more so than he'd been at any time in their marriage. It was a change that would've been a huge triumph for Michele if it weren't for one thing.

The book in his heart held nothing but pensive sorrow and broken lives.

Half the time Connor seemed consumed with guilt over what he'd done. The way he'd hurt so many people. The rest of the time his sadness came from a place he could neither hide nor deny.

A place that ached for his son.

She no longer hated him for caring about the boy. The connection she'd made with the child his last night in their home was enough to at least feel empathy for her husband.

Even the girls had struggled since Max's departure.

"He was so funny, Mom." Susan found her on Sunday, her tone whiny and frustrated. "No one else'll climb the tree in the front yard with me, except Max. Can't he come back again? Please?"

Elizabeth was more introspective. "I think Dad misses him, don't you?"

"Yes, honey. That's bound to happen. Max was here for two weeks."

"But I think Max wanted to stay longer than two weeks."

"You may be right, but Max has a future in Hawaii. They found a family who wants to adopt him."

"I know." Elizabeth looked out the window at the sky beyond their backyard. "Daddy told me." Then she found Michele's eyes again. "A couple isn't a family, Mom. Not like *we're* a family."

There were times when she wanted to stand on the kitchen counter and yell at all of them. *Get over it, already!* Max wasn't part of their family; he belonged in Honolulu with the couple who wanted to adopt him. It was time to move on.

Other days she wondered what the girls would think if they knew the truth, that Max was actually Daddy's son. That their daddy had been with another woman even after he promised never to do that. Would they like Max as much then?

Every few hours the thought crossed her mind that maybe they should call Mr. Ogle and tell him they'd been wrong. They wanted Max, after all. But that thought would only make a fleeting appearance in her mind. The situation was so much bigger than that, so much more complicated. Long after forgiveness had done its work, Max would still be that dreaded reminder of Connor's worst days.

And what about the kids at school, or their friends at church? "This is Max, Connor's son. Yes . . . we just found out about him. That's right, Connor had an affair and never called the girl again. Mmm-hmm, this was the first we knew about the boy."

The idea of trying to explain it made Michele's stomach hurt.

Of course, it would be different if Max had no one, if Mr. Ogle couldn't find anyone to adopt him. But the Hawaiian couple sounded nice enough. So what if they ran a bed-and-breakfast and wanted Max to help out around the grounds? Work was good for kids, and certainly they'd shower him with love, as well.

By Tuesday, Connor was back at work with a layover in Atlanta and a flight home the next afternoon. Then on Thursday he set off for a series of longer legs that would take him away from home until late Sunday afternoon. The assignment was one Connor had asked for, extra hours to make up for the time he'd taken off when Max was with them.

With the girls at school and Connor gone, Michele figured the best thing she could do was clean the house and talk to God about how they were supposed to move on. She worked her way from the kids' bathroom to the guest room where Max had slept while he was there. The sheets had already been changed, but now she dusted the windowsill and the headboard.

She was wiping the rag across the bedside table—the place where Max had kept his white Bible—when she saw it.

A small white envelope lay on the floor beneath the table. Michele knit her brow together. How come she hadn't seen it before, when she changed the bedding? She reached down, picked it up, and brought it where she could see it better. The three words scrawled across the front made her breath catch in her throat.

For Mrs. Evans.

Michele made a slow drop to the edge of the bed. Who could it be from? Not from ... not from Max's mother, was it? She slid one trembling finger beneath the flap and made a careful tear along the top. Then she pulled a single page from inside, unfolded it, and began to read.

To Mrs. Evans:

Hello. My name is Ramey, and you don't know me. I've been Max's baby-sitter for all of his life. Whenever his mother was out of town on a flight, the boy was with me. During that time I haven't been much of a believer. In fact, I haven't believed in God at all, really.

But now as I watch Max, as I think about the months and years he has ahead, I want to believe, ma'am. With all my heart I want to believe.

Marv Ogle tells me that you and your husband are Christians, the same way Kiahna was a Christian. I've read through some of Kiahna's journal so I might understand Max's situation better, and what I found has given me the beginning of belief. Enough so that I've asked God for a forgiveness miracle for Max.

You see, ma'am, I might not be very educated, but I know it will take a forgiveness miracle for life to work out the way Kiahna and even, I think, God wants it to work out.

The reason I'm writing is because all of this will be hardest on you, Mrs. Evans. You might not have known about Connor and Kiahna's time together. If not, then I'm sure you won't want Max, not at first. He would be a reminder of everything you want to forget.

Michele's hand fell to her lap. She gripped the edge of the bed with her other hand and closed her eyes to ward off the sudden stinging. This . . . this Ramey woman had known her heart exactly. Her soul was heavy, soaked in sadness as she opened her eyes and found her place on the page.

But I found something in Max's Bible that maybe might help. It comes from a part called 1 John, and it says, "As Jesus laid his life down for us, so we must lay our lives down for other people. Anything else is not really love. Not love for God and not love for people."

I don't know if that will help you make a decision, Mrs. Evans. But I can tell you this. Max has been the greatest light in my life for all of his seven years. I'm old and my heart won't go on much longer, but I want Max to be in a family where they know the treasure they are getting. Max is a treasure. I'm praying that you will see so for yourself.

Please call me if you have any questions. Again . . . I'm sorry for whatever pain this has caused you, but Max needs a home. I'd do anything to see that he gets one.

Sincerely,

Ramey Aialea

At the bottom of the letter was the woman's phone number.

Michele reminded herself to exhale. Her hands were shaking so much now that the notepaper made little noises. *Okay, God . . . why? Why do I find this now? What do you want from me?*

Daughter . . . be still and know that I am God. My ways are not yours . . .

The words were straight from Scripture, a part of the Bible Michele hadn't read for years. But now they blew across her terrified soul like a gentle balm. Again and again they came until her hands were no longer trembling.

When she was finally still, the way God wanted her to be, she read the note one more time. The part about Max's Bible and the words from 1 John sliced at her convictions like a sword. A double-edged sword.

Had she laid down her life for anyone? Ever?

For her children, yes, at one point or another. But that was the definition of parenting, giving away self for the sake of your own. Somehow, Michele was certain that wasn't the meaning of the verse. After all, Jesus had laid down His life for people who mocked Him and spat on Him. People who were cruel and biting and unforgiving.

People like her.

Tears formed a layer over her eyes, and she blinked so she could see the words in the note more clearly. She hadn't cried much these past few weeks, and when she had, the tears had been selfish. Even the night before Max left, her sorrow had been for herself, for the agonizing decision that had been placed squarely on her shoulders.

But this time, the sadness that rose in her heart was nothing but pure God-given remorse.

No, she hadn't laid her life down, not at all. Though Connor had started this ordeal that summer night eight years ago, he was willing to lay his life down whatever way God called him to do it. If that meant taking in Max, then he'd take him. If it meant letting Max go forever, he'd do it.

Even the girls seemed to understand the Scripture better than she did. Yes, they were confused by Max's arrival. But they'd put aside their fears and concerns and uncertainties and almost from the beginning they'd loved him for who he was.

Your ways aren't my ways, God? Does that mean . . . does that mean Max was never supposed to go? She sniffed and set the note back in the envelope. Then she covered her face with her hands and wept for how wrong she'd been, how blind and cold and selfish.

Ramey's words stayed with her throughout the day. After a few hours she washed her face and reapplied her makeup. She didn't want the girls thinking something else was wrong. But a decision was taking shape in her soul, a decision that felt more right than springtime.

She began making phone calls. By Thursday morning, after Connor left for the airport and his four-day trip, she called the girls into the living room and sat them down. She explained that she was taking another trip, a visit to Hawaii. Her friend Renee would be there in half an hour to stay with the girls until whenever Michele got home.

"Will you see Max, Mommy?" Susan clapped her hands. "Tell him we miss him!"

"But don't be gone very long, okay." Elizabeth bit the inside of her lip, always the serious one. "I don't like when you're gone."

Then Michele drew a slow breath. *Okay, God . . . give me the words . . .*

"This is the important part, girls. I have something to tell you about Max . . ."

⌒

Ramey wasn't sure, but she thought maybe this was the miracle she'd been praying for.

Michele Evans was set to arrive at her apartment any minute. Her plane came in at two o'clock, and she hoped to arrive before Max walked home from the bus stop.

Ramey waited in her chair, mulling over the events of the past twenty-four hours. The call from Michele Evans came yesterday afternoon. The woman explained that she hadn't read Ramey's letter until the day before; she found it while she was cleaning Max's room.

"I want to talk to you about laying down my life," she said on the phone. "Can I come talk to you tomorrow?"

"Yes." Ramey had almost felt the floor buckle beneath her feet. She had to pinch her knee to convince herself she was even having the conversation. But she had to be honest at the same time. "Mrs. Evans, Max's adoption is already underway. I'm not sure what good it'll do now."

"I'm letting God take care of everything else." The woman's voice had been strong and sure. "He wants me to come, so I'm coming. I want to know more about Kiahna, I want to see pictures of her and Max, so I can know what the boy has lost."

Ramey wasn't sure whether to laugh or cry, but she told Mrs. Evans by all means come. Now, with only a moment or two before the woman arrived, Ramey took the chance to talk to God again.

Okay, so maybe You do hear me up there. And You must love Max a whole lot, because I'm not much of a letter writer. But this woman says my letter made her want to come. She gave a slow shake of her head. *I'm not sure what You're doing, God, but I want a front-row seat to see it happen.*

A gentle knocking sound broke the moment. Ramey whispered a hasty good-bye to God, and then changed her mind and asked Him to stick around. As long as possible, actually. She huffed her way to the door, opened it, and before she could welcome her, they looked at each other for a long moment, and then the Evans woman was in her arms. "Thank you, Ramey. Thank you for opening my eyes."

"Nah . . ." Ramey drew back first. She batted at an errant tear. "It was nothing."

"It was, though. It was everything." The woman stepped inside. "I'm Michele Evans. I wouldn't be here if it wasn't for you."

Buddy rounded the corner and dropped down on his haunches. The heat from the afternoon made his tongue hang out a bit. "That's Buddy."

Mrs. Evans walked up to the dog, scratched him behind the ear, and gave a gentle twist on his blue scarf. "He looks like a nice dog."

"Max loves him to death." Ramey studied the woman for a minute. "Why didn't Mr. Evans come?"

The woman's face fell a bit. "He doesn't know I'm here."

Alarm bells went off in Ramey's soul. "Then you can't exactly make a decision about—"

Mrs. Evans held up her hand. "My husband made his mind up about Max a long time ago, Ramey. And I talked to our girls this morning. Our decision is unanimous."

They talked for a short time before Michele wanted to see pictures of Kiahna and Max. Ramey pointed at the old bookcase. "At the bottom there, the photo albums—they belonged to Kiahna.

One is put together from her childhood; the yellow one with the butterfly on the cover has pictures of her and Max."

The woman took the yellow book and held it up. "May I?"

"Sure." Ramey struggled around the sofa and joined Michele. A catch sounded in her voice. "They were something together."

Michele lifted the cover and worked her way through the beginning of the book. "She was very beautiful." She studied a photo of Kiahna holding baby Max. "I knew she would be."

"Yes . . . she could've had any man on the island." Ramey tapped the photograph. "But she wasn't interested. Not once."

The Evans woman caught her eye. "How come, Ramey? I thought . . . I figured she would've had lots of men."

Ramey fought off the defensiveness for Kiahna that pierced her. The woman's misunderstanding wasn't her fault. All she knew of Kiahna was the affair she'd had with Connor. "You don't know the story? What happened with her and your husband?"

Mrs. Evans's face grew a few shades paler. "No. I . . . I never wanted to know until now."

"Kiahna was a rare girl, Mrs. Evans. She was twenty-one when she met your husband, and she'd never been with a man." Ramey squinted at the photographs, as the story came back.

She told the Evans woman everything, details even she hadn't known until reading Kiahna's journal. How the two of them had met at the airport, and Kiahna had trusted something about him. When the storm came up there wasn't a hotel room anywhere on the island. Kiahna offered her couch only as a way of being kind.

"That's the part I don't understand." The pain in the Evans woman's eyes was deep and tormented. "She had to know what she was getting herself into."

"Fair enough." Ramey nodded her head to the side. "But her journal tells a different story. She was alone; her parents had recently died when she met Connor. He told her he was a Christian, that he shared her devotion to God." Ramey hesitated. "And he told her he lived alone."

"Alone?"

"Yes." Ramey raised an eyebrow. "He said he was married, but his wife lived in Florida and he lived in LA." She lowered her voice and leaned in. "You know something else? He didn't have on a wedding ring, either."

"What?" Mrs. Evans ran her tongue over her bottom lip and leaned back, gripping the sofa arm so tight her knuckles turned white.

Poor woman. Ramey waited before going on. Obviously Mrs. Evans's husband hadn't told her the details. Her face was as pale as her knuckles, and anger and hurt no longer took turns with her expression.

Rather, the woman's face was blank, wide-eyed and desperate.

The look of a person in shock.

THIRTY-THREE

Michele's head was reeling.

All this time she'd blamed Kiahna for what had happened. But now . . . Connor hadn't been wearing his wedding ring? He'd told her he lived alone? She felt a gaping hole in her chest where her heart had been. Was that what he'd been trying to tell her in the days before Max's visit? Even the day she returned from California? He'd said it was all his fault, and now the picture was clear as water.

She looked around Ramey's apartment, desperate for a way to make the room stop spinning. Finally she released her hold on the sofa arm and squeezed her eyes shut for a moment. She still wanted to lay down her life, but she hadn't expected it to be this painful.

When she opened her eyes, she looked at Ramey. "Kiahna had no idea he was married?"

"Not till it was too late." Ramey hesitated. "Kiahna wanted to be a doctor, Mrs. Evans. She didn't want love or marriage or kids until after she finished med school."

"When she found out she was pregnant, why . . . why didn't she tell Connor?"

"He was a married man, Mrs. Evans. He had no plans to see her again; he told her that much before he left the island. Why would she tell him about the baby?"

"So she never did."

"Right." Ramey stared at the photo album. "After Max was born, she had time only for her son and for God."

Understanding flooded Michele's heart. The poor girl! Alone and pregnant, her dreams of med school shattered. Yes, Connor's revelation after the camping trip had been right on. The affair, the entire mess, was all his fault.

And now . . .

Now she could choose to forgive him or make him and Max and all of them pay a lifetime for his sins. She could lay down her life in love, or hold tight to it even if it meant living in misery and bitterness the rest of her days. A soft huff sounded in her throat. She'd already made her decision; it was the reason she'd spent the entire day on a flight to Honolulu.

She thought about her conversation with the girls. They had taken it far better than she'd expected, nodding and listening while she talked to them.

"Remember how Max wanted to find his daddy, the one he knew was somewhere out there?"

"Yes." The girls looked at each other, and then back at her.

"Well, we found out something about that. It turns out that your daddy is Max's daddy, too."

Susan's reaction was instant. "Really! Great, Mom! That means Max has to come back here and be our brother, right?"

A frown shaded Elizabeth's eyes. "So Daddy did love Max's mommy?"

Michele could do nothing but be honest. "For a short time, yes."

That seemed to be all the information they needed. Whatever had gone on with Max's mother and their father, the details didn't matter. Their daddy had always been there for them, would always be there. If it meant Max was their brother now, then all the better.

"Will he come live with us?" Elizabeth's eyes danced with the beginning of a smile. "I think he should, Mom. If he's our brother and Dad's his daddy."

There it was; the simple childlike love that had open arms no matter the situation.

"I want him to. But you both need to pray, okay?"

They agreed to pray, and that was that. Discussion closed. The details she and Connor had fretted about prior to Max's visit were laid out and accepted in as much time as they might've decided what to eat for dinner that night.

The memory of that morning dissolved, and Michele kept flipping pages in the yellow photo album, stopping at certain key shots. Near the back of the book she saw one of Max and Kiahna holding hands at the beach next to Buddy. The photo was taken on a day that must've been not long before her death. Max's hair was windblown, his cheeks tanned from a day in the sun. Kiahna wore a tank top and shorts, and a smile that told the world how she felt about the little boy beside her.

Max had been Kiahna's whole world. She'd made one mistake and paid for it all her life, growing closer to God, teaching Max about the ways of faith, and spending as many hours in the air as it took to take care of her precious son.

Michele shifted her gaze to Max's image and the look in his eyes. It showed a tender mix of confidence and faith, a trusting that his happy world would keep on that way forever. Beside him, even Buddy looked content with life. Max's love for his dog was clear. He had his hand on the dog's collar, and the dog was leaning into him.

Michele studied the boy, surrounded by all he loved most.

Then in one awful morning everything changed.

Michele could have hidden herself in a hole for the way she'd treated Max while he was with them. If only she'd known this part of the story before . . . Michele swallowed back a wave of emotion. This wasn't the time. She had too much work to do.

"Okay, I need your help, Ramey." Michele closed the photo album and locked eyes with Ramey. "Tell me about the couple, the one that wants to adopt Max."

"They were nice enough." Ramey made a grunting sound and brushed her hand in the air. "But the lady's allergic to dogs."

"No Buddy?" God's ways grew another degree clearer.

Ramey shook her head. "The man said dogs were out of the question." Ramey was breathing hard. She waited until she had control again. "I thought what with Max running out of the room, that they'd change their mind. Maybe agree to keep Buddy outside or something."

"They didn't?"

"No. They thought Max would get over it, adapt or something."

Michele looked at the clock on the wall. According to Ramey, Max would be home in a matter of minutes. "Ramey, I need a favor."

"Whatever I can do." She coughed twice, and her face stayed red.

"I need you to call Mr. Ogle and ask if we can do something drastic."

The older woman seemed to hold her breath. "Drastic?

"Yes. I need him to stop the adoption."

Max walked home from the bus stop with Jerry from the apartments 'cross the street. Ramey was more tired now, so she couldn't come get him like she used to, but that was okay, even on hot days like this one. As long as he could go back to her and Buddy he would walk a hundred miles.

He slid his feet along the ground and stared at the sidewalk as he went, because he didn't feel much like looking up.

Any day, Ramey had told him. Any day Mr. Ogle could work out the details and he would be packed up and sent to live with the Mollers. He told Ramey it wasn't fair. But it didn't matter what he thought.

Yesterday night Mr. Ogle even came over and said a 'pology about the Mollers not wanting Buddy.

"They liked you a lot, Max. I've talked to their friends and people in their family. I believe you'll learn to love them."

Max didn't think so. And if they wouldn't take Buddy, Max was sure he wouldn't love them. He'd be too busy missing everyone else. Mommy and Buddy and Ramey. And the Evans family.

Thinking things made the walk go faster. His feet came up to Ramey's door lickety fast this time. He lifted his hand to knock, when he saw a strange sight. The door was open the smallest size, the size of his little finger.

Max shrugged. Maybe Ramey left it open for him so she wouldn't have to get out of her chair. Getting out of her chair was harder for her every day, and sometimes that put a new spot of worry in his heart next to all the other spots of worry.

He pushed open the door very quiet, and he was going to call out her name when he heard some voices. A scared feeling grabbed him by the neck and made his arms start to shake. Was it the Mollers? Had they already come to take him away?

With silent steps he walked into the hall and saw Buddy. "Shhh." Max gave Buddy a serious look. The dog walked up to him, licked his fingers, and lay down on the floor near his feet. That was when Max could finally hear what the people inside were saying.

"Well, I made the call." The person was Ramey, because her breathing was hard and plus it was her voice.

"So . . . what did he say?"

Max froze in place. Even his heartbeep didn't want to work for a breath or two. Because that voice sounded familiar, that's why. He almost thought it was the voice of Mrs. Evans, except that wasn't even possible since Mrs. Evans lived in Florida.

"He called the Mollers while I was still on the phone." Ramey chuckled some. "They weren't very happy at first, but then the truth came out. They didn't really want a boy at first, anyway. They wanted a girl. An older girl."

The woman who sounded like Mrs. Evans made a long breathy sound. "Oh, thank God, Ramey! That's what God was telling me all day yesterday. I knew I had to fly out here and see for myself if Max was supposed to be with them." She stopped and a cracking sound came in her voice. "Or if he was supposed to be with us."

Max felt his heart beeping just fine now. Very fast and very fine. Because now he was sure as could be that the woman in the next room really was Mrs. Evans! She had to be. His feet couldn't stand there another minute. He dropped his backpack and raced speedy fast around the corner and yes. There she was.

"Max!" Mrs. Evans turned and saw him.

"I . . . I heard what you said." His words were short and breathy because he couldn't believe what was happening.

"Is that what you want, Max?" She sank down to the floor and sat on the backside of her shoes. "Do you want to live with us?"

"Yes. I want that with all my heart. Buddy wants it, too."

Mrs. Evans held out her hands and said only, "C'mere, Max."

Tears filled up his eyes, but he didn't care. He ran to her and gave her the tightest, bestest hug in the world. When he pulled back he rubbed at his eyes so he could see better. "You mean it? You want me to be part of your family?"

Long rivers of wet came from Mrs. Evans's eyes, but she smiled anyway. "Yes, Max. We want that forever and ever."

Max thought for a moment, and he remembered something. The rock for Ramey! "Be right back."

He ran into the room where he was staying and dug beneath his pile of clothes. There it was, shiny black with four snowy white stripes.

His fingers slid around it and he ran it back to Ramey. "Here." He opened his hand. "So you don't forget me."

Now wet was in Ramey's eyes, too. She took the rock and hugged him so hard her big arms made his breathing hard. When she let go, she rubbed his head and said, "I could never forget you, Max. Not as long as I live."

"Know what, Ramey?" Max pointed to the rock. "Only God can make rocks like that."

Ramey smiled a special smile, the one she used only for him. "You're right about that, Max."

"So . . ." Max felt his eyebrows raise up. "I'm really gonna live with the Evans family?"

"Yes." Ramey smiled and two tears fell from her eyes. "You got your miracle after all."

Mrs. Evans reached out and took hold of his hand. "Let's get your things, okay?"

And just then, Max could almost see his mommy smiling at him from heaven, because she was right, after all. God really did give second chances, because right then he knew he would never scoot along the ground again.

Forever more, just like his mommy, he would fly.

All the extra emotion wasn't really good for her, but Ramey didn't care.

She wiped at her cheeks as she took in the scene, Max tucked safe in the arms of Mrs. Evans, a perfect picture of the one thing Kiahna believed most in.

Love happens when people forgive.

So what if her heart hurt a little. Love did that to a person every now and then, didn't it? Besides, she was too busy thanking God for sticking around that afternoon, thanking Him for doing the very thing she'd asked of Him. No, the thing she'd demanded, really.

He'd given them a forgiveness miracle.

And even if she lived only another week or two, she would go to heaven a happy woman. Because God had indeed given her a front-row seat to watch it happen.

Thirty-Four

Connor pulled into the driveway at four o'clock Sunday afternoon and made a mental note to himself.

No more long trips.

Even with the strain he still felt around the house, he hated being away from home more than a night or two. Besides, if he was going to work things out with Michele—and he was determined to do so—he needed to spend as much time with her as possible.

He pressed the garage door opener and eased his truck into the space beside Michele's minivan. His body was more weary than usual, tired in a way that couldn't be explained by the long series of flights these past four days. He knew what it was, of course.

It was Max.

He missed the boy so much it was a physical pain, an ache that made him wonder if maybe people could notice a limp in his gait. The scene at the lake when he taught Max how to fish, the one on the big rock when the butterfly landed on Max's pole, the time in the recliner when Max had fallen asleep against his chest . . .

The good-bye at the airport.

All of it played over in his mind a hundred times a day, and no amount of prayer had done anything to dim the pictures. Time would have to handle that task. Or maybe he was doomed to relive the memory of the boy the rest of his days. Punishment for his mistakes, his unbelievably bad mistakes.

He parked the truck, turned off the engine, and climbed out. His bag was in the back, but he could get it later. Right now he needed to see Michele and the girls, needed to know that God had left him with at least the family he'd betrayed. He loved them more than ever before, loved Michele for sticking with him. Her support was more than he deserved.

The garage was cluttered, a job he could tackle in the morning. No doubt the grass needed mowing in the backyard, and tomorrow would be the time to do it. He had two days off before he had to fly again. As he stepped between the cars, another familiar thought came to mind.

How was Max doing? Had he already gone home with the Hawaiian couple, and was he getting to know them? Did he think much of his time in Florida, or the way he'd wanted Connor to be his pretend daddy? Or was he mad at them, smothered in feelings of betrayal and abandonment by everyone who had made an impact on his life?

Connor sighed and it sounded like it came from the heels of his uniform shoes. Thoughts about Max would have to wait. Right now he needed to see his family, needed to feel their arms around him, the reassurance of their love for him even after all he'd put them through.

He heard something coming from the backyard, voices of the girls and maybe even Michele. Normally he would go through the house, but he'd been gone so long this time. Why not go straight into the backyard and surprise them?

The door stuck some, another project to add to the list. But on the second try he pulled it open and stepped down a single stair onto the grass below. The chimney stood like a barrier on his left, blocking out the view of the yard. He was about to move around it and catch the girls off guard when from around the corner something charged him.

Before Connor could react, a yellow Labrador retriever bounced up and licked his hand. Connor stared at the dog, his brow furrowed. What in the world? Had the girls found a stray? That had to be it, but the dog looked familiar, somehow. Maybe he belonged to a neighbor or someone they knew, a house they'd visited sometime.

Then it came to him. He looked exactly like Max's dog, Buddy. Max's best friend. The one in the picture, the one his son had missed so much while he was visiting. Connor leaned against the chimney wall for support and ordered his mind to focus.

Of course this wasn't Max's dog; his mind was merely working overtime.

"C'mere, boy. Let's see if you have a collar." Connor held out his hand and the dog came closer. He had a blue scarf around his neck, and Connor had to run his fingers beneath it to figure out that yes, the dog did have a collar. And a tag, too. He twisted the tag to the top of the dog's back and leaned closer to read what it said.

The tag held just one word.

Buddy.

"Buddy . . ." His heart slipped into an unfamiliar rhythm and with a burst of adrenaline he rounded the corner—

And there they were.

"*Surprise!*" The voices rang out in unison, and Connor took in the faces before him.

Michele and Elizabeth and Susan—and *Max*—all running toward him with open arms. And there in the back, eyes locked on him, was his father. He was older, grayer, but seeing him now erased the eight years they'd been apart in as much time as it took to speak a single word. For an instant he remembered the car accident. If the man inside had been his father . . .

God . . . thank You for giving us this second chance. Thank You.

"Dad . . ." Connor mouthed the word, and across the yard the old man nodded his head and gestured toward the others. His turn could come later.

"Oh, Daddy . . . you're home, and look who's here!" Susan and Elizabeth reached him first, and Connor swung them around. As he did he caught Michele's eyes in the back of the group. She was crying and laughing all at the same time.

"Yes." Connor looked at his son and stooped down to his level. It had to be a dream. The scene was too amazing, too wonderful, to be taking place in his own backyard. "Max . . ."

The boy ran to him and jumped into his arms. "I'm back, Mr. Evans! Forever and ever. Mrs. Evans came to Hawaii and got me and Buddy, and Ramey called Mr. Ogle and said no, I didn't want to live with the Mollers, and now here I am. Isn't that a *miracle?*"

Again his eyes found Michele's. She only nodded to him that yes, it was all true. He wasn't dreaming at all, because he could feel Max's hands around his neck. "Yes, Max." He hugged his son tight to his chest. "It's the biggest miracle I could ever imagine."

Elizabeth yelled for the others to join her on the swings, and the children skipped off together. Connor didn't know what to do first, but he saw Michele motion toward his father. With his eyes fixed on the strapping man at the other end of the yard, Connor went to him and the two did something they'd rarely done.

They embraced.

His father placed his hand against the back of Connor's head and held him as if he were a little boy again, held him the way Connor had always wanted to be held. But before his dad could say a word, Connor drew back and searched the man's deep blue eyes.

"I'm sorry, Dad. I . . . I didn't say it the other night, but I'm sorry." His throat was thick, but he was too stunned for tears. "What happened between us . . . it was my fault."

In all his life he'd never seen his father cry. But now, tears fell onto his weathered cheeks, and when he opened his mouth, nothing came out. Instead, while the kids played in the distance, he pulled Connor close one more time and held him as if he might never let go.

When they pulled apart, Connor's brain began firing some of the questions that had been flash frozen in the shock of the moment. "I can't believe you're here … how did … ?"

His father only nodded at Michele. "She called me, Son. From Hawaii. She told me what was happening, what she wanted to do." This time his father leaned close and kissed him on the forehead. "I told her I wouldn't have missed this for the world." He paused. "Your son's beautiful, Connor."

He looked over his father's shoulder at the boy running in circles around Susan. "Yeah, he is, isn't he?"

"But that woman"—his dad pointed toward Michele—"is beautiful inside and out."

"I know it." Connor glanced at Michele. "I think I need to go tell her so myself."

His father patted him on the shoulder. "Yes, Son, I believe you do."

Connor left his father with the children and pulled his feet through the grass to where Michele stood, not far from the patio door. She still had that sheepish grin, the one that told him yes, everything was exactly how it looked. She had done it all while he was gone on his trip.

"Michele … how did you … ?" He shook his head. His thoughts formed a logjam in his heart, and he couldn't make himself voice even one of them.

She came to him then, slipped her hands along his sides and wrapped them around his lower back. Her lips met his, but the kiss was a quick one, promising more later on when they were alone. She drew back and placed a single finger to his lips. "Shhh. We can talk about it later."

"But how did you—"

"Later." She smiled at him again, her eyes swimming. "First there's something you have to tell that little boy." She looked beyond him to the children playing near his father. Buddy was frolicking at their feet, thoroughly enjoying his new home. "The girls already know you're his daddy. I told them Thursday morning." Her eyes met his again.

"Were they . . . were they okay? The girls, I mean?"

"Yes." She gave him a look that silenced his fear. "They're fine. Now it's time for you to tell Max."

What? His heart was beating so hard he expected it to burst from his chest and do flips across the yard. Was she serious? Right now? Thirty minutes ago he was trying to figure out how he'd live the rest of his life missing a green-eyed little boy with a face like his own, and now . . . He gave a shake of his head and forced his mind to think straight. What had happened to her in the past few days? A miracle, no doubt, but why?

"Michele . . ." His heart broke for all she'd been through, the price she'd paid for his selfish decisions one night an ocean away from her. "I'm so sorry. Do you believe me?"

"Yes." Her voice was tight with emotion, but her smile was as genuine as he'd ever seen it. "And I forgive you, you know why?"

He had no idea. "No . . . I guess I don't."

"Because love happens when you forgive." She held her finger to her nose and made a sound that was more laugh than cry. "Max told me that."

Once more he looked at her, but she only nodded toward the children. "I have dinner ready inside. I'll bring everyone else in. That way you and Max can be alone for a few minutes." She cupped her hands around her mouth. "Okay, guys, everyone inside to wash hands."

His father must've been in on the plan, because he looped an arm around each of the girls and whispered something to Max. Connor watched the boy grin and look straight at him. Connor nodded and used his finger to call Max to his side.

As soon as they were alone together, Connor begged God for the right words. *Don't let him hate me for not telling him sooner. Please, God...*

"Max ... I have something to tell you." He sat back on his heels, ignoring his dry mouth and the way his throat kept tightening.

"Can you believe it, Mr. Evans?" Max raised his hands high in the air and hooted. "I get to stay forever, and Buddy, too."

"I know." He gave his son an impulsive hug, and then tried again. "What I want to tell you, Max, is that—"

"And guess what!" The boy was vibrating with excitement. "You get to be my pretend daddy now, Mr. Evans. Isn't that just the bestest thing you ever heard?"

"Max." Something in his tone made the boy settle down and catch Connor's gaze.

"Yes, Mr. Evans?" A worried look flashed in his eyes, and Connor had to hold back a smile. He needed to get the news out fast, before the boy misunderstood.

"Remember how your mommy told you that maybe one day you'd find your daddy somewhere out there?"

"Yes." Max's eyes were wide, his breathing still fast. "I remember."

"Well, Max ... Mrs. Evans and I found out something you should know."

"Okay, but guess what?" Now the boy's eyes were almost full circles. "I don't want that daddy anymore, Mr. Evans. I want you."

"Good." Connor allowed the smile to fill his face. "Because we found out I'm your daddy, Max. The one your mommy told you about."

For a long time, Max only stared at him, searching his face as though maybe this was a joke or perhaps he'd heard wrong. Then he did a giant gulp and his voice fell to a whisper. "You're ... you're my daddy? My real daddy?"

"Yes, Max."

"So you mean . . ." Max did a little laugh. "You mean God answered all my prayers, every single one?"

Relief spilled across Connor's soul. The boy wasn't upset with him. "Yes . . . and I know why, too."

Max looked bewildered, giddy with joy and stunned all at the same time. "Why?"

"Because somewhere up in heaven, your mommy has been bugging God probably every day to make sure things worked out just like this."

The boy looked like he might soar around the yard and never come down, but instead he flung his arms around Connor's neck and whispered not far from his ear. "Can I call you *Daddy?* Like 'Lizabeth and Susan do?"

"Yes, Son. You can call me that the rest of your life."

Connor was thinking how he'd never been happier, never felt more free, when the girls rushed into the backyard. "Daddy, Daddy . . . look what Grandpa caught!"

With careful movements, Connor's father stepped into the backyard behind the girls. His hand was cupped over something on his wrist, something impossible to make out.

Michele stood a few feet behind him, and Connor winked at her, silently telling her that yes, he'd talked to Max; mission accomplished. She grinned, her face glowing in a way that spoke volumes about their future.

Max ran to the girls. "What is it?" He peered between them at the thing that had stirred up so much attention.

"Well?" Connor chuckled at the sight of his father surrounded by his children. *All* his children. "What'd he catch? A bumpy brown toad?"

"No." Max turned to him and their eyes held. "You won't believe it, Daddy." The boy's face broke into a smile that seemed to go on forever.

"Tell me." Connor stood and made his way closer to the group. The sound of Max calling him *Daddy* still echoed in his heart.

Max took his hand and pointed to the monarch on his father's wrist. "It's a butterfly."

And so it was.

The prettiest butterfly Connor had ever seen.

READER NOTE

Dear Friends,

As always, thank you for traveling with me through the pages of *Oceans Apart*. I pray that the story of Max and Connor and Michele and the steadfastness of Kiahna has touched you as you've read. And I pray that in the process you've felt God working on your own heart.

I certainly felt Him working on mine.

From the beginning I knew *Oceans Apart* would be about forgiveness. I asked myself how it would feel to be Michele, to have a husband I loved and to suddenly, in a moment's time, be asked to forgive him for something as monstrous as unfaithfulness.

Then I let God complicate the story. What if a child was involved?

Suddenly I knew I had to write it out, process the idea by placing it on the pages of this book. Only then would I see that yes, forgiveness is possible. Even when the greatest wrong of all has been committed against you.

Those of you reading this know what I mean. Some of you have rips and holes in your own marriages. Admissions of affairs, unexplained absences, and other areas of pain or betrayal, areas that will never be fixed without forgiveness.

Others of you aren't struggling in your marriage. But perhaps you've been the victim of gossip or unfaithfulness on the part of a friend. I think we can all relate to that, and like Michele, we won't find peace until we forgive. Forgiveness doesn't make a problem go away; it simply gives you the peace Christ intended. Often, when both parties are willing to work on a relationship, healing will come. But sometimes it doesn't.

Even then, forgiveness is the only way to the freedom Jesus wanted for us, the freedom He died for. Without forgiveness, bitter roots grow in our hearts and choke out any good fruit that would otherwise grow there. And we can't have that.

So yes, forgiveness was the obvious life lesson from *Oceans Apart*.

But while I was writing it, God showed me another lesson, one that became almost as important. The lesson of second chances.

Second chances.

The idea that all of us are caterpillars, really. Furry little creatures scooting along the ground wondering why we can't seem to fly. And then God, in all His goodness, encourages us to crawl in a hole, bury our old selves, and die to the life we once knew. If we'll do that, if we'll trust Him with our entire existence, then He'll give us something beautiful in exchange.

He'll give us wings.

The ultimate wings come when we give our lives to Christ and let Him be Lord of our lives, our Savior. Without those wings, a person cannot see heaven—a tragedy none of us need face if only we accept God's gift of grace.

If this idea is confusing to you, if you've never considered Jesus' second chances, then make a phone call. Find a Bible-believing church and find out more about the God who made you, the One who created a plan for your salvation.

But if you've known God and find yourself stuck on the ground again, remember this. Second chances happen throughout our lives. Jesus told us to forgive seventy times seven—in other words, to always forgive. And in return He promised us the same. No matter where you're at in life, no matter what you've done, God waits with open arms, ready to give you that second chance. Even for the seven-hundredth time.

It's a good idea to take Him up on the offer. Because only then will you be able to use the wings He's already given you.

On a personal note, my family is doing very well. Donald is coaching our own boys these days, and loving every minute. He is considering starting a private team, anchored in Bible study and prayer, a team that would involve the families of players and help shape young men not only as basketball players but also as godly, contributing members of society. I remain in awe of his gifts.

Our children are growing like weeds, and this year they seem to have slipped into a warp speed of growth, a kind Don and I have never seen before. Kelsey is beautiful, with long hair and longer legs and a smile and determination that proves she is a one-in-a-million girl. Tyler is still singing and acting, and thrilled that this year Kelsey has joined him on the stage in our local Christian Youth Theater.

As for the four youngest boys, sports remain their top priority. We manage to slip a bit of reading and arithmetic in as well, but they're happiest when they're playing basketball or soccer, swinging a bat, or rollerblading in our driveway. They have each become professional frog catchers, and I delight to see them run through the back door with a special catch in their hands. I try to take pictures of the best frogs, and if they sometimes hop onto the kitchen floor, well then, that's okay. They'll forget about the frogs soon enough.

This year we also had another addition to our house, two boys—nineteen and twenty-one, respectively. These young men both played sports for Don in years past, but didn't know each other before coming to our house last spring. Each was desperate for structure and Christian guidance. My heart is full beyond belief today as I see the changes they've made, and the godly men they are becoming. And what a blessing to know that God has trusted us—even for a short time—with two more of His own.

As always, I covet your prayers for my writing ministry and especially for my family. You are the other half of this writing life I lead, you who read the books and tell others about them, you who pray for me that I will hear God before each and every book I write.

Thousands of you have written to me in the past year, and I've read every letter. Sometimes with tears, sometimes with a smile, always with a grateful heart that Christ would give me a story that might touch your life. Amazing. Please contact me and let me know how you're doing. I love hearing from you.

In Christ's amazing grace,
Karen Kingsbury

Email address: *rtnbykk@aol.com*
Website: *www.KarenKingsbury.com*

Visit my guest book to see what other readers are saying about this and other books.

Study Guide

1. Think of the beach scene where Michele first learns that her husband has been unfaithful to her. Describe a time when you discovered someone had hurt you. How did you react to the news initially?

2. What role did God play in how you handled that news?

3. Read Romans 8:28. God tells us that all things work to the good of those who love Him. Did hurtful events in your life end up bringing about good in your life? Explain.

4. Kiahna loved to talk to Max about second chances. Describe the time in your life when you first understood God's gift of grace and salvation. Share your personal story with someone, or write it in a journal.

5. Kiahna felt that she needed a second chance with God because of what major event in her life? Did she fall easily? What led to her sin?

6. Think back and remember a time when you fell short of God's best for your life. Describe that time. How did you feel immediately after falling?

7. What did God bring about to help you realize you could be forgiven?

8. Describe your second chance after that difficult time.

9. Read Colossians 3 and 4, and list seven rules for holy living that will help you avoid the type of situation Kiahna and Conor fell into.

10. Do a search on forgiveness in Scripture. List four verses that act as guidelines on how to handle broken relationships, whenever possible.

BETWEEN
SUNDAYS

DEDICATION

To Donald, my Prince Charming ...

I smile as I write those words because of our recent trip to Ohio. I would take the stage at my speaking events and say, "So, this probably isn't a good time to mention that I'm a Michigan fan." When the boos died down, I would hurry and tell them, "But my husband's a huge Ohio State guy." After the hearty applause, I would say, "See ... he really is Prince Charming!"

We made great memories with the kids, and Kim and Keith, and we gained thousands of new friends. But here's the thing: you really are my Prince Charming, Donald. I mean it. I love you more with every passing day, understanding as we settle into these middle years that time is not a guarantee. Today is a gift, and tomorrow uncertain. And so I treasure these beautiful, loving days, looking forward to our intimate moments in a quiet walk or laughing over something only we would understand. The ride is breathtakingly beautiful, my love. I pray it lasts far into our twilight years. Until then, I'll enjoy not always knowing where I end and you begin. I love you always and forever.

To Kelsey, my precious daughter ...

You are eighteen now, a young woman, and my heart soars with joy when I see all that you are, all you've become. We prayed that through the teenage years you would stay true to who you are, to that promise of purity you made when you were thirteen, once upon a yesterday on a bench over-looking a sunlit river. But I never dreamed you'd so fully hold true to that promise. You look forward to that far-off day, when you can share with your future husband the gift you've saved for him alone. But in the meantime, you trust God that laughter and friendship and dancing and singing and spending time with your family is enough. More than enough. Honey, you grow more beautiful every day—inside and out. And always I treasure the way you talk to me, telling me your hopes and dreams and everything in between. I can almost sense the plans God has for you, the very good plans. I pray you keep holding onto His hand as He walks you toward them. I love you, sweetheart.

To Tyler, my lasting song . . .

So many wonderful things are happening in your life right now, things we once only dreamed about. You're the Cat in the Hat in *Seussical*, but not once have I seen you act arrogant about the fact. Worried, yes. Something that makes me smile, because I know . . . I know you'll be the absolute best ever at that part when the show opens later this month. I'm proud of you, Ty, at the young man you're becoming. I'm proud of your talent and your compassion for people, and your place in our family.

But two things will stand out when I look back on this time. The way my heart melts when you sing "Proud of Your Boy," and the earnest look in your eyes when you told me last week that maybe . . . just maybe, you'd want to be a teacher like your dad. A drama teacher, of course. Giving kids the skills to be successful on stage. You're fourteen and six-foot-two, Ty, no longer my little boy. But even as I see the future in your eyes, I'll treasure my memories of all the stages of your life. However your dreams unfold, I'll be in the front row to watch it happen. Hold onto Jesus, Ty. I love you.

To Sean, my happy sunshine . . .

Today you came home from school, eyes sparkling, and you told me you'd tied the school record for the high jump at track practice. The fact that your mark didn't count because it wasn't in a meet didn't dim your enthusiasm even a little. I was struck, as you recounted your jump, how much the story symbolized everything about you, Sean. You're so happy, so optimistic. You have a way of bringing smiles into our family, even in the most mundane moments. I pray that God will use your positive spirit to always make a difference in the lives around you. You're a precious gift, son. Keep smiling, and keep seeking God's best for your life. Make sure the bar's set high — not only at track practice. I love you, honey.

To Josh, my tender-hearted perfectionist . . .

Watching you work on your social studies project today, I saw again what always amazes me about you. Your work is so careful, so detailed, it would almost seem you'd traced pictures straight from the textbook. I couldn't turn in the work you do if I took all week. And yet — even with track and soccer and homeschool tests — you still take the time to seek perfection. Along with that, there are bound to be struggles. Times when you need to understand again that the gifts and talents you bear are God's, not yours. And times when you must learn that perfection isn't possible for us, only for God. Even so, my heart almost bursts with pride over the young man you're becoming. You have an unlimited future ahead of you, Josh. I'll be cheering on the sidelines always. Keep God first in your life, and who knows ... one day maybe you and Alex Smith will be teammates. I love you always.

To EJ, my chosen one ...

We had a family meeting the other night, one of those talk sessions you kids sometimes tease us about. The subject was a reminder that sitting around the dinner table each night are the very best friends you'll ever have. Your sister and brothers. And also that everyone needs to pitch in more. We talked about giving a hundred percent, because some day far too soon, when all you kids are grown and in families of your own, you'll need to give a hundred percent always. That's what love looks like. In the days that followed our family talk, Dad and I were thrilled to see you truly stepped up your efforts at helping out. We'd see you standing at the sink, washing dishes and singing a happy song, and you'd grin at us. "A hundred percent!" you'd say. EJ, I pray that you hold onto that very small lesson always. You're a wonderful boy, son, a child with such potential. Every day, every season, just give a hundred percent, okay? Because God has great plans for you, and we want to be the first to congratulate you as you work to discover those. Thanks for giving your heart, EJ. I love you so.

To Austin, my miracle boy ...

I was editing this book when you came into my writing room yesterday and smiled at me. "You're the most beautiful mom in the whole world," you said. "I really mean it." Then you plopped down on the sofa beside me and put your arm around my shoulders. "I think I'll cuddle with you here all day." I smiled, "Okay ... you can watch me edit." And then — here's how I know you're getting older — you jumped up and giggled. "No, Mom. Just kidding. I have schoolwork to do." You kissed me and patted my cheek, and then you were off.

But in the storage room of my heart, I had a memory I'll hold onto forever, sweet son. That, and the one from this afternoon. You're taking voice lessons, and this week your song is from Casting Crowns—"Who Am I." When the teacher was gone, you came upstairs with Dad, and from the other side of my writing room door, I heard Dad start to play his guitar. I stopped editing for a moment and stared out at the forest beyond my window, holding tight to the precious sound. You're my youngest, my last, Austin. I'm holding onto every moment, for sure. Thanks for giving me so many wonderful reasons to treasure today. I thank God for you, Austin, for the miracle of your life. I love you, Aus.

And to God Almighty, the Author of Life, who has—for now—blessed me with these.

ACKNOWLEDGMENTS

A book of this magnitude does not come together without help from many, many people. And so, here I humbly take a few minutes to thank the family and friends who partnered with me to bring you *Between Sundays*.

First, a special thanks to my dear friends at Zondervan Publishing. Without a doubt, in the world of Christian publishing, the team at Zondervan understands best my dedication to writing Life-Changing Fiction™. They are completely committed to getting these books to you, and to praying along with me that somewhere between the first and last pages, people will find their lives changed by the power of story. I am blessed beyond words to work with you. Thank you to Sue Brower, my truest supporter. And to Leslie Peterson, my editor on this project. You pushed me and challenged me, Leslie. I need so much more of that. Let's work together again soon!

Also, thanks to my amazing agent, Rick Christian, president of Alive Communications. Rick, you've always believed only the best for me. When we talk about the highest possible goals, you see them as doable, reachable. You are a brilliant manager of my career, and I thank God for you. But even with all you do for my ministry of writing, I cherish most your prayers. The fact that you and your wonderful wife, Debbie, are praying for my family and me keeps me confident every morning that God will continue to breathe life into the stories in my heart. I could never find the words to truly thank you.

A special thank you to my husband, who puts up with me on deadline and doesn't mind driving through Taco Bell after a baseball game if I've been editing all day. This crazy wild ride wouldn't be possible without you, Donald. Your love keeps me writing, your prayers keep me believing that God has a plan in this ministry of fiction. And thanks for your help with the guestbook entries on my website. I look forward to that time every night when you read through them, sharing them with me and releasing them to the public, praying for the prayer requests. Thank you, honey.

And thanks to all my kids who pull together, bringing me iced green tea and understanding about my sometimes crazy schedule. I love that you know you're still first, before any deadline.

Thank you also to my parents, Anne and Ted Kingsbury, and to my sisters, Tricia, Sue, and Lynne. Mom, you are amazing as my assistant — - working day and night sorting through the mail from my reader friends. I can picture you and Dad sitting there in your family room, while you interrupt his paper or news show every few minutes. "Wait, Ted ... listen to this one!" I love that you and Dad still get tears in your eyes — the way I do — - when you hear that another life has been touched, a heart healed through what God's doing with fiction. Amazing.

Tricia, you are the best executive assistant I could ever hope to have. I treasure your loyalty and honesty, the way you include me on every decision and exciting website change. My website has been a different place since you stepped in, and along the way, the readers have so much more. Please know that I pray for God's blessings on you always, for your dedication to helping me in this season of writing. And aren't we having such a good time too? God works all things to the good!

Sue, I believe you should've been a counselor! From your home far from mine, you get batches of reader letters every day, and you diligently answer them using God's wisdom and His Word. When readers get a response from "Karen's sister Susan," I hope they know how carefully you've prayed for them, and for the response you give. Thank you for truly loving what you do, Sue. You're gifted with people, and I'm blessed to have you aboard.

Thanks also to my forever friends and family, the ones who have stood by loyal and true through the years. Worldly success does strange things to people who watch it happen, even though that success is transient and pretend. I always say there'll be no autograph lines in heaven, so this is only about helping people see a little brighter glimpse of God and making friends along the way. Thank you for not seeing me or us differently, and for your love and laughter. You know who you are!

A very special thanks to San Francisco 49ers quarterback Alex Smith, who helped me research an inside look at the NFL and at the country's foster care system. Thanks for writing a foreword for *Between Sundays*, Alex. Our children's books are going to be a lot of fun over the next few years. And one of these days, we'll have to see that fox-trot we're not telling anyone about.

And the greatest thanks to God. The gift is Yours. I pray I might use it for years to come, in a way that will bring You honor and glory.

FOREVER IN FICTION™

A special thanks to Candace Rathbun, who won Forever in Fiction™ at the San Ramon Valley Christian Academy auction in Northern California. Candace chose to honor her daughter, Paige Judith Rathbun, by naming her Forever in Fiction™.

Paige Rathbun is nine and loves bringing sunshine to the lives of her family, including her older sister Katie, and her younger brother, John. Paige has blue eyes, blonde hair, and a contagious smile. She loves Disneyland, swimming, playing with dolls, and spending time with the people she loves. She wishes her four cousins still lived next door.

In addition, Paige loves to sing in her church choir and she prays for anyone with a need. Everyone who knows Paige, knows she's a hugger. And while she's passing out hugs, she's also likely to pass out her toys or books, anything someone else takes a liking to. Her huge heart is part of what makes her special.

When her family rescued a golden retriever last year, Paige took him under her care. They named him Shakespeare, and he and Paige have become best buddies. Paige asks a lot of questions, but only because she's intelligent and knows there's an answer.

In *Between Sundays*, Paige Rathbun's character is the niece of the 49ers head coach, Chuck Cameron. During a season when Chuck's career is on the line, Paige makes weekly phone calls to her uncle, encouraging him, and helping him keep his focus on Jesus. Because that's the sort of thing Paige would do in real life.

Candace, I pray your daughter Paige is honored by your gift, and by her placement in *Between Sundays*, and that you will always see a bit of Paige when you read her name in this novel, where she will be Forever in Fiction™.

For those of you who are not familiar with Forever in Fiction™, it is my way of involving you, the readers, in my stories, while raising money for charities. To date, this item has raised more than $100,000 at charity auctions across the country. If you are interested in having a Forever in Fiction™ package donated to your auction, contact my assistant, Tricia Kingsbury, at Kingsburydesk@aol.com. Please write *Forever in Fiction* in the subject line. Please note that I am only able to donate a limited number of these each year. For that reason, I have set a fairly high minimum bid on this package. That way the maximum funds are raised for charities.

NOTE TO THE READER

While set against a very real backdrop, the characters in *Between Sundays* are completely fictional. There is absolutely no resemblance between 49ers quarterback Alex Smith and the fictitious Aaron Hill, nor is there any resemblance between any of the characters in *Between Sundays* and any real professional football player.

As with any novel, I have taken poetic license in some areas of research, in an effort to create not only believable football players, but relatable characters. I was very careful in my NFL research, but it would be impossible to be completely accurate in my depiction of professional football.

That said, any inconsistencies between this novel and the real-life world of the NFL are entirely mine.

Foreword by Alex Smith,
San Francisco 49ers Quarterback

As an NFL quarterback, I spend my Sundays during football season calling plays, reading defenses, and avoiding sacks. All of this takes place in front of a national television audience and eighty thousand screaming fans. However, my Sundays were not always spent this way, nor were my days in between. That is why my time spent "between Sundays" is so important to me.

Back in San Diego, California, where I grew up, Sundays were spent with family. Sundays were "game time." Sundays were times spent talking and laughing and being together. We were able to create a supportive team and that team did not rest during the week. Team Smith consisted of my mom and dad, my older brother Josh, and my sisters Abbey and MacKenzie. I would not be where I am today if it were not for the love and support of my family and the invaluable time we spent together, caring for one another.

My family always believed in the importance of love and encouragement, the necessity of an education, and the value of reading. As a reader, I've seen the power of story. Sometimes a story is the only way to touch the heart of a person, to help them see the truth through something that isn't true at all. That's the case here. Though *Between Sundays* tells an entirely fictitious story, it is set against the backdrop of a very real problem facing our country today—the problem with our foster care system.

I chose foster care as the focus for my Alex Smith Foundation because most foster children do not have what I have. My "team" structure, my upbringing, and my family life, is the antithesis of what most foster children have. More important, my family's love and support did not end when I turned eighteen. Foster children are taken from their homes and families for reasons of neglect, abuse, and abandonment; and on their eighteenth birthdays, they are abandoned again by the state.

Less than half of foster kids in our nation graduate from high school. Within a year of leaving the system at eighteen years old, a third end up homeless and another quarter end up incarcerated. College is out of reach for most of these youth. Recent studies indicate that just 7 to 13 percent enroll in college, compared with 62 percent of high school graduates nationally. Less than 2 percent of former foster youth who begin college complete a bachelor's degree. This is compared with 27 percent of the general population. We as a society are failing these children, and, sadly, their stories and struggles go unnoticed today. These children deserve a better opportunity at life. They deserve a chance for a successful adulthood, and they cannot get that on their own. Which of us—alone and poor at the age of eighteen—- would be able to succeed?

Giving these foster youth a chance at life, a chance for success, is so much more important to me than improving my passing rating, scoring touchdowns, and wins and losses. I play a game on Sunday for a living, and I have a great team to support me on and off the field. These kids don't play a game for a living. Their game is survival and they need and deserve all the support they can get.

We all need support. Whether that support comes from running backs, receivers, linemen, coaches or parents, siblings, teachers, or mentors, we all have a responsibility to work together. As a quarterback, I know this firsthand. I would be nothing if it were not for the players around me. Likewise, I would not be where I am today if it were not for the love and support I received from my family and friends off the field.

I appreciate Karen Kingsbury for allowing me to share my story, and I appreciate her willingness to expose the positive side of a professional athlete's life between games. But most important, I appreciate the opportunity to create awareness for my foundation and to increase support for foster children everywhere.

It's not what we do in front of eighty thousand people on Sundays that defines who we are. Just as we are not defined by what we do on Sundays in church. It's what we do and how we live Monday through Saturday, when no one is watching, that defines our legacy. It's more than a game, it's life, and we all have a chance to make a difference as we live our lives between Sundays.

For more information about my foundation, you can go to AlexSmith Foundation.org.

See you there!

Alex Smith

PROLOGUE

The ache in Amy Briggs's chest hurt worse than before, and every breath came with a frightening wheeze. A wheeze no cough could loose. Not that she had the strength. She'd taken ibuprofen an hour ago, but still her fever raged. It made the air in their boxy apartment feel hot and stuffy, and it blurred her vision. She tried to sit up, but her body was too tired.

Cough syrup, that's what she needed. Cough syrup to break up whatever was suffocating her. She stared at the rickety table next to the worn-out sofa. The bottle of Robitussin lay on its side, empty, next to a stack of bunched up tissues and a half-empty box of Kleenex.

"Cory ... " Her voice barely lifted above the sound of the TV. "Can you get me ... some water?"

Her little boy was six, mesmerized by a special on the San Francisco 49ers. He jumped up. "Yes, Mommy." He stopped near her face, and his eyebrows lowered. "Are you better?"

She struggled for her next breath, but even so, she forced a smile. "A little." The lie was all she could manage. Cory couldn't help her. If things grew worse, she could call Megan, her friend and coworker at the diner. Megan could take her to the hospital if her cough got bad enough.

Her eyes closed and the sounds of the announcer dimmed in the background. Days like this, the battle was almost more than she could bear. Being a single mother to Cory, wondering where next week's food was coming from. Especially now that she was sick. Three missed shifts this week and she wasn't any better. A week without pay would mean she'd be bargaining with the superintendent at the end of the month.

"Mommy ..."

Amy opened her eyes, but it was a struggle. She nodded to the table. "Set it there, okay?"

He held the table so it wouldn't wobble, and waited until the glass was steady. "Need anything else?"

"Yeah." She took his hand in hers and met his eyes. "I need you ... just you, Cory." She tried to fill her lungs, but failed. A series of coughs came from deep inside her, and she turned away.

"Your skin's really hot." He touched his fingers to her forehead. "Maybe you should go to the doctor."

Maybe, she thought. But she was too tired to move. "After my nap, baby ... all right?"

He wrinkled his blond brow. "You sure?"

"Yes." She coughed into the pillow. "You watch your team."

For a heartbeat, Cory seemed torn. He looked at the TV and then back at her. "Feel better."

"I will, baby." She inhaled, but it sounded like she was underwater. "I love you."

"Love you too." He still looked worried, but he turned and moved a few feet closer to the TV, then he dropped down cross-legged and stared at the screen.

At his 49ers.

Since Cory was born she'd made the team her single obsession, even moving to San Francisco so that her son might have the chance he deserved, the one she prayed for every day.

The chance to know his father.

Of course, there were other reasons for leaving Los Angeles, reasons that had nothing to do with Cory or football. Those suffocating, terrifying minutes in the dark bushes that lined the campus parking lot that night had changed everything. Even if she hadn't told anyone then, or now.

A thousand bricks lay stacked across her chest. She had to sit up, had to find a way out from under the pressure. With her elbows, she used all her energy and slid up onto the arm of the sofa. A burst of oxygen filled her airways, and suddenly there was sweet relief.

She felt herself relax and again the sounds around her grew dim. She was falling, drifting into sleep. In the background, the announcer was saying something about Aaron Hill and how this was going to be his best year yet. *Aaron Hill ... the one everyone's watching*, the voice said. Or maybe it wasn't the announcer talking at all, but her heart.

Aaron Hill ...

Her heart slipped into a rapid, pounding rhythm and she tried to push herself up again on the sofa arm. This time, there was no relief. She felt hotter than before, her lungs heavy with fluid. She wanted to cough, needed to find a clear breath. But there was none.

"Mommy …" Cory's voice held an increasing sense of alarm. He stood over her and ran his little boy fingers along her forehead. "You look sicker."

"I'm … I'm okay." She had to be. Cory didn't have anyone in all the world but her. "I'll tell you … if I feel worse."

He frowned, nervous and frightened. Slowly he turned back to the TV, to the special still on. The 49ers. Ready for another season. Amy tried to focus, tried to listen to the announcer, but panic pulsated through her veins. Why couldn't she breathe? What was happening to her?

Strange voices filled her head. Voices from the TV. Or from Cory. She wasn't sure.

" … Aaron Hill … the quarterback to beat."

" … maybe the best year ever … a team desperate for a championship and …"

Amy rolled onto her side. She sucked in a breath, but she couldn't tell if any air entered her lungs. She needed to call Megan. Her friend would find her a ride to the hospital. Amy clenched her teeth and dragged back the smallest bit of air. *Relax*, she told herself. *Everything's going to be okay.*

A siren sounded in the distance, loud and louder, and after a minute Amy realized the sound wasn't coming from out on the streets. It was coming from her throat, her chest.

"Mommy, I'm calling Megan." Her boy was standing near her again, his breath soft on her face.

She tried to open her eyes, but the effort was more than she could make. Instead, she moved her lips and forced just enough air through her lips so he could hear her. "Please … call her."

Spots appeared before her eyes and danced in tight circles. The sounds around her blurred more, and time froze. *Aaron, you should be here …* She wanted to breathe, but the sound scared her. If it weren't for Cory, she would've moved on, as far from San Francisco as possible. But Aaron and Cory belonged together.

And this was the year.

Right, God …? Please, God …

I am with you, daughter … and I am with your child, now and always.

Peace filled Amy's heart. *Good, Lord. Thank you.* One benefit of leaving her parents' house six years ago was this—she'd found a friendship with God. Not the critical, narrow-minded God of her mother's world. But a God who had sent His Son to open the gates of heaven for her, a God whose Word was alive with hope and promise and direction for her future.

Cory's future.

"Wake up, Mommy." His little hand was on her head again. "Don't go to sleep."

I won't, baby … Mommy's okay. Jesus is here with us.

She said the words, but she wasn't sure they made it past her lips. The sounds around her faded a little more, and even the whistling coming from her lungs didn't seem as loud.

Amy wasn't sure if she slept or fell into a dream, but suddenly around her there was a burst of motion. Someone picked her up and she was on a long bed, moving fast, faster down a hallway. And she was in a car and there were sirens again but this time they weren't coming only from her throat but from everywhere, all around her, and she was moving on the bed again and a little boy was crying.

Cory! Cory was crying, and she had a sudden burst of energy. Her eyes opened and there he was, right beside her.

"Mommy, don't go to sleep … please." His eyes were red and damp and scared.

She brought his fingers to her lips and kissed them. "I'm okay, baby. Keep praying."

"I am." His breaths were fast and uneven, his features overtaken with fear. "Don't leave me! I need you!"

"You're okay." She pressed his fingers against her cheek. She wanted to do as he asked, but she was so tired. Her eyes blinked twice, three times. Then they closed. "I … love you." Her words were the softest whisper, and the darkness settled in around her again, a darkness thicker and more complete than any she'd ever known.

Something was pulling at her. Something or someone, and suddenly she couldn't fight it a moment longer. She let go, let herself be drawn in, and the feeling was wonderful. But as she did, as she moved toward whatever was calling her, she was seized with alarm.

Cory!

She had more to tell him, more to say. Her son needed her. Who would care for him if she wasn't there? The pull was stronger than before, and instead of the darkness, she was surrounded by a warm glow, a living light that was unlike any she'd ever known. With everything in her, she understood that her future was here, in the light.

But, God ... what about Cory?

At that instant, sound and sight returned to her world and she could see Megan, her arm around Cory, comforting him, and a knowing filled her. Megan would take care of Cory. And one day, she would hold her son again and he would understand that God kept His promises. This was the waiting room, all of earth. The real adventure was on the other side. The adventure she was going to take. Cory would be okay, just like she'd told him.

There was something else Amy was sure about, more sure than ever before. Almost as if God Himself were making the future suddenly clear. Her son would always have Megan, but very soon he would have someone else too.

Cory would have his father.

ONE

Two Years Later

Sometimes Cory Briggs took the long way home, pedaling as fast as he could so Megan wouldn't worry about him. Because Megan said eight-year-old boys should come straight home from soccer practice, especially on late afternoons. San Francisco was the sort of city where it was best if you were in by dark.

But that early August day, Cory did it again. He slipped his backpack onto his shoulders, left the soccer field at McKinley Elementary, and rode his bike up the hill and a few blocks out of the way, to Duboce Park. He would make up time on the downhill, so he stopped just outside the fenced-in play area and stared.

Shadows made it hard to see the bench, the one where he and his mom used to sit. But Cory shaded his eyes with his hand and squinted, and suddenly there it was. The same bench, same brown wooden slats, same way it looked back when he was a first grader, back when they came here every afternoon. He didn't blink, didn't break the lock he had on the bench, and after a minute he could hear her again, her happy voice telling him everything would be okay.

"God has good plans for us, Cory." She would kiss his cheek and smile at him. But her eyes weren't always happy, even when she smiled. "We'll find our way out together."

He remembered her still. He blinked now because he didn't want to cry. A bit of wind blew against his back, and Cory squinted against the tears. The day was hot, but already the bay breeze was cooling it off, which meant it was time to go. He climbed back up onto his seat and looked at the bench one more time. His mom was buried in Oakland somewhere. Megan took him once in a while, but Oakland was far away. When he needed to see her one more time, when he wanted to hear her voice, he came here.

Duboce Park.

"Take good care of her, God," he whispered. Then without another look back, he set off along the sidewalk pedaling hard as he could, turning down Delores to Seventeenth, and the third story apartment where he and Megan lived.

Cory knew the streets between his school and his apartment. He even knew the way to Monster Park, where the 49ers played. But Megan would never let him ride his bike all the way to the stadium. That was okay. It was enough just knowing it was close. Because once a year he and the kids from his neighborhood entered a drawing for tickets to a game, and this year ... this year he was going to win.

He focused on the ride. He knew which alleys to stay away from, and which areas had gang members standing around. He took the streets with the least traffic lights, because that was smarter. He had to stop for only three before he reached their building, jumped off his bike, and walked it through the doorway.

Bikes were allowed in the elevator if they fit, and his did. At the third floor he stepped off and already he could hear it. The sound of happiness. Laughing and loud voices coming from the Florentinos' apartment. He walked past two doors and stopped. The smell of spaghetti and garlic bread slipped beneath the door and filled the hallway. Sometimes, when Megan had to work late, he would knock on the Florentinos' door and they'd invite him in for dinner.

They had seven kids, but Mrs. Florentino said she always had an extra plate.

Cory raised his hand to knock, because Megan might not be home yet. Then he remembered. She'd made a Crock-Pot dinner this morning because she got paid first of the month. He walked his bike to the end of the hall to No. 312. The newspaper was there, opened, and a little scattered. The Florentinos got the paper every day, and after they read it, they set it outside his and Megan's door. Megan might deliver the paper, but that didn't mean she could take a copy free. That's what she said.

So instead, Mrs. Florentino brought over hers, and that way Cory could read about the 49ers. Especially now, in the preseason.

He used his key and walked into their apartment. Then he set down his backpack and the paper, walked across the room, and opened the front window. Nothing but alleys and winos below, but Cory loved having it open. A little bit of summer came in with the breeze.

Oreo, the cat, rubbed against his ankle.

"Hi, boy." Cory bent down and rubbed his fur. He was black and white with a lot of gray around the whiskers. Some days he was Cory's best friend. Cory straightened and looked around. The apartment was small, but it was clean. Megan liked clean. And almost every day she left a snack for him. Cory went to the table, and there on a napkin, were two chocolate chip cookies and an empty glass.

"So you'll remember to drink your milk," Megan always told him.

At the other end of the table was the Scrabble box. Each day was a different game. Sometimes Yahtzee or a deck of cards or Memory. But Scrabble was their favorite. They'd eat dinner first and then they'd play a game before homework. Megan was nice that way. Plus, the TV only got four channels clear. So board games were good.

Cory poured himself a glass of milk and sat at the table. The cookies weren't warm, of course, but they tasted like smooth vanilla and Hershey bars. Because that's how Megan made them. Which was nice because Megan didn't have much time. Early mornings, before he was awake, she delivered the *Chronicle*, and after that, she worked all day at Bob's Diner downtown. Two jobs because she said that's what it took to keep food on the table.

There was the sound of a key in the door and then it opened.

"Cory!" Megan stepped inside. She had a grocery bag in her hands and her cheeks were red, the way they got when she walked fast. She held up the bag. "Fudge brownie ice cream."

"The best!" Cory stood and ran to her and hugged her tight. When he'd first come to live with Megan, he didn't like to hug her because she wasn't his mom. But she was his mom's friend. And after two years, hugging her was almost as good as it used to feel to hug his mom. Plus, Megan liked the 49ers. So that made her and the apartment feel like home. Especially during football season.

Cory took the grocery bag. "Thanks." He grinned at her. "The Crock-Pot smells good."

"Not as good as Mrs. Florentino's dinner, but ..." She grinned. "It's the best we can do."

"Yep."

He helped put the ice cream in the freezer, and he held the door shut extra long because it didn't stay closed that good.

"Salad?" He opened the fridge and looked at her.

"Of course." She lifted the lid on the Crock-Pot. "Always salad."

He took out the head of lettuce and a worn-out knife from the drawer. If he had money of his own, he'd buy Megan some new knives. Forks too. And maybe a warmer sweater for the days she had to walk fast after dark.

They worked together, and Cory smiled to himself. It felt nice having Megan there. When they were sitting at the table eating the Crock-Pot dinner, Cory watched her a couple times when she wasn't looking. She was pretty, and she loved him like he was her own. That's what she said. And maybe she could keep him for good if the court hearings went okay. So far Megan said it was nothing but red tape and the runaround.

Whatever that meant.

Megan put her fork down. "I talked to the social worker again." A half smile lifted her lips. "I told her I want to adopt you, Cory."

He finished chewing a bite of potato. "What'd she say?"

"She said"—Megan raised one eyebrow and looked straight at him—"you told her the same thing. About having a dad."

Cory shrugged. "Yeah." He studied the pieces of meat still on his plate. Then he looked into her eyes. "Everyone has a dad."

She gave him a look that said no-funny-business-mister. "You know what I mean." A sad breath came from her. "If you tell her your dad's in the picture, we'll need his signature. I can't adopt you until he says so."

"Right." Cory checked his dinner again. He poked his fork around and pushed the carrots to one side. "If we get his signature ... I can meet him."

Megan waited for a second. Then she breathed long and loud and looked at her plate. "Let's talk about something else."

They talked about soccer practice and the other guys on the team and about her work at the restaurant, because she had a rich guy come in today, a big baldy, who left her a twenty-dollar tip.

"That's why the ice cream!" Cory raised his fork in the air.

"Exactly."

After dinner, they played Scrabble, but Cory couldn't think about big words. Some turns he couldn't think about any words at all. He wanted to read the newspaper, the sports section. Because the 49ers were getting ready for the season and he didn't want to miss a single story.

Megan won with the word *zebras*, and Cory hugged her. "Good job." He took a few steps back. "I'm gonna read the paper."

"How about the dishes first?" Megan had dark hair, and she tossed it over her shoulder when she stood up. It was easy to think of her as older, sort of his mom's age. Maybe twenty-nine or thirty. But she was twenty-five. Megan said that wasn't exactly young and that she had an old soul.

The two of them washed dishes, him scrubbing the plates and Megan rinsing. When they were finally done, he grabbed the paper and ran it to the couch. He was halfway through the sports section when he saw it. The headline read, "Derrick Anderson Hosts Pizza Party at Youth Center."

Cory raced through the short story. It talked about how Derrick Anderson loved foster kids, and that he was having a pizza party on Friday night at the youth center. All foster kids and their parents were invited.

"No way!" Cory shouted. "Megan, look at this!"

She was washing off the counter and made a little laugh. "Must be big. Read it to me."

"It is big!" He read her the story, every line, and then he let the paper fall to the floor and he ran to her. "Please, Megan. I could meet Derrick Anderson! He's the backup quarterback for the 49ers, the famous one who used to play for the Bears. Remember him?"

"The whole world knows Derrick Anderson." She did a sad sort of smile. "Well, they used to know him. Back in his prime."

"What?" Cory jumped around. "He's still *in* his prime, Megan! He's thirty-nine, and he's still one of the best quarterbacks in the league." He jumped some more. "I can't believe we can meet him." He stopped, his eyes wide. "We can, right? Can we? Please, Megan?"

Her eyes twinkled. "Are you kidding?" She messed her fingers through his hair. "That's the best Friday night offer I've had for a year, at least."

"Did you know about this, the pizza night?" Cory blinked at her. Megan volunteered at the youth center three times a week. She should've heard about this long before the newspaper.

Her eyes danced. "I had an idea. But I wanted to be sure before I told you. The 49ers' front office set it up. I guess the team wants to do whatever it can for the city. With all the talk about building a new stadium thirty miles south in Santa Clara."

"Yeah." Cory didn't like thinking about a new stadium. The 49ers had played at the same place since 1971. They were the best pro sports franchise in the state. Anyone knew that. Plus, Megan said if the mayor convinced the 49ers to stay in the city, they were going to build a bunch of new houses and stuff. Cory and Megan would have to move for sure. He blinked and tried to forget about the whole stadium thing. "Besides, Derrick's doing the pizza party for a different reason."

"Oh, really?" Megan gave him a half smile.

"Yeah, because he likes foster kids. And that's all."

Megan tilted her head, and her eyes said she was done teasing. "I think you're right."

"So"—he felt his heart dance around inside him—"We're going?"

A laugh came from Megan. "Definitely."

He grinned and held out his hand, official-like. "Okay, then. It's a date."

"Date." She shook his fingers, and then she laughed and went back to wiping the counter.

Cory picked up the paper again and stacked it on the sofa. Friday was only four days away. Which meant it wasn't too soon to do what he'd done a hundred times before. He ran to his room, pulled a box out from beneath the bunk bed, and grabbed a piece of paper and a pencil. He took out a dictionary to use for his table, and he started to write.

Every other time he'd done this, he never actually gave the letter away. Because when his mom was alive, she told him he couldn't just send it off without knowing where it would go, or if it would even be opened. So usually, he wrote the letter and threw it away. Or tucked it into his box, or his backpack. In case he ever ran into the guy at the park or something.

But this ... this was the most exciting thing to ever happen, because Derrick Anderson could deliver his letter, Cory was sure. And maybe these were the good plans from God his mother had always told him about.

Cory thought for a long time. He would write the best letter yet, stick it in the nicest envelope, and write across the front. So Derrick would know who to give it to. And Derrick would do it, because he loved foster kids. The *Chronicle* said so. And the letter was for one of Derrick's teammates, one of the most famous football players in the country. A man Cory prayed every night he might someday meet.

The man was quarterback Aaron Hill, but Cory didn't want to meet him because he was the city's favorite football player. He wanted to meet him for a different reason.

Because Aaron Hill was his dad.

Two

M egan couldn't go five minutes without Cory asking her about the time or how long it was until they left or some other question about the pizza party. Now it was five-thirty, almost time to leave, and Megan was in the bathroom running a brush through her hair. In the other room, Cory was talking to himself, going on about how this was the big day, the time of his life, the chance he'd been waiting for.

A smile tugged at Megan's lips. Cory's excitement was refreshing, and it gave both of them a reason to look forward to the night. But Megan worried about the boy too, about the letter he'd written for Aaron Hill.

Megan stared at the mirror. "You hear that boy out there, right, God?" She kept her conversation quiet, the way she always did when she talked to God. Cory's mother may have been a churchgoer, but Megan wasn't — she didn't trust organized religion. But from the time she'd been out on her own, God had been her closest friend. She held her breath. *Please, God ... don't disappoint him.*

"Almost ready?" Cory popped into the doorway. His eyes were wide, his smile so big, his freckles stretched ear to ear.

"Almost." She set the brush down and studied her look. She didn't wear much makeup, and tonight was no exception. She dabbed on fresh lipstick and tossed her hair. Then she turned to Cory. "Okay ... let's go."

"Yay!" He wore his best 49ers T-shirt, a 49ers baseball cap, and blue jeans. He grinned at her. "Do I look like their number-one fan?"

She tugged at the bill of his hat. "Definitely." Something bulky stuck out from his back pocket and she raised her eyebrow at it. "The letter?"

"Yes." His voice was practically trembling with anticipation. "Derrick'll get it to him, I know it."

Megan didn't want to dim the boy's enthusiasm, but she had to keep him grounded in case he never had a moment alone with the veteran quarterback. "You know, Cory, he might be too busy. It'll be packed tonight."

He grinned, unfazed. "I only need a few minutes."

"Hmmm." Megan walked past him into the kitchen and found her bag on the counter. The center had called on every volunteer to help with tonight's event. "You might only get a few seconds."

Cory thought about that for a heartbeat. "Perfect! That's just enough time to give him the letter and ask him to get it to Aaron."

Megan opened her mouth to say something about Cory having too vivid an imagination and setting himself up for heartbreak, but she changed her mind. There were a dozen ways Cory could get hurt or disappointed by the end of the night. The whole idea of a letter for Aaron Hill telling the star player that he was Cory's dad was crazy in the first place. If Aaron Hill was Cory's father, Amy would've said something about it. Megan and Amy talked about everything. The two were together all the time. And though they were both 49ers fans, the subject of Aaron in connection with Cory never once came up.

The notion was nothing but a little boy's fantasy. Megan could understand that much. There was no father in his life, so Cory had dreamed up a Hollywood movie scenario, the idea that his favorite quarterback was also his dad. But every time Megan tried to correct him, Cory was adamant. Lately she'd stopped trying to convince him. Life would take care of that all too soon.

This was the biggest thing to happen to Cory all year, maybe ever. "Okay." She smiled at him. "Let's go."

They took the stairs, since the elevator was being repaired. Once they were on the street, Cory ran a little ahead, turned around, and waited for her to catch up. "You think he'll be bigger in person?"

"Derrick Anderson?"

"Yeah. He's six-two, but I mean"—he patted one of his shoulders—- "bigger because of his muscles."

She stifled a laugh. "I'm sure he'll be big."

Cory walked backward, so he could see her. "Yesterday's paper said Derrick wants more foster kids at the games."

"I saw that. I'm glad he's thinking about it." The sidewalk was busy, full of people getting off work and loosely assembled groups sharing cigarettes and swapping stories outside the row of shops that made up their street. Megan took gentle hold of the boy's shoulder and turned him forward. "You're going to back into someone."

The party was at the Mission Youth Center on Market Street, an eight-block walk uphill from their apartment. They had twenty minutes, and Megan wanted to be there a little early—so they could get a seat close to where Derrick would be set up. Cory wasn't the only one who wanted a few minutes with Derrick Anderson.

Megan had her own reasons for wanting to meet the man. Ever since he arrived in San Francisco, he'd been passionate about foster kids. In that way, they had much in common. Foster kids were everything to her, and reform in the system was something she dreamed about.

But she was lacking everything it took to make a difference—time, money, and influence. Everything Derrick Anderson had in reserve.

Megan took long strides and thought about her life, the difference she wanted to make for kids like Cory. It was something she dreamed about in the predawn hours when she walked her fifteen-block route delivering the *Chronicle*, something that played over in her mind between serving plates of scrambled eggs and club sandwiches at Bob's Diner.

Most of all, she thought about her vision for foster care during the three days a week she volunteered at the center. The state had no money for the program, so the center was kept open largely by volunteers and donations from private citizens. Megan was an after-school coordinator, and in her spare time—at night after Cory was in bed—she worked on a grant proposal, one the director hoped to present to the state legislature.

Cory skipped ahead and then stopped himself and waited for her. "Two more streets!"

Megan pushed herself, the way she always did when she walked the steeper hills. No money for a gym, and no time for an exercise hour, but Megan did more walking in a day than most people did all month. She pressed on, picturing the kids who would be at the party today. Most of the foster kids who hung out at the center were fourteen, fifteen, even sixteen. A few were nearly eighteen.

Which meant that in a few months, on their birthdays, government services for those kids would suddenly stop. A shiver ran down Megan's arms. The kids could feel the deadline coming, and most of them were talking about it. Turn eighteen, and then what? Megan felt the familiar pain in her heart. She'd been there once herself, not that long ago. The answer for many of them lay in the statistics. Half ended up unemployed, a third became homeless, and one in four wound up in jail or prison.

"We're here!" Cory practically shook, he was so anxious to get inside.

The door was propped open and a chorus of voices spilled out onto the street. Megan stayed behind Cory as they walked inside. Already the place was packed. Many of the faces were familiar, kids who spent more time at the youth center than at their foster homes and group homes. Derrick Anderson had brought out every foster child in the city.

Megan peered at Cory. "Kinda crowded."

"Not too much." He stood on his tiptoes and stared past the milling people into the double gymnasium. "Do you see him, huh? Is he in there?"

"Let's get closer." Megan took hold of his hand and moved through the crowd. They should've come an hour ago. She reached the doorway and scanned the front of the room. It was still quarter to six, so Derrick might not be here yet.

"There he is!" Cory released her hand and ran toward the front of the room.

She saw the quarterback at the same time. He was near the front corner, and already a line of kids stood waiting for a chance to meet him. Cory was right; he was bigger in person. His dark brown skin stood in contrast to his white polo shirt, and even from this far away, the guy's warmth shone from his eyes. Megan worked her way closer, between the cafeteria tables that had been set up across the gym floor. She found an open spot at a table three rows from the front.

The atmosphere was frenzied, foster kids packing the place as if this single event was every birthday and Christmas rolled into one. She placed her elbows on the table and leaned into them. The line of mostly boys formed a thick crowd around the veteran player, and a string of volunteers worked to straighten them into a single line. Across the room, another batch of workers came through the side doors, each carrying a stack of pizzas. Pauline's Pizza had given them half off, and Derrick Anderson picked up the rest of the tab.

A few tables over, a little girl sat with an older woman. Both of them looked lost, overwhelmed by the chaos. The girl had dark hair and blue eyes, and a wistfulness about her that made her seem far older than her young age. Something haunting and familiar shone in the girl's eyes, and it took a few minutes to realize what it was. The girl looked like Megan, the way Megan had looked at that age.

The sounds around her faded as Megan was drawn back in time, back to the days when she came to this same youth center, attended the same community pizza parties.

"Your mother isn't stable," Megan's social worker had told her just before they took her from her downtown apartment and placed her in the first foster home.

Megan didn't need anyone to tell her that. She'd taken care of her mother from the time she was five years old, back when she first realized how troubled the woman was. Her mom was a crack addict and a binge drinker. She loved Megan with all her heart and always promised she'd find treatment. Once in a while she did, but only for a season. Megan spent her life in and out of foster homes.

At least until she turned eighteen. That year, she was released from foster care and returned to her mother. Megan had the highest grade point average in her graduating class, and for a year she managed to care for her mother and carry a full load of university classes. But her mother's health deteriorated the summer before her sophomore year, and Megan had no choice but to drop out.

By the time her mom died at the end of the next year, Megan had the paper route and the job at the diner, and college was little more than a distant dream.

Megan blinked and searched the line of kids until she found Cory, not far from the front. Amy would've loved this, a chance for Cory to meet a player from his favorite team. Megan squinted against the glare of the past. Hard to believe two years had passed since her death.

Cory looked over his shoulder and gave her a nervous grin. Her heart responded, the way it always did around the boy. What would've happened to him if she hadn't taken him in? His grandparents in Southern California were both dead, and he had no father in the picture. An image of Aaron Hill filled her head. No realistic father, anyway.

During her long talks with God, Megan concluded she'd been placed square in Amy's life for the sole purpose of taking care of Cory. Who else in Amy's world would've understood foster care the way she did? That was one of the reasons she wanted to adopt Cory—as soon as possible.

She blew at a wisp of her bangs. Maybe Cory's letter really would make it all the way to Aaron Hill, and maybe he'd get a message back to the boy that, well, he simply wasn't the boy's father. Cory believed it with all of his heart, so the truth was bound to hurt. But at least then he'd stop telling the social worker that he knew who his dad was, and in time, the adoption would go through and they'd both be happier.

Megan took a long breath. The smell of warm cheese and pepperoni was making her hungry. But she couldn't eat, couldn't move or blink or do anything but watch the line of kids and the big, strapping quarterback at the front. This was the first step toward the moment of truth.

Cory was next in line.

—

Finally Cory could hear Derrick Anderson's voice.

Because he was only four more kids away from his turn.

Cory put his hand over his heart like when they said the Pledge of Allegiance before a game. It was pounding hard, right close to his shirt. He swallowed and stared at his old tennis shoes. Derrick would give Aaron the letter, right? He would do that sort of thing because he was a nice guy. Otherwise he wouldn't be here having pizza with a bunch of foster kids.

They moved up another spot and he could hear Derrick laughing, the same sort of laugh he sometimes had when he was on TV and the news people talked to him. "Well, I don't know about that," he told the kid at the front of the line. "I'm there for Aaron, certainly. But I can't say I want his job."

Derrick Anderson didn't need anyone's job. He could retire now and be in the Hall of Fame in no time. That's what Megan said, and it was true. Derrick already had two Super Bowl rings, and that was more than Aaron Hill. Derrick was steady and dependable, year after year. The newspapers always wrote that about him. Aaron was flashy with a lot of big touchdown passes. Plus, he had good looks and a lot of endorsement deals. That's what they said about Aaron Hill.

Cory felt the letter in his back pocket, and his heart beat even faster. Maybe since he was closer now, he should take it out and have it ready. So he wouldn't waste any time once he got to the front. He reached back, but then he changed his mind. Better to keep it in his pocket where it was safe.

The letter wasn't super long, but it had all the stuff Cory wanted to say, like how his mom always told Cory that Aaron was his dad, and how they moved to San Francisco so they could be close to him and so that Cory could meet him one day, and how this might be the year because he never was able to get a letter to Aaron until now. The letter had Cory's phone number, plus some other good stuff at the end, but Cory couldn't think of the exact words right now.

He swallowed again. The nervous feeling in his stomach was worse than before any soccer game. Plus, the line wasn't moving very fast, and he was shorter than most of the guys in front, so he had to keep leaning sideways and trying to see exactly what was happening to make it take so long. Maybe some of the kids were filling out their raffle ticket for the prize basket. All the guys were talking about it. Five ticket packages with two seats each were being given out tonight. The best gift ever. Cory had already filled his out, and he wrinkled the slip of paper up a little in his hands so maybe Derrick would feel his more than the others, and Cory's name would get picked.

The line shuffled a few feet closer. Two more kids, that was all. Cory gave a little wave to Megan, because she was watching him. She didn't like it that he was giving Derrick a letter. She didn't say so, but Cory could tell. He smiled at her and looked back at his shoes. Then he tried a trick to make the time go faster. He thought about his last soccer practice, and the drills, and he pretended in his mind that he was going around the cones and dribbling the ball and passing it to the other guys on the team.

And then, just like that, it was his turn.

Derrick smiled at him. "Hey, partner, how's it going?"

His throat was dry, but he licked his lips and stepped forward. "Good." He stuck out his hand, proper like the way his soccer coach did when he met one of the other coaches before a game. "I'm Cory Briggs."

"Hi, Cory." Derrick shook his hand. Up close, his face looked a little bit like Michael Jordan's. He had a friendly smile and nice eyes and a smooth voice. "I like a young man who can look me in the eyes and give a proper handshake."

The rumbling in his stomach settled down. "Megan says you're the best quarterback who's ever played the game." Cory waited a few extra seconds before letting go of Derrick's hand.

"Megan?" He looked behind Cory, and his eyebrows bunched together, confused.

Cory giggled, because Derrick seemed like a guy who laughed easy. He pointed at Megan sitting three tables away. "Over there. She's my foster mom."

"Oh." Derrick waved at Megan, and then he took a photograph from a stack and signed it to Cory. "Here you go."

All of a sudden, Cory felt panic because maybe Derrick was going to tell him goodbye, and that it was the next kid's turn. But he put his hands on his knees and looked right into Cory's eyes. "You play football, Cory?"

"I want to." Cory felt his shoulders sink a little. "I play soccer. Megan says football has to wait." He didn't stay discouraged for long. "I'm gonna be a running back in high school."

"Running back's a tough position." Derrick sized him up. "I think you'll be a good one."

His words made Cory feel twelve or thirteen, instead of eight. He stood super tall, and then in a flash, he remembered the letter. "Oh." He twisted around and pulled the envelope from his back pocket. For a second he stared at it. The name Aaron Hill was across the front. *God, please ... let Aaron get this.* He felt a little shy all of a sudden, and embarrassed because maybe he should've brought a letter for Derrick too. He bit the inside of his cheek and gave Derrick a worried look. "Can I ask a favor?"

Derrick put his hand on Cory's shoulder. "Sure, partner." His smile looked real, like it came from inside his heart. "What's the favor?"

"This." He held the letter out to Derrick. "It's a letter for Aaron Hill."

Derrick took the envelope and looked at the front. "Aaron Hill ... yep, it says so right there." He gave Cory a look, the sort of look a dad might give a son. Because Cory had seen it when the dads talked to the other guys on his soccer team. That kind of look. "Is Aaron your favorite player?"

Cory wanted to say no, Aaron wasn't his favorite player. He was his dad. But Megan said that was the sort of detail that Aaron had to find out before any of his teammates did. So Cory shrugged one shoulder. "Kind of." He rushed on. "Course, you're one of my favorites too." He gave a nervous laugh. "I liked you before I liked Aaron, and that's the truth. 'Cause I've been watching football since I could walk."

Derrick did one of those grown-up kinds of laughs. Then he held out his hand again, and Cory shook it. "Tell you what. I'll make sure Aaron gets it." He leaned in a few inches closer. "Promise."

Everything inside Cory lit up all at once. "Really?"

"Really." Derrick tapped the envelope on his knee, and then slid it into his own back pocket. "I'll give it to him tomorrow at practice."

"Okay." Cory licked his lips again. "Thanks, Derrick. I mean it a lot. You're the best."

Derrick nodded toward Megan. "I think she's saving you a seat."

"Yeah." Cory looked at her and waved again. "She's good about that."

"Get yourself some pizza and maybe you'll win the tickets. We'll pick the winners in about half an hour."

"Okay." Cory was going to shake Derrick's hand a third time, but he changed his mind. Too much of that sort of stuff bugged people. So he took a step back and pointed to his letter in Derrick's pocket. "Tomorrow?"

"Yep." Derrick gave his pocket a few light pats. "Soon as I see him."

A few kids in line were saying hurry up, and that Cory was taking too long. He took a step backward. "Thanks again."

Derrick winked at him, and then just like that, the meeting was over. Cory walked back toward the table where Megan was but he didn't remember taking even one step. And he didn't want pizza either. All he wanted was to sit there and watch Derrick and imagine that sometime tomorrow he would take the very same envelope that held Cory's letter and hand it over to Aaron Hill.

The whole event was a dream come true.

"That looked like it went well." Megan gave him a hopeful smile when he reached her. "He took the letter, at least."

"Yeah." Cory's voice was full of victory, the way it was after he scored the winning goal in the first soccer scrimmage a few weeks ago. "He said he'll give it to Aaron tomorrow at practice."

Megan told him to get some pizza, and even though he wasn't hungry, he obeyed because maybe he'd be hungry later. Plus, he had to find something to do to make the time go faster between now and the drawing for the preseason game tickets. This was his best chance ever to see the 49ers play in person.

Cory kept his eyes on Derrick, even when he was eating his sausage pizza. Finally, the director of the youth center stood on a platform and tapped her microphone. It made a loud sound and she backed up a few inches. "Okay, kids, settle down."

The kids weren't that good at settling down, not usually anyway. But today everyone settled very fast because the director was going to tell them about the tickets. Derrick came over to her, and another lady gave him a big basket of names.

"Now boys and girls, you know there's only five sets of preseason game tickets available tonight. But Derrick brought lots of water bottles and 49ers T-shirts and bumper stickers. So after I draw the winning names, stay quiet. You still might win something."

Cory crossed the fingers on both hands, and then, just for a little extra help, he crossed his hands and set them on the table next to his empty pizza plate. *Come on, Derrick … pick me. You gotta pick me.* That would be perfect because then he could meet Aaron, and by then Aaron would've read the letter and they could get right down to business and talk about how Aaron was his dad.

Derrick swished his hand around in the basket and pulled out a slip of paper. It looked wrinkly as he handed it to the director.

This is it! Cory held his breath.

"The winner is … Tommy James."

All the air in Cory's lungs came out. Now how would he ever get a chance to go to a game and meet Aaron Hill? Across the room, a big kid jumped out of his seat and shoved his fists straight into the air. He hooted a few times as he ran to the front of the room. Someone took a picture of him and Derrick, and then Derrick gave him a package.

Four more times Derrick picked a name, and four more times it wasn't Cory's.

When all the excitement calmed down, the director handed the microphone to Derrick. "I know there's a bunch more of you kids out there who'd like to see a game at Monster Stadium."

The kids clapped and cheered.

"So, here's the good news. I'll have a pizza party like this every Thursday or Friday night through the preseason—depending on whether the 49ers are home or away. And each time we'll give away five pairs of tickets and a bunch of other stuff."

Cory's heart felt light again. If Derrick gave away five sets of tickets at every pizza party, one of them was bound to go to him and Megan. It had to.

Of course, there was one other way they could make it to a 49ers game this year. Derrick could give the letter to Aaron at practice tomorrow, and Aaron could read it, and he could be glad that he had a little boy named Cory living just a few miles from the stadium. And he could call Cory up and invite him and Megan to a game. Then he could ask if Cory wanted to come down to the locker room afterward so they could hang out. And that, Cory told himself as they left the youth center that night with nothing from the prize table, would be even better than a water bottle or a T-shirt or even preseason game tickets.

Because that's what a dad would do.

THREE

Derrick walked out onto the field at the Santa Clara practice facility fifteen minutes before any other player. Today would be light, since the past week was one of the hardest so far. Derrick headed to the warm-up track and planted his feet, shoulder width apart. He put his hands on his hips and leaned to the right for ten seconds, then to the left. Stretching took longer than it used to, his bones and muscles and tendons holding tight to the memory of a hundred NFL games.

He drew in a long breath and stared at the place where the brown rolling hills met the sheer blue sky just beyond the field. This was it. His last chance at a game he'd loved since he was in kindergarten. He could feel the finality as surely as he felt the constant ache in his throwing arm. After a standout career and a dozen playoff wins, after two Super Bowls and the roar of the crowd one touchdown pass after another, the whole glorious ride was about to come to an end.

He squinted toward the afternoon sun. *God, show me how ...*

Another deep breath and he started to jog. He took the first lap slow, just fast enough to get the blood flowing through his body. Retirement would be nice, no question. His wife, Denae, had all sorts of plans for him and their three young teenage kids. Trips to Hawaii and Mexico and a cruise to Alaska. And of course, coaching. Two of the three were boys and Derrick rarely saw them without a football. He would coach them as long as the local high school allowed it.

Derrick had a pretty good hunch they would.

But all that could wait. Here, now, he had just one goal that mattered, one that had consumed him since he took his place with the 49ers. He had to help this team reach the big game, had to win one more Super Bowl. He'd made a promise, after all. If Derrick wanted to be remembered for one thing when he hung up his helmet, it was for being a promise keeper.

Fans of Derrick Anderson never had to worry about opening the pages of the sports section and finding his name linked with drugs or drunken behavior or police activity. He might not be flashy like Aaron Hill, but he was dependable. God alone had given him the ability to play, and when he went out, he would do so with the sort of tribute his God deserved.

If he could only figure out exactly what that tribute was.

He rounded the first lap and picked up his pace. The run was easy, second nature. With every lap he felt his body waking up, falling into a familiar rhythm and quickness that he would need if he was going to make a difference this season. And he would, because God had told him so. Derrick's only question was how that would happen.

Near the entrance to the facility, a few other players were arriving. But Derrick kept his focus. This season was going to be special, maybe the most special of all. There was the foster program, of course. The city was inundated with foster kids, most of whom had no plan outside their eighteenth birthday. Derrick wanted to change that. The pizza parties were only the beginning. He wanted to pass on his love for foster kids to the other players. Get the whole team to embrace the city's parentless kids.

That wasn't all the next four or five months were about. Coach Chuck Cameron's job was on the line, for one thing. He'd taken the team to the playoffs four of the last seven years. But he hadn't won a conference championship, and he hadn't made it past the first round in five years. This year, once again, the best thing going for the team was Aaron Hill, the top-ranked quarterback in the league, but the 49ers were weak at the line and two of their top receivers had undergone surgery in the off-season. No one expected them to break records this year. Grumbling was coming toward the coach loud and clear from the front office. Win it this year, or pack up and leave. The owners expected a new stadium in five years—whether it was in Santa Clara or at Monster Park. They wanted a championship team long before that.

Coach Cameron wasn't the main reason he was here, though. The main reason, Derrick believed, was the team's hotshot quarterback, Aaron Hill. Coach Cameron thought so too.

"Get through to him, Anderson," Coach had told him last week. "Guts and talent aren't enough in this league. Never mind his reputation, Aaron Hill won't go to the next level until he plays with heart."

So maybe that was his primary job, the formerly great Derrick Anderson: Help Aaron Hill play with heart. When he prayed about the season, about what God wanted from him, he sensed it didn't have much to do with his own on-field contributions. Derrick was realistic about the coming schedule. He might not play a down all season. But he knew the secret to winning, and Coach was right. It had everything to do with the inside of a man, the life that happened off the field. Between Sundays. If the 49ers' starting quarterback would slow down enough to realize that, they might all win in the end.

The first fine layer of sweat broke out on his forehead and the small of his back. It was eighty degrees and breezy, the sort of late summer day that hinted of fall. Derrick kept his breathing even as he pushed himself. Four more laps and he could join the others.

He watched Aaron strut onto the field, then he shifted his attention straight ahead. Aaron was a nice guy, likeable. After seven seasons in the NFL, he was one of the most liked players in the league. The guy played through strained ligaments, back spasms, and concussions, and that made him a hero to his adoring public. As long as he could score a touchdown in a two-minute drill, the world loved him.

Off the field, Aaron was shallow and cavalier. He partied hard, though the press hadn't caught wind of the fact. A different stunning blonde or brunette waited for him after practice every week or so. He drove a Hummer and prided himself on being a slick dresser. All neat and put together, just like his reputation.

Derrick had a feeling Aaron had lost something deep along the way. No doubt, Aaron Hill was one of the reasons God had moved him to the 49ers.

"Hey, Anderson," Coach Chuck Cameron waved him over. "It's time."

"Okay." Derrick wiped his brow and jogged toward the others. The two-mile run was his own doing, a way of compensating for the years.

The sound of the guys drifted across the field, most of them talking about Friday night or laughing about something. As Derrick rounded the final curve, Coach Cameron blew his whistle and waited. The guys pulled up around him and silence fell over the team.

Derrick found a spot near the back, his stomach muscles pushing through his shirt from exertion.

One of the linebackers leaned toward him. "Show off."

"Yeah, you're jealous." He grinned and focused on Coach.

"Things are heating up." The coach paced a few steps. "I don't think I have to tell you all that's riding on this season." He tucked his clipboard against his side and studied them. "*Sports Illustrated* says ten teams have the chance to go all the way this year." He paused. "We're not one of them. The media thinks we're a quarterback, nothing else."

A disgruntled mumbling came from the group.

"Best offensive line in the league." Aaron Hill grinned and gave a nod to a few of his linemen. His support of his line was widely touted throughout the league. Aaron treated them to steak dinners and bought them iPods during the season.

Smart guy, Derrick thought. Without the line, Aaron would be like any other quarterback, scrambling for his life and winding up on his back half the time.

"So here it is." Coach Cameron's voice rang with sincerity. "We need to come together this year. Because the media's not God. *Sports Illustrated* isn't God. This year"—he walked along the front of the group, his eyes never leaving theirs—"I have a feeling. You know what I mean?"

The guys shifted, their attention fully on the coach.

"Let's get out there and prove some people wrong."

He didn't mention that his own job was on the line, but the intensity of his brief talk remained as practice began. Derrick lined up between Aaron and rookie quarterback Jay Ryder—a fourth-round draft pick out of Texas A&M. The three of them were taking snaps and firing consecutive short-pattern passes.

Aaron threw another one and grinned at Derrick. "I was waiting for Coach to say, 'Aaron Hill isn't God.'" He laughed. "Since he got all religious on us."

Derrick caught the snap and released it in a single fluid motion. "Well"—he kept his tone light—"you're not."

"Not what?" Aaron looked at him.

"God."

Jay Ryder grinned, but he didn't say anything. Jay was twenty-one, and he stayed quiet most of the time. Still figuring out his place on the team.

The center snapped the ball and hit Aaron in the chest. Frustrated, he snagged it off the ground and threw a bullet at the receiver. "I'm kidding, Anderson. Take a joke."

Derrick didn't push. Half the team was made up of people strong in faith, and Coach Cameron was one of them. His message wasn't meant to be humorous. Derrick spent enough time talking to the guy to know that much. Most likely, in his ongoing communication with the Lord, Coach had come to the realization once more that with God, all things were possible. All things.

Even a Super Bowl.

He and Aaron didn't talk again until after practice when they headed for their lockers. Derrick's was near the back, between Aaron's and Jay's. Coach made sure of that. Aaron took the lead down the aisle between the lockers. He'd been brilliant on the field today, probably spurred on by Derrick's comment.

Derrick kept pace with Jay. He was impressed with the young player. Four or five years and he would be a major contributing force in the league. "Good job today."

A smile lifted Jay's lips. "Thanks. My arm felt good."

They reached their places, and Aaron seemed to keep his back to them.

Derrick opened his locker and slipped off his cleats. As he did, his eyes fell on the photo that hung on the inside door of his space. A photo of his wife and him, and their four beautiful children.

"Your kids coming to practice next week?" Jay sat next to him and began working the laces on his shoes.

"They'll be here. Denae took them to Anaheim last week." He chuckled. "The two boys would rather be here than riding a rollercoaster. But she wants them to know more than the game."

"Wise woman." Jay slipped off his practice jersey. "So hey, I saw your name in the paper. What's that thing you did last night?"

Derrick pulled his shirt over his head and leaned on his locker. "Pizza party for some foster kids. The city's full of 'em."

Aaron turned and grinned at Jay. "Good old Derrick Anderson, saving the world one project at a time." He faced his locker again.

Jay raised his brow, as if to say maybe the comment was a little harsh. He pulled off his socks. "I did a report on you when I was in seventh grade. You did a lot of work with foster kids, even back then."

Derrick tried to focus. Aaron's reaction bugged him, but he kept his frustration to himself. The starting quarterback's cockiness covered up something deeper—that had to be the reason. He glanced at Jay and then at the photo of his family. "I learned something a long time ago." Derrick pulled his duffle bag from his locker and set it on the bench. The smell of sweat and ripe shoes was strong, the way it always was after practice. "Something that stayed with me."

"About foster kids?" Jay pulled his pads from his pants and hung them at the back of his locker.

"About life."

"Do tell us …" Aaron turned around again. The frustration was gone, and in its place the easygoing smile known to sports fans around the country. "Oh, great and mighty one."

Derrick laughed to keep things light. At the same time, he remembered the kid's letter, the one the freckle-faced boy had given him last night at the youth center. He pulled it from his bag. If God wanted him to influence Aaron Hill, he'd have to get the guy to trust him. Easy for a rookie like Jay Ryder. Much more difficult for a proven player.

He cocked his head and stared at Aaron. "Who you are as a man, as a player, isn't about what happens out there on game day." He held up the envelope and then handed it to Aaron. "It's what you do between Sundays. That's what matters."

"Between Sundays." Jay drew out the words, as if they were hitting him in slow motion. "I like that."

Aaron took the letter. "What's this?"

"A kid gave it to me last night. Wanted me to give it to you."

Aaron gave the envelope another look and then tucked it along one side of his locker. "That's really how you spent your Friday night, Anderson? Having pizza with a bunch of kids?"

"And a whole roomful of foster parents."

Aaron whistled. "Doesn't get any better than that."

"You're doing it again this week, right? Didn't I read that?" Jay finished undressing and wrapped a towel around his waist.

"Every Friday or Thursday night throughout the preseason." Derrick hesitated. "Come with me this week. The kids'll love it."

"I was thinking that." Jay nodded, thoughtful. He looked like a taller version of Tiger Woods. Same lanky body, same easy smile. He would've been a hit with the ladies, but his family kept a tight circle around him. "Might help me connect more with the people of the city."

"Exactly." Derrick was almost ready for the showers too. "How 'bout you, Hill. You up for a Friday night at the youth center?"

Aaron chuckled, then he squinted and looked at the ceiling for a moment. "Let's see ... Friday night." He raised his eyebrows at Derrick. "Booked solid. Sorry."

Jay slipped his bag back into the locker. "Why foster kids? I mean, the city's got sick kids too. And a bunch of other causes."

The reason didn't come up often. Most people never asked. Derrick tucked his towel around himself. "When I was young, my best friend was a guy named Mikey, a foster kid. He moved around, three or four homes, but he always stayed in the area." Derrick shut his locker. "'Cause of him."

"You stay in touch?" Jay leaned against his locker.

"No." Derrick felt the familiar pain, the one that never quite went away. "Mikey turned eighteen and started selling drugs. Got messed up with a gang. Two years later he was killed in a drive-by."

Jay groaned and stared at the rubber mat beneath his feet. After awhile he looked up. "Makes sense now."

"Hey, man," Aaron patted Derrick's shoulder. "I'm sorry. I didn't know."

"It was a long time ago." Derrick didn't want to talk about Mikey. "When I'm done with football, maybe I'll run for office. Get a bunch of programs in place so foster kids'll have some way to transition into real life."

They headed for the showers, and the conversation stalled. Even if Aaron made light of the idea, and despite the fact that his Friday night was booked, Derrick had seen something change in his teammate's eyes at the mention of Mikey. Whatever caused the difference in Aaron's expression, it was enough to give Derrick a glimmer of hope. The purpose God had in connecting him with Aaron Hill might not be something Derrick had to wonder about for weeks on end. Rather, it might be on the verge of showing itself.

For that reason, as he showered, he switched up his prayer for the starting quarterback. Rather than praying for an inroad to the guy's heart, he prayed for something else.

An open Friday night.

FOUR

Saturday night was a disaster, and Sunday was looking worse. Now on his day off, Aaron pulled into the parking lot at the 49ers facility in Santa Clara and climbed out of his Hummer. He never should've taken the girl up on her offer. She was gorgeous, but she wore a low-cut shirt and too much eye makeup. The trashy kind of girl he'd been good at staying away from.

Saturday night he got careless, and Sunday the story was on the front page of sports. He pulled a baseball cap low over his eyes and headed for the side door. The meeting today was between his agent and Coach Cameron. Not that Aaron had much to worry about.

His agent, Bill Bonds, had already briefed him earlier that morning.

"How bad is it?" Aaron was standing in the kitchen when the call came in. "What's the buzz?"

"No one's happy." His agent sighed. There was no hiding his frustration. "Cameron wants to bench you for the first preseason game. Teach you a lesson."

"Great." Aaron downed a glass of orange juice. "What about the front office?"

"They're against the idea. A little good publicity, a batch of stories off the subject, and they think everything'll be fine."

"The bar girl?" Aaron leaned against his kitchen counter. He could've had his pick from the women that night. A sigh squeezed through his clenched teeth. "Any news from her lawyer?"

"Not yet. I'm waiting for the call." Bill paused. "I'm pretty sure she'll drop charges, but it'll cost you, Aaron."

"That's fine. Whatever."

"Yeah, whatever." His agent gave a bitter laugh. "We'll talk about it at the meeting today, and listen …"

He waited.

"I've been looking out for you since you were a college kid, Hill. Image is everything. We can't afford this sort of thing."

"Yeah, well … I met with my financial guy last week." He chuckled. "Pretty sure we can afford it."

"This isn't funny." Bill sounded tired. "Don't be late today, Hill. I mean it."

"Yeah, yeah. I'll be there."

His agent's tone put a cloud over the morning, one that stayed now as Aaron walked through the door, down the hall, and into the meeting room next to the cafeteria. He wasn't late, but he wasn't early either. Coach Cameron, two assistants, the offensive coordinator, and Bill were already seated around the table.

His agent took the lead. "Sit down."

"Listen." Aaron found the right sort of tone. He took the spot next to Bill and met the eyes of the coaches. "This whole thing's being taken out of context."

Coach Cameron's anger showed in the lines on his face. He stood and paced along a bank of windows overlooking the practice field. "A seventeen-year-old girl's giving out interviews like candy, telling the press you made out with her in the parking lot and tried to pressure her into having sex in the back of your Hummer." He stopped and stared at Aaron. "What exactly is being taken out of context?"

"Look," Aaron sighed. "She told me she was twenty-three. A girl wears that much eye shadow and anyone would believe her."

Coach's forehead creased with concern. "She said you forced your hands up her shirt and pushed her toward the back door of your car."

"Come on." Aaron tossed out a few weak chuckles, but stopped. No one else was laughing.

"Are you saying you didn't do those things?" Bill's tone was kinder now, gentler. He was working the situation for Aaron's benefit, the way he always worked it. No matter how Bill felt about Aaron's Saturday night, his agent wouldn't let the team know he was worried.

"Of course not." Aaron rocked back in his chair. "I kissed the girl, okay. I invited her back to the house. But forcing her?" he huffed. "Not bragging, guys, but I'm a gentleman with my dates." He tried a weak smile. "I don't have to force myself. Just doesn't happen."

Bill shot him a look, as if this maybe wasn't the time to talk up his off-field conquests.

Coach Cameron leaned against one of the windows. "You're amazing, Hill. Whole world thinks you're a hero, when you're nothing but a jerk."

"Listen." Bill was on his feet. "We didn't bring him in here to call him names. He was out having a little fun, and he's allowed that much." He returned slowly to his seat. "I'm expecting the girl to drop charges today."

"Four days before preseason?" The offensive coordinator shook his head. "I'd like to think my multimillion-dollar starting quarterback was home studying plays on the weekend. Not hitting up girls at the local bar."

Silence hung over the room. Coach Cameron finally drew a long breath and took his place at the table again. "The penalty holds. Derrick's starting at quarterback the first preseason game." He leveled a look at Aaron. "Maybe for the first two games."

"Look." Aaron felt a flash of anger rip through his gut. "That's ridiculous. I told you the girl's—"

Next to him, Bill Bond's cell phone rang. *Good*, Aaron thought. Maybe it was the girl's attorney.

Bill stood and excused himself. While he was gone, Coach Cameron talked about his plans for the season, his dreams. "We have no room for this kind of garbage, Hill. Not a minute of it." He tapped his fingers on the table. "You're not the only guy on this team." He gestured toward the window. "We got guys who'll get cut if things don't go well this year. Guys whose future depends on you. Ever think of that?"

Not even the slightest regret rattled around in Aaron's head. He shrugged, his tone light. "I didn't think I was on the clock."

"You need to start thinking." Coach sneered at him. "You're the quarterback of this team. You're always on the clock."

Before Aaron could think of another way to defend himself, his agent returned. Victory screamed from his expression. "Done!" He held up his cell phone as he took his place at the table. "She dropped the charges. Her official statement's going to say she must've misunderstood Aaron's intentions."

"What'd that cost you, Hill?" The offensive coordinator shot him a look.

"If you paid her off, the press'll find out." Coach Cameron glared at him.

The team had nothing to worry about. Bill had paid off women before. No one would ever find out. Besides, he really had thought the girl was older. She lied to him, trapped him. Now she had what she wanted. She was a snake, and Aaron should've seen through her. But it didn't matter now. The incident was behind him.

"Hey, listen." Aaron kept himself from smiling. This wasn't the time to act smug. He never meant to hurt the team. "I'm sorry, Coach. Really."

Bill looked surprised and somewhat relieved. He cleared his throat. "Exactly, gentlemen. Aaron meant nothing by this. Taking away his starting position at the beginning of the season won't be good for him or"—he looked straight at Coach Cameron—"for any of you."

"It'll be my decision." Coach's answer was quick. He stood, and the other three coaches followed suit. "We have another meeting. But we'll be watching." He narrowed his eyes. "I won't have a team marked by moral failure."

Aaron wanted to ask him whether the front office agreed on Coach Cameron's definition of morality. "Can I say something?"

"What?"

He could feel the warning look from his agent, but he didn't care. "I never asked to be defined by my moral character, only by my play on the field." He crossed his arms. "I don't want or deserve my reputation as a good guy." His voice filled with intensity. "The fans did that, not me."

"Oh, yeah?" Coach Cameron uttered a bitter laugh. "You're unbelievable, Hill." He walked to the door, stopped and looked back at Aaron one last time. "Rather than complain about your good reputation, maybe it's time you start earning it."

The coaches left the room and Aaron turned to his agent.

"Way to go." Bill raked his fingers through his hair. "You don't tell the head coach it isn't your fault people like you. Fan support is huge to the 49ers." Bill exhaled hard. "I spend my whole career investing in you, Hill. But you still don't get it, do you?" He stared hard at Aaron. "You shatter the image, and it'll all disappear. The fans, the endorsements, the autograph parties. All of it."

Aaron stared out the window at the stretch of grass beyond. An image, that's all he was. He knew it and Bill knew it. The coaches knew it. Maybe it would be easier if the fans knew it too. Derrick Anderson's words came back to him. *It's what you do between Sundays. That's what really matters.* That was fine for guys like Derrick Anderson, but Aaron had already had his chance at doing things right. Way back when Amy Briggs was still in his life. Since then, the only thing he wanted to do between game days was push himself harder in the weight room, faster on the field, always looking for the edge.

"Look"—Aaron turned to his agent—"I give everything I've got on that field. The 49ers aren't paying me to be nice."

"Yeah, well, maybe you'd like to take a look at this." He reached into his briefcase and pulled out a few pages stapled together. "AOL did a vote last night over a six-hour window." He moved the document close enough for Aaron to see. "They asked the public if the story about you and the teenage girl lowered their opinion of America's favorite quarterback."

His heart beat a little faster than before. "They did that?"

"Look at the results."

Aaron peered at the columns beneath the question. Sixty-three percent said the story had harmed the way they saw him. He winced. "Who verifies that garbage?"

"It doesn't matter." Bill flicked the paper. "Everyone who reads it takes it as truth, and in the process it becomes truth. Whether it's true or not."

"What's the second page?"

"Two faxes from your top sponsors. They're advising you to clean up your image or else."

Aaron flipped the first page and stared at the first fax. "They're threatening to cut me? Because of one story?"

"They can do that." Your sponsors are in the business to sell tennis shoes and sportswear. They make their money on a clean-cut image. The good kids, the athletes—they wear the stuff."

Aaron understood. He pictured himself sitting at the table with his offensive line Saturday night. The blonde vixen had lured him into the parking lot in no time. But who could've seen it leading to this? He sighed. "So what's next?"

"Damage control." He pushed the papers toward Aaron. "Keep that as an incentive."

"Meaning what, an autograph session after practice?"

"You're supposed to be doing that anyway." The stress showed in the shadows on Bill's face. "I was thinking more like this pizza thing Derrick Anderson is doing. Helping out with foster kids."

Aaron tightened the muscles in his jaw. Derrick Anderson. The coaching staff had run the acquisition by him before they hired him: "He'll be like a mentor, Aaron. Someone to help ground you a little." From the beginning Aaron didn't like the idea. Derrick was a legend. He would hardly go quietly into the night, so what place did he have on the 49ers? Aaron was the star quarterback of this franchise.

But the front office suits had their minds made up, and in the end Aaron had little choice except to make the best of it.

Aaron rocked back in his chair again. "So, go to the next pizza party with him? That's what you want?"

"It'd be easy. The team hosts the Bears Thursday night, so Friday'll be light practice. Spend the evening with a bunch of kids at a youth center, and people will think a whole lot more of you than they do today."

Hanging around a bunch of kids no one else wanted? He had nothing to offer kids like that. He could think of a dozen ways he'd rather spend a Friday night, but the letters from his sponsors were serious business. He didn't care about being good, but he cared about his sponsors. He could go with Derrick once, couldn't he? Put in an appearance.

Bill was moving ahead, talking about the logistics. "I've already asked Derrick. He says you can join him, no problem. Once you commit, I'll tip off the media. Tell 'em if they want to see the real Aaron Hill, they can catch him by surprise at the Mission Youth Center."

"Won't they see through that?" Aaron didn't like the idea, but there was no other way. If the stunt was going to work to improve his image, then the media had to capture it.

"This city loves you, friend." He gave a wary laugh. "Even now. Give them a reason to catch you doing something good and it'll be front-page news. I promise."

Aaron didn't need long to think about it. He had no choice. "Fine. But just once. If I need a charity, it'll be something less personal, raising money for a Little League park, something like that." He raised one eyebrow. "Kid charities are for the married guys, right? That's what you always told me, right?"

"That was in your first few years." The lines at the corners of Bill's eyes looked deeper. "To be honest, you'd be better off meeting a nice girl and settling down. You stay single much longer and people will peg you a playboy. I told you that last year, remember?"

Bill was probably right. He usually was. The agent had been with Aaron from the beginning, back when he was a sophomore in college. Bill couldn't legally sign Aaron until after college, but he hung around, handing out free advice and connecting Aaron with the best trainers and dieticians and financial planners. His UCLA coach warned him about Bill and anyone else too anxious to step in and help Aaron make decisions. But by the time he graduated from UCLA, Bill was more a father to him than his own dad.

Which was why, when Amy called and said she was pregnant, Aaron talked to Bill first.

Good thing. Bill did some checking and found out Amy was seeing other guys on the side. Aaron was shocked, stunned. If Bill hadn't had exact times and places where she'd been, Aaron wouldn't have believed it. He had loved Amy, and the news crushed him as nothing else ever had.

Bill apologized for bringing the truth to light, but Aaron didn't fault him. In fact, after losing Amy, the hint of doubt Aaron had harbored about Bill and his motives disappeared. Aaron moved into his pro career trusting Bill Bond completely. Everything Bill said made sense. And Bill had a lot to say — especially about Aaron's private life.

"You're better off single," Bill had always told him. "More marketable. A relationship will threaten your role as America's heartthrob." And always he would add, "Whatever you do, Hill, don't get someone pregnant. It'd be a death knell to your image."

His agent doled out advice almost daily, and always it was intended to help Aaron some way. Bill looked out for him, and when he had an idea — - the way he often did — he talked about Aaron as if the two of them were a team. "We should think about that …" or "We would never consider such an offer." That sort of thing.

Now Aaron watched as Bill made a few quick phone calls, the tips to the media he'd promised. Bill would lay down his life for Aaron, no question. If he thought Aaron needed to spend a Friday night with Derrick Anderson and a gym full of foster kids, so be it.

Aaron stood and motioned to Bill that he had things to do. Before he left, he needed to check his locker. He was missing a pair of running shoes, and he had a feeling they were mixed with the junk at the bottom of his space.

The locker room was empty, everyone else enjoying the day off. Aaron hurried down the long aisle to his spot and opened the door. As he rummaged around, he felt the envelope—the letter from the foster kid. He pushed it toward the back. No time for fan mail today. He wanted to spend an hour in his pool and get his Hummer cleaned up. He had a date tonight with a French bikini model, the sort of girl he could picture himself settling down with. For a few months, anyway. Or maybe forever. Which wouldn't be the worst thing. Because maybe settling down would do the one thing seven years and a string of women had never quite been able to do.

Make him forget about Amy Briggs.

FIVE

Megan had been up since just after four that morning, but she wasn't tired. Today was Monday, and she had a shift at the youth center that afternoon. These were the best days of the week, the days she felt closest to God. On occasion, she read her worn-out Bible, the one that used to belong to her grandmother. From what she could gather, Jesus wanted people to serve. More than that, maybe the entire reason people were created was to serve. So the world would get a better picture of Jesus, the way He had worked when He was on earth.

Megan had known church kids when she was in high school. Mostly the kind that spent Wednesday nights at youth group and Friday nights slamming back a six-pack of Budweiser. Popular kids from the right families, kids who had convinced their teachers and parents that being part of a church meant they were the good kids. They stayed away from Megan because she didn't have the right clothes or the right home life. Not one ever tried to be her friend.

No, Jesus wouldn't have hung out in stuffy wooden pews with mostly hypocrites, reciting an hour's worth of songs and prayers once every Sunday. He would've been at the youth center, shooting hoops with the kids who didn't have anyone.

She finished her paper route and put in her time at the diner. Then she hurried home and ran up two flights of stairs to her apartment. She had thirty minutes to be at the youth center, where Cory had gone after school, just enough time to grab a yogurt and an apple. She rushed through the door and when she finished eating, she made a quick cup of coffee, poured it into her travel mug, and changed out of her uniform.

Cory hadn't stopped talking about the pizza party, of course. When he was home, he checked the answering machine three times an hour in case he might've missed a call from Aaron Hill. Megan almost wished the guy would call. Then, for all time, Cory could put aside the fantasy that the quarterback was his father.

She tucked a loose strand of hair behind her ears and ran down the stairs. She was five minutes later than usual, and she wanted to make up the time. Which she would. She was used to making up time. Her jobs kept her running, and today was no exception. She hurried out onto the street, and five blocks later she zipped down the stairs and bought a ticket to Mission 24th Street. Some days she walked the whole way, but not this afternoon.

The kids expected her at a certain time. They counted on her.

Megan liked taking the BART—the Bay Area Rapid Transit system. It gave her a few minutes to think about the day and the grant proposal she was working on. She pulled it from her bag and studied what she'd written so far. It started with the scenario of a fictional foster boy, the year after his eighteenth birthday. In a short sequence of events, the boy graduates from high school and learns there is no longer room for him at his foster home. Not long afterward, he's stealing from the cash drawer at a convenience store and being locked up for theft. When they let him out, he connects with a drug dealer, running deals, collecting cash.

The story was compelling, and Megan had a suspicion that if she could get the proposal into the hands of the right people, the grant money might actually become available. Maybe a person didn't need to be highly educated or famous or wealthy to ask for government funding. Maybe they only needed passion.

She tucked the papers into her bag and surveyed the other passengers. At the back of the car were a mother and daughter, both of them hollow-eyed and silent. The girl was maybe ten or eleven, and she had her head on her mother's shoulder. Megan didn't want to stare, but for a moment she was looking at herself, just as she had at the youth center, the way she looked the few times she was reunited with her mother during her childhood. The brief flashes when she'd been granted the privilege of laying her head on her mother's shoulder. Anyone who'd seen Megan back then would've known from her eyes what she was thinking. How, if only she could freeze time, she would never, ever leave her mama's side again.

Megan looked away. The car was slowing, coming to her stop. She stood quickly and was the first one off. Whatever the story between the mother and daughter, Megan didn't have time to stick around and find out. The city was full of sad stories.

She ran lightly up the stairs and down the sidewalk toward the center. The sidewalk teemed with people, folks of every color, size, and shape. San Francisco was a melting pot of nationalities. The shops along the way told the story. A Korean thrift store, a Chinese dry cleaner, a Vietnamese grocer.

Megan pushed open the door to the center and glanced into the gymnasium. Four older kids were playing Ping-Pong, but most of the regulars weren't here yet. She set her bag under the desk in the office and found her whistle, the one she wore when she worked the pickup games.

On the way into the gym, she spotted a kid sitting on the floor in the hallway, leaning against the brick wall. His knees were drawn up, his head down, resting on his forearms. Megan looked closer and recognized him. He was a stocky black kid, loud and cocksure, a junior football player in high school. He'd been placed in a group home a few months ago — an event that triggered trouble for many foster kids. Last she heard, the boy was on academic probation, his place on the football team in jeopardy.

A trio of teenagers entered the building and grinned at her. Megan returned the smile and waited until they moved on into the gym. Then she headed down the hall until she reached the boy on the floor. "Rudy?"

He didn't look up. "Leave me alone."

Megan dropped slowly onto the floor in front of the boy. She sat cross-legged and made her voice softer, gentler. "Can't do that, Rudy. You know me."

A sigh slid through what sounded like clenched teeth. "Doesn't matter."

These were the same things she heard over and over again at the center. *Doesn't matter ... leave me alone ...* Kids who weren't coping, kids already jaded and betrayed by the system. The future was crashing in all around these kids. Of course it mattered or Rudy wouldn't be here.

Megan wasn't in a hurry. "Is it school?"

He was silent.

Details came back to her, a conversation she'd had with one of the other volunteer counselors. "You had a big math test Friday, right?"

"Yeah." He looked up, his eyes distant and defiant. Fear was there too, the way it was for most foster kids. But like the others, Rudy was good at hiding fear. He exaggerated a shrug. "Left my math book on the kitchen table and one of the kids took it. Couldn't study without a book."

Megan winced. "How'd you do?"

Rudy clenched his jaw. "Failed it." Another shrug. "Who cares, man? What's it matter?"

"A lot, Larry. You're going to college, remember?"

"For what?" He narrowed his eyes and shook his head. "Man, you talked to Toby lately? Got hisself a scholarship until Christmas break. Then what? School closes and he winds up in a mission, mixing with the homeless." Rudy shrugged again. "Didn't go back, 'cause what's the point? He wasn't staying in no homeless shelter all summer, you know?"

Megan felt her heart breaking. This was the exact scenario that needed addressing. Why wasn't a counselor at the college made aware of the situation for foster kids? What would it take to give them year-round housing through college? She stifled her frustration. "You can't give up, Rudy. Education's the only way out of here. You know that."

They talked a few more minutes, and Megan patted his shoulder. "Bring your math test Wednesday. You and I are going over it one problem at a time. I'll call your teacher so you can take it over."

He lifted his eyes, apathy and doubt meeting in his expression. "Then what?"

"Then we spend a few minutes every day going over it until the semester's over and you have a grade you're proud of."

Rudy looked at the floor for a few seconds. "I saw my picture the other day."

"Your picture?" A surge of hope pulsed through Megan's veins. He was listening to her, and that was progress.

"Yeah." He narrowed his eyes. "On a photolisting."

He might as well have slipped a knife between her ribs. The photolisting was part of the state's adoption website. Rudy was among hundreds of kids listed with a photo and a short bio. Kids who were a stone's throw from adulthood, still waiting to be adopted. She resisted her desire to tell him the photolisting was a good thing, that an adoption could happen. He had a better chance of winning the lottery. Instead, she sighed and put her hand on his big worn-out Nikes.

"They got it all fancy and everything." He spoke through clenched teeth. "Says Rudy Booker's a friendly young man with great athletic ability and much potential. Rudy's still hoping that you'll be his forever family." He threw his hands up. "What a lie, huh?"

There was no clearing a path through the jungle of disappointment Rudy was venturing toward. Instead, Megan took a quick breath and smiled. "You got me, Rudy. Me and your math book, which you're bringing Wednesday." She stood and reached her hand out to him.

For a few seconds he hesitated, but then he clasped her hand and pulled himself slowly to his feet. "Still don't know why."

"'Cause I said so." She wasn't nearly as tall as him, but that didn't matter. Rudy was a kid, and he, like so many of the teenage foster children who acted tough, really wanted a parent figure. Megan wasn't nearly old enough to be Rudy's mother, but the years had given her a wisdom that belied her age.

Rudy must've sensed that, because he gave her a reluctant grin. "Fine. But don't be surprised if I show up at your door with my suitcase someday."

"Any time, Rudy." She stopped and faced him. She was too young to adopt him, but she would never stand by and let him fall through the cracks. Not as long as there was a spot on her sofa. "I mean it."

This was the part of her job Megan liked most of all. Learning about the kids who were about to become a statistic, and doing whatever she could to show them a way to succeed. A way to survive.

After an hour of heated pickup ball, Megan retreated to the lunchroom. She needed to call a couple social workers, and the youth center had a phone in the small eating area. Communication between the adults who cared for foster kids was crucial.

An old TV sat on a rickety stand at the corner of the room, tuned in to ESPN. As Megan sat down, the story on the set changed and Aaron Hill's face filled the left half of the screen. A concerned-looking anchorman announced that charges initially pressed against San Francisco's star player for the 49ers were no longer an issue. "Early today, the teenager who first reported sexual harassment by Hill withdrew her complaint. A statement, issued through her attorney, said the girl was confident she misunderstood Hill, his actions, and his motives." The anchor looked down at his notes. "In other NFL news ..."

The girl misunderstood him? Megan rolled her eyes and focused on the phone calls. She could only guess how much money Hill had paid for the misunderstanding to come to light. Stories like this about Aaron Hill were rare. Megan had only caught wind of an occasional tabloid headline where the quarterback had been seen at this bar or that party.

But the story wasn't a surprise.

Aaron Hill's arrogance shone through in every interview. He acted as if he were invincible, king of the world, an island. Rarely did he talk about his teammates or share the light with his supporting cast. He'd been careful with his reputation — or someone had carefully looked out for him. But that didn't change the guy's character. Megan was glad for Cory that Aaron Hill wasn't his father. The sooner Cory became convinced, the better.

As for the news, thanks to Mrs. Florentino, the story had slipped by without Cory noticing it. The woman down the hall had called Megan, concerned about the bad press surrounding Cory's hero. "I keep the paper tonight, yes?" she asked.

"Yes." Megan's heart warmed. The woman was beyond thoughtful. "You keep the paper. Thank you."

Megan finished her phone calls. One to a social worker about a teenage girl who'd come to the center last week with bruises on her arm. Megan had called the social worker the first time that same afternoon. Today the girl hadn't shown up, and Megan needed to talk to her social worker to hear the news.

"We moved her to a different foster home." The caseworker sounded encouraged. "Apparently she was sneaking out to meet her boyfriend, and last week they got into a fight. The guy's just a junior in high school, but already he has a history of abuse."

Megan was confused. "So they pulled her from her foster home?"

"No supervision. Something like this, we figure she needs a new environment." The social worker hesitated. "It wasn't a great match in the first place."

Megan wondered if she could add another sofa to her already crowded apartment. "Where is she today?"

"With a counselor. She's pretty upset."

The call ended with Megan more discouraged than ever. The girl gets abused and loses her foster family all in one week. Of course she was upset. Megan would make a point to pull her aside and talk to her when she returned to the center.

The second call was to Rudy Booker's social worker. Megan gave the man an update on the teenager and asked for the phone number of Rudy's school.

"I'll follow up on the math test." Megan found a pad of paper in her purse and jotted down the school's number. "I'm sure they'll let him take it again."

"Thank you." The man sighed. "I'll make a call too. But if you've got time to tutor him, that could make the difference."

"Yes." Megan looked out the door and into the adjacent gymnasium. Twenty-five kids were lined along the walls waiting for a turn on the court. "Sometimes the smallest things make the difference for these kids."

When she was finished, she hung up the phone and headed back to the gym. Cory met her in the hallway, his eyebrows raised high into his forehead. He still had his backpack slung over his shoulder.

"Any phone calls?" His eyes were so wide she could practically see the whites around them.

Megan wrapped her arm around his slim shoulders and pulled him close. "No."

Cory was antsy. He pulled back and searched her face. "Some kid told me Aaron Hill's in trouble with the police." Anger flashed in his eyes. "That's crazy, right?"

She wanted to be careful how she handled this one. Honesty was everything to kids like Cory. "The news said a girl accused Aaron of doing something wrong. But she changed her mind yesterday, so everything's okay."

Cory made a face. "Probably a Raider fan."

"Probably." Megan wanted to change the topic. "How was school?"

"I aced my spelling test." He stuck his chest out. "Mrs. West said she wouldn't be surprised if I'm the smartest boy in third grade."

"Of course." Megan's voice was ripe with teasing. "Look who's helping you with your homework."

"True." Cory hugged her again. "Hey, my bike got a flat tire. I walked it all the way up the last hill."

Megan thought about the money she didn't have. "I think there's a patch in one of the drawers in my office. Seems like someone donated a pack of patches a few months ago."

"So ... not a new tire?" Cory didn't look disappointed, just matter-of-fact. As if he wanted to be sure about his options.

"Nope, buddy. No new tire this year."

"Okay." He skipped ahead of her a few feet and then turned around. "Let's fix it later. The guys want you to ref the next game."

Megan laughed. "Last time they told me I need glasses."

"That's only 'cause they love you." Cory gave her a silly grin. "But I love you more, know why?"

This was the best part of her day, no question. The teasing and laughter she shared with Cory. Now if only he would let go of his insistence that Aaron Hill was his father. That way she could adopt him and he'd never again have to wonder where he belonged.

She played with the bill on his baseball cap. "Why do you love me more?"

"Because"—his eyes twinkled—"you're going to take me to Derrick Anderson's pizza party again this week." He folded his hands, his eyes pleading with her. "Please, Megan?"

The organizers of last week's party had already talked to her, and like before, she had promised that both she and Cory would help with cleanup. "Tell you what?" She took hold of both Cory's hands. "Every time Derrick Anderson has a pizza party at the youth center, you and I will go. I promise."

"Wow!" Cory's eyes lit up. "You're the best ever! I mean it." He began turning in a circle, still holding her hands until they were both dizzy. Then he threw his fists in the air and danced around. "I can't believe it!"

Megan watched him, and her heart filled with love. Sometimes Cory seemed so old for his age, so worldly and wise. He was only eight, but on his bike he could navigate through the roughest parts of the city, getting himself to and from school every day, and to soccer practice and home again. The vehicle code suggested an independent bicyclist should be eight or in third grade, which Cory was. More than that, he was savvy to bicycle safety, more than most older kids.

Here, though, his face filled with hope and wonder, the truth was very clear. Cory was still just a young boy, a child. Weekly dinners with one of the 49ers was a dream come true.

After he settled down and they were on their way into the gymnasium, Megan stopped him. "One thing though ..."

"What?" Cory was still buzzing with excitement. He bounced in place while he waited for her to continue.

"No more letters for Aaron Hill." She raised her eyebrows just a little. "Derrick Anderson's a good guy. He passed on your letter, I'm sure."

"But ..." Cory's face fell, "Aaron hasn't called."

Megan wasn't sure how to say this, but it had to be said. If not now, then later. "Cory ..." They were in the entryway into the gym, and she leaned against the doorway. The pickup game could wait. "What if Aaron isn't your dad? Remember, we talked about that."

A shocked look flashed in Cory's eyes. "But I told you ... " His tone was filled with hurt. "My mom said it was true, and my mom never lied to me. Not ever."

Great. Megan steadied herself. *Any ideas, God? I'm fresh out here.*

Do not worry, daughter ... every day has enough worry for itself.

The words seemed to come from somewhere deep inside her, but Megan had heard them before. They were from a Bible verse, something she'd read from one of the Gospels. She uttered a silent thanks to God. "You're right, Cory." She smiled at him. "Your mother would never lie." She put her arm around his shoulders again. "Let's not worry about it right now." The guys were picking teams on the other side of the gym. "We have a game to play."

For a few beats, Cory looked wary. As if he wanted to bring the subject up again. But Megan jogged with him over to the guys. The kids were a mix of ages and colors, both boys and girls. A few of the older kids had made sure the teams were fair, and for the next hour Megan did her best to officiate.

By the time the game was finished, Cory was himself again, but he didn't bring up Aaron Hill or the phone call that never came. Not that day or the next, or Saturday night when the 49ers played the Bears in the first preseason game. Aaron stayed on the field the entire first half until they were winning 21–0. Derrick played the second half and threw another three touchdowns.

Even then, Cory asked nothing about whether Aaron had called. Megan wasn't sure what to make of his silence. Most likely, he didn't want her to question the issue again. Whatever the reason, Cory believed with all his heart that his mother had told him Aaron Hill was his father. Even so, she hoped his silence on the issue might be a sign of something else. That no matter what he believed or even what his mother believed, the truth was clearer with every passing hour. Aaron Hill was a talented quarterback.

But he wasn't Cory's father.

SIX

D errick felt better than he had in years.

The last game was proof he wasn't past his prime, and though the starting job would of course go to Aaron, Derrick stood ready to fill in whenever needed. The newspapers shouted loud about his efforts, calling San Francisco the only two-quarterback show in the NFL. For a time, it had looked like Derrick might even get the start for the game against the Bears. But in the end, the front office made the call. Aaron was the franchise. One shady news story wouldn't put him on the bench.

All that and this: Aaron Hill was sitting shotgun in his Ford F–150, ready to spend an evening at the youth center. When he first found out from Coach that Aaron wanted to come along, Derrick almost laughed out loud. The idea couldn't have been Aaron's. Miracles didn't happen that fast.

"It's the girl, right?" Derrick had raised a wary eyebrow at Coach Cameron.

The man massaged his temples and frowned. "He needs a little good PR."

"So the press'll be there?" Derrick bristled at the idea. "This isn't about us, Coach. You know that."

He put up his hand. "The media wants in on anything Aaron does. I can't believe they'll send a camera crew. But a reporter or two are bound to show up for a slice of pizza."

Derrick choked back any further complaints. This was what he'd prayed for, that Aaron Hill might have a Friday night free to visit with foster kids. Anything to help him see past his own reflection in the mirror. However it had come about, Derrick had a feeling his teammate was bound to make progress tonight. The kids had that effect on everyone they met.

"That's it, right?" Jay Ryder was in the backseat. He leaned forward and pointed straight ahead. "The big brick building?"

"That's it." Derrick pulled into the parking lot, found a spot near the back of the lot, and cut his engine. He looked at his teammates. "There'll be a lot of kids tonight." His voice held the slightest warning. "Be patient. Most of them haven't ever been to something like this."

Jay got it. His expression said so. He gave a firm nod and climbed out of the truck. Then he heaved the oversized duffle bag over his shoulder. "That's a lot of water bottles and bumper stickers."

"T-shirts too." Derrick grinned as he stepped out. "Kids love T-shirts."

Aaron looked uncomfortable as he fell in next to Derrick. He looked at his watch. "So, what's the story? These kids are wards of the court, or homeless ... or what?"

Derrick stopped and stared at his teammate. "You're serious?"

"'Course I'm serious." Aaron looked embarrassed and irritated all at once. "I've been in a football uniform since ninth grade, Derrick. What do I know about this?"

No matter how far Aaron had to go, he needed to start somewhere. Derrick steadied himself and took a slow breath. "Foster kids don't have permanent families. Most of the time they were taken from their biological parents because of drugs or abandonment or criminal activity."

"That's where foster parents come in." Aaron nodded as if this was the part he understood. "They take care of the kids until someone adopts them." He hesitated. "Right?"

Derrick jerked his thumb toward the big brick building. "Ain't nobody gonna adopt the kids in that youth center. They're too old and too jaded. They've been passed from one foster home to another. We got thousands of them right here in San Francisco."

"I studied that in college." Jay moved closer, so the three formed a loose huddle. "People want to adopt babies, not middle-school kids." He stuck his hands in his pockets. "Makes me wonder ... I never woulda got here without my parents' support."

"Exactly." Derrick frowned at Aaron. "You understand a little better now?"

The walls in Aaron's eyes became a little thicker. "It isn't my thing, but yeah. I understand."

Derrick paused, but only for a moment. Then he looked past Aaron and started walking again. "All right, gentlemen. Let's go love up on some kids."

They moved into the building and the buzz through the gym was instant. Derrick had brought along two other players! Jay Ryder and ... and

Aaron Hill! Derrick waved at the kids as he directed his teammates to the front of the room. They set up near each other, so the kids could form one line and visit with each of the players all at once.

Just as the first kids reached the front of the line, Derrick remembered the boy's letter. He was sitting next to Aaron, and he nudged him. "Hey, what'd you do with that letter?"

Aaron leaned closer and held his hand up to his ear. The room was loud with the sound of excited kids.

Derrick raised his voice just enough to be heard. "The letter I gave you last week—what'd you do with it?"

The blank look on Aaron's face told the story. "Letter?"

"From the boy." Derrick scanned the room, but in a sea of kids, the freckle-faced boy with the big eyes didn't stand out. "I gave you a letter from a boy I met last week."

Aaron's expression changed. "Oh, that." He hesitated. "It's still in my locker."

A frustrated sigh forced its way through Derrick's lips. "If I see the boy, I'll tell you. At least you can fake it."

Aaron looked bored. "Whatever."

The kids were forming more of a mob than a line, and volunteers were trying to straighten them out. With that, the director of the center announced the players had arrived—in case anyone had missed their entrance—and they'd be meeting kids and signing autographs for the next couple hours. Pizza would be there in just a few minutes, and after dinner there would be another drawing.

A pair of little girls, clearly sisters, stepped forward. "Hi." The voice of the taller one was barely audible over the roar of the group.

Derrick reached out and took her hand. "Hi, I'm Derrick Anderson. What's your name?"

"Susie." The girl held tighter to the hand of her sister. "We love the 49ers."

"Yeah." The smaller one beamed a smile at Derrick and then at Jay and Aaron. "You guys are the best."

The three signed photos for her the girls, and as they walked off, Jay leaned in toward Derrick and Aaron. "This is amazing. I love it already."

Derrick felt his heart soar. He kept scanning the line, looking for the freckle-faced boy, so Aaron wouldn't be caught off guard. All the while, he couldn't help but think that finally ... finally he could feel God smiling down on him. Maybe the whole team really would get behind the idea of helping the foster kids in their city. No matter the deep pain of his past, Derrick had to believe God had a plan for his life.

And here, now, he could almost feel it taking shape.

⟶

Aaron was just getting the swing of interacting with the kids when he spotted her. Across the gym and a third of the way back, sitting by herself was a woman who took his breath. At first he looked away, focused his attention on the kids in front of him. After all, he was here because of his wandering eye for women. The last thing he needed was an infatuation over a foster kid volunteer.

But every few minutes, no matter how hard he tried, Aaron couldn't help but look. The woman had pale skin and striking features. Her dark hair shone in the light that still streamed through the side doors. All of that was nothing to the look in her eyes. She was talking to a thin black woman seated beside her, and all the while, her expression was strong and independent. He would never find someone like that in a bar or hanging around the player exit after a game.

She wasn't dressed flashy, and when she stood and went to the pizza line he got a better look. She wore jeans and a long-sleeved knit shirt, simple and subtle, but the strength and character she exuded stirred something inside him. Derrick had to elbow him to get his attention.

"Focus, will you?"

He stared at the woman once more. "Sorry."

Derrick followed his gaze and squinted. "That's her."

"Who?"

Jay was busy signing an autograph and chatting with a teenage boy, a football player. Derrick pointed to the woman. "Remember the kid with the letter? That's his mom."

"Oh." The feeling of disappointment was crazy. Of course she was married. A woman like that, someone would've fallen for her years ago. "So where's her husband?"

For the fifth time that night, Derrick gave him a look like he'd asked where to find a dress for next week's game. "Who said anything about a husband?"

Aaron ignored the comment and did his best to welcome the next child. A little boy, maybe four years old. "Hi, pal. How's it going?"

"Are you really Aaron Hill?" The tyke looked suspicious. "'Cause I thought you were taller. My foster dad says you're bigger than life."

A flash of pride swelled in Aaron's heart. He didn't want to be here, but the adoration wasn't a bad thing. "Tell him I said thanks, okay?"

He didn't want to connect with any of the kids, even the cute ones. Do the time and fix his image. That's all he wanted from tonight.

Aaron waited until the young boy had moved on to Jay. "You said she was the boy's mom. That must mean there's a dad, right?"

"Aaron, you're the dumbest quarterback I ever met." Derrick laughed under his breath. "She's his *foster* mom. I have no idea if she's married or not." A warning sounded in his tone. "I wouldn't worry about it. Get my drift?"

"I get it." Aaron held out his hand and shook the much smaller one of a quiet girl. He didn't like being reprimanded by Derrick Anderson. Guy was a do-gooder, worse than his reputation had it. He found a smile for the little girl. "Hi, I'm Aaron Hill ..."

Even as he welcomed the child, he caught another glimpse of the woman. What was it about her? The combination of strength and beauty. He didn't want to take her into the parking lot and kiss her. He wanted to meet her. Somehow he had an unexplainable sense that just talking to her, standing in her presence, would be an honor.

The line of kids was still halfway across the building, and finally an hour into it, after a pair of reporters and a photographer had come and gone, Derrick nudged him. "There he is. Five kids back." He nodded toward a boy with a 49ers baseball cap and a face full of freckles. "He's the one who gave me the letter."

"Perfect." Aaron felt his heart skip a beat. Ridiculous, he thought. He was Aaron Hill, most well-known football player in the country. Why was he getting nervous over meeting a grade-school kid? Even as the question passed through his mind, he knew the answer. It wasn't the boy who made him nervous, but the dark-haired beauty watching the child from a distance. She hadn't looked his way once, not that he'd seen. So she probably had no use for football players. That only made her twice as attractive. And if he was ever going to meet her, it would be because of how he handled himself in the next few minutes.

With a boy whose personal letter he hadn't even bothered to read.

———

Cory could barely stand still. The night was going better than he ever dreamed. And now ... now he finally knew why Aaron Hill hadn't called him. He'd decided to come to the center and meet Cory in person! Of course! It was a much better idea than a phone call.

He'd been helping Megan, setting up the last row of tables at the back of the gym when Derrick and Jay Ryder and Aaron walked in.

"Look!" He wasn't the only kid to react to the sight of three 49ers quarterbacks entering the gym.

Megan looked up and something changed in her eyes. "Hmmm. Aaron Hill."

"He came for me!" Cory felt his arms and legs start to shake. "Why else would he come?" He pounded out a little rhythm on the table. "Can you believe it?"

A tired expression came over Megan's face. "Help me with the rest of the chairs, okay? Then you can get in line with everyone else."

Cory helped with the chairs. He could hardly stand waiting, but he did it anyway. Because what was his rush? Cory's heart slammed hard against his shirt, lots harder than last time. Finally, the tables and chairs were where they needed to be and Megan told him he could go. "But don't say anything about the letter." Her look said she meant serious business. "I mean it, Cory. If he says something, fine. But leave it to him."

Her last words were barely out before Cory raced to the back of the line. That's where he stayed, inching forward a little more every minute or so, until now. Now, when there were just four kids left in front of him before it was his turn. He tried to look casual and normal, like any other boy.

But his armpits were sweaty and his eyes were stuck on Aaron Hill and no one else. He hadn't noticed it on TV before, but he and Aaron had the same nose. The exact same one. And the hair too. Cory's was a little blonder, but still ... they both had blond hair. And so, of course his mother was right all this time. Not that he was mad at Megan for not believing it. What foster kid wouldn't want Aaron Hill to be his dad? It was just that in his case, it was true.

Otherwise, Aaron wouldn't have read his letter and come tonight.

Three more kids and then it was his turn. The kids in front of him moved up a little, but before Cory could take a step, two sixth-grade boys slammed into the spot. They turned and made a face at him. The bigger of the two got close to Cory's face. "Don't say anything, punk. Not if you wanna make it to the front of the line alive."

Cory pushed the kid. "No cuts, loser." He wasn't afraid of the boys. The director already said no cuts, and he'd waited long enough to meet Aaron Hill. But the big kid meant what he said, and when he got his balance back, he grabbed Cory by the shirt and threw him onto the ground.

Kids came running up yelling, "Fight ... fight ... fight."

Even now Cory had no fear. The kid sat on him, pinning his stomach to the ground, but Cory kicked at his back. Just then a bunch of volunteers came rushing up and someone grabbed the kid off.

"That's enough from you boys." The director snarled her words at the big kid and at Cory too. "You boys will go sit at the back of the gym. No player meetings for you."

As she finished talking, Megan hurried over and put her hand on the director's arm. "I saw what happened. If you don't mind."

The director gave her a mean face. "I show no favoritism, Megan Gunn. Your boy was part of the scuffle. He has to follow the rules same as anyone else."

"I saw it too." The voice was familiar.

Cory looked up and his mouth hung open. It was Aaron Hill. His father had left his seat up front and come to his rescue!

"Those bigger guys cut in front." Aaron looked at the older guys. He smiled, but his voice was serious. "You shouldn't pick on kids smaller than you. Didn't anyone teach you that?"

The boys looked stunned too. Cory wanted to laugh. They probably never figured they'd be getting a talking-to from Aaron Hill before the night was over. The director had no choice now. She took a step back and pointed the older kids to the back of the gym. When they were gone, she looked at Cory. "Next time someone upsets you, tell a volunteer."

Cory wanted to say that telling a volunteer would never have worked. Because he woulda had to get out of line to tell someone, and then he wouldn't get his place back. Even if he was right. But he had the sense this wasn't the time to say that. Instead, he gulped and gave a quick nod. "Yes, ma'am."

"Very well." The director smiled at Aaron. "Thank you for stepping in."

The kids who had been in front of Cory were talking with Derrick and Jay Ryder. Megan put her hand on Cory's back and looked at Aaron. "Thank you." She sounded very professional. Not fun like usual. "Cory's waited ... a long time to talk to you."

"I know." Aaron put his hand on Cory's shoulder. "Last week he sent me a letter through my teammate Derrick."

If Cory could've frozen time, if he could've blinked and made all of life stop right at this very point, he would've. Because all his life he wondered what it would be like to feel his dad's touch. And now ... with all the kids racing through the gym and grabbing slices of pizza, he finally knew. Suddenly he realized what Aaron had said and he gasped. "You mean, you read it? I knew it!" He grinned at Megan. "I knew that's why he was here."

Aaron laughed, but not the sort of laugh like when something was funny. He faced Cory and held out his hand. "I'm Aaron Hill, Cory. Nice to meet you. Officially."

Officially. Cory liked that. He shook the man's hand and again he felt the connection, the feeling only a father could give. He returned the shake. "Nice to meet you." He wasn't sure what to call him. Maybe it was a little soon for "Dad." "Aaron" didn't sound exactly right either. Because no one called a father by his first name, right? So he didn't use any name at all, and that felt like a good decision.

Then, before he could ask Aaron what he thought of the letter or whether all the stuff inside was a total surprise or how long he had loved Cory's mother, Aaron Hill did a funny thing. He turned to Megan and held out his hand again. "You must be Cory's foster mom."

She took his hand, but she took a step back at the same time. And she released his fingers right away. "Nice to meet you, Mr. Hill."

"Aaron." He smiled. "You can call me Aaron."

"Very well." She angled her head. "Kicker, right?"

Cory couldn't believe his ears. Megan knew every player at every position on the 49ers. She'd been a fan even before Cory was born, that's what she said. So how come she was acting like she didn't know? Just then she gave him a look that was fast and clear. Whatever she was doing, he wasn't allowed to ask her about it. Not here and now.

"Uh..." Aaron did another soft laugh. "Actually, I'm the quarterback."

"Oh, right." Megan nodded. "You back up Derrick Anderson, right?"

Cory watched the conversation through wide eyes.

Aaron opened his mouth, probably to explain that it was the other way around. Because he was the starter, not Derrick. Then he smiled and nodded, real slow like. "Okay ... yeah."

Neither of them was making sense. Cory tapped on Aaron's arm, real polite like. "You coulda called me. I gave you the number at the bottom of the letter."

For a few seconds, Aaron looked confused. Then he crouched down so he was more at Cory's level. "I figured I'd see you here." He held up his hands. "And now it all worked out."

It all worked out? The room started to spin and Cory's whole mind raced like the hundred-yard dash. So he read the letter and he believed every word? It all worked out, meaning he was here to claim his role as Cory's father? Was that what he was saying?

The line was just about finished, and the remaining kids were all around Derrick and Jay. Cory had Aaron all to himself, but just then, the director asked for quiet because she had to do the drawings.

Aaron held up his finger. "Just a minute. This is my part." He jogged over to the director, and one at a time he picked five names. Five lucky kids. But Cory's name wasn't one of them. When Aaron was done, he came back and looked right at Cory. "You didn't win, huh?"

"No." Cory didn't want to sound sad. No one liked a spoilsport. That's what Megan always said. "I'll win one of these days." He said that because it was the right thing to say. But inside, he was hoping Aaron would have a different idea. Because he was Cory's dad, after all.

Aaron smiled at Megan. "How 'bout you two come to the next game as my guests? We're home against the Raiders a week from tomorrow."

"The Raiders?" Now Cory was sure he must've died and gone to heaven. Three weeks ago if someone would've told him he'd be standing in the youth center getting invited to the 49ers game against the Raiders by none other than Aaron Hill, he wouldn't have believed it. Not for a minute. His throat was dry, and he tried to swallow. "We'd love to." He turned a quick look to Megan. "Right?"

Megan looked only mildly interested. "I'm off that day." She shifted her attention to Aaron. "Thank you, Mr. Hill. How should we get the tickets?"

Cory couldn't understand why Megan wasn't being nice to Aaron. Maybe it was because of the adoption thing. She couldn't adopt him unless Aaron said it was okay. But all that was too much to think about right now. All that mattered was Aaron, here, right here where he was always supposed to be! He'd read the letter and now he wanted Cory and Megan to go to a game as his guests!

Aaron found one of the raffle tickets and turned it over. "Give me your address. I'll send the package overnight. You'll have it by Monday."

Megan didn't look happy, but she gave him their address. "We'll do our best to make it, Mr. Hill. Your offer's very kind."

Cory waited for Aaron to correct her. He already asked Megan to call him Aaron. But he only smiled at her. "After the game maybe we can go out for burgers."

Her look got a little stronger. "All this because you read Cory's letter?"

He looked a little embarrassed. "I guess it really touched me."

"Yeah." She thought about that for a few seconds. "That's what I figured." She nodded at him the way she looked at the cat when he missed the litter box. Then she took a step back. As she did, she took hold of Cory's arm and gently led him away from Aaron. "Cory has to help with cleanup."

For an instant, Cory thought Aaron was going to offer to help too, but just then Derrick and Jay Ryder came up. Aaron seemed to realize he wasn't here by himself, and that Cory and Megan weren't the only people in the room.

"Time to go." Derrick patted Aaron on the back. Then he waved at Cory. "Good to see you again."

"Thanks." Cory smiled at him and then at Jay. "I'm Cory." He held out his hand. "Nice to meet you."

"You too." Jay shook his hand. "Fun night, huh?"

Cory's heart was still doing somersaults. "The best ever!"

Aaron was looking at Megan and there was something funny in his eyes. "I'll be seeing you." He held one hand up toward Cory. "High five?"

Even though Megan still had hold of his arm, Cory stretched and high-fived Aaron. "See you next Saturday."

"See you then." Aaron smiled at him, but once more he looked at Megan. "I'm looking forward to it."

She nodded, more at Derrick and Jay than at Aaron. Then she turned Cory around and walked him to the kitchen. Cory waited until they were behind the swinging door before he tugged on her sleeve. "Megan?"

She groaned and he heard the tiredness in her voice. "What?"

"Why'd you ask if he was the kicker?" Cory was worried about her. If she was having trouble remembering that detail, maybe something was wrong with her brain.

She looked a little angry at first, but then that look went away and her face was soft again. "I was just playing around." She leaned in and kissed Cory's cheek. "It's good for big shots to be humbled once in a while." Megan kept on toward the double sinks. There weren't many dishes; pizza wasn't that messy. A few cutters and the salad forks and bowls from the serving table. That was all.

Cory tagged along behind, but he was confused. Making Aaron feel humble didn't seem like a very nice thing for Megan to do. "So, are you, like, you know, mad at Aaron for some reason?"

"No." She rolled up her sleeves and turned on the water. Then she looked at him. "I have my doubts about him, okay? That's all."

"Why would you have doubts?" Cory took his place next to her at the sink. He scooped up a handful of forks and put them in a bowl of sudsy hot water. "Aaron read my letter, he came here to meet me. And now he wants us to go to the Raiders game as his guests."

"I know." She sounded tired again. "I'm sorry, Cory. You're happy, I know that. I don't want to spoil your night."

"Good." He swished the forks around in the water. His voice got a little quieter. "My mom prayed about this night all my life. Ever since I was born." He stopped swishing. "That's what she told me."

Megan smiled. "Then I guess God answered her prayers."

Cory stared at the soapy water. He liked the way that sounded, and even more, he liked how it felt inside him. Because that's exactly what had happened. Two years after she died, God answered the prayer that mattered most in his mother's whole life. Now he only hoped that wherever she was in heaven, his mother was watching.

Because Cory had a feeling the answers had only just begun.

SEVEN

He hadn't read the letter; Megan was sure of that much. The nerve of the guy to show up and lie to Cory, and for what reason? If she didn't know better, she'd think he was hitting on her, that the whole invitation was more about that. Whatever it was, the lie made Megan furious.

That Monday she made sure she left with enough time to walk the whole way to Bob's Diner. She needed the fresh air to clear her head. The conflict between her real thoughts about Aaron Hill and the sheer adoration Cory had assigned the guy was driving her crazy. When Cory was home, all she could do was smile and nod and agree that Aaron was the greatest man ever. Why else would he have come to the pizza party?

But Megan saw through the guy from the beginning. If Aaron had read Cory's letter, if he knew Cory thought that Aaron was his father, he wouldn't have made a casual appearance at a pizza party, talking about how Cory's letter had touched him. Rather, he'd be panicking. He would've either ripped up the letter and never given it another thought. Or he would've called and tried to clear up the whole mess. At the very least, he would've pulled Megan aside and explained how Cory's beliefs were mistaken. Instead, he said nothing about it, which could only mean one thing. He hadn't read the letter.

Megan dodged a group of people gathered outside a liquor store.

"Hey pretty lady," one of them called out.

Megan ignored the comment. The city didn't scare her. She delivered papers before dawn. She knew her way around every bad alley and gang territory. A couple of catcalls from a bunch of winos weren't going to make her skip a step.

So had Aaron actually been interested in her? The idea was ridiculous, but why else would he pick the two of them to be his guests? She slowed her pace. Guilt maybe. He might've been feeling badly about not reading Cory's letter. Still, the way he'd watched her all night made her suspicious. Then, when Cory had the run-in with the older kids, Aaron stepped up and seized the moment. Rescuing Cory from punishment and meeting her all at the same time.

Now Cory was absolutely certain that the invitation meant Aaron was claiming his role as Cory's father.

Megan had ten minutes and only two blocks left. She stared up between the buildings toward the blue sky beyond. *God, I don't get it. If Amy prayed about Cory meeting Aaron Hill, why didn't she tell me? Cory must have his facts wrong. He must. He was only six when Amy died.*

She kept to the outer edge of the sidewalk. Fewer pedestrians to veer around. *So we go to the game and then what? Should I pull Aaron aside and tell him the content of the letter? Or just let him stumble along until Cory says something?*

Her heart felt a wave of peace as she silently voiced her concerns to God. He was her Savior and her friend. He listened whenever she had things to work through. *Thanks for being there, God. I need Your help on this one. I can't stand by and watch Cory get hurt.*

There was no answer this time, no Scripture that came to mind. But a sense of God's bigness came over her. She would stay quiet and let the details play out at this week's game. God would take care of the details because He cared deeply for each child.

Including Cory Briggs.

Megan's work at the youth center that afternoon put her emotions on a rollercoaster. There was the success of helping Rudy Booker study for his math test retake, and knowing he was ready to ace it first thing tomorrow morning. Then came the breakdown by the bruised teenage girl, as she told Megan about the difficulty in transitioning to her new foster home.

"I don't want to be a boarder," she admitted, tears streaming down her cheeks. "I want someone to love me."

"God loves you, sweetheart. He has plans for you, even if they're hard to see right now." Megan whispered her response. If the legislators could see this, foster reform would be a cinch. Megan sighed. She pulled the girl into an embrace and let her cry.

On the way home, Cory was quieter than usual, and even now with dinner over and the dishes nearly done, Megan could feel a tension between them. Normally Cory would help with the cleanup, but he had homework. Megan didn't mind. She was still thinking about Aaron Hill and his motives.

She wasn't interested in Aaron Hill, no matter what he had in mind. In high school she'd dated a guy from a wealthy family, and in the end she'd walked away more jaded and independent than before. Society had drawn lines and Megan understood her place. Pro football players didn't date women on food stamps.

Not that it mattered. Megan had no interest in committing her heart to a quality guy, let alone a playboy like Aaron Hill. Even if he lived in Nob Hill.

Bottom line, on Saturday the delusions Cory was carrying around were going to come crashing down around him. Because Aaron Hill wasn't Cory's father, and she wasn't interested in dating him. So this Saturday would likely be the last time Aaron would invite the two of them to be his guests at a 49ers game.

She thought about her high-school romance again. Her life had never been normal, not in the way it was for other girls her age. Now she was twenty-five, and nothing scared her more than the idea of relying on someone else.

Even the right guy.

The dishes were finished, so Megan dried her hands. She wandered into Cory's room and found him sitting on the floor near his bed, working on math. He didn't look up as she approached, and Megan was worried. Maybe her skepticism was seeping through, troubling Cory more than she'd realized.

"Hey, buddy." She sat on the edge of his twin bed. "Whatcha doing?"

"Times tables. Fours and fives."

Oreo walked into the room, meowed, and came to Cory. "Good boy." Cory patted his black and gray face. "You're a good friend." The cat curled up on the other side of Cory.

Megan smiled at the picture they made together. She pointed to the math paper. "You can count by fives, right?" She put her hand on his head and softly twirled a piece of his hair.

"Five, ten, fifteen, twenty, twenty-five, thirty ..." Cory looked up at her. "Yeah, I can do that."

"Then you know your fives times tables. Five times three, count three fives. Five, ten, fifteen." She held up her hands and smiled. "See? Three times five is fifteen."

The corners of his lips lifted a little. "Hey, that's cool. I get it." He thought for a bit. "Six times five, count it six times. Five, ten, fifteen, twenty, twenty-five, thirty! Six times five is thirty."

"Right." She brought her hand back to her side. "You're a good boy, Cory. I'm happy for you. About the game this Saturday."

"Really?" He wrinkled his nose and looked at her. "You don't seem like it."

She slid down onto the floor beside him. "I'm sorry." She took hold of his hand. "I don't want you to get hurt, that's all."

"I won't get hurt. I can't." Cory smiled at her as if he were the caring parent, trying to comfort *her*. "Aaron asked us to be his guests so he could talk to us about what happens next."

Megan kept herself from any show of disbelief. "And what do you think will happen next?"

"Well, that's what I'm thinking about." He drew a small football on the corner of his math paper. "'Cause if he wants me to come live with him"—Cory looked up, his eyes glistening—"then what about you, Megan? You're all the family I have."

Never mind that the idea of Aaron Hill asking Cory to live with him would never happen. The dilemma was a real one for Cory. Megan squeezed his hands twice, their sign for "Love you." She kept her tone even. "Don't you think Aaron would know that? How I'm the only family you have?"

"Yeah, but ..." Cory bit his lip. "I always wanted my dad too. So I don't know what to do or who to live with. You know?"

Megan closed her eyes. *God, are You catching this?* She held her breath and then let it out slowly through her tight lips. All of a sudden she remembered the verse from the last time she didn't know how to answer Cory. She opened her eyes. "Remember how we talked about not worrying about anything more than we can handle in any one day?"

"Yeah." Cory didn't sound sure. "What does that mean for today?"

"Well..." Megan pulled Cory's math paper a little closer. "It means today we work on times tables. And Aaron Hill can wait till Saturday."

Cory nodded. He still had his hand in hers. "Can I tell you something, Megan?"

"What?" She felt her heart breaking over the child's angst.

"I love you."

Megan understood. This was his way of saying he was still worried about whatever might happen Saturday, but for her sake, he wouldn't talk about it right now. Not more than to simply let her know what was in his heart. "I love you too."

For now, that was all that mattered.

EIGHT

They were running forties when Derrick felt a snap in his right knee. Like a sudden wild fire, the pain exploded through his leg and up into his gut. He fell to the ground as a rush of legs passed him in a blur, and from somewhere near the middle of the field he heard a whistle.

"Stop. Everyone stop!" It was Coach Cameron.

No, God ... not now. Please...

Coach was coming closer. He was a big guy, a former tackle, and he didn't so much run as waddle toward Derrick. At the same time, Jay Ryder was at Derrick's side, kneeling beside him. "What happened, man? What is it?"

"Nothing." Derrick grimaced and held his knee, gripping it, willing the pain to subside. Even so, he couldn't say the words, couldn't articulate that the worst possible scenario was playing out. His right knee already bore scars on both sides from those times when a surgeon put back together what a linebacker had dismantled.

"One more injury to that knee and you're done," the doctor had told him last time.

So this couldn't be it, not here at the beginning of his last season. He released his knee and sat upright. By then, Aaron Hill and a few other guys were making their way slowly back to him.

Coach Cameron reached him, huffing hard, his face creased with concern. "What happened, Anderson, talk to me."

"I ... I took a wrong step." He felt the sweat beading up on his forehead, felt the nausea that came with the worst injuries. But he wasn't giving in to it, not this time. He straightened his legs out in front of himself. "It's nothing." He ordered his lips to lift just enough for the slightest smile. "Really, Coach. I promise. Give me a few seconds."

Doubt flickered in the coach's eyes, but he gritted his teeth and took a step back. He waved at the others. "Keep running!"

Derrick leaned back on his hands and nodded to one of the trainers. "I'm fine, man. Really. Go on."

Aaron watched from his place in line, but when their eyes met, he looked away. Even in the midst of a series of pain waves that took his breath, Derrick felt his frustration rise. Aaron had kept his distance since the pizza party, and once Derrick overheard him talking to a receiver about some hot brunette he'd met at the event. If that's all he got from the outing, then where Aaron Hill was concerned, Derrick still had his work cut out for him.

Looking reluctant, Jay stood and joined Aaron. The two walked off, and Derrick stared at his right leg. *Come on, God ... let me move it. Please.* He focused all his energy on the knee and then bent his leg and straightened it again. It hurt like crazy, but his ligaments weren't torn. The injury was nothing like the two others that had sent him to the hospital—one during his third year in the NFL, and the other on the eve of his ten-year anniversary in the league. He'd been playing seventeen years now. Seventeen years. He knew better than anyone what his body was capable of.

The late afternoon sun beat down on his shoulders, adding to the sick feeling in his stomach. *You can do this, Anderson. Get up.* He pulled his good leg underneath himself, and with all his weight on that foot, he stood. The blood pounded through his injured leg, a half second slower than the pounding in his heart. *Please, God...*

He looked across the practice field at the team. Everyone taking long swigs from their water bottles between their sprints. Off to one side, the coaches were gathered, talking, watching him. They'd paid a big chunk to get Derrick Anderson as their backup quarterback. So was this it? Was he through? Even from half a football field away, Derrick knew what they were saying.

Derrick still stood on just his left foot. The weight of his dangling right foot put pressure on his knee, as if his foot were being stretched away from his leg by some sort of mechanical vice grip. He rested his toes on the grass. How did it happen, anyway? They were running forty-yard dashes. The most basic drill in all of football.

The guys were starting their last set, so it was now or never. He was going to make his knee work, whatever the pain. The first few steps he stayed light on his right foot. The pain radiated out from his knee with any bit of weight, but it was a pain he could tolerate. Nothing was ripped or torn or broken.

Derrick was convinced. One foot in front of the other, he moved toward the team and took the last twenty yards at a jog. No wincing, no tears. Nothing but forward movement.

Coach Cameron met him first. He stared at Derrick's knee and then into his eyes. "You feel as good as you look?"

"I'm fine." He ran a few steps in place. The pain throbbed through his body, but he could tolerate pain. He was a pro football player. The only question was whether the knee would hold him up, and it was. It would.

"Okay…" Coach raised his voice. "But get it checked out today." He gave Derrick a final wary look, then turned his attention to the team. "Let's line up … same groups."

Derrick's group was last, and he was glad for every minute of the break.

The quarterbacks ran in the same group with the kickers. They had four groups before it was their turn. Aaron came up beside him. "You okay?" His tone wasn't exactly friendly, but his interest seemed genuine.

"What's this? Aaron Hill gone soft?" Derrick laughed, and the release felt good. It was better than screaming.

"Never." He gave Derrick's shoulder a shove. "I want you at the top of your game, that's all." They were stepping up to the line, waiting for the whistle. Aaron winked at him. "Someone's got to push me."

The whistle blew and the group was off. The pain took Derrick's breath, but he could still run. He finished middle of the pack and then jogged off to the sidelines for a drink. His season was still intact. If he had to play the next four months with pain in his knee, he would do it. Because this was his last chance. God had brought him here for a dozen reasons — but none of them would take place if he was on crutches.

Practice was long that day, and even without the injury Derrick would've felt the drain of it. That's not what he was thinking about, though. For the past two weeks, with his family gone to Southern California, he'd come home from practice, sat in the hot tub for an hour, and then watched Sports Center while he stretched on the living room floor. Then he'd eat chicken and vegetables and hit the sack.

But not tonight.

⟻

Derrick pulled his Ford into the driveway of his hillside home. He'd been looking forward to this moment all day. His family had flown in during practice, and tonight he would see them for the first time in way too long. He babied his right leg as he swung his bag over his shoulder and headed for the front door. But before he could reach it, the screen swung open.

"Dad!" Larry, the oldest of his kids at almost sixteen, flew through the doorway, his arms outstretched.

Derrick braced himself and caught the boy in a full embrace. "Mmmm, you don't know how good this feels." He pulled back and put his hands on his son's shoulders. "Look at you! You're an inch taller!"

"Really?" Larry straightened himself. "Mom measured me. I'm almost six foot."

Before Derrick could respond, the door opened again. His thirteen-year-old twins, Lonnie and Libby, came bursting out at the same time. There were more hugs and joyful shouts as the kids celebrated the fact that they were all together again. As they headed into the house, Libby circled her arm around his waist. "I met a boy at our hotel, Daddy."

Derrick raised his eyebrows at her. "You're thirteen, young lady."

"Yeah, and the guy was seventeen." Larry rolled his eyes. "He barely noticed she was alive."

Relief eased his fears. He grinned at his daughter. "You trying to give me a heart attack, or what?"

Libby batted her eyelashes at him. "He was cute, that's all."

"Cute boys can wait." Derrick kissed the top of her head. "Till you're thirty-five or so."

"Daaaaddy." Libby giggled. She was straightening her hair now, and the little-girl look he so dearly loved had been replaced by a beauty that hinted at the way she would look as a woman. She stood on her tiptoes and whispered near his ear. "Mom can't wait to see you. She bought a new pair of pants just for you."

Butterflies danced around Derrick's heart, and he realized in the rush of emotions that his knee didn't hurt as bad as before. The pain would probably be gone in a few days. He caught a glimpse of blue sky as he walked into the house. *Thank You, God ... for all of this, and my knee too. Thank You.*

They walked straight to the kitchen, and there she was. Denae. The love of his life. She was tall and shapely, not one of those skinny women who usually made up the group of players' wives. Denae carried a little extra on her hips, but the curves only made her more beautiful. She wore a pair of black slacks that flared out at her ankles. The moment she saw him, her eyes lit up. "Derrick, baby ..." She had a dishtowel in her hands, and she tossed it on the counter.

"Denae ..." He caught her in his arms and held her close to his chest. "I missed you, honey. So bad."

She nuzzled against his neck. "That's too long, Derrick. The last few days I almost jumped on a plane and came home early."

He took a step back and surveyed her. "The pants are sexy."

"Just for you." She struck a pose, and the look in her eyes said more than her words. She took hold of his hands and pulled him close again. "Mmhmm. You're a sight, Derrick Anderson. I never get tired of looking at you."

"Mmmm." He rocked her gently one way and then the other. "Nothing was the same with you gone." He took a long sniff. "The house hasn't smelled this good since you left."

Denae flashed him a satisfied look. "The kids and I are making your favorite lasagna." She picked up the spatula from the counter and held it in the air. "Right, kids?"

"Homemade noodles and everything." Libby skittered past them and opened the oven door. The casserole inside looked like something from a magazine cover. "See, Daddy? Isn't it perfect?"

"It is!" He stretched out his arms and shifted his weight. A pain shot through his knee, but he ignored it. He looked behind him at Larry and Lonnie, and then at his girls. "C'mere you guys. You don't know how glad I am to see you."

The excitement created a buzz that stayed with them through dinner. The lasagna was the best he'd ever had. Or maybe it just tasted that way since it felt so right to have his family home again. Halfway through the meal, Denae asked about the milk, but Lonnie made a sheepish face. "Sorry, Mom. I left it in the kitchen."

"I'll get it." Derrick was used to helping out during the meal. If he was serving his family, he was loving them. His mama had taught him that, and she was right. But not until he pushed back his chair and tried to stand did he remember about his knee. He took a stutter step, and then settled into a more natural rhythm.

When he returned with the milk, Denae had one eyebrow raised. "Thank you, Derrick." Her look said she was on to him, on to the fact that he'd hurt himself.

Derrick smiled and did a light shake of his head, telling her not to worry, he was fine. The silent, subtle communication between them was something else he loved. How they knew each other as well as they knew themselves.

When the boys were finished with their third servings of lasagna, Larry pushed his chair back and faced Derrick. "We have two-a-days all this week. Can you believe it?"

Two-a-days. Derrick could remember when he was in high school and the team would hold practice twice a day for a week. He and his teammates thought it was such a big deal, working out that long. It always felt something like boot camp. And now his oldest son would have his first chance at the experience. He grinned at the boy. "You excited?"

"So excited, Dad. Coach says I'll be a starter on the freshman team, for sure." His eyes danced. "And if I tear it up, I might have a shot at varsity."

Derrick exchanged a high five with his son. "That's my boy."

"I prayed about it." His look grew more subdued. "If God wants me on the freshman team all year, that's fine. Wherever I can do the best for the team."

Emotion welled in Derrick's throat. That he was living his dream, still playing football after seventeen years in the NFL, that he had a family others only dreamed of having—all of that was enough to drop him to his knees each night in gratitude to God. But this ... the faith of his oldest son ... overwhelmed him. At a time when other kids were experimenting with dope and drinking, Larry was asking God to place him where he could do his best work for the team.

Derrick reached over and gave his son's knee a squeeze. "Keep that attitude, son. In the end, that's all that matters."

Larry shrugged, as if there couldn't possibly be any other way to think about life. "Like you always say, it's how we live our lives between Sundays that really matters." A mischievous look came over him. "Speaking of which, could me and Lonnie come to practice this week? When I'm home from two-a-days?"

"Please, Dad?" Lonnie had been quiet, wolfing down one piece of lasagna after another. The boy was going to be six-five if his appetite was any indication.

"Sure." Derrick shot a questioning look at his wife. "If it's okay with your mom?"

"It's fine." She waved her fork in the air in mock frustration. "Not like I have any say in the matter. I wanted them to play the piano, march in the band." She made a dramatic roll of her eyes. "But no ... not for my boys. Football and only football."

"And shopping?" Libby turned a hopeful smile at her mother. "Since school's almost here, and since the boys'll be busy?"

"You can roll your eyes at football," Derrick chuckled in the direction of his wife, "but you two have turned shopping into a full-contact sport." He winked at her. "I guess that makes us even."

The conversation continued, the good feelings of the homecoming coloring everything about the evening. Not until the children were out back, Libby on the phone to one of her girlfriends, and Lonnie and Larry tossing a football, did Derrick carry a load of dishes into the kitchen and find Denae watching him.

She put her hands on her hips. "How'd you hurt it?"

He stopped, his expression as innocent as he could make it. "Hurt what?"

"Your right knee." She motioned for him to come closer. "Come on, lift up the sweat pants. Let me see the swelling."

His shoulders slumped forward and a defeated chuckle sounded in his throat. "Good thing I don't have much to hide." He came to her and pulled up his pant leg. "You see right through me every time."

Denae stooped down. She touched her fingertips to the swelling on either side of his kneecap. "Derrick, look at that." She stood and stared straight at him. "How'd it happen?"

He tried to minimize the situation. "Simple sprints. Something popped, but I wasn't down more than a minute or so." He let his sweat pants fall back down again. "I'm fine."

"Fine." She tossed her hands in the air. "How many times have I heard that, Derrick." She mumbled something under her breath. "You need to have it checked."

"Baby, listen." His lighthearted attitude was gone. "I did. X-ray's fine." He needed her on his side if he was going to get through this season. He put his hand on her shoulder and looked deep, all the way to the center of her heart.

Something in her expression softened. "Okay." She worked her arms around his waist, and tenderly, with all the love the years had built between them, she kissed him. When she eased back, a shadow fell over her eyes. "Does it hurt?"

He could be honest with her. Slowly he nodded, never breaking eye contact. "Bad." He clenched his jaw, warding off the pain and disappointment at the same time. "But I can play on it, Denae. I know I can. God's gonna get me through this one last season."

She searched his heart, his soul. "You don't have to make good on the promise, baby." She pressed her face against his chest. "He would understand. You know he would."

A sea of sorrow welled inside him, but he swallowed it, held it at bay. "If I have anything to say about it ... I'll keep every word." He kissed her this time. "It's now or never."

The voices of their children outside drifted through the open kitchen window, mingling with the smell of late summer, hydrangea and honeysuckle. Derrick smiled, but he could feel his chin quiver. "You have to believe, baby."

She breathed in slow through her nose. "I do." Her eyes closed and she held him tight, clinging to him. "I believe with everything I am, Derrick."

For a long while, they stayed that way, swaying to the sounds of the children they loved so dearly. Sounds that wouldn't be around forever. Life had already given them proof of that much. When finally he took a step back, he grinned at her, finding the light and happy mood from earlier. "Now let's say we get some dishes done."

"No." Her eyes were still soft, still full of a love that knew no limits. "Go sit down and put your leg up. I'll bring you an ice pack."

He was about to protest, but her look stopped him. "All right." He blew her a kiss, and moved into their bedroom for a sweatshirt. That way he could sit out on the upstairs deck, the one that offered a panoramic view of the San Francisco Bay, and not feel too chilled.

As he walked into the room, his eyes fell on his family's picture, the one framed on the wall next to the closet, from six years ago.

Derrick slowed his steps, and as he reached the picture, he studied the faces. He and Denae, in love with all the world ahead of them. Their eyes told the story, really. Confident and full of joy. As if nothing in the world could dampen the happiness surrounding them. The relaxed look of untested people.

His eyes drifted down along the faces of his children. Nine-year-old Larry, straight and proud beside him, and the twins, just seven, standing in front of their mama. And in the middle, eyes bright with innocence, was five-year-old Lee.

Forever five.

With the softest touch, Derrick brushed his thumb along the image of Lee's arm, his face. "I miss you, son." His words were a pained whisper. He closed his eyes, and for a minute he was back again, back at the hospital holding his son's hand for the last time.

"You're gonna … win it all, Daddy! The … Super Bowl." His words were scratchy and strained, his eyes barely able to stay open.

This had been the running talk between him and Lee. Derrick had a Super Bowl ring for Larry and another for Lonnie. Now he needed one for Lee. Derrick couldn't see for the tears flooding his eyes. "Okay, little man. I'll win it all."

"For me." His breathing was labored, shallow and weak. "Win it … for me, Daddy. Like … we talked about."

"I will, baby. I promise."

"Daddy…" Lee's eyes opened once more, one final time. He looked like an angel, his eyes bright with childlike love. He patted Derrick's hand, soft and tender. "You're my best … friend."

The memory lifted and Derrick opened his eyes. That single promise had stayed with him every year, every spring training, and every summer camp. At the middle of every huddle, in the midst of every play, every game, he carried the promise in his heart. *Win it for me, Daddy.*

No one knew how hard he'd tried, but every year his teams had come up a few plays short, a few wins shy of the title. The well ran dry in Chicago, and this past February he and his agent talked about it.

"Maybe it's time to hang it up, Derrick. Go out standing tall." His agent was a good guy, one of the last in the business. Not once did he make a deal unless it was right for Derrick, whether it was good for the agency or not.

But all Derrick could see were Lee's eyes and the way he looked in the hospital bed that October day, an hour before he died. "No." He worked the muscles in his jaw and gave a strong shake of his head. "I wanna play. One more season." His look pleaded with his agent. "Find me the right team, man. I gotta win it all. One more time."

Derrick ran his thumb over the framed photo again. His agent had settled on the 49ers. The big game had eluded them long enough, he said. "You might be the missing factor, Derrick."

"How do you figure?" Derrick wasn't convinced about San Francisco. There were other teams more likely to win a Super Bowl—teams like Indianapolis or New England.

"Because ..." His agent smiled a knowing sort of smile. "You're a champion. You know how to be a champion." He wagged a finger in the air. "If you can teach that to Aaron Hill, the 49ers will be unstoppable."

Derrick took a step back from the photograph. He walked into his closet and grabbed the first sweatshirt on a stack halfway up a row of shelves. He slipped it on and went out through the patio slider on the far side of the room. The kids were still playing outside, grabbing at every last minute of sunlight. He sat down and gingerly lifted his right leg onto the footstool.

They'd won their first preseason game, but what would happen from here on? Especially if Aaron needed backup? As if in answer, Derrick's knee throbbed with every heartbeat. Here in this moment, futility breathed its hot breath on him. He could hardly picture winning a league game, let alone a Super Bowl. Doubts crowded him like so many cold shadows. He was a thirty-nine-year-old man with a bum knee. What could he possibly teach Aaron Hill about becoming a champion? And how—short of a miracle—could he keep his promise to Lee in this, his final season?

Derrick drank in a long gulp of fresh air and lifted his face to the sky. *I have nothing to offer, Lord. Nothing that'll make a difference this season. But You've got my little boy, Father. And You know the promise I made him.* He blinked back tears, just as a breeze drifted over him. It stung at his eyes, and he squinted. *I want to win it for him, Lord. So bad. So very bad.*

My son, when you are weak ... then I am strong.

Almost as if they were carried on the wind, the words spoke to his soul, calming him, assuring him. The verse was engraved on a wooden plaque that hung in the hallway near the boys' bedrooms. It was something he talked about with his kids often. How they shouldn't fear weakness, because only in the impossible moments could God truly show His power.

Suddenly he was overwhelmed with a sense of hope and direction, determination and courage. He wouldn't let an injury discourage him for all the games yet ahead. The season hadn't even officially begun. He sat up straighter in his chair. He would help his team, if it took everything he had. Somehow, he would help them, and in the end his efforts would make all the difference. He could feel it in his aching bones. God shone best in impossible moments, right?

Derrick ran his fingers gently over his right knee. It was one more thing the Lord wanted to teach him through the coming season. Learning how to be weak, so that God could be strong.

Because as moments went, the idea of an old man with a bum knee helping a team win the Super Bowl was about as impossible as it could get.

NINE

C ory watched out the window of their apartment, looking for the cab.
Megan didn't want to take BART today. Sometimes it got too crowded
on game days, and this was a big game—preseason or not. Every time San
Francisco played the Raiders, it was a big game. So all week she'd been saving
her tips, putting a little extra aside. That way they'd have money for a cab,
which was really special.

Only here was the weird thing. Aaron didn't come to the pizza party last
night. Cory got there early and so did Megan, and they waited. Because what
was taking Aaron so long to talk about being a dad? He hadn't called, so all
week Cory figured he'd see Aaron at the youth center. Derrick was there, Jay
Ryder too. But no Aaron.

Cory waited his turn for Derrick. The lines were shorter every week,
since kids were getting used to the idea of Derrick Anderson. When Cory
was next, he stuck his hands in the pockets of his jeans and lifted one shoulder a few times. "Aaron didn't come?"

"No." Derrick looked sad at this. "He had other plans."

"Oh." Cory's eyes fell to the floor for a few seconds. When he looked up,
he tried to sound hopeful. "Maybe he's getting ready for tomorrow."

"Tomorrow?"

"We're his guests for the Raiders game." The words felt good to say. "He
read the letter I gave him. That's why." He didn't want to say too much.

Derrick patted Cory's arm. "Maybe that's it, then. Maybe he's getting
ready."

"You're gonna win tomorrow, right?"

"Of course."

The conversation stayed with Cory all night and into this morning, but
the part about Aaron didn't really make sense. What would he need to do to
get ready? After the game they were going out for burgers. So why would that

make him busy on a Friday night. He talked to Megan about it when they walked home, but just a little.

"He probably had a hot date." She laughed and took a few running steps ahead of him. "Come on, race you to the top of the hill."

Megan was always doing that, changing the subject when the subject was Aaron. Cory still wasn't sure why. She had to believe that Aaron was his father now. Otherwise, he never would've come to the youth center last week, and he wouldn't have invited them to be his guests. Her doubts made him mad, so he didn't bring up Aaron again last night.

"Cory? Any sign of the cab?" She was in the bathroom, doing something with her hair.

"Not yet." He planted his elbows on the windowsill and stared down the street in either direction as far as he could see. "You almost ready?"

"Almost."

Cory thought about wearing his Aaron Hill jersey, but he changed his mind at the last minute. First, he didn't want Megan saying anything about how he was trying too hard. And second, that was his special jersey. The one he slept in. He couldn't risk spilling mustard or Coke on it. Instead he wore the new 49ers T-shirt, the one he got in the drawing yesterday. That and his old faithful San Francisco baseball cap.

A yellow cab pulled up out front, and Cory jumped off the couch. "It's here. The cab's here!"

Megan stepped out of the bathroom, and for a minute Cory felt like he was seeing her for the first time. She wore a white shirt and jeans, but she had some of her hair pulled back. The rest was curlier than usual. Plus she had a little eye makeup on. At least it looked that way. "Wow." He whistled at her. "You look pretty."

"It's a big day for us." She took her bag from the table and held her hand out to him. "I've wanted to see a game in person forever. Just like you."

Cory took her hand and they hurried out the apartment and down the stairs, 'cause the elevator was still on the fritz. He couldn't help but think as they jogged out onto the street that maybe some of the reason why Megan looked pretty was because of Aaron. The way he'd looked at her that night a week ago at the pizza party.

But he said nothing. Instead, he took his seat, his heart pounding, and fastened his belt. The trip into the stadium was like the beginning of an adventure. He didn't want to miss a minute of it. They drove down a few streets and up a few more, and then they turned onto a freeway, and then another freeway, and finally they got off at a street right next to the water.

Cory checked the sign and it said Gilman Avenue, Monster Park. 'Cause that's what some people called it now, but not faithful fans like Megan and him. Candlestick. That's what it was, and that's what it would always be. The cab driver stayed on Gilman down toward the water and around the lower parking lots. Then he circled up and suddenly all the cars stopped. From every direction, cars were coming toward the stadium, hundreds of them. Maybe thousands even.

"Lots of traffic." Megan looked out her window. "Hard to believe all these people fit into that stadium."

The cab driver looked over his shoulder at her. "So right." He had dark brown skin and an accent. "That's why we need new stadium." He brushed his hand at the traffic. "Crazy people sit in traffic three hours for game."

Cory didn't mind the line of cars. The waiting gave him time to watch the people. Everywhere he looked, cars were parked in the lot on the other side of the big fence. Barbecues were set up along every aisle. Cory rolled his window down, and the smell of cooked burgers and hotdogs filled the cab.

"Tailgating." Megan leaned toward him and looked out his window. "People park early in the morning and eat their meals in the parking lot. It's called tailgating."

Cory stared at the people, at the celebrations they were having near one car after another. It was like a whole other world, the idea that people spent all day Sunday here. Back when his mom was alive, they spent Sunday at church. But Megan didn't like church that much. So they spent Sundays cleaning the apartment and getting ready for Monday.

Cory could definitely do this, spend all day at a 49ers game. The barbecue smell made his stomach growl. Megan told him they'd get hot dogs before kickoff and then, of course, they were having dinner with Aaron. Cory looked at the faces scattered across the forever parking lot. *And I'm the only one having dinner with Aaron Hill.* The thought made him feel good again. Aaron wouldn't have dinner with just any old kid from the youth center. It was on account of he was Aaron's son.

He tugged on his baseball cap and studied the sidewalk. Streams of people walked along both sides, heading for the gate. It was easy to tell who were the Raider fans and who were the 49ers. People wore jerseys and carried flags. They had black painted on their faces or red, and some of them had big hats with *Raiders* or *49ers* on them. When a car passed by, some of the fans would wave their flags and shout through colorful megaphones something not so nice about the Raiders or 49ers. 'Cause this was a serious game.

Aaron had sent a special pass for the parking lot, and Megan took it from the envelope.

"Here." She gave it to the cab driver. "This will get us up pretty close."

The man looked at it, and his eyebrows shot up. "You must know someone important, lady. This is VIP."

Cory wasn't sure what VIP meant. Maybe something about Very Inside Parking. The cab driver switched lanes, and in a little while, he pulled up to a gate with no one in line. He showed the pass to the man stationed there, and the man waved him into the parking lot where all the other people were having their barbecue tailgating. They drove slowly past one little party after another, until they reached a gigantic sign with the letter *A* on it.

The driver stopped. "Here you are, lady." He checked the red numbers on the box attached to his dashboard. "Eighteen dollars, fifty cents."

Megan made a slight face, like it was hard for her to pay that much money for a car ride. But she pulled out a twenty-dollar bill and handed it to the driver. "Keep the rest."

"Thank you." He took the bill and grinned. "Have very good time!"

Cory's eyes met the cab driver's in the rearview mirror. "Go 49ers!"

"Go team." The man waited until they were out, then he drove away.

Cory suddenly felt small. The crowd was all around him, and people were shouting and carrying drinks and food. A row of portable toilets stood close by, and Cory looked at Megan and made a face.

She nodded. "Me too."

They walked to a line of six people waiting for a turn, and that gave Cory more time to watch the people. A man was shouting something about wanting tickets, and a trailer was set up close to the bathrooms. Inside was every kind of 49ers shirt or hat or souvenir a person could ever want. And everyone was eating something or drinking something.

A boy and his dad walked past, both of them chewing on corndogs, and headed for the big gate marked *A*. At the same time, a helicopter flew overhead, and behind it was a sign flapping in the wind. The sign read, *Here's to Another Great Year! Go 49ers!*

The place was like 49ers heaven.

After they used the bathrooms, they got in another line, the one going through the big gate. The man taking tickets looked at Megan's and grinned. "Well, well … you've got the good seats!" He pointed up an escalator and told Megan to turn right at the top. "Box seats have a private elevator. The attendant will be just outside."

A private elevator? Cory's stomach did flip-flops inside him, and he was sort of out of breath. Like when he played soccer and it was the last minute of the game. He licked his lips and took Megan's hand.

"Amazing, isn't it?" She was watching everyone, just like he was.

"It's perfect. Everything about it."

The man in front of them wore a Raiders jersey. He turned around and noticed Cory's 49ers T-shirt. He had a big cup of something, probably beer. When he raised it in the air, a little bit sloshed out. "May the best team win."

Cory wanted to say that would be the 49ers, but he kept quiet. Megan told him some people took football very serious. So serious they might want to fight about their team. So Cory only nodded and smiled.

They reached the top of the escalator, and then after a little walk around to the right, they saw the private elevator.

"Should we get food first?" Cory stared at a food counter a few feet away. Lots of workers were busy handing out hot dogs and nachos and giant pretzels with creamy cheese. The people were loud all around them, so he raised his voice. "Huh, Megan, should we?"

"Not yet." She took his hand and walked him to the man standing outside the private elevator. "Let's find our seats first."

The private elevator took them to a much quieter walkway. It was all cement, and it went in a circle around the stadium. A woman in a red suit led them for a little walk and then pointed them to a small flight of stairs and a door. "That's Aaron Hill's box." She nodded to them. Then she went back to find the next people, probably.

Cory's heart was beating so hard he wondered if Megan could hear it. She led the way down the few stairs and opened the door. The box turned out to be a little empty room with three rows of seats. Maybe twelve or fourteen spots altogether. And across the front was all glass and a fantastic view of…

"That's the field!" Cory jogged down the last few stairs and put his face up close against the thick glass. He checked around it. "Is there a way to open the window? So we can hear what's going on?"

Megan looked up and pointed. "They have speakers, so you can hear the announcer."

"Oh." Cory didn't want to look disappointed. This was Aaron's special spot, after all. But he wanted to be out there where the people were, where the action was. As close to the field as possible.

He dropped into the middle seat on the first row. "This is like a miracle, right Megan?"

"Pretty close." She laughed. And just then, two men came into the little room. They both had on fancy suits and ties, and when they spotted Cory and Megan, they stopped.

The shorter guy looked at Megan. "Hi." He made a strange face. "I'm Bill Bond, Aaron's agent." He nodded at the other guy. "This is Albert. He's Aaron's financial planner."

Cory didn't say so, but already he didn't like Mr. Bond. He sounded not altogether nice, and maybe a little suspicious. Like how did Megan and Cory get in there, anyway.

"Megan Gunn." She held out her hand and shook his. "Aaron invited me and my son to be his guests today."

"Oh." The man hesitated. After too long a pause, he smiled. "I see." He switched his attention to Cory. "And what's your name, young man?"

"Cory." He stood, because his mom taught him that was polite when someone new came into the room. "Nice to meet you."

"Yes." He looked back at Megan and frowned. "Nice to meet you too."

Megan took a few steps toward the door. "We were just going back up for a couple hot dogs." She smiled, but it wasn't in her eyes. "Would you gentlemen like something?"

"Uh…" Mr. Bond glanced over his shoulder at a big counter at the back of the room. "Catering will bring us whatever we want." He did a curious laugh and looked strange at Megan. "That's always how it is in the box."

"Oh." Megan didn't look upset. "Well, Cory and I haven't ever been to a 49ers game. Let alone in box seats." She shrugged one shoulder. "Now we know."

Megan walked back to the first row, and at the same time, the two men sat down.

"I wanna be outside," Cory whispered. Only, because it was such a small little room, Mr. Bond heard him.

"You wanna be closer to the action, is that what I heard you say?" He walked down the couple steps and looked straight at Cory.

Cory gulped. Anything would be better than watching the game with this guy. "Yes, sir. But that's okay."

"Look." He took a pair of tickets from his pocket. "I've got fifteenth row, fifty-yard line. Saving 'em for a buddy of mine." He did a quick look back at the other guy. Then at Cory again. "How about you and your mom take these, and my buddy can sit up here with us?"

"Really?" Cory felt his heart beat hard again. Because that would be a perfect swap. He turned to Megan. "Can we?"

"Sure." Megan did a little eyebrow raise at the men. "I think that would be better anyway."

"Except," Cory remembered something. "What about after the game? We're supposed to meet Aaron here at the box."

"Hmmm." Mr. Bond looked uncomfortable, like he had a rock in his shoe or something. "I hadn't heard about that." He frowned in a way that was mean again. "I guess you should come back up after the game. I'm sure your name's on his list, if he invited you."

Cory couldn't wait to be out of the small room and back on the cement walkway toward the elevator. "What a creep!" he whispered to Megan when the guys closed the door to the room. "He didn't like us."

Megan laughed. "I don't think he was expecting us."

"Still ..." Cory took long steps to keep up with her. "He didn't have to be rude."

"No. That's the way some people are when they're around someone famous. They start to think they're better than everyone else."

"That's stupid."

"Don't say stupid." She kept her eyes straight ahead, 'cause they were almost at the elevator. "It's not something your mother would want you to say. Me neither."

Megan was right. "Sorry. It's just"—he followed her into the elevator—-"everyone's the same. So no one should think they're better."

When they were back with the crowds of people, Megan bought them each big, juicy hot dogs and giant cokes, and when they walked to their seats, Cory couldn't believe it! They were down so close to the field, he could see the looks on the faces of the 49ers. They were warming up on the field, and he could see if they looked frustrated or if they laughed about something. They were so close he felt like he was part of the team, practically.

He scanned the group, and then he pointed. "There he is." He shaded his eyes, because the baseball cap wasn't enough in this sun. "It's Aaron, Megan! Look!"

"I see him." She sounded calmer than him. But she was a grown-up, so that was okay.

For a minute, he stopped stone still on the steps and watched every move Aaron made. He wanted to jump around and wave until Aaron noticed him, but that probably wouldn't happen. 'Cause Aaron thought he was sitting up in the box.

"Come on, Cory. People are trying to get to their seats."

"Sorry." He followed Megan down one of the rows and they sat down. "Wow!" He pulled his baseball cap low and shaded his eyes again so he could look way up high to the glass windows of the box seats. "This is tons better than up there." He took a big breath. "You can breathe down here."

Megan smiled. "I agree."

Cory grinned. He liked Megan more all the time. Sometimes she was so much like his mom that he almost forgot she wasn't her.

The stadium was filling up, and Cory sat on the edge of his seat. He didn't want to miss a single thing, like the marching band, which was coming out onto the field.

Pretty soon the team jogged back to the bench and Aaron and Derrick Anderson moved close to the first row. They put some space between them and threw a pair of balls to a couple of receivers. "They're warming up!" Cory pointed at them. "Just like in high school."

"I see that." Megan asked to borrow the program of the woman sitting beside her. She began looking through it, as if she wasn't too concerned about the warm-up process.

Loud trumpets filled the stadium, and the marching band took the field. There were drummers and trumpeters and flute players and big horn-type things. Everyone stayed all together, one foot after another, just like on TV.

"It looks bigger in person, the whole band out there on the field." He had to shout so Megan could hear him. "See, don't you think it looks bigger?"

Megan finished looking at the program book, and she handed it back to the lady. "Yes," she leaned her head close to his. "It's all very big and loud. Much more than on TV."

The band stopped at the middle of the field, and then a big voice told them to stand for the national anthem. A heavy kid in a nice suit and tie came over to a platform and someone gave him a microphone. Cory could see all of it, just as it was happening. The boy didn't look that old, but he could sing like someone on *American Idol*. Cory put his hand over his heart, and he thought of his mom up in heaven watching this, and suddenly he felt tears in his eyes and he wasn't even sure why.

No, he did know why. 'Cause this was the happiest day in his whole life.

When the song was almost done, the most amazing thing happened. Streaking jet fighter planes zoomed over the stadium. They were so fast and loud, Cory's heart skipped a beat, and he gasped. "Wow!" He couldn't say it enough. When the planes passed and he could hear again, he felt his eyes get perfectly round and he looked at Megan. "Wow! Did you see that? Those were jet fighters. Probably keeping us safe for the game!"

Megan laughed a little, but the loud voice was talking again and Cory couldn't hear what she said. The coin toss happened, and San Francisco won. "They'll receive, I know they will." He bounced in his seat, and he was right. The 49ers would have the ball first!

Aaron was talking to Coach Cameron, nodding his head and looking very serious. After a few seconds, he turned and jogged out to the field where the rest of the offense was waiting for him. From the huddle he looked back at the coaches one more time, and it almost seemed like he was looking straight up at Cory.

Dad, Cory thought … *You're really my dad. Thank You, God, for hearing my mom's prayers all those times. I can't believe it's really happening.*

Aaron's first pass was a completion to one of the veteran receivers, the guy who was injured last year. "See!" Cory clapped his hand against Megan's knee. "I knew he'd be okay this year. I knew it!"

Six more plays, and on third and eight, Aaron threw a pass to the same receiver, right in the corner of the end zone. Cory was on his feet. "Touchdown!" He jumped around and high-fived Megan. "Touchdown, 49ers!"

Once the fans all settled back into their seats, Cory remembered his hot dog. It tasted better than any hot dog ever in his whole life, and by the time he finished it, Aaron had thrown a second touchdown pass. Just like their first preseason game, by halftime San Francisco was so far ahead, Coach Cameron took Aaron out of the game and put in Derrick Anderson. Cory was glad, because Derrick was a great player and a nice guy. Plus, how many teams had two quarterbacks who could win a game? Derrick kept things at a little slower pace, and in the end, the 49ers won 24 to 3. Like the man on the escalator said, the best team definitely won.

It took ten minutes to walk along with the crowd and find their way back to the elevator. This time they went up to the empty walkway, and when they reached the small room, there were four other guys with suits standing around talking. A TV set hung from the ceiling—something Cory hadn't noticed before.

"Let's stay out here," Megan came close so just Cory could hear her. "We might breathe a little better."

Cory giggled. Just then, one of the guys in the room stepped out and smiled at Megan. "You must be friends of Aaron's?"

"Yes." Megan looked uncomfortable, as if maybe they should've stayed down in the outside seats a while longer. "New friends."

Mr. Bond seemed to hear that part. He gave Megan a look, and then turned back to the men he was already talking to.

The friendly guy waved them into the box. "Come on, there's a tray of hot cookies in here."

Even with the hot dog and pop, Cory was still hungry. He raised his eyes at Megan, and she waited a few seconds. "Okay. Get a cookie, then come out here."

He skipped down the stairs, and the man was right. A tray of the biggest chocolate chip cookies ever was waiting right on the counter. They were still warm! He took two and a napkin, then he thought a minute and took a third. In case Megan wanted some. He was still getting the cookies balanced in his hands when someone walked up beside him.

He lifted his eyes and his breath caught in his throat. It was Mr. Bond, and he didn't look happy. "Hi." Cory tried a smile, but it didn't feel very strong.

"Hello." The man leaned against the counter and stared straight at Cory. "So, uh, how exactly do you know Aaron?"

"We met a few weeks ago." Cory was never afraid of anything, and right now he had to remind himself about that. He stood straighter and lifted his chin. "At the Mission Youth Center."

The man looked a little less mean at that information. "So, what … Aaron singled you out of all those kids and asked you to be his guest today? Is that it?"

Cory looked over his shoulder, but he couldn't see Megan. She was probably up the stairs on the empty cement sidewalk, waiting for him. He turned to the man again. "Not exactly." Megan didn't want him to talk about Aaron being his dad. But this guy was getting on his nerves. "I guess I was special to him."

Mr. Bond narrowed his eyes. "Why?"

"Because…" He licked his lower lip and took a step back. *Be brave, Cory, be brave.* He stuck out his chest. "Because I wrote him a letter and Derrick Anderson gave it to him."

"A fan letter?" The man looked very suspicious this time. Like when his teacher caught Zoe Walters cheating off Cory's paper in math last week. "You wrote him a fan letter, so he invited you to sit in his box?"

Cory needed air. He took a breath, but it didn't seem to help. There was only one way to get the guy off his back. He pulled the cookies to his chest. "I think it was more 'cause of what I told Aaron in the letter."

"What'd you tell him?" The other men were all talking to each other. No one even looked their way or tried to interrupt.

So Cory had no choice this time. He didn't blink. "I told him he was my dad."

Until that moment, Mr. Bond had a sort of tan type of face. But now his mouth opened up, and little by little his face turned gray. Like maybe he was going to pass out. "Listen, kid." He made his words small and tight and angry and threatening. "Don't ever say that again, you hear me? Aaron Hill has no children." He hissed the words, quiet so no one else could hear. "Don't ever tell a lie like that again, do you understand?"

That's when Cory realized something. He didn't need to stand here and explain himself to Mr. Bond. He knew the truth and so did his mother, and so did Aaron Hill. That's why they were his guests today. Instead of saying anything back, he took his cookies and the napkin, and marched past Mr. Bond and out the door. To the place beside Megan, where finally he could do what he hadn't been able to do once inside the small room.

He could breathe.

TEN

Megan was just about to give up on the idea that Aaron was ever going to meet them, when she heard commotion at the far end of the hall. Trailed by a few of his linemen, Aaron appeared, and she could tell by his expression that he was looking for them.

Cory spotted him at the same time, and he ran to meet him. "Great game!" He gave Aaron a side hug. Aaron gave Cory a quick glance, then did the same, but it didn't last long.

"Thanks." He was dressed in dark jeans and a neatly pressed light blue buttoned down shirt. He looked past Cory to Megan. Their eyes met and held for a long instant. "Megan … Did you like the box?"

"Well …"

They were closer now, and Megan crossed her arms. That's when she saw it. There was a striking resemblance between Aaron and Cory. She dismissed the idea. How could she keep the boy grounded if she allowed herself to fall into his fantasy? She smiled politely at Aaron. "Actually … we took a couple tickets from your agent. Closer to the field."

"Perfect." He grinned at Cory. "I like the view better from down there too."

Three of the linemen stopped, curious looks on their faces. "Come on, Hill, introduce us." The biggest guy, a black man with a shiny bald head, grinned at her. "You keep all the pretty ones to yourself."

Cory was still stuck to Aaron's side, but now Aaron stepped away and put his hand on Megan's shoulder. "This is Megan Gunn. I met her at the youth center." Again he held her eyes.

"Hello." Megan made a subtle move away from Aaron, and he dropped his hand. She wasn't sure what to make of Aaron's attention. She smiled at the lineman and shook his hand. But at the same time she spotted Bill Bond, Aaron's agent. He was standing just outside Aaron's box, glaring at her, listening to every word. She focused on Aaron's teammate again. "Great game!"

"Thank you. If I'd known you were watching, I woulda been more nervous." He looked at Cory. "And who are you?"

Not now, God . . . please. Make him keep it simple. She held her breath.

"I'm Cory." He bit his lip and nodded at Megan. "She's my mom."

They made small talk with the three linemen for a few minutes, and then Aaron took gentle hold of Megan's arm and led her toward the steps to his box. "Okay, guys. Enough. They're my guests."

She didn't like the way he had a hold of her, as if she were his property. But she didn't pull away, didn't want to make a scene. Aaron's teammates made a few more teasing remarks, and then bid goodbye to Megan and Cory. As they left, Aaron put his face near hers. "Now you get to meet the suits. It won't take more than a few minutes."

Megan wanted to say that she could pass. She'd already met two of them and she wasn't impressed. But making an issue out of the moment would only take longer. They spent the next five minutes mingling with the men in suits, and during that time she watched Bill Bond pull Aaron aside. Throughout their whispered conversation, Mr. Bond didn't look happy.

Whatever. If Aaron's agent didn't like him associating with people he'd met at the youth center, so be it. She held her head high and kept her attention on Cory, and whatever person was in front of her. Finally, Aaron broke free of the discussion with his agent, and he motioned to Megan. "Let's go."

She was more than ready. On the way out of the stadium, Aaron didn't act any differently. Whatever his agent had told him, he wasn't letting it change his plans for the evening. The three of them headed into the players' parking lot, and Aaron led them to a jet-black Hummer.

"Wow!" Cory ran ahead and then stopped a few feet shy of the vehicle. "Is this really yours?"

"Yep." Aaron pulled his keys from his pocket. He stopped and admired the vehicle. "It gets me around."

"I've never even been this close to a real Hummer!" Cory waited until Aaron opened the door. Then he climbed into the backseat.

Aaron led the way around to the passenger side. He stood a little too close to Megan. "So you had fun?"

"I did." She wasn't impressed by his chivalry, but as he held her door open she couldn't help but feel the slightest bit attracted. No wonder so many girls fell for him. She stepped into the car, and the smell of leather surrounded her.

On the way to the restaurant, Cory chattered on the whole time, breaking down the game one play at a time. Twice, Aaron looked at her and grinned.

"He's excited," she whispered.

"I know." He kept his eyes on the road. "It's fine. But later … I hope there's time to get to know you better."

The comment dissolved her attraction. She'd been right; he was hitting on her. That's why the invitation to the game and dinner. He couldn't care less what Cory said, as long as he had the chance to get to know her.

Megan steeled herself. She'd make her lack of interest known as soon as she had the chance.

They drove to a diner not far from Nob Hill. Megan didn't have to ask if that's where Aaron lived. Anyone in the city knew that much. The restaurant was small, only four tables and a drive-thru window, but Aaron seemed to know the older couple who ran it. Megan hadn't thought about it before, but life as Aaron Hill wasn't as glamorous as it might seem. He probably ate at small family-run places like this so that he could finish a meal without being asked for an autograph.

Halfway through their burgers, a group of teenage boys came in and almost immediately, recognized Aaron. He spent the next ten minutes signing autographs and posing with one or two of them while the others snapped pictures with their cell phones.

When the boys had their food and were gone, Megan looked at him. "Is it like that often?"

A slight laugh came from him. "All the time." He gave her a look that said he didn't mind. "Goes with the territory."

They talked about the upcoming away game at Denver and the one after that in San Diego. Megan was waiting for him to ask about her personally, but he kept the conversation light. Maybe he already sensed her resistance.

"So." Cory sucked on his straw, slurping up a mouthful of chocolate shake. "Who stays at your house when you're on the road?"

Megan felt a wave of panic. Cory would only ask the question for one reason. He was fishing, doing the one thing she'd told him not to do. She shot him a look that ordered him not to take the conversation one step further.

"No one most of the time." Aaron picked at his french fries. "I have a housekeeper, and she has her own key. That's about it."

Cory must've caught her message, because he switched topics again, this time talking about Coach Cameron and how important the season was if he wanted to stay with the 49ers.

Megan didn't mind that the conversation centered mostly around Cory, but she wished the night were over. Where could it possibly lead?

When they finished eating, Aaron drove them back to their apartment. Megan didn't care if he saw how they lived. She was much too independent to worry what people thought of her or her low-income housing. She was doing the best she could.

"Wanna come up and see Oreo?" Cory's enthusiasm hadn't dimmed all night. "He's our cat. He's a 49ers fan too."

"Cory, I'm sure Mr. Hill has to get back home." She could sense Aaron next to her starting to protest. "Besides, we have to go over your spelling words." She turned to Aaron and held out her hand. "Thanks for a wonderful day. Cory enjoyed it very much."

"You can call me Aaron." He looked disappointed, and slightly dazed. He took her hand, but instead of shaking it, he held it. His eyes lifted to the apartment building outside and then back at her. "And yeah, if Cory has homework, then, sure. You better go."

Her heart reacted strangely to the feel of her hand in his, especially for so long. A part of her wanted to stay there beside him. But common sense had something to say about the situation, so she eased her fingers from him and uttered a nervous laugh. "Maybe we'll see you at the youth center."

"Hey, wait." He fumbled around the center console until he found a pen. Then he dug into another compartment and pulled out a pad of sticky notes. "Can I get your number? Maybe we can have dinner sometime?"

"You already have it!" Cory poked his head between the two front seats. "Remember? It's at the bottom of my letter."

Aaron's eyes showed his surprise. He hesitated for a second or two. "Of course." He cast a weak smile at Cory. "I almost forgot."

Cory put his arm around Aaron's shoulders. "This was the best day in my whole life. Thanks so much."

"You're welcome." Again Aaron's expression was slightly uncomfortable. As if he didn't quite know what to make of Cory's behavior. Cory slid across the seat and stepped out onto the sidewalk. Aaron turned a sheepish look toward Megan. "I really want to see you again."

Her, not Cory. A sudden anger consumed her. She lowered her chin and aimed her gaze straight at Aaron. "Well, then … Mr. Hill … I guess you might want to read his letter."

He did a short laugh. "Wait a minute … I read it a few weeks ago. I already told him back when—"

She held up her hand. "Don't lie to me, Mr. Hill. And don't lie to that little boy." She kept her tone kind and gracious, but she could see her words were hitting him hard. "You can fool him, but you can't fool me. You haven't read his letter." She opened the door and gave him a final look. "I'm pretty sure we'll all know when you actually do." She stepped onto the ground. Her smile was the type reserved for annoying customers at Bob's Diner. "Thanks, again. Cory wasn't kidding. This was the best day of his life."

With that, she turned and took Cory's hand. They were through the apartment door and halfway up the stairs before Megan exhaled. She was right about Aaron Hill, and she couldn't believe it. He wasn't interested in Cory at all. For whatever reason, he'd taken a liking to her. Whether he was a banker or a pro football player, it didn't matter. The feeling wasn't mutual. Because for all his kindness and manners tonight, he'd broken Megan's cardinal rule. He'd lied to a child. And not just any child either. Because Cory never belonged to Aaron Hill, no matter what Amy had told the boy, and no matter how much they looked alike. He belonged to her.

The way he always would.

Eleven

Aaron barely paid attention to the road as he made his way from the Mission District north to his home in a gated area of Nob Hill. His heart and head were spinning in different directions, making him wonder at his sanity.

Megan Gunn had turned him down flat. She wasn't the least bit interested, and that was a first. For as long as Aaron could remember, girls had been easy for him. Women lined up to talk to him after games and practices, and in hotel lobbies across the country.

That's why Amy had been so special. She wasn't a groupie. Amy knew him in the deepest places of his soul, but since then he'd never let another woman get that close. There hadn't been any need, and besides, he never wanted to let anyone that close ever again.

Until now.

Megan wasn't glamorous or done up, the way the girls in his world were. She was too thin to be a cheerleader and her makeup would never stand out in a photo shoot. But her beauty stopped his heart each time he saw her. More than that, he was taken by her sheer determination and utter independence. The way she refused to call him Aaron, even.

He pulled into his driveway, parked his Hummer, and headed inside. Most game nights he dropped into his recliner and turned on ESPN. But not tonight. Tonight he needed quiet, so he could sort through the conversations from his time with Megan and Cory.

Mostly Megan. The boy was nice, but he was like any other kid. His constant chattering made it hard for Aaron to get to know Megan, hard for her to see who he really was. Still, until the very end of the evening, Aaron thought things were going great. Megan seemed relaxed and happy, like she was enjoying his company. Then at the end she pulled out the Mr. Hill thing.

And that's when the whole night crashed and burned.

He wanted her number, of course. How else could he set up a date or have a conversation without the kid interrupting the whole time? He'd planned from the moment he suited up before the game to ask her if he could call. Not that he was very good at getting numbers. They were usually given to him, unsolicited.

Not once when he tried to imagine how the evening would go had he thought that when he'd ask for her phone number, Cory would pipe in and say he'd written it on his letter. How could he have remembered the boy's statement about writing his phone number at the bottom of the letter? Or known that Megan would figure out the minute he asked her for it that he hadn't read the letter?

He groaned and let his head fall back against the recliner. Now that he thought about it, he vaguely remembered the kid saying something about a phone number back at the youth center. How could he be so stupid? The first time he'd lied to the kid about the letter, he'd made a mental note: next time he opened his locker, he'd dig around the bottom and find the envelope. Then he'd read it, so the next time he saw the boy he could look him in the eyes and talk about whatever he'd written.

After spending an evening with the kid, Aaron could pretty well write the letter himself. *Dear Aaron, you're my favorite player ... I've been watching you since I was two ... I've waited all my life to meet you ... I'm the biggest 49ers fan in the whole city,* etc., etc., etc.

The last part of the night hadn't worked out at all like he planned. He actually figured maybe he'd walk her and Cory up to their front door — or as it turned out — up to their apartment. He imagined Megan getting Cory off to bed, and the two of them sitting around her dining room table drinking coffee and getting to know each other. A kiss wasn't out of the question the way he first imagined it.

Frustration simmered in his belly. The boy would've loved it if Aaron came up with them. Megan had cut the possibility short. It was only nine o'clock when he dropped them off. And they had all day Sunday to get his homework done, but Aaron could hardly argue with her. Megan had her mind made up before they pulled up in front of her apartment.

He closed his eyes and imagined her home, her neighborhood. It was only a few blocks from the youth center, a neighborhood that was rough in the daytime. At night a single mother like Megan shouldn't even consider going outside. He'd read once in the *Chronicle* that the Mission District — - the poorest in San Francisco — was also home to more kids per square block than any other in the city.

Kids like Cory.

He opened his eyes, stood, and wandered into the kitchen where he poured himself a glass of water and leaned against the dishwasher. The housekeeper must've started it before she left, because the door was still warm. He thought about Megan and Cory. They didn't have a car, clearly. Like so many people, they probably walked and took the BART everywhere. No telling how they'd made it to the game earlier that day.

He sighed. Maybe that's why he was taken with Megan Gunn. She was a fighter, a survivor. How else could she be a single mom to Cory and still keep food on the table?

He realized then that he hadn't once asked her what she did. As if somehow being a foster mother might be her only job. But that wasn't possible. Otherwise, they wouldn't have any sort of home at all. Money from the state for foster care paid only enough for a few trips to the grocery store. Derrick had told him that.

Suddenly he knew what he had to do. He took his cell phone from his pocket and found Derrick's number. Coach had made them swap numbers first day of spring training. Before he hit the Send button he stopped himself. He had nothing in common with Derrick Anderson. He had it bad for a pretty girl, that's all. The whole foster thing meant nothing to him.

He snapped his phone shut, but he could hear Coach Cameron's voice. "Hill, make sure you have Anderson's number. You never know when you might need advice from a champion."

At the time, he couldn't imagine himself ever picking up the phone and making that call.

And that was still how he felt even a few days later when practice was back in session. The confusion with Megan Gunn and the secret to understanding her might be something Derrick could help with. But Derrick was a smart guy. He'd know that Aaron wasn't interested in foster kids. He'd probably accuse Aaron of seeking another conquest. And Megan was more than that. At least Aaron thought she was more.

Practice was drawn out and Aaron found himself watching Derrick. No question, on the field he could learn from Derrick. The guy had already won more games than most quarterbacks win in a lifetime. But now, with the sting of Megan's words still echoing in his mind, a conversation with Derrick Anderson wasn't going to make him feel better. Because the guy wasn't only a champion on the field. He was a champion at life.

Something Aaron hadn't ever wanted to be.

Chuck Cameron stepped into his office and grabbed his water bottle. He walked to his window, the one overlooking the practice field. Whether this was his last season or not, he would always be grateful for his time in San Francisco. He couldn't hold it against the owners if they fired him this year. A team led by Aaron Hill should win the Super Bowl at least once in so many years of dominance. The temperature outside was cool, though the clouds overhead had broken up an hour ago. The break in the heat was nice. They'd gone through a lot today, and they had much more still to do tomorrow. If they were going to finish the preseason strong and make a serious run at the title, the team needed to be prepared.

And they would make a serious run. Management had left them no option.

He turned his back to the window and leaned on the sill. A week ago, he could almost feel their slim chances at a Super Bowl season dissolving like sand through his fingers. Aaron Hill was hanging out at bars, getting in trouble with girls, and distracting the team. But now … well, now at least the media recognized a show of character in the team's franchise quarterback. Hill's Friday night stint at the Mission Youth Center was a good start. But that had more to do with Hill's pushy agent. If they were going to make a run at a championship, the changes in Aaron would have to be more than smoke and mirrors, more than an agent making a call to a few local reporters. No, he couldn't change Aaron Hill any more than he could will his team to win every game. But he could pray about both situations and let God bring the victories.

Chuck sighed, and a tired laugh slipped past his lips. The front office could fire him if they wanted. He wasn't going to change his ways now. No, he hadn't won the big game, but not every win could be notched on a playing field.

His precious niece Paige had reminded him of that just this morning. Chuck's kids were grown, but Paige, at eight years old, had taken a special liking to her uncle. Her mother—Chuck's sister—must've told the girl that this year was especially important for her Uncle Chuck. Whatever the reason, Paige had been calling him once a week. Just to say she was praying for him.

In the off-season, Chuck and his wife had spent time at his sister's house, so he had a chance to watch Paige. The girl had long blonde hair, blue eyes, and a heart of gold. When the good Lord talked about having the faith of a child, Chuck's guess was that he had Paige Rathbun in mind. The child was a ray of sunlight for her older sister, Katie, and her little brother, John. She sang in the church choir and prayed as easily as she breathed, and whether she knew a person or not, Paige's hellos were accompanied with a hug.

During Chuck's visit, Paige was instrumental in rescuing a golden retriever from an animal trap in the woods behind her family's home. Paige didn't see the dog as an inconvenience. "He's a gift from God," she said.

The same way Paige was a gift.

Chuck remembered the child's words from earlier today. "Sometimes God gives us hard things, don't you think so, Uncle Chuck?"

Chuck thought about Aaron Hill. "Yes, Paige. I think He does that sometimes."

"You know why?"

"Why?"

"Because He loves us enough to help us grow up."

Chuck let the words run through his mind again. He might lose his job this season, but he wouldn't lose his faith. Paige's phone calls always helped him remember that much.

As for Aaron, if he came out of the season a changed man, a man driven to make a difference in his community, and with even half the faith of Derrick Anderson, then Chuck would have the victory he'd been looking for. He grabbed his clipboard and flipped off the office lights. No matter what the outcome, he didn't need a trophy in the front office at the end of the season to prove he'd done his best with this group of athletes.

But it would be nice to have a job.

TWELVE

Aaron was headed toward his locker after practice when Jay Ryder caught up to him.

"I gotta tell you something." Jay's jersey was damp, his face streaked with sweat. He'd taken more snaps than usual today and spent a lot of time at the bottom of the pile. "I like that you're real, Hill. I can learn from you."

Aaron shifted his weight. He looked around to see if Jay's comment was some kind of a prank. "How's that?"

"The whole foster kid thing. I'm really into it, man. Just like you. Talked to my financial guy, and I might actually start a foundation, set up scholarships."

Aaron grabbed a water bottle from a passing trainer. He had no idea where his teammate was going with this. "Where do I come in?"

"I hate to say it"—he looked at the ground, a grin pulling at his lips—- "I thought that first time you went to the youth center it was just a media stunt." His smile faded. "But I heard the coaches talking about you going again tonight, and I was impressed. Seriously, man."

Aaron twisted the cap off the water bottle. He'd considered going back—so he could see Megan again. Only he couldn't find the letter, the one from Cory. At least not near the top of the junk in his locker. And he could hardly face Megan without finally reading what the kid wrote. Not only that, but two voice mail messages from his agent and a comment from Coach Cameron had soured him on the idea of another visit to the youth center. Everyone wanted him to have this save-the-world image, but why? Wasn't it enough that he stayed out of trouble without turning into a bleeding heart? He wasn't Derrick Anderson. No one could push him to be something he wasn't.

Jay was looking hopeful, and Aaron wasn't sure what to say. He could go, couldn't he? Jay was counting on him, apparently, and if Megan was there, then maybe he could turn things around for the two of them.

"Yeah …" He took a long swig of water. "Wouldn't miss it. You, uh … you riding with Derrick?"

"Not tonight. Derrick wants to get right home afterward."

"I can drive. You live close." And like that, Aaron and Jay worked out the details.

A few hours later Aaron picked up his younger teammate and the two headed for the youth center. Jay was pensive from the beginning. "I mean, I think about my life and all. How good I've had it." He hung his elbow out the open window. "I'm only four years older than some of those kids. Four years."

Aaron wasn't in the mood for a talk on charity work, but he had no choice. Jay was a nice kid, and Aaron cared what the guy thought. They could be playing together for a long time still.

Jay stared out the windshield. "Four years ago if someone wished me luck and sent me out on my own, I never woulda made it. And that's what happens to these kids."

"Sad." Aaron switched lanes and picked up speed. Maybe he could find Megan and pull her aside, tell her she was right. He hadn't read the letter because he lost it. That might help.

Jay tapped his fingers on his thigh. "Makes me wanna do something, you know? Join up with Derrick and you and really make a difference. Change some laws." He shook his head. "Something."

"I know what you mean." Aaron checked the time on the clock radio. Five more minutes and they'd be there. He'd look for Megan first off.

"I keep thinking about what Derrick said. You know … how in the end people won't remember us by our wins and losses on game day, but for what we do between Sundays. It's true, isn't it?"

Aaron glanced at his rearview mirror. "Definitely."

Jay kept up the conversation until they were walking through the youth center's double doors. By then Aaron had tuned him out, tossing back a few single syllable answers to give Jay the sense of an attention span.

Sure enough, he spotted Megan as soon as he walked into the gym, and she saw him too. She looked his way, but then she turned her attention to another of the volunteers. About the same time, Cory spotted him. The boy lit up and ran toward him, and for the slightest moment, Aaron felt the pings of regret. The kid probably thought Aaron was there to see him.

"Aaron, you came!" Cory hugged him around the waist. "How was practice?"

"Good." He stared past the boy and watched Megan disappear through a door at the back of the gym. "How 'bout you?"

Cory's eyebrows sprang up. "You remembered? About my soccer?" He took off his baseball cap and ran his fingers through his hair. "Wow, yeah ... practice was great."

Aaron wasn't really listening. He found Cory's eyes again. "How's your foster mom?"

The kid's expression fell. "She's good. Really busy, that's all. I asked if we could go watch a practice, but she had to work."

Aaron had a dozen questions. Where did she work, and what were her hours, and how would she have taken Cory to the practice facility in Santa Clara in the first place. But he held back. Instead, he patted Cory on the head. "Gotta get up front with the guys." He motioned to the pizza table. "Bring me a few slices of pepperoni, okay?"

"Sure!" Cory took off as if getting pizza for Aaron was a timed event.

The first hour blended into the second, and the whole time Aaron kept his eyes on the far end of the room. Whatever Megan was doing in the back of the building, it was taking all her time. Surely, she had to have seen him, but she was making herself clear. She wasn't interested in talking to him.

He was frustrated, ready to leave with Jay, when Megan entered the gym with a dishrag in her hand. She tossed it on the first table and dried her hands on her jeans. Then for the first time that night, she looked directly at Aaron.

Cory was still hanging around, asking questions and getting a little annoying. He stood a few feet away from Aaron most of the night, waiting while Aaron talked to the other kids, and interjecting whenever he had the chance. Now, though, as Megan approached, he ran to her and joined her as she walked up.

Aaron wanted the kid to take a break, go to the restroom or something. But before he could say something, Megan put her hand on his shoulder. "Go see if they need more help in the kitchen, okay?"

"Okay." Cory looked ready to protest, but he set his jaw and jogged toward the back of the gym.

"He's a good boy." Aaron meant it. Even if the boy was a little too determined, he was considerate of Aaron's time with the other kids, and he was polite. "Best manners of any kid at the center."

The gym was almost empty. Megan kept a few feet between them and she crossed her arms. "His mother did a great job with him. She left big shoes when she died."

Jay was finishing up with the last few teenagers. As they left, he turned to Aaron and Megan. "I'm going to find the director, talk about some other ways I could help."

Aaron felt his heart rate quicken. With Cory and Jay gone, maybe he could finally figure out what was bugging Megan, why she'd kept her distance all night. He found her eyes, and tried to see past the walls there. "You were busy tonight."

"I was." She didn't break eye contact, and while her voice wasn't angry or bitter, it was definitely cool. "Did you read his letter?"

"I wanted to talk to you about that." He leaned against the wall and slid one foot up. "I can't find it. Should be in my locker, but maybe I dropped it that first day. Janitors might've found the envelope and tossed it."

"Well." Megan shrugged one shoulder. She smiled, but it didn't reach her eyes. "I guess that's your loss, then." She hesitated.

Aaron's mind raced for something to say. He wanted to salvage the moment, but their conversation was unraveling like a cheap sweater. "I'd still like to take you and Cory out again, if that's okay?"

"I'm sorry, Mr. Hill." She took a step back. "I don't see the point. But thank you for coming tonight. The kids loved it." With that, she nodded her goodbye, turned and walked across the gym to the back. She found her dishrag and began wiping down a table.

Aaron watched her, and his frustration mixed with anger. She made him feel like a socially inept schoolboy. Never mind that her face haunted him day and night, or that she was the first woman to actually turn him down. If she didn't want anything to do with him, so be it. He would leave the situation alone. But he would do one thing when he hit the practice facility Monday. He would take a few minutes and really dig through his locker. That way he could find Cory's letter and finally read it, the way he should've done from the beginning. And whether he ever used it or not, he would have the one thing he'd wanted for the past few weeks.

Megan Gunn's phone number.

—

Aaron ran out of time before practice, but now their final set of sprints was wrapping up. He finished the last of three runs and jogged toward the locker room. All day he'd felt uncomfortable, frustrated with himself. The weekend had been a total waste. First, the pizza party at the youth center, and then a loss to Denver on Saturday. If that wasn't enough, he'd spent Sunday evening at a party thrown by his agent, Bill Bond. The guests were a mix of financial planners, stock brokers, and real estate investors. That sort of thing.

"Glad to see you made another appearance at the youth center." His agent stayed by his side for most of the party. "You did your good deed for the weekend. Now you wouldn't want to be anyplace but here." He nodded at a group of guys across the room. "Big hitters, Hill, all of them. A couple of these real estate giants could turn five million into ten in a year."

Aaron grabbed a towel from the rack, flung it over his shoulders, and headed for his locker. He'd met every last one of the suits before the party was over. Because he always did what Bill said, and most people told him he was smart because of it. Bill was respected industry-wide, and whether his advice came on personal or financial matters, Aaron had always prospered because of it. But a dozen times through the night, he'd found himself wondering why it was so important that he turn five million into ten. And in just one year?

Last night the power guys at Bill's party droned on in one conversation after another, and Aaron barely caught any of it. He was too busy thinking about Megan Gunn and Cory, about the life they lived, and about Megan's determination to keep Aaron at bay.

There were women at the party too. Not the groupies he'd been known to hook up with, but sophisticated women, smart women. Daughters of senators and daughters of bankers. Women who handled the financial accounts of Fortune 500 companies. Aaron talked to ten of them, at least. But not one of them had a fraction of the passion he'd seen in the dark-haired foster mom. By the time he left the party, he was sure of just one thing.

If he could find the kid's letter, he was going to call her. After all, she hadn't really given him a chance.

Aaron's phone rang just as he reached his locker. He checked the caller ID and felt his irritation rise. What was it with his agent? The guy was calling every day lately. "Hey, Bill."

"Aaron, my man." His agent laughed. Bill was always laughing. "Did you see the paper?"

"The *Chronicle*?"

"Yep, the big dog. Front page sports." Another chuckle. "Looks like our publicity stunt worked."

Aaron leaned against the bank of lockers. Everything about Bill was getting on his nerves. Until this year, he worried that he wouldn't know what to do without Bill Bond, how to interact with the 49ers front office or the media, or even how to spend his money. But now—ever since Bill showed his disapproval of Megan at the Raiders game—the guy was bugging him. Aaron glanced at his teammates. A few feet away, Derrick and Jay had their lockers open too, but they were lost in conversation. Even so, Aaron didn't want to be heard. He dropped his voice. "What stunt?"

"The youth center. The 49ers beat writer picked up on it. Headline reads, 'Aaron Hill Shows His True Colors.' Story talks about how your image took a hit a week earlier, but days after the girl dropped charges against you, there you were, giving back to a bunch of foster kids. The fact that you were there this past Friday night, too, only makes you look more genuine." He snickered. "Almost sounds like it was your idea."

Aaron shielded his eyes. He took a big breath and held it for a few seconds. Then he puffed out his cheeks and exhaled slowly. "First of all, it wasn't a publicity stunt." His tone was seething, but he kept his voice low. "I went because I wanted to go."

Bill was silent for an extra beat. "This is Aaron Hill, quarterback of the 49ers, right?" He paused. "'Cause I thought I called Aaron Hill."

"Shut up." Aaron turned so his back was to Derrick and Jay. "Nobody makes me do something, got it? You suggested it, okay. But if I didn't want to go, I woulda stayed home."

"Okay." Bill drew the word out, like he was talking to a troubled child. "Point made. Either way"—his tone lightened halfway to where it had been before—"it worked. The paper loves you, the city loves you. Your fans love you." His laugh sounded defensive this time. "That's all I was trying to say. A little thanks might be nice."

"Do they know about the other night too?"

"You didn't tell me you were going. Otherwise I could've made a call."

"Do me a favor." Aaron evened out his tone. His agent was only looking out for him. "Tell me before you contact the press on my behalf, okay?"

Bill drew a loud breath. "All right, then. Good talking to you. Don't forget to call the real estate guy. He's waiting for you."

"Sure … fine." Aaron snapped the phone shut, and for a few seconds he stared at the floor, calming himself down. He hadn't thought about it before the Raiders game, but he was sick of being managed. He was going to be thirty this spring, and still he was like some sort of puppet. Whatever string Bill Bond pulled, Aaron jumped. With Megan that day at the park, Bill had lowered his voice and looked in her direction. "A foster mom, Hill? That the best you can do?"

Aaron hadn't wanted to get into it. "I met her at the youth center." He kept his voice light. "She and the boy have never been to a game."

Bill nodded, his distaste showing in his expression. "Well, then … one game should be enough, right?" He patted Aaron on the back. "Good deed done!"

His agent's message that day was unmistakable. Bill didn't want to see Aaron hanging around a woman he thought beneath him. Period.

Normally Aaron would've understood. Some women were bound to chase him for his money, but not Megan. And ever since the incident, Aaron's attitude toward his agent had soured some.

"Everything okay?" Derrick bumped him on the shoulder. Jay was gone, and they were the only two left in this section of lockers.

A weary smile tugged at his lips. "My agent … he's pushy."

"Bill Bond?" Derrick chuckled. "It took you this long to notice? Rumor back when you entered the league was that you didn't burp without asking permission from your agent."

"Great." He positioned himself in front of his locker. "I guess I never saw it before."

When Derrick was gone, Aaron hung his head against the frame of his locker. Was that really how people saw him? Putty in the hands of Bill Bond? And why hadn't anyone said something? The answer came to him as soon as the question hit his mind. He'd been nothing more than a college kid when Bill first came into his life. His own father wasn't interested in football. He traveled the globe as an international marketing director. His only advice when the media started hinting about a pro career for Aaron was this: Find a good agent.

Which was exactly what Aaron had done.

But lately he'd been wondering about more than the parties and publicity stunts. He wondered about Amy too. Amy had been everything to him before UCLA, before Bill broke the news that she was seeing other guys. But what proof had Bill really had? At the time, he remembered thinking he should ask. Because maybe Bill had pictures or a contact he could refer Aaron to. But he never did. He trusted Bill, and that trust parlayed into one of the biggest contracts and signing bonuses of his day.

The familiar locker room smells of sweat and rubber matting filled his senses. One year of football after another, and Bill had controlled his every step, something Aaron had always thought was a good thing. And maybe it was.

He closed his eyes and all he could see was Megan Gunn, her passionate determination, her eyes so deep he could fall into them. There probably wasn't a hundred extra dollars in Megan's bank account, but he had a sense she knew more about life than Bill and all his clients combined.

He opened his eyes and reached into the locker. The letter was in there somewhere, probably near the bottom. He moved his fingers past a few baseball caps and a pair of old socks, and then he felt it, the envelope. The one that had eluded him last week. He pulled it out and stared at it. Aaron's name was scrawled across the front in kid writing. It didn't matter that he could predict what it said. The letter came from the kid's heart. Here, in the silence of the locker room, he would read it with all the importance that had clearly gone into it.

He slid his thumb beneath the flap and gently pulled out the piece of paper from inside. It was folded four times, but once he opened it, Aaron could see the letter wasn't long. He leaned against the locker next to his and started at the top.

Dear Aaron Hill,

> *I've wanted to write this leter for a long time. Lots of days I started it and then I threw it away. Because how was I going to get it to you? But now I think maybe this will work. Derrick Anderson will be at the youth center Friday night, and he's your backup.*

Aaron smiled. The kid definitely knew his 49ers football. He kept reading.

So Friday night I'm going to ask Derrick to give it to you. See, I have something really important to say. Because a long time ago my mom told me that you weren't just a nice football player. You're my dad. That's what she told me.

Aaron scrunched up his face and read those last few lines again. What was this? A strange feeling spread through his chest. The kid actually thought he was his son? He felt like someone had punched him in the gut. No wonder Megan knew he hadn't read the letter. But did that mean she believed he was Cory's dad?

A sad laugh filled his throat and it became a groan. "Poor kid." He picked up where he left off.

My mom always prayed I could meet you, because a boy should have a father. Don't you think so? Anyway, now that you know, could you call me at my house? Thanks very much.

Your friend, Cory

Sure enough, at the bottom of the letter was a phone number scribbled larger than the rest of the words. Probably so Aaron wouldn't miss it.

He read the letter once more and stared at it a minute longer. He'd seen a lot of fan letters, but nothing like this. Where a kid got so caught up in adoration that he actually believed Aaron was his father. He took a long breath and thought about the conversation he needed to have with Megan. The boy wasn't his, obviously. He would start there. But he also needed to know what role Megan played in all this. As smart as Megan was, as clear-minded as she'd shown herself to be, he couldn't believe she would support Cory writing this type of letter.

That was probably why she was distant around him. She wanted to see how he'd react to the child's fantasy. Aaron added the phone number into his cell. Then he folded the letter, slipped it back into the envelope, and tucked it near the back of his locker. He felt a mix of sorrow and frustration over the boy's claim. Aaron didn't know Cory's past, other than the small bit Megan had shared the other night. That Cory's mother had been wonderful, and that she was dead.

He finished changing clothes, and then grabbed his duffle bag. If Megan thought the boy's letter was going to scare him off, she was wrong. The child didn't know any better. So he'd made a mistake? What if he did see Aaron Hill as his father ... or the father he never had? If Megan would see him again, Aaron would treat the boy the way he, himself, would want to be treated if he were in Cory's shoes. Not necessarily like a father. But like a friend.

Even so, he felt strangely uneasy. These were waters he hadn't navigated before, and maybe he'd be better off sharing the details with someone else first. Or maybe he just needed to hear Megan Gunn's voice again. He set his bag down, opened his phone, and pulled up Megan's number. But before he hit Send, he changed his mind. Instead, he pulled up Bill's number, and then — at the last second — he dialed the number of a guy he hadn't planned to call all season, let alone now.

Because no matter what he thought about his teammate, one thing was certain. Derrick Anderson was a straight shooter. He would listen and he would respond in truth, something Aaron wasn't sure he could get anywhere else.

And suddenly — where Megan and Cory were concerned — truth was something he desperately wanted.

Thirteen

Derrick was putting his ice pack back in the freezer when Denae padded into the kitchen in her bathrobe and slippers. Her smile lit up his heart.

"How did my man do in practice today?" She took a tea bag from a drawer and dropped it into the Starbucks mug from Houston. Derrick collected them for her when he was on the road.

"Held my own."

She looked at his knee and raised her eyebrow. "How's it feel?"

"Hurts. Bad." He felt the pain with every step as he came closer to her. "But I can play. No matter how much it hurts."

"Ah, baby …" She took hold of the back of his neck and pulled him in for a kiss. "I wish you could see someone." She sidestepped him and filled her cup with boiling water from the hot tap near the sink. She turned and held the cup close to her middle.

"I will." He smiled. "After the season. For now …" he chuckled, "nothing feels better than beating the Raiders."

"Except maybe beating the Seahawks." Her eyes sparkled, the way they did when she played with him.

"Seattle will be tough." He patted his thigh. "I might see a little more rest. As long as Aaron stays strong. And Coach wants Jay to take a few snaps."

"Never mind. God's got it all covered." She sipped her tea. "I already asked Him."

"Well…" He limped to the fridge and grabbed a string cheese. "Ask Him about Aaron Hill too. I think God's up to something big with that guy."

Before Derrick could finish his sentence, the phone rang. He was only a few feet away, and he forced himself not to favor his right leg. His strength had to carry him on and off the field. Otherwise, he wouldn't give his all when it was asked of him.

He picked up the receiver. The caller ID was blocked. "Hello?"

"Derrick?" The voice was familiar. "Aaron Hill. You got a minute?"

A chill ran down Derrick's arms. How weird was that? He asks his wife to pray for his teammate, and at the same instant the guy calls? He tried to focus. "Yeah, man. No problem. What's up?"

Derrick heard Aaron exhale, and with it came the certainty that something wasn't right. "You remember the woman at the youth center, the pretty one with dark hair?"

"The foster mother." Derrick lowered his brows. She was the one he'd invited to the Raiders game. What was Aaron doing thinking about a woman he'd met several weeks ago? At his pace, he should've moved on by now. "Her son gave you that letter."

"Right … her." He took a quick breath and rushed ahead. "I read it … I guess the kid thinks I'm his dad." He laughed, but it sounded forced. "How weird is that?"

Derrick braced himself against the counter. "Is it true?"

"Definitely not. Some sort of fantasy, I guess."

Aaron explained the main details, how he'd asked for her number. Only the boy had written the number at the bottom of the letter. "Megan knew I was lying. She saw right through me."

Since he'd joined the team, Derrick had been careful when he talked about his faith. For the most part, people wanted to see a sermon, not hear one. But if Aaron was asking for advice, Derrick was going to give it to him. He held his breath. "She's not the only one."

"What?"

"Who sees right through you. She's not the only one." He kept his tone easy, relaxed. "You've never talked about God, Hill. You ever give Him much thought?"

His teammate hesitated. "Not really. I mean"—he allowed a nervous laugh—"what's that got to do with Megan Gunn?"

"Everything. You start thinking about God, and I'll tell you what. You'll read letters from kid fans the first time around. Because you'd understand you don't play a down—on or off the field—without God letting you play it."

Aaron thought about that for a few seconds. "Yeah, well … anyway, this letter thing. I guess I'm not sure what to do next. I want her to think I made the right response."

"Sounds like this should be more about the boy than his foster mother." Derrick looked at his wife. He covered the phone and whispered, "Can I ask him over for dinner?"

Denae held her teacup up and gave a dramatic nod. "Get that boy over here. I'll tell him a thing or two."

Derrick nodded and uncovered the receiver. "Hey, Hill … we're barbecuing. Why don't you stop by for dinner? Maybe we can talk a little."

Aaron's hesitation lasted only a moment. "Tonight?"

"Sure, right now. We're a low-maintenance outfit. Just head on over."

"Okay … can I bring something?"

"Nah." Derrick reached out and patted his wife's lower back. "Denae's got it covered."

When the conversation ended, Derrick hung up the phone and looked at Denae. "Like I was saying, ask Him about Aaron Hill too."

"Just so you know … my stud husband"—she came to him and set her teacup on the counter—"I'm one step ahead of you."

"You've been praying for Aaron Hill?"

She smiled. "Since your agent first started talking about San Francisco."

Derrick kissed her on the forehead, and then on the lips. God had given him a start to this season he would remember always. Beating Oakland and then, against anything he might've imagined, the unreachable, unflappable Aaron Hill calls him for advice. That, more than anything else, was proof God was hearing their prayers.

And that maybe, He'd only begun handing out answers.

Fourteen

The doorbell rang just as Derrick was basting Denae's secret recipe barbecue sauce across a pan of raw chicken. He cupped his free hand around his mouth. "Somebody … get the door!"

Denae was doing her face in the bathroom upstairs, but Larry and Lonnie were in the other room in the middle of a mad NFL PlayStation game. This was the first time Aaron had been over to the house, the first time his kids would hang out with his teammate other than the quick hellos they'd exchanged at a few spring practices.

Larry sprinted past the kitchen and Derrick heard the door open, and then Aaron's voice. "Hi … your home's beautiful."

"Thank you, sir." Larry's voice held a degree of awe. "My dad's in the kitchen."

"Using one of my other skills." Derrick's voice was ripe with teasing. "Which is more than I can say for you, my bachelor friend. All those Taco Bell wrappers in your locker!"

Larry and Lonnie headed out to the backyard, where Libby was curled up on the patio sofa doing her homework. Aaron entered the kitchen and came up alongside him. He held out his hands. "What, you took the chicken out of the package?" He waved his hand at Derrick and walked around the counter to the bar on the other side. "Even I can do that."

"No." Derrick tried to find a dignified look. "I've mastered the art of applying barbecue sauce." He dabbed the brush at the sides of one of the pieces. "Chicken has a certain amount of natural juice. You have to seal it in just so, especially if you want—"

"Don't listen to a word he says." Denae walked into the kitchen, came up behind Derrick, and took the basting brush from his hand. "Mmm-hmmm. Boy's been telling stories since the day we met." She snapped her fingers at him. "Don't you be taking no credit for my secret chicken, Derrick Anderson."

Derrick started to protest, but before he could say a word, Aaron shook his head, as if he were sorely disappointed in his teammate's duplicity. "I had a feeling." Aaron donned the innocent look of a choirboy. "You should've heard him. How he's been working over the stove all morning, and ever since he got back from practice. How he does all the cooking for the family."

"Thanks." Derrick feigned a defeated look. "The barbecue guy gets no respect."

Denae laughed, and as she finished basting the chicken, she smiled at Aaron. "I'm Denae Anderson. Welcome to our home."

"Thanks for having me." He winced. "Kinda last-minute."

"Don't go talking about last-minute. You come through the front door, that makes you family. No reservations needed."

"The invitation came at a good time."

Aaron sounded kind. A person meeting him for the first time could never have known he had a reputation for being a cocky braggart.

"I'm glad." She gave her husband a warning look. "Since *I've* been slaving in the kitchen all day."

Derrick held his hands out, palms down, and bowed to his wife. "Absolutely. Let the record show that all delectable meals made in this kitchen come from my lovely wife. I only do what I'm told. All of it under the fine direction of one of the best cooks in all of California."

A satisfied look crossed Denae's face, and she grinned at Derrick. "That's better." She took a potholder from the counter and opened the oven door. "The potatoes have another forty minutes." She waved the potholder at her husband. "Shoo ... I got this! You and Aaron go out back with the kids."

Aaron stood and motioned to Derrick. "Let's take a look at that view of yours." He wandered toward the back door.

"I'm right behind you." Derrick put his arm around his wife's waist. "You're amazing, you know that?"

"My chicken, you mean?" She leaned up and brushed her lips against his. He felt the familiar desire, the feelings only she could ignite in him. "Not the chicken. Because you put Aaron at ease without even trying."

"God works best in comfortable places."

Derrick studied her. "You're something else." He kissed her this time, and then he headed for the back sliding door. "Let me know if you need anything."

"Just you, baby." Her smile warmed the whole house. "Just you."

Outside, Derrick stopped and watched the happenings in the backyard. Their home was centered on a two-acre square bluff overlooking the San Francisco Bay. Off to the right side was a half-court for basketball, complete with extra-high netting so no one had to chase a ball all the way down to the beach. The middle yard, the part that took off from the house toward the back landscaping, was plush, manicured grass. And on the left was a shop garage with a large patch of asphalt where over the years he expected to watch his kids play with remote control cars and bikes and skateboards. It was the sort of backyard any kid would love to have, and Derrick looked forward to hundreds of hours out here with his family.

"Come on, old man." Aaron held up a basketball in Derrick's direction. Then he passed it to Lonnie, who passed it to Larry. "Let's go two-on-two."

"Yeah, Daddy." Libby looked up from her homework. She had her legs curled up beneath her, and she wore an oversized USC sweatshirt. "I love when you play basketball."

Derrick made a funny face at his daughter. He felt like Bill Cosby. "You like when I play basketball?"

She giggled. "Football too. It's just you don't play basketball that much anymore."

"Well, young lady…" He walked past her toward the court. "I guess I'll have to change that."

Again she giggled, and the sound made his heart soar. He loved having a daughter, loved the way she adored him. She always said that one day she'd marry a man just like him. If she wanted him to play more basketball, he would. But there was no way he was playing two-on-two right now. He might be getting around without a limp, but the pain in his knee was still constant. He couldn't risk a worse injury in a pickup game.

For that matter, Aaron couldn't either.

He reached the court and moved just inside the fence. "Don't tell me your contract lets you play hoops during the season." Derrick raised his eyebrows at his teammate. "I know mine don't."

"Ah, come on." Aaron's grin proved he'd been caught. Of course, his contract forbid pickup games during the season. "You're just afraid."

Derrick pointed to himself and let his mouth hang open. "Me?" he mouthed the word. Then he wagged his finger in the air. "*Au contraire*." He added a French accent for effect. "I don't need a pickup game to beat you at B-ball." He held his hands out and caught a pass from Larry. He was outside the three-point line, but he eyed the basket, launched the ball, and swished it.

"Nice, Dad." Lonnie grabbed the ball and passed it to Aaron.

Derrick tipped an invisible hat toward Aaron. "You got something to say about that?"

"Yeah. Step back." Aaron waved him out of the way. He took aim and shot an air ball, one that missed even the backboard by a foot.

"Oooh…" Derrick studied his teammate with an exaggerated look of concern. "Sorry, man. Did you think we were shooting left hand?"

"That's an *H*, and I don't mean for Hill." Lonnie ran after the ball and took a shot from the corner. When it swished, all four of them shouted their approval, and the game grew competitive quickly. Larry got the letters in HORSE first, and then Lonnie. Derrick and Aaron were neck and neck for the last five shots, until finally Derrick shot a basic free throw, underhanded.

"How's that from an old man."

Aaron shook his head and grabbed the ball off the ground. "Doesn't get any more old-school than that." He dribbled the ball to the free-throw line, set his feet apart, and swung the ball back between his legs and up toward the hoop. The ball ricocheted around the rim, bouncing three times before popping out to the side.

"Dad wins!" Lonnie raised both fists in the air. "Way to go, Dad."

"Good try." Larry patted Aaron on the back.

"Yeah," his grin showed his defeat. "Remind me to come over every week. I usually need to file taxes to get this sort of abuse."

The boys launched into a half-court game of one-on-one, and Derrick and Aaron walked across the yard and up a slope to the rock fence at the far end. They sat on it and stared at the ocean beyond.

Aaron narrowed his eyes. "You can see halfway to Hawaii."

"We love it." He looked over his shoulder at the boys. "I plan to watch the kids grow up in this yard."

A comfortable silence settled over them. In the distance, a jet flew over the bay. Derrick was grateful for the laughter and the game of HORSE. But that wasn't why Aaron wanted to talk to him. Something was changing just the slightest bit in his heart, Derrick could sense it. He found a softer tone with none of the teasing from earlier. "So … about the boy's letter."

"I still can't believe it." Aaron kept his eyes on the view. "Kid thinks I'm his dad. I mean, how crazy is that?"

Another possibility entered Derrick's mind. "It's not the pretty foster mom, is it? Trying to get money from you?"

"Hardly." Something softened in Aaron's eyes. "I think she's a little baffled by the boy's thoughts too. Her name's Megan, the foster mom. Maybe she's waiting to see how I'll handle it."

"That's heavy stuff."

"Yeah." His voice grew distant. "I don't know if it's meeting all those foster kids or what, but … I don't know. I feel crummy lately." He pulled one leg up onto the rock wall and circled his knee with his arms. "And my agent's bugging me. Pushing more than usual."

"What about this Megan?"

Aaron started to say something and then stopped. A frustrated groan came from him and he shook his head. "She turned me down. She knew I lied about the kid's letter, about reading it."

"Hmmm. Not good."

"No. It's a bad time to feel like things aren't going right. I need to be at the top of my game, you know?"

"Either you or me." Derrick allowed a smile into his voice.

"Yeah. I guess." Aaron laughed, but it sounded tense. "You know how many girls I've been with, Derrick?"

"Lots." This wasn't the time for a funny line. Derrick's soul ached for the emptiness he was sensing in his teammate.

"A whole lot." He narrowed his eyes and looked deep at Derrick. Deeper than ever before. "But not one of them ever made me smile the way you smiled when Denae walked into the room."

"So maybe this is the year." Derrick patted Aaron's back. He stood and nodded at Aaron to follow him.

"The year?"

"Yeah." Derrick tossed him a smile over his shoulder. "The year you figure it out."

They went inside and took the tray of chicken out to the barbecue. Lonnie and Larry stayed nearby, getting pointers on the fine art of grilling chicken. When they were seated around the table, Derrick said the prayer.

"Father, we thank You for this food and the hands that prepared it. The female hands."

"Got that right," Denae muttered.

A few giggles sounded from around the table, and Derrick cleared his throat. "Seriously, God, we're grateful for all You've given us, and for the love You've blessed us with. We ask that Aaron would take a little bit of that love home with him tonight. In Jesus's name, amen."

Derrick wasn't sure, but he thought maybe Aaron was a little pensive after the prayer. If he was, he didn't stay that way for long. Dinner was a blur of one-liners and extra helpings and the sort of warmth that marked every day Derrick spent with his family. Throughout the meal, he would catch Aaron mid-bite, his fork in his hand, studying the kids and Denae and the way they interacted with each other.

God, You're touching his heart, aren't You? Right before my eyes. A shiver ran down Derrick's spine, and he tried to imagine what the Lord was doing in Aaron's life and how that process must've been directly connected to Derrick's decision to play for the 49ers. It was more than he could get his mind around.

After dinner, when the kids were busy with the dishes, Derrick and Aaron walked out to the upstairs balcony. From there, the view was breathtaking—-especially with the setting sun.

"Man, how do you ever leave?" Aaron sat on one of the cushioned patio chairs.

Derrick took the one next to him. "The view?"

"All of it." He allowed a single laugh, one that expressed his amazement. "Your family's like something from a TV show. I didn't have a single meal like that one when I was a kid."

"We're blessed." Derrick used the word on purpose. Because luck had nothing to do with the evening Aaron had just shared in.

"I'd say so." Aaron leaned over and dug his elbows into his knees.

Just watching him made Derrick cringe. With great care, he lifted his right leg up and rested it on the footstool.

"You're a churchgoer, aren't you?" Aaron craned his neck and stared at him. "I mean, you talk about God, but it's more than talk for you, right?"

"It is." He felt a surge of joy. He'd prayed for this chance, this opportunity to help Aaron see that faith in Christ was the only way to tackle the emptiness. "My family and I go to a Vineyard church in the city. Meets Saturday night and Sunday mornings. Rockin' choir … big potluck dinners. Lots of ways for the kids to stay involved." He nodded. "And preachin' right from the Good Book. Every week I learn something."

"What about when we're on the road?"

"During the season, I go when I can make it. But Denae's there with the kids. The stability's good for 'em."

Aaron squinted at the setting sun. "So you believe the whole story, God made the earth and sent His son, the crucifixion and resurrection. All of it?"

"I do." He pictured Lee, the way he'd looked that day in the hospital. "Even in the worst of times."

They were quiet, both of them focused on the sun as it dropped beneath the horizon, casting brilliant rays of light across the Pacific. In the glow of pinks and pale blues, Aaron turned to him once more. "Tell me about the family picture. What happened to the fourth kid?"

The pain in Derrick's knee was nothing to the sudden ache in his heart. He pressed his lips together. "You notice more than you let on."

"Sometimes."

Derrick sucked back a long breath. If telling the story about Lee would help Aaron understand faith, help him get a picture of what it was to truly believe, then he would tell it now. No matter how much it hurt. "It was seven years ago. October. My tenth season in the NFL."

Aaron shifted slightly in his chair, his attention completely on Derrick. The look on his face said he hadn't meant to bring up something too deep, too personal. "Hey, man, I didn't mean to pry."

"It's okay. Sometimes it's good to go back." Derrick steadied himself and the years rolled away. "I was boarding a plane in Dallas that Sunday night after a game against the Cowboys, when my phone rang. The flight attendant was saying something about shutting off our cell phones, but I took the call. Denae was on the other end, hysterical."

He could hear her still, the way her voice sounded frantic, desperate. "Derrick, it's Lee … it's our baby, Derrick. Dear God, it's Lee …"

All around him players were chatting about the game and positioning their airline pillows and buckling their seatbelts. But Derrick was trying to catch his breath. "Denae, baby, calm down." He placed his hand around his mouth so his teammates wouldn't hear him. "I can't understand you, baby. Talk to me."

"Someone ran the red, Derrick. Dear God, no." She let out a loud wail, one that echoed in his heart still today. "I need you, Derrick. Please. Dear God, not my baby. No!"

Derrick could feel his heartbeat double, and for a moment he considered tearing down the aisle and getting off the plane. But then he realized that would be crazy. He couldn't get to Denae any faster by leaving his seat. Instead he gripped the phone as tightly as he could. "Is there ... is there someone else around? Someone I can talk to?"

She was still weeping, but she must've heard him, because she handed the phone to a man with a calm, professional-sounding voice. "Hello, this is Doctor Lander. Is this Derrick Anderson?"

"It is." His heart slammed against his chest and panic choked him. "What happened?"

"I'm sorry, Mr. Anderson. There's been an accident. A speeding car ran a red light and broadsided your wife's van. We've checked out your wife and oldest three children. They're all fine."

Get to the point, Derrick wanted to scream. What about Lee? "Our ... youngest?"

"He took a severe blow to the head. He's in critical condition." The doctor's voice was heavy. "You need to get here as soon as possible."

No, God, please not Lee. Derrick closed his eyes and bent over his lap. He pictured Lee, jumping into his arms as he left for the airport the day before the game. "Daddy, I love you ..." *Please, God, not little Lee.* He found his voice. "I'm on my way. Please ... put my wife back on."

Denae was still sobbing when she came back on the phone. "Pray, Derrick. I can't ... I can't lose my baby."

The flight attendant could sense something was very wrong. She didn't ask him again about his phone, but the plane was moving. Derrick promised he would pray and then he hung up and turned off his cell. Nearly four hours later when they landed in Chicago, Derrick took a Town Car straight to the hospital.

The story was always difficult, but Derrick hadn't realized till now that there were tears on his cheeks. He swiped the backs of his hands across his face. "He was still conscious when I reached his room. The other kids were huddled on the floor against one wall, crying. Denae was standing by the bed, holding Lee's hand."

Derrick's breath caught in his throat, the way it always did when he allowed himself to go back to that horrific moment. His eyes fell on Lee, the way his head and face were swollen. At that point, Derrick didn't know his son's prognosis, but he didn't need a doctor to tell him the situation was grave. He hurried to the side of the bed and tenderly, carefully, he took hold of his son's other hand. "Baby ... Daddy's here."

Lee blinked slowly, the blink of heavy sedation. "Daddy?"

Sorrow flooded Derrick's heart and soul and he struggled to speak. "Jesus is with you, Lee. Everything's going to be okay." His words were as much for himself as they were for his son.

Across the bed, Denae met his eyes. Tears were streaming down her face and she shook her head. "It's not good," she mouthed. Then she squeezed her eyes shut, released Lee's hand, and turned so he wouldn't see her break down. After a minute, she motioned for Derrick to follow her.

An ocean breeze washed across his face and he looked at Aaron. His teammate was gripped by the story, stunned by it. Derrick sat up straighter in his chair. "The news was worse than I imagined." Derrick's voice was distant, lost back in that long ago fall. "You know, you figure he's talking, he's coherent. He must be okay." Derrick shook his head. "He wasn't."

Denae led him into the hall and she collapsed in his arms. "He's bleeding," her face twisted in a gut-wrenching sorrow capable only from a parent losing a child. She fought for her voice. "Doctor says he can't stop it. Blood's coming from too many areas."

For the first time that awful night, anger sliced through Derrick's grief. "So what? We're supposed to stand by and watch him die?" All his life Derrick had tackled adversity, as a high school player at a school where black kids were looked at with disdain by alumni, and at college when he had to battle for a starting position. He worked hard for his success, every touchdown pass, and dollar earned. Always Derrick believed a person had control over his destiny.

But not here, not in a hospital room.

The panic was back, and suddenly Derrick didn't want to debate Lee's prognosis in a cold, sterile hallway. He wanted to be in the room beside his boy, holding his hand. And that's what he did. He kissed Denae's tears and then returned to Lee's side.

The media touched on the story of Lee's death, but no one but Denae and the kids knew about the part that came next. Aaron Hill wasn't family. He wasn't even a close friend, not yet, anyway. But if he was the reason God moved Derrick to San Francisco, then he'd tell the story.

He massaged the muscles above his right knee. "We had one more conversation, me and Lee." His voice was choked with a hurt that was never far from the surface.

He reached the boy's side and took his hand again. "How're you doing, little man? You hanging in there?"

Lee squinted at him. "Daddy?" He clung tight to Derrick's fingers. "My head hurts."

"I know, baby. I'm sorry." He felt more helpless than ever in all his life. *God, no ... not Lee. Stop the bleeding, please.* "What can I do, baby?"

For a few seconds, Lee was quiet. Then his little boy smile lit up his swollen face. "Win ... a Super Bowl, Daddy! ... Okay?"

The statement was the strangest thing. Lee had only recently become aware of Derrick's status, the fact that he'd won two championships. A few weeks before the accident, Lee asked to see his rings, the rings he kept in a bedroom drawer. Derrick had showed him, and Lee had done his own figuring. One ring for Larry, one for Lonnie, so now all he needed to do was win one for Lee.

Derrick had asked him about Libby, but Lee wrinkled his nose. "Girls don't care about Super Bowl rings, Daddy. That's for boys."

And now, with his brain bleeding uncontrollably, his youngest son remembered.

Derrick bent over the hospital bed, and with his free hand, he ran his knuckles over the boy's swollen cheek. "A Super Bowl, baby? That's what you want?"

A tired little laugh breezed across his lips. "Yeah. You're gonna ... win it all, Daddy! The ... Super Bowl." His words were scratchy and strained, his eyes barely able to stay open.

Tears blurred his vision, but Derrick did the only thing he could do. He lifted his boy's hand to his face and tried to hold on, tried to will life and healing into him. Then in a rush of determination unlike any he'd ever felt before, he nodded. "Okay, little man. I'll win it all."

"For me." Lee's breathing was getting worse, shallow and weak. "Win it … for me, Daddy. Like … we talked about."

"I will, baby. I promise."

Derrick had heard about cases where a dying person had one last shining moment, the final flicker of a fading fire. For Lee, that moment happened then. His expression lit up once more. "Daddy …" his eyelids opened wider than before. He looked like an angel, his eyes bright with childlike love. He patted Derrick's hand, soft and tender. "You're … my best friend."

"You're mine too."

Denae was back on the other side, stroking Lee's arm, his legs. But no amount of love or prayers or willing him to be healed could change what was happening. Lee's eyes closed, and after a few minutes, his breathing grew slower and then finally stopped. And the bright ray of sunlight that had been their youngest son was snuffed out before he ever really had a chance to shine.

Derrick sniffed. The tears didn't embarrass him. If recalling Lee's death didn't make him cry, he'd be worried about the condition of his heart. He wiped at his face again. "I miss him."

For a long time, Aaron didn't say anything. He stared at the sky, at the fading pinks and lengthening shadows. When he finally put words to his thoughts, they were strained with confusion. "You still believe? Even after that?"

"More than ever." The determination in his voice was the same he'd felt that day in the hospital room. "I never coulda survived losing Lee without Jesus. Woulda died from sadness, man. No way." He pressed his fist to his chest. "In here, I believe with everything I have that Lee…" His voice broke. He took a few seconds to find control again. "Lee is with Jesus. Happy and whole, helping get things ready till we're all together again." He felt drained from telling the story. "What would I have if I didn't have that?"

They sat a long time in silence, and then Aaron thanked him. "I had no idea."

"Everyone has their struggle."

"Yeah."

Without another word, Aaron stood and shook Derrick's hand. Derrick followed him to the stairs and listened as Aaron moved down into the kitchen. He thanked Denae and told the kids goodbye, then let himself out the front door. With someone else, Derrick might've been worried about the abrupt exit. But this was Aaron Hill, and the exit could only mean one thing. The evening, the story, their family, had made an impact on the guy. So much that Derrick guessed Aaron didn't know what to do with his feelings.

When he was gone, Derrick went to his bedroom, to the photo that hung on the wall by the closet. God used all suffering to build character, right? Wasn't that what the Bible taught? Because losing Lee changed everything for Derrick.

After that, his faith could never be something passive, a pleasant outing to a friendly church service. Faith became everything, because heaven held one of his own. He was passionate about making sure his family all wound up together in heaven.

But here on earth, winning another Super Bowl ring was important too.

He kissed his thumb and pressed it next to Lee's precious little face, beaming at him from the photograph. Nights like this, he could still hear his son's last laugh, see his last smile. "It might happen, baby. This might be the year."

Either way, he was certain of one thing. Aaron Hill had listened to every word tonight, and if God was going to change him, the journey might just begin right here.

In the legacy of a little boy who never really had a chance to live.

FIFTEEN

Aaron drove without thinking, without processing even one bit of Derrick's story. He drove until he came to Baker's Beach, the stretch of rocky sand just west of the Golden Gate Bridge. It was almost nine o'clock, but a few couples still dotted the sand. Aaron didn't want to talk to anyone.

He walked away from the bridge, toward the part of the beach that drew fewer people. Feelings were building in him, weighing on his heart, but he couldn't think about them, not yet. He pushed himself. Long strides, his hands in his pockets. Only when he was far away from anyone else, did he walk toward a craggy boulder near the surf. He climbed to the top, drew his knees up, and sat facing the water, and finally ... finally he stopped.

He rested his arms on his knees and let his head fall against his fists. And there, for the first time Aaron could ever remember, he felt his eyes tear up. Anger and sorrow and guilt and helplessness welled up inside him. Strange and deep feelings for Derrick and the precious child in the family photo, and for Megan, who had dedicated her life to helping kids without families. And for Cory, who wanted a father so badly he was willing to make up the idea that Aaron might be his dad.

All of it mixed together in his heart until he could barely breathe for the sadness. He had always respected Derrick Anderson. Yes, when the 49ers brought him on board, Aaron had felt threatened. How could the franchise have room for two star quarterbacks? But from the beginning, Derrick had made it clear. He was there as much to mentor Aaron and Jay Ryder as he was to make any real contribution on the field.

The story Derrick told him tonight changed everything about how he saw the man. Aaron lifted his face and let the ocean breeze dry his eyes. He didn't cry; he wasn't sure he could cry. Even so, his heart ached for the thoughts weighing on him. He stared at the moon's reflection on the bay and tried to imagine what that night in the hospital room must've been like.

He'd never been a father, never cared for anyone as much as he cared about himself and his career. No one except Amy Briggs.

When Derrick told that story, Aaron felt like he was there, like it was his own son Derrick was talking about. The hurt somehow transferred deep into his heart, to a loss he'd never registered before tonight. The loss of a different child that maybe, just maybe, was his own. The one Amy had told him about his sophomore year at UCLA.

By then Bill Bond had already been saying how Amy was seeing other guys on the side, and how she was only sticking around for the money. When Bill heard about Amy's claim to be pregnant, he scoffed at the idea. "She's playing you, Hill. You're a star, and you're letting a girl play you. Come on, now."

Aaron even wondered if maybe his agent had talked to Amy, discouraged her from fighting for their relationship. Aaron had asked him, but Bill only dismissed his question. "You take care of the football," he would say whenever the subject came up, "and I'll take care of the riffraff. And there will always be riffraff." At the time, Bill's comments were comforting. Aaron couldn't trust Amy, but he could always count on his agent.

Every day, every year since then, he'd told himself the same thing. He couldn't have been the father. Amy was seeing other guys and maybe she wasn't even pregnant. He never saw proof, never saw her with a bulging middle. And he certainly never heard anything about the child.

A boat passed by, and from somewhere out on the water he could hear laughter. He waited until it faded, until only the lapping of the water against the shore remained. The smell of seawater filled his senses, and he hung his head again.

What if he was wrong? Aaron gritted his teeth. What if Amy had really been pregnant? What if she'd had a child, Aaron's child, and he'd spent all these years not knowing it?

How could he have turned her away, let her fall out of his life without even a hint at closure?

What was he thinking back then? He was a kid, a boy whose dream was unfolding faster than night traffic on the Ventura Freeway. Strangers waited for him every time he left a class or headed out to his car in the UCLA parking lot. Bill Bond was the one who stuck, the one who seemed like the friend and father he'd never had.

Bill thought Amy was bad for his career, so that settled it. Aaron gave her some lame words and a lot of cold shoulder, and after a blur of seasons, he signed a pro contract. By then, Amy was so far gone from his life, it was like she never existed at all.

But she had existed, and he'd wronged her.

Hearing Derrick's story tonight stirred his memory and his conscience and brought to light wrongs that had been eating at him since the last time he talked to Amy. Even if he hadn't acknowledged it until now.

He opened his eyes and Megan Gunn's face filled his heart. She was crazy for that little boy of hers, even if she was only his foster mother. In that way, she was the opposite of everything about him. When he'd heard about a fatherless child, when Amy had come to him with news of her pregnancy, he'd taken a quick door and disappeared from her life. When Megan heard about a child without a father, she stepped up and gave her whole life, everything she had. Her freedom and reputation, her dating life, her time and finances. All of it.

His face was dry, but the ache in his heart stayed. What sort of person was he, to let all these years pass without even calling Amy? If she really was seeing guys behind his back—however Bill Bond knew that—then no, they wouldn't have worked out. But he could've at least had a final conversation with her. He could've asked why he hadn't been enough for her.

Then, as if the events of the evening had crystallized his memories of Amy, he realized for the first time that something didn't ring true: Amy hadn't dated a single guy all of high school until the two of them went to his prom. Why would she have suddenly done any differently? He should've pressed his agent harder about his evidence, his proof that Amy was cheating.

A crazy thought hit him, and his gut tightened in a sick feeling. What if Bill had made up the whole story about Amy? He might've done it in a twisted attempt to protect Aaron, right? It was possible. Even now, nearly a decade later, the breakup didn't make sense.

He slid down off the boulder and walked to the water's edge. Amy was probably married with three kids and a wonderful life. Whatever had happened back when he was a sophomore in college, she was certainly over it by now. Over him.

He couldn't do anything about the past, but he could try to figure out his future. He needed to talk to Bill, get more details about whatever he'd found out about Amy. Bill didn't like Amy, and now he didn't like Megan. Maybe Aaron had spent enough time listening to his agent and not his heart.

He turned and began walking back to his car, his Hummer. Nothing felt right, not the way he carried himself or the way he looked at tomorrow. Something needed to change, but he wasn't sure exactly what. He pulled out his cell phone and punched in Derrick's phone number. His new friend answered on the first ring.

"Hey, man, you forget your doggie bag?" It was the Derrick he was more familiar with, the one with a ready one-liner.

Aaron didn't feel like smiling. He kept walking. "You doing that pizza party thing for the youth center again this week?"

"Yep." The teasing dropped from Derrick's tone.

"Can I go?" He was breathless, but not from the walk. "I'm serious, I can't explain it. Being with those kids ... it made me feel good."

"I don't know, Hill. No one at the center wants a media circus."

"No press. I didn't bring any last time. I won't even tell my agent."

Derrick was quiet for a beat. "Okay. The kids would like it."

"Good." A hint of relief sparked in his soul. "Thanks, man."

The drive home took longer than usual, Aaron's mind running through the details of everything he'd seen and felt that night. He needed to be stronger, needed to stand up to his agent a little more often. He couldn't go back and make things up to Amy. But he could spend next Friday night at the Mission Youth Center, working alongside a woman unlike any he'd ever met. And maybe this time he wouldn't try so hard to hit on her. It might be enough just to watch her, study her.

Maybe in the process, some of her strength would rub off on him.

Sixteen

M egan wasn't sure what to make of seeing Aaron Hill enter the youth center next to Derrick and Jay Ryder that Thursday night. But here he was, and something seemed different about him. Every time she stole a glance in his direction, he was locked in sincere conversation with a child, not just giving out an autograph and a practiced smile, but actually caring about them. At least it looked that way.

Megan grabbed a dishrag from a bucket of hot soapy water. She wrung it out and worked it over the food table. It was six-thirty and most of the kids had already eaten since the party started at five tonight. Megan lifted her eyes to the front of the room. It was Cory's turn to talk to Aaron.

Megan straightened, because this was her boy. He could catch her watching and that wouldn't be a problem. Without looking, she dropped the rag on the table and took a few steps forward. Cory was standing directly in front of Aaron, and Aaron had his hands on Cory's shoulders. Whatever the quarterback was saying, the atmosphere looked happy and upbeat. Which left only one explanation. The guy still hadn't read Cory's letter.

Megan sighed and returned to her cleaning. What would it take, five minutes? Could Aaron really care so little about the boy that he wouldn't give even that much time to read the letter of a young fan? She tucked a strand of hair behind her ears and took her anger out on the messy table. She was finishing the job when she heard Cory run up behind her.

"Megan, quick ..." He was breathless and excited.

She set the rag back in the bucket and turned to him. He needed to get home and work on his times tables. "Ready to go?"

"No." He came to a sudden stop and his expression fell. "Aaron wants to go to the park." Cory pointed toward the open gym door. "It's still light."

Megan hesitated. She didn't want Cory spending time with a guy who couldn't be bothered to read a kid's letter, but maybe the park was a good idea. That way she could pull Aaron aside and tell him what she thought of him. Megan nodded slowly. "Yes." She brushed her hands on her jeans and smiled at the boy. "Let's go to the park."

The line of kids was much shorter today, so Aaron had no trouble leaving early. He said a few words to Derrick and Jay, and then he looked at her and smiled. It wasn't the come-on smile he'd flashed at her the first time they met. Now there was depth and something else in his look. A bittersweet sadness. Whatever it was, Megan's heart reacted to it, and she chided herself. The next hour had to be about Cory, not about some misguided infatuation the guy had for her.

They met up at the door and he kept his eyes on her. "Thanks for doing this." He glanced at Cory. "I know it's a school night."

"That's okay." Cory placed himself between them. "I only have a little homework."

"You have your sevens." Megan gave him a teasing frown. "Let's not forget that."

"Right. My sevens." Cory managed to seem subdued for a moment before bursting into a big grin again. "Still, the sevens will always be there. Right, Megan?"

Despite the seriousness of what lay ahead—at least from her perspective—Cory's comment made her laugh. She put her hand on his shoulder as they walked. "You have a point."

They were passing the youth center parking lot when Aaron motioned to his Hummer. "Just a minute." He jogged over, opened the door, and snagged a football from the front seat. He smiled at Cory as he shut the door. "Wanna play catch?"

"Wow! Really?" Cory ran to him and held out his hands. Aaron tossed him the ball, and the two caught up with Megan again and headed up the street. Again Megan was baffled. No matter how she tried, she couldn't figure Aaron out. If he'd read the letter, then why was he taking them to the park? Why offer to play catch with the boy? If he hadn't read the letter, then his actions were all a well-put-together show, intended to impress her that he was someone he wasn't.

Megan redirected her thoughts. The sky was blue, the day warmer than usual. "Indian summer," the customers at Bob's Diner had called it earlier today. It was still warm enough that none of them needed a jacket. Cory kept the conversation going as they made the five-minute walk. "Derrick's pretty good." Cory squinted up at Aaron. He had the football tucked beneath his right arm.

"Derrick's very good." Aaron's tone held a level of respect that hadn't been there before. "He's teaching me a lot."

Megan listened, interested. The papers had hinted that Aaron had been frustrated when Derrick was acquired earlier this year. She let her eyes meet Aaron's. "Derrick could help the team this year."

"He could." No defensiveness rang in his tone. "No question. I'm glad we have him."

They reached the park and walked until they came to a large patch of grass. Aaron took the ball from Cory. "Okay ..." He drew his arm back, ready to throw. "Go long!"

Cory ran as fast and hard as he could, his eyes never leaving Aaron. "Ready!"

Aaron winged a perfect spiral straight into Cory's hands. "Nice catch." He jogged a little closer and held out his hands. Cory threw the ball back and Aaron chuckled. "You're pretty good, Cory."

"Thanks."

Megan felt guarded and jaded, and she wondered at her sanity for allowing this trip. Still, Cory would remember it as long as he lived, the chance to play catch with Aaron Hill in a city park. She moved to a nearby bench and sat down, mesmerized by the picture they made. Again, she noticed a resemblance between them. The same sandy blond hair, the same cheeks.

Ridiculous, isn't it, God ... why am I thinking that way? Cory isn't Aaron's son, so why sit here and get caught up in the fantasy? Just because they look so natural together? That's not a good reason, and I know it. So give me a clear mind, God. Please ...

She filled her lungs and kept her focus. This wasn't about Cory, not a bit.

When ten minutes had passed, a boy from Cory's soccer team called to him from across the small park. The boy was with his dad and brothers, and he wanted Cory to join him on the climbing structure. The boys didn't seem to recognize Aaron through the long shadows and trees that marked the distance between them, and when Cory hesitated, Aaron tucked the ball under his arm. "Go ahead. I want to talk to Megan for a minute anyway."

Her heart skipped a beat. What could he want to talk to her about? Cory headed off to play with the kids, and Aaron ambled over to her. The bench wasn't long, and now she slid toward the side, giving him plenty of room. He sat down and caught his breath, his eyes still on Cory. "I like that kid."

"He likes you." Megan folded her hands. It took everything she had to keep her tone pleasant. "But I think he'd like you even more if you read his letter."

Aaron set the football down between them and leaned over his knees. "I read it." He was still watching Cory. "That's why I wanted to come here. So we could talk."

Megan gripped the edge of the bench. "You understand, right? Cory thinks you're his father."

Aaron looked at her. "You and I both know that isn't the case."

There it was. Never mind the resemblance, Aaron Hill was not Cory's father. "Of course." She hurt for Cory, for the disappointment ahead. "That little boy wants a dad so badly, he somehow created this … this idea. And now he believes it."

"I know. I can tell." Aaron sat up straight and shifted so he could see her better. "I've never had this happen." His words were thoughtful, not rushed or nervous. "I figured you'd know best what should take place from here."

Megan tried to understand. She angled her face. "You don't owe him anything, Mr. Hill."

Her use of his last name hit its mark, but this time Aaron didn't correct her. Instead, his eyes danced with a teasing that made him seem warm and familiar. "I realize that … Ms. Gunn." He paused. "But I like him. And I sort of like you too." He grimaced. "Though I'm not sure why, really."

The awkwardness of the moment and the emotions battling each other came together in a nervous laugh. She leaned back on the bench and turned her attention to Cory again. "I'm not sure either."

"Anyway … Cory has to know the truth." His teasing faded. "I've learned a little about kids lately. Someone told me the other day that I shouldn't lie — not to kids or adults."

"True." Megan stifled a smile. "So Cory needs to know, and you're not sure how to tell him?"

"Or if I should tell him." He sighed. "Maybe it should come from you."

"Maybe." A pair of birds flew past and landed in a tree a short distance from the bench. The sounds of the boys on the play equipment made the atmosphere feel comfortable and familiar. "Actually, I've told him before. Lots of times."

A curious look came over Aaron. "So he's believed this for a while?"

"Since his mother died." Megan felt the familiar sorrow. "Two years ago, when Cory was six."

"Oh…" Aaron closed his eyes for a moment and groaned. "I wondered… about his background, what led him to the foster care system."

"His mother and I were friends. We worked together."

"Did she …" He sounded slightly uncertain. "Did she ever mention me?"

"No. Not once." Megan gave him a sad smile. "She was single as long as I knew her. Never dated. Spent every spare moment with Cory." Her attention shifted to the boy, still playing in the distance. "If she thought you were her son's father, she would've said something. I have to believe that."

Aaron was quiet, taking in the details of Cory's life.

"I want to adopt him, Mr. Hill. I'm all the boy has." She felt the futility of Cory's situation, deep in her heart. "The system won't let me make him my own until they get his father to sign off. He insists you're his father, so his social worker isn't ready to label him abandoned."

"Wow." He raised his eyebrows. "It's that serious, then."

"It is." Her tone lightened some. "That's why I knew you hadn't read his letter."

"Yeah." He winced. "I got that pretty much the minute I read it." He stretched his legs, linked his hands, and placed them behind his head. "How did you wind up with Cory?"

"His mother came down with pneumonia. She called me, but it was too late." She shrugged. "Cory had nowhere to go, no family, so he stayed with me during the funeral week, and that's when I realized it was up to me. I went through the training and became a foster mother."

For a few seconds Aaron said nothing. Then he looked at her and his eyes seemed to see deeper, past her heart and into her soul. "You must love him very much."

"I do." She felt the weight of her responsibility, the way she felt it often. "There're so many kids like Cory. Someone has to do something to help them."

They talked some about the system, and how younger children could get by okay. "But when no one steps up and adopts these kids, then what?"

She told him the statistics, how hard life was on the older teenage foster children and how they were often left to fend for themselves once they became adults. "Derrick told me at the last pizza party he's talking to Jay Ryder about the two of them starting a foundation. Derrick and Jay might testify before the state legislature and see about getting laws changed."

"I'm impressed." He sounded sincere. "I didn't know much about foster kids until a few weeks ago."

"And now a foster boy thinks you're his dad." Her smile was intended to show him empathy. This talk was good for her. He wasn't the bad guy she'd made him out to be. Deep inside he cared more than she gave him credit for, or at least he was starting to care.

"Cory deserves a dad." Aaron picked up the football and rolled it around in his fingers. "Every kid does."

They talked a few more minutes, and then Cory came sprinting over. Megan wanted to finish the conversation. "I'll tell him. It's okay."

"That'd probably be better."

Cory reached them, a smile stretched across his face. "Ready?"

"More catch?" Aaron stood and patted Cory on the back. "You bet."

For another fifteen minutes, they tossed the ball. Megan watched, and in the distant part of her heart, the part that still believed in happy endings, a sorrow took root. Because the moment Cory was having was all make-believe. Aaron Hill was a busy guy. Just because Cory had some strange delusion that Aaron was his father didn't obligate the quarterback to spend time with him. Megan hoped Cory was holding on to every moment of this magical afternoon. Because the odds of it happening again—now that the truth was out on the table—were next to nothing.

Aaron walked them back to the center and gave them a ride home. Again, he looked like he wanted to come up, maybe share coffee or more conversation. But he didn't ask. Cory told Aaron goodbye. "Let's play again sometime, okay?"

"Definitely." Aaron reached into the backseat across the console and gave Cory a hug before the boy stepped out onto the curb. Then he turned and faced Megan. "We're away this week and next."

"I know. Cory told me." Megan's mouth was dry. Why was she letting him have this effect on her? She wasn't a football groupie, and she didn't want to date him or anyone else. So why did he make her heart beat faster every time he looked into her eyes? "And no more pizza parties, right?"

"Not for now. Derrick said he might put something together mid-season on our bye week, but it'll be pretty busy." His eyes lit up. "After the season, though. Derrick and Jay are talking about making a regular event out of stopping by the center."

"That's right." Megan had heard the director talking about the possibility. Nothing was for sure yet. "Anyway, thanks for reading his letter." She looked intently at him, trying to figure him out. "I sort of thought we wouldn't see you again, once you knew what Cory thought about you."

"Why?" His smile was easy. "Little boys create fantasy worlds all the time. It's part of being a kid." The smile faded. "I don't want him hurt, that's all."

"I'll tell him. Maybe not tonight, but before the weekend."

Megan wasn't looking forward to the moment. Cory wouldn't believe her at first, but if she explained that she and Aaron had talked, then as sad and difficult as the truth would be for a while, the boy would have no choice but to believe it. She took a quick breath and reached for the door handle. "The good news is I can adopt him now. If he tells the social worker he doesn't know his dad, and since there's been no father in the picture all these years, the judge will clear him for adoption."

A depth shone in Aaron's eyes. "I don't envy you, having to tell him the truth."

"Yeah. I'll be doing a lot of talking to God this week."

For a moment, it looked like Aaron might ask about that, about God. But Cory was waiting on the sidewalk, and Megan had to get going. Aaron put both hands on the steering wheel. "Can I call you? After the road games?"

There was no reason for Megan to say yes. But before she could stop herself, she grinned at him. "I'm not sure why, Mr. Hill." She could feel her eyes sparkling. "But you can call. I can let you know how Cory took the news."

"Okay." He started to reach out, as if he might take her hand or touch her shoulder. Then he pulled back and smiled. "I enjoyed today, our talk. Learning about Cory and getting to know you better."

She smiled before she could stop herself. "Me too." Then, with her heart racing at triple time, she stepped out on the sidewalk, shut the door, and gave him a final wave.

On the way up the stairs, Cory tapped on her arm. "Hey …"

500 ⟶ KAREN KINGSBURY

"What?" She stayed a step ahead of him, because if she moved fast enough, maybe she could outrun the strange emotions whirling in her heart, the feelings she was starting to have for Aaron Hill.

"You looked sorta happy in there, talking to Aaron." He was teasing her, using the voice kids use when they think two people like each other. "I think he has a crush on you, Megan."

"He doesn't." Her answer was quick. She reached the third floor and made a straight line for the apartment door. "He's just trying to be nice."

"Hmmm." Cory had to run every few steps to keep up. "I don't think so."

Once they were inside, Megan directed Cory to get his backpack. "Take your math papers. I'll be in your room in a minute."

He did as he was told. When she was alone, she fell against the door and closed her eyes. Her heart was still racing, still betraying her. She should've said something to stop the madness. She could've told him that, by the way, she wasn't interested, or she could've asked him not to call. Most of all, she could've avoided saying "Me too" when he told her he enjoyed their talk that day. But then that would've been going against her own beliefs, and that's what troubled her most.

Because lying wasn't right, no matter what.

Seventeen

A aron didn't call her after the road games, and he wasn't sure why. Mostly just that he had a lot to figure out about himself, and someone like Megan Gunn deserved a guy with his act together.

It was Monday night, first official game of the season, and the 49ers were hosting the Cardinals. Anticipation and energy were at an all-time high, and the entire team felt it. All week, sports announcers and media members had guessed about the game and about the coming season. Indianapolis would be strong again, and so would the Bears and the Patriots. Most talk shows liked San Francisco in tonight's game, because the team had buffed up its defense with the draft and traded well for a receiving team that would complement Aaron's abilities. But the team was still picked to place just third in their bracket. Sports media believed Aaron didn't have what it took to win the big game, and oddsmakers in Vegas had them a twenty-to-one shot to win the Super Bowl. The worst odds since Aaron had joined the team.

They were on the field, finishing warm-ups, and Aaron surveyed the stands. Cory would've loved it here tonight, but Aaron couldn't bring himself to invite the boy, to lead him or Megan into believing something that he wasn't sure he could carry through. Aaron wasn't worthy of a girl like Megan Gunn, so maybe it was best to take a step back. Besides, the boy had to know by now that Aaron wasn't his father. So a phone call to Megan or an invitation to the game could've come across as patronizing or charity. Still, Aaron wished they were there.

No matter his own shortcomings, he hadn't stopped thinking about either of them since he dropped them off at her apartment.

Aaron tried to clear his head, tried to focus on warm-ups, which were nearly finished. He took the snap from the center, danced back a few steps, and fired it at a passing receiver. This time, instead of the neat tight spiral he was known for, the ball soared past his teammate and landed ten yards on the other side of the guy.

"You with us, Hill?" Derrick was taking snaps a few feet away. "I mean, come on, you never call, never write. We have one dinner and you ditch me."

Aaron laughed. "I'm here. It's just my head."

"Yeah, well." Derrick stared at him, just as one of the coaches blew a whistle. "Game's starting in five minutes. Might be a good time to reattach it."

"Right." He slapped Derrick's helmet as they jogged back to the sidelines. "I'll do that."

They lost the coin toss, and Aaron was glad. He needed a few minutes to focus on the game. The hype and commotion was all a distant roar compared with the thoughts in his head. Every spare moment since his talk with Derrick, he'd been more and more aware of the life he'd been living. How many people had he used since he'd come into the league? The more he thought about it, the more the trail of his success as a player seemed paved with a stream of nameless, faceless girls, none of whom had meant anything to him.

And for the most part, he probably meant nothing to them. At least that's always what he'd told himself. The girls he hooked up with weren't the types to get broken hearts. They were the type that marked their night with him as another conquest, another line on their résumé. The sort of girls Bill Bond approved of—as long as none of them was underage—because they came and left in the shadows. Girls that didn't hurt his image as a bachelor.

"Keep your play toys in the closet, Hill," Bill would say, "and everything will work out fine for us."

But the more Aaron thought about foster kids and the statistics, how so many became street people, he had to wonder. Some of the women he'd used over the years were probably looking for a way to feel needed. Even for only a night. Did his agent ever think about that?

Aaron knew the answer, and the weight of his sin, his responsibility to those women, stayed on his shoulders like a lead blanket. Even here on the sidelines. Beneath the weight of it, he struggled to find the carefree, cocksure athlete he'd been before showing up that first night at the youth center.

Aaron focused on the unfolding game. The 49ers' defense held the Cardinals to three plays and a punt. Now it was his turn, whether he felt good about himself or not. He jogged over to Coach Cameron and listened for the plan.

"Hill, what's eating you?" Coach's eyes were dark with worry.

"Nothing." Aaron let his gaze fall to the ground. "Just some things I'm working through."

"Work it through later." Coach gave him a hard pat on the back. "I mean it, Hill. We need you a hundred percent tonight."

"Yes, Coach." Aaron steeled himself against the crud in his heart, the weight on his shoulders. Coach was right. This was their opening game. The team needed him. He ran out to the huddle and shot a look of intensity at his offense. "All right guys ... let's do this!"

He sounded convincing, but the drive stalled at the Arizona thirty-yard line. A field goal put them ahead by three, still no matter what he tried, Aaron couldn't engage his heart in the game. He'd played football since high school, and not once in all that time could he remember a game where he struggled to give his all. Until here, opening night. A game televised to the entire country.

The team battled Arizona all night, and Aaron threw an uncharacter-istic three interceptions. Before the fourth quarter, Coach pulled him aside and threatened to put in Derrick or Jay. The talk was enough to give Aaron the push he needed, and in the final five minutes, he threw two touchdown passes, giving the 49ers a three-point victory. His performance was pathetic by any measure. He threw for just over a hundred yards and his touchdown to interception ratio was his worst in four years. But it was a win, and Aaron was grateful.

Media flooded the locker room after the game, but Aaron had noth-ing to say. What could he tell them? That he felt like a creep? That his self-centered past suddenly felt shallow and empty and the result left him with little desire to even play the game, let alone win it? All of America would think he'd lost his mind.

He found Coach Cameron and begged off from the post-game inter-view. "I'm not feeling good."

"Is that what you call it?" Coach's expression went from sarcastic to con-cerned. He pursed his lips and shook his head. "Don't worry about the press. I'll handle them. Get home and get some rest. The schedule won't get any easier."

Aaron stared at the ground. "I'm sorry." His eyes met his coach's. "I'll figure it out."

Coach held Aaron's look for a long moment. Then he nodded and headed off to face the press.

Aaron shuffled toward the showers, dizzy from the strange feelings plaguing him. After a game like tonight, it wasn't always smart to dodge the press. They expected the key players to show up after the game. His missing the interview would give them reason to speculate that something was wrong, that Aaron Hill was maybe fighting an illness or an injury. Two or three games like the one he'd played tonight and they'd start talking about whether he'd lost his edge, whether he should be replaced.

He undressed and stepped into the shower. The hot water felt good on his shoulders, but it didn't wash away the heaviness surrounding him. At some point, he needed to talk to his agent, have a sit-down with him, and get to the bottom of the situation with Amy — even if it had been years since her name had come up. Plus Bill had called a couple times in the past week, telling Aaron about a few A-list actresses and one country singer who had expressed interest in him.

"Say the word and I'll set it up, Hill." Bill sounded beyond excited at the prospect. "We could use a connection like that."

Aaron had made himself clear both times. "I'm not interested. I can find my own relationships."

Bill didn't act offended. He only chuckled, dismissing Aaron. "You'll come around. Guys like you need to mix with your own kind."

Aaron ended both calls before things got too strained. The conversation he needed to have with Bill wasn't one they could have with his agent chuckling on the other end of a phone line.

Aaron ran the bar of soap over his aching biceps and under his arms. If he didn't know better, he'd think the fog in his head was depression. Something he'd never even considered.

When he was dressed, he grabbed his bag and kept his head low. Derrick caught up with him just as he was heading out to the parking lot. "Hey, man... talk to me."

"I'm okay."

"You're doing it again." Derrick put his hands on his hips. "You're lying to me."

"No." Aaron tried to find a smile. "I need some time, that's all." He appreciated his teammate more than the guy knew. But he needed to be alone now. Being in Derrick's presence only made him feel worse about himself. All he had to offer was glitz and looks and athletic ability. The deeper places—the places that shone brightest for Derrick Anderson and even for Jay Ryder—were for Aaron draped in cobwebs.

Derrick studied him. "All right, but I'm warning you, man."

Aaron waited. He wasn't quite able to look his friend in the eyes.

"I'm talking to God about you, Hill." He shook his head. "Mmm-hmmm, let me tell you, when someone starts talking to God about you, look out."

"Yeah?" He looked at Derrick.

"Oh, yeah. Changes start happening so you don't recognize yourself in the mirror." He took a step closer and gave Aaron the sort of hearty hug typical between athletes. "I'm here if you need me, man. Seriously."

He coughed and tried to find his voice. He wanted to thank his friend, but all he could manage was, "See ya." Then he hurried outside to his Hummer.

As he neared it, a slim blonde woman wearing a short dress and heels stepped out from behind one of the other player's cars.

She blocked his path and batted her eyes at him. "Hey, Aaron."

He vaguely recognized her. Once maybe a year or so ago they'd shared a night together, he was pretty sure. Now the thought of that, the way it was empty and meaningless, made him sick to his stomach. But the familiar temptation was there too. He stopped and shifted his bag a little higher onto his shoulder. For a few seconds he gritted his teeth, forcing himself to get control. He lifted his chin and averted his eyes. "Hey."

"It's been too long." She ran her finger down the length of his arm. "I'm free tonight … let's find somewhere quiet for dinner."

Aaron worked the muscles in his jaw. He'd used the blonde for his own selfish pleasure, and she wasn't even bothered by the fact. Not outwardly, anyway. And worse, his body was responding to her touch, reminding him of the pleasures that could lay ahead tonight if he were willing. He breathed in sharply through his nose and then looked straight in her eyes. "Look, I can't tonight." He broke eye contact and stared blankly at a point beyond her. "I'm busy."

The girl's face turned red, and she stumbled for something to say. Her expression grew softer, sexier. She took a step closer. "What I have in mind

... won't take all night, Aaron." She put her hand on his shoulder, her fingers working small delicate circles on his upper back. "You sure you're busy?"

The familiarity of the moment intensified the struggle. Aaron stared at his shoes and considered her offer, the way a night like those he had experienced so often before might ease his burden for a while. But then what? He pictured Megan, her determination to make life right for an orphaned boy, and he pressed his lips together.

In a rush, he pushed the young woman's hand off his shoulder and took a step back. "Go find some other football player." He snarled at her, the feelings of temptation quickly giving way to disgust. "I told you I'm busy."

Without another look at her, he walked past her to his Hummer.

"Aaron ..." He could hear her walking toward him. "I'm sorry if I came on too strong ... maybe we can just have coffee somewhere ... maybe we—"

He climbed into the driver's seat and slammed the door before she could finish her sentence. He hated the girl for trying to make him give in, and he hated the fact that he'd slept with her before.

As he drove off, he realized something else. He hated his car. Everyone in the city knew he drove a Hummer, and at stoplights he was often recognized by other drivers. For what? So he could make it clear to the world he was Aaron Hill, that he had enough money to drive an expensive car? So he could feel bigger than life on the field and off?

The cell phone on his console vibrated and he punched a button.

"Hey, Hill ... good game." Bill Bond's voice filled the car.

"It wasn't good, and you know it." Aaron gripped the wheel and picked up speed as he entered the freeway. "I've been in the league seven years, Bill. You don't need to blow smoke at me."

"So it wasn't our best showing." Bill's voice was upbeat as usual. "Got the whole season ahead, friend ... not to worry!" He barely paused. "Speaking of which, I'm your best friend and you don't make it up to the box to say hello after the game? I mean, come on, Hill. I had three brokers I wanted you to meet."

"I didn't feel good." Aaron switched lanes and settled back into his seat. He needed a meeting with Bill, but he would let his agent do the talking first. "What's up?"

"Strategy." He dropped the friendly tone, and his voice took on an urgency. "This is a big year for you, Hill. Very big. Everyone in the business is whispering about it being time. You prove yourself now, or maybe you're not all America had you cracked up to be."

"Maybe I'm not."

Bill paused, and then he let loose another short burst of laughter. "Yeah, well, this isn't a joke, friend."

In college, and even in the years after signing his pro contract, Aaron had liked how Bill called him friend. The word seemed an accurate reflection of the relationship he shared with his agent, the way the guy looked out for him. Aaron usually felt comforted by the fact, reminded that Bill wasn't only interested in making money off him, but in caring for his career, his future. The way a friend would care.

Lately the word grated on Aaron's nerves. It felt cheap and forced and saccharin. Bill never asked how he was or how he might be feeling, why his game had struggled tonight, for instance. His calls were always about strategy and key meetings and endorsements. Things good for Bill's bottom line.

His agent was going on about a new plan, something he'd discussed with some marketing people at one of his big sports clothing sponsors. "Here's the deal…" Bill picked up speed as he went along, practically stumbling over his own words in his excitement over this new venture, whatever it was. "Okay, so at the meeting we all decided your image needs an update. The foster kid thing was nice short-term, but it's not enough."

Anger rose quickly in Aaron's gut. He was tempted to push the Off button, but strangely Bill's monologue fascinated him in a twisted sort of way. It was like looking in the mirror and seeing what he'd become, what he'd let himself become.

"So …" Bill was clearly winding up, "we all agreed it was time you got married."

"Married?" Aaron was so caught off guard he nearly rear-ended the car in front of him. He hit his brakes. "Are you kidding me? A marketing meeting can't decide my personal life."

"Of course not." His agent rushed ahead. "You'll pick the lucky lady. I mean, come on, Hill." He laughed. "You have some say, after all."

Aaron clenched his jaw and waited.

"Here's the reason. You've been single all these years and it's been a good thing. Good for your image. Boys and teenagers and college kids, all of them could relate to you. Best quarterback in the league, a fearless gunslinger admired by women around the country. Around the world!" His tone changed. "But you're almost thirty, my friend. Stay single after thirty and you lose some appeal. Guys have less ability to relate to you, understand?"

Aaron gritted his teeth. "That's garbage, Bill. No one makes a corporate decision to get married. I'm not even dating anyone."

"Good." He sounded beyond relieved. "As a side note, I did some checking at the Mission Youth Center on that woman you asked to the Raiders game. Megan Gunn."

Aaron couldn't remember giving Bill her name. But he wasn't surprised that his agent found out. He had a way of knowing whatever Aaron was involved in, something that even a year ago had brought Aaron comfort. Not anymore. He felt his anger double. "I don't believe this."

"She's not your type, friend. She's a single mother, of course. But more than that—her mother was a drug user, a street person. You probably don't know, but this … this Megan has several jobs—none of them high paying. She dropped out of college and she apparently has no plans to complete her degree."

"So basically she's poor." Aaron's voice seethed with rage.

"Slow down, there. It's more than that. She's a single mother." He paused. "How would that look? Everyone who saw you together would wonder if maybe the kid was yours. Otherwise why would you spend so much time with him?" He whistled low. "An illegitimate kid, I'm telling you that would be bad, Hill. Very bad."

Aaron wanted to know about the rest of the marketing meeting. "So your little strategy session, who do you think I should marry? Did you figure that out?"

"Not exactly." He laughed again. "But I've been telling you about the A-listers, the actresses and the singer. I know you don't agree yet, but Hill, you have to think about it. There's some real potential there."

"Potential?" Aaron felt his face growing hot. More amazing than his agent's plan was the fact that he was serious. He truly thought he could plan Aaron's marriage at a marketing meeting.

"Starlets. That's the trend. Big name entertainers have their agents contact the agents of certain star football players. A meeting is set up and voila! Instant romance." Again, he barely stopped long enough to breathe. "The marketing gurus think a wedding with one of the top stars could raise your endorsement worth a million dollars a year or more. I mean, talk about your win-win situations. It'd be the top news for a month."

His anger became a sick feeling that hit with a vengeance. Aaron needed all his concentration to focus on the road. "So just flip through the tabloids and pick out a starlet?"

"No." Bill sounded hurt. "Nothing like that." His voice changed, as if this next part was top secret information. "The fact is, those inquiries I told you about, they're legit, Hill. A couple phone calls and the first meeting's a done deal."

That was it. He couldn't take another minute. "Look, Bill. I'm on the road. I'll call you back." He stabbed his finger at the Off button. Was his agent out of his mind? Or was this how Bill had always acted? His agent thought nothing of telling Aaron this was the year he should get married, that he might be worth another million or so if he did. Because he'd been making calls like this one since he first gained Aaron's trust.

A starlet? Aaron shook his head, his breath hissing out in disbelief as he replayed the conversation in his mind. A big wedding, something the newspapers and ESPN and the tabloids could all get excited about. Everyone but him. He leaned back in his seat and exhaled long and slow.

He didn't want to marry a movie star, someone more self-centered than he'd always been. If he were going to marry some day, he would choose someone different.

He thought about that for a moment. He'd never really explored his feelings before, but he suddenly realized he'd prefer a woman who couldn't care less that he was Aaron Hill, famous quarterback. He'd had enough of the shallow women he picked up in bars across the country. Women like the one he'd pushed away in the parking lot tonight. No, he wanted someone with depth. A woman with strength and determination and intellect. Perhaps a woman who understood the virtue of volunteer work and helping the less fortunate. Someone whose faith and honor shone from the depths of her heart. Who was willing to work three jobs so she could pay rent and keep food on the table. A woman with dark hair and fine features and unforgettable blue eyes.

The sort of woman he'd been avoiding every day for the past few weeks. A woman named Megan Gunn.

Derrick and Denae prayed with their kids and went out on their upper deck to talk. It was late, and already they'd told the kids they could miss the first half of tomorrow's school day. That was their tradition whenever Derrick's team played a Monday night game.

It felt good to fall into the patio chair outside their bedroom slider. Derrick worked his fingers into the muscles above his right knee. "Long day."

"Definitely." She made a curious face. "Something's wrong with Aaron. Did you feel it tonight?"

He sighed and gripped the arms of his chair. "Baby, I think the whole country felt it."

"I was ready to walk down there and give Coach a piece of my mind." She huffed. "Keep my baby on the bench when the game's falling apart."

Derrick smiled. "Mighta helped."

She crossed her arms. "That Cardinal team isn't so great. You could've won the game with one hand tied behind your back."

"That's my baby." Derrick allowed a quiet bit of laughter. "Still my number one fan."

"No one loves you better." Her attitude still sounded in her voice. "I could barely sit there watching that young guy mess things up."

A softness filled Derrick's heart. "Aaron's got it bad, that's for sure."

Denae's tone lifted some. "So what's the problem? Do I need to talk to the boy?"

"No." Derrick stared out at the moon on the water. The bay was so beautiful. It was one more way he felt God's favor on him this season — even if winning the Super Bowl was a long shot. "Remember, baby, we talked about how God brought me here for a reason."

"I know." She still had some frustration in her expression. She brushed her hand in front of her. "So why does He park you on the bench through a nail-biter like tonight?"

His answer was slow in coming. "Because maybe He brought me here for Aaron Hill."

"Yeah. You've said that before." She sounded doubtful. "You really think that, baby?"

"I do. God's working in that young man." He made a fist and pressed it to his heart. "I can feel it deep inside."

"Could be indigestion after a game like that." She muttered the words under her breath. Then she turned and faced him. "Don't get me wrong, I like the guy. But tonight … he wasn't trying, baby. You'da done better."

"I don't know." Derrick leaned his elbow on the arm of the chair and stroked his chin. "This season's something special, Denae. It's like God's working out a bunch of miracles all at once." He turned to her. "Really."

She was quiet for a long time. Then she reached out and took his hand. "So maybe next time Coach'll put you in?"

Derrick smiled again. "Maybe even that."

Neither of them said anything about Derrick's promise to Lee, or the fact that this was his last season to make good on it. Winning a Super Bowl wasn't something a player could control by himself. It wasn't something a team could will, either. Every team in the NFL wanted a trophy at the end of the run. Besides, Denae was right—Aaron looked weak out there. He'd struggled bad against a team that figured to finish in the bottom half.

Maybe that's exactly the way God wanted tonight to go. Maybe it would get worse before things started moving full speed ahead. That way when they all stood around at the end of the season marveling at the victories on and off the field, they would know for certain they hadn't found their way there by hard work and determination.

But by God alone.

Eighteen

Megan was making macaroni and cheese in a pot on the stove, and Cory was sitting at the kitchen table reading *Tom Sawyer* from the school library. The radio was tuned to a country station, and a song about miracles was playing. Megan hummed along, but even then, Cory's silence hurt.

Megan had told him the truth about Aaron, and since then, Cory had been much quieter, less excited and talkative. The furor over Aaron Hill's involvement in their lives had dropped off now that it had been three weeks since their outing to the park. Megan understood Cory's disappointment. But she wished there was a way to get through to him that the truth wasn't her fault.

The problem was he still believed the fantasy. Which was exactly what Megan had feared all along. She was beginning to wonder if maybe she'd taken the wrong approach with the news. Maybe Aaron should've been the one to set him down and explain that no, he wasn't Cory's father. That way, maybe Cory could hardly refute the fact.

She glanced at him, but he was lost in the book. He'd been reading more lately, books and not the newspaper. He still tuned in for the games, glued to every play — especially Monday night when Aaron pulled the game out in the last quarter. But Cory didn't talk about the 49ers as much as usual.

They'd been at the youth center late tonight, taking part in an informal tournament of three-on-three games. It was after seven, and she and Cory were both hungry. She stared into the pot and willed the water to boil.

"Megan?"

"Yes?" She looked up, careful to smile at the boy.

"Did Tom Sawyer have a dad?" He planted his elbow on the table and cocked his head.

The question took Megan's breath. *God, do You hear this child? How can I ever be enough for him when all he wants is a father?* She sighed, but not so loud that he could hear her. "I don't know, buddy. What do you think?"

"Well…" Cory looked back at the open book on the table. "He musta had a dad somewhere. Because everyone has a father." He lifted his eyes and met hers.

His point was well-taken in a biological sense. "That's true." She stirred the spoon through the water and noodles again. "But not every father knows how to be a dad. Sometimes they miss out on their child's entire life. A boy like Tom Sawyer might never have known his dad, not ever."

Cory furrowed his forehead and studied the book again. "I think Tom Sawyer had a dad. Maybe the author didn't write that chapter."

"Maybe." Megan stared at the noodles again, but this time her vision blurred. How could she adopt a boy who was so desperate for a daddy? She was still pondering the question when the phone rang. She set the spoon on the countertop and picked up the receiver. "Hello?"

"Ms. Gunn?" Aaron Hill's voice filled the line.

Megan's heart skipped a beat. Why was he calling now, after three weeks of silence? "Yes?"

"I'm parked out front." He sounded unsure of himself. "It being a Friday night and all … I wondered if you and Cory would like dinner out at Pier 39?"

She stared at the packet of powdered cheese mix on the counter. Then she caught herself. It didn't matter how good dinner at the pier sounded. They didn't need Aaron's charity, and there could be no other reason why he was here. She turned her back on Cory. "Tell me why."

"Why what?"

"Why dinner? Why now?"

He exhaled and his frustration was evident. "Can you come down here, Megan. Please."

She hesitated, but then she felt herself giving in. He'd driven all the way out here. He deserved the chance to explain himself. "Just a minute." She hung up the phone, turned off the stove, and stared at Cory. "Be right back, okay?"

"Where're you going?" He'd been too lost in the book to figure out who was on the phone.

"Downstairs. I have to talk to someone."

"Okay." Cory didn't look interested. He focused on the book again. "Is dinner almost ready?"

"Almost." She slipped on her sandals, and as she hurried out the door and down the stairs, she ran her fingers through her hair. No matter how she'd reacted on the phone, it felt wonderful to hear his voice again. But what was she thinking? She reached the last few stairs and slowed her pace as she moved toward the door. She was as bad as Cory, fantasizing that Aaron Hill had changed into a gentleman, and more, that she could ever trust a guy like him with any piece of her heart.

More likely, the youth center had showed him a side of life he hadn't acknowledged before. Now he was focusing his attentions on Cory and her as a way of making up for times when he hadn't thought of those less fortunate than himself. In other words, he probably saw them as a charity case. She took a steadying breath. She would thank him profusely for coming and explain that they were getting along fine. They didn't need his favors.

She opened the door and scanned the street for his Hummer. It took a few seconds to realize he was right in front of her, in the driver's seat of a light gray pickup truck. It was newer, a full-size with rear doors and a long bed. But it had none of the sparkle of the Hummer. She wrinkled her eyebrows, curious, just as he stepped out and met her near the doorway of the apartment building.

He must've realized she was looking for his Hummer, because he nodded to the truck. "I traded it."

"Really?" Megan narrowed her eyes.

"Yeah." He kept a polite amount of distance between them. "I needed a change." His eyes met hers and held. "In a lot of areas."

Megan wasn't sure what to say in response, so she crossed her arms and looked down at the cement for a few beats.

"Now." His voice was soft. "You were saying?"

Something about his tone washed over her like a caress, and her cheeks suddenly felt hot. She was saying? She swallowed hard and tried to remember their conversation from a few minutes ago. But his nearness was unnerving, breaking down her defenses and leaving her unsure of even a single reason why she and Cory wouldn't have dinner out on the pier with him. She lifted her eyes. "You don't have to do this, Aaron." It was the first time she'd used his given name, the first time she hadn't been completely on her guard. Because there was no reason now. She wanted to be transparent before him. "I told him you're not his father."

Aaron slipped his hands into his jeans pockets. Pain shaded his expression. "How'd he take it?"

"He didn't." She laughed, but it held a hidden cry, a sound of defeat. "He told me he'll believe forever that you're his dad."

Aaron hesitated and then turned halfway around, his eyes raised to the sky. After a few seconds, he looked back at her. "That's so sad."

"I know." A chill hung in the air, and she crossed her arms more tightly. "That's what I mean. You don't owe us a night out." She lifted one shoulder. "You've done enough."

The muscles in his jaw flexed and he took a step back. He seemed to be searching for the words. Finally he came closer again, his eyes locked on hers. "Maybe this isn't about Cory. Maybe I just want to take you out to dinner."

"Why?" Again, she felt defeated. She uncrossed her arms, held up her hands, and let them fall to her side. "I'm not your type. You ..." She looked into the air between them, as if the answers might be drifting by on the breeze. "You're a celebrity, Aaron." She thought about her life, her paper route and her shifts at Bob's Diner, and she uttered a sad laugh. "We couldn't possibly be more different."

"Except one thing." He reached out and touched her bare arm.

The feel of his fingers against her skin sent shockwaves through her body. A part of her couldn't understand why she was fighting him so hard, when all she wanted to do was feel his arms around her. Her teeth chattered and she bit down to still them. "What?"

He looked deep at her, and the tenderness in his eyes was as real as the air they were breathing. "I can't stop thinking about you." He made a lighthearted face. "Believe me, I've tried. Nothing works."

She wanted to say that she knew the feeling. Because as sensible as she was, as much as she prided herself on being intelligent and a realist, she saw his face everywhere she looked. Even when she wasn't watching the 49ers on TV. Instead she bit her lip. "I'm not ready, Aaron. I can be your friend, that's all."

Nothing in his expression changed, but the hint of a smile brightened his face. He let his hand fall back to his side. "I can handle that."

"So." She tilted her face, studying him, trying to figure him out. "Dinner at the pier?"

He nodded, and he looked up to the windows in the apartments above them. "Better go get Cory."

Megan giggled. She stepped back, and then turned and ran lightly through the door and up the stairs. She had questions about herself. Why was she agreeing to this night when it couldn't possibly lead anywhere, and how could she allow Cory to live out his fantasy by spending more time with Aaron? And when did Aaron become the sincere, genuine guy she'd just talked to down on the sidewalk? She silenced the questions as soon as they hit her. She had no answers, anyway. For now, maybe it didn't matter. She and Cory didn't have much, after all. And if this was the last time the two of them hung out with Aaron Hill, so be it. They'd at least have this: A night they would remember the rest of their lives.

~~

Cory could hardly believe it.

Megan came rushing into the apartment and told him to get his shoes and his sweatshirt. They were having dinner with Aaron Hill. He took a minute to catch his breath over the idea, but then he closed his Tom Sawyer book and jumped up from the table. He wanted to say, "See, Megan, I told you so. Told you Aaron is my dad. 'Cause otherwise why would he come to take us for dinner?"

But he didn't say that. He only hurried with his shoes and his sweatshirt, and tried to make his heart stop pounding so hard. The strange thing was that Aaron hadn't said anything about the letter yet. Megan said he talked to her about it, and that he really wasn't Cory's dad.

Cory wasn't so sure he really said that, 'cause why wouldn't he just tell Cory and not Megan. Plus, if Aaron really didn't believe Cory was his son, then that only meant it was Cory's job to convince him. His mother hadn't lied to him, definitely not. She would look right straight in his eyes every time she told him, "Aaron Hill's your daddy, Cory. But it has to be our secret."

He remembered those words coming from her as much as he remembered her saying that Aaron had been her friend in high school and how Aaron was only her friend until he asked her to some dance when they were seniors. A prom or something. Aaron Hill was his dad. That's what she said. Megan always asked then why didn't his mother ever tell Megan? That was a good question. Why didn't she? That would've made everything much easier, 'cause then when she died, there wouldn't be any confusion.

But his mother hadn't expected to die. She got a cold and it went to her lungs and she died without making any plans about Cory's father. That's what happened. And so after Megan's talk with him about Aaron not being his dad, Cory pulled out his special box, the one with the things from his mom. He had some letters she wrote to him, about how much she loved him and how she would always be there for him. Because that's what she wanted, but God had other plans. That's what Megan said.

Also in the box were the newspaper articles, the ones about Aaron. There was one from when he was doing great at UCLA his junior year, and people were talking about him being a pro one day soon. His mom went to a different college. Junior college. But still, she and Aaron were boyfriend and girlfriend. And there were a couple articles from the next year when Aaron won a lot of games and he got drafted in the first round, third pick by San Francisco. After that, she had two in the box from his first couple years as a 49er. Then she stopped cutting out stories about him.

Pictures were in the box too. Pictures of Cory when he was little and when he was learning to walk, and one of him and his mom on the first day of kindergarten. But that was all, 'cause she died after that.

But in the box there was also a big yellow envelope, and inside were three envelopes with Aaron's name written across the front. Another one just said the word "PRIVATE." All three were sealed tight, the way his mother had left them. A long time ago she taught him that you don't open other people's mail. So, even though lots of times Cory was tempted, he never opened the letters. 'Cause they belonged to Aaron.

And that sent a wave of excitement through him, because now Aaron came back! And maybe tonight, or maybe very soon, he would give Aaron the letters and then that would clear up any confusion. He tied his shoes and grabbed his sweatshirt, and then they hurried out the door.

Because it wouldn't be nice to keep his dad waiting.

NINETEEN

Aaron felt like a schoolboy. The sense of victory over convincing Megan to spend an evening with him rivaled the feeling he had after a playoff win. They drove out to Pier 39 and parked, with Cory chattering in the back about Monday's game.

"I never for minute thought you'd lose." He leaned forward and gripped the corner of Aaron's seat. "Not for a minute."

"I did." Aaron rolled his eyes and cast a quick look at Megan.

She put her fingers to her lips, covering a light laugh. "It didn't look good."

"It didn't feel good." He kept his tone easygoing, but only to cover up how he'd really felt that day. How he'd felt every hour since, until now. Later, if the night worked out the way he hoped, he'd have a chance to talk to Megan about the changes happening inside him. He had a feeling she'd understand.

Pier 39 was busy, but that worked in Aaron's favor. With so many people milling along the walkways, between the shops and restaurants and street performers, the crowd would help hide his identity. He wore a baseball cap and a jacket with a high collar. Most of the time he could get away with being in public if he dressed like this.

"You've been before, right?" Aaron walked beside Megan, with Cory on his other side.

"Not often." Her smile held a distance again, the caution that had marked her conversations with him since the beginning. "But yeah, once in a while."

"I've never been," Cory piped in.

They were hungry, but on the way to the restaurant, as they walked along the soft worn slats of wood, they passed the carousel. Cory slowed to a stop and watched it go round a few times. People of all ages sat atop the painted animals and benches, most of them laughing, enjoying the ride. Cory looked at Megan. "I thought merry-go-rounds were for little kids."

"Not this one." She put her arm around his shoulders. "See that." She pointed at the paintings that made up the perimeter of the attraction. "Look close. There's Coit Tower and the Golden Gate Bridge, Lombard Street and Alcatraz." She turned her attention to Aaron. "I read somewhere that this is the only carousel in the country with paintings of its home city."

"I didn't know that." Aaron had the sudden impulse to take her hand, but he resisted. She wasn't ready, that's what she'd said. She wanted a friend, and for now, that's what he would be.

"Wow ..." Cory took a step closer. "That's cool!"

That was all Aaron needed to hear. He saw a ticket booth a few feet away and he motioned to Megan that he'd be right back. As crowded as the place was, the carousel had no line, probably because it was the dinner hour. He bought three tickets and returned to Megan and Cory. "Everyone should ride once."

Cory wasn't about to act too excited. Aaron understood that. At almost nine, he already had a sense of machismo, especially in a crowd. He was a kid who understood the streets and navigated the Mission District on his bike, like he'd told Aaron the first time they met. But there was no mistaking the thrill in his eyes as they got in line and then as they boarded. They chose a trio of painted horses, and Megan climbed on the outside one. Aaron helped Cory onto the inside horse, and he took the middle.

While the carousel made its rounds, Aaron had the strangest thought. What if this was really his life, here between this endearing child and the woman who took his breath away? They were coming to a stop when a teenage boy in the crowd pointed at him. "Aaron Hill!" He looked around and then back again. "Hey, that's Aaron Hill!"

"Looks like we need a fast get-away." Megan climbed off her horse first. She whispered the words to Aaron. "Got a plan?"

"Be my date." He held his elbow out to her. Then as Cory jumped off his horse, Aaron took his hand. "Come on ... let's get out of here."

Megan looped her hand around his bicep, and they hurried off. A little family, with no idea why some kid was yelling at them from the crowd. They slipped between a couple shops and walked out toward the water, toward a walkway that took them to the west end of the pier. The evening was beautiful, the way mid-September always was, but the weather and the fading blue sky had nothing to do with the way he felt. Megan was still holding onto his arm. Aaron released Cory's hand and reached over to cover Megan's fingers with his own. If he had his way, she would never let go. "Thanks." He tried to smile at her, but he got lost in her eyes. "That doesn't happen all that often."

"I'm sure." Her look said she didn't believe him. But she didn't mind, either. She seemed to notice that she was holding onto him longer than necessary, longer than she should. She withdrew her hand and allowed a little extra space between them. "Where are we eating?"

"Yeah." Cory ran a few steps ahead, turned around and walked backward. The way he had a habit of doing. Before either Aaron or Megan could say anything, he backed straight into a wooden post. But he only laughed at himself and gave his back a quick brush-off. "Like I was saying, I'm so hungry I'm dizzy."

"We're almost there." Aaron's heart felt light and free, better than it had felt for weeks. He had no idea where his feelings might lead, especially when he hadn't dealt with his past. But he had to find a way to keep Megan from running out of his life. She was right about their differences. Still, other than his agent's control tactics, there were no rules saying a pro quarterback had to date certain people and avoid others.

Unless that wasn't the reason she was keeping her distance. Maybe she'd read about the teenager in the parking lot of the bar a month ago, or the ongoing tabloid talk that he was a serious bachelor, playing the field outside the stadium as much as he played it inside. The possibility was enough to bring the fog back around his mind and soul. He deserved his reputation. If she'd already made her mind up about him, then he wasn't sure what he could do.

They were at the west end of the pier now, and a crowd gathered off to one side. Even from where they stood, they could hear the barking of dozens of sea lions, perched on an outcropping of rock halfway between the pier and Forbes Island. The farther they walked out onto the pier, the more nervous Megan looked. She checked over her shoulder and stared at the length of the pier. "Is the restaurant up there?"

"No." He pointed out to a small island not far from the end of the pier. "It's out in the water."

"The island?" Megan turned her eyes to him. Her alarm showed in her eyes. "Aaron, I … I can't."

"There's a restaurant out there? On that island?" Cory walked a little closer toward the crowd. "That's so cool! How do we get across?"

"A shuttle boat." Aaron had eaten there a number of times with his linemen. The restaurant had gourmet food, but more than that, it had an intimate atmosphere. He was much less likely to be recognized. "I know the owner."

"Great!" Cory ran toward the edge of the pier and grabbed onto the wooden railing. He pointed at the sea lions, then looked back at Megan.

Only a slight nod came from Megan. She anchored her feet and stared at the wooden slats beneath them. Her face looked pale, and she shook her head a few quick times. "I can't … do it." She kept her voice low, as if she didn't want anyone else to hear.

"Why?" Was she sick, was that the problem? "It's the best food here."

"No, it's the …" she gulped, "the boat. I'm afraid, seriously."

He considered laughing, but he had a strong sense she wasn't teasing. He put his hand on her shoulder. "Really? You're not kidding?"

"I'm not." She shivered a few times and cast wide eyes back at the water. "I'm scared to death of boats."

"How come?"

"I'm not sure." She bit her lip. "I can't swim, for one." She was being painfully honest, because the walls from earlier were down now. "And I saw a show once when I was a little girl, about a boat lost at sea without a captain."

He studied her, and he liked what he saw. In the strength that made up the woman before him, he'd found a chink, one small slight weakness. Cory was still over at the railing, whistling at the sea lions, mesmerized by them. Megan wanted Aaron to keep a certain distance, he was aware of that. But here, now, he only wanted to reassure her. He took a step closer, put his arm around her shoulders, and pulled her close. The hug was the same type he would give a sister, but it sent feelings through him so strong they made him dizzy.

"We'll go somewhere else." He swayed slightly with her. "I didn't know, okay?"

She nodded her head against his chest, and after half a minute she stepped back. "Sorry. I guess I don't think about it that often." Her cheeks were redder than before. "I don't understand it, to be honest. I can do a pa-per route in the dead of night, but I can't step onto a boat."

A paper route? In the city in the dark? Aaron felt a rush of adrenaline release through him. Megan was young and beautiful, hardly someone who should be out on the dark streets delivering papers. He hoped she was kid-ding, but he made a note to ask her about it over dinner. Again, he wanted to take her hand, but he only motioned toward Cory. "Let's take a look."

She followed him to the edge of the pier, but even there Megan seemed nervous. She gave Cory a thumbs-up when he said he'd like to dive off the pier and swim around with the sea lions all day. "Me too." She made a seasick face at Aaron. "Can't think of a better way to spend an afternoon."

Aaron laughed. "Come on, let's go eat." He touched the small of Megan's back and directed her and Cory toward a flight of stairs. "There's a place up here that's all windows." He looked at Cory. "You can watch the sea lions the whole time we eat."

Cory's eyes opened wide. "Wow! This is the best day ever."

They were the same words the boy had said after the Raiders game, and again Aaron knew without a doubt, the boy was telling the truth. Megan didn't say so, but the reason she hadn't been here often — the reason Cory had never been here — was because of money. It had to be. Something Aaron hadn't thought about since long before he signed his pro contract. But if his agent was right, if Megan worked three jobs, then certainly every dollar mat-tered.

They walked up the stairs and into the Sea Lion Café. The food wouldn't be what it would've been on Forbes Island, but that didn't matter. He was here with Megan and Cory. They could eat leather burgers and he'd have a good time. As they entered the restaurant, he leaned close to Megan. He needed her to help hide his identity. "Do the talking, okay?"

She seemed to understand and she took the lead. The hostess sat them next to the window, and Cory took the seat closest to the glass. "Wow, you can see forever from here."

Aaron looked at Megan across from him. Cory's statement suddenly took on a different meaning, and Aaron wanted to tell Megan he felt the same way. Just maybe he could see forever from here too. But he couldn't say so, not now.

They ordered fish and chips, and during dinner, with Cory distracted by the view, Aaron told Megan about his visit to Derrick's house. "He has it all." There was no mistaking the wistfulness in his voice. "His family is amazing."

"I've always liked him." She pulled her iced tea closer and fiddled with the straw. "He has a strong faith, from what I've read."

"He does. I wanna be just like him when I grow up." Aaron grinned and rested his forearms on the table. The noise in the restaurant was less than it had been, so he kept his voice low. "He doesn't make a big show of it, but it's there . . . in everything he does."

"I like that." She grinned at him. "I don't believe in church. But I talk to God all the time."

Aaron mulled over the strength of Megan's opinions. She didn't want a relationship and she didn't believe in church. Clearly, she struggled with trusting people, and that raised his sensitivity level. He drew an even breath. "Derrick says church isn't so bad. Sort of where it all happens — the teaching, the worship . . . the growth. But he calls it 'talking to God' too."

She stirred her straw through the ice cubes in her drink. "That's all it is. Just like you and I are talking right now."

"Hmmm." The idea of talking to God still felt intimidating, but it seemed less foreign all the time. "Derrick's talking to God about me a lot." He gave her a guilty look, one that made her laugh. "No question I need it."

Megan looked out the window for a few seconds and her eyes grew distant. "I saw a TV special on him once, how he's been through every set of emotions possible. The highest highs, and the lowest lows."

Aaron pictured the little boy in Derrick's family photo. "He lost a child six years ago."

Sadness colored her expression. "A car accident, wasn't it?"

"Yes." Aaron took a deep breath and he recounted the gist of Derrick's story. Then he told her about Derrick's promise to little Lee.

Megan looked worried. "You can promise a child a lot of things, but winning the Super Bowl?"

"It's a big order." Aaron leaned back in his chair. "He's pretty serious about it. He's committed to doing everything he needs to do." Aaron looked at his empty plate. "It's his last season."

She sipped her tea and lowered her eyebrows. "I didn't know that."

"He doesn't want a lot of fanfare."

A smile pulled at her lips. "That's fitting. For the sort of guy he seems to be."

They finished eating, and Cory wanted to go back to the edge of the pier, so he could get closer to the sea lions. They headed back down the stairs and closer to the water.

Aaron spotted a bench, one in a much less crowded area. He nodded toward it. "Want to sit there?"

"Sure." The shy look was back in her eyes. Which was better than the walls she'd had earlier.

The sun had set, and now in the dusk it was harder to make out the sea lions on the rocks off the pier. Cory didn't seem to mind. He took his place next to a boy his age, and they appeared to start up a conversation. Aaron sat down on the bench, leaving plenty of room for her. She joined him and gazed out at the water, toward the lighthouse on Forbes Island. She seemed intent about something, so he waited for her to talk first.

"Sorry about the boat thing." She gave him a side glance and then looked back out at the water. "It's ridiculous."

"Don't worry about it. Fear has a mind of its own."

"This one does." She worked her fingers into her hair and shook it out around her shoulders. "The air out here feels so good." She leaned against the armrest and met his eyes. "Next time I'm out here, I'm taking a boat ride. I hate limiting myself."

Aaron wasn't surprised. If he knew her as well as he was starting to, having any fears at all was probably a thorn in Megan's side. "Tell you what ... I win the Super Bowl, and we'll take a boat ride around the bay."

"The whole bay?" She looked like a child, considering the idea of crossing a major street for the first time.

"The whole bay." He loved this, having fun with her this way. He raised his hands, feigning innocence. "That's what you want."

"It is." She didn't look too happy with herself. Then she raised an eyebrow at him. "Of course, you have to win the Super Bowl first."

"You have doubts?"

She angled her head from one side to the other. "Let's just say I wouldn't buy the boat tickets quite yet."

"Thanks." He put his hand up on the back of the bench and studied her profile. She was watching the water again, and he let the silence wash over them for half a minute. Then he asked the first question that came to mind. "What do you do when you're not at the youth center?"

For a split moment, it looked like she might put walls between them again, then she pulled one foot up on the bench, hugged her knee, and faced him. "Well..." Her eyes shone with a newfound trust. "I deliver the *Chronicle* before dawn, and then I go home and get Cory up and ready for school. After breakfast, he sets off on his bike, and I walk to my main job."

Shock hit him hard in the face, but he didn't flinch. Megan actually delivered newspapers before dawn every day. His heart softened, but he kept his tone even. "And your main job?"

"I'm a waitress at Bob's Diner." She said it the same way a quietly confident person would say they were a surgeon or a professor. Her eyes shone with pride and determination. "It's sort of like working as a counselor." She grinned. "We have a lot of regulars."

He didn't know Bob's Diner, but he could imagine a greasy spoon nestled between a dry cleaner's and a drugstore somewhere in the Mission District. And Megan, treating each day like another wonderful counseling session. He ordered himself not to feel sorry for her and instead grabbed at some sort of response. "You've worked there a while?"

"I have. That's where I met Cory's mother. We were coworkers for almost five years before she died."

"So you've been there seven." He smiled.

"Exactly." She looked out toward the water again. "I was a foster kid." Again, she had no shame in the fact. "Did I tell you that?"

"No." He wanted to say he wasn't surprised. That would explain a lot. Her independence and her resistance to relying on other people. Her compassion toward kids like Cory. "Was it hard? Growing up?"

"Sometimes. They moved me around a lot because they kept giving me back to my mom."

There was much Megan wasn't saying, but Aaron didn't want to pry, so he waited. They weren't in a rush. Cory was still busy talking with the kid beside him, and now that darkness had settled over the pier, there was an intimacy between them, a feeling he didn't want to push.

She stretched both legs out in front of her. "My mom loved me very much. I was lucky that way." She found his eyes again. "She had a terrible addiction."

Aaron could imagine what Bill Bond would say about Megan now. A single foster mother working three jobs and struggling with a broken past, a mother who was an addict. It made him want to put his arms around Megan and keep her safe, protect her so no other bad thing could ever harm her again. Protect her, even, from the judgment of his agent.

"The drugs and alcohol killed her in the end. By then I was a college sophomore. I dropped out of school to care for her." She smiled at him and her eyes told the story. She wasn't bitter, but the disappointment remained. "She died later that year."

He breathed in slowly through his nose, letting the story find its place in his heart. "I'm sorry."

"It's okay." She pulled one foot up onto the bench. "We were very close when she died. At peace with each other."

Aaron couldn't begin to grasp the sorrows that had made up Megan's life. He crossed his arms, unable to shake the way he hurt for her. "And your schooling?"

"I'll go back someday. Maybe."

"What were you studying?"

"I was still finishing the pre-reqs, but I knew I wanted a degree in sociology. That or psychology. I always figured I'd be a counselor or a social worker. Without some of my foster parents, I don't know where I'd be." She paused. "I guess I figured I'd use my degree to give something back to the system."

"You're doing that now. Without a degree."

"Thanks." Her eyes filled with kindness. "That's what I tell myself."

Again, Aaron had the urge to take her hand, or rub her shoulder. Connect with her some way so she would know how touched he was that she trusted him with her story. How sorry he was for her. The fact that his agent wouldn't approve of the amazing woman sitting beside him was proof that just maybe Aaron had put his trust in the wrong person. Thinking about the man's words now only filled Aaron with a simmering rage. He dismissed the thoughts. In this precious time, with Megan opening her heart to him, he wanted only to be available for her.

He stretched his arm along the back of the bench again, and as he did he inched a little closer. More to keep their conversation intimate than to gain any advantage with her. "Tell me about your paper route."

She giggled and sat up a little straighter. "It's not glamorous. I get up at four o'clock and walk a few blocks to the drop-off point. Lots of us get our papers there, but it's on the edge of my route." She did a dainty shrug. "I'm the only one without a car."

He silently struggled against the unfairness of Megan's life. She really didn't have a car? She and Cory had virtually nothing, a problem he could remedy in an afternoon. But the strangest part was Megan didn't seem like she needed anything. As if her simple life suited her just fine. "So ... you walk around handing out papers?"

"Exactly." She held her thin arms out and flexed. "It's better than going to the gym every morning."

As she brought her hands back to her sides, her arm brushed against his fingers. Maybe it was his imagination, but she seemed to notice it too. Because she looked down at the pier for a few seconds, and she swallowed. As if she was trying to pretend she wasn't feeling it, the unbelievable attraction between them.

"Anyway, yeah, I wear a bag stuffed with papers and I walk my route. Up and down about four blocks, and then I go home."

He could picture bums and crazy people lurking in the shadows as she passed by, beautiful and vulnerable. "You've ... you've never had a problem?"

She laughed. "I'm not afraid of street people. They leave you alone if you know where you're going. Even the gang members. I carry pepper spray, just in case." Another wave of easy laughter came over her. "One time I used it on a trashcan."

He gave her a crooked grin. "A very aggressive trashcan, I'm assuming."

"It seemed that way. I was tossing a paper and the can tumbled toward me. I thought I was being attacked, so I grabbed the spray and unloaded."

"And ..."

"A tabby cat ran out from behind the can, sneezing his head off." She gave a single understanding nod. "Last time I was ever attacked by a tabby cat."

"Or a trashcan."

She leaned over her knees, laughing at the memory. "I can only imagine what the wino across the street must've thought. He probably ran for the shadows for the next month whenever I came along."

"Crazy papergirl."

"Yep."

Aaron had a hundred things he still wanted to talk to her about. Her hopes and dreams and her goals for the foster care system. But Cory was walking back toward them. The crowd had thinned considerably, and only a few couples strolled along the edge of the pier. Even the sea lions had quieted.

Megan stood to greet the boy. "Ready to go, buddy?"

"Yeah. The sea lions are falling asleep."

They were walking back when Megan stopped and stared out at the ocean. "It's so big."

Cory stood beside her and shaded his eyes. "Someday I wanna sail around the world."

"I always wanted to do that when I was a kid." Aaron took the spot on Megan's other side, and at the same instant, they took hold of the wooden railing. As they did, their fingers touched. In half a second, Aaron made the decision not to move his hand. She must've done the same because she kept her hand where it was, slightly beneath his.

"It's beautiful." She was so close he could smell her subtle perfume. Their shoulders touched, and again she didn't move.

"Can we do this again next week?" Cory peered past Megan to Aaron. "This is the greatest place. Better than the park."

"That'd be fun." Aaron winked at the boy. "It's a lot better than sitting around an empty house by yourself." Which was what he'd been doing lately, ever since his first visit to the youth center. Actually, it was since he first saw Megan. He thought of only her and dreamed of spending an evening like this with only her. Their fingers were still touching, and instinctively Aaron looped his pinky finger around hers. She gave his the slightest squeeze, and the sensation made his head spin. She couldn't know how badly he wanted to take her in his arms and love her, protect her. But he couldn't rush her. If he did, she would fly from him like one of the seagulls at the end of the pier.

And that would be that.

Cory yawned and Megan gave Aaron a knowing look. For a moment, there was only the two of them, and Aaron could see the one thing he'd wanted to see all night. The fact that she felt the same way—if only for an instant. She released his finger and took a full breath. "All right, then … I guess we better get going."

They made it all the way to the truck without stopping this time, and Aaron held the door open for her and then for Cory. He was so glad he'd traded in the Hummer. The truck suited him much better now, the person he was somehow trying to become. When he dropped them off, Megan hesitated. Then she took his hand and held it for a couple heartbeats. "Thank you. For tonight."

Aaron had to use all his strength to keep from leaning close and kissing her. Instead, he held back and nodded. "Thanks for talking. I could've listened all night."

She smiled. "Next time we'll talk about you." She climbed out and waved one more time, and then she and Cory were gone. It occurred to him then that Cory hadn't said anything about being his son. The boy didn't believe the truth, and so Aaron had half expected him to bring the issue up during dinner. But Cory was well-mannered and quieter than usual most of the night.

Maybe next time they were together, Aaron would talk about the subject. And there would be a next time, Aaron was sure. Whenever that was, if Cory knew that Aaron was going to be his friend, it might not hurt so much that Aaron wasn't his dad. He grinned as he pulled his truck back into traffic and headed home. His heart was full, and he hadn't felt this good in a long time. Maybe ever. Whatever the season brought, through intense workouts and hard-fought competition, he would hold tight to the memory of this night.

And if he found the courage, he would ask God to help Megan feel for him what he felt for her.

However slow he needed to move from here.

TWENTY

S omewhere along the course of the night, Megan had lost her ability to stay distant. She had fewer reasons to dislike Aaron, now that he knew about Cory's fantasy and even so, he was still coming around. News accounts and *Sports Illustrated*, televised post-game interviews and gossip columns all showed Aaron being arrogant and indifferent. He was fearless on the field, yes, and he won often. But he never showed the sort of humility and compassion that made sports so compelling.

But tonight, he was someone entirely different. Walking beside her and listening to her, holding her when she let her crazy fear of boats stop him from taking her to a gourmet restaurant ... that guy intrigued her. And when he showed up at her apartment again the following Friday, she and Cory went with him back to the pier without hesitation.

They ate at the Sea Lion Café again, and Cory and Aaron had their picture taken in the arcade. Afterward Cory spotted the Turbo Ride. Megan didn't care for amusement park rides, so she wasn't sure she should attempt it, but Cory took the lead, bouncing and talking loudly about how he'd seen this on TV once and it was the best ride ever and how they had to all three ride it because the seats went straight across and Aaron could sit in the middle.

"What exactly is it?" Megan was relieved it had nothing to do with water. It was inside a building, after all.

"It's amazing!" Cory grinned. "That's what."

"Which one should we ride?" Aaron put his arm around Cory's shoulders and they stared at a sign listing the possible adventures.

"Extreme Log Ride!" Cory turned and high-fived Aaron. "That's gotta be the best!"

Megan hung back as Aaron and Cory moved up to the front of the line, ordering tickets. "Hey, guys ..."

The music from inside the Turbo Ride was so loud they didn't hear her. She moved to Aaron's side. "Not the Extreme Log Ride, okay?"

Cory giggled. He held up three tickets, each of which read, "Extreme Log Ride."

"Come on." Aaron was being pulled toward the entrance line by Cory. He waved for her to follow. "I'll keep you dry!"

She let her shoulders slump forward. "Fine." Her heart thudded in a strange off-beat pattern. *Ridiculous*, she told herself. *It's a simulator*. She caught up to them just as the double doors were opening. "I'll have you know"—she leaned close to Aaron, so Cory wouldn't hear her—"I'm scared to death."

"You said you wanted to get used to being on the water." Aaron touched his hand to the small of her back and let her go in front of him. Teasing colored his voice.

The theater was dark with only eight rows of eight seats. They chose the third row and Aaron took the middle, like Cory had planned. Megan buckled her seatbelt and wondered if everyone in the theater could hear her pounding heart. She gripped the arms of her seat, pursed her lips, and exhaled. It was only a movie with special effects. If it felt too crazy, she could close her eyes and she'd be fine. She took a steady breath, just as Cory leaned around Aaron.

"It's not real," he whispered. "You won't get wet."

"I know." Her returned whisper was marked with light sarcasm, and she caught Aaron grinning into his fist. "Thanks, Cory."

The lights faded to black and the screen came to life. Immediately the seats lurched forward and Megan swallowed a scream. "I'm not made for this sort of ride." She muttered the words, and as she did she felt Aaron's hand cover her own on the armrest.

He leaned close. "I won't let you drown." He breathed the words against her cheek. "It'll be okay."

Instantly they were on the water, sitting in a flimsy-looking log. At least it felt that way. The seats rocked gently in time with the rhythm of the water, as the log at first floated across calm waters toward what looked like a steep drop-off. Whatever lay ahead wasn't nearly as frightening with Aaron's hand over hers. Megan pressed herself toward the back of the chair. "Here we go ..."

The log reached the edge of the waterfall and the nose went straight out at first before gravity sucked it straight down. Megan's stomach dropped, and suddenly the feeling inside her wasn't silly amusement park nervousness. It was outright fear. Without thinking, she grabbed onto Aaron's arm and buried her face in his shoulder. *Breathe, Megan ... come on, breathe.*

Almost instinctively, Aaron put both arms around her and cradled her close to his chest. "I told you I wouldn't let you drown." His words were velvet against her face.

She peeked at the screen, and now the log had reached the bottom of the drop and was jerking and fighting its way through thick, frothy white rapids. The simulator jolted and jerked and bumped as they hit various rocks and pushed their way forward. But with Aaron's arms around her, the irrational fear that had seized her a few seconds ago eased. She turned back toward the screen. It was incredible. It truly felt like they were on the log, surrounded by angry water on every side.

Then the strangest thing happened. Megan was actually enjoying the ride. Safe in Aaron's arms, she didn't care if they hit a rock or dropped off another waterfall. Because her mind was only partly focused on the adventure on the screen. The greater adventure, the one happening in her heart, was all but consuming her. Here, her head against him, his arms around her, she could smell his cologne, feel his heartbeat and the rise and fall of his chest with every breath. The sensation was intoxicating, unlike anything Megan had ever known.

"Feeling better?" His words were like a soft caress, filling her senses.

"Much." She was grateful for the darkness, grateful he couldn't see the heat in her cheeks.

She wasn't sure how Aaron could have such an effect on her so quickly. No matter how she felt right now, the thought of falling for him was more terrifying than any boat ride. But no matter what common sense had to say, Megan was only certain of one thing.

She didn't want the log ride to end.

After another minute of rapids, their vessel survived and floated into still waters once more. Aaron released his tender hold on her, but again he covered her hand with his and gave it a single squeeze.

The lights lifted and Cory jumped from his seat. "That was so cool! See, Megan, no problem!"

Megan thought about the feelings tumbling around inside her, her attraction to Aaron and the senselessness of it. She smoothed her T-shirt and smiled at the child. "I'm not sure."

"I kept you from drowning." Aaron winked at her. They left the theater with Cory in the lead, and Aaron reached back and took her hand. Softly, he ran his thumb along her palm. Before they walked into daylight, he grinned at her. "Personally, I think we should ride it again."

She kicked lightly at his tennis shoe. "So you can see me scared to death."

For a moment, she thought he might turn around and pull her into his embrace. But he only hesitated, still looking over his shoulder. "Was it that bad?" His smile sounded in every word.

She held his eyes, knowing that whether or not she wanted them to be, her feelings were laid out for him to see. "No." She tightened her fingers around his hand, mesmerized by the feel of his skin against hers. "It wasn't."

They finished the night with ice cream, and Aaron maintained a comfortable distance between them. A couple times he suggested another go-round in the Turbo Ride might be smart, but his comment only allowed him to exchange a knowing smile with Megan.

As they licked their cones, Megan studied Cory. She was impressed with him, both tonight and last week when Aaron took them to the pier. The boy still believed Aaron was his father, but he hadn't mentioned the idea even once. She sensed the subject would come up eventually.

It happened on the ride back to their apartment. Cory leaned up between Aaron and Megan and gave a troubled sigh.

Aaron reached a red light and glanced back at Cory. He seemed to sense Cory was thinking about something other than sea lions and turbo rides. "So did you ace your spelling test?"

"One wrong." Cory sounded disappointed. "I hate getting one wrong."

"Me too." Aaron snuck a quick look at Megan. "All the other ones might be easy, but you miss out on that one that's most difficult, and it ruins everything. Because really that's the only one that matters."

"Right." Cory didn't look too deep into Aaron's statement.

Sitting next to him, Megan was trembling. Aaron's message was unmistakable, and it sent a warm, tingly feeling through her body. Was that really how he saw her? The one woman in his life who was difficult, the only one who mattered? She looked out the windshield and tried to imagine what might become of her if she actually let herself fall, if she trusted Aaron Hill with her heart. Cold terror ran through her veins, but it mixed with a warmth she'd never known any other time in her life, a warmth that only being with him could bring.

Cory was talking about school and his upcoming soccer game. "You can come if you want. I play tomorrow morning."

"Well…" Aaron thought for a minute. "We have another away game this weekend, so I'll leave early tomorrow." His eyes lit up. "But let's try for next Saturday."

They talked about Cory's game time and set a plan. Cory was still leaning forward, and again Megan could practically feel him thinking. "You know what else I've been doing?"

Aaron kept his eyes on the road. "What?"

"Going through the stuff my mom left for me. It's all in a box, so I can pull it out and look through it any time."

"That's good." Tenderness crept into Aaron's tone. "I'm sure the things in the box are very special."

"They are." Cory sounded more nervous with every few words. "She wrote some letters for you in there too. They have your name across the front, but I never opened them 'cause you don't open other people's mail." He was picking up speed. "So I can get 'em to you if you want, 'cause maybe you'd like to read what she wrote sometime. Plus she cut out articles of you in college and when you signed with the 49ers and—"

"Cory …" Megan looked at him. "That's enough."

The implied warning in her voice made his expression fall. "I was just saying …"

"Cory …" She mixed compassion with a no-nonsense tone that put an end to the conversation. She faced forward again, afraid to look at Aaron. Megan had heard from Cory once a long time ago about the letters, but she hadn't seen them. Just one more part of Cory's imagination where Aaron was concerned. Now though, she felt sorry for the boy. He knew he wasn't supposed to talk about this, but it must've been building inside him all night. Finally, she met Aaron's curious look, and she mouthed a silent apology.

Aaron looked in his rearview mirror. "Letters like that are a very important thing, aren't they, Cory?"

"Yes." His voice was small.

"Maybe you can show me sometime." His voice was relaxed, casual. It was clear he didn't believe anything in the letters was really written by Cory's mother specifically to him. But he must've wanted to validate Cory's feelings.

Megan's admiration for him doubled. When Amy died, when Megan made her decision to take Cory as her own, she knew the sacrifice she was making. Guys would have to like Cory if they were ever going to like her, which ruled out most of the men she would ever meet. Megan could still hear the determination in the voice of one business guy, a man she'd met at Bob's Diner: "You've got a kid …" He held up his hands like a traffic cop stopping traffic. "Never mind. Too much baggage."

Megan didn't care, really. She would've been fine if she remained single — for a year or a decade. Forever, if that's the way things worked out. That's what she'd always told herself. She'd made a good life for Cory and her, and that, combined with her friendship with God, was enough. No one to rely on, no one to let her down.

As Aaron dropped them off, he leaned over and hugged her, holding on a little longer than necessary. He drew back and looked deep into her eyes. "When can I see you again?"

"Aaron … I don't know." She couldn't think straight, couldn't imagine a way to answer him without diving into waters she couldn't escape. Her mind was dizzy with his nearness, and she couldn't catch her breath. Everything inside her screamed for the chance to kiss him, to get lost in his embrace without thought or reason interfering. Instead, she thanked him for the night, and her eyes held his as she climbed out and headed inside with Cory. Only then did she exhale.

By the time she fell into bed that night, she realized something about herself. Maybe she didn't want to be single, after all. Because more than air, she wanted Aaron Hill beside her again, protecting her from a simulated log ride, their arms touching.

She rolled over in bed and willed herself to fall asleep. Her paper route was in five hours, and she wasn't thinking straight. No need wasting sleep over Aaron Hill, no matter how she'd felt in his arms, no matter how her heart soared when she was with him. Everything Aaron did was newsworthy and public—the sort of life Megan never wanted for herself. Aaron Hill falling for a papergirl? That sort of thing simply didn't happen. Even if she could stand the thought of letting herself fall.

A sigh came from her soul and filled the quiet room. These past few Fridays were just a chance at friendship, and Aaron, a person who was breezing through their lives at a time when she and Cory needed the diversion. But no matter how she tried to convince herself that her feelings for Aaron couldn't possibly amount to anything, she came up short. It was too late to question whether she was falling for Aaron Hill. She'd fallen. Totally and completely. Whatever became of the situation, she would hold tight to the memory of today. The conversation, the laughter, the sunset.

And the thrill of a log ride that would stay with her forever.

Cory was glad Megan wasn't too mad at him. She tucked him in and told him it wasn't good to break the rules, but she understood why he did it.

"He's a very nice man," she told him. "But he's not your dad, Cory. You have to believe that."

This wasn't the time to tell Megan, even politely, that she was wrong. So he nodded and set his picture of him and Aaron from Pier 39 on the windowsill next to his bed. When he had it balanced just right, Megan prayed with him, and she asked God to work out all the questions that didn't have answers. Cory wasn't sure what that meant, but it had to do with Aaron. He knew that much.

When Megan was gone and the door to his room was closed, he crept off his bottom bunk and turned on the flashlight by his bed. 'Cause the main light might shine through the door and Megan would know he was up. He moved really quiet and aimed the flashlight under his bed toward his box of special things. Then he pulled it out and shone the light straight inside.

There had to be a clue, right? When he read mystery books, there was always a clue. And since Megan didn't believe him and even Aaron didn't believe him, he had to find something. He pointed the light at one of the envelopes with Aaron's name on it. What would be the best thing, the best way to prove he was telling the truth? He bit hard on his lip and thought for a minute. A picture, of course. A photo of his mom and Aaron together. But he only had a handful of pictures and they were of him or his mom and him. That's all.

He sifted around and found the envelope marked with only the word "PRIVATE." His fingers felt it on the top and the bottom, and then he picked it up. It was lumpier than the other envelopes, so it might have something other than a letter inside. Something that might be a clue.

All this time Cory always figured this letter was for Aaron too. But it didn't say Aaron's name, actually. Private didn't mean only Aaron could open it. His heart jumped around a little more than before. Private only meant his mom didn't want lots of people passing it around and making it public. Yeah, that's right. Because in English they studied opposites and public was the opposite of private. So if he didn't make whatever was in the envelope public, he would still be obeying his mom's wishes.

Cory held his breath and suddenly he was convinced. He blew the air out of his lungs and ripped a small rip down the side of the envelope, which wasn't easy since he had the flashlight in one hand. Carefully he shook the envelope and out came just one thing. A picture. Cory's heart beat like a loud drum and he could hardly hear himself think. He picked up the photo with his left hand and aimed the light at it with the other. He did a long gasp, so long he had to press his lips together so Megan wouldn't hear him in the next room. This was the clue he'd been looking for, a clue he would save for just the right moment.

The picture was of a teenage girl and a guy in sort of a slow dance kind of pose. They were dressed in nice clothes next to some flowers, and beneath it in gold letters were the words, "Prom, 1995." And the people in the picture were his mom and a guy who looked almost the same all these years later. A guy who matched with the newspaper clippings in his special box, and so Cory had no doubts at all.

The guy was Aaron Hill.

Twenty-One

Derrick took his seat on the private jet preparing to fly the 49ers home to San Francisco, and he hung his head. He was as dazed as the rest of the guys, trying to fathom how they'd lost two straight road games to mediocre teams. He clenched his jaw and willed himself back in time, back to that first Monday night when they had one win and unlimited potential.

He leaned his head against the cool window. What had gone wrong? How could they be 1 – 2 now, with the season in a tailspin just three weeks in? Derrick had no answers for himself, no more answers than Coach Cameron had for the media. But one thing was certain. Derrick had underestimated how it would feel standing on the sidelines, helpless to make a difference. The competitor inside him knew without a doubt he could've won those games. Instead, he and Jay Ryder had been forced to watch while Aaron and the rest of the team imploded.

Aaron was trudging up the aisle, one of the last on the plane, his expression set. Derrick lifted his head and watched his teammate, studying him. Aaron had been open and genuine at the dinner Denae cooked after practice a month ago. Derrick felt certain God was going to use the season to build a bond between them, to give Derrick the chance to mentor Aaron, if not on the field, then certainly off it. But since then, Aaron had been distant with everyone on the team—even Derrick.

The empty window seats were gone by the time Aaron reached Derrick's row. He said nothing, but he stopped and tossed his bag into the overhead bin. Then he took the aisle seat, leaving one between them. He buckled his belt, closed his eyes, and leaned his head back.

People could sit wherever they wanted on the flight home. The fact that Aaron chose to sit by him was a sign; it had to be. No matter how he acted or how little he said, Aaron needed advice, strength. Derrick looked out the window at the ground crew, busy tossing bags into the belly of the plane. *Okay, God ... things don't look too good. But Aaron's here.* He felt a ray of hope. *Give me the words. Please, God ... it's third and long. I'm counting on You.*

Derrick waited until the plane was in the air, and by then it looked like Aaron was asleep. A few minutes into the flight they hit sharp turbulence, and Aaron blinked his eyes open. He pulled a magazine from the seat in front of him and flipped through it. Derrick watched him, and he could feel God with him, feel His Holy Spirit giving him the words and tone and timing to finally say something to his teammate that might really matter.

"Lookin' for the answers?" Derrick stared at Aaron, his voice not quite teasing.

Aaron looked slightly confused at first, but then he shifted his attention from Derrick back to the magazine. With an exaggerated breath, he closed the magazine and slipped it back in the seat pocket. "I'm beginning to wonder." He mumbled the words, and he avoided looking at Derrick again.

"Beginning to wonder what?"

"If there are any answers."

Derrick had a feeling he wasn't just talking about the losses. "My daddy once told me you can't play football with a head full a' trouble. You gotta pick your battles and play 'em out one at a time." Derrick kept his words slow and easy. "Daddy was a wise man."

"Yeah." He hesitated for a few seconds, then he turned his eyes to Derrick. "The woman at the youth center, remember her?"

"Megan, right?"

"Right." Aaron's heavy heart left fine lines around his eyes and mouth. "I'm falling for her, man. In a big way."

Derrick let that sink in, and nodded slowly. "I can see that. Guy finds a great girl and all of a sudden he walks around the locker room frowning and slouching and making a beeline for the showers." The sarcasm helped keep the moment light. "Makes good sense."

"It's not her." He gazed into nothingness. "She thinks I'm someone else."

"Hmmm." Derrick tapped his knee. "You mean like Jay Ryder? 'Cause if she thinks you're Jay Ryder, girl needs glasses. Jay's a black man, Hill, and that ain't right if you're out there all walking around and stuff, letting her think she's got a chance with a guy like Jay Ryder."

Aaron didn't want to laugh, that much was obvious. But he could only pinch his lips together for a few seconds before a low chuckle slipped. He shook his head. "I'm serious, man." He took a long breath and his half smile faded. "She thinks I'm a gentleman. But until I met her, I wasn't even close. And that's what's not right. It's like…" He stared at the controls above their seats and adjusted the airflow. "It's like I have to fix the broken parts of me before I can move forward with her. You know?"

"Truth is, I usually charge for this kind of thing, but"—Derrick leaned against the window—"I happen to have a little time on my hands. How much broken are we talking about?"

Aaron ran his fingers through his hair. "A lot of broken." He closed his eyes for half a minute, and when he opened them his expression grew distant. "Her name was Amy, first girl I ever loved. Only girl until … well, until recently."

The story started slowly, sputtering from one detail to another in a way that wasn't chronological or compelling. But what Derrick learned from it was enough to give him the widest window yet into Aaron Hill's soul. His teammate talked about Amy and her pregnancy and how his agent had steered him away from her.

The sum of it was similar to what Aaron had talked about that night after dinner. The fact that he'd been with more women than he could remember. Always under dark and shady circumstances, always with a different blonde or brunette whose name he would forget a day later.

"Not to be rude"—Derrick raised one eyebrow—"but that's a lot of risk." He whistled low. "You ever get yourself checked?"

"Lots of times." Aaron sighed. "I'm careful. I learned how to play the game early on."

"Rules change all the time in that game." He looked at Aaron significantly, with a dramatic shake of his head. "People losing every which way every time you turn around. I mean, all those touchdowns you've thrown, that's one thing. But if you're still passing your blood tests, I'd say you're luckier than most people think." He made a wry face. "Seriously, man."

"Anyway…" Aaron was quick to move past the gritty details. "I'm finished with that. Just thinking about the things I've done … it makes me sick. I feel empty and terrible." He pressed his hand to his chest. "Like my insides are filled with rotten potatoes."

Derrick made a face. "No wonder you head for the showers so fast."

"Exactly." Aaron wasn't laughing. "It's affecting my game. I can feel it."

Suddenly Derrick knew it was time. "Remember I told you ... maybe this is the year you'll figure it out?"

"Yeah." Aaron stared at him. "You're right. I'm figuring it out, but the truth's only making me feel worse, so now what?"

"That, my friend, is the right question." Derrick's smile was genuine, the teasing from earlier entirely gone. "Everyone has a load of garbage from their past." He touched his fingertips to the place above his heart. "Sits in here, twisting and hurting and stinking up a man's life until nothing's right."

Aaron was gripped. He didn't blink or breathe, even.

"Here's the secret." He pointed at Aaron. "Only God can take the garbage out, man. Only God."

Tears shone in Aaron's eyes, and he blinked, steadying himself. "I know all about God." A sad laugh sounded low in Aaron's throat. "Believe me, God doesn't owe me any favors. So how am I supposed to get Him to take away the garbage?"

"That's easy." Derrick's gaze was intent, and he prayed silently his words would pierce the fog of guilt and confusion surrounding his friend. Then he smiled. "You ask Him." He tossed his hands. "That's it, Hill. You take yourself to a quiet place where you can think and you tell Him about all your garbage. Then you ask Him to get rid of it. And when it's gone, you ask Him to fill in all the empty, cleaned out places."

A nervousness came into Aaron's eyes. "But that's like, I don't know, talking to God. You have to know what you're doing for that."

"You don't have to know nothing at all." Derrick rested his forearm on the seat in front of him. His tone was lighter now, because he could sense Aaron pulling away. "Know why?"

Aaron looked at him.

"Because it isn't about how good you are, Hill. You and me, we'd fail that test first thing." He smiled, as if this next part was a secret. "It's about how good *God* is. And when you figure that out, everything else will line up the way it's supposed to."

They were quiet for a while, and Aaron asked a few questions about the short patterns, the ones that were giving him fits so far this season. After that, Aaron closed his eyes and in a little while he was sleeping. Derrick stared out the window and realized how drained he felt. He wanted, this season more than any other in all his life, wanted to win and keep winning.

But after tonight, something else would drive him to push harder, sending him early to practice on a knee that burned with every step, encouraging him to be a positive voice for his teammates even when everyone else was down. Because there was something he wanted even more than a Super Bowl ring this season, and that … that thing was suddenly very possible.

He wanted Aaron Hill to find healing in Christ.

TWENTY-TWO

Megan took her spot in the bleachers and pulled her wool coat tight around her shoulders. Across the park, four games were getting started under a thick layer of clouds, and Megan felt the chill to her core. The temperatures that day would reach the seventies—typical for September—but Cory's ten-thirty soccer games felt colder every week.

Cory was warming up with his team, looking every minute or so toward the parking lot. This was the game Aaron had said he could attend, and Megan expected he'd show up, which was bound to be awkward. She looked out across the field, but all she could see was the article in the *Chronicle*, the one that hit Monday, just a few days after their last night at the pier.

Between her paper route and her shift at the diner that day, she read the sports section. Partly because she wanted to know what Aaron was doing, how he was doing. But also because she wanted proof that he was who he seemed to be when they were together. And until last Monday, she was becoming convinced. Maybe the rumors about him before were only that. Maybe he hadn't been the sort of playboy the press hinted at all the years he'd been in the NFL.

But last Monday, buried in a compilation of sports briefs, was Aaron's name, and it caught her attention. The story was just a few lines, but it was under a small headline that read, "Playboy Aaron Hill Has His Eyes on the Stars." Megan didn't want to move beyond the headline, didn't want her image of Aaron shattered. But she had no choice. She slid the newspaper closer and consumed the next few lines. Basically, the story said various A-list actresses had inquired about Aaron, and that Aaron was very interested in one of them. His agent was putting together plans for a first meeting. Details, the story promised, would be pending.

Megan had sat down, unable to draw a full breath as the news hit her. She read the story again, and a third time. He was interested in an A-list actress? So the whole time he'd been acting interested in her at the pier, he'd only been waiting for a call from the actress? She folded the paper and pushed it to the other side of the table. She'd been a fool for letting herself fall for him in the first place.

He called her on Wednesday, but she let it go to her answering machine. She had nothing to say to him, not if he was only playing her the whole time. She and Cory would be just fine without him in their lives; in fact, they'd be better. Safer. Megan turned slightly to ward off the wind. Cory wouldn't talk about his reasons, but he was more insistent than ever that Aaron was his father. Of course he would feel that way. Their two Friday nights at Pier 39 had made even Megan feel like they were a family. What was an eight-year-old boy supposed to make of the situation?

Monday's article stayed with Megan all week, convincing her that the next time she saw Aaron, she would have no choice but to break things off. He called again yesterday, but she didn't pick up. She couldn't. For Cory's sake, and for her own. No matter how attracted he was or how he seemed to feel about her, his people were busy connecting him with some actress. Which was a better fit for Aaron, anyway. Still, he didn't have to lead her on, not her or Cory.

Now she would protect the two of them from getting more involved. She lifted her eyes to the clouds overhead. *God, this won't be easy. You've always given me strength whenever I need it.* She breathed in slowly through her nose. *Well, I need it more than ever.*

Daughter, I am here ... I will never leave you or forsake you.

The verse that breezed through Megan's soul was one of her favorites. It was the Scripture that convinced her she could be single forever, if that's what God had for her. Because even single she was never alone, not for a minute or an hour. Not even in the darkest times. God was with her. He would never leave her or forsake her.

Peace came over her, and the chill in her bones eased. A pickup truck like Aaron's pulled into the parking lot, and a man with Aaron's build climbed out. As he walked across the far field, Megan had no doubts. He'd come to the game, just like he promised, and he was looking for them, trying to figure out which field Cory was playing on.

She stood and waved, and he spotted her immediately. He broke into an easy jog as Megan sat back on the bleacher. She shifted her attention to Cory, and sure enough, the boy had spotted Aaron, probably at the same time Megan did. He was waving and jumping, his whole face taken up by his smile. He even took a few running steps toward Aaron, before he seemed to realize he was in the middle of a warm-up drill.

Aaron reached her, and his eyes danced the way they had the last time they were together. "Hi." He took the spot beside her, slipped his arm around her shoulders, and gave her a quick hug. "Did I miss anything?"

"Not yet." She smiled because she wasn't angry. He'd made her no promises, after all. But she could feel the walls in her eyes. "His team's warming up."

"Good." He rubbed his hands together. He wore a sweatshirt and sweat-pants. "It's colder than I thought."

She looked up. "It'll warm up when the fog breaks."

He hesitated and she could feel him look at her. As if he understood something had changed between them. "Everything okay?"

"Fine." Another smile. Then she turned her gaze to the field. "I love watching Cory play soccer." She kept her tone light because she didn't want to give her feelings away, not completely. This wasn't the place to cut ties with him. That could come later. For now, it was more important that they focus on the game.

Aaron's body language showed his concern, but he must've realized there was nothing he could do. Not if Megan wasn't willing to talk about whatever was going on. So instead, he cupped his hands around his mouth and shouted. "Let's go, Cory ... Make it happen!"

Then, and throughout the game, as Cory scored first one goal to tie the game, and then a second to win it with a minute left, Megan savored the feel of Aaron beside her. For just one more hour, it felt good to believe they might've had a chance, that maybe he really had feelings only for her. And it felt good to have a man cheering for Cory, something the boy had never experienced.

When the game ended, Megan felt herself being pulled back into reality. She congratulated Cory, and Aaron did the same.

"Thanks for coming!" Cory's cheeks were red and the joy in his eyes knew no limit. He slipped his arm around Aaron's waist as they walked to-ward the parking lot. "Wanna get lunch and take it to the park?"

"Sure." Aaron cast her a questioning look.

"Sounds good." She averted her eyes, but only so she'd stay strong. She'd already made up her mind about what would happen after today. Now she had to act on her decision.

They picked up subs from a deli and made their way back to the same park, a few blocks from the youth center. They sat at a sturdy picnic table, and while they ate their sandwiches, Cory talked about the game and how his teammates passed better than ever before, and how a few of the guys knew it was Aaron Hill cheering for him, and how one guy even asked for Cory's autograph because of it.

Megan barely ate her lunch. Her stomach was in knots, and now she had no doubt Aaron had picked up on the fact that something was wrong. When they were finished eating, Megan put her hand on Cory's shoulder. "Hey, buddy, could you do me a favor?"

"Sure." He grinned.

A flash of pain ripped through Megan's heart, because maybe Cory would not look as happy as he did right now for a very long time. She steeled herself against the hurt of what lay ahead. "Could you go play on the equipment for a little while? I need to talk to Aaron alone."

Cory's smile dropped off some, but not in a way that showed he was truly worried. He looked at Aaron and then back at her. "Sure. I wanna get on the swings, anyway." His smile was back in full force. "I'm trying to set a personal best on how far I can jump."

Megan could feel Aaron watching her and sensed that he wasn't willing to make another minute of small talk. She forced a smile for Cory. "After that amazing soccer game, today's probably the day to do it."

"Yeah." He climbed off the picnic bench and took a step back. "Thanks." He started his familiar backward running, and he waved at her and Aaron. "See you in a little bit." Then he turned around and sped off to the swings.

They were sitting across from each other, and for a few minutes, neither said anything. Already the air between them was dramatically different. Awkward and strained. Aaron broke the silence first. "Did I miss something?"

She sighed and turned her eyes to him. "I've been thinking …"

"Oh." He hesitated, and then a nervous laugh sounded from him. "Why does that seem like a bad thing?"

"Because …" She hated this. If only she could slide over to his side of the table and cling to him the way she had during the Turbo Ride. This part of the adventure was even more frightening than going over a waterfall. She searched his eyes. "It could never work, Aaron. Me and you."

His expression froze, and for a few seconds he only stared at her. "You're kidding, right?" He let loose a single, bitter laugh. "I'm gone for a week and everything changes?"

She wasn't sure she wanted to get into the gritty details, but she had no choice. She couldn't let him wonder why her feelings had changed. She lifted her chin and breathed in long and slow. As she exhaled, she faced him again. "I read Monday's paper."

Aaron blinked, as if he were still waiting for her to make sense. "Okay…" He laughed, but it sounded tense and desperate. "We lose a couple games and you're ready to give up on me?"

She hesitated. "You know what I mean. The piece about you and the Hollywood actress."

He couldn't have looked more surprised if she'd suddenly started speaking Japanese. "What piece?"

Megan's head began to spin. She gripped the edge of the bench with both hands and stared at him. He had to know about it, right? The truth behind the story, if not the article itself. Her mouth felt dry as she tried to find the words. "The article about you and some actress being interested in each other." She met his eyes straight on. "Your agent's working to set up a first meeting."

For a few seconds, Aaron looked stunned, too shocked to move or speak. Then his face grew red and anger blazed in his eyes. He stood and turned his back to her, and he walked to the nearest oak tree. He clenched his fist and drew it back like he was going to send it deep into the tree trunk. At the last second, he stopped himself and then released a few controlled hits against his other palm. Every muscle in his body looked tight with rage.

He walked a few steps to the side, stopped and took two more steps in another direction. He was the picture of pent-up fury and Megan couldn't understand. Didn't he think she'd find out, that she'd see it in the *Chronicle*? Even if he didn't know about the article, he had to understand that the media would find such a story sensational.

Aaron finally relaxed his hands and stared up through the trees at the still foggy sky. He groaned, and after a little while, he turned and faced her. Fifteen yards separated them, but from where Megan sat, she could see the turmoil in his eyes. He came to her slowly, and as he reached the bench he narrowed his eyes, looking at her more intently than ever. "I had nothing to do with that article, Megan. You have to believe me."

Confusion swelled inside her. She wanted to believe him, but his words didn't make sense. "You didn't know about it?"

"No." He dropped back to the edge of the bench, still facing her. "My agent must've called it in. That's all I can figure."

His agent. Megan shifted her eyes away from him and onto the ground near her feet. The same agent who showed such disdain when she and Cory showed up for the Raiders game during the preseason. If he was Aaron's agent, he was in constant contact with Aaron, constantly working deals for him. The article meant the guy either had no knowledge of Aaron's feelings for Megan, or he disapproved of them. A sad weariness came over her as she found his eyes again. "There has to be some truth to it, Aaron."

Anger changed his expression. "There is." The muscles in his jaw flexed. "My agent *wants* me to date a Hollywood actress. Thinks it'll be good for my image. Which is something I'll be talking to him about when I'm done here." He seemed to catch the fact that he was talking too loud. He lowered his tone, his eyes pleading with her. "But I don't want that kind of setup. I never authorized him to run the story."

Megan studied him, the sincerity in his eyes. Slowly, gradually, she felt herself changing her mind about the incident. So maybe he didn't want to date an actress, and maybe his agent was responsible for tipping the paper about the story. "Still…" Her voice was softer than before, more vulnerable. "He's your agent. He knows you better than I do. He must."

Aaron's breathing came faster, in short bursts. He shook his head slowly, clearly warring with his emotions. Finally, he shrugged his shoulders and looked hard at her. "He doesn't know me at all. Not who I am today … who I want to be."

His statement rolled around in her heart, but in the end, the answers came from her soul. She reached across the table and put her hand over his. "We're too different, Aaron. Can't you see it?" Her heart thudded against her chest, because she hated this, hated breaking away from him. But God had allowed her to see the article for a reason, to warn her. "Look … you're a nice guy, Aaron. A different guy than I had you figured to be." Her voice mixed with the sorrow inside her. "I had a great time." She turned her attention toward the distant swing set, and Cory, pushing himself as high as he could go. "Cory had a great time too."

"And that's bad?" Aaron was deeply upset, his voice told that much. He pulled away from her touch and stood, his back to her again. "It's just like I thought."

Her heartbeat came harder, faster. "What?"

He put his hands on his hips and stared into the sky. The fog was clearing, and he seemed to find a blue patch. For a long while, he only gave an occasional shake of his head, a few sounds of disbelief. When he finally turned to her, he met her eyes straight on. "It's my past, right? You can't see around it, and you know what?" He put one foot up on the bench where he'd been sitting. He leaned over it, his eyes intense. "I can't see around it either."

Aaron had never gone into detail about his past, but he must've figured she knew, that his public persona hadn't escaped her. "It doesn't matter, Aaron. I don't want to fight." She stood and walked around to his side of the table. She sat on the table and set her feet on the bench. "You've been a good friend, but …" She felt a rush of tears, and she hesitated until she had control. "It has to end sometime. I'm just saying it might as well be now. Before it gets harder for either of us. For Cory."

He let his shoulders fall forward, and he turned and sat next to her on the table. Their knees touched, but only for half a second. Aaron seemed intent on keeping some distance between them. "I knew this could be difficult, Megan." His anger was gone, and in its place was a sorrow so strong it hurt to look in his eyes. "But I didn't think it was impossible."

She held her hand out to him, and for a moment, he hesitated. Then, reluctantly almost, with both hands he took hold of her fingers. She couldn't fight her tears much longer. "I'm sorry. I think we better go."

At first it looked like he might argue again, try to convince her that she was wrong and that he'd never let go of her hands no matter what she thought. But then defeat came over him like a wet blanket, changing his expression and his posture, and in that single change, Megan could sense it was over. Because deep inside, he must've realized that she was right.

"Okay." He brought her hands to his lips, and he kissed her fingers. "I'll take you home."

The kiss burned through her, because it wasn't the kiss she had longed for just a week ago. And because it was goodbye, no question.

She went to get Cory, and like every other time they'd been together, Aaron dropped them off at their apartment. Cory must've sensed something was wrong, but he didn't ask a lot of questions. When it came time to get out of the truck, Aaron parked and gave Cory a hug. But by then she was already waiting for Cory near the front door of the building. No sense dragging out the inevitable.

She waved a quick goodbye, because she couldn't speak, and she waited until she hit the stairs inside the building before she let herself break. The whole way up, she navigated with the stair rail, because she couldn't see for the tears.

"What's wrong?" Cory trudged along beside her, his voice somber. "Did something happen?"

How was she supposed to explain the situation to Cory? Better to let the passing of time tell the story. She sniffed. "I'm just ... sad. That's all."

He didn't ask again, and when she reached the apartment, she set her bag down. "I need a nap, okay, buddy?" Tears were still filling her eyes, but she was holding back on the sobs.

"Okay." He kicked his foot a little. "I'll take a shower."

With that, Megan went into her room and locked the door behind her. She didn't make it to the bed before the sobs washed over her. Wave after wave after wave of disappointment and hurt and regret. She'd actually let herself believe that it was possible, that the famous 49ers quarterback might sweep her off her feet and give her the love and the life she never dared dream about. And look where it had gotten her.

She squeezed her eyes shut and willed herself to feel God's presence. He was here, just as He promised. Always. Never forsaking her. It took everything she had, but finally as the sobs slowed she could sense Him in the room with her. Her God and Father ... her Friend. And good thing. Because with God she could survive this, the pain of saying goodbye to Aaron Hill.

Even if she was never the same again.

TWENTY-THREE

Aaron had Bill on the phone a minute after he pulled away from Megan's apartment.

"Hill, my friend ... I was just thinking about you and how we need to get dinner at Morton's one of these — "

"Shut up, Bill." Aaron's tone was sharp and mean. He didn't care. "Tell me about the article. The one in the *Chronicle*."

Bill uttered an indignant chuckle. "What about it? I got another one coming out in a few weeks. Reporters are crazy for this stuff, man. I mean, we're talking celebrities, Hill. You're in the big time now. There with the other young guns fresh off the draft."

His rage made it hard for him to focus. "Another article? Bill, I never authorized the first one."

"Right, so thank me." His laugh became more of a huff. "I mean, someone has to look out for your image. Leave it to you, and you'll drag in some single mother on welfare."

"Wait!" Aaron seethed, his blood running hot through his veins. He pulled his truck over and slammed it into park. "You don't know the first thing about Megan Gunn, so leave her out of this." He planned to meet his agent in person, but now Aaron was glad a phone line separated them. Otherwise, he might've knocked the guy senseless. "Stick to the subject, Bill. The article." He raised his voice. "You called the *Chronicle* and told them a bunch of lies?"

"Listen." Bill's voice held some attitude now. "I've been doing that since you were a sophomore at UCLA." Bill allowed a momentary burst of anger. "I don't have to run everything by you, Hill. You got enough to do on the field. That's why you hired me, right? To handle your contracts and your connections and your image." He paused, his disgust obvious. "You're welcome."

Bill went on about how a little appreciation would be nice since he basically spent all day and every night thinking up ways to help Aaron have an edge in the public eye and with other endorsement companies who might be—

"Bill!" Aaron gritted his teeth. "What's the next article say?"

His agent hesitated. "Same thing. You're interested in one of Hollywood's young elite. Just enough to keep you on the cutting edge."

Aaron clenched his teeth and gripped the steering wheel with both hands. "Call the paper, Bill." His voice was calmer now, almost frighteningly so. "If the article runs this week, I'll sue you. I swear I will." He lifted his head and stared straight ahead. But all he could see was Megan, the hurt in her eyes. "Are you listening, Bill?"

"I am, but you've got this whole thing wrong, friend, this is the best—"

"Stop." He wanted to ask about Amy, about the tricks Bill must've pulled back then. But this wasn't the time. He needed to focus on the season. That conversation, and his decision about whether Bill would remain his agent after a stunt like this, could wait until he hung up his cleats—hopefully, well after the New Year.

Aaron sat up straighter and every word dripped in cool venom. "Pull the article, Bill. Or my attorney'll have an official notice on your desk next week and we'll be through. Understand?"

"Listen, call me later." He sounded frantic. "I'll pull the article. Come on, Hill, don't get crazy on me. I'm your friend, the guy who made you what you—"

Aaron hung up. He'd expected that after he told off Bill he'd feel better about the situation. At least his agent would know not to manipulate the media on his behalf ever again, and that should have brought some sense of satisfaction. But as Aaron pulled back onto the highway, he didn't feel even a little better. Because, amidst the trash piling up in his heart, was one more piece he didn't know how to deal with. The fact that somehow, without meaning to, he'd done the one thing he couldn't forgive himself for doing.

He'd lost a dark-haired, blue-eyed girl whose soul was as clean as his was full of filth, a girl who would take with her a piece of his heart.

Even if they never spoke again.

⌐

Cory sat in his room, staring at the things in his special box. Something had gone very wrong, but he wasn't sure what. He went over the events of the day again and again. The soccer game was a winner, and the lunch was good. But sometime when he was on the swings Megan and Aaron musta had a fight. Sometimes that happened when people had questions, and Megan definitely had questions. Why did Cory still think Aaron was his dad? And Aaron probably had questions too. Why was Cory holding onto something that wasn't even true? Those sorts of questions.

So now, he couldn't sit back and wait on his clue any longer.

He pulled his backpack to him and took out a piece of paper. Then he wrote Aaron another letter. This one was shorter than the first one. He folded it, and then he tucked the photo of his mom and Aaron inside. He would have to get an envelope later, because they were in the kitchen, and he was supposed to be taking a shower.

No matter what happened, even if Megan was mad at him, the next time he saw Aaron he would give him the letter and the picture. Then maybe whatever was wrong between Megan and Aaron would clear up, because that's what happened when people had proof. Cory smiled, even though he didn't feel like it. 'Cause when Aaron looked at that picture, that would be that.

And there wouldn't be any questions at all.

—

The season went from bad to worse. Derrick had no choice but to stand by and watch as the team won just eight games over the next thirteen weeks. He and Denae prayed about the team and the season, the pressure on Coach Cameron, and the struggles in Aaron Hill's head. In the end, they had to agree with the headlines in the *Chronicle*. The 49ers wild card berth in the playoffs was nothing short of a miracle. Even more, they had to admit, along with everyone in the sports world, that a team with a 9–7 record had the same chance as snow in Phoenix.

Which was where the Super Bowl was being held.

According to the announcers on ESPN, San Francisco would be knocked out in the first round. Derrick figured most of his teammates felt the same way, including Aaron Hill.

But no matter what Derrick tried, Aaron wouldn't say more than a few words. The demons that haunted him earlier in the season had apparently gotten meaner, because without question it was Aaron's worst regular season performance ever. He threw more interceptions than touchdowns and battled speculation from the press after every game. Internally, there was talk of replacing him with Derrick or Jay, but now that they'd made the playoffs, the front office didn't want to rock the boat. Replacing Aaron would be a major news story. It would take the focus off the playoffs and place it squarely on the conflicts San Francisco was facing.

With each passing week, Derrick worked harder to control his anger at his teammate. This was Derrick's last season. His last chance. Aaron knew it and still he couldn't get his head in the action.

The wild card game took place on a cold, cloudy afternoon at Soldier Field against the defending NFC champion Bears. During warm-ups, heaters were set up along the sidelines and a temperature gauge showed below freezing conditions. Snow was in the forecast. Derrick tried not to feel the frustration from the season as the team huddled together in the locker room around Coach Cameron.

"You guys know as well as I do ... only God could have brought us here. Not once all year did we play to our potential." He managed to sound intense and positive, something even he had struggled with during recent chalk talks. "But now that we're here, I don't care what the media says." His voice built with the sort of passion that simmered deep inside Derrick, even after all the ways the 49ers had struggled. Coach looked around the room, singling guys out, staring them down. "Now that we're here, we have as much a chance as anyone else. Three wins." He held up three fingers, his gaze intense. "Three wins and we're there, suiting up in Phoenix for the big game."

Coach didn't mention the unlikelihood that they'd win those three games. ESPN had been spouting the statistics all week. Since the wild card system began in 1970, only eight wild card teams had advanced to the Super Bowl. Of those, only four had won the title. Coach seemed to read his thoughts. "I don't care what the statistics say." He pointed at Aaron Hill and then two of the team's top receivers, and their leading running back. "This team has what it takes." He paused. "Now go out and win that ball game."

By kickoff, a ten mile-an-hour wind had started up, sending bitter cold along the sidelines. The 49ers were first on offense, but Aaron led a stuttering drive that stalled around the fifty. A punt put the Bears back deep into their own territory, and on San Francisco's next possession, Aaron chipped away a few yards at a time before he handed off for the first score.

Derrick paced the sidelines, trying to stay warm. *Thank you, God … come on, help us out…*

But the victory on the field was short-lived, and by halftime Chicago had a ten-point lead. Aaron was one of the first players into the locker room, and Derrick caught up with him next to his locker. He slammed his palm against the metal door and glared at his teammate. "Talk to me, man! What's happening out there?"

Aaron braced himself against his locker and hung his head. "Nothing's clicking."

"Yeah, starting with you." He leaned closer and brought his voice down to a low hiss. "You were supposed to talk to God about the garbage, remember?"

He shook his head, his response tortured. "There's more now."

Derrick clenched his teeth and slammed his hand on the locker again. He did a half turn and then spun around and faced Aaron. "That's your fault." The anger inside him surged to the surface. "This team needs you, Hill. Today. This afternoon. I don't care if you got a mountain of garbage in that cold heart of yours. Just play your game."

For a few seconds, Aaron said nothing. Then in a rush he slammed shut his locker and stormed off. Derrick didn't feel bad. They didn't have a chance if Aaron didn't rise to the occasion. If he wasn't going to talk to God, so be it. Either way, he had a responsibility to the team.

Coach said basically the same thing before they went out for the second half. And this time, the Aaron Hill who took the field was the fighter, the warrior. He threw a touchdown pass three minutes into the third quarter, and then again in the fourth, as the sky broke open and released a blinding burst of snow onto the field.

"There it is." Derrick's knee throbbed in the freezing cold, but he didn't care. They could do this, they could win it despite everything. He found Aaron on the sidelines after the score and slapped him hard on his helmet. "Come on, Hill … make it happen."

Aaron didn't say anything, but his expression told the story. Whether it was Derrick's talk or a switch that flipped inside his brain, Aaron wore his game face now. The snow continued, and with five minutes to play, Chicago kicked a field goal. By then the lines on the field were all but impossible to see, and the officials called a timeout so they could clear the snow off the yard markers. Derrick could hardly watch from his place next to Coach Cameron. *Please, God ... keep Aaron focused ...*

The last few minutes of play were an icy battle. Aaron struggled to move the ball, but a few close first downs and another touchdown pass tied the game. A beautiful kick in the waning seconds, and the 49ers squeaked by with a one-point win.

The atmosphere in the locker room after the game could hardly be called celebratory. Guys were exhausted, mentally and physically. The idea of taking on the Seahawks next week seemed daunting. But as Coach pointed out, they still had life. And at this point, anyone with life had a chance.

At O'Hare International Airport, Derrick boarded the private 737 and looked for an empty row near the back. He had business to do, so he didn't want to talk to anyone. But as he passed Aaron, whose eyes were closed, he stopped. Then he bent close to his teammate. "Hill ..."

Aaron blinked his eyes open, and for a moment they only looked at each other.

"Talk to God, man. I'm serious." He straightened again. "No one can do it for you."

With that he kept walking. There wasn't anything else to say, really. In light of all they'd been through to get here, and all that lay ahead, if Aaron didn't figure out how to break free, they might as well hang up their cleats now. Telling Aaron what to do would never be enough. It hadn't worked once all season. That was the business he had to do. So, for the next four hours Derrick talked to God almost constantly, begging Him that someway, somehow, Aaron would cry out for help. And in doing so, a miracle would happen.

The miracle he'd come to San Francisco to see.

Twenty-Four

A aron ached all over from the Chicago game. He'd been sacked four times—not once because of his linemen falling down on the job. He alone was the problem. He didn't need Derrick to tell him. He was so distracted, so burdened by whatever it was, that he could barely focus. Even in the middle of a play.

He slept in late Tuesday, and when he climbed out of bed, everything hurt. Now he was supposed to get right back into shape and battle it all over again on Saturday. Just five days. He staggered into the kitchen and by the time he'd had breakfast and unpacked his bags, it was two o'clock when he reported to the 49ers training facility.

The trainers were waiting for him. He alternated between sitting in hot water and ice, and then they worked him through a series of stretches—all designed to keep him loose. His body, anyway. But through every minute of it, he could hear Derrick's voice in his head. Since Megan backed out of his life three weeks into the season, the garbage inside him had only gotten heavier. Some days he was sure the burden would do more than affect his game. It might strangle the life from him.

He told himself he could handle it, he could work through it. If Megan didn't want anything to do with him, fine. He could get along without her, same way he'd done before he met her. He had offers, and if he wanted to, he could have a warm body in bed next to him tonight.

Only he didn't want to. Not with Megan's eyes and heart still consuming him.

Now as he finished up at the training facility, he had the strongest desire to run, to get into his truck, pick a direction, and drive until sunup. Even then he couldn't outrun himself. He started to head home, but he drove past his exit and didn't pull off until he reached Pier 39 and a parking place at the back of the lot. He rolled down his window and stared at the carrousel in the distance.

How had things gotten so bad? Aaron couldn't find an answer, and when he set back out on the road he thought about going to Derrick's house. But he knew what Derrick would say. So instead, he drove back home and wandered around his house. Therapy had taken the edge off the aches, and good thing. Aaron wouldn't take pain meds. He'd seen too many players get addicted, popping pills between downs. His second year with the 49ers a player he'd hung out with at the Pro Bowl died in his sleep after a three-year battle with pain pills. The guy was thirty-one years old. No, when the pain got that bad, Aaron wouldn't look for a prescription. He'd simply call it a day.

But his trainers couldn't do anything to touch the pain inside him. So maybe the end of his career was coming, after all. If he couldn't get his head in the game, he had no right being on the field, no matter what Bill Bond said.

Aaron walked into his backyard and sat in the chair overlooking the pool. His agent still called every few days.

"I pulled the article, so come on, man. What's wrong? Talk to me, friend … we need a dinner out, a chance to relax."

Aaron always cut him off before he could get going. "I'll figure it out." That was his answer to everyone. Everyone but Derrick. Aaron stared at the gray sky and tried to feel something. But his mind, his soul, all of him felt stone cold, and finally — around eight o'clock when darkness lay thick over his home and his heart, he climbed into his truck and headed for Baker's Beach, the same place he'd gone before, back when it first occurred to him that Derrick might be in his life for a reason.

He parked and climbed out. The air was damp and cold, which wouldn't be good for his aching shoulder. He grabbed his leather jacket from the driver's seat, slipped it on, and zipped it up to his chin. Then he buried his hands in his pockets and started walking. This time the beach was completely empty, which suited him. He turned left, like before, and walked to the big rock.

Somehow he had a sense that here, in the cold black of night, it might finally happen, he might finally find the courage to talk to God. He walked hard and fast, breathing deep, stirring something new and uncertain in his blood. When he reached the rock, he climbed up and found the flat section at the top. Then he drew up his knees and stared out at the shiny black water. No moon pierced the sky tonight, no sign of stars. In the far distance, the soft hum of traffic on the bridge mixed with the hushed sounds of a nearly still surf. Here, there was no last-minute wildcard win, no playoff game five days out. No world watching and waiting for him to fail. He was alone.

Just him and God.

Because after all his running and trying to figure his pain out on his own, it had come to this. Him and God. He stared into the emptiness and thought about the Creator, the all-knowing Savior, the One he'd been running from. His parents never talked about faith or belief. Small wonder. They lived for their jobs, creating a void in Aaron when it came to relationships of any kind — God included. But his high school coach had been a Christian. It wasn't something the man talked about much, but after hours, when Coach gave him a ride home, he would drop him off and say, "Keep your eyes on Jesus, Hill."

As long as he played for Coach, Aaron never really knew what that meant. But his junior year he went with a group of teammates to a church summer camp. The things he heard from the speaker that week floored him. Jesus was alive? His Spirit was moving among them? He had died on the cross for their sins, for Aaron Hill's sins? Night after night that camp week, kids came forward after the speaker finished — some of them weeping. And the counselors talked about how many students were giving their lives to Christ.

Aaron came close. The last night when the speaker was talking about the emptiness inside, and how every one of them had a hole in their hearts that only Jesus could fill, when he told them Jesus was calling them, and that only someone very foolish would fight the pull of Jesus Christ, Aaron felt himself start to get up. Then he looked a few feet over and spotted some of his teammates. Weakness wasn't tolerated among the guys, not for a minute. Whether the teammates had come forward for Jesus at some point, Aaron didn't know. But in that moment he couldn't admit his emptiness and he couldn't admit the hole in his heart.

He didn't come home from camp a Christian, but he came home a believer. Jesus was Mighty God, Wonderful Counselor, Prince of Peace. He had no doubts. But every day since then he came to believe something else. That the holy God of the universe couldn't possibly want anything to do with Aaron Hill. After all, he'd had a chance to make a commitment to Jesus before, and he'd failed. What would God want with him after that?

The wind off the water was cold, and Aaron slid one leg down along the craggy, cool rock. His thoughts about God only grew worse as time went on, as he walked away from Amy and began believing he was something special, someone famous. For years it wasn't so much that he felt ashamed before God. He simply didn't think about Him because there was no need. Between him and Bill, life was going along just fine without God.

All that changed with Megan Gunn.

The junk in his heart, the emptiness, the guilt and regret—all of it had been there before that fateful day at the youth center. He thought about her, about the way she'd caught his attention and taken his breath from the beginning. It wasn't just her beauty that shone a spotlight on the ugliness inside him. Rather, it was something in her eyes, an innocence and kindness that stood brightly in contrast. That's when the trouble started. After getting to know Megan, he saw himself differently, felt differently. As if every awful, mindless, self-centered thing he'd ever done was suddenly and painfully clear.

He hung his head and tried to find a warm bit of air for his lungs. When he looked up, he stared past the Golden Gate Bridge to the waters beyond, to Alcatraz Island.

He'd always been struck by the ghost of the prison, the way the captives must've felt knowing there was no way out. He wondered about the futility of being a prisoner in a place like Alcatraz. But here, tonight, he didn't have to wonder because he knew. He was just like them. Trapped in a prison of his own guilt and humanity with no way out.

Derrick's words filtered through his heart, his soul. *Maybe this is the year ... talk to God, man ... He's the only one who can take out the garbage.* He stared down at the rock beneath him, and like a volcano building steam, every wrong thing he'd ever done, every empty hour came to mind, filling him, torturing him, until finally ... finally he slid off the rock and fell to his knees.

"God! I can't bear it!" He shouted the words and the darkness around him swallowed them without an echo. He couldn't catch his breath, couldn't hold his body up under the weight of his own guilt. "I've done it all wrong, God. All of it." And then, his sides heaving, he silently recounted everything he could remember. Every time he'd ever used a woman, and every promise he'd casually broken. Every selfish decision and careless attitude toward people less fortunate than him. The cockiness and arrogance, his judgmental spirit. Even the way he'd pushed the blonde woman aside in the parking lot that night earlier in the season. Callous and careless, as if only he mattered. One by one by one, he laid the burdens of his heart flat before God until the array of trash stretched out before him was staggering, overwhelming.

Dampness from the sand soaked through his jeans, but he didn't care. He bent over his thighs, his head hung low. "Take it, God … take it from me. I can't live another hour with the guilt. It's strangling me."

And then he remembered things spoken by the speaker, the one from the final day at church camp his junior year of high school. Things he'd blocked out until here, now.

Jesus died for your sins … He was God in the flesh … He could've commanded a hundred thousand angels and His rescue would've been certain… He went to the cross for you, and you alone. The speaker's voice had filled the lodge, and now the memory was alive again. *If you were the only person in all the world, He would've gone to the cross anyway. Your sin sent Him there … yours, and yours alone. He loved you that much.*

Aaron felt the full extent of his choices, his years of selfish living. And finally, gratefully, tears erupted from the smoldering mountain of his sin. His tears became deep sobs, deep and tortuous and silent until he understood clearly what he needed to do. He straightened, standing on his knees, and raised his hands to the starless sky. "I'm sorry, God. I'm sorry!" His sobs rang out in the winter air. He could do this, he could talk to the Creator of the Universe. "Forgive me. Take my life and set me free!"

A gust of wind washed over him and he fell silent, awestruck. After a long while, when his tears were dry and his hands were down again at his sides, he realized something. He actually felt different. Something wonderful and alive was happening inside him. The heaviness was gone, and in its place, he felt new and light and whole and healed. The prison bars were broken and he would never, ever be captive again.

He had God in his heart, and he would hold onto Him forever. He would ask Derrick about going to church because he wanted a place where he could learn and grow and connect with people who had found this hope ages ago. He breathed deep, and joy he'd never known filled his lungs and flowed into his veins. Until this moment, the season had been a drain, a burden. But now, all his days stretched out before him like an amazing adventure, one he would live for God. Whether Megan joined him or whether he never found another woman like her, he would be complete, whole.

Slowly, carefully, he rose to his feet. His knees were cold and wet and aching, but he barely noticed. For the first time in his life, the holiness of God consumed him, taking his breath, showing him he was nothing next to Jesus Christ. Nothing and everything. Because the place that had only an hour ago been filled with a mountain of trash, was clean and full once again. Full with the power of God now and forevermore. All because of what Jesus had showed him here on a cold stretch of winter beach. Aaron smiled to himself as he turned and headed back for his truck. Only one thing could make this night any better.

A call to Derrick Anderson.

———

The phone rang in Derrick's house late Monday night, just as he and Denae were getting into bed. Denae gave him a look, and Derrick shrugged. He picked up the receiver and stretched his legs out across the layers of sheets. "Hello?"

"I did it." The voice on the other end released a few bursts of happy, carefree laughter. "I did it, man. I really did it."

He recognized the voice. "Aaron?"

"I drove out to the beach and I talked to God. Just like you said." He laughed again. "I can't believe it, man. I never felt this good in my whole life."

Derrick motioned to his wife and pointed to the phone. "He did it," he mouthed. He could feel his grin filling his face. "Aaron talked to God!"

"What? Are you too shocked to speak?" Aaron sounded five years younger. "You shoulda told me to do this months ago."

"Now wait a minute …"

"I'm kidding you, man. I called to thank you." The laughter in his voice dropped off and he was silent for several seconds. "You saved my life, Anderson. I couldn't have waited another day."

"You know what I think …" Derrick's voice choked with emotion. "I think the Seahawks better watch out."

———

As it turned out, Derrick might as well have been a prophet. Led by a changed Aaron Hill, the 49ers swept into Seattle and dominated the Seahawks in the Divisional Playoff game that Saturday. They started strong and never quit, and when they notched a 24–3 victory, Derrick was less surprised than anyone. Because Aaron had been a talented quarterback before. But now he was a talented quarterback operating by the power of God.

And nothing on heaven or earth could come against that.

Twenty-Five

Megan's volunteer shift at the youth center Monday night was more wearying than usual. One of the older foster teens, a sixteen-year-old boy, had been picked up for selling drugs. When the details came from the director that afternoon, the story made more sense. The boy had been through three foster homes since school started in September, and now—because of bad behavior—he was facing expulsion from school.

The story was sad, because the people close to the boy had seen the train barreling toward the cliff. With no stability, no one to believe in him, and no future, the boy had gone the way of the street, found his place among drug dealers always looking for the newer, younger guys to do their dirty work.

Back at the apartment, she finished washing the frying pan, dried it, and put it away. Oreo walked into the kitchen and rubbed against her ankles. "I know ... time for your milk."

Cory was watching Sports Center, mesmerized by the dramatic retelling of the showing by the 49ers against Seattle. Megan tried not to watch, but when she heard his name, she stopped and leaned her elbows on the counter. If she'd had her way, she would've stayed away from sports all season. It had been too hard to watch, knowing that Aaron was struggling so badly.

Once in a while, she even wondered if maybe she had something to do with his terrible season. Certainly, he hadn't connected with any movie stars, at least not that the *Chronicle* had picked up on. Whatever details were pending never came, except in the tabloids. When she was at the market, she'd see a small headline about Aaron Hill finding solace with this actress or that one. But there were no photos, and the reputable news and sports agencies only talked about his game.

It had been more than three months since she told him goodbye, long enough that she should've been over him. They only spent a few days together, after all. Even still, she thought about him constantly, when she did her paper route early in the morning and when she fell into bed at the end of the day. Part of it was Cory. Never mind that Aaron wasn't Cory's father, Cory held to his beliefs. As far as the boy was concerned, Aaron was his dad and his hero all at the same time, and he talked often about missing Aaron and hoping for another night at the pier. Whenever the 49ers were on TV or when there was a story in the *Chronicle* that Mrs. Florentino brought over, the boy was consumed.

And so Megan had kept tabs on Aaron Hill without wanting to.

The image on the TV screen changed and Aaron's face appeared. Cory was sitting a few feet away, cross-legged on the floor, his head blocking part of the picture. The TV wasn't very big to begin with, but with Cory in the way, Megan could only make out half of the image. She sighed and moved into the next room so she could see better. As she came closer, Megan froze in place.

His eyes were different. Even from last week, when his interview after the Bears game had been short and terse. Yes, she was sure of it. Something about his eyes and his expression was different now. Almost like through the sweat and grime he was glowing from the inside out. She took a step closer. "Turn it up, Cory. Please."

He looked over his shoulder at her and smiled. "Yeah, listen to this. I already heard it three times, but listen."

The volume came up and Aaron's voice filled her home, her heart. "I can't take the credit ... it was a team victory."

The announcer was next. "You can say that, but three touchdowns for more than four hundred yards with no interceptions? Did you ever think you'd come out against the Seahawks and have your best game of the season?"

Aaron smiled and there it was again ... a clarity and vulnerability in his eyes that she'd never seen before. He laughed like a high-school kid without a worry in the world. "Yeah, I guess I sort of did." His eyes shone. "Something happened this week. I guess it made all the difference."

There was a knock at the door, and Cory jumped up. "Mrs. Florentino's bringing us some chocolate cake." He darted past her. "She promised."

"Okay." Megan remained unmoved, glued to the interview. The announcer didn't look like he knew what to make of Aaron's statement. "You wanna let us in on the secret?"

"Yeah." Aaron grinned. "I took Derrick Anderson's advice."

Cory opened the door and before he could say anything, a voice sang out. "Cory! You grew an inch since I saw you last!"

Megan felt the blood drain from her face. The voice was the same one coming from the television. She turned quickly in case her mind was playing tricks on her, but there he was. Aaron Hill, standing in her doorway, looking past Cory straight at her. Now, in person, she could see the change in his eyes more clearly. Adrenaline raced through her, and she took a moment to feel her feet on the floor. When she did, when her lungs were working again, she took a step closer, her eyes locked on his. "I have a question."

He looked deep at her, past the lonely months to the place that had made the decision to say goodbye. "What's your question?"

"What did Derrick Anderson tell you to do?"

Cory seemed to remember something important. He gasped and raced into his room. Megan was ten feet from him now, and Aaron closed the gap, moving toward her until they could hear each other breathing. A crooked smile lifted his lips and he shrugged one shoulder. "He told me ... to talk to God."

A knowing came over her and she grinned at him. "So that's it."

"What?"

"Your eyes." She made a half turn toward the TV and then back to Aaron. "You were just on Sports Center, and I could see it. Something was different." A light laugh tickled her throat. "Now I understand."

He wore a tan-colored coat, and he reached inside his pocket and pulled out a thick envelope. "Here."

She wasn't sure what to say. He might've figured out how to talk to God, but that didn't mean they'd found common ground or that she should open up her heart to him again. The reasons that existed before still existed today. But the only words she could say were the ones she felt most deeply. "I can't believe you're here."

His grin softened. "I sat outside for half an hour trying to get up the guts."

Her heart melted. She looked at the envelope still in his hand. "What is it?"

"Open it up." He handed it to her. At the same time, Cory came into the room with an envelope of his own.

Megan stared at the boy, and then at Aaron. Whatever was going on, she was completely in the dark. She took the envelope from Aaron, opened it, and as she pulled out the contents, as she sorted through the documents and realized the extent of his gift, she brought her fingers to her mouth.

"What?" Cory raced to her side and peered up at the papers in her hands.

"Tickets." Her eyes found Aaron's. "To the conference championships in New Orleans."

Cory raised his fist in the air and jumped in a full circle. But then he stopped and cocked his head. "How'll we get there?"

"It's all here." She didn't blink, didn't break contact with Aaron. "Plane tickets and a hotel room. Everything."

"A car will meet you at the airport and take you to the hotel, and then to the game." He took a step back, his expression humble. "It's all taken care of."

She handed the tickets to Cory, and stared at him. "Why, Aaron? After so long?"

"To thank you." He still wouldn't take his eyes off her. "For helping me see what I'd become."

"Wow!" Cory held the tickets out. "We're going to the NFC championships!"

Megan was speechless, but more because Aaron was really here, standing in her apartment giving them an opportunity like they'd never had all their lives. She heard what he'd said, but she wasn't sure she understood it. "For helping you see?"

"I'll tell you later." He laughed. "I won't keep you." He took another step back toward the door. "I just wanted to make sure you'd be there."

She hesitated, the reality still sinking in. "We will."

"How will we meet up with you?" Cory ran to Aaron and took hold of his arm. "There'll be so many people."

Aaron thought about that. "Let's have a sign." He hesitated. "I know … when they put the cameras on me, I'll do this." He held up his first two fingers and did a little wave. "That'll mean I'm looking for you."

"Okay!" Cory clapped his hands. "Perfect!" He was still for a second. "But will we see you?"

"Probably not." His smile dropped off some. "We'll get right on a plane after the game. But I'll know you're up there."

"Oh." Some of Cory's excitement dimmed, but not for long. "We're going to New Orleans!"

Megan wasn't sure what to say. "Thank you, Aaron."

He put his hand on the door. Clearly, he wasn't going to hug her or push her in any way. Even if a part of her wanted him to. He looked deep at her again. "I want to talk later, when the season's done."

"Okay." She could hardly wait.

Aaron was telling Cory goodbye when he gasped. "I almost forgot!" He held out his envelope to Aaron. "This is for you. I need you to read it."

Easy laughter came from Aaron and Megan at the same time. They swapped a look, and then Aaron took the envelope. "I will. As soon as I get to the car."

"Good!" Cory hugged him. "Talk to you soon."

Aaron mouthed a gentle goodbye in her direction and raised his hand. She did the same, and then he was gone. It took a minute for Megan's shock to wear off, and when it did, she remembered Cory's envelope. He was back in his room. "Cory, come here."

He darted out and looked at her. "Yes?"

"What was in the envelope?"

"Proof."

She gave him a curious look. "Proof of what?"

"That Aaron's my dad." He said the words calmly, matter-of-fact. "I found a picture of my mom and him at a dance. I wanted him to have it."

A chill ran down Megan's arms. "Don't joke with me, Cory. I mean it."

"I'm serious." He looked hurt. "I found it a few months ago, but I didn't want to show it to anyone but Aaron. Because he's the only one who has to know the truth."

The surprises from the night were beginning to add up. Megan sat down at the kitchen table and put her head in her hands. She was suddenly breathless, the possibility only beginning to make its way through her mind. Even then, it was too big to get her head around all at once. If Cory had a photo of his mother and Aaron, then ... then could it be that all this time he'd been right? That what she'd thought was a fantasy was the truth all along? And how could it be true when Amy had never once mentioned that Aaron was Cory's dad, or even that he might be.

She felt dizzy and giddy and like she was dreaming all at the same time. Whatever was happening—between Aaron's change of heart and Cory's proof—there really was only one explanation.

God was up to something bigger than all of them.

TWENTY-SIX

As he walked down the stairs of her apartment and headed for his truck, Aaron felt God's presence stronger than at any time since his night at the beach. He'd done what he'd come to do. Megan had the tickets, and now she and Cory could have a weekend like nothing they'd ever had before. And in a few weeks, Aaron would tell her what his comment meant, how God had used her to open his eyes to all of life. Real life.

He stepped into his truck, but before he turned the key, he opened Cory's envelope. He'd learned his lesson about lying to kids, or anyone else. The rest of his life he wanted to live out the change in his heart. This was one small way he could make that start. Inside the envelope were two others, both with his name written across the front. Aaron narrowed his eyes, confused. The writing was cursive, definitely not Cory's. Third in the package was a piece of folded paper. He opened it and a wallet-sized photo fell on his lap. Before he picked it up, he read the words on the page.

"Dear Aaron, I figered you needed proof. So here it is. Tell me if you believe me now. Love, Cory."

A strange sensation came over him, and without drawing a breath, he picked up the photo from his lap and turned it over. He stared at it, not believing his eyes. It couldn't be … it couldn't … Slowly, certainly, the bottom fell away and he began to freefall. This wasn't happening.

The people in the photograph were he and Amy Briggs.

His Amy.

His heartbeat doubled and a layer of sweat broke out across his forehead. Amy Briggs was Cory's mother? He'd talked about her with Megan, but never once had either of them mentioned her name. Megan had always been intentionally vague, rarely even calling Aaron by his first name. There would've been no reason to ask about Cory's last name. Until now, Aaron hadn't even thought about the fact that the boy didn't share Megan's name.

The whole foster kid thing was too new to him. If Amy was Cory's mother, then …

But the truth was … the truth was as clear as the picture in front of him. Cory was his son! His very own! He drew a sharp breath and wondered if he might explode from the shock … the shattering realization and the joy bursting inside him. Cory was his son? He looked at the photo again. Cory was his son! Amy had been pregnant with Aaron's child, just like she'd told him all those years ago. So, Cory had to be his son.

His emotions shifted. What had he put the boy through? All these months Cory had stood by his story, that he was Aaron's son. Period. And the whole time — for years in Megan's case — nobody had believed him. Aaron Hill, the father of a foster kid? A kid whose mother never even mentioned the idea? He and Megan both chalked it up to the boy's overactive imagination and his deep desire for a dad.

Aaron groaned out loud. His heart broke for the boy who wanted his dad so badly he would never, ever give up. What must he have been thinking when Aaron made so light of his insistence? And all those recent times when he'd thought about Amy, how he'd never given her a proper goodbye and how he'd turned his back when she'd come to him, pregnant…

And then another reality hit him, devastating him.

Amy was dead.

The girl he still thought about, the one he figured was married and living a wonderful life with some other guy, had in reality raised Cory by herself in a poverty-stricken environment, and then she'd died of pneumonia two years ago. The blow tore at him, stirring fresh debris into the gutters and alleyways of his heart. Amy had lived poor and alone, working at a diner while he signed his contract for millions of dollars and moved on without her. He hung his head and pictured her, the girl he'd loved so much back in his early college days. His Amy was gone. She'd died without his ever making things right.

He remembered the envelopes, the ones with his name written in cursive. His stomach churned as he sat up straighter and picked up the first of the two. There was no time to waste. The boy in the third-floor apartment was his son, and he didn't want another ten minutes to pass without going back up and making things right. He opened the envelope and held the paper tenderly, as if it still contained a little piece of Amy.

Dear Aaron,

He stopped and closed his eyes. Her voice, her face, all of it was there in front of him again. "Amy ... why didn't I see it?"

There were no answers; there might never be. He opened his eyes and started over again.

Dear Aaron,

Yesterday our son was born. The experience was more miraculous than anything in my life, and I only wish you'd been there to see for yourself. He's beautiful, Aaron. I named him Cory Joseph Briggs. The first time I held him I saw you in his face. He has your eyes and your cheekbones. I can practically see the strapping boy and athlete he'll become.

I know you're going through a lot of changes. I'm not even sure how I'll get this letter to you. You must know about your agent, how he called me and told me to stay away from you. He threatened legal action if I contacted you again ...

What? Aaron's heart skidded into a strange rhythm. Bill had contacted Amy? Threatened her? Heat filled his face and pulsed through his body. He reached for the buttons on his phone, but then stopped himself. He would deal with Bill, but not yet. From this day on Cory would come first.

He drew a jagged breath and found his place again.

... but somehow I must find you. Especially now. Either that or I'll wait forever for you to come back, to find Cory and me. Because I've asked God to get your attention, to touch your heart and help you remember who you used to be. Before your world went crazy.

This time Aaron set the letter down on his lap. Tears blurred his eyes, and he blinked so he could see again. That's exactly what had happened. Directed and fed by his agent, Aaron's world had gone crazy and he'd allowed every minute of it. He lifted the letter and kept reading.

Don't feel bad, but my mom gave me a few weeks to get out. She was very upset about the baby, which I can understand. I just wish she would help me. But either way Cory and I will be fine. I'll get a job and an apartment and I'll pray for the day when you come back. I promise you, Aaron, as long as I live I'll wait for you. Wherever you go, I'll go. So that when you're ready to find me, I won't be far away. I love you, Aaron.

Amy

The air left his lungs and he let his head fall back against the seat. So that was why she moved to San Francisco, the reason she and Megan wound up at the same diner. Amy had moved here because she was following him, waiting for him. He pressed his fists to his eyes and swallowed a series of sobs. How could he have missed out on this, on her?

With all his remaining strength, he picked up the other envelope and opened it. Cory was waiting. He needed to get through this so that he would have all the information available when he went for the first time to his boy, his son. He studied the letter, and the date. It was written first, before the one talking about Cory's birth. He began to read.

Dear Aaron,

You're acting different these days, and I don't know what's happening. Maybe it's your agent, pulling you away from me, into a new and glamorous future. Or maybe it's something worse.

I know what my mother would say. Now that I've given you what you want, you're finished with me. My friends tell me you're seeing other girls, but I can't believe that. Not after the promises you made to me a week ago. I can't believe you'd listen to your agent over me, so I can only think of one reason why you would turn away from me, Aaron.

What I'm about to tell you, I've never told anyone else. I never will. Three nights ago, I was at Pierce College walking back to my car when a man grabbed me and pulled me into the bushes. I won't go into detail, but I want you to know the truth. He raped me. He wore a mask and he only said a few words. When it was over, he left me on the ground and he ran away. By the time I pulled myself together and reached my car, I didn't have the strength to go to the police. I was ashamed and sick inside. When morning came, I knew I could never tell the police or anyone else. I had no way of identifying the guy, nothing at all. He was tall and he was white. That's about it.

Aaron had to stop. He was furious and sick to his stomach. Amy had been raped? Was she serious? And where had he been, out to dinner with Bill Bond? Believing suddenly that everyone—even Amy—was hanging around to share in his money and power and fame? He clenched his fists. Amy had been attacked, and he hadn't so much as been a crying shoulder for her.

Aaron willed himself to draw a breath, and he realized how amazing the timing was. Because if he'd gotten this news before his talk with God, it might've sent him over the edge. It was difficult enough now. He didn't want to read another word, but he lifted the paper, anyway.

I have to tell you about what happened to me, because I'm afraid that somehow you know. Not that anyone would've told you. But maybe you know instinctively. Maybe the last time we talked you sensed something different in my voice. And maybe that's why you're acting different. That's why I have to be honest. I want no secrets between us, Aaron. I've never been with anyone but you. If I have my way, I never will again. Not until the day you marry me. Okay ... now you know. Because I believe you, Aaron. That someday you'll come back and marry me. I love you.

Amy

His hands shook as he folded both letters and placed them carefully back in their envelopes. He knew without a doubt that Amy had kept her promise. She was that type of girl, no matter what lies Bill Bond had told about her. If he was right, then she had died loving him, waiting for him. The truth was bigger than all his other poor choices combined. Aaron trembled as he gripped the steering wheel. His breaths came shallow and fast, and he felt a layer of sweat bead up across his forehead. How could he be such a creep, believing Bill Bond over his precious Amy? Had the glare of fame and fortune been that blinding? The truth was unbearable, and he grew sick to his stomach.

But then ... gradually, a greater truth dawned on him.

He didn't have to carry this sort of pain anymore. First, because Amy was safe now. In heaven with Jesus. And second, because he could ask God to take away his guilt.

Lord, I messed up so bad. I didn't watch my little boy grow up, and I lost the chance to tell his mother how much I loved her, how wrong I was. No matter what my agent said. Forgive me, God … please forgive me. I can't bear the guilt otherwise.

It took a while, but an otherworldly peace came over him. A peace that was not without deep sadness. An urgency built in him, then, and he grabbed the small photograph, rushed out of his truck and back upstairs to the sparse apartment Megan shared with Cory. He knocked on the door and when Megan answered it, he launched into an explanation.

"He's telling the truth …"

She searched his face, trembling. "He told me. Is it … is it really possible?"

"Look at this." He handed the photo to Megan. "Amy was my first love. I was … I was going to marry her." He could've cried, but his excitement had the upper hand. "What's his last name?"

"Briggs." Megan's words were fast and anxious. She was as blown away by the turn of events as Aaron was. "Cory Briggs."

The reality was still sinking in. "He's my son, Megan … he really is." There would be much to talk about later, notes to compare. But for now all that mattered was—"Cory!"

The boy came running up to the door. His smile held none of the drama and intensity both Aaron and Megan were feeling. He simply looked into Aaron's eyes. "Do you believe me now?"

Something amazing and marvelous was happening in Aaron's heart. He stepped past Megan, touching her hand without looking at her. Then he dropped to his knees for the second time that week, and he held out his arms. "Cory …" Happy tears choked his voice, but he didn't care.

The boy hesitated for only a second, then he ran the few steps that separated them and landed hard in an embrace that was eight years coming. "So…" Cory sounded small, still not quite sure. "You're my dad, right?"

"Yes." Aaron held him to his chest, stroking his small back and rocking him. Something inside him told him to be careful. Tests would be needed before he could know for sure. But he and Megan would take care of that right away. Not that he needed tests. They would be merely a formality. Cory really did look just like him, something he hadn't seen before today.

Aaron squeezed his eyes shut. "I'm sorry …" He pressed his son's face to his heart and managed the most precious words he'd ever said. "I'm your dad, Cory. I never knew until today."

They hugged for a long time, and Aaron stayed and tucked him in when it was bedtime. Aaron rubbed Cory's back for a minute or two. He'd missed so much, but tonight was the first of many times when he would be with his son before he went to sleep.

He and Megan would work out details of a paternity test in the morning. Aaron would look into it. When he left, he hugged Megan and his feelings for her came back in a rush. "Can I ask you something?"

"Anything."

"Did Amy ... as long as you knew her, did she have someone special, a boyfriend?" The question made things somewhat awkward between them, but Aaron needed to know.

"No one." Megan's answer was quick and heartfelt. "She never even dated. Said she didn't have time because Cory needed her."

Aaron reacted physically to the news, hunching slightly and struggling for his next breath. Everything Amy had told him in the letters was true. She had waited for him until her dying day. Aaron took Megan's hand and held it for a beat. "I have a lot to think through."

Her eyes danced. "I can't believe it."

"Me neither." There was something else he was only now realizing. Megan wanted to adopt Cory. She'd told him so. But now that Aaron had found him, he couldn't possibly let him go. The fairytale ending was obvious, but so far, Megan hadn't wanted to think of him that way, as someone she'd date. They had much to work through.

For now, it was enough that they parted with smiles and promises to talk tomorrow. He walked slowly back to his car, playing over the night's events. They were so far beyond unbelievable, even he couldn't quite grasp his new reality. But the sad truth about Amy was what stayed with him most as he drove home. He would always regret the decisions he made surrounding his breakup with Amy. And he needed to have a much overdue conversation with his agent. But there was something he could do now, while there was still time. He glanced at the photo once more. He might not have gotten the chance to tell Amy he was sorry.

But he could spend the rest of his days loving their little boy.

Twenty-Seven

More than 70,000 fans packed the newly renovated Superdome for the NFC championships the third Sunday in January, but Derrick's attention was on just one person. His teammate, Aaron Hill. The pageantry of the contest caused the pregame to be drawn out an additional half hour — more time to focus on the task ahead.

Before the coin toss, Derrick found Aaron on the sidelines and grabbed his arm. "You play with the power of God today, understand?"

"No other way." Aaron's eyes held a fire Derrick hadn't seen since he joined the team.

Derrick slapped Aaron's helmet and then walked down the line, yelling encouragement at players and groups of players. "This is it, boys … this is our day!" He stopped at Jay Ryder and spoke a few inches from his face. "Whether you play a down or not, you're a winner, Ryder, you understand me?"

Jay nodded, but he wasn't quite focused, his feet antsy. The team's two punters were questionable, and Coach had told them Jay might have to step in. Jay, who hadn't punted in a game since high school. Derrick slapped Jay's shoulder a few times as the announcer's voice echoed through the building, driving the fans into a frenzy.

"You hearing me, Ryder?" Derrick shouted above the roar of the crowd. "You're a winner, man. You get the whole between Sundays thing." He gripped the back of Jay's helmet and met him straight on. "When the season's over we're gonna change some lives, but right now … right now we're taking no prisoners!"

This time Jay's eyes were clear and intense. He nodded and then he smacked Derrick on the arm. "I'm ready … ready, man. Let's get it!"

Already they had made history. No wild card team since 1989 had even made it to the NFC championship game. But here they were. Derrick moved closer to the field and watched as his team won the coin toss and elected to receive. They would have the chance to draw first blood. Derrick bounced on his toes. His knee hurt but not as much as before. If Aaron needed him, he'd be ready. His eyes moved up to the seats of the packed stadium, to the vast sections of red and the handmade cardboard signs that said, "49ers Faithful" and "We Believe!" and "It's Our Turn!"

The Superdome rocked with noise, roaring with the excitement. The marching band competed with the announcer, and TV cameras were everywhere. Derrick eyed the roof of the structure. This was the first time he'd been here since the stadium reopened after Hurricane Katrina. He smiled. The city had done a great job on the storied building, improving it in record time so that it stood as a beacon of hope and determination to all who passed by. The city would rise again. The way the 49ers might win today and also rise again. And with the changes in Aaron...

Be with him, God ... guide his hands.

Derrick stretched his arms one at a time, and then rattled off twenty high-knees. The nervous energy and noise in the building was infectious, and up and down the sideline Derrick could tell his teammates felt the same way. Antsy, anxious, ready to get the show on the road. The San Francisco offense was on the field ready for their leader. A few more seconds with Coach Cameron and Aaron jogged to the middle of the huddle. Even the way he carried himself was different than earlier in the season. The story was on all the sports news shows, the change in Aaron Hill and how it couldn't have happened at a better time for the 49ers.

Derrick grinned in the direction of his friend. If his sense about the game was right, the sports anchors would have more to talk about after today. "Come on, Hill ... take it to 'em!" He shouted the words as loud as he could, not that Aaron could hear him. In the Superdome, noise had nowhere to go. Aaron would have an almost impossible time calling plays today. But that was okay too. Coach Cameron had worked on hand signals all week, not just with Aaron but with the entire team.

Aaron took the first snap, danced around the pocket for what seemed like forever, and then fired an eighteen-yard bullet to one of the rookie receivers. Derrick jumped along the sidelines, high-fiving his teammates and smacking shoulder pads. They could do this ... he could feel it. He stopped and bent over his knees watching as the next play started. Aaron handed off and the rusher dodged two tacklers for a five-yard gain. Derrick paced a few steps in either direction, clapping his hands, hard and intense. "Keep it going, boys ... keep it going!"

The drive didn't stall once. From the New Orleans twelve-yard line, Aaron took the snap and tossed a floater into the end zone. The receiver had no one near him, and he reeled it in for a touchdown. San Francisco 7, Saints 0, and only two minutes had fallen off the clock. But the Saints weren't about to be outdone. They'd gone most of the history of the franchise without playoff success. They battled back, nicking away at the yardage and using up seven minutes to notch a twenty-four-yard field goal.

During the Saints' drive, Aaron came up to Derrick and grinned. "I feel great, man. I can see the field, every player." He shook his head, amazed. "I just wish I would've listened to you sooner."

"Yeah, ya dummy." He smacked Aaron's shoulder pads. "That'll teach you."

A TV timeout, and then Aaron and the offense were back on the field. Aaron threw beautiful passes and with first and nine, goal to go, he took the snap and watched his pocket collapse, watched the Saints defense move into the end zone to cover the receivers, and suddenly the only thing in front of him was green. Without the slightest hesitation, he tucked the ball to his side and ran toward the goal line.

At the same time, the star linebacker for New Orleans realized what was happening. He ran to stop Aaron, and at the last minute the linebacker left his feet and grabbed at the quarterback. In the process, their two helmets made a sickening crash, and Aaron fell limp into the end zone. The officials had their hands raised straight in the air, signaling the touchdown. But already Coach Cameron was waddling out onto the field, his face stricken.

A hush fell over the crowd, and people rose to their feet. Derrick wanted to run out, too, but he couldn't. Coaches needed to assess injuries first and then — if the player was down for several minutes — other players might be allowed out to offer encouragement or to pray. Derrick moved along the sideline as far as he could, so he was parallel with his friend. Aaron was motionless, Derrick could see that better now. His legs were sprawled out just the way they'd been when he first collapsed.

"Get up, man ... get up!" he shouted, his voice tight with fear. He'd seen hits like this before, and once in a while a guy never got up again. A shudder ran through him, and he shouted again. "Get up, Hill!"

The linebacker was already up, his hands on his hips, head hung, pacing dizzy circles a few feet from where Aaron lay. One of the New Orleans coaches ran out to meet him, and the two walked off the field to the Saints' sidelines.

On the JumboTron screens, the network was showing the replay in slow motion. Derrick didn't want to look, but he had to, had to see how serious the hit was. At the point of impact, Aaron's head reacted violently, snapping sharply back. As the replay ran, a horrifying gasp came from the crowd. Derrick's eyes darted back to his teammate on the field. "Get up, man!"

But Aaron still hadn't moved. Coach Cameron was surrounded by other coaches and a host of trainers, and now Coach waved frantically at the paramedics on the opposite sideline. His message was unmistakable. Get here. Fast. The paramedics pushed a stretcher between them as they jogged out to the place where Aaron lay. One of them had his arm tucked around a backboard and a brace.

God, please … not Aaron. Wake him up, God … this can't be happening!

Aaron had told him earlier that he'd invited Megan, the woman from the youth center, and Cory, the boy. There was more to the story, Aaron told him. They'd have to talk about it later. Now Derrick looked into the stands, wondering where they were, knowing they were also praying for Aaron.

Finally, after several minutes, the paramedics lifted Aaron and strapped him to a backboard. Carefully, they lifted him onto the stretcher and as they did, Aaron moved his feet. As if he wanted to get the message out to everyone in the stadium, he flexed his toes and then pulled his knees up.

Derrick bent halfway over and exhaled. "Thank you, God." The hit hadn't done permanent damage to his spine, that much was obvious now. Derrick straightened again, just as Aaron raised one thumb into the air. Slowly at first, the shocked fans began to clap and cheer, and over the next few seconds their show of support for Aaron grew into a thunderous roar. Aaron Hill might be down, but he wasn't out.

Only then, as they wheeled Aaron toward the tunnel, did Derrick snap back to reality. They still had a little more than three quarters to play, and Aaron was out! Derrick was so worried about his friend that he hadn't remembered until just now that suddenly he was the quarterback, the one the entire team would be looking to.

Derrick sucked in a quick breath and jogged in place for a few seconds. He was ready. Never mind the pain in his knee, he'd been playing on it all season. And back home in San Francisco, Denae and the kids would be pulling for him, cheering him on, covering him in prayer.

He was stretching his arms again when Coach Cameron yelled for him.

The game was in progress, the Saints offense on the field, but it was stalling fast. The 49ers' defense was fired up, determined to pay back New Orleans for its debilitating blow to their quarterback. Derrick jogged closer. "Coach?" Derrick could see desperation in the man's eyes. Even getting this far, if the 49ers lost today, Coach Cameron's job in San Francisco was likely over.

As they stood facing each other, their eyes locked, Coach Cameron's fear turned to sheer determination. "Warm up, Anderson."

"Yes, Coach."

Derrick grabbed a couple of receivers and a ball and moved to a clearing on the sidelines. On the field, the Saints punted and the network called a TV timeout. Derrick ran his tongue over his lower lip. This was his moment, the one he'd come to San Francisco to play. He had time for just six warm-up throws and a few words with Coach before he ran out onto the field.

He expected to see wide eyes in the huddle, and that's exactly what he found. But it wasn't the big-eyed look of fear and uncertainty. The offensive line, the receivers, the tailbacks … all of them were intent on victory for one reason — they trusted Derrick Anderson. Most of them were young enough that they'd probably grown up watching him play on TV. If Aaron Hill was out, Derrick could lead them. There wasn't a San Francisco player on the field who didn't believe that.

Derrick took the snap and straightened in the pocket. Whatever pain his knee had felt all season, faded in the rush of the moment. He was playing the game, his game! He had a chance to make good on a promise he'd made six years ago, and nothing … nothing was going to stand in his way. He dominated through the second quarter, but three drives fell short of a score. The Saints, having collected themselves, rallied for ten points, giving San Francisco just a four-point lead going into halftime.

Derrick wasn't worried. He'd found his rhythm. After more than a quarter on the field, he could see the weaknesses in the Saints defense. The long ball was open, and after halftime, Derrick planned to connect on a handful of dramatic passes. He jogged toward the tunnel and into the locker room, where the team was given a report on Aaron. He had a concussion, and he'd been taken to the hospital for tests.

A murmur ran through the players huddled around Coach Cameron, and the coach raised his hand. "Listen, he's okay. I talked to him before he left. The tests are only for precaution. I've been contacted by hospital personnel, guys. He may be out for the season, but he'll be back here in the locker room before the game ends."

Relief came over Derrick like a burst of sunshine. *Thank you, God … You're beyond merciful.* Derrick could picture Aaron, hurrying the technicians up, wanting the tests to be finished so he could get back to his team. When he did, Derrick wanted the victory well within hand.

He ran out onto the field for the second half feeling as good as he'd ever felt. God was carrying him, holding his knee together for this, his last season. With that in mind, he tore into the third quarter and had an easy time in the fourth, despite a couple touchdowns by the Saints. As time ran out, Jay Ryder was called onto the field where he booted a forty-eight-yard punt that put the ball on the one-yard line. Half the team embraced him as he ran back to the sidelines, and moments later the 49ers won the game and the NFC championship, 32–25. Derrick looped his arm around Jay's neck, and he raised the ball to the stands with one hand and pointed to God in heaven with the other. All around him, the San Francisco crowd went crazy. Never mind the 9–7 regular season. The 49ers were in the Super Bowl, and the miracle Derrick had believed would happen was on the brink of coming true.

He was almost to the locker when he spotted Megan and Cory pressed against a rope, amidst a mob of fans. The two were probably the only San Francisco fans not celebrating.

"Derrick!" Cory shouted to him. "We need to see Aaron. Please… the security people won't let us in."

Derrick looked from the child to the woman. Aaron would've wanted to see them more than anyone else. He pursed his lips and took the lead. He spoke to the gatekeepers, and Megan and Cory were given temporary passes and allowed to cross the line. Derrick gave Megan a reassuring smile. "Follow me."

When he'd cleared them through another few security points and into a room where they could see Aaron, Derrick saw Coach Cameron signal him. "Be ready, Anderson! A hundred reporters want a piece of you."

Derrick nodded. "How's Hill?"

"Groggy. His head hurts, but he's propped up in the locker room. Doctors say he'll be fine."

Derrick pictured the hit again, the way it rocked Aaron and knocked him unconscious. "Wicked hit, man." He met the coach's eyes. "God was with him."

Coach Cameron smiled. "He was with you too."

A smile started at the corners of Derrick's lips and ran all the way through him. "Tell the press I'll be there in a minute."

He jogged to his locker, acknowledging the congratulations along the way. He didn't need anything, but he wanted a moment alone before the crazy aftermath began, before speculation started and the media began reminding fans every hour that the odds were vastly against San Francisco for the big game in two weeks.

Before any of that, he needed this. He opened his locker, braced himself against it, and hung his head. *God Almighty, today … today was for You. And it was from You.* He wiped the sweat off his forehead and brushed it on his damp jersey. He'd given everything he had out there, and even now the ache in his knee was only a distant throb. He breathed hard, worn out from the exertion. *So, I wondered if You could do me a favor, God?* Tears stung his eyes and mixed with the sweat on his face. *Could You tell my little boy … his daddy's trying to keep his promise? Please, God … and kiss his face, okay? Because if he were here, that's what I would do. And You're a better Dad than I could ever hope to be.*

He sniffed and grabbed a towel from inside his locker. He scrunched it in a ball and pressed it to his face, drying the tears and grime and sweat. *Oh, and also …* He dragged the towel across his cheeks and tossed it back in the locker. *Tell Lee one more game. Just one more game.* As he slammed the locker door shut, he willed himself to find control again. *Thanks, God.*

With that, he walked through the locker room to the waiting press, where for the next half hour he did something that came as natural to him as suiting up for a game. He hung with the reporters, fielding questions and smiling and giving entertaining answers, careful to give all credit for the unlikely win to God alone.

Where it would always belong.

Megan's stomach had been in knots since Aaron took the hit, but even then, she couldn't let her fear show. Not with Cory sitting beside her. The only reason she hadn't tried to come down to the locker room sooner was because the announcer had given occasional updates on Aaron's condition. He had a concussion, he'd been taken to the hospital, his tests were negative, and now he was back at the stadium in the locker room. The last update said he was expected to make a full recovery, but his prognosis for the Super Bowl was uncertain.

With each announcement, Megan felt her fears ease, but still she wanted to see for herself. Even then, without Derrick, they never would've gotten through to see Aaron. Now, though, they waited in a room across the hall from the lockers. Ten minutes passed, and then the door opened and Aaron's agent poked his head through. He stared at Megan and then at Cory and his expression changed from confused to irritated. "What are you doing here?"

Megan steeled herself against the man's disapproval. "Aaron invited us."

Next to her, Cory started to say something, but Megan put her arm around his slim shoulders and gave him a squeeze. Cory took the hint and grew silent.

Bill sneered at her. "Fans aren't allowed behind security lines."

Cory took a step forward, his voice defiant. "Derrick let us through. We want to see Aaron."

The agent steadied his gaze straight at Megan. "Aaron doesn't have time for charity work during the season. I'll speak to him about this disruption." He held her eyes for a moment longer, then he was gone.

Megan realized she'd been holding her breath. She exhaled hard and turned to Cory. "Thank you."

Cory's eyes blazed. "That guy's mean."

"Yes, he is. But no one can know about you and Aaron until it's time, okay?"

"Okay." Cory looked dejected, but not for long.

Before Megan could say anything else, a man with a shirt marked "trainer" wheeled Aaron into the room. The wheelchair must've frightened Cory at first, because he hesitated, staying close to Megan. But his joy at seeing Aaron sitting up, his eyes open, must've won out because Cory ran to Aaron's side and gently touched his arm. "Are you okay?"

"I'm fine." His eyes were only half open, his voice groggy. But he smiled at Cory and then winced as he shifted his attention to Megan. "Do you need a ride home?"

Megan blinked. A ride home? She looked at the trainer, and the guy mouthed the word, "concussion." Megan nodded, but her stomach churned with renewed fear. She pictured him on the field, unmoving, unconscious. At the time, she couldn't draw a breath, couldn't move or speak for all the horrible scenarios playing in her head. He could've been paralyzed, or if his neck had broken in the exact wrong spot, he could've died without ever getting up. By the end of the game, the announcer made it sound like Aaron was doing so well he was probably joking around with the trainers in the locker room.

The truth was far from that. Aaron rested his head in his hand and massaged his temples. Cory stood beside him, rubbing small gentle circles into his back. "I prayed for you."

Aaron's face twisted in pain. "Me too." He tried to focus on Cory. "I prayed on the beach."

Worry filled Cory's eyes, and Megan gave him a calming look. "It's okay. He'll be all right." But at the same time she shot another frantic look at the trainer.

The guy moved around Aaron and came close to Megan, so close Cory couldn't hear what he was saying. "He'll hurt for a while. He's dizzy and he can't see clear. It'll take some time."

"Shouldn't he be in the hospital?" She was shocked that medical professionals had seen Aaron's condition and released him.

"He has no bleeding in the brain; the tests were clear. The emergency room doctor wanted to hold him overnight for observation, but the team doctor promised someone would stay with him for a couple days. Make sure he doesn't develop any new symptoms." The trainer glanced at Aaron, and then back at Megan. "He's on pain meds too. So he's a little loopy."

Megan swallowed hard. "Okay." Her knees trembled, and her hands shook so bad she could barely tuck her hair behind her ears. "I shouldn't worry, then?"

"No." The trainer's tone was reassuring. "This happens in football."

Great, Megan wanted to say. But instead she moved past the trainer to Aaron's other side. She put her hand on his shoulder and stooped down so her face was near his. "We're here, Aaron. You're going to be okay."

He squinted at her, and then he stretched his arm out. "Megan ... take my hand."

A surge of hope welled inside her. He knew who she was! *God, let him be okay. Please ...* She reached out and gently took hold of his fingers. They were much larger than hers, but his touch was as gentle as the breeze off the bay. "You're in the Super Bowl! Can you believe it?"

He looked like a person trapped in a room with too much noise. He made a face and stared at his knees. When the pain or whatever had passed, he bunched up his eyes and stared at her, as if he were trying to see through thick fog. He brought her fingers to his lips and kissed them. The way he'd done at the park that day. "You're so beautiful, Megan."

The trainer nodded at her, and stepped toward the door. "I'll be out here when you need me."

"Thank you." Megan wanted this time alone with Aaron, though she had no idea where it would lead. She didn't belong here, the woman linked with the team's star quarterback. Aaron's agent was right. That role was reserved for the elite and famous, the actresses hinted about in the *Chronicle.* Which was something she wanted to ask him about, whether anything had come from his agent's efforts. But Aaron had only stepped back into their lives a few days ago. And now...

She looked at Cory. He was glued to every word, every move Aaron made. "You'll be fine by tomorrow." The boy looked at her and nodded, probably trying to convince himself. "Right, Megan? He'll be fine tomorrow?"

"He will." She wasn't sure, but it was the only answer for now. They stayed a few minutes longer, and all the while Megan could hardly think, hardly breathe for the feel of his hand against hers. She prided herself on being smart, on knowing when a situation wasn't good for her. But here, when all the signs told her to run, she was stretching out the moment as long as she could.

When she went to leave, she put her arm gingerly around Aaron's shoulders and gave him a side hug. "We'll talk when we're back home, okay?"

For a few seconds he didn't look like he knew what to make of that. Then he dropped his voice to a whisper, his eyes clearer than they'd been since he came into the room. "I love you."

Megan's breath caught in her throat, and she took a step back. "We'll … we'll talk, okay?"

He held her eyes for a second or two, and then he let his head fall into his hand again. Megan shifted her attention to Cory, but he was bent over, tying his shoes. Megan was almost certain he hadn't heard Aaron's statement. If he did, he was bound to have questions.

They were out of the stadium and in the Town Car on the way back to the hotel when Cory grinned at her. "You should marry Aaron."

Megan's heartbeat quickened, but she kept her composure. "I'm not marrying anyone." It was the safest answer she could give. If she wanted to keep what was important to her, if she wanted to protect herself from getting hurt, then she'd stay in her apartment with Cory and their cat, Oreo, and nothing about her life would ever change.

Cory frowned at her. "But you should. Then everything would be perfect." His features relaxed. "You and Aaron could get married, and then I'd have a mom and a dad! And we could eat dinner at Pier 39 every Friday night!" He paused. "Plus he loves you, Megan." His tone took on the familiar sing-song sound. "I heard him tell you."

She brushed off the possibility. "He didn't know what he was saying." Despite her alarm and the flush in her cheeks, Megan felt for the child. In his world, the answers really were that simple. She stared out the window and tried to think of something to add that would put the idea to rest, a sensible response.

But she had none to give, and a knowing came over her. The ride ahead was going to be difficult for her. Difficult and painful. Because Aaron didn't want to marry her, not if he was thinking clearly. But one day soon he would want to bring Cory home. The boy was Aaron's son, Megan had no doubt. The resemblance between them was uncanny now that she knew the truth. Where would that leave her? Especially when all she could hear were his whispered words of love, words that had touched the most private places in her heart.

Whether he knew what he was saying or not.

Twenty-Eight

Aaron sat in the lobby of the clinic a few miles from Cardinals Stadium and closed his eyes. The injury had happened more than a week ago, but his head still hurt and that worried his doctors. Even so, he was getting a little better every day. The double vision was gone, and his short-term memory was almost back to normal. The day before the flight, the doctor had cleared him for certain tasks—driving and light workouts.

He was doubtful for Sunday's game against the Chargers, but Coach wasn't sharing that with the press. Aaron was in his hotel room last night when he heard the coach interviewed on a special edition of Sports Center. "Aaron Hill's making a very fast recovery. The coaching staff expects him to be the starting quarterback this Sunday."

Aaron had stared at the TV screen, confused. Three doctors had weighed in with their opinion earlier that day. Only one of them thought he had even the slightest chance of playing in the big game. But then, Coach was praying for him. Coach and Megan and Cory and everyone in Derrick's family. If he kept improving, anything was possible. For now, though, the game was not the first thing on his mind.

He leaned his forearms on his knees and clasped his hands. There was no reason to be nervous. He'd set up this meeting a week ago, arranged to take the blood test here in Phoenix—so they wouldn't have to wait longer than necessary. Cory was his son, he had no doubt. But in case the issue ever was called into question, Aaron wanted the paperwork. When it was finished, he would frame it and set it where he would never forget, never go a single day without appreciating the gift he'd been given in finding his son.

A nurse stepped into the waiting area and smiled. "Mr. Hill?"

The clinic was known for its high-end clients, and for its ability to be discreet, even keeping the information from his agent if necessary. Bill Bond had no idea his star client was about to take a paternity test. The news would've pushed him over the edge for sure. Bill was in town for the game, but Aaron had kept their time together to a minimum. His agent was upset by the presence of Megan and Cory at the conference championship in New Orleans. Just yesterday, Aaron met Bill in a private meeting room at the hotel to discuss offers for more endorsements. When the short meeting ended, Bill shook his head, clearly disappointed. "You're giving people the wrong impression, bringing that woman and her son to the game." Bill paused. "When the season's over, we need to talk, friend."

"Yeah." Aaron hadn't wanted to get into it, but he could agree on that much. "We definitely need to talk."

Now Aaron followed the nurse into a small room, and with little fanfare, she swabbed his arm and asked him if he was aware that the test was for a DNA paternity match, and he confirmed the fact. If she knew who he was, she didn't say so, and as she drew a vial of his blood, she didn't make small talk. When she was done, she slipped a small bandage across the needle mark and went about her business.

Aaron appreciated her silence. He couldn't risk having news of this visit in the press, not this week or ever. A minute later, when the nurse had labeled the vial and filled out a piece of paperwork, she gave him another polite smile. "That's all, Mr. Hill. The sample will be sent to the lab, and when the other one comes in, a test will be performed to see if there's a match. You'll be notified of the private results by courier." She checked her notes. "If things go the way they're set up, you should have results in a week. Next Wednesday."

Aaron thanked her. As he left he pictured Megan, who was taking Cory into a clinic in San Francisco this same afternoon. He didn't know if the boy was afraid of needles, but for a strong moment he wished he were there beside him. It wasn't Cory's fault Aaron had walked away from the boy's mother. But at least some of the blame belonged to Bill Bond. Bill, who had made Megan feel uncomfortable, and who had threatened Amy, warning her to stay away from Aaron at all costs.

On the drive back to the hotel, his frustration and anger toward his agent grew to a boiling point. For weeks he'd been putting off the talk he wanted to have with Bill, all because he wanted to stay focused on the season. Because he didn't want a news story about him and his agent to take anything away from the team and its run at the title.

What did it matter now? Aaron wasn't likely to see a minute on the field, and the press was in such a frenzy about the pending game, they wouldn't run a story about Aaron's agent until a week after the contest. At the earliest. He waited until he was back in his hotel room before he took a long breath and pulled his cell phone from his pocket. It was time to do what he should've done months ago. Years ago. He opened his phone and uttered a bitter sigh. His agent was one of his top speed dial choices — not a friend or a wife or any family members. The others were all reserved for business contacts. Aaron's heart felt heavy at the realization and what it said about his life until now.

His agent picked up almost immediately. "Hill, my friend." His laugh sounded phony and forced. "It's about time. I was beginning to think you'd forgotten about me. How 'bout dinner tonight down the street?"

Aaron had wasted too much time for small talk. "Where are you?"

"Uh…" Bill hesitated, "all right, we'll forget the niceties." He kept his tone upbeat. Whatever Aaron wanted, Aaron got. "I'm in the lobby with a few financial guys. You can join us, in fact I was hoping you'd — "

"Get up here, Bill. Now." Aaron kept his tone even, otherwise his head would hurt too much. "You know my room number."

Bill dropped his voice a notch. "Everything okay?"

"No." Aaron massaged his temples. "Just get up here."

"Okay." He paused, his voice suddenly nervous. "Give me five."

The call ended and Aaron's head pounded from the pain. In less than five minutes there was a knock at the door. Aaron let his agent in, and he led the way to the living room of his suite. They sat facing each other. Bill sat deep against the corner of one sofa, and Aaron balanced on the edge of the other. He dug his elbows into his knees and fired an intense look straight at his agent.

Before he could talk, Bill started in. "Hey, how's your head, by the way? I meant to ask, but you were, you know" — he tried a short laugh, but it didn't quite work out. He waved his hand around — "distracted by whatever this is." He grabbed a quick gulp of air. "You still in pain or what?"

"I'm fine." Aaron kept the intensity in his stare. "I have a question."

Bill ran his tongue along his lower lip. "Okay." His throat sounded dry. "Shoot."

He didn't hesitate. "How'd you know Amy Briggs was cheating on me?"

Bill blinked and went stone still. His look said he was maybe worried about Aaron's sanity. "Amy Briggs?"

"Yeah, remember her? Girl I was dating back when I was a sophomore in college?"

"Amy … hmmm." Another laugh. "You've dated a lot of girls, Hill. You gotta give me more than that."

"Think hard, Bill." Aaron could see in his agent's eyes the guy was lying. "I knew her from high school. She lived in the Valley." He pictured her, the gentle way she had about herself. Her kind eyes and loyalty. "She was my girl when you and I met. She and I talked on the phone a lot." Sarcasm crept into his tone. "You told me it wasn't good for my image to be so serious about a girl, remember? You wanted me to think about football and my classes. Period. Because image was everything."

"It worked, didn't it?" Bill rarely took a tone with Aaron, but now his voice mixed defensive frustration and arrogance. He straightened and leaned a little closer. "You checked your bank account lately?"

Aaron felt like he'd been punched. Had he really traded whatever he might've had with Amy for a bigger bank account? The comment cut Aaron to the depths of his soul. "That's all you ever cared about, isn't it? The bottom line." His headache pounded, and he willed the pain to ease. "Tell me about Amy, Bill. I want an answer. You told me she was seeing other guys behind my back, and I want to know. What was your proof?"

After a long beat, Bill huffed his indignation. "Come on, Hill. I wasn't exactly a detective. Girls like that, the needy ones. They're with a different guy every weekend. You were too young to see it." He stroked his chin, nervous-like. His chuckle said he could hardly believe he was having this conversation. "What's it matter? You got what you wanted."

Aaron's head spun, and the edges of the picture Bill made began to blur. He closed his eyes and pressed his free hand to his brow. "So you're saying … you had no proof on Amy?"

"Okay, so it was a feeling." For the first time since he'd entered the hotel room, Bill sounded truly nervous. He tried to lighten his tone. "I remember the girl. She was trash next to you, Hill. You couldn't see it, so I had to see it for you."

Aaron wanted to throw up. He'd walked away from Amy because he was young and jealous of other guys. And because Bill knew that, he knew what buttons to push, what to say to make Aaron break up with her. And all of it had been nothing more than a feeling? He wanted to throw the guy out of his room, but he wasn't finished. "Amy wrote me a letter."

Bill looked doubtful, and Aaron had to use every ounce of his restraint not to fly across the coffee table separating them and pummel his agent. Aaron opened his mouth to tell Bill that he didn't have to worry about Amy any longer, because Amy was dead. But he caught himself. He didn't want to give his agent even the slightest chance to feign sorrow. He breathed in through gritted teeth. "She told me you threatened her." His words were slower now, each one fired at their target. "You told her she wasn't to contact me. Sound familiar?"

His agent's face was paler than before. He squirmed and shifted his position. "Of course I told her that. You were about to be famous, Hill. Someone had to protect you."

Aaron had all the information he needed. He stood, his head thudding with every heartbeat, and he stared down at Bill. The man he'd relied on and looked to, the one who had controlled the puppet strings of his life for so many years, looked suddenly small and pitiful. "You can go now, Bill. We're finished."

Bill didn't make a move to leave. His brief laugh made him sound dazed. "What're you saying?"

Aaron thought about Amy again, and he clenched his fists. "You're fired, Bill. We're through."

"Look, we can talk about this." Bill inched to the edge of the sofa. "You're not thinking straight, Hill. It's the concussion."

"You're right." Aaron took a step back and pointed to the door. "If I were thinking straight, I would've done this months ago."

Bill had no choice but to stand. "Hill, look, we can figure all this out when we get home. You and I can sit down and crunch numbers. I can show you the difference I've made being in charge of your endorsements and your image and the media connections and—"

Aaron closed the gap between them and grabbed Bill by the arm. Not hard enough to leave a bruise, but hard enough to get the guy's attention. "You're fired, Bill. End of discussion." He led Bill to the door. "My attorney will have paperwork on your desk tomorrow morning officially severing our ties."

Bill started to speak, as if he might list his accomplishments one more time. But instead he jerked his arm free and moved to the door. "You're sick, Hill. When you come to your senses, call me." He left and slammed the door behind him.

Aaron stared at the door for a few seconds until he was sure Bill was gone. Then slowly he went back to the bed and lay down. After a few minutes, the pain in his head let up. Before he could truly relax, he found Derrick's number in his phone and he hit the Send button. Derrick picked up after several rings.

"Okay, Hill, I'm a busy guy; just give it to me straight." There was a smile in his teammate's voice. "Press says you're the man. You ready to play?"

"Sure." Aaron grinned. "I was gonna ask you the same thing."

He chuckled. "The answer's yes. Now if we can just make it past the media circus."

"Yeah, well, I'm dealing with another kind of circus. Which is why I called." He massaged his eyebrows again. "Can you give me the number of your agent?"

Derrick paused. "Sure." He rattled it off by heart, and the teasing in his tone fell away. "Time for a change?"

"You have no idea. Bill Bond's controlled my life long enough."

"Yeah, well … guy is a genius, but he has the worst reputation in the whole league."

He thought about Amy, and his heart hurt. "I'm always the last to find out." He didn't want to go into details now. He could catch Derrick up later, after the game. They talked about the week's schedule and about Aaron's headaches. After the call, Aaron stared out the window and willed the pain that was returning to his temples to go away. On the list of things he needed to do—now that he was a father—he'd taken care of the first one. Next, more than anything, he wanted to see Megan. The last time they were together, his head was fuzzy and he couldn't think straight, but when they wheeled him into that small room in New Orleans and she and Cory were there, he wanted to take her in his arms and ask her to be his. Forever. The feeling had stayed with him ever since.

His past was an issue, certainly. And there was Bill's publicity stunt about the nonexistent young actress. He rolled onto his side. He couldn't blame her if she didn't think their worlds would mix, if she didn't want to take a chance on him. But whether she did or not, he wanted to be a father to Cory. The fact that Megan wanted to adopt him complicated things. So lately, Aaron had been asking God for another kind of miracle. That someday there might be room in Megan's heart for more than hurting people and foster kids.

But for him too.

TWENTY-NINE

Their light practice was over and Derrick was getting his things from the locker room when he got the word. Coach Cameron wanted to talk to him. He shoved his bag back into his space and returned to the front of the room, where the offices were. Derrick's knee was feeling better, but the official word coming from the 49ers was that Aaron would start on game day. Which was fine with Derrick. He'd done the job when his team needed him, and that's all that mattered.

That and his promise to Lee.

He reached the office door and went inside. "Coach?"

Coach Cameron looked troubled. "One of the doctors treating Hill just gave me his report for tomorrow. He doesn't want him to play."

"I thought ..."

"We were guessing." He sighed. "The reporters were like a pack of wolves this week. And if Aaron wasn't playing, we didn't exactly want San Diego knowing." He picked up a report on his desk. "Jay Ryder's our starting punter at this point." There were bags under his eyes. "Bottom line, Anderson, we need you. More than you know."

A surge of adrenaline hit him. "I'm starting?"

"Starting and finishing." Coach's smile hid the stress he must've been feeling. The front office still wanted all or nothing from the coach, according to the press. "You can do it, Anderson. You can. You've done it before. If you want my thoughts, it's a coin toss on which of you I'd rather have leading the team tomorrow."

Derrick listened, not sure what to say. This was it, his chance to win it all one last time. Not just as a bystander, but as the guy making the plays. Win or lose, the results would rest squarely on his shoulders. He gathered himself and stood a little taller. "I'm ready, Coach."

"The way I figure it, none of us should be here anyway." He stood and slipped his hands into his pockets. "As long as God's smiling down on us, there's no reason for Him to stop tomorrow."

Derrick grinned. "Exactly."

The meeting lasted a few more minutes while Coach went over a few slight changes in the game plan. When Derrick shut the office door behind him, he steeled his mind against any of the hype and hoopla of the past few weeks. All that mattered was tomorrow and the job he had to do.

A job he wanted to do just one more time.

When Derrick woke up Sunday morning, he smiled. God was with him, and He would be with the team that day. Not that God cared about winning, so much. But in getting them here, God had opened doors that should've been bolted shut. Derrick had the feeling He wasn't finished just yet.

The morning routine was familiar, but that didn't ease the nervous energy coursing through him. As he and Aaron suited up, they were quiet, each lost in their thoughts about the game. Before they circled around Coach Cameron, Aaron faced him.

"Waited my whole life to be here, man." His smile didn't hide his disappointment. "Dreamed about it since I was a kid. But right now ... right now I only want you to go out there and win it for your boy." He smacked Derrick's shoulder. "I mean it. Do your magic, Anderson. This is your day."

Derrick stared at the concrete floor and rubbed the back of his neck. When he looked up, his eyes found the photo of his family at the back of his locker door. The one that always stayed with him, the last one ever taken of Lee. Derrick felt his chin quiver, but he steadied himself. His emotions were high, filling his senses, driving him to play at a level he'd never found before. After seventeen years in the league, this was his last game. The very last. He turned his attention to Aaron. "Thanks. I'll remember that."

The pregame talk was what Derrick would've expected. Coach Cameron kept his words brief and full of punch. "I've been asked a hundred times this week what this season has taught me, and every time I say the same thing. It's taught me the importance of faith." He locked eyes with Aaron and then one player after another down the line. "Faith in a Creator with whom all things are possible ... and faith in our ability to come together as a team. Faith that no one ... no one can write our story except us."

In the end, his voice rang with passion. "Believe, men! Believe you can win this game." He raised his fist in the air, his face etched in determination. "Let's go get us a Super Bowl trophy!"

Derrick felt better than he had all season as he jogged down the tunnel and took the field. The new stadium's retractable roof was open and the roar of the crowd echoed in the cooling desert air. Derrick tuned out the sound—all of it. This was his game. When the 49ers won the toss, he took the field, and on the first drive he threw an eighty-two yard touchdown bomb to give San Francisco a 7–0 lead.

The game stayed close into the second quarter, and with fifteen seconds to go in the first half, the 49ers were up by three. Derrick was driving the offense, looking for at least a field goal before time ran out. With the team well into Chargers territory, the play was a fake handoff and a down-and-out pattern to the left side of the field. The ball was hiked and Derrick faked left and then planted his right leg for the pass.

As he did, a sickening snap shot through his knee and he crumpled to the field. The pain was immediate and blinding hot, and for the first few seconds all Derrick could do was try to breathe. *No, God ... not now! Please ...* He didn't need a doctor to tell him what had just happened. The ligament in his knee, the one that had been strained all season, was shot. Ripped apart. He rocked his head one way and then the other, his face twisted up. A scream built inside of him, but he swallowed it, pursing his lips, and forcing himself to exhale. *No! This couldn't be happening.*

Coaches were running out to him now and he had the sudden urge to get up. Never mind what he'd felt in his knee or the pain burning through him. If he could get up, he could play again. He sat and tried to move his right leg, tried to pull it up beneath him. But even the slightest movement tripled his pain and made spots dance in front of his eyes. He couldn't pass out. He had to stay strong, had to figure out a way.

"Anderson, don't move it." The trainer was at his side now, just ahead of the coaches. "I saw it happen. It's not good."

Derrick squeezed his eyes shut, because he didn't want to hear it. This couldn't be all there was. When he pictured himself taking his last snap ever, he saw it as a touchdown pass or a beautiful completion. He hadn't played nearly two decades to have it all end like this. But as the trainer carefully positioned his leg, and as he called for help, Derrick shut those thoughts from his mind. Only one thought mattered.

His little boy.

He couldn't give up, not when the game was half over. Maybe they could give him a brace or a shot of cortisone, anything to numb the pain so he could run again—just for thirty minutes more. But it was too late. He couldn't move his leg, and the pain was turning his insides into knots.

A cart was driven up by someone on the training staff, and a couple of them helped him into the back. As they did, every person in University of Phoenix Stadium rose to their feet. Chargers fans and 49ers Faithful alike sent up a round of applause that filled the air and washed over him. The rumors had come out in the weeks before the Super Bowl. After this game, Derrick Anderson was calling it quits. Here, then, the fans understood what they were watching.

This was their last time to show him how they felt about him. Their chance to tell him goodbye.

Derrick blinked back tears, and as the cart drove off for the tunnel, he raised both hands and waved to them. He had loved every minute playing quarterback in the NFL. He'd heard the cheers so many times, the sound of their applause was like meeting up with an old friend. But this was the last time he would hear it. Suddenly, the pain in his leg was dimmed by an even greater pain. The pain of knowing that the final lines in this chapter of his life had been written. Somewhere in the stands, Denae and the kids had to know too.

It was over.

The cart pulled into the area adjacent to the trainers' station and Derrick started praying. Not for his knee. That could come later. But for whoever was about to take his place.

Because right now, the entire season rested on the shoulders of that one guy.

⟻

Aaron knew the moment Derrick went down. The rest of the game was his. He was standing next to Jay Ryder, the third-string quarterback, and the two exchanged a look. "Coach wants me to punt. But I can do both, Hill. I can do it."

"No." Aaron clenched his jaw and patted Jay on the shoulder. "This one's mine."

Jay was a competitor and he would've done his best. But he hadn't taken a snap in a game all year. Besides, they needed him at punter. Jay grabbed him by the shoulders. "Okay, then. Win it, man. Finish it up."

Aaron nodded. There was no hurry. When Derrick was taken off the field, the 49ers let the clock run out on the next play. On the way into the locker room, Aaron jogged up alongside Coach Cameron. "I'm ready. Put me in."

Coach gave him a wary look. "The doctor ..."

"I know my own body." They reached the tunnel and Aaron stopped and faced his coach. "I'll be careful."

He hesitated. "Let's talk about it with the trainers."

In the end, there wasn't much discussion. Aaron was clear thinking and adamant. He could take the field and he could lead the team. When the decision was made, Aaron hurried from the office and into the training room. Derrick was there, laid out on a table, one arm raised over his head and covering his eyes. Aaron went to his side. "Anderson."

Derrick lowered his arm and their eyes met. Derrick's were red and watery, and his chin quivered. For a few seconds neither of them said anything. "I'm sorry, man. I wanted to finish it." He dug his elbow into the padded table and held up his hand. "You're in, aren't you?"

Aaron reached out and clasped Derrick's hand around his thumb. "Yeah." He swallowed, struggling. "Sorry about your knee." He didn't say that he was sorry about his career ending this way. That much was as evident as the tears brimming in both their eyes.

Derrick set his jaw and gave a sharp shake of his head. "Don't be sorry. Get out there and win it for my boy."

For the first time since Derrick fell to the ground, Aaron smiled. "For yours ... and for mine."

The trainers were out of the room now, and Derrick's brow became a series of deep wrinkles. "Yours?" He managed a nervous laugh. "You're still loopy, Hill." He nodded toward the door. "Go tell Coach to put Jay in."

"I'm serious." Aaron grinned. His mind was incredibly clear, actually. He pictured Cory and Megan, somewhere in the stadium witnessing the drama play out. "I have a son, Anderson." He looked at the clock. The team needed him on the field. "I'll tell you about it later. Just trust me. I've got more reason to win this thing than you know."

With that he gave Derrick's hand one more squeeze. "Talk to God for me, man."

"The whole time."

When Aaron took the field, the Chargers had scored and were up by four. On the first snap, Aaron got the ball, took three backward running steps deep into the pocket, and looked at his options. But as his eyes darted from one receiver to another, the ground seemed to tilt and his vision blurred. The rush of dizziness made him feel sick to his stomach, and he could see the linebacker barreling down on him. He released the pass just before the sack, but before he hit the ground he saw the ball fall far short of his man.

He shook off the hit, but he was slow getting to his feet. His teammates were coming together in the next huddle when San Francisco called a time-out. Coach was pacing the sidelines as Aaron reached him.

"No more passing. You're not ready." His voice was gruff, but his eyes were marked with fear. Another concussion at this point could leave permanent damage. Everyone knew that. "We're going to a running game." He barked a few orders at one of the halfbacks and two of the running backs.

Aaron couldn't argue. If that last pass was the best he could do, they had no choice but to switch up their game. But as the third quarter wore down, San Diego scored again, and at the start of the fourth, the 49ers trailed by eleven. During the TV timeout between quarters, Aaron pulled off by himself. It wasn't working, the revised strategy. He needed help and he needed it fast.

Then suddenly it hit him. The idea of praying was still so new to him, he hadn't realized something. Derrick was praying for him, but Aaron hadn't prayed for himself. So he sat on the edge of the bench, dropped his head into his hands, and cried out to God the same way he had at Baker's Beach.

I don't deserve this, God. I don't deserve anything from You. Aaron concentrated on finishing the prayer. *I can't play the rest of this game without You, God. I'm not asking for a win, just that You'd clear my head. Take away the dizziness. Let me see the field like never before.* The words settled deep into Aaron's soul. A strange peace and a knowing came over him. He'd done what he could do. Now he needed to play his game.

It didn't happen all at once, but with third and eight on their own forty-yard line, Aaron called an audible. Long pass to the end zone. A few of the players raised an eyebrow, but they didn't argue. Based on the third quarter, San Diego was probably lulled into thinking Aaron wasn't going to do anything more tricky than a quick dump pass. But this time when he stepped back in the pocket, he saw with a clarity that could've only come from God. His receiver was all alone, streaking down the field, and Aaron hit him with a pass that rivaled any he'd ever thrown. The touchdown closed the gap to four, and the networks called another timeout.

"Hill!" Coach Cameron's face was beet red. He stormed over to meet Aaron as he jogged off the field. "What're you doing? I told you no passes."

"Something happened." Aaron put his hands on his hips and tried to catch his breath. "I can see clear now. I promise, Coach."

"I don't want you sacked, you understand? No blows to your head."

"My line's holding. It was my fault before." Aaron gripped his coach's shoulder. "I asked God for vision, and He gave it to me. We have to play our game."

Coach looked like he was about to pass out from the stress, but he nodded. "Okay. Go with your gut. If it's there, if you feel it — call it."

The Chargers opened the fourth quarter with a touchdown, giving San Diego an eleven-point edge. Aaron felt himself narrowing in on what was needed, on the job ahead. With six minutes left, he used a couple audible passes to take San Francisco quickly into Charger territory. A running play for a touchdown meant the 49ers still had a chance.

San Diego wasted three minutes on short runs for little yardage. Their punt put San Francisco on the four-yard line. One more chance … they had one more chance. Aaron's head throbbed from the intensity and exertion of the game. He had to hold on, had to find a way to dig deep for one more drive.

"Okay, Hill." Coach shouted at him above the roar from the crowd. "Less than two minutes and ninety-six yards to go. If anyone can do it, you can!"

Before he took the field, Aaron imagined Megan sitting in the stands. Megan who got up every morning before dawn to deliver papers on foot through the streets of San Francisco, and who walked miles each day to her job waiting tables.

God, if You would give me half the determination of that woman, I know I can do this. Help me find it … please, God.

A verse came to mind, something Megan had told him about during a phone call a few days ago. It was from the book of Isaiah. *Those who hope in the LORD will renew their strength. They will run and not grow weary, they will walk and not be faint.*

That was it! He would take the field with all the determination Megan had shown him, with the experience of mastering the two-minute drill season after season. But he would do it by waiting on the Lord. He sucked in a full breath as he ran out to the huddle. He still felt weary and faint, but God would have the final say over whatever happened in the next few minutes.

A field goal wouldn't be enough, so everyone in the stadium knew Aaron was looking toward the end zone, and only the end zone. From the first snap, he followed Coach Cameron's game plan. A short run, a breakaway for seven yards, another short pattern. Gradually, in what felt like painful slow motion, the team trudged up the field while the seconds fell away. Aaron could feel himself running on some power other than his own. Even still he wasn't sure if he could pass. The dizziness was back, and he couldn't hurt the team. The risk was too great.

Finally, they inched into the red zone, the last twenty yards leading up to the goal line. Another few runs, a short pitch pass, and they were first and ten at the twelve with forty-six seconds to go. The next three running plays fell short, netting only a yard or two each.

Aaron huddled the team and glanced at the clock. Five seconds to go, fourth-and-two. There was no point going for the first down — time would run out in the process and the game would be over. It was a touchdown or nothing. A TV timeout bought them a breather. Aaron looked at his team, and he knew what he had to do. San Diego had to be expecting a pass, no matter how exhausted Aaron looked or seemed. With the eyes of his teammates locked on him, Aaron took the risk of his career. "Quarterback keeper." He felt the intensity in his stare. An intensity borne from the determination he'd witnessed in a woman he would long for all the days of his life.

Again, the guys didn't react. Never mind that this was how Aaron had been hurt in New Orleans. It was the last play the Chargers would be expecting, and for that reason, it had a chance. "We need just four yards." He shouted his encouragement. "We can do this! Come on guys, hold the line."

His teammates nodded, gave a single clap, and lined up for the play. Aaron felt his knees shake as he dropped back with the ball and faked like he was going to pass left, and then right. Then as the slimmest window opened in front of him, he took off. One yard, and then two … and Aaron could see what was happening. His line was rising to the challenge, covering him, holding off the swarming defense like never before.

Aaron kept pumping his feet, running, pushing for the end zone. Three yards … and then suddenly, he was across the goal line without being touched by a single Charger. The officials raised their hands and seventy-three thousand people were on their feet, screaming and cheering and hugging each other, crazed by what they had just witnessed. Aaron still had the ball tucked beneath his arm. They'd done it; they'd won the Super Bowl. As his teammates circled him, hitting him on the back and shoulders and lifting him in their arms, he pressed his hand to his helmet and let the tears come.

Because somewhere in heaven, a little boy named Lee was dancing with the angels and grinning down at his daddy. And in the trainer's room in the depths of the stadium, Derrick Anderson was grinning too. Because no matter who made the winning score, Derrick had done something a father was supposed to do.

He'd kept his promise.

—

Megan and Cory were exhausted and thrilled. They'd laughed and cried and hugged each other and everyone in Derrick's family during those first wild moments as the 49ers won the Super Bowl. Cory had been beside himself. "He did it, Megan!" he shouted over the chaos around them. "They won it all!"

The celebration had lasted long after the score and after the final seconds ticked off the clock. First, they'd waited as Coach Cameron accepted the Vince Lombardi Trophy, the one handed out each year to the winner of the Super Bowl, and now they watched while Aaron was awarded Most Valuable Player.

Someone handed him the microphone, and a teammate slapped a Super Bowl Champions baseball cap on his head. Aaron grinned, his face ten stories high on the JumboTron screen. "First I wanna thank God Almighty … not so much for the win"—he looked at the trophy and chuckled—"though the win's pretty great. But I wanna thank Him for opening my eyes." He spoke another minute, thanking the fans and his teammates and the coaches. Then he put his hand on the smaller MVP award and raised the Super Bowl Trophy high in the air. "This one's for Lee."

Megan felt the slightest confusion. Then she remembered the conversation she'd had with Aaron early in the season, before their falling out. Lee was Derrick Anderson's son who had been killed in a car accident. Her eyes welled with tears again and her heart swelled with compassion for the man on the podium. A man who seemed at times like two different people — the one the world knew, and the one she alone had connected with.

Aaron was about to step down from the platform when it happened. He faced the crowd and looked in their general direction, then with his first two fingers, he waved. Megan brought her fingers to her lips.

"There it is!" Cory jumped as high as he could, pumping his fist in the air. He tapped the man next to him, shouting to be heard. "That was for us, did you see that? Aaron Hill waved like that just for us."

The man — decked in red and gold — gave him a mildly disapproving look and then returned to cheering for the 49ers. Cory didn't care. He turned to Megan and hugged her, and then he waved at the screen — as if Aaron could see them. The sounds around her — still loud and full — faded as Megan, too, set her attention on the big screen. As he waved once more with their secret signal, two things hit her. First, he was Cory's father and that wasn't going to change. It wouldn't happen overnight, but he would want Cory to live with him.

And second, maybe he really was in love with her.

As the celebration wound down and she and Cory finally arrived back at the hotel, Megan called the airlines and switched their flight to one leaving in a few hours. Though Aaron had hoped to meet up with them, she knew that would be impossible. He would be bombarded with TV and print interviews, and after all that, he would want to be with the team.

Aaron needed his space. Besides, she didn't want Cory around a horde of media, not with the DNA test results pending. Cory didn't really understand the reason for the blood test. She'd told him it was necessary and that it had to do with matching his blood with Aaron's.

"We don't need a test." Cory had been upset in the waiting room of the clinic, thinking he was being doubted again.

"I know, buddy. You look just like him." She patted his knee. "But the test might help other people believe."

But now, if it became public knowledge somehow, the scrutiny would be unbearable.

Megan waited until they were about to board their late-night flight before she texted Aaron. *Congratulations! We went home early, but we'll talk to you when you get home. Thanks for everything…*

Once she sent the message, she turned off her phone and rested her head against the window of the plane. Cory was tired, and he closed his eyes as soon as he was belted in beside her. The flight was full of fans headed home, most of them deliriously happy with the team's fifth championship. Megan watched them, and then turned her attention to the slight boy in blue jeans beside her. The DNA results would come this week. And so, while for every other 49ers fan the adventure had come to a wonderful, miraculous ending, the same couldn't be said for Cory. Whatever the test results, his adventure was hardly over. It had just begun.

She smiled to herself and once more she could feel Aaron's arms around her, his eyes melting into her own. She stared at the seat in front of her and allowed herself to imagine. Because if she could learn to trust Aaron Hill, maybe the adventure ahead wouldn't just be true for Cory.

But for both of them.

THIRTY

Aaron paced from the kitchen to the front door of his house and back again. It was Wednesday and the results would arrive any time, that's what he'd been told. A courier service was supposed to bring by the sealed envelope just after three o'clock. He stared at the clock on the microwave: 3:10.

He took a glass from the cupboard and filled it with cool water. His headache was fading, but it wasn't entirely gone. He downed the glass and gazed out the window at his backyard. He wasn't worried about the results, but they mattered. Because once they were in hand, he knew what he wanted to do. What he had to do.

Even with the tension of waiting, he felt fantastic. He'd had time to think things through. During the media circus and yesterday's parade down the fan-lined streets of downtown San Francisco, he couldn't have been clearer about what he wanted next in his life.

Very simply, he was in love with Megan Gunn. Once he had the results, he had the rest of the afternoon and evening all planned out. Not just what he wanted to tell her, but where he wanted to take her. After all, he'd kept his part of the deal by winning the Super Bowl.

There was the rumble of an engine from the front of the house, and Aaron caught his breath. He spun around and darted to the front door. A yellow delivery truck was pulling into his driveway, heading up to the front door. Aaron watched it park, his heart pounding, every breath just the slightest drink of air. This was it ... In a minute he'd know for sure that Cory was his son and then he could get on with the rest of his life.

He opened the door, signed for the package, thanked the driver, and shut the door behind him. His palms were sweaty as he clutched the cardboard mailer. He swallowed hard against his dry throat, and a lightheaded feeling came over him. Dazed and dizzy, he wandered into the kitchen and dropped onto the first barstool. He pulled the tab at the top of the envelope and then he stopped.

The blood rushed from his face and his stomach dropped. He set the cardboard container down and stared at it. Cory was his son; he could see it the moment he looked at the prom picture. Amy hadn't loved anyone but him all her life. That's what she'd told him in her letters, and Megan had verified the fact. Amy hadn't been with anyone but him…

But then, slowly, like an unavoidable car wreck happening right before his eyes, a possibility hit him. Amy had been raped. A week after she'd given in and slept with Aaron, she'd been attacked on the Pierce College campus. It was a detail he hadn't acknowledged over the past couple weeks, because it was too hard to accept. Somehow, it seemed his fault that she'd been alone that night, walking to her car. That if he'd been more supportive, more available, maybe she would've already been home, talking with him on the phone rather than working late at the library.

The idea was crazy, of course, and Aaron knew that in reality he couldn't have helped her that night. Either way, there was no point holding onto the truth that his special girl had been viciously attacked. Until now. He grabbed the slightest breath and considered the possible results that lay in the envelope. What if the precious boy who looked like him and longed for him had been fathered by a cowardly rapist? His heart pounded and his stomach twisted in knots. If that were the case, how could he ever tell the child the truth without destroying him? The boy would go from being the son of an NFL quarterback, to being the son of a twisted and depraved criminal. Aaron shuddered. He pictured Cory, the way the news would feel like a lie at first, impossible. If the results went that way, no matter how involved Aaron stayed in his life, eventually Cory would understand the reality of his situation. He would be the son of a rapist.

Anger choked Aaron, and his breathing came uneven and fast. He should've been there all along. If he wouldn't have turned her away, he would've been by her side when Cory was born and there never would've been a question, never a paternity test. He would've married Amy. He looked around at the luxury surrounding him, the granite counters and travertine tile floors. They would've lived here in this house, raising their son, and Amy would still be alive.

He picked up the cardboard mailer one more time. Slowly, like the first light at the crack of daybreak, an understanding dawned in his heart. The results were confidential, and he alone had received a copy. Weeks ago, he ordered the test and paid for it, and at the time, he figured Megan didn't need a copy. He would tell her the results as soon as he could see for himself, because of course Cory was his son.

Only what if that wasn't how it played out?

He stood and gripped the package, and he headed down the hall and into his office. With each step, he felt his fear lifting, dissipating, because he knew what he was going to do. He walked through the double doors of his office and toward the corner. There on the counter was a machine he used only once a month—when he had statements he didn't need, statements he didn't want anyone finding, to protect himself from identity theft, credit card theft.

Now, with a sense of right that consumed him and breathed new life into him, he took the contents from the mailer, and without looking at them, he stacked the two pages back-side up, neatly one on top of the other. Then he lifted them to the top of the machine and watched them dissolve through the mechanical teeth of the shredder.

And like that, it was over. He was Cory Briggs's father.

No matter what the test results said.

⟨⟩

He found them at the youth center, where he'd known he would find them. He parked his truck, and already he heard the sound of a basketball pounding the old parquet floor. He strode through the entryway, on a mission like none other in his life. When he reached the gym, he leaned on the doorframe and watched them for a minute. Megan wore a sweatshirt and jeans and she had a whistle around her neck. She was officiating a pickup game that seemed to have no rules, and few boundaries.

After a minute or so, she spotted him. She'd been about to blow the whistle, but now she let it drop back into place. "Timeout," she shouted. Her voice echoed in the big old building. "Everyone, take five."

Cory noticed him then, but Megan stopped him from running over. She said something to him, and he nodded. But as he headed for the drinking fountain he grinned and waved at Aaron.

A lump formed in his throat as he waved back. Cory hadn't wanted the test in the first place. Aaron never should've pushed the point, but none of that mattered now.

Megan's eyes looked worried, and Aaron understood. She must've been more concerned about the results than she let on. She could vouch for Amy's lonely single life in the years she lived in San Francisco. But she hadn't known Amy back when Cory was conceived. A week ago, over a phone call, Megan had admitted that she was afraid for Cory. Afraid that he'd never recover if the results showed Aaron wasn't his dad.

Aaron stood straight and grinned. No worries now.

Megan reached him, her face slightly pale, lips parted. She searched his eyes. "You … you got the results?"

"I didn't need them." He wrapped his arms around Megan and held her, loving her. "He's my son, Megan. He's my boy."

"So … so the results didn't come?"

He wanted to lie to her, tell her that he'd read them and everything was just as he'd suspected. That Cory was his son, no question. But he was through lying. He put his hands gently on her shoulders and searched her heart, willing her to understand. "I didn't open them. I shredded them."

"But—"

He held a finger to her lips and dropped his voice to a tender whisper. "I don't need test results, Megan. Cory's my son." He turned his gaze to the boy. "He looks just like me."

She started to cry and she pressed her face against his shoulder. "Thank you … for not looking." Relief mixed with the emotion in her voice. "I wanted … I wanted him to be your son … so badly, Aaron. So badly."

"He is … it's okay." He stroked her back, and he had the sense something else was on her heart. That she wasn't entirely happy about the news. He eased away enough to see her eyes. "What else, Megan? What're you thinking?"

"I don't know." She looked down, and the color came back in her cheeks. "I love him too."

He wanted to tell her not to worry, that between the three of them, there was enough love to go around. But Cory was racing up to them. Aaron released Megan and turned to the boy. His boy. He held out his hands and swept him up in a hug that lasted a long time. When Cory was back on his feet, Aaron stooped down so they were eye level. "Remember the blood test?"

Cory looked confused for half a second. Aaron and Megan hadn't told him that the results were coming in today. He still didn't understand the significance of the test, other than its ability to match the two of them, once and for all. A worried look flashed in Cory's eyes. "I remember."

"We didn't need it after all." Aaron grinned. He kept his voice low, because the other kids weren't too far away. "You're my son, Cory ... just like you always thought."

Cory hesitated, and then he pumped his fists low at his waist. "Yes! I knew it! This is the best news in the whole world!"

For the slightest instant, Aaron imagined how differently this scene might've played out. He swallowed the possibility, stood, and exchanged a high-five with Cory. The boy peered over his shoulder and grinned at Megan, as if to say — in the most polite way — that he had certainly told her so. He'd told both of them. Then he flung his arms around Aaron's neck. "So what're we gonna do now?"

"That's why I'm here." He smiled at Megan. "I was thinking dinner at Pier 39."

"The Sea Lion Café?" Cory's eyes lit up. "That's a great idea!"

"Well," Aaron chuckled. "Not the café." He kicked the toe of his shoe lightly against hers. "Forbes Island. Because one of us made good on our deal. And now it's time for the other one to step up to the plate."

Megan raised her hands in mock surrender. "You're right."

"Cool!" Cory held up his pointer finger. "One sec ... I have to get my things."

When they were alone again, Megan's expression turned shy. "It's going to be a wild ride, isn't it?"

"It could be." He took hold of her hands and the feel of her fingers against his own melted his heart. "But ... we'd be crazy to miss it."

Megan smiled and her eyes danced. Because she clearly knew they weren't talking about the ferry ride over to Forbes Island, a trip that would last only a few minutes.

But about a ride that from tonight just might last forever.

THIRTY-ONE

Megan's heartbeat was anything but normal as Aaron helped her into the small cruise ship. Cory helped them decide that it would be better to eat at the Sea Lion Café where they had the best fish and chips in the world, and then take a boat ride around the bay. One that lasted an hour long.

As it turned out, most of the bay cruise lines were closed until April. The one that was open had a sunset cruise at five o'clock, so they saved dinner for afterward. The sun was splashing a waterfall of diamonds across the water as they boarded the three-story ship, and Megan fought hard against her fears. She wanted to conquer them, and that helped. They moved inside on the main deck and sat at a booth near the back along a row of windows. Megan gripped the tabletop and Cory giggled at her.

"We won't sink, Megan. Really." He kneeled on the seat so he could see out the window. "I always wanted to sail on the ocean at night."

"Oh yeah." She blew at a wisp of her hair and slumped against the back of her seat. "Me too. Always."

"Plus, if you think about it, you're not really afraid of the boat, right?"

"I always thought I was."

"Yeah, but without the boat you'd have to swim back."

"He has a point." Aaron took the spot on the bench beside her.

"Right." Cory giggled again. "So that means you're afraid of water. Only you drink water all the time, Megan. So you're not even afraid of that." He held up his hands as if he'd solved her problem.

Aaron hung his head and tried to hide his quiet laughter. He wore a UCLA baseball cap pulled low over his brow, because he'd told her he didn't want to be recognized. Not tonight. Not that there was much of a chance that would happen. The cruise was nearly empty, and most of the passengers appeared to be from a group of Russian-speaking foreigners.

Aaron picked up a brochure on the table and studied it. "Hmmm." His eyes shone as he looked at her. "Sunset's at 5:43."

"Great. So seventeen minutes of sailing under dark skies." Megan leaned her head back against the cool glass. "I might need help."

Under the table, Aaron reached for her hand. Always, he'd held her hand like a friend might, the way a father held the hand of his child. But this time, he worked his fingers slowly between hers and his eyes found the most anxious places in her heart. "I'll stay beside you the whole way."

"I won't." Cory grinned. He bounced a few times and pointed to the front of the deck. Where the bow of the boat came to a point, the ship was solid glass. Pillows had been placed on a carpeted area there, inviting guests to enjoy the cruise from a comfortable, secluded spot.

"Can I sit up there once we get moving?"

"Sure. You can go up there now if you want." Aaron settled against the back of the seat so that his shoulders were touching Megan's. "As long as we can see you, it's fine."

"Really?" Cory's eyes lit up. He was so full of life, so appreciative of the things he'd never had a chance to do before. "Okay"—he pointed again—"I'll be right there. You can watch me."

Megan tried to think of something to say, but she was completely consumed with the look in Aaron's eyes, the sensation of his fingers between hers. She forced herself to breathe out. "He's right, don't you think?"

Aaron hesitated. "About sitting at the bow?"

"About not sinking." She gave him a weak smile. "I can't believe I'm doing this."

For a moment, he looked concerned for her. "You don't have to." He glanced at the loading area. The doors were still open. "We can get off."

"No." Her answer was quick. Classical music clicked on just then and filled the boat with soothing sounds. With Aaron strong beside her, his fingers between hers, her fears were already easing. "I want to do this. You're with me, that makes me feel better."

"Right." He grinned. "That way, I can help you if we sink."

"Thanks." She allowed herself to melt into his arm a little more. "I might have to close my eyes."

"You better not." He ran his thumb along her hand. "You'll miss the sunset." Something in his eyes told her he wanted to say more, but he seemed to be holding back.

The engines moved into high gear, and one of the crew shut and locked the door. Whether she wanted to or not, there was no turning back now. As the thought crossed her mind, she wondered if that was true not only for the hour cruise, but for her and Aaron as well. There was no mistaking the look in his eyes, the gentle way he spoke to her, or the way he held her hand. He had feelings for her, and now that he was convinced he was Cory's father, a casual dating relationship would never work.

Because Cory belonged to both of them.

They would either need to move ahead as friends and nothing more, or they needed to consider jumping in. Otherwise, Cory would be confused, and that wasn't fair. He'd had enough confusion in his life already. She rested her head on his shoulder and stared out the window. She pictured the scene from earlier: Super Bowl MVP Aaron Hill walking into the Mission Youth Center and whisking them off for a cruise?

A part of her kept wondering when the director was going to yell cut.

"I never get tired of looking at the bay." His voice held a quiet joy. "Especially this time of night."

"It's beautiful." Megan sat up straighter and realized they were near a mostly glass door, one which led to a small deck that apparently wrapped around the main cabin. With so many windows, they could go outside and still have a clear view of Cory. Also, it was the only door that led out to the deck. So if Cory went outside, he'd have to come this way.

Aaron must've noticed at the same time, because he nodded toward the door. "Let's stand out there. Until we get too cold."

A shiver ran down her arms, but it had nothing to do with a chill in the air. The inside was plenty warm. No matter how tempting the idea, standing on the deck with Aaron seemed dangerous in a host of ways. Still, when he stood, she stood with him. Two other kids—a boy and a girl—were sitting by Cory now. They were dark skinned, from India maybe, and probably on vacation. Most locals would be home getting ready for school in the morning.

They slipped outside and Aaron paused. "Are you okay?"

She breathed in sharply through her nose and studied the water—so close she could feel the spray from the wake. In her imagination, this would be the most terrifying moment of all, standing outside on the deck of a boat, feeling the sway of the waves beneath her feet, knowing the water was only a few feet away. But something about the moment felt fresh and invigorating in a way she hadn't expected. "I am." She sounded as surprised as she felt.

There was a wooden bench down a little ways, and near it two heaters, warming the area for nights like this. Aaron led her to it. They sat and he slipped his arm around her. For a long time he said nothing. They were facing west off the rear of the boat, and the feel of the sun on their faces and the rhythm of the ocean was enough. But after a while he whispered near her ear. "Do you trust me, Megan?"

Her heart skipped a beat. She didn't want to seem nervous or startled, but she had to wonder. She turned slightly so she could see his eyes, and there, without a doubt, lay the answer. "You're not talking about the boat."

"No." He moved his hand off her shoulder and brought it to the side of her face. "I missed you ... not seeing you."

She wanted to talk, but she couldn't catch her breath. If he was going to kiss her, she wouldn't stop him. Whatever that said about her. "Aaron ..."

With his hand still sheltering her face, guarding against even Cory seeing what he was about to do, he leaned in closer and lightly touched his lips to hers. The kiss started slowly, marked by innocence and uncertainty. But it ignited a smoldering fire for both of them, because instead of coming up for air, the kiss grew deeper, slow and passionate.

When they drew away, there was breathless desire in both their expressions. Megan allowed herself to get lost in his eyes, swept away by the moment. "I can say one thing." She brushed her nose against his and he pulled her into his embrace. She kept her voice low and near his ear. "You made me forget the boat."

He nuzzled his face against hers. "You need the boat, remember?" He kissed her again, smoother, slower still. "I made you forget the water."

"Mmmm." She kissed him this time. "Whatever." She felt herself falling, getting lost in his embrace and his touch. And suddenly she wanted to know why ... why they were doing this and what it meant and what about the actresses that waited in the wings. She slid a few inches from him and searched his face. Her cheeks were hot, and suddenly the heaters were overkill. The occasional cold breeze from the ocean felt good. "What ... " She held her hair to keep it from blocking her view of him. "What're we doing, Aaron?" She looked over her shoulder at Cory, still sitting facing the windows at the other end of the boat. Then her eyes found his again. "What's happening?"

She hadn't wanted to be catty or jealous. It had never been any of her business until now. She gripped the bench seat. *God, give me the words ...* "What about the actress?"

At first he looked baffled by her question, but then his expression changed and sorrow darkened his eyes. "That was my agent. I told you." He ran his thumb along her cheekbone. "I fired him last week."

Megan's heartbeat jumped around again, and this time it had nothing to do with the boat or the water. With Bill Bond out of Aaron's life, the future was that much more possible. "Really?"

"I don't want an actress, Megan." He worked his fingertips up into her hair, and the sadness in his eyes grew stronger. "That's why you stopped seeing me ... right?"

"It is. I didn't want to keep you from someone ... someone more your type." She should feel guilty for dismissing him so quickly that day at the park. She'd missed him every day since. But she couldn't, not when she was consumed with joy here beside him. Those days were gone. She brought her hand to his face, his rugged jawline. "I'm glad you don't want an actress."

The sun was setting, sinking into the water, and the reflection on the bay was stunning. Together they went in and checked on Cory, chatting with him and his new friends for a few minutes. When they went back outside, the sun had dropped below the horizon, and the sky was washed in pink. They found their places and kissed again, and then Aaron stood and looked down at her, smiling. She watched him, wondering. Maybe he was too cold and he wanted to go in where it was—

Slowly, Aaron dropped to one knee and held his hands out to her.

She started to shiver, but she took his fingers. What was he doing, and why did it feel like it was all happening in slow motion? "Aaron ..."

"I love you, Megan Gunn." His words mixed with the sound of the wind and water, but they were clear and thought out. "I love the way you know who you are and how you don't need material wealth to be happy, and I love your dedication." He wasn't in a hurry. "I love your passion for foster kids, for changing the system." His eyes shone a little brighter. "I even talked to Derrick and Jay Ryder about putting something together to present to the governor ... or to Congress. You could help us."

She held his hands a little tighter. His words spoke deeply to her because they proved that ages ago she had become more than a conquest. He didn't love her for her looks or because she was needy. She realized even now with Aaron declaring his love to her, she looked more like a college co-ed than the sort of woman the public would expect to see with a celebrity quarterback.

He wasn't finished. "I love everything about you, and maybe most of all, I love that you're my son's mother."

She felt her eyes begin to dance. She wanted to hug him, to let him know that she believed him and trusted him and that she didn't ever want him to leave. But she needed to hear him out. So she only gave him a slight grin. "*Foster* mother."

A dampness filled his eyes, but he never broke contact with hers. He reached into his pocket and pulled out a small velvet box. "Not if you marry me."

She brought her fingers to her lips and her soft gasp died on the wind. The air was getting colder, but she wasn't shivering like before. She was too shocked.

He opened the box, and a stunning solitaire diamond ring lay neatly inside. It wasn't overly large, but simple and understated. Like her. "Marry me ... be a family with Cory and me. Please, Megan."

She looked from the ring back to him, and there were tears in both their eyes. *God, is this really happening?*

My daughter, I know the plans I have for you ... to give you hope and a future ...

The verse spoke tenderly to her soul. It was one that hung on the wall in the youth center. Megan believed the promise with all her heart, but a long time ago she'd come to believe that God might not mean good plans here, on earth. Maybe the good plans were more like heaven, and that was great too. A hope and a future didn't have to mean the same exact plans a person might dream for themselves.

Aaron was watching her, waiting. He laughed, his eyes wide with a nervousness that was uncommon for him. "If ... if you need more time you can get back to me."

She stood and he did the same, facing her. Through her tears, she felt herself surrounded by a feeling she'd never known before, a feeling she'd run from whenever she thought it might be catching her. Especially where Aaron was concerned. But now, in the waning light, with the cruise ship making its way back to the dock, she framed his face with her hands and looked deep into his eyes, to the places of his heart and soul that she understood now belonged only to her. "Yes, Aaron Hill. I'll marry you and be a family with you." She tilted her head back and her laughter rang out in the air. She was crying as hard as she was laughing.

He caught her hand and he shook as he slid the ring onto her finger. It fit perfectly. "It's gorgeous."

"It reminded me of you that way." He eased his arms around her waist. "You're beautiful, Megan." He brushed his cheek against hers. "I about died when you stopped seeing me. I couldn't quit thinking about you."

"Me too." She leaned up and kissed him the way she'd wanted to earlier. Not sitting side by side, but like this, wrapped in his embrace. When they drew back, she smiled and it became a full-hearted laugh. "I can't believe this."

He caught the back of her head and brought her close to him again. His lips touched hers once more and he breathed against her. "Believe it. I'm never letting you go. Not again."

Just then Cory came running out. "I made a new friend from India and his name's —" He came to a sudden stop and seemed to notice the way Megan and Aaron were standing, face-to-face, their arms around each other. He giggled. "What's going on out here?"

"Well..." Megan turned so they were both facing Cory. She kept her arm around Aaron's waist, and he kept his around her. They exchanged a quick look, and then Megan showed her ring to the boy. "Aaron asked me to marry him."

"What!" Cory hadn't ever looked so surprised. "Really?" He turned to Aaron. "You did that?"

"I did." Aaron put his hand on Cory's shoulder. "I figured since I'm already your dad, and since she's your mom, it seemed only right that we should get married." He winked at her. "Because she's pretty terrific and because that way you can be with both of us at the same time."

Cory sucked in a fast breath, his eyes wide with excitement and thrill and shock. "Like a family!"

"Yes, son." Aaron looked like he savored the chance to say the word. "Like a family."

That's when so much about the day and the night came together for Megan. *I'm not afraid anymore, God. I'm here on a boat and I'm not afraid.*

Ah, my daughter, there is no fear in love. But perfect love drives out fear…

This time she almost had to sit down, so she clung more tightly to Aaron. Because God had rarely spoken so clearly to her. His quiet whispers reminded her of a verse she'd read after telling Aaron goodbye back in September. Perfect love drives out fear. She pressed in close to Aaron, and when the boat docked, the three of them walked off holding hands.

Megan wasn't afraid of boats anymore, at least not if she was with Aaron. And she wasn't afraid about how she would share Cory. She wasn't afraid to love, and she wasn't afraid to trust. As they headed for the Sea Lion Café, the reason was as clear as the night sky above them. She wasn't afraid anymore because the unfamiliar feeling that had come over her when she was with Aaron on the back deck of the boat wasn't passion or nervousness or uncertainty.

It was love, a love strong enough to drive away any sort of fear. A love only God could've given her.

Deep, profound … and perfect.

⟼

Derrick was watching a Bill Cosby rerun in the TV room, with Denae and the kids gathered around him. They'd spent more time together than usual this week, catching up on the stories Derrick had from the Super Bowl.

Already he and Denae had planned a trip to Chicago, to the cemetery where Lee was buried. Derrick was on crutches, but he wanted to make the trip anyway. He and Denae would bring a photograph and tape it to the edge of the boy's tombstone.

The photo wouldn't be of the ring he'd just won, because that ring would take months to come in, so he'd take a photo of one of his other Super Bowl rings. That way he didn't have to wait.

Lee wasn't really in the ground at that faraway Chicago cemetery. But the baby he'd cradled and held, the one he'd swung up onto his shoulders—that body was in the grave. And so if he had to go to a place to make good on his promise, he would go to the cemetery.

On the television, Cosby said something funny about chocolate cake, and the rest of the family burst out laughing.

"Daddy," Libby whined at him. "You're not paying attention."

"Sorry, baby." He let the images in his mind fade. "I was drifting."

Derrick had his knee in a full brace, elevated. Surgery was coming at the end of the week, but the doctor had said the ligament tear was clean. A full recovery was possible. He wasn't too worried about it. As long as he could play catch with his kids and keep up with the boys when he coached. The episode was just ending at 8:30 when the phone rang. He picked it up from the arm table next to the sofa. "Hello?"

"Anderson … what are you doing?" There was the sound of wind or waves in the background.

"Hill … is that you?"

"It is." Aaron laughed. "What are you doing?"

"Watching Cosby. What else?"

"No you're not!" The familiar teasing rang in Aaron's tone. "Without me?"

"Just this once." Derrick chuckled. "That why you called? To ask me what I was doing?"

"No, something even more important." The noise in the background made it hard to hear. "I asked Megan to marry me, and you won't believe it! She said yes!"

Even with the noise, Derrick heard that. He leaned his head back against the couch and felt his friend's happiness to the core of his being. "I'm proud of you, man. First you talk to God, and now to Megan. We'll be talking to the president before you know it. Fixing things for those foster kids. You and me and Jay."

"And Megan. She's in too." He chuckled. "Hey, Anderson … be my best man, will you?"

"I already am. That's why you won the MVP, 'cause you finally started listening to me."

Derrick teased so he wouldn't let his emotions get the upper hand. There would be time for that later, when he pondered all the season had wrought. For now, he wanted to celebrate with his friend. "But sure, Hill. I'll say yes and make it official."

They laughed some more and the call ended half a minute later. Aaron had to go. He was finishing up dinner with Megan and Cory, bonding with his new family.

"Tell me that wasn't Aaron Hill?" Denae sat beside him. She kept her voice low so the kids could hear the beginning of the next episode of Cosby.

"Yeah, baby." He grinned at his wife, at the woman who had stood by him and prayed with him not only for the season, but for Aaron as well. "Talking about getting married and asking me to be the best man. Can you believe it?"

She'd looked like she was listening to Derrick's side of the conversation, and now her eyes shone. "Now, don't that just beat all?"

By then they both knew the story of the boy, and how he was the son of Aaron's high school girlfriend. The miracles of the past season were so much more complex than either of them could've dreamed. They'd won the Super Bowl, yes, and Coach Cameron was offered a five-year extension on his contract. But more than any of that, Derrick had made a friend. One he'd get the chance to tease and pick on and hang around with not just here in San Francisco, but for all eternity.

And that, by far, was the greatest miracle of all.

EPILOGUE

Cory looked at himself in the mirror and straightened his tie. It didn't look right, but that was okay. His dad would fix it for him before the wedding started. He lifted his chin and grinned at himself. He was the ring bearer, and that was a great job for a wedding. It wasn't too hard and there wasn't a lot of stuff to remember.

"Mom! Should I put my shoes on now?" He still smiled when he called her Mom. It sounded funny and good, but he was getting more used to it. Not that she would ever take the place of his first mom. But his first mom was in heaven, and Megan was here. He had a lot of years left to need a mom, so he was glad. Plus, he loved Megan.

"Yes, Cory," she called to him from her room. "We leave in five minutes. Definitely put your shoes on."

Megan was wearing regular clothes to Derrick's church that morning. The place had something called a bridal room, so Megan was getting dressed nice there. Which was good, because Cory didn't think her big white dress would fit in the Town Car.

They met near the door and Megan was practically glowing. Cory lifted his eyebrows. "Wow ... you look beautiful."

"Thanks." She smiled and adjusted her veil. Megan already had a girl over to the apartment that morning who curled her hair more perfect than ever before, and then she attached the veil. Now whenever Megan turned her head, the veil flew along behind her. It made her look like an angel.

Which Derrick said she was when they were together last Sunday at church. Megan had changed her mind about church, because she and Cory's dad and Derrick had a talk, and now everyone understood. Church was someplace where they could all come together and figure things out.

Sort of like a team huddle.

Once they reached the Andersons' church, everything happened fast. His dad found him and helped him straighten his tie. And they talked a little while about this being a day they would never forget. Cory knew that was true for him maybe most of all. Lots of people got married, but how many foster kids wound up with a mom and a dad all in one day?

The wedding started right on time, and the church was full of people. Lots of guys from the 49ers and people from the youth center too. When Cory reached the front, he stood next to his dad, and his dad put his arm around Cory's shoulders. Then they waited and special music started.

And nice and slow-like, here came Megan. She definitely looked like an angel now, and the whole crowd of people stood up and watched her walk down the aisle. Derrick was beside her, 'cause Megan didn't have a dad, and no dad ever showed up in her life the way Cory's dad did. So Derrick did the job.

Cory watched it all — the walking part and the part where Derrick let Megan go. He watched the part where his mom and dad said words to each other, promises about health and time and standing by each other forever.

Finally they said the "I do" part, which was the best part of all. Because his dad had said that after that, him and Megan were married for good. Sort of the happily ever after part. As that happened, as his mom and dad and him became an official family, Cory thought of something he hadn't before. It made his eyes sting, and he had to wipe away a little wetness on his cheeks.

'Cause his first mom had prayed so hard for Cory to find his dad. But Cory wasn't sure if his mom would've wanted Megan to marry his dad. That was something his first mom had wanted to do, Cory was pretty sure. That's why the tears were on his face. But all of a sudden he could see his mother again, see her the way she'd looked before she got sick, the way she must look now — in heaven — smiling and laughing and loving him with all her heart. And what he saw made him happier than he'd been all day.

Because somewhere up in heaven, his first mom wasn't sad at all. She was smiling. The way he and his new family all were.

The gushy kiss came next, and a whole lot of pictures. On the ride to the reception, Cory thought about the next week. He was staying with Derrick's family while his parents went on a honeymoon to Hawaii. A week wasn't very long, and it was good for his dad to have some time alone with Megan. Cory already had her for the last two years, so it was okay for his dad to have some time with her.

Plus, he liked Derrick's family, and Derrick best of all. Cory and his mom and dad spent a lot of time visiting at Derrick's house because it was the off-season. April. And that meant his dad had just short workouts each day until summer camp. Last week, Derrick talked some more with Cory's dad and Megan about church. He told them church is just a bunch of people who know they messed up. Also, it was easy to feel close to God at church. Sometimes that feeling could carry over on the other days, which would help. And Cory's dad said he understood, because life didn't happen only at church.

It happened between Sundays.

A Note from Karen

Dear Reader Friends,

What an adventure, writing a book set in the NFL! All my experience as a former sports writer came rushing back as I tried my best to set this story in the very real world of professional football, while creating characters that were completely fictional. Lots of details—you may have noticed—were accurate: the names and locations of teams and stadiums, the schedule as it relates to this football season, and some of the rituals that go along with the game.

On the journey to writing this novel, I enjoyed getting to know San Francisco 49ers quarterback Alex Smith. We first met, many of you know, when our family attended a game in San Francisco as Alex's guests. We visited with his parents—Pam and Doug, and his fantastic sisters and brother. All of them, we learned, were excited not just about what Alex does on the field, but off the field. Between Sundays. His passion for helping foster kids sparked in me the idea to write *Between Sundays*, and he graciously agreed to help me have an inside look at the NFL and the positive things some players do with their time away from the game. Alex has an amazing family, a family full of love and hope and wisdom and guidance.

That's where this story really hit me, the importance of having a family. It was something Megan Gunn understood—whether it was just her and Cory forever or whether God helped her drop the walls around her heart so she could love someone like Aaron Hill. At our house, we see the benefit of family every single day. We laugh and love and listen to each other, and when disagreements come up, we talk about how right here—around the dinner table—are the best friends of all. The people who will love us no matter what. But the truth is, sometimes we can't love even our families until we let God clean out the garbage in our own hearts.

I'll let you in on a secret. At first I was going to have the test results show that Aaron wasn't really Cory's biological father. He was going to shred the results and keep the truth a secret forever. But my editors and I agreed that the new Aaron wouldn't have wanted to keep something like that a secret. Just so you know, in the process of changing this part of the story, I decided something else. Aaron really was, in fact, Cory's dad. There. Now you don't have to wonder.

I pray that as you read this book, you saw a little of what Megan saw about foster kids, a little of what Aaron saw about God's grace. And a little of what Derrick understood about miracles and the importance of keeping a promise—whenever possible. Life really is about how we live it between Sundays. I know I'll remember that a little more carefully after writing this book.

As always, please stop by my website at www.KarenKingsbury.com and leave me a comment on my guestbook. I love to hear your thoughts, and I'd especially like to know how this story touched your heart. At my website, you can also leave photos of your military loved ones so that people around the world can pray for them. In addition, you can leave a prayer request, or stop by and pray for the needs of others. Finally, pass this book on to someone you know, someone who hasn't read one of my books. As you do, enter my ongoing Share-A-Book contest. Winners are picked every spring. Details are on my website.

I pray that God holds you and yours close, and that you'll feel His touch a little more in the days to come. Until next time ...

In His light and love,
Karen Kingsbury

Reader Study Guide

1. How did fame and sudden wealth at a young age change Aaron Hill? Was it his fault or the fault of his agent, Bill Bond? Explain.
2. In what ways were Megan Gunn and Amy Briggs alike? Talk about their similarities and their differences.
3. Where did Megan find the strength to take on responsibility for Cory after Amy's death? Discuss Megan's faith through most of this novel.
4. Cory had a firm belief that Aaron was his father. Compare Cory's adamant belief to something a child in your world believes.
5. Discuss what it means to have a child's faith.
6. What do you know about the foster care system? Talk about your experience with this system.
7. Did you learn anything about the plight of foster children? How can you be part of the solution for these kids?
8. Bill Bond was a manipulative man. What motivated him to control Aaron Hill? Discuss our nation's fascination with celebrity.
9. Derrick was a strong presence of faith in *Between Sundays*. Talk about Derrick's faith, and how it impacted the people around him.
10. What tragedy did Derrick carry with him? How did it affect his faith?
11. How has tragedy affected your faith? Is it possible to have difficult times and still believe in God? Talk about this.
12. Talk about Derrick's marriage to Denae. What were signs that their marriage was a deep and wonderful one?
13. How important is humor to a successful relationship—friendship or marriage?
14. One of the people Derrick affected was young quarterback Jay Ryder. How important is it that people of faith also act as mentors for those around them? Give an example from your life.
15. Megan Gunn had a difficult time trusting people. Why do you think that was?

16. Have you ever had a hard time trusting someone? How did you resolve that situation?

17. Aaron wished for a chance to apologize to Amy. When he learned of her death, he knew it was too late. Are there people you need to apologize to? What is stopping you?

18. How would you define wealth? During most of the story, who was richer — Megan or Aaron? Explain your answer.

19. What did you think of Aaron's decision to shred the DNA test results? Explain why the role of mom or dad can't always be defined through a biological connection. Give examples.

20. Aaron Hill asked God to clear his heart of the garbage that had piled up. Talk about a time when you or someone you know reached that point with God.

ABOVE THE LINE SERIES

Take One

Karen Kingsbury,
New York Times *Bestselling Author*

Could they change the world — before the world changes them?

Filmmakers Chase Ryan and Keith Ellison left the mission field of Indonesia for the mission field of Hollywood with a dream bigger than both of them. Now they have done the impossible: raised enough money to produce a feature film with a message that could change the world.

But as Chase and Keith begin shooting, their well-laid plans begin to unravel. With millions of dollars on the line, they make a desperate attempt to keep the film from falling apart — even as a temperamental actress, a botched production schedule, and their own insecurities leave little room for the creative and spiritual passion that once motivated them. Was God really behind this movie after all? A chance meeting and friendship with John Baxter could bring the encouragement they need to stay on mission and produce a movie that will actually change people's lives.

In the midst of the questions and the cameras, is it possible to keep things above the line and make a movie unlike anything done before — or is the risk too great for everyone?

Hardcover, Jacketed: 978-0-310-31843-9

Pick up a copy today at your favorite bookstore!

Every Now and Then

Karen Kingsbury,
New York Times *Bestselling Author*

A wall went up around Alex Brady's heart when his father, a New York firefighter, died in the Twin Towers. Turning his back on the only woman he ever loved, Alex shut out all the people who cared about him to concentrate on fighting crime. He and his trusty K9 partner, Bo, are determined to eliminate evil in the world and prevent tragedies like 9-11.

Then the worst fire season in California's history erupts, and Alex faces the ultimate challenge to protect the community he serves. An environmental terrorist group is targeting the plush Oak Canyon Estates. At the risk of losing his job, and his soul, Alex is determined to infiltrate the group and put an end to their corruption. Only the friendship of Clay and Jamie Michaels — and the love of a dedicated young woman — can help Alex drop the walls around his heart and move forward into the future God has for him.

Softcover: 978-0-310-26615-0
Unabridged Audio CD: 978-0-310-288183
Audio Download, Unabridged: 978-0-310-288190
ebooks:
Adobe® Acrobat® eBook Reader®: 978-0-310-28821-3
Microsoft Reader®: 978-0-310-28823-7
Palm™ Reader: 978-0-310-28825-1
Mobipocket Reader™: 978-0-310-28822-0
Sony® Reader: 978-0-310-29045-2
ePub: 978-0-310-29623-2

Pick up a copy today at your favorite bookstore!

Even Now

Karen Kingsbury

Sometimes hope for the future is found in the ashes of yesterday.

A young woman seeking answers to her heart's deepest questions. A man and woman driven apart by lies and years of separation ... who have never forgotten each other.

With hallmark tenderness and power, Karen Kingsbury weaves a tapestry of lives, losses, love, and faith — and the miracle of resurrection.

Softcover: 978-0-310-24753-1
Unabridged Audio CD: 978-0-310-25404-1

Ever After

Karen Kingsbury

2007 Christian Book of the Year

Two couples torn apart — one by war between countries, and one by a war within.

In this moving sequel to *Even Now*, Emily Anderson, now twenty, meets the man who changes everything for her: Army reservist Justin Baker. Their tender relationship, founded on a mutual faith in God and nurtured by their trust and love for each other, proves to be a shining inspiration to everyone they know, especially Emily's reunited birth parents.

But Lauren and Shane still struggle to move past their opposing beliefs about war, politics, and faith. When tragedy strikes, can they set aside their opposing views so that love — God's love — might win, no matter how great the odds?

Softcover: 978-0-310-24756-2
Unabridged Audio CD: 978-0-310-25405-8

Share Your Thoughts

With the Author: Your comments will be forwarded to the author when you send them to *zauthor@zondervan.com*.

With Zondervan: Submit your review of this book by writing to *zreview@zondervan.com*.

Free Online Resources at
www.zondervan.com

Zondervan AuthorTracker: Be notified whenever your favorite authors publish new books, go on tour, or post an update about what's happening in their lives.

Daily Bible Verses and Devotions: Enrich your life with daily Bible verses or devotions that help you start every morning focused on God.

Free Email Publications: Sign up for newsletters on fiction, Christian living, church ministry, parenting, and more.

Zondervan Bible Search: Find and compare Bible passages in a variety of translations at www.zondervanbiblesearch.com.

Other Benefits: Register yourself to receive online benefits like coupons and special offers, or to participate in research.